Vasiliy I

GOA

Confession of the Psychedelic Oyster

Vasiliy Karavaev

Goa. Confession of the Psychedelic Oyster.

My e-mail address: vasiliykaravaev@mail
https://www.vasiliykaravaev.com

An ordinary Russian guy named Vasiliy lives in the north of the Indian state of Goa. He has a beautiful wife, a smart daughter, and his own restaurant on the shore, where you can have a taste of hash cake and wash it down with real kvass – an old Russian beverage – for just 100 rupees. Vasya and his friends consider themselves psychedelic 'Che Guevaras,' and help their fellow citizens – both true downshifters and 'two-week trippers' – make a quantum leap in consciousness. But Vasya's prolonged journey through wonderful India, where desires tend to materialize and time is 'as thick as a mango smoothie', gradually turns into a bad trip.

It is a narrative about how 'heaven without hell can unnoticeably turn into hell', which is fascinating not only to the wide gallery of characters that took a direct part in the described events, but also to the new generation of psychedelic Jedis, willing to learn from their mistakes of their predecessors.

Dedicated to my daughter Vasilina

Contents

Chapter 1. Part One. Inside.

I slowly take my palms, which smell of oysters, away from my face. I open my eyes. Damn!!! This isn't a dream – reality remains unchanged. Ten to twenty... The phrase echoes in my temples. From ten to twenty years in jail! No, this can't be real, they've got to get me out of here! So this is what it's like, my first night in jail. I have never been locked up before. I need to get some sleep and try to eat. The iron plate of rice garnished with dal isn't appealing in the slightest. A ginger cat with bald patches sneaks through the barred window, sniffs my food lying on the floor, and continues walking past it with disdain, in search of something edible. A massive gray rat pops out of its hole in the corner of my cell, jogs unhurriedly across the room, wagging its tail as if to say 'goodbye' to me, and disappears behind the toilet door.

What am I doing here? This is just a nightmare and I need to wake up fast. God... What an excruciating heat has set in this time of year! It feels no less than one hundred degrees Celsius. Every slight flutter of a breeze brings orgasmic joy. I'm sure I look like a caged animal. The only thing missing is a sign reading 'Big White Ape. Habitat: areas with a cold climate. Does not reproduce in captivity.' The cage is quite spacious for a species such as myself. Ten feet wide and four feet long. There are iron bars instead of a door.

The last zoo I went to was in Bangkok; it looked much cleaner and there wasn't such a stench coming from the lavatory. Can they really have such big quarters for each inmate here? Now I can understand the animals that strut from corner to corner every day in their zoo-jail. It's just impossible to stay still. I've been walking around the cell in circles for four hours. I note the guard's indifferent stare: he watches me pacing around my concrete box with a mean grimace.

"Hey you, I'm thirsty! Where do you get drinking water here?"

The guard grins, passes me a plastic bottle through the bars, and silently points to the toilet door. I take the bottle with disgust, push the grimy door open with one finger, and stand paralyzed with horror, hesitant to step inside. I never thought I'd have to drink water in such conditions. I still have to get to the water itself... The whole floor is covered with a layer of mucus, urine and shit. I can't force myself to step forward barefoot.

"Hey, guard, give me my shoes, I'm not some kind of animal, I need to get to the water tap."

The guard smiles again and throws my sandals through the bars.

"After you've finished, give them back, or else you'll never get them again," the young man says, resting his elbow on his long old rifle.

What's wrong with his face? He seems to always be smiling, and that's a relief. It's good that they don't get physical with the inmates here; I'd rather they always smiled.

Carefully making my way across the layer of greenish-brown slime to reach the water tap, I feel happy for the first time since I've been here. Water!!! The warm liquid coming from the dirty tap in a thin trickle reeks of chlorine. Hopefully, I won't have to drink it for long in here... They've got to get me out of here. I have a thousand friends, and surely they will do something about this. Now I need to keep myself busy. Doing nothing drives me insane. I'm dying for a cigarette! Maybe, an inmate could've stashed some tobacco or at least a cigarette butt somewhere. The uneven concrete cell floor can't have been swept for two hundred years. I might have a better chance of finding something in the pile of trash in the corner. I start rummaging through the old plastic bags and crumpled pieces of newspaper and come across a suspiciously neatly-folded piece of toilet paper. I hope it's not some kind of joke, and somebody didn't just put a piece of shit in it. Wary of contracting a contagious disease, I unroll it with two fingers and discover three cigarettes, yellow from time and humidity, and five matches. There you are!!! My luck is coming back!!! The cigarettes, judging by their color, have been sitting here for over a month. Oh Lord, bless the man who took the trouble to stash this for me! The setting Sun adds to my joy, but the concrete that has been exposed to the heat all day is not willing to part with the heat. I'd love to poke my head through the bars and breathe the air from the street; it is much cooler than in the cell. Another problem appears – mosquitoes. The light lures them, like a magnet. There are thousands of them in the cell, maybe even a million. My shirt and shorts are soaked through with sweat. The mosquitoes sense the smell of sweat and swarm towards the uncovered parts of my body. Randomly slapping myself with my palm I kill a handful of the bloodsuckers. I don't exactly dream of contracting malaria, which not everybody is capable of surviving. Driving the mosquitos away with a newspaper, I light the first prized cigarette. The burning acidic smoke of the cheap Indian tobacco has an effect on me comparable to a hash joint. The light dizziness and feeling of acute fatigue throughout my body force me to lie down and forget about my problems for a moment. If only I could fall asleep now. The smiling guard notices me lying on the floor; without a sound he throws a pile of old newspapers at me. Evidently they are my bed sheets now, a plastic bottle being my pillow. One newspaper is my mattress, another is my blanket. I wrap the newspapers around my head and neck, lie down and for a while I listen to the sound of mosquitoes near my ear; they are looking for ways to get closer to me. It is unlikely that I'll manage to survive in such conditions... However, my exhausted mind collapses and I manage to fall asleep for a few seconds. I dream of when I was a fifteen year old boy fishing in the Volga river and trying to sleep in a tent full of mosquitoes. The mosquitos from my dream finally wake me up. I look at the ceiling. The sticky heat and mosquitoes don't bother as much anymore, gradually giving way to another disturbance – my inflamed brain doesn't stop looking for a solution to the problem. Working at a very high speed and producing negligible results, it starts to overheat. "I've got to do something, I've got to do something," the phrase is pulsing in my head, making my consciousness seek ways of getting out of this situation. "That's it. You're facing ten to twenty years" the casual phrase of one of the cops that struck my life like a lightning bolt.

What am I doing here? This shouldn't have happened. This is some sort of misunderstanding, an accident, an injustice... I've been framed! I'm filled with a burning fury, making my whole body tense up like a compressed spring. I need to start walking around the cell and concentrate on my breathing, that should pacify my troubled mind. If I start walking fast enough, the damn mosquitoes won't have enough time to land on me. For a while one of my problems disappears. Thousands of mosquitoes follow me in a buzzing gray cloud, trying to pierce my flesh.

Where did I go wrong? Why am I here? Like a broken record, my brain again begins to repeat: "I've got to do something, I've got to do something, I've got to, I've got to, I've got to." First I need money, because money always solves everything. Where can I get some cash? The cops took my last five grand. I need to somehow contact my wife and tell her to sell our apartment as soon as possible. I wonder when they'll let me make my first phone call. What will I tell my family? "Sorry, my darlings, but now you have to move out of your three-bedroom apartment into a one-bedroom." What an idiot I am! Well... I may be an idiot, but at least I'm still alive. Let's just say that now is the time to part with the real estate that I considered my last resort. Maybe I should have done it long ago. If I had done it, I wouldn't be here now. When did this all start? When did I take the wrong path that led me here? Dymkov. The name springs to mind. Maybe it started with him. Maybe sooner, maybe later, but it is his image that my mind is producing as an answer to the question "why am I here now?" The whole story must have started with him. This man, whom I met by accident, had a great effect on me. Or you could say that my whole life changed dramatically after I met him.

Chapter 1. Part Two. Outside.

Without going into details of the causes and consequences, I can assume that the bad luck that turned into an avalanche of trouble started to come about just before I became acquainted with Dymkov in the mid-1990s. The turbulent times of political change in Russia were coming to an end, although we were not aware of this back then. My life had just begun. Earning money was easy and fast, and as a result my days were filled with all kinds of pleasures. I craved more and in greater variety, so earning easy money brought a lot of joy. I was just a small entrepreneur in a big, but provincial city. Back then half of the country's population were entrepreneurs, surviving thanks to their own initiative. During the Perestroika[1] years, the profit from my small business went from zero to a quarter of a million dollars. I kept reinvesting and making new money. There wasn't a thing I didn't invest in! I traded everything that it was possible to trade, and provided all kinds of services, anything and everything that the law allowed. All of my life I have considered myself to be a law-abiding citizen. My obedience was not based on fear, but rather on the morals and ideals that I received from my parents. My mother was a clothes designer and I inherited my good taste from her. My father worked as an engineer in a factory all his life; he taught me how to survive in this world with my hands and my brain. And even though I spent my childhood in working class areas of the city, I was raised on the principles of good morals and abiding by the law.

It was the peak of the nineties. Quentin Tarantino's "From Dusk To Dawn" had just hit us. Like thousands of other young people infected by the fast-spreading virus of freedom, I wanted to get

---

[1]Perestroika - the political movement for reform within the Communist Party of the Soviet Union during the 1980s, widely associated with Soviet leader Mikhail Gorbachev.

a tattoo, just like the cult movie's main hero. As having half of one's body covered with tattoos was costly, in order to minimize the expense, I opened the first tattoo salon in the city. I rented a small office, did the redecorating myself, hired two tattoo artists, and started tattooing my body while we waited for the first customers.

Dymkov, a short guy wearing a rocker-style leather jacket, turned up in my salon and immediately became one of my clients. Wearing glasses with large lenses, his long dark hair tied in a ponytail, he looked like a pre-Perestroika punk rocker who had outgrown his time. Back then he worked fixing watches in a small shop and had plenty of free time that he spent on his favorite occupation: music. He played the guitar in a small, unknown rock band, collected records by Time Machine and even wrote reviews on new records for music magazines. That year he had a tattoo on his shoulder in the form of the 'peace sign' on a globe background. United by our love of rock music, motorbikes and tattoos, we quickly became friends. We spent a few wonderful years together surrounded by girls, alcohol and marijuana. They were fun times. Easily accessible girls flocked around the tattoo salon, alcohol flowed like a river, and the marijuana and money never ended.

A few carefree years passed before Dymkov inherited an interesting job from his mother. During the Soviet regime she had worked for the philharmonic and brought many stars of the stage to the city. Dymkov quit his watch repair job and became famous in the city as a producer: a trendy profession at that time. I sold my tattoo salon to my friends, but remained on good terms with Dymkov. Every weekend we would see each other on our regular visits to prostitutes. Our wives were both ten years our senior, and that gave us something in common. Our spouses were smarter than us. They were educated, entrepreneurial, self-sufficient, and therefore didn't appear to us as objects of sexual desire. Maybe we were poor lovers, incapable of turning our wives into hot goddesses who craved us all the time, or maybe our wives, overloaded by their careers and daily routine, didn't exude as much sex appeal as we wanted. That is why Dymkov and I regularly visited prostitutes. Prostitutes united us.

Slowly but surely the era of Perestroika came to an end. The turnover of my two Turkish-Italian clothes stores was still about a quarter of a million dollars, but I hardly saw any of it. I had to pay huge monthly bills for business expenditures, taxes, rent; all of which resulted in me having not more than a thousand dollars a month in my pocket. The situation was getting out of control. My brain had gotten used to bathing in waves of ecstasy and was demanding new sensations. By that time I had divorced my first wife and bought a motorbike, and I started to live the life of a Russian biker. In summer I would travel across the country and in winter I would hang out in rock bars, spending money on hard liquor and easy women. The way my business was arranged, I only worked two hours a day collecting the money generated by my two stores. Unlike me, Dymkov less and less frequently found free time to spend on himself.

The times of uncontrolled 'freelance producers' passed, and Dymkov was taken under the wing of a large, prosperous corporation. He was given the role of director of a nightclub in the Center of Culture and Entertainment, and he had his own office, where we would gather almost every evening to smoke a joint. The office was guarded by a security service, so we could comfortably get stoned, knowing that we didn't have to worry about anyone disturbing us. It was there that I met one of the owners of the corporation, who we respectfully and fearfully referred to as 'Sam[2]' between us. By then Sam had quit the common, detrimental habit of getting drunk every day and seriously took to fighting the all-out debauchery that surrounded him. Thanks to him, all of the top managers and other management personnel in his corporation abstained from alcohol. But he fought hard drinking in his own way, one that had at one time helped him to stop the terrible habit of taking a hair of the dog every morning. Even before Perestroika, when being an independent contractor or making any money under the table was illegal, he fooled his countrymen playing the thimblerig at an auto market. The job was rough, and he had to drink a lot. He had to drink with bandits and he had to drink with the cops, there was no way around it. The years passed and we changed. Eventually he quit his criminal activities and focused on legal business. Producing plastic windows was his next endeavor, and later on he managed to get a hold of a relatively big share of Autovaz, which manufactures Lada cars. Several major factories and plants across the country were bought for next to nothing. Post-Soviet industry was inefficient and dilapidated; a drunken stupor ruled the country. Everybody was drinking: from simple folk to the elite and even the president. Hard drinking had penetrated every aspect of people's lives. With that in mind, Sam, who was now the owner of a big corporation, made up his mind to switch his staff from drinking alcohol to smoking marijuana. Sam was able to get off the bottle with the help of the miracle herb. No, he didn't start buying wholesale marijuana by the ton; he didn't even get into the drug business. He just set an example of how it was possible to enjoy life without drinking. As a moderate smoker, he managed to be a superb businessman and lead a healthy life. He was the picture of a successful businessman who knew how to live with a taste.

That fall the Russian version of *Forbes* magazine, which writes about the richest people, published an article on the year's most successful corporation, featuring an interview in which Sam declared that he was the first legal billionaire in our city. At that time, in order to be independent of drug dealers, I was growing different strains of hydroponic marijuana under lamps on my balcony. It was enough for my personal use and to treat my friends. Every two months I harvested it and we tried it in Dymkov's office, discussing the advantages and disadvantages of new Dutch marijuana strains. Occasionally Sam would join us. He was always laconic and seemed preoccupied with other things. After smoking with us, he would rate the herb, discuss the club business with Dymkov, and after an hour he would leave, accompanied by armed bodyguards.

One evening Dymkov calls me and asks me to come urgently, because he has something interesting to share with me. Not having anything else to do, I grab a bud of White Widow[3] and reach his office in fifteen minutes. In his office I see that a couple of my friends are with him, all connoisseurs of good weed, lying on the sofa, watching Dymkov. First of all he rolls a joint, passes it around and then starts to talk excitedly.

"Vasya, can you imagine, I was smoking with Sam an hour ago…"

---

[2]Sam - there is a subtext to this name in Russian, which could be translated as 'himself' (as in 'Elvis himself'), reflecting the respect that this character is held in.

[3]Black Widow - a potent cannabis strain developed in The Netherlands.

"That's no big deal, Dymkov, you smoke with him every day," I try to make a joke, making use of the pause while he takes a puff.

"Listen to me, Vasya, and don't interrupt," Dymkov doesn't let me finish, passing the joint to me, "Do you know what Sam has got on his mind?"

"I'm afraid to even think about it," I say, smiling at him and exhaling a stream of sweet smoke, "Is he running for President?"

"Oh, Vasya, if only… Yesterday he went to hang out with the big shots at an official town banquet. He told me that, as usual, everybody got shitfaced and he had to sit like an idiot listening to all the crap those colonels and businessmen were talking, after they had all turned into drunken animals in just a few hours. He said he couldn't even step outside and have a smoke, as it could have been misunderstood."

"And… so?" I interrupt him, intrigued by the beginning of his story.

"So, Sam has decided to promote the legalization of marijuana. Vasya, when he said that, I almost dropped my joint. If I didn't know him so well, I would have thought it was a joke, but he never wastes his breath."

"And what did he decide to start with?" I ask with irony, not taking his story seriously.

"What he wants, Vasya, is to change our society's attitude towards marijuana, for starters. He wants it to be like Europe, he wants ganja smokers to be treated as normal human beings, and not registered junkies. So, Vasya, right now he is willing to fund any project that will lead to a change in people's attitude towards marijuana. Before you came, Ilya Beech was here, and Sam gave him money to go to Amsterdam and shoot a ten-minute video about the annual ganja festival and the people's attitude to marijuana."

"Yes, it wouldn't be bad to go to Amsterdam for a week and visit the Cannabis Cup[4], " I say enviously and immediately my mind draws a picture of me sitting in a coffee shop[5] in the Red Light District.

"Vasya, what's stopping you from doing it? Come to think of it, what could you do to promote the legalization of marijuana?" Dymkov says, making a straight-faced parody of Soviet Second World War propaganda posters.

"You know, Dymkov, I'm a trader, I can sell anything and everything, but I won't sell drugs."

"Nobody is asking you to sell drugs. Think of something. What are you, thick or what?"

After hesitating for a second, I feel like I'd been struck by lightning.

"Look, Dymkov, I was ordering new strains of Dutch marijuana online recently and by accident I clicked on a very interesting link. A Moscow firm offers clothes made from marijuana to wholesale buyers, it is called Hemp."

---

[4]The Cannabis Cup - the world's foremost annual cannabis festival.

[5]Coffee shops - establishments in the Netherlands where the sale of cannabis for personal consumption by the public is tolerated by the local authorities.

"Vasya, that's exactly what we need!" Dymkov exclaims, jumping out of his leather armchair. "Start putting together a business plan tonight. If you say that this project will pay off in three years, you'll get funding for it."

As I drive my Jeep back home I turn on cruise control, not paying attention to anything going on outside. I am absorbed in this new idea; a plan for a new exciting life is being born in my head. I don't get a wink of sleep that night. I browse all of the Internet resources that have anything to do with Hemp, I sit down with a calculator and by morning I've put together a preliminary business plan that requires seventy-five thousand dollars to realize. My heart beats like a bass drum and I feel like I am Che Guevara. That night I start to believe that everything in this world was possible; one just had to really want it. Dymkov calls Sam and gets preliminary approval for the budget. Everything starts to spin so fast, that in a month I am in Amsterdam to get some overseas experience.

Walking down the beautiful Dutch streets, I enjoy the spirit of European civilization. The absence of aggressive, dismal faces is inebriating. The spirit, taste and smell of freedom can be felt everywhere. One can legally smoke marijuana and hashish in coffee shops and eat psilocybin mushrooms, peyote and other psychoactive plants in smart shops. In bars one can drink tasty beer, and on the streets one can legally enjoy love for sale. What strikes me most is that nobody bothers anyone else. Everybody seems to enjoy life and not keep others from enjoying it. Everything that is banned in Russia is for sale here, either legally or semi-legally. Street dealers selling banned drugs freely offer passers-by their goods right in front of the cops without any fear of being arrested. "Will this level of democracy ever be achieved in Russia? What can be done for me to be able to see it during my lifetime? Can this be achieved in the near future?" I think, recalling my homeland. Day and night, I can't get this thought out of my mind.

Cruising from one coffee shop to another, I observe the people hanging out in those places. Some of them are old Rasta men and Jamaicans. In their faith smoking ganja is a religious ritual, so they always take smoking very seriously. Listening to reggae music, I watch with great pleasure how the Rasta men roll joints filled with Jamaican ganja. Pot smokers in Russia never put any effort into making smoking look good. My countrymen usually put a mix of ganja and tobacco in a Russian cigarette, and the taste of cheap paper prevails over the sweet marijuana smoke. In general, Russian smokers hardly ever use aesthetic accessories, preferring to insert the mix into an empty cigarette with their fingers, sitting in their houses or cars, or some hiding place where they will go unnoticed by the police. In Holland one feels class and style everywhere, including in smoking. Some coffee shops are gathering places for creative people, and have a great assortment of marijuana and hashish from all over the world. Paying careful attention to the smell of Turkish hashish smoke, we compare it to Moroccan, Nepali, Afghani, Pakistani, Kashmiri, Indian and other strains. Each one has its own smell, taste and effect.

We spend a whole day in an underground squat at a trance party surrounded by interesting and creative people. Lying peacefully on leather sofas, some of them were paint, while others just socialize. The availability and affordability of intellectual, as well as party drugs, is phenomenal. Everywhere there are 'Common interest clubs' packed with people united by the love of ganja and light drugs. In smart shops it is completely legal to buy organic analogues of virtually all synthetic drugs. Substitutes for ecstasy, LSD and other psychoactive substances are on sale, sharing a shelf with hallucinogenic cacti and psilocybin mushrooms. We spend hours on end hanging around small stores selling drug paraphernalia, staring at the shelves and forgetting about time. The whole city of Amsterdam consists of very well cared-for houses inhabited by beautiful, intelligent elves. The democracy that our government talked about now seems a hoax. All of a sudden our country seems a haven of evil goblins, who live in tastelessly built apartment complexes and don't smile at each other on the streets. It is hard to imagine free municipal bikes with ten sets of pedals being ridden on Russian streets. At a station in Amsterdam I see a man with a case get off one such bike and another man get on in his place, turning the pedals to reach his destination for free with ten other passengers. Nobody slacks off. Everyone turns their pedals, humming a merry Dutch tune together.

One month after I return to Russia, I hold a business plan endorsed by Sam in one hand, and a bag with seventy-five grand in the other. All of the official papers are in my name, as Sam refuses to involve his corporation in such a compromising project as Hemp, which he explains as due to it being too soon to reveal the real forces behind the 'Legalize' project. "First we need to change society's attitude towards smokers, and afterwards: legally decriminalize marijuana. The first step will be to make the penalty for possession of light drugs less harsh, after that we'll be able to promote the legalization of marijuana," Dymkov explains, handing the bag with the money to me. During the first stage I am to promote hemp clothes. Sam wants everybody in town to be talking about the brand. According to Dymkov, Sam is funding and supervising our project personally. My business plan stipulates that most of the funds are to be spent on advertising and promotion. I fit myself into the business plan budget as a manager with a modest monthly salary of eight hundred dollars. If they had refused to pay me, I probably would have agreed to work for free. I felt like a hero.

"It's a risky enterprise, as far as business is concerned," I say to Dymkov, a few days before the grand opening of the store. "It's a new business, and it's virtually impossible to predict what's going to happen in the future."

"Don't wet your pants, Vasya, we'll make it!" Dymkov replies, tipping a pile of ganja sitting on a folder with the heading 'Hemp Business Plan' into an empty cigarette. "You probably understand, Vasya, that this project is political rather than commercial. It's just like a big toy for Sam and he understands that. Do you know what he told me yesterday when he stopped by the office for a smoke?" Dymkov suddenly says in a low voice, taking out his Zippo cigarette lighter, which always smells of gasoline. "He told me, Vasya, that if the initial investment pays off in three years, he will give us Hemp as a gift. I've been dreaming about owning a store with unique goods and being able to promote the legalization of cannabis all my life, Vasya."

"Yes, we're standing on the verge of big changes and making history with our own hands," I reply to Dymkov, inhaling the sweet fumes of White Widow. "We might open the first coffee shop in our country someday."

"That wouldn't be too bad," Dymkov adds with a smile, staring at the thick cascades of smoke floating towards the open window. "You do know, Vasya, that the first coffee shop in Amsterdam was opened by Russian emigrants and it's called 'Moscow'?"

"I sure do," I reply with a big grin on my face, recollecting the times we smoked AK-47[6] in Amsterdam, on the street right across from the 'Moscow' coffee shop. We had been warned that we could only smoke in coffee shops while in Holland. If caught smoking in the streets, you can be fined. But as we were used to smoking in the streets in Russia, we rolled a couple of joints and started walking down the street under the autumnal yet pleasantly warm sunlight. We stood at a Dutch canal, smoking sweet cultivated marijuana and dreaming about the time when we'd be able to do the same in our home country, slowly and easily, just like we did in Holland, without having to watch out for cops, in fear of getting locked up for a few years for just one joint. We stood and smoked our joints right on the sidewalk; two policemen rode their bikes right past us, not paying any attention to the sweet smell mellowing down the street, that made passers-by smile at us with understanding.

"Stop smiling," Dymkov says all of a sudden, interrupting my sweet reminiscence of that wonderful country. "Do you understand what I'm saying? We'll be gifted Hemp, if we return the money in a timely manner," Dymkov repeats, shaking my shoulder.

"Of course we will return the money, whatever it takes. If Sam is supporting our project, everything will be alright. Jah Rastafari[7] is on our side."

---

[6]AK-47 - a potent strain of marijuana.

[7]The Rastafari movement - an Abrahamic religion that developed in Jamaica in the 1930s, following the coronation of Haile Selassie I as Emperor of Ethiopia in 1930. Rastafari are monotheists, worshiping a singular God whom they call Jah.

Chapter 2. Part One. Inside.

Sometime in the morning I manage to fall asleep for about an hour. As they keep the lights in the cell on all night, thousands of mosquitoes gather together from all over the place to taste my blood. Every inch of my skin not covered by clothes is bitten many times. The long-awaited coolness of the morning lasts only half an hour. No sooner has the Sun appeared above the trees than the bloodsuckers that had been terrorizing me all night are gone. All living beings outside the window must be searching for shade now. Having slipped off into a sweet morning slumber for a few minutes, I am roughly awakened up by the clang of the opening iron bars. A sleepy guard points at the door without saying a word. "Vovan must have done something!" I think with joy as I head towards the exit, picking off pieces of newspapers that have stuck to me during the night on the way. While I put on my sandals I notice two armed guards standing behind the bars, which doesn't seem promising at all. Squinting my eyes, I enter a short corridor leading to the street. After the gloom of the cell, I have to cover my eyes with my hands for a moment, to give them a chance to adapt to the bright sunlight. The first thing I am able to see clearly are camera lenses aimed at me. Journalists and cameramen with three TV company logos on their cameras eagerly record every step I take. Damn!!! I guess it is unlikely that things will get sorted out quietly. I guess Vovan couldn't help me, it's too late.

After that, everything is a blur. In a state of complete frustration, I only vaguely understand what is happening. Silent, pretending not to understand their questions, and for some reason covering my face from the cameras. Then the TV crews are gone and the chief of the drugs police, Pashish, begins to interrogate me.

"So you wanted to fool us? You thought that if you changed your bike, clothes and cell phone, you would become a different person? Did you want to screw with us? Well, you've screwed yourself! You're looking at a minimum of ten years, man. Why are you silent? You've got nothing to say, Russian? If you want to keep silent, that's okay – I'll do the talking. First off, thanks a lot for the money. It is good you didn't have time to spend it; look, my boys are happy," Pashish says, pointing at the corner of the room where four Neanderthals in police uniform are playing cards.

"Thanks for the money," one of them says, turning to me as he takes his winnings and puts them into his pocket.

"Don't put that money away, bid another five hundred," says another thug in a uniform with a scar on his face, jerking him by the sleeve.

"Don't spend it all in one day, you lot, bidding five hundreds," their boss shouts and turns to me.

"So, Vasiliy, are you going to tell me the story or are you going to carry on with your 'not understand' bullshit? Should I treat you to a line of cocaine? My boys have some really good stuff. Last week we snatched it from a nigger; you've never had it this pure."

"No, thanks, I don't do drugs, but I wouldn't mind a cigarette," I say, looking at a pack of Marlboro sitting on the table.

"As a matter of fact, smoking in here is prohibited, but you may smoke. Have a smoke and go back to your cell. Everything we could take from you, we've taken, so you're of no interest to us. Bear with our conditions for a while, in a few days you'll be transferred to a different jail. I will go ahead and finish typing your charge sheet and we'll see each other in court in a year or so. That's all, my job is done. Take him back to his cell," Pashish says with content, stretching in his armchair.

Left alone in my cell, I smoke the last half-cigarette in three puffs. It seems like I am in trouble, serious trouble. It doesn't get more serious than this.

Chapter 2. Part Two. Outside.

The grand opening of Hemp is mind-blowing. The city is flooded with banners advertising our hemp clothes. 'Hemp: and no addiction...', our slogan declares boldly in capital letters on all of the main intersections of the city. The phrase 'Magic wear from hemp' is to be found everywhere. All of the TV channels and radio stations tell the population that hemp is not only a drug, but also high quality, fashionable clothes. 'Hemp - magic wear' shines in big neon letters every evening on the facade of a new business center. The best creative designers worked on the image and interior of our unusual store. Inside tall glass cases, large pictures of cannabis flowers are displayed. The huge buds covered with white and golden crystals of tetrohydrocannabinol[8] make the eyes of youngsters passing by glisten merrily. I see those eyes. For many people hemp wear is associated not only with the light drug that all of the 'advanced' world is having a good time with, but also with the spirit of freedom that our country lacks. For many years our society dictated to us a slave philosophy, suppressing our individual identity for the good of the system. Whole generations of Soviet citizens spent their lives doing monotonous jobs, which were often unnecessary. Those privileged enough to go abroad would occasionally meet 'abnormal' people there. Having reached certain minimal goals in life, those 'abnormal' characters stopped and refused to keep running along with the others, after the Golden Fleece. To the 'ordinary' people's mind, those 'weirdos' were spending their time in a very questionable way. They traveled, they were creative, they tried to develop themselves spiritually.

After the USSR collapsed, our country was finally, legally invaded by the seeds of alternative information. All of my friends and acquaintances who stopped devoting their life to making more money, got infected by the virus of 'freedom'. Most of my friends primarily associated 'the spirit of freedom' with cannabis, or the beautiful Latin American word 'marijuana'. Looking at the glittering eyes of the alterative thinkers hanging out in my store, I become increasingly convinced that marijuana smokers and the non-smokers who are lenient towards this drug are by no means some sort of marginal people. They look nothing like the 'fallen' junkies that we were used to watching in the criminal chronicles of the Russian mass media. In spite of the high price of hemp clothes, one piece

---

[8]Tetrahydrocannabinol (THC) - the active chemical in cannabis and one of the oldest hallucinogenic drugs known.

costing about $100, they sell fast. I see people of different ages look at our huge pictures of the banned seven-leaf plant and enter the store with glowing faces. It makes no difference to them what to buy: they would buy anything. People touch the clothes thinking that their eyes are deceiving them. 'Can the spirit of freedom have made it here?' the expression on their faces says. But, unfortunately, delegates from the 'opposite camp' visit us as well. Sometimes drunk cops appear in the store and, unable to find anything illegal, verbally abuse the salesmen. "Got yourself some freedom over here, have you? Watch us come and get you. This is not Europe. We'll find a way to shut you all down, anyway," the cops say with an evil sneer. One can understand them. Raised in a totalitarian state, they can't see their role in a society where individuality and creativity do not have to be suppressed. Their main argument is the standard: "Who is going to work, if everybody smokes?" Watching the customers I realize that the majority of the people who are lenient towards marijuana are not 'asocial personalities', despite the stereotype. They are just different. Within the first three months of opening we sell almost all of the merchandize. Our net profit is much higher than we planned and totals ten grand. Dymkov stops being nervous and reminding me that we have to return seventy-five thousand dollars in three years. Our store becomes the entire city's pride and joy. In the nightclub run by Dymkov, regular promotional parties take place. Every day local newspapers and journals publish interviews with me, in which I explain that magic hemp can be not just a drug, but also clothes. And every night, before falling asleep, I realize that I am making history, changing the mindset of a million people.

25

Chapter 3. Part One. Inside.

"Vasya, Vasya, come to the window," I hear Vovan's familiar voice in my sleep.

"Vovan, what took you so long?" I shout happily through the bars, touching the cold metal with my forehead.

"Hush, Vasya, don't shout, I am here illegally," Vovan whispers, looking around. "I gave the guards two hundred bucks in order to get to the window. We only have five minutes."

I take cigarettes and matches from Vovan and start smoking right away.

"Don't worry, Vasya, I have good connections with the ministry, I might be able to get you out of here. Although you will have to spend some time here, whatever happens. First and foremost, you need to hire a good lawyer. He'll be able to close your case in six months and you'll get out of here."

"Have you lost your mind, Vovan?! What six months are you talking about?" I shout, unable to hold in my anger, forgetting that Vovan could be jailed for being there illegally. "Get me out of here right now. Didn't I give you five thousand bucks two weeks ago. Give it to somebody, it's big money for the cops."

"I don't have it anymore, Vasya, I spent it on safrole oil, nitroethane and other chemicals. And when the police arrested you, I flushed it down the toilet."

"Well, Vovan, what else is there to do? Call my wife, tell her to sell our apartment and come here. Something has to be done."

"OK, I'll contact Lena today. Look, the guard is pointing at his watch, it's time for me to go, time's up. Don't worry, it's going to be alright. The day after tomorrow you'll be transferred to a better jail. Be strong, hold on. I hope to see you soon. Don't worry, you'll soon be out of here. We'll do everything we can to get you out," Vovan says, waving his hand before he disappeared into the darkness.

"I'm counting on you," I shout after him, for some reason not believing his words.

Chapter 3. Part Two. Outside.

"Dymkov, I told you everything will be alright. Here's a report for the three months, and here is the profit – ten thousand dollars. Not too shabby, don't you think?"

"Ten grand is not bad," Dymkov replies, making a serious and slightly discontent face. "But this sum will go to Sam. You received a salary of sixty thousand rubles for the three months and returned ten grand to Sam, and what about me?"

"And this is for you. Here, as we agreed, your ten per cent commission off my salary," I take a bag of money out of my pocket with a smile.

"That's much better," Dymkov says with a big grin, stashing the envelope in his table drawer. "If we're done discussing money, why don't you go ahead and tell me about your relationship with GosNarkoKontrol[9]?"

"We seem to have settled everything, why?"

"They've been checking the club frequently, recently. We have nothing to be afraid of, we've got no drug circulation. But I wouldn't want them to shut Hemp down."

"Why would they shut it down? I don't have drugs in my store either. We have three months of negotiations behind us, everything has been settled. They tried to shut us down for propaganda, but I have some connections in the city that helped me straightened that out. Too bad they didn't let us use the seven-leaf marijuana symbol in commercials."

"Damn bastards!" Dymkov says, inhaling a joint that he has just fired up. What about 'Red Poppy' candies? Isn't that propaganda right there, Vasya?"

"The GosNarkoKontrol people told me that these are the last days of 'Red Poppy' candies. They are about to be renamed 'Red Valley' later on this year."

"They must be out of their minds. Instead of fighting heavy drugs, they're involved in some sort of nonsense."

"Damn it! Forget about the candies. I had to sign a paper saying I won't give any interviews without a comment from GosNarkoKontrol. Now I have a female officer who gives interviews together with me. These days any article about Hemp in the mass media ends with her comment: "GosNarkoKontrol cannot ban sales of clothes made from hemp, as it does not contain any narcotic substances. However, our youth should understand that hidden promotion of drugs is attached to it. This wear is not magic; entrepreneur Vasiliy Karavaev is using this infamous drug to make his dirty money on it."

"Assholes! It's okay to advertise booze and cigarettes, but it's not okay to sell clothes made from hemp. They want everybody to be alcoholics. They want everybody to be dumb. Look at their faces, Vasya," Dymkov says, all excited, pointing at a group of young people outside the window, drinking beer at the club entrance.

"Yeah….it's kind of hard to call that a face. They don't seem to be fortunate enough to be blessed with intellect. All they care about is getting some booze after work and getting in a fight. I can't see any other desires in their eyes."

"Exactly…" Dymkov adds after a long pause, taking a sweet cannabis bud out of a bag.

"It's good that Lisyutsky schmoozed GosNarkoKontrol for us. If it weren't for him, we wouldn't be able to sell our merchandize."

"How do you know Lisyutsky, Vasya? Tell me how you managed to make an appointment with the chief of GosNarkoKontrol?" Dymkov asks, reclining in an armchair, handing me an empty cigarette ready to be stuffed with marijuana.

"I've known Konstantin Sergeyevich Lisyutsky for a long time. A highly intelligent person, a professor, he opened the Psychology Department at the State University. He used to be my professor

[9]GosNarkoKontrol - Federal Drug Control Service of Russia.

at university. He wrote several books on drug abuse and drug addiction. For many years he's been actively fighting hard drugs, opening free rehabilitation centers and offering psychological support to former drug abusers around the city. Once when I was a student, he invited me to watch him work with junkies in one of those psychological support centers. He showed me some miraculous things. He was able to get registered junkies back from the other side, inducing a trance to make them believe in a happy life without drugs. He really put his soul into helping people and gave each of them a bit of his heart, receiving a pittance for his work. At that time I was exporting Chinese stereos from Poland. I was eager to help those people, so I gifted a stereo to their center. At that time minimal funds were allocated in the federal budget for such social projects. Lisyutsky has a good command of a unique technique of hypnosis. Giving up drugs is easy, he says, it only takes a week of going cold turkey. It takes a strong will not to resume taking drugs, and this strong will is usually something drug abusers don't have. And that is what he focuses on: making those people strong willed. Former junkies come to him during their hard times and tell him about their problems. He listens to them, puts them into a trance and sets them on leading a happy life without drugs. For somebody to fall into trance, he needs to listen to special relaxing music at that moment. To cut a long story short, my gift was just what was needed. It was then that Lisyutsky told me: 'If you are ever in trouble, give me a call. I will help you with anything I can.'"

"I just wonder, Vasya, how is it that your drug-fighting professor agreed to help our Hemp? Marijuana is a scheduled drug, isn't it?"

"Well, unlike GosNarkoKontrol, Lisyutsky knows the difference between light and heavy drugs. I've talked to him. He thinks that marijuana does less harm than alcohol or tobacco. One should beware of heroin and cocaine and their derivatives, everything else is toys."

"I wonder, Vasya, how did he manage to convince a GosNarkoKontrol colonel to let you sell your merchandize?"

"Oh, that was a hell of a circus. I can tell you, if you have time."

"I never do, Vasya. But I am interested to hear about your visit to GosNarkoKontrol."

"When Lisyutsky and I came GosNarkoKontrol and entered the colonel's room, he was in a meeting. The cops were sitting there with sour, hungover faces, drinking water and discussing the possibility of getting our store banned. They didn't expect me to show up with Lisyutsky. When the colonel saw us he jumped to his feet: 'Good morning, Konstantin Sergeyevich, we didn't expect to see you here. How should we take it? You are the main anti-drugs ideologist in town and you are here to defend this individual here today?' He pointed his finger at me. Lisyutsky said: 'Vasiliy has done nothing wrong. He doesn't sell drugs, one may say, he's on our side.' 'We don't understand you, Konstantin Sergeyevich,' the colonel made a face that was half surprised, half dumb. 'You shouldn't be surprised, comrade colonel. You've seen banners around the city advertising Hemp. Did you look at the slogan that's written there?' 'That's what we are here for, Konstantin Sergeyevich. We're having a meeting to discuss whether or not Hemp is propaganda of the drug cannabis,' the colonel said, pointing at a newspaper on his table that featured my picture and the heading 'How entrepreneur Karavaev became a cannabis dealer.' 'It's too bad, comrade colonel, that you haven't read their slogan. It says right there: 'Hemp… and no addiction.' Do you have any idea how the average Joe becomes a drug addict?' Lisyutsky asked him, and not waiting for him to reply, started to explain. 'Usually, a young person decides to try an illegal drug because it is considered cool in his circle of friends. He is not a child anymore, and by doing this he proves that he is an adult and he's not afraid of punishment. 'I also want to be cool' he declares to the world outside when trying ganja for the first time. So there, thanks to our 'entrepreneur Vasiliy', young men have an alternative for being cool without having to do drugs. Putting on clothes supposedly made from a 'drug', they automatically associate themselves with the 'cool, adult and advanced' category of people. Now they don't have to prove how cool they are by smoking these drugs. Not everyone wants to be a junky when they are young, but everyone wants to be cool. Nowadays almost every main character in contemporary movies and books smokes a joint at least once. Otherwise, he's not cool! That's our reality these days.' "There is some truth in your words, Konstantin Sergeyevich. Had you not come along, we would have made it illegal for your protégé to sell his merchandize,' the colonel said grinning, and looked at me with disdain. 'But since you've come today, Konstantin Sergeyevich, would you please rate our project,' the colonel said. "We want to lobby a law in the State Duma, according to which all students applying to university would have to pass a drug test in order to be admitted. Whoever doesn't pass would be turned around and kicked the hell out of the higher education system. How do you like our new project?' Lisyutsky opened his mouth with astonishment. 'This is a blatant abuse of human rights,' he said. The colonel replied: "What rights are you talking about? We shouldn't waste our time on junkies. You write books about the harm of drugs, Konstantin Sergeyevich. We should all fight this vice any way possible. Human rights will remain untouched.' Lisyutsky did not argue, he only added: 'Well, well, we will see. Then we left GosNarkoKontrol, got in my Jeep, and sat there in silence for a while. I took out my Amsterdam pipe and put some ganja into it. 'Would you like to try, Konstantin Sergeyevich, I grew this strain of marijuana myself. In Canada, California, Israel and some European countries they sell it in pharmacies, it is considered medicinal marijuana." Do you know, Dymkov, what his answer was? He said: 'I do it very rarely, but sometimes I allow myself to smoke with good people.' We had a puff of hydroponic ganja, reclined and started to discuss a group of young people passing by our car with bottles of beer in their hands and cursing. They looked exactly like the people who are drinking cheap booze outside the windows at your club entrance now. Once they finish, Dymkov, they will enter your club to smash someone's head in. Smoking pot is not a matter of 'like – don't like' for Lisyutsky. It's not a matter of mental helplessness or a matter of flirting with anarchists such as myself. For him, it's a matter of understanding the fact that the world we live in is not simple. Smoking pot with me is an opportunity for him to get to know the reasons behind mental struggles and methods of salvation and demise…"

"Vasya, why did you switch to talking about the club? What did your conversation with Lisyutsky result in?" Dymkov interrupts me after I lose my train of thought.

"Yeah, do you know what Lisyutsky told me? 'You're doing a good thing, Vasya. If somebody gives up alcohol thanks to weed and uses it to relax instead, the world will change for the better. Weed has helped many people abstain from the terrible habit of getting drunk every day. Many people have given up hard drugs thanks to it. Lots of people, smoking it occasionally, lead a socially responsible life and take care of their own business. And the most important thing is that everybody who quits drinking, also changes their social circle. If all they used to talk about was business, vodka and prostitutes, now they go to the movies and read books. They have increased their level of spirituality, so to speak. I wish the GosNarkoKontrol people could understand it. You have just seen yourself how they fight drugs. They put all drugs into one category. Heroin and marijuana are one and the same thing to them. How does the youth react to that? What can a young person think about it without the necessary information? 'If marijuana and heroin are the same thing, why not indulge in the latter?' This is how the new generation gets addicted to heavy drugs. We will see, Vasya, what your Hemp will turn out to be. Personally, as a Psychology Doctor, I don't see any threat to society coming from your project.'"

"If I didn't stop you, Vasya, you could go on talking for hours on end," Dymkov interrupts my story. "Well, Lisyutsky is a diamond, such wise people are rarely to be found in our city. Okay, Vasya, go take care of your business; I've plenty of things on my to-do list. Good job, I'll give the money to Sam later today and tell him about Lisyutsky."

31

Chapter 4. Part One. Inside.

For the first time in the last ten years I haven't been stoned for three days. It's my third day of a crystal clear, inflamed mind. I have no craving for anything that would get me high. My brain processes different options for getting out of this dead end, working at maximum speed. It seems like my brain is about to freeze, like an overloaded computer. Something has to be done. I have been denied a lawyer and a phone call, yet I am not accused of anything. What am I doing here? It's been three days since I've touched food – I have no appetite. The guards are starting to worry about me. The smiling guard brought me a cigarette and told me I would get it if I ate. I had to force myself to eat some rice with spicy dal sauce. I eventually managed to take a shower using a plastic bottle to get some warm water out of the tap and pour it all over myself with one hand. The heat is still excruciating. The gods must have joined forces to torture me to death for my sins. Only two weeks ago I bought a new expensive air conditioner for my house. I wish I had it here now. My overheated brain refuses to think about anything. I've been staring at mold on the wall for a few hours. I get brought out of my coma-like state by some familiar Russian speech. If it isn't Psyu, if it isn't crazy Psyu! How did she get here? Her loud blabbermouth voice is hard to mistake for anybody else's. Psyu is a long-term junky. She's been on cocaine for the last ten years or so; which is nothing out of the extraordinary, considering that her husband is the number one drug dealer in Goa. It is virtually impossible to talk to her about anything; you can only listen to her non-stop monologue of nonsense. Yet now it sounds to me like the voice of hope. You always hear her first, then see her.

"Psyu, how did you find out I got arrested?!"

"How? Your ex-wife called me from Thailand and told me you were in trouble. Somebody told her; I'm not sure who it was. I've bought you toothpaste and underwear. Now tell me, what happened?"

"Psyu, it looks like I'm in big trouble, I would even say, in deep shit."

Chapter 4. Part Two. Outside.

"Dymkov, it looks like we're in trouble."

"What now, Vasya, are GosNarkoKontrol after you again?"

"No, everything seems to be alright with them, although they are also a pain in the ass. Yesterday there was a good party in the club. Besides us, it was sponsored by another company that sells cannabis-flavored beer called Hemp."

"Vasya, why are you telling me about the party. I was there last night, we had a good crowd in."

"Dymkov, you left earlier, as usual, and later on that night the GosNarkoKontrol people visited us. Undercover cops were chasing me around the club all night. Wherever I went, they were after me. I didn't smoke a single joint all night. Towards morning they detained two of my friends. Thank God, they didn't have anything illegal on them. They interrogated them for two hours, asking questions about me. They asked them who I was and how long they had known me. They asked them if I was a drug dealer and so on and so forth."

"You should be more careful, Vasya. Are you still growing hydroponics[10] on your balcony?"

"Do you take me for a fool, Dymkov? I stopped doing it right after our store opened. I gave all the equipment to my friends. Now I get a share of the harvest. It's not much, but it's enough for my personal use. That's not the problem. We have sold almost all of the summer collection, and the new fall delivery is delayed."

"It's good that everything has been sold, but what's the problem with the new delivery?"

"Three months ago we had to return our winter collection because everything that had been shipped to us was defective."

"What do you mean, defective? Had they been smoking at the factory?"

"I don't know. They promised to redo everything in three to four months."

"Three to four months? Have they lost their minds? Who's going to need it in three months? People buy clothes for the upcoming season in advance. Our rent is five thousand dollars a month. We'll go bankrupt while they are redoing it."

"That's what I'm saying. We are in trouble."

"Trouble? I'd say we're in deep shit! What sort of contract did you conclude with them? Who is going to take responsibility for the delay with the collection?"

"I did warn you, Dymkov, that it's a new business and it's risky. Our suppliers totally understand this and they have refused to take responsibility for the term of the delivery. It's also a new business for them. They told me upfront: 'If you want to buy it – do; if not – don't!' So there is nobody to put the blame on; we'll have to think of something ourselves. But I think I have found a way out of this. Yesterday I spoke to an old friend who had just returned from India. He said that there is hemp merchandize everywhere in India."

"Yeah, I know their hemp merchandize: Manali charas and Kashmiri hashish, we'll get locked up for fifteen years for that kind of trade."

"No, he said it's clothes and accessories, all made out of hemp."

"Have you ever been to India, Vasya? They say it's dirty, with disease everywhere."

"I've always wanted to visit India but I've never had an excuse to go before."

"So why don't you go? The only thing is, who will manage the store?"

"Don't worry, my wife is pretty smart, she'll fill in for me while I'm gone."

---

[10]Hydroponics - a subset of hydroculture and a method of growing plants using mineral nutrient solutions, in water, without soil.

Chapter 5. Part One. Inside.

"Don't worry, everything's going to be alright," Psyu rattles like an exploding firecracker, handing me a bag with toothpaste and soap through the bars. "I'll help you find the best lawyer; here is your toothpaste, towel and a book called "The Unbearable Lightness of Being" by Milan Kundera. At least you'll have something to do in your spare time. I have already informed the embassy and called your family. Your wife will arrive soon, I've told her everything. What happened to you? Tell me quickly, we've only got two minutes."

"To cut a long story short, I didn't touch anybody, I was at home. The cops came to my place, arrested me, didn't find anything, said I was a drug dealer and locked me up here."

"Alright, that's enough. I will try to find out the details through my connections in the police department. I'll come back tomorrow at the same time and tell you everything. Hang in there, I'm off. Kisses."

Having watched the blonde disappear, I go back to counting paces around my cell. Psyu's words, even though she is a certified crazy junkie, give me a little hope. Her husband is a long-term cocaine dealer with a reputation. Hopefully, she knows how to get people out of jail in such situations. Three years ago Murtinian, her husband, was arrested with a kilogram of cocaine and three hundred grams of MDMA. Having served only one month, he was released after bribing the authorities with thirty thousand dollars. Maybe I can get out that way, too. Sure enough, I don't have thirty grand, but I am no Murtinian either.

The damn Sun is setting, finally. On a beach down by the ocean, you think of the Sun in a very different way. Sitting on the warm sand, enjoying the beautiful show, watching the huge ball of fire slowly sink into the water below the horizon, it wouldn't occur to anybody to refer to the Sun like that. Now it is as if it's mocking me, as it hides behind the tops of the trees. No matter what, today it has failed to nuke my brain. It becomes cooler and all of the scents become sharper. Ah there, it has finally disappeared behind the horizon. It smells of mold and shit in the cell. The stench of exhaust fumes coming from the street acts like a deodorant, masking the odor of human feces.

Chapter 5. Part Two. Outside.

Every country has its own inimitable smell. It is felt more acutely if you arrive in a new place by air. Every time I land in a new place, right after coming out of the plane I take a few seconds to inhale the new unfamiliar smell, so that it stays in my memory. My brain interprets it as foreign for only a few hours. Then it gets used to it and stops noticing the difference. Stepping onto the runway, I immediately feel the smell of this country. It smells of shit, exhaust fumes, incense and spices. The air is so hot and humid that it makes me cough.

"Well, hello, India!"

I need to take a cab and find a hotel. One week before my departure, I spent the whole evening sitting in my house in Russia with Alex Nicaragua, listening to the stories about his incredible adventures in India. As a result, I made a very important conclusion – you cannot trust anybody in this wonderful country. Looking at a crowd of cab drivers at the airport exit, I immediately recall the story about his first experience of getting around India. "Upon arrival, be sure to only take the government cabs," Alex told me, making a very serious face, as if somebody could kidnap me. "Otherwise they will take you miles away to visit their distant relatives who have a couple of vacant rooms. They can put a 'Hotel' sign on any booth and rent it out." "No, it won't happen to me," I thought then, laughing at Alex's adventures. Nevertheless, I took notes of the hotel names, districts, cities and various pieces of advice from the experienced traveler, Nicaragua. Coming out of the big glass doors, I realize that I have made my first mistake. All the government-owned companies providing cab services are located inside the airport, the area I have just left behind me. Well, well, Alex, thanks a lot for your advice, but it looks like I will have to make my path on Indian soil. No sooner have I stopped for a couple of moments to think it over, than a crowd of Indians gathers around me, making a lot of noise and grabbing me by my sleeves. "Hare Rama hotel, Hare Rama," I hear a familiar name that Alex had mentioned. "Hare Rama, Main Bazaar," a Muslim, terrorist-looking cab driver shouted loudly.

"Hare Rama, how much?"

"Five hundred."

Hearing this, all of the surrounding cab drivers, like a bunch of parrots, start to shout "Hare Rama" and "five hundred."

"OK," I say, pointing my finger at the bearded Muslim, who is wearing a white cap that somehow sticks to his head. In a moment, the crowd surrounding me becomes silent and I am no longer of interest to them.

"It won't fall apart, will it?" I ask the driver in Russian, pointing at a big rusty hole by the passenger seat.

"Don't worry, sit down please. Welcome to India."

Driving around Delhi at night reminds me of a scene from a horror movie, with the main character landing in a city where all the people are zombies. The Full Moon, mist crawling along the ground, a suspicious looking cab driver with red half-closed eyes, and people outside the window, moving slowly like zombies. The exhaust fumes make my throat itch. People wrapped in newspapers and dilapidated clothes are to be seen on most of the sidewalks. The piles of trash make me think that the city doesn't have any street cleaners. Only the sleepy cows wandering about destroy the harmony of this scene of urban collapse. How did they get here? What do they eat? A city with a population of twenty-five million people. It is hard to imagine cows wandering around Moscow at night. According to my friend, we should have reached the hotel within fifteen minutes, yet we have been driving for half an hour along suspicious narrow streets surrounded by Indian slums.

"Hey, monster, where is Hare Rama hotel?" I reach for the driver's shoulder in panic, suspecting him of some sort of trick.

"Don't worry, five minutes," the Bin Laden look-alike driver mutters, rubbing his red eyes with his fists.

In a few minutes the driver stops the car at a strange building, on which 'Mohammed Hotel' is written roughly in English on a grimy wall.

"Very good hotel, toilet, hot water, good quality, cheap," the driver says in an Indian accent, giving me a smile that exposes his mouth full of rotten teeth, pointing at a door that hangs off its hinges.

"What do you mean, Mohammed hotel? You bastard, take me to Hare Rama, right now!"

"Don't worry, this is my brother's hotel, good quality. Hare Rama bad, no room in Hare Rama."

Immediately he dials a number on his cell phone, handing it to me with the explanation: "This is the number of the Hare Rama hotel, you can ask them yourself, they will confirm that they don't have any vacant rooms." I take the cell phone and hear someone telling me some bullshit in Hindi.

"What the hell is going on, you bastard? Where have you taken me? Take me to Hare Rama right now, or else I will call the police."

"No police, sir, I will take you right to Hare Rama. It is nearby, only a fifteen-minute drive."

The Hare Rama hotel proves to be even scarier than the Mohammed hotel. My friend must have played a joke on me, sending me to this hole, I think, getting out of the rusty car. I should pay him back next time I see him. The hotel, if you could call it such, is situated on a street that was about a yard-wide. I have to drag my stuff down the dark street for another hundred yards from the place where the car stopped. Alright, well, I'll have to spend the night here. According to Alex, this is the place where all travelers stay at the beginning of their Indian trip. Observing the degree of cleanliness and general level of feng shui in the foyer, I conclude that people traveling around India are ascetic and not very demanding. The walls in the hotel must have been painted once in a hundred years, with the paint chosen by name rather than by color. Judging by the mold and chunks of paint falling off the walls, it has not been redecorated in at least fifty years. I give the receptionist five dollars and receive a key to a room with unwashed bed sheets with holes in them, and a noisy fan above the bed. It's a good thing there is water. I need to take a shower and get a bite to eat. "Hot water must be a luxury here," I think as I turn on the only tap, with water that is barely warm. Having taken a shower, I go downstairs in order to find out whether a foreign tourist can get any food at one am. The receptionist is lying in a chair, sleeping peacefully.

"Excuse me. Hey, dude, wake up! Eat, eat, is there anything I can eat here at this hour?" I say to the sleepy man, who stares back at me.

The Indian, who is only wearing an old shirt with holes and underwear, regains consciousness and starts trying to work out what I want. I have to explain it to him using mime. At last, the Indian laughs and shakes his head from side to side.

"Yes, yes, go up," he point his finger at the roof of the hotel. "We have a restaurant there; if the cooks are not asleep, they will feed you."

What I find on the roof reminds me of the hole-in-the-wall places from the pre-Perestroika era, which were never swept or mopped. It must be generally accepted in this country to only remove trash when it blocks the way, I think, moving empty bottles from the nearest table. The place is empty. Stepping toward the passage leading to the kitchen, I see several characters in oily clothes with holes, lying down on the tables preparing to go to sleep. Usually every time I travel abroad I manage to explain everything I need to people using my bad English. Here, for the second time in one night, I have to demonstrate my skills in mime to get my message across. This time it lasts twice as long as the conversation with the receptionist. The kitchen zombies refuse to understand what I am demanding, or pretend not to understand me, enjoying the free midnight performance. They must take me for somebody else! Russians don't give up so easily. Trying my hardest not to touch the oily kitchenware, I squeeze through the door and point my finger at a huge black pan with fried rice and vegetables: "For me, one." A fat Indian realizes there is no escape, spits his chewing tobacco onto the floor and starts to warm up some food for me. God, where the hell am I!? The fried rice with vegetables is completely devoid of taste. The only thing I can feel is hot chili with an odor of rancid oil. "How can they eat this?" I think, chasing each spoonful with water. "Or did they put so much chili in on purpose, so that I wouldn't bother them again at night?" I decide to find a good place to eat first thing in the morning. And buy some hashish, too. I can only accept this type of reality if I'm high. Just like any other kind of reality. Hundreds of flies buzzing in a cloud over my plate try to get into my mouth. After force-feeding myself half of the dish, I proceed straight to my room to escape the pesky flies and smiling cooks watching me eat. I need to go to sleep. I've got a new interesting day ahead of me. Hopefully, this nightmare will end when I leave the hotel building.

Chapter 6. Part One. Inside.

I could definitely use some sleep now, but my brain just won't switch to relaxation mode, like a broken record it's repeating: "From ten to twenty, from ten to twenty." Blood is pulsing in my head. I've got to do something. What do Russian inmates do when the cops harass them? In my childhood I heard stories from my older friends about inmates slitting their wrists. Back then I couldn't understand what they did it for. But now I'm coming to realize why. Should I do it, too? I'd be able to get some sleep in the hospital. Tomorrow they will take me to the court for the first time. A suicide attempt would impress the judge. This is bullshit! I didn't have any drugs at home! I may be able to explain to the judge that my case has been falsified. I could tell the judge that I slit my wrists because I saw no way out of this situation. But what can I use to do it? I probably won't be able to chew my wrist with my teeth. There is a good chance of finding something in the trash lying on the floor. I'm lucky again! A small piece of tin that used to be a stand for mosquito coils, rusty and dirty, is sitting in the middle of the trash pile. But, I don't intend to die. And this piece of tin must be home to all known bacteria, from syphilis to hepatitis. Although, I must admit that syphilis and hepatitis are still better than ten years in jail. I need to try and sharpen this thing. The concrete floor, polished by the bare feet of inmates over the course of many years, is an ideal whetstone. My small knife looks more like a fragment of a saw with rare teeth. A few moments later, I'm still looking at my veins, hesitant to touch them. But, like a damaged hard drive, my brain keeps repeating: "From ten to twenty." I need to go for it. I must. My skin won't cut; it tears. It is strange indeed that I don't feel any pain. First, second… now the fifth cut. With every strike, my brain calms down a little. A vein finally appears in my split-open skin. Another few strikes and thick red liquid starts to pour from my vein, pulsing to the sound of my heartbeat.

"Hey you, monkey!" I shout to the sleeping guard through the bars. "I need a doctor, hospital," I show him my bleeding arm.

The sleepy guard slowly starts to realize that I have just caused him some trouble. The expression of his face tells me he is not too worried about the blood on my arm. He must be visualizing being reprimanded for falling asleep while on duty and letting a foreigner make a suicide attempt. The blood is starting to clot, becoming a thick wound. I have to act fast, or else I won't be taken to the hospital.

"Doctor! Hospital! I am khatam[11]!!!" I start to shout, lying on the floor pretending to be having a fit.

Reaching for his cell phone, the guard starts justifying himself into it. The sleepy person on the other end interrupts him and starts to shout loudly, accusing him of all sins.

"Ok, ok, sir," the guard finishes the conversation, looking at me threateningly. "In fifteen minutes they will take you to the hospital. You got me in a load of trouble now. I won't get my bonus and it's likely that I'll be punished. Did you hear my boss shouting?"

---

[11]Khatam - 'done', 'over', 'end' (Hindi).

"Oh, it's you who's in trouble is it? What do you need money for? You're guarding my cell all the time. You get food and clothes for free, and your salary is enough to buy booze. I am the one who is in trouble here. I am looking at ten years. And my family is left without money, who is going to feed them?"

Pouring some water over my open wound, I see the blood running down my arm again. My blood streams down onto the concrete floor, mixing with water and forming patterns. I'm sure I've seen this picture before somewhere.

Chapter 6. Part Two. Outside.

Blood is pouring all over the curb, down to the sewer, where it becomes a dirty pink liquid. I am standing a few yards away from my hotel, dazed and confused by what I have just seen. I have just watched an old man begging for money, cough and fall down on the ground. His coughing immediately turned into the roaring of an animal. Dark red clots of blood started coming out of his mouth. And there he lies with glass eyes and blood streaming out of his mouth. For the first time in my life I am watching somebody die in front of my eyes. I stand paralyzed, not knowing how to react to this. Passers-by are knocking into me with their shoulders, elbows and bags. Nobody is paying any attention to the man lying in a puddle of blood. I reach out for the sleeve of a salesman in the store across the street, pointing at the corpse. Without expressing any astonishment or fear, the salesman looks at the dead man and calmly concludes: "Khatam." What a wonderful country, where nobody pays any attention to a man that has just died on the street. What a nice start to my journey! It is strange that not only are the locals not paying attention to the person lying in a puddle of blood, but the tourists aren't either. Trying not to look into each other's eyes, they hurry on. Wearing weird clothes, the white-skinned tourists remind me of medieval characters. Simple, one-size-fits-all pants and plain, collar-less shirts. I get the feeling that they all want to look like locals. Only the huge rucksacks on their backs give them away as tourists. Out of the whole flow of people, I am the only one who looks like he just arrived yesterday. I should get rid of my trendy velvet pants. Compared to the simple clothes that other tourists, wear I must look like a millionaire.

Chapter 7. Part One. Inside.

To my disappointment, I don't manage to get any sleep while in the hospital. Having fixed my wounds with a rusty medicinal needle, the doctors declare that I will survive, give me some sedative pills and send me back to my cell. "I've got to do something!" my poor brain starts playing the usual tune again. Should I try to escape? Jump out at the intersection and run for my life? But where to? I must get out of here somehow. My chances of doing it right now are equal to zero. I'll get caught and then ten years in jail will be guaranteed. There are three cops from the drug police and two jail guards together with me in the police car.

"Hey, Neanderthal, will you see your boss today?" I ask a tall Indian with a scar on his hand.

"Yes, why? Do you want me to tell him something?"

"Tell him that I've understood everything. I'm ready to pay him money, just like Tamir. Tell him that."

"OK, he will stop by your cell before the hearing," the officer smiles and hands me a cigarette.

Before leaving me alone in my cell, each of the people accompanying me makes me promise that I will not try to slit my wrists again. The Indian guard gives me a cigarette. Having taken two Valium pills that the doctor gave me, I quickly fall into a deep sleep. I dream of a house: a big, spacious Indian house with lots of rooms. I'm standing at the window and notice police cars pulling up outside. The cops get out and start to knock on my door.

"Open the door, sir, this is the police. Don't resist, your house is surrounded."

At this moment I realize that I have a suitcase full of drugs in my possession. I start rushing about the house. I must hide them somewhere! No, I must run! No, I must hide the drugs first! The loud sound of the iron door drags me out of my sleep, relieving me of the need to make such a serious decision – whether I should run or hide the suitcase full of drugs. Pashish himself, the chief of the drug police, is standing in front of me. Before entering the cell, he starts shouting something in a language I don't understand.

"Why did you do this?" he points at the bandage on my arm. "I will arrange for another five years in jail for you, if you ever attempt to do it again."

"I understand everything, sir. It will not happen again."

"Why did you do this?"

"I have a little daughter going to school here, in India. My wife has a breast tumor; she needs money for her surgery. You've taken all my money, how am I supposed to look my child in the eyes and tell her she can't go to school? What will I tell my wife? Should I tell her I don't have the money for her surgery, that I'm looking at ten to twenty years in jail, and that I don't have money to hire a lawyer?"

"You gave us a problem, you've only got yourself to blame," Pashish deadpans, giving me a very serious look.

"Everybody makes mistakes, give me a chance. I am ready to pay you any amount of money every month, just like Tamir."

"I don't need anything from you. Tamir is my friend. Of all the Russians, he's the only one who pays me money. Promise me that you will never try to commit suicide again, and I will help you."

"I promise."

"What did you use to cut your hand?"

Pointing at the pile of trash and hundreds of flies buzzing around it, I feel like a schoolboy that has just messed up and gotten himself into trouble.

"I found it there."

Pashish frowns scornfully, turns around in silence and steps out, leaving me alone in my cell again.

Chapter 7. Part Two. Outside.

There are flies everywhere, thousands of them. The moment I stop moving, the nasty creatures begin to tickle my face in the most disgusting manner. I am hungry. However, everything sold on the street is surrounded by a cloud of flies, which swarm over from the nearby sewage pipes to land on the food. The memory of the puddle of blood is still resonating in my head. The restaurant menus contain names of dishes that are unknown to me. Each time I enter a restaurant, I point at a random item on the menu in the hope of getting something tasty. After waiting half an hour I am finally brought a cup with a liquid of a questionable color and a piece of local bread. Having taken a few sips, I start coughing due to the huge amount of chili they have put in it. I start to gasp, my eyes full of tears. It looks like I need to start getting used to chili. I try to chase down my meal with some tea, only to realize that they have also put spices in my tea. Just like the restaurant personnel, the street sellers refuse to understand me. I can only buy whatever I can point my finger at. I have been to many countries, but this is not like any other country I've seen before. Everything is different here. The dirty narrow streets are overcrowded and stuffed with everything that moves. A lively crowd drifts past the shabby shop-windows, filled with God-knows what. The moving mass consists of bike-cabs, pedestrians, dogs, cows, and wagons with all kinds of crap. Sometimes I see elephants and blue sheep pass by me, and all of it is diluted with a multicolored mass of humanity. It is impossible to stop in the middle of this living stream. No sooner do I stop, than gaping tourists immediately start bumping into me. You can't even stand on the sidewalk-shores of the stream. Seeing me as a potential customer, workers of street stalls, hotels and restaurants immediately start to drag me by the hand. Drug dealers and street touts are the most annoying. They follow me through the crowd and continually try to get me to buy something. I can only get rid of them by entering a store, as hard as it is to call these wretched premises located on the ground floor stores. Nevertheless, there is a lot of buying and selling of some weird merchandize going on inside them. There are no European style stores at all. Everything sold in these stores looks like it is either defective or a laughable fake. I see clothes made from hemp, but their quality leaves much to be desired. They aren't meant to be sold in my hemp store. They aren't fit to be sold anywhere. In the end I manage to find some appropriate hemp clothing, having walked around the whole Main Bazaar area. After going through a hundred kilos of different stuff that is either discolored, moldy or with holes made by rats, I am able to put together a package to be shipped to my homeland. I am surprised to see 'Made in Nepal' labels on the hemp clothes. "I might have to go to Nepal," I think, for some reason realizing that I haven't been stoned in a long while. Too bad I only have one month; that isn't enough. I'll go to Nepal next time.

And now I need to get some food and some hash. No, first I need to get some hash, then some food. It's taking me too long to establish a connection with the local dealers. Either my basic English is too basic, or the local pidgin language is too pidgin. It doesn't take long before I find the drug dealers. No sooner do I stop moving within the living stream and look around, than two unshaven characters came up to me and offer to sell me some hash. I follow them down a back alley, where one of them takes a matchbox-sized piece out of his sock. The drug dealers, who looked like Azerbaijanis, turn out to be Kashmiris who have come to Delhi to work from the territory disputed by India and Pakistan. Having told me how neither Pakistanis nor Indians like Kashmiris, they offer me a price of thirty dollars. Knowing that a piece this big would be worth no less than three hundred dollars in Russia, I still knock the price down to twenty and, happily, run to my hotel to get stoned in peace. On the way to Hare Rama I finally spot some food that doesn't look disgusting. In a big cast iron pan, a street food seller is frying potatoes, onions and tomatoes in filthy brown oil and swiftly making sandwiches out of them. A crowd of Israeli tourists has gathered around him, hungrily devouring the sandwiches. Squeezing through the crowd and pointing my finger at the pan, I tell the seller: "One." The Indian, as though making fun of me, asks: "What one?" Losing my temper, I point again at a slice of fried bread. The Indian swiftly wraps a newspaper around the slice of bread, hands it to me and pronounces with a smile: "Two rupees."

"You could have put something in the sandwich," I say in Russian, pointing at the wrap.

The Indian unwraps the newspaper, waiting for additional instructions. I point at the pile of fried vegetables, but the seller keeps waiting for something else.

"Why are you staring at me? Put the filling into the sandwich," I say in Russian, trying to keep cool.

The seller quickly puts a fried tomato on the bread, covers it with another slice and starts to wrap it up.

"Stop, stop," I start to shout, showing my discontent, pushing away the wrap he is handing to me. "Look at the sandwiches you made for the Jews, why are you giving me this empty one?"

The Indian unwraps the sandwich once again, puts a fried egg in and pours some ketchup on it.

"Ten rupees."

"Here's a twenty, give me change."

"No change," the Indian makes a gesture with his hands that is apparently supposed to denote the absence of change.

What kind of country is this? They are all crooks!

"Choke on your change," I say, taking my sandwich.

When I get back to my room, I unwrap the sandwich and discard the oily newspaper, happy to have something to eat. To my disappointment, the smell of the rancid oil kills my appetite completely. A big fat drop of ketchup falls off the sandwich onto the floor. Instantaneously, my brain retrieves the fresh memories of the morning's corpse and the stream of blood flowing down into the muddy sewer. Sudden stomach spasms cause me to dash to the toilet. Having roared into the toilet bowl for some time, I calm down and flush the disgusting sandwich away. I must do something. It would be a disgrace to just go back home. I need to smoke. Smoking has always helped me find a way out of hopeless situations. Having put together a device for smoking from foil and an empty plastic bottle, I take my first two puffs in this country.

47

Chapter 8. Part One. Inside.

It's strange. I haven't smoked hash for four days and I don't feel like it at all. I only have one desire – to get out of here as soon as possible. I am ready to do anything. I need to promise the cops that I will give them all the drug dealers, if they'll just let me go. And once I am free, good luck on trying to catch me. I'll cross the border with Nepal, and flee to Russia from there. To hell with this country. Of course, I won't really give them anybody. Although, the bitch that I owe for my current place of residence surely deserves the same kind of punishment. If only I could get out of here. I'll never use anything again. The damn drugs have led me here to this prison cell. I don't want to spend the rest of my life in this place. The whole pink, illusory world in my head is starting to fall apart. What have I been doing here for the last five years? Who am I? A psychedelic revolutionary trying to change the world for the better, or a coward who fled from the hardship and complications that he didn't want to deal with in Russia? Why am I here, in jail? Do I actually deserve this? Or is this some ridiculous mistake? The door opens loudly.

"Get ready, we're going to court," a skinny cop, looking like an Indian monkey, says to me.

"That won't take long, I have nothing to get ready. Let's go."

The building I'm escorted to looks like a poor copy of an English court. Of the primness and grandeur that the Indians inherited from the Portuguese, only badly repaired shabby furniture and worn out tiles on the floor remain. The judge, wearing a classic English gown, looks more like a parody of a judge and does not inspire any trust. The chairs squeak and the fans rotate noisily.

"Drugs were found in your possession. Would you like to say anything?" the judge turns to me, observing me critically.

"What drugs? Show me my drugs? I did not have any drugs!"

The judge, an aged Indian wearing glasses, starts to laugh out loud, pointing his finger at me. The policemen join him.

"What kind of circus is this? Give me a lawyer and an interpreter! I don't understand a damn word you're saying," I begin to shout angrily in Russian.

Chapter 8. Part Two. Outside.

"Excuse me, do you speak Russian?" I ask a young couple making out at the hotel entrance.

"No, we don't speak Russian" a guy with a long black hair replies in broken Russian. "When I was in the military, there were a lot of Jews from the former USSR, so I can curse well in Russian," he says, trying to stroke his girlfriend's ass inconspicuously.

"There's no need to curse. My name is Vasya. I came from Russia yesterday and my English is very bad. I can't even buy food. I've just bought some hash and I don't feel like smoking it alone. Would you like to join me?"

"Why not? We like to smoke. We're staying in Room seven."

"And I'm in Room nine. We're almost neighbors, come to my room."

After his pretty girlfriend nods in approval, the young man gestures for me to enter the hotel.

"My name is Yair, and my girlfriend's name is Edi. We've just bought a good chillum and we want to try it. Do you smoke chillum?" he asks, taking a clay pipe out of a nice leather case.

"I've been smoking for a long time, but I've never used this kind of pipe."

"This is the traditional way of smoking here in India. If you've never done it, watch carefully and repeat after us." Yair nips off a small pea-size piece of hash and begins to crumble it into a small bowl made of polished coconut.

Then he takes out a cigarette and dries it thoroughly with a lighter, blackening the paper. After that he breaks the cigarette open with one elegant move and empties it into the bowl with the hash.

"Mix it well, while we're preparing the chillum," with a quick, elegant movement he tears two thin strips of cloth from the kerchief he is wearing around his neck. Edi takes one piece and wraps it tightly around a thin bamboo stick.

"This is called a 'stick', you wrap a 'safi' around it, so that you can clean the chillum after you smoke it," Yair takes the second piece of cloth and wraps it around the narrow end of the clay pipe. He puts a clay hexagonal stone into the wide end of the chillum and stuffs it with the mixture I have prepared.

"Here, now the chillum is ready for smoking. You usually start by reciting mantras and then smoke in high spirits. They smoked this way a thousand years ago, they still smoke this way today; so let us not depart from tradition. You take one deep puff and hand it to whoever is on your right-hand side, round the Shiva circle," I start to ask why it is passed to the person on your right-hand side and not the other way round, but Yair interrupts me, continuing his interesting lecture.

"The most important thing is to not touch the chillum with your lips. If you ignore that rule, nobody will ever smoke with you. The piece of cloth at the end of the chillum serves as a filter. You put your hand around it and it becomes an extension of the chillum, then you inhale, only touching your hand with your lips. You can suck your fist all you want."

Showing me by example, Yair first puts the chillum up to his forehead, closing his eyes for a second, and then to his lips. Edi starts to recite a mantra, loudly and melodically, enchanting me with unknown, melodic sounds: "Bom Bolenath, Sabke Sath, Bom Shiva, Bom Shankara, Bom!" Firing the chillum up, Yair rapidly takes several shallow puffs, transforming the tobacco and hash into a small red ball of fire sticking out of the clay pipe. Yair goes first, then his girlfriend, then me. "These people in India are pretty hardcore," I think, trying not to faint. I feel as if the smoke is penetrating my brain directly, in a cool concentrated state. Mesmerized by this magic effect, I sit motionless for several minutes, watching them clean the chillum thoroughly.

"Not bad at all, to inhale a dried cigarette and one third of a gram of hash in three puffs."

After cleaning it, Yair proudly hands the still warm chillum to me.

"Here, look: an Italian master's work."

I hold the clay pipe up to the sunlight and see that the space inside is as even and polished as the barrel of a gun.

"It is made for one cigarette, exactly three puffs. We bought it today for two hundred dollars, a good chillum can't be cheaper than a hundred," Yair proclaims, proudly taking back the clay pipe. "There are lots of three-dollar chillums everywhere around here; don't be in a hurry to buy them, that crap is for the tourists. Once you have traveled across India for a while, you'll be able to tell the difference."

"So, you are traveling, are you?" I ask them, surprised, watching the Israeli carefully putting the chillum back into the case.

"What else is there to do in India? We worked as waiters in Israel for a year and now we plan to travel around India. We're headed down South now. We lived in the Himalayas for three months before. If only you knew, the kind of charas there… All of the Himalayas are covered with cannabis, all the locals deal in charas. That's all the local economy is based on."

"What is charas?" I ask, expecting it to be something made from cannabis.

"We've just smoked hashish, it is made in Kashmir. Kashmiris climb the mountains, rub the hemp flowers with their hands, then collect everything that has stuck to their hands and wrap it in palm leaves; that's why it is hard and you can discern traces of palm leaves on it. Charas is a freshly picked kind of hashish. They don't dry it, it is as soft as cream, it smells like Himalayan grass, and it gets you higher than any hashish. So why did you come to India. Aren't you traveling?" Yair asks me suddenly, checking out my trendy pants.

"As a matter of fact, I'm on a business trip. I'm looking for hemp, have you heard of such a material. It is made from marijuana."

"Of course we have. They sell hemp clothes in Israel, too. It's very fashionable now and relatively expensive."

"I own a store in Russia called Hemp. I've come to India to buy something new for my store."

"You want to go to Nepal to look for hemp. It's all exported from there. Nepal is a beautiful place."

"I've already realized that I'll have to go to Nepal; next time I will get there, for sure. I have pretty much bought everything I need. I'm thinking about going to Goa for a couple of weeks and then back to Russia. By that time the package with hemp will have reached Russia, and I'll have to sell it."

"Actually, we're also headed to Goa. We wanted to stop by in Pushkar in Rajasthan for a week on the way. You can come with us, if you want."

51

Chapter 9. Part One. Inside.

"Psyu, what's going on? The judge said that drugs were found in my possession."

"Yeah, dude, you're in trouble – the cops stated in the charge sheet that twenty grams of MDMA were found. If it had been less than ten grams, you would have been released on bail. With more than ten grams you're looking at ten to twenty years in jail."

"The cops told me that, but they didn't find anything on me."

"You must have stepped on their toes at some point."

"I can guess where, but this is getting completely out of hand."

"There is nothing you can do about it, you've been framed. You're in trouble, deal with it. How is your hand? Why did you slit your wrists? Don't you want to live anymore?"

"I do. It's an old prison trick. I was trying to scare them so they wouldn't add drugs to my case."

"And? How did that go? Did you succeed?"

"They couldn't care less," I say sadly, sitting down near the bars.

"Take it easy, the day after tomorrow you'll be transferred to another jail with better conditions and less mosquitos. William is the best lawyer for drugs cases. He got my Murtinian out of here with a kilogram of cocaine. Here, sign the papers. If he gets you out of here, you'll pay him five thousand bucks."

My lawyer standing next to Psyu, who looks no different to the Indian cops, hands me a pen and some paper through the bars.

"Sign this, it is your contract for his services."

Having taken back the papers with my signature, William starts quickly explaining something to me, pausing so that Psyu can translate what he is saying to me.

"Listen carefully. Tomorrow you and the witnesses will go to your place with a search warrant," Psyu starts to interpret what the lawyer is saying, trying not to miss a word. "Do you have anything illegal at home?"

"But they have already been to my place and didn't find anything, right?"

"According to the official charge, you were detained in the morning selling drugs on the street opposite the school."

"Psyu, you're not confusing things, are you? This is bullshit. Have you used anything this morning?"

"I haven't used anything yet," Psyu interrupts me resentfully, rubbing her nose. "As a matter of fact, I have made up my mind to give up drugs. I'll soon be leading a healthy lifestyle."

"Yeah sure; I've been hearing that for five years now."

"I can't do it anymore, now that I'm an official representative of the Russian Embassy in India. I didn't graduate from the FSB[12] school for nothing."

"So what do you do at the embassy?" I ask her doubtfully, imagining Psyu snorting cocaine with the consul.

"I am an official interpreter with our embassy now. I even received a certificate. In the case of a nuclear war or some other calamity, I will be evacuated to Russia on the first plane, along with the embassy officers."

"Psyu, can you go on with interpreting, I'm not all that interested in hearing about nuclear wars right now."

"So listen and don't interrupt. In order to be released on bail, you can have on you less than one kilogram of hashish, less than one hundred grams of cocaine, less than two hundred and fifty grams of heroin, less than twenty kilograms of marijuana, or less than ten grams of MDMA. Anything higher than that is considered a commercial quantity, and thus a serious offense. That is why I'm asking you again, do you have anything illegal in your house?"

"I have a small marijuana plant and some mushrooms. The plant is young, about twenty grams, not more. A hallucinogenic mushroom has started growing, but as far as I know, psilocybin mushrooms are not illegal. Synthetic psilocybin is scheduled, but nobody has bothered to learn how to extract it from the mushroom. The chief of the drug police, Pashish, didn't even notice the hydroponics cupboard or the mushroom plantation when he came to my house."

"Don't worry, tomorrow they will notice. But so much the better. The quantity is below the minimum, you won't be locked up for this. Your mushrooms and weed won't be added to your case, on the contrary, they may distract their attention during the search. You don't have anything else in there, do you? Where did you buy the MDMA? Was it Apollo, by any chance?" Psyu suddenly switches to a different subject.

"I didn't have any MDMA on me. Psyu, don't you believe me? I didn't buy anything from Apollo either.

"I don't give a shit about whether you're lying to me or not. You've fallen foul of Pashish somehow. If you choose to, you will tell me. I'll see you next time, in another jail. I've got nothing more to say. Say goodbye to William. Kisses. I've got to run."

Chapter 9. Part Two. Outside.

Traveling halfway across India with my new friends, I smoke chillums with them virtually everywhere. We smoke in cars, bike-cabs, buses and trains. The acceptance of smoking hashish in a chillum can be felt through the reaction we get from the people surrounding us. Sometimes the people traveling on the same bus with us would say something against a cigarette being lit up, but never against a chillum. No sooner have we recited the mantra praising Lord Shiva (to whom a divine bird is

---

[12]FSB - (Federal Security Service of the Russian Federation) - the principal security agency of the Russian Federation.

said to have brought a cannabis leaf) than a neighbor joins in our praise of the Indian gods. "Bom Shiva, Bom Shankara," every Indian knows phrase this from childhood. Were currently making our way through the empty state of Rajasthan, enjoying smoking Himalayan charas. The couchette car with shabby seats we are in seems terribly exotic, I can't recall the last time I was in one. Three dirty, noisy fans buzz overhead. Sweet and aromatic, the cloud of charas is instantaneously sucked out the open window, blending with the dull desert scenery. Policemen passing by us don't pay any attention. I feel the inebriating smell of freedom again. Just like in Amsterdam, people smoking hashish don't bother anybody. Will I ever see times like these in Russia? I think I might, but definitely not in the near future. I could start out by opening Hemp clothes stores in all the major Russian cities. If I succeed in this, people will become more tolerant of cannabis in a few years. If hemp was freely talked about across the country, marijuana would cease to be considered a drug. Indeed, many countries have acknowledged that tobacco and alcohol are far more dangerous than ganja. It's too early for our society to legalize marijuana, but we could at least decriminalize it, like they did in Amsterdam. When society is ready for it, Sam will be able to lobby a bill in the State Duma allowing citizens to possess a minimal quantity of hashish or marijuana. Will it ever be possible to see happy faces in the streets instead of gloomy ones? Right now it's hard to believe. The alcohol magnates will do anything to stop that from happening, as marijuana could become serious competition for their business. But, as Lisyutsky puts it, it only takes ten per cent of the population to officially admit to smoking, for the rest of the people to reconsider the necessity of alcohol in their lives, provided there is such a wonderful alternative available. If that happens, no alcohol oligarchs will be able to stop us. I gaze out the window thinking about my role in life – could it be possible that I will be able to influence events in my country? A butterfly spreading its wings in Japan can cause a tornado in Brazil. I must take my chances, I am ready to become that ganja-loving butterfly. Strange pictures, unusual people and animals, slide past the window; but I am not seeing them anymore. In my thoughts I am in Russia. I feel like Che Guevara. I love my homeland but detest the scumbags living there. Since my childhood my soul refused to relate to all the shit that my compatriots radiated. We saw different countries on TV, both near and far. The faces of those people on the black-and-white screen looked more human than those around me. It seemed to me that the gloomy faces that surrounded me everywhere were endemic to Russia only. The rest of the human world had built a border so that they didn't have to see the dumb grin of the Russian drunkard. Many years later, when I went abroad for the first time, I confirmed my theory that the center of all evil is located in Russia. The further I got from Russia, the more happy and joyful were the faces I met. I could always tell my countrymen from other foreigners, regardless of which country I was in. The main differentiating factor was in their eyes. Their confident step and condescending attitude to everyone else around them hid the darting, self-conscious eyes of a slave. Their eyes lacked freedom. The freedom that makes people open their heart and smile at other people. My fellow countrymen's eyes almost always expressed a hidden fear and uncertainty, which they masked with aggression. Our spirit of freedom was suppressed by tsars, prime ministers and presidents for way too long. In order to get rid of this fear, the whole nation drank, and drank hard. Ever since the times of Peter the Great, our people had been alcoholized on a government level. People's freedom was taken away and replaced with booze. If my country had an alternative to alcohol – light drugs, psychedelics to be precise, substances that alter the human mind – people would be able to make a quantum leap in their perception of reality and catch up with the progressive world. The train keeps rolling on and I dream that, one day, free happy people will inhabit my country. The same way that the first psychedelic gurus dreamt some thirty or forty years ago. Many of them traveled across India, just like me, trying to find answers to the questions that they couldn't answer at home. Just like me, they probably took this train headed to the psychedelic capital of the world – Goa. The names of the pioneers of the psychedelic movement pop into my head: Dr. Timothy Leary, a Harvard professor; Stanislav Groff, a doctor and scientist who introduced holotropic breathing to the world; Robert Anton Wilson, a philosopher who changed my perception of the world; Terrence McKenna, a scientist who devoted his entire life to studying psychedelic plants and their effect on the human mind. All of them and their many supporters dreamed about changing the world around them for the better. Can I be holding a means of changing the world in my hands, too? My heart begins to beat faster, and my brain, covered with cannabinol crystals, paints pictures of a happy future for the whole country. I can see my happy countrymen smiling at each other, I can see a president with clever and honest eyes. I can see my country not being involved in any wars, and not having any hungry or homeless people. But, of course, a millennium will pass before society reaches that level. Is it possible to speed up the process of evolutionary development? Once upon a time, after the ice age, Neanderthals made a quantum leap in their perception thanks to the micro-doses of psychoactive compounds that got into their food. During a short period of some three millennia, the human brain tripled in size. Maybe now is the time to make another quantum leap, and break the stagnation that our society is drowning in. All we need is to alter the perception of ten per cent of the population. Shortly thereafter, it will hit the rest of the population, like an avalanche. But that is a concern for the future; right now I have a real task – hemp. I have a plan and I will succeed.

Chapter 10. Part One. Inside.

Today I will be transferred to another prison. I recollect scenes from movies where the main character gets locked up and continues struggling for his life and for justice to prevail. It's weird; I never thought I'd end up in prison. Every time I had to do something illegal, I would find out what it would cost me beforehand. What do I know about prison? From the childhood stories told by my neighborhood friends' older brothers, I know that a lot of unwritten laws exist. I know that the weak and the 'bitches[13]' sleep by the toilet. I know that you shouldn't have anything to do with the bitches, otherwise you'll be made into a bitch yourself and will be sent to live by the 'can'. According to my friends' brothers, the life of the bitches is hell. They are called 'roosters' and play the role of slaves. They are raped, beaten, and forced to wash everybody's clothes and mop the toilets. No, that kind of life is not for me. I need to find the piece of metal that I used to slit my wrists; I may need to use it as a knife. What is waiting for me in the new prison? I must behave appropriately right from the beginning. If anything happens, I'll smack whoever it is in the face without thinking about the consequences. What if the only vacant space is by the toilet? I'll have to find the weakest person in the cell and make him move. Are these really my thoughts? What have I become? Who am I? I must calm down; everything will be alright. I will succeed in everything. Having found the piece of metal with stains of blood from my veins in the pile of trash, I hide it inside the sole of my rubber sandal.

"Vasiliy, ready! Go transfer, Mapusa Lock Up Jail," an Indian guard shouts, opening the door.

At last, to get away from this hell. I climb into a small Mahindra car, a caricature of a Jeep, and drive into the unknown, with freedom shimmering through the windows. What is freedom? Everyone has their own definition: for some, it is synonymous with pleasure that is obtainable upon request. For others, it is the ability for unrestricted movement. So what is my definition of freedom? What have I been deprived of? I'm coming to realize that for me freedom is being able to be close to my loved ones. How's life treating my girls? My daughter, Vasilinka, and my wife, Lena? They must be going out of their mind at the news about me. What an idiot I am. To hell with the psychedelic revolution. Who needs it? Those idiots that have surrounded me lately? Evolution of perception, a quantum leap, freedom, independence… Did they ask me to alter their consciousness? Do I know the meaning of these beautiful words? Did they want freedom as much as I want it now? I'll probably have to explain to my baby why she can't go back to school this year, because we have no money. What an idiot I am!

"We're here, get out," the guard says, slowly opening the back door of the car.

---

[13]Prison bitch - an otherwise heterosexual prisoner forced into sexual submission to one or more stronger prisoners.

A one-story Portuguese building with a brick roof and a facade surrounded by chiku and mango trees growing around it. Iron bars instead of doors. Approaching the entrance, I recall crazy Psyu's instructions: "You can barely speak English, that is your biggest advantage for the court. And don't sign anything without me or your lawyer." The jail warden, a five foot tall Indian with a strong body and faggy voice, asks me in English: "Sir, do you understand where you are?"

"I don't speak English."

"You are in jail, do you have anything illegal on you?"

"I don't speak English."

"This Russian, just like all the rest, doesn't seem to understand a word I am saying. Search him and bring in his stuff."

A guard takes a pile of dirty laundry, a metal plate, a mug and half a bar of soap out of the locker.

"Here's a towel. Wrap it around you, take off all your clothes and sit down on the floor," the guard explains to me with gestures.

An Indian inmate that has just been brought in is doing the same thing. Having refused to sit down on the floor for some strange reason, he gets slapped so severely that he falls over. A small bag of tobacco drops out from between his legs. The guard slaps him again a few times and throws his things at him. Following his instructions, I sit down on the floor.

"You may put your clothes back on," the jail warden smiles and throws some dirty rags at me. "This is your bed now. Welcome to Mapusa Jail."

I need to be very careful and pay attention to details. The first day in a new jail. I am escorted down a corridor with cells along it. They all have iron bars instead of doors. I notice a pair of human eyes glaring in the dark. Somebody is shouting: "Foreigner, foreigner, Russian!" Everything reminds me of a zoo, with big apes sitting in cages.

"Cell number four," the guards open the door with a clang.

Seven pairs of eyes stare at me curiously. I silently look around the cell. It is slightly larger than the balcony on my house. How can it hold so many people? A window with three different layers of iron bars, a toilet in the corner with a small door covering only the bottom. A loud color TV sitting on a metal shelf nailed to the wall. An old Indian with a mongoloid face points at a space near the window, pushing his mattress aside. "Not a bad place, by prison standards," I think, putting my stuff on the floor. Sitting along a barely lit wall, seven people eagerly watch me in the darkness. It is unlikely that I will see a bed again soon. Indians like to sleep on the floor.

Chapter 10. Part Two. Outside.

"They don't seem to care where they sleep," I say, pointing at the locals lying directly on the sidewalk.

"Indians must be the laziest people after Arabs," Yair answers after a short pause, lifting his feet so as not to step on a person sleeping in the shadow of a tree. "They sleep most of their life. They sleep at night, they sleep after meals, they sleep at lunchtime. They really don't care where they sleep.

Wherever they feel like sleeping, that's where they sleep. Wherever they can find some shadow, they make themselves comfortable."

"That's why it's so dirty all around here. They prefer sleeping to collecting their own trash," Edi adds, stretching her thin lips to kiss Yair, "I love you, my darling."

Yair embraces Edi around her narrow waist, trying to catch the moment and enjoy the spontaneous feeling of love, as often happens with lovers, but he stops suddenly. Elderly Indians sitting in the shadows of the trees and houses start to shout aggressively from all corners of the street: "No kiss! No kiss! Go home, kissing at home!" They instantly transform from kind old people into evil dwarves, shaking their fists at us and shouting something that is obviously really offensive.

"Why don't we go back to the hotel, drink some tea and smoke a chillum on the roof. Nobody will disturb you kissing there. And there's a magnificent view over Pushkar from up there," I suggest, unwilling to get into a conflict with the locals.

"Savages," Edi tells the old men in a low condescending voice, hugging her boyfriend.

"To hell with them, let's go. They can't have been able to get it up for years, that's why they're angry with themselves," Yair replies, taking his girlfriend by the hand.

Pushkar is wonderful; a city of vegetarians and camels. A small town situated around a small round lake full of fish. We pay a few rupees for a plate of boiled peas and spend some time watching carp jostling each other, trying to swallow as much food as they can with their fat lips. It's surprising that you can't buy meat or fish in this town. It is illegal. Meat and fish are not on sale anywhere. The city, which is home to so many Hindu temples, is considered holy in India. Just like in Delhi, the narrow streets look like a stream of biomass. Camels, cows, elephants, monkeys, tourists, locals; the entire motley mass flowing between a dozen temples, leaving hundreds of pounds of shit beneath their feet. A wonderful city, where it is easier to buy opium and hashish than meat and fish.

"At the lake shore there is a nice place where we can smoke. Shall we crash there for a while?" Yair suggests, wiping the sweat off his face.

"I don't mind, we need some shade, somewhere close to the water," I agree, waving a hand fan that I bought along the way.

We walk some fifty yards and find ourselves in a cool place by the lake with dozens of concrete benches. A few hundred people of all kinds are standing and sitting, all of them waiting for the show that happens every day. The show called 'sunset'. The people around me don't look like those you normally see in touristy coastal areas. Almost everyone is wearing simple yet colorful Indian clothes. Most of them, regardless of sex or age, have long hair or dreads. I feel like I am on a different planet, as if I have traveled by time machine and ended up in the era of the hippy heyday. The sound of drums is to be heard everywhere. People are drinking tea, dancing, and talking to each other. Nobody is in any hurry. I can hear mantras praising Indian gods coming from all sides. It's surprising, but nobody is drinking alcohol; everybody is smoking chillums. Everyone looks happy and carefree. The Sun touches the hill and Yair hurries to finish preparing his chillum. The best time for meditation with a chillum is sunset. During sunset, it is much easier to understand that nothing lasts forever in this world. Out of the blue, two police cars pull up to the lake and cops wearing sunglasses jump out of them. "Oh, here it goes," I think, recalling the Russian police. Oddly enough, nobody except me is even thinking about hiding their charas and chillums. Nobody seems to care about the presence of the police. Yair points at a strangely important looking Indian getting out of a jeep and reassures me.

"Do you see the guy wearing the suit? He is one of the ministers of India, he was written about in the newspapers. He's come to Pushkar to meditate for a while. Every evening he comes down here with his security to watch the Sun go down."

I can only imagine what would happen in Russia, if somebody tried to smoke hashish with a Russian minister present. He'd probably be arrested and jailed for ten years as a terrorist. And here babas[14] smoke hashish at every temple.

All of a sudden, as if on cue, the sound of the drums coming from different parts of the shore starts to blend into one rhythm. This means that the Sun has touched the horizon. Edi lights up the chillum for Yair and recites a mantra. "Bom Bolenath, Sabke Sath, Bom Shiva, Bom Shankara, Bom." At the same moment, I can hear mantras praising Shiva for creating charas coming from all around. Nobody but me seems to be paying any attention to the minister and his security. It seems like nothing exists for him in such moments, either. He is watching the tired Sun going down with everyone else. Dozens of chillums proudly point at the sky amid a huge cloud of sweet charas smoke; an incredible sight. I deeply inhale the Himalayan charas and think that I may be falling in love with this country. Poor freedom is better than glamorous slavery. Do what you want, but don't disturb others. This is arguably the authentic democracy that was replaced in my country by the deceptive phrase "Everybody has equal rights". Nowhere else have I ever felt equal to others in terms of rights like here in Pushkar, smoking hashish next to a minister and watching the Sun go down. Next comes a moment of silence. A gust of wind blows a small palm leaf out of a cart full of leaves used as disposable plates. Time seems to stop for a moment and it feels like the leaf is falling endlessly in the silence. In slow motion, it falls as if dancing, and I stand in silence absorbing the magic. The moment it touches the ground, somewhere on the opposite side of the city a loud bell starts to toll, as if somebody has pushed an invisible 'Play' button, and everything comes alive again after the divine pause, filling the world with thousands of sounds. The Sun has set; life goes on.

---

[14]Baba - a person who has given up the material world and pursues the path of spiritual development and enlightenment. Also used as respectful form of address for an older man.

Chapter 11. Part One. Inside.

Well, anyway, life goes on. Everyone seems to be healthy around me, no one is dying.

"My name is Vasiliy."

Seven men state their foreign-sounding names, and I don't remember any of them. Making mistakes, they try to pronounce my name.

A shower would be good. I've eaten virtually nothing for 5 days, and instead of taking a shower I've poured water over myself from a bottle. The toilet, which is also the shower, is a small square about five feet wide and six feet long surrounded by a low wall. The walls and the floor are covered with brown tiles. An Indian toilet is an astonishing thing. Despite the dirt everywhere in the houses of the Indians, their toilets remain the tidiest place. This prison cell is my new home now, and this is my toilet. A clean toilet is a relative concept. Of course, this toilet is much tidier than the one in the previous jail, where no one seemed to have cleaned it for ages; and it is spotlessly clean compared to any public restroom back in Russia. But it is of course not a home toilet with white marble tiles. Since footwear is left outside the cell, I can only hope that my immune system will not let fungus colonize my feet. There is a bucket of water near the hole in the floor. A tap hangs from the wall, with water dripping from a piece of wet, slippery cloth at the end of it. Apparently, this serves as flush, sink, shower, bidet, and drinking water at the same time. Judging by the bagginess of my clothes, I must have lost around 10 pounds. When I get undressed, I notice that my whole body is covered in red scratched mosquito bites. Thank God I haven't caught the malaria these little bloodsuckers carry. Alright, it is not that bad, the conditions are bearable; it could be much worse. I can handle three months easily, and then someone should get me out of here. After having a shower and changing, I sit on the floor; this is my place now. Thank God I don't have to fight for it. I can see a chessboard in the corner of the cell. It will be easier to kill time with chess. "To kill time," it sounds so horrible. This is my lifetime, and someone took it away from me. A lifetime is not that long and the Lord only knows when it will come to an end. It is hard to imagine that several months of my life will be taken away from me. And it will only be several months, provided that my friends and relatives get me out of here. What if it's ten or twenty years? No, I'd rather not think about that; it can't be possible. Money should do its job in this country, since it is the most corrupt in the world. Half a year at the most and I'll be out of here. I wonder what the other inmates do to kill the time. There is some Indian show on TV. Some are watching it, some are reading the newspaper. I need to think of something to do for the next few months. I don't want to waste them. As I have the chance, I need to spend this time on myself. Tomorrow the doctor should take the stitches out of my arm. I will start doing sports, and learning English and Hindi. These things should come in useful in my life. Books and chess I will keep for my spare time. I have to make a schedule for myself and keep busy so that I don't get a chance to think of anything stupid.

"Hey, Russian," a strong skinny Indian addresses me. He is wearing a T-shirt with the arched lettering of the 'Adidas' brand on it. "We read in a newspaper about you. You are here for twenty grams of MDMA and cultivating marijuana. As for me, I robbed a petrol station, but they should release me on bail soon. You got unlucky with the quantity, if it was ten grams you could get out of here soon, too. But do not get upset about it, you won't be bored here. My name is Dominic. Do you see that man with long hair in the cell opposite us? He is Russian, too."

"Russian??!"

It is good that he's Russian, it will be much more fun together.

"His name is Viktor and he has been here for three months. He's here for drugs, too."

"Oh, I know him. There was a Russian guy called Vitka, also known by the nickname Dusya."

He was said to be in jail, but I thought he'd already been released. He turned up in Goa a few months ago. Sometimes I met him at parties, usually once or twice a month. I wasn't interested in where he lived or what he did. He was one of those people who considered themselves psychedelic gurus without having read a single book about psychedelics. The last time I saw him was in East End, the only trance club that survived the repressions. It happened just three months ago. He looked like an old crazy Russian in his late fifties. Without any suntan, round-shouldered, with a sagging belly, he wandered around the party giving away cheap amphetamine from the pharmacy, mixed with tooth anesthetic. He proudly called his powder 'my cocaine' or 'magic powder.'

"Viktor!" I yell across the platform separating our cells. Somebody dressed in a lungi approaches the barred door. His body is suntanned and lean.

"Vasya, is that you?" he replies laughing and reaching his hand toward me. "We read about you in a newspaper just a week ago. What brings you here?"

"They want me to serve ten years," I answer, having recognized his voice, happy that I'm not alone in here.

"Don't shit your pants, they want everyone to serve ten years here."

"Thanks, that sounds comforting. How are you doing in here?"

"Not bad, it is like a health resort. Let's talk tomorrow during walking time; I can't hear you well enough now. Besides, I am busy at the moment, I'm doing yoga, sorry."

"Khana agya[15], khana agya," suddenly these weird, unknown words begin to be chanted by all the inmates, while they hastily take their plates and mugs out of the pile of dishes.

---

[15] The food is coming (Hindi).

Chapter 11. Part Two. Outside.

"Khana agya, khana agya, tea, tea, tea, omelet-cutlet, cutlet-omelet," various food hawkers cry, trying to outshout each other.

"The train is approaching Bombay, we should eat something," Yair tells me, sleepily rubbing his eyes. "Today, when we arrive, we need to get to another station. It is at the other end of Bombay. If we are lucky and buy tickets for today, tomorrow we will be in Goa."

"Oh, the sooner the better; I'm tired of travelling, I want the sea." I reply, looking at the unusual types of food in the hands of the passing merchants.

"What's the matter with you, Russian? Why have you gone sour? How can you get tired of a journey? Especially when the adventure is only just beginning. It is unlikely that we will be able to buy tickets on the train today. The whole of India reserves tickets during the peak season two months in advance. There are more chances to buy tickets for the bus than the train."

"Well, then maybe we should go immediately to the bus station? It is alright for you, you still have half a year to travel. But I have only a week left and I'd like to see Goa."

"You'll see it eventually; but now we need to eat, we don't know when we'll get a chance again."

Having paid a young food peddler thirty rupees, I receive a plate of rice, a chicken drumstick covered with pea sauce, two flatbreads and a plastic bag with drinking water. A crippled cleaner, crawling on the floor of the car, stops sweeping the floor and watches hungrily as I try to open the tray of food. At intervals of several minutes, different kinds of cripple crawl past me on the floor. The majority of them are children of seven to ten years of age. Some do not have eyes, some can't walk, but all of them have something resembling a broom in their hands. Crawling on the dirty floor of the car, they sweep up the dust and beg for money. Having tried to eat, I realize that only the rice and flatbreads are edible for me. From the chicken and gravy my mouth burns and tears flow. Although I have already been in India for a week, I have a great deal of difficulty eating the local food: burning chili peppers are a major component of any dish. On an Indian diet I have managed to lose ten pounds. Having bought myself so-called "fishermen"[16] pants and a simple Indian shirt for three dollars in Pushkar, I look like a typical traveler in India. We used my expensive, fashionable clothes for rags to clean the chillum after smoking. Deciding to throw away my half-eaten plate of rice and chicken, I stand up and head towards the end of our car. A boy with mutilated legs who has been watching me carefully, immediately crawls after me, quickly moving his hands across the floor, trying to get ahead of another boy – another beggar – who was cleaning a few meters away from me.

"God, how horrible."

Until now, I have never given anyone my uneaten food. Is it really possible that desperate hungry children are ready to crawl on the floor to finish someone else's food? No, I'd rather throw away my leftovers, and give them some change so that they can buy a normal meal. At the end of the car, I notice another couple of beggars, who, seeing the uneaten food on the plate, immediately rush to

---

[16] Fishermen pants - one-size-fits-all pants.

my side. One of them, having noticed that I was going to throw away my almost untouched food, grabs the plate with his little hands, and abruptly pulls it towards him. However, the plate does not move because on the other side two pairs of small hands are already pulling the food to their side. Releasing the plate, I barely have time to jump out of the way. The food is instantly scattered all over the floor and the walls of the car. The children crawl around the dirty, spit-covered car, eating the leftovers of my meal straight from the floor. Shocked, I return to my seat and stare out of the window, trying to divert my thoughts from the intense sense of guilt at seeing these little cripples.

For some reason I feel guilty that I sometimes complain about the injustice of fate, that I whine about the things that I feel I lack. Would these little kids ever understand me, if I told them about my problems? Not having the latest model cell phone and a mink coat for my wife, the need to constantly repair my old jeep, or the roof that leaks in my two-bedroom apartment in the spring. These problems, which seem illusory now yet at times make me depressed, would seem ridiculous to these children. Where is the magical India that Roerich drew? Endless piles of garbage and slums float past the window. The slums of Bombay begin a few hours before the entrance to the city. Small houses made of cardboard, sticks, stones, cow dung and other debris start to stretch along the tracks. The first thing that catches your eye is the hundreds of slum dwellers quietly squatting and defecating along the railway tracks. Having no qualms about doing such an intimate act in public, they look curiously at people in the windows of passing trains. Some manage to brush their teeth at the same time, or quietly talk to a neighbor while the latter is washing his ass with a plastic bottle. Despite the lack of a personal toilet, almost everyone has a happy, cheerful face. Why do we, who have all of the possible benefits of civilization, constantly live under the yoke of a lack of things, which are in fact useless? A little cripple crawling down the aisle of the car smiles at me, thanking me for my unfinished food. I would like advise all those gloomy people who commute to work in the morning to learn how to enjoy life from this little cripple.

Chapter 12. Part One. Inside.

Judging by the receding darkness, it's currently around five am. Woken by a horrible growl coming from the bathroom, it takes me a while to figure out where I am. Is someone being strangled in there? Ah, I remember: Indians have a silly tradition of starting their day with their toilet. First thing in the morning they rush into the bathroom to take a dump and brush their teeth, doing this simultaneously most of the time. After they are done brushing their teeth, they shove the toothbrush down their throat to scrape the base of their tongue, making this horrible loud growl. I had the same awful nightmare again, of me running away all night. I had a suitcase full of some kind of drugs, I was surrounded by the police and had no idea what to do. But I feel like I have finally got a good night's sleep. After using newspapers as my bedding, the filthy rag with holes – which the inmates cherish and call a 'bed sheet' – seems as soft as silk now. The jail is gradually waking up. I hear the noises of inmates clearing their throats in the neighboring cells. In every single cell someone is growling. The oldest inmates, who are used to not sleeping for long, are the first to wake up. My cellmates roll up their bedding, take their teacups, and squat, waiting for their morning tea. Then the floor is cleared to create a free space for movement. An Indian in a greasy shirt and dirty pants appears on the other side of the door. "Good morning, Mangaldas," Dominic greets him, taking a pile of round buns through the bars. Mangaldas pokes the spout of an aluminum kettle between the iron bars and slowly pours tea for everybody, one by one. My neighbor is thoughtful enough to bring two hot buns and half of a cup of tea with milk to me in my bed. No one has brought me breakfast in bed for a long time.

"What's your name?" I ask the old man, who looks like an old Eskimo.

"Budaram, my name is Budaram."

"Thank you, old man Budaram."

I examine the cell, while tearing off chunks of the hot bun and dipping it into the tea. Some inmates take butter from their bags and spread it over the bun, others place tea-soaked cookies in the middle of the bun. Nobody is in any hurry. The sunlight coming through the bars leaves a checkered pattern on the floor and the walls. The peeling walls are pretty much completely covered in mold and fungus. "I better not catch some sort of infection while I'm in here," I think to myself, looking at the feet of my neighbor. Budaram finishes his breakfast first, and is now fully concentrated on dipping a rag into red fluid in order to rub it on the rotten area between his toes. The nails on his toes are almost completely consumed by fungus. A disgusting sight. If I was on the outside and I witnessed something like that, I'd run for the hills. But there is nowhere to run in prison, so you just have to accept it. I wash my teacup, and once again immerse myself in memories. That's the only thing that no one can take from me. I'm doing my best to pretend that I am fascinated by the TV program about this year's crop of Indian carrots. Just so nobody bothers me with their questions. The space that surrounds me gradually melts away. My memories — much like a time machine — take me back a few years in an attempt to find what led me to this place. I can once again smell the sea and see Goa the same way I did when I saw it for the first time, back when I looked at things through large rose-tinted glasses. Glued to the TV screen, I lie on the floor and smile like an idiot. The loud noise of the door opening jerks me out of the illusory reality.

"Walking time!!!" the guard's shout brings me back to the prison.

A square yard: fifteen steps long and fifteen steps wide. Seven cells line the perimeter. There are iron bars instead of a ceiling. The inmates are slowly coming out of their cells. Nobody is smiling; nobody is in any hurry. I'm the only one who walks briskly around in circles, not paying attention to anyone. I'm filled with so much energy. I've got to let it all out during the hour allocated for walking. I will have to sit here for another three, maybe even six months, because of some Russian asshole. No, I shouldn't even be thinking about six months. If I walk for two hours each day at a rapid pace, I might even lose a few pounds. Oh, and I should build some muscle. Big muscles are one of the essentials in prison. I just need to look for the positive in everything. I need to concentrate… I'm in a health resort, I'm being healed, and when the monsoon ends and I get out of here, I'm going to be handsome and healthy.

"Hey, Vasya," I hear my name pronounced correctly. "Welcome to Mapusa Five Star Hotel."

"I see you're not wasting your time around here, Vitya. You look good, I barely recognized you."

"Well, Vasya, I've been free of drugs for three months. I do aerobics and yoga every day. I don't smoke, I don't drink, I sunbathe every day, and I've already lost twenty-two pounds. I feel like I'm in some kind of medical-labor clinic — we had those in the USSR, if you remember. Let's go for a walk and I'll tell you everything. First rule: don't be afraid, it's not a Russian prison. Nobody wants anything from you here. You don't bother anybody, and nobody will bother you. Second rule: learn to wait, that's the best meditation around here. Nobody knows when you will get out of here, except the Lord."

"Actually, I'm counting on getting out of here in three months," I say with a serious face, but Viktor begins to laugh hysterically.

"Yeah… I was counting on that, too," he says, still smiling, with his eyes filled with tears from laughing, chuckling like an idiot. "Come on, Vasya, I'm going to introduce you to my friends, they've been here for over a year. And all of them were counting on getting out of here 'in three months', too. Please meet our doctor, David, he delivers medicine to the prison cells."

An old Iranian man who looks like an Azerbaijani, stares into my eyes, then points his fingers like a gun at my head and says with a straight face, "Bang! Bang!" The Iranian pauses for a few seconds, and, smiling with his toothless mouth, extends his firm hand to me.

"My name is David. Welcome to hell. Viktor told me that you are here for twenty grams of MDMA. That's too bad. I've been here for two years. If I'm lucky, I'll get out of here soon. If not, well, then it's going to be from ten to twenty, but I'm ready for anything at this point. They got me with five kilograms of charas and eighty grams of cocaine. A Russian snitched on me, otherwise the police would never have caught me. I'm a professional drug dealer. I've been doing it my whole life.

If I get out of here, I'm going to start dealing again. But first, I'm going to find that Russian guy, I'm going to make sure I find him. He is a dead man, and that's a promise."

David goes silent for a few moments, tensing his jaw muscles. Inmates of European origin slowly approach us from every direction.

"And this is 'Milano'. His name is Alexandro, he is from Sicily," Viktor takes advantage of the pause in our conversation with David, and points at a muscular Italian with an aquiline nose. "Look at his great physique. He is 52, but he looks better than most 40-year olds. He has been selling drugs his whole life, too."

"My name is Alexandro," Milano utters in a sing-song voice, like all Italians, and extends his firm hand to me. "I had only nine hundred and fifty grams of charas, but the police added fifty more grams of their own, and so now I'm looking at ten years."

"C'mon, Milano, don't start that again," Viktor interrupts our conversation with a displeased, tired face. "Please feel free to tell Vasya your story when I'm not around. Ever since I got here, all I've heard is his endless talk about the police being unfair. Milano shouldn't have touched the drugs in the first place, then he would be on the outside now."

Without taking offence at Viktor's words, Alexandro turns to David and continues to tell, probably for the hundredth time, the sad and unfair story of his arrest.

"Well, I'm not a drug dealer, my name is Adam. I'm from Poland," a ginger-haired guy of about my height says in Russian with an accent. "I'm a professional killer, I was tracked down by Interpol. I'll be sent to Germany soon. I killed some fritz for twenty-five grand there, and wanted to serve my sentence here, in India. But, well… it didn't work. The only thing that cheers me up is that they have nice prisons in Germany compared to this one. When I'm there, I will eat and rest for fifteen years, and then, when I get out, I will get back in the business."

"You see, Vasya, all that one talks about is his killings. He was a hired mercenary and can't do anything but kill," Viktor whispers to me so that the Pole doesn't hear him. "We only have an hour to walk, so let's get walking!" Viktor pulls me by the elbow away from hearing the whole of the Pole's story.

We walk briskly around in circles. Sitting in clusters in the corners, Indian inmates observe us curiously.

"What are you in here for, Vitya? If I'm not mistaken, you were selling pharmaceutical amphetamines. Do people go to jail for that now?"

"You won't believe it, Vasya, but I'm in here for a jar of Indian Novocain."

"How is that even possible? Isn't Novocain an over-the-counter drug, like an anesthetic?"

"Vasya, it's India, everything is possible here. Do you recall the freak carnival in Arambol back in March?"

"Of course I do, Vitya. We had a great time on the beach to the sound of the drums."

"Well, listen to this, Vasya – the next morning I woke to the sound of the police knocking on my door. Some plain-clothed Indian policemen came to my house and started a shakedown. And I had a 200-gram jar filled with anesthetics in my refrigerator. They opened it up, smelled it, and the powder looked exactly like cocaine. They tasted it: it freezes the gums just like coke. So they sent me here, to prison. As for the powder, they sealed it and sent it for an expert analysis to Hyderabad, the other end of India. Well, I've been waiting for the results of the analysis for three months now. The judge won't set me free until the results come back. Once every two weeks they drive me to the court, where I am given an extension, and then they drive me back here, to this health resort. If the police didn't frame me and didn't mix anything into my powder, they should set me free. If those assholes did frame me, then I'm looking at ten years."

"To your cells, go to your cells!" the guards start to shout, banging their bamboo batons against the bars.

"Vasya, after lunch, from three to four pm, we have another walk. I'll show you Mapusa beach[17] then," says Viktor, who smiles and heads toward his cell.

Chapter 12. Part Two. Outside.

"Where is the beach?" I ask Yair, looking around.

Is this really Goa? We are in complete darkness on a deserted street, watching the rickshaw that brought us here heading off into the night. It probably looks funny: three silhouettes with a heap of backpacks illuminated by the dim light of the only working restaurant. A painting entitled "This is Goa?"

"The sea is somewhere nearby, I can smell it," Edie says soothingly, hugging Yair. "Tomorrow morning, we will figure it out."

We've made it! A two-week trip across India is enough to tire you out and make you just want to lie on the beach.

It's nighttime. The smell of some strange flowers makes the air slightly sweet. We stand at the entrance to a place called Manchis, a fairly large establishment by local standards, built out of sticks, bamboo and palm leaves. Having waited until the Israeli couple finishes kissing, I suggest going to a restaurant to eat. We carry our belongings into Manchis, and finally hold a normal menu in our hands, with understandable names of dishes. After travelling across the whole of India, I have realized that Indians have an unhealthy love of all things plastic. This Indian love manifests itself in this place in all its glory. Can it really be that here, in a place where bamboo grows everywhere, plastic furniture is cheaper? Red and blue plastic tables and chairs are everywhere. Can it be true that I'm going to eat normal food, by European standards? I imagined Goa differently. After visiting Kazantip[18] many times, and listening to seasoned freaks[19] and trancers, I imagined Goa as something

---

[17] Mapusa beach - as the town of Mapusa is not located on the coast, it does not actually have a beach.

[18] Republic of Kazantip (in different years it has also had the names Republic of Z, KaZantip) - an annual international music festival that was held in Crimea until 2013, the most famous electronic music festival in the former USSR. Club and electronic music is played at the festival, with DJs and musicians from all over the world performing on its dance floors.

[19] Freaks - a counter-culture group uniting punks, hippies, etc. Happy, colorfully dressed hedonists, frequently not opposed to the use of drugs, who live outside the normal social matrix.

similar. The sea, the beach, dancing people everywhere, dozens of bars and restaurants, loud music all night. I can't see any of this now. One restaurant, darkness, and no music. And this is the so-called capital of freaky Goa – Anjuna?

"Look, there's the first flipped-out[20] character," Yair interrupts my thoughts, moving a bowl of hummus closer to him and pointing at the entrance.

Out of the darkness, like a ghost, a tall European with a strange facial expression and light, waist-length dreadlocks, comes into the restaurant. Gently swinging his hands as if to the tune of music, he paints an intricate, invisible mosaic in the air. He suddenly stops, locking eyes with me, as if seeing something very important in them. Without taking his gaze from me, the strange character begins to approach our table. Scrutinizing me carefully for a few seconds, he abruptly falls on his knees and starts praying, trying to kiss my feet. Not knowing how to react, I sit with my mouth wide open, and try to hide my feet under the chair. Several couples from different tables eat their meals, indifferently observing the show. As if it is normal for a man to kiss another man's feet.

"Ok, alright, alright, go away, go," Yair comes to my aid just in time and begins to drive the crazy guy away.

"What's wrong with him?" I ask, watching the strange man, who as if nothing happened, once again starts to draw a pattern in the air that is visible only to him.

"Don't mind what just happened. Here, in Goa, there are a lot like him: they stuff themselves with drugs and go crazy."

"And what, they just wander around like that?"

"Who needs them? They have neither money, nor brains. If they are lucky their relatives come to collect them, but usually they get hooked and die."

Pushing the empty plate away, I understand that finally, for the first two weeks, I have had a delicious meal. This, of course, could not be called a first-class meal. It's more like some cheap food from a roadside eatery, but it is undeniable: compared to what I have eaten for the last two weeks, it was just wonderful!!!

---

[20] Flipped-out character - a person who has gone mad, usually as a result of excessive drug use.

Chapter 13. Part One. Inside.

"Vasya, they cooked crabs for us today. Can you imagine that? Have you ever heard of crabs being served in prison? Just today I had a dream about oysters. The oysters didn't work out, but I managed to manifest some crabs," Viktor shouts to me from his cell, smiling.

"Crabs – that's good. I am fed up with peas; at least it's something new. I want to eat something tasty, I have already lost twenty pounds," I shout back to him across the prison.

"Khana, khana agya," the prison begins to echo in different voices.

"Mangaldas has come, brought food, you better eat, or you be thin. What are you in here for, son?" mangling the language, my neighbor, old man Budaram, is trying to talk to me, using his meager vocabulary.

For some reason I want to call him Old Man Mudra. His whole face is covered with wrinkles like a soaked apple, and instead of eyes he has narrow slits. Twelve hours a day he endlessly mutters a mantra, apparently asking Buddha to release him outside.

"The cops planted twenty grams of MDMA on me," I say with a sigh, once again feeling a surge of fury that I only manage to calm a little thanks to my morning meditation.

"Wai-wai-wai," Old Man Mudra sympathetically shakes his head from side to side. "Bad, very bad. You will not be released on bail. More than ten grams – you will not be released."

"It's you, you old blister, who won't be released; I'm getting out of here in a couple of months," I say angrily, feeling the need to meditate again.

"What are you doing your time for, anyway?" I ask angrily, knowing that it's unlikely he is capable of anything other than selling charas.

"Charas, two kilos. I have already been here for nine months, commercial quantity. I'm here for the same thing you are – from ten to twenty, no release on bail."

"How did you get caught, old man?"

"I brought charas from the Himalayas, wanted to make some money. My grandfather made charas, my father made it. My whole family gathered this charas for a month. And here, in Goa, the police grabbed me and they want to lock me up for ten years. And I have a family in the Himalayas, four adult children, eight grandchildren, my own corn field, a horse."

"And how did you get here from the Himalayas?"

"He came on a horse; he got on his mountain horse and galloped down here," A bald Indian of thirty years answers for him, laughing out of his corner.

"He's a little wild, like all mountain people, but he's kind. He got here by car; transporting his charas for a whole week. And here one of his people tipped him off to the police."

"And what are you doing your time for?" I ask, trying to guess what this innocent looking young man, who prays from morning till evening, could have done to get in here.

"Murder," the bald guy answers, sighing and lowering his eyes for a moment. "I killed one with a pistol and wounded the other. It's a pity that the second one didn't die. They are my enemies – I should have killed them. Our families have been feuding for a long time. My uncle works in the ministry, he was running for office, and the opposition party set me up. The bastards organized everything so that I could not leave them alive. But I'm going to be released from here soon. I will serve half a year and get out of here. My name is Disay," he says, coming closer and extending his hand to me.

"And I am Vasiliy. You can call me Vasya."

"Vashya, you have a difficult name. Can I call you Vasa?"

"Call me Vasa, I don't care."

"Look," Disay points at a man covered from head to toe with a blanket. "That's a cop from Calangute. Hey, police, show us your face."

Turning to the wall and muttering something in Hindi, the policeman becomes silent again, having no desire to talk.

"He is depressed. He was denied bail again. And he's here for the same reason you are – "commercial quantity of drugs." His name is Chetsi. Hey, Chetsi that's enough moping around. Pull yourself together; you're a cop. You must set us an example."

"Look at him," Disay laughs, addressing the other inmates. "And this is our police? Stop embarrassing us and get out from under your blanket. You've had a lie-in for half of the day. Not only is the cell small, but on top of that you're sprawled all over the place."

"And this is your namesake, his name is Vasu," the cheerful bald Indian continues to introduce me to the other inmates. "Vasu is a soldier. Together with Chetsi they dragged a kilo of heroin from Rajasthan. And here they were grassed up by their own cops."

A guard approaches the door and opens it with a clang, smiling. My neighbor, Old Man Mudra, shudders, ceasing to mumble his mantras. Why does he need to rattle the bolts so much? Is it really that much fun to watch as the prisoners flinch from this awful sound? Although, on second thought, what normal man goes to work as a prison guard? It's lifelong, voluntary imprisonment.

The inmates go out into the corridor, holding their plates and mugs. I follow them. In the hallway, an Indian is sitting in dirty, greasy clothes on a small stool. Surrounded by three pots, he deftly dishes out rice, vegetables and gravy. In a moment, a few spoons of rice and boiled cabbage appear on my plate. In the iron mug: a thick brown mixture consisting of small crabs, peas and coconut. Returning to the cell, everyone immediately begins to eat. No one has a spoon, everyone eats with their hands. Old Man Mudra, having poured all of the gravy into his rice, quickly begins to eat. Everyone is sitting on the floor eating. After a few minutes the floor around Mudra is covered with rice and drops of gravy. He immediately places the large lumps of rice that fall on the floor back into his mouth, without a thought for the dirt on the floor. He swallows the small crabs whole, including the shells and bones, almost without chewing. I should practice using my fingers instead of a spoon so deftly. The rice slips through my fingers, the gravy drips from my hands, and my mouth burns. How much pepper do they put in the food? I desperately want to wash it all down with water.

"Where do you get water here?" I ask my neighbor with gestures.

"Over there," Mudra calmly points to the empty bottles near the toilet.

From the bucket near the hole, I scoop warm liquid into the empty bottle with a dirty, slippery ladle. Who could have thought that I would ever drink water like this? Holding the bottle up to the light, I can see some sort of sediment floating in it. But there is no other water and it seems that there isn't going to be. I have to get used to it. I am very thirsty.

Chapter 13. Part Two. Outside.

It is morning. I am very thirsty. The fan no longer provides salvation from the heat. So here it is, my first morning in Goa. A chorus of wild sounds produced by awakening birds, animals, and insects is coming from the street. Stepping onto the porch, I knock on Yair's room next door, hoping to find something to drink.

"Yair, are you asleep?"

"No, come in, my Russian friend," I hear from the inside. "We're not asleep."

Edie opens the door, wrapped in an colorful Indian sheet like a sari. Smiling widely, she holds a chillum in one hand, and a bottle of water in the other.

"Will you have a chillum with us this morning?"

"For two weeks my morning has started with smoking a chillum in your company, why would I change this tradition now? Of course I will! Just give me some water to drink first. It was so hot all night, I thought I would die of thirst. I had to take a shower three times during the night, but I still didn't dare to drink from the tap."

"That's right; it's easy to get water poisoning here. When buying water, always make sure there is a plastic seal on the lid. The smart-assed Indians don't even care about our health, selling water from the tap under the guise of mineral water. At first, I didn't pay attention to the seal, but having been sick a couple of times, I've begun to carefully examine what I buy. So be careful if you value your life."

"Greetings from Shiva. Bom Bolenath," says Yair, holding out the smoking chillum. "Will you come to the party with us today?"

"Are you asking me seriously? I made this trip to Goa specially to see the world-famous trance parties with my own eyes. I'd like to take a drop of real LSD and meditate in the dance. In Russia, it is very difficult to get LSD-25. They sell Shulgin[21] substitutes: DOB, DOET, PSP, and PCPY. But I want LSD-25, the effect of which was described in the writings of Timothy Leary, Stanislav Grof, Robert Anton Wilson, and the other founders of the psychedelic movement."

"Well, then you have a great opportunity today to see the latest generation of psychedelic 'flower children'. Rent a bike or scooter, tonight we're going to Paradiso.

---

[21] Shulgins - a family of world-famous chemists who invented more than 160 psychedelic drugs.

***

"Hello Lena, how are you? I'm alright; I'm finally in Goa. How is Vasilinka, how is Hemp?"

"Everything is Ok. I received your parcel with the Hemp stuff. It's shit quality, but we have already sold half of it. When are you coming home?"

"I'm thinking of hanging about for a couple of weeks, maybe I will buy some more hemp goods, and then I'll come home."

"How is Goa? Is it everything you dreamed of?"

"I don't even know what to tell you, Lena. It's not like Kazantip at all, and not like anything I imagined. There is dirt everywhere, and during the whole day I have been here I haven't heard any trance music. I'm going to a trance club tonight. If that sucks too, then we can assume that all of the rumors about Goa are total baloney. But still, there is something about Goa that I cannot quite put my finger on. It may be its energy, or the people, who aren't like those that surround us in Russia."

"They are probably all crooks and drug addicts."

"In some way, you're right, Lena. Almost all of the Indians are crooks. But they are sort of good rogues. Everyone is trying to trick you in relation to the smallest things. And the Europeans who have been living here for a long time look like aliens. Everyone walks around and smiles at each other. And their faces are all clever and kind. You want to meet them and talk to them."

"The most important thing for you is not to meet any girls. I miss you so much; come home soon."

"I will do my best, kiss Vasilinka for me. I'll call you in a few days. Kiss you, bye."

***

"Well, here it is – now I can see the real Goa. I'd started to think that everything people say about it is bullshit," I say to Yair, who is descending the stairs of the club.

Paradiso is the oldest open-air trance club. Open-air trance parties have recently been banned, but here people party hard every day. The club is located in a sort of a cave with a view onto the sea. Having spotted a number of his Israeli friends, Yair forgets about me and heads directly to the center of the dance floor, getting out his chillum in the process. Beautiful trance music plays loudly and clearly. Hundreds of people are sitting on mats around the dance floor. Old Indian women are constantly making coffee and tea on paraffin burners. It feels like everyone around me is smoking charas non-stop. A large, sweet cloud hangs over the club. Goa parties are so different from anything I've seen before. Hundreds of happy people, not burdened by any problems. It is as if the air is imbued with the spirit of freedom. It's surprising that this freedom doesn't get out of hand: that it doesn't turn into alcoholic chaos, as so often happens in Russia. Beautiful girls and guys dance in their own unique style across the floor, moving around the club. It's not even a dance. It's a special kind of language that people who have gathered from all over the world in search of their own kind use for communication. I am glad that I understand this language of signs and gestures. I also want to immerse myself in this dialogue, because I also have something to share. This is my tribe. This is my language. Finally I've found you! Overwhelming feelings of joy make me want to laugh and cry at the same time. It feels like I have been brought to a meeting of shamans, who have come to share their knowledge. The people resemble characters from futuristic movies, where the protagonists experience a global catastrophe. Tattoos, piercings and dreadlocks are an integral part of each of them. Unusual, weird clothes glow in the ultraviolet light. There are very few Russians. Most of them are Israelis. You can spot the Russians from a mile away. The majority of Russian men have white 'Dolce Gabbana' shirts and shorts, pulled up to the navel, with aggressive, but at the same time frightened, looks on their faces. Most of the Russian girls look as follows: gaudy, short tight skirts, puffy white thighs and make-up. They look like prostitutes, like aliens. Aliens from the planet of the white monkeys.

"Hi, where are you from?" A tall, beautiful girl, not at all like the standard Russian girls, suddenly knocks me out of the flow of my thoughts. "I am from Russia."

"I'm Russian too."

"My name is Nadine. Let's go find a mat, have a smoke and a chat. We have a nice crowd. Everyone is from our tribe," Nadine says laughing, as if reading my thoughts. "Do you want tea?" The Russian girl asks me, motioning to sit down.

"Yes, with pleasure; I don't like booze, but I respect psychedelics with tea."

"Mama-chai, one masala chai for our fellow countryman." She calls loudly to an old woman with a kettle, and sits down next to me on the floor. "Did you come here long ago?"

"Last night."

"Well done! You look good; you don't look like a Russian. You can spot the recently arrived Russians a mile away."

"We've been hanging out here for two weeks already. By the way, this is Lyokha."

A tall, thin guy extends his hand to me.

"Everyone calls Lyokha 'Sponsor'. You can call him that too. And this is Ira, she has been hanging out here for a year."

Ira, waving her head and smiling seductively, straightens her long pink dreadlocks.

"You lot don't look like Russians at all. My name is Vasiliy. You're not dressed like Russians."

"Yes, we quickly realized that we get treated like mugs in European clothes." Lyokha answers, hugging both girls around the shoulders at the same time. "So we drove to the Night Market and got dressed up in line with the latest freaky Goa fashion. Now the locals have started treating us like humans, 'cause when they see an 'Armani' T-shirt, they immediately try to sell you something, and the price skyrockets five-fold. And you, Vasya, you don't look like a Russian, either. You're dressed like an Israeli."

"I've been travelling with some across India for two weeks. I met them in Delhi and we came here yesterday."

"It's obvious at first sight; they have their own separate Goa fashion. Do you want something to bring you up?" Lyokha asks with an enigmatic smile, holding out his open palm to me.

In it are several pills with 'Mitsubishi' signs embossed on them and a small bottle.

"Help yourself, don't be shy. That's why he is called 'Sponsor'. He loves to treat everyone to sweet things." Nadine says cheerfully, placing a pill into my mouth.

Chapter 14. Part One. Inside.

My Lena arrives tomorrow. Maybe she will get me out of here. My mom has given us six thousand dollars from her retirement savings, and so now there is money for a lawyer. On one hand, I've missed my beautiful wife terribly; but, on the other, I feel a terrible sense of shame. I am ashamed that I was such an idiot that I managed to get locked up, leaving my girls to survive alone outside. I madly want to hug my Lena. But how will I be able to live in peace after that, here in prison, unable to touch her, knowing that she is somewhere near? How can I go about my business, remembering her smell, her touch? I'll be so glad to see my Lena, but how much misery will I have to suffer after I return to the cell? How can you learn to turn off your memory and feelings? Having created a schedule for my day, I have almost learned not to think about my loved ones. Waking up at six in the morning, I start the day with my morning procedures, and then I read books by Indian philosophers. Aurobindo, Krishnamurti, Osho, Rabindranath Tagore – their books help me tune into the perception of the illusory nature of our existence. Then breakfast and a walk follow, during which I discuss the duality of philosophical reflection with Viktor. After the walk: gymnastics, learning Indian and English, lunch, chess, a walk with Viktor again, gymnastics, dinner, reading Russian books, and finally, sleep. There is no time at all for doing nothing.

"Walking time!" the guards shout, once again opening the door with a loud noise. But I do not shudder, for me it has already become as familiar a sound as the endlessly screaming noise from the TV or the humming of the fans.

"How are you, Viktor?"

"Open Mapusa Beach!" Viktor yells loudly in response across the whole prison, dragging a plastic bucket with water. "Such a good day today! What about starting with water procedures, Vasya?"

Stripping down to our shorts, we pour a scoop of cold water onto our heads, and go for a walk around our little courtyard.

"Where shall we go today? From Arambol to Mandrem[22], or from Mandrem to Arambol?"

"It's exactly an hour," Viktor answers, smiling and, as is traditional, standing on my left.

"It's strange: if you go on my left side when we walk, we go in parallel. But if you go on my right, we constantly bump shoulders. But with David it's the opposite. Maybe every person has his own attraction to the right or the left. What heat! Usually at this time, in May, I walk along the seashore every day. I love this time. The tourists are leaving; the beaches are deserted. You walk along the edge of the water, and when the waves roll back they leave a thin layer of water on the sand, turning the beach into a huge mirror. I like to walk, looking at the clouds reflected under my feet. The

---

[22] Arambol and Mandrem - villages in North Goa.

sky is overhead; the sky is underfoot. On one side: the endless sea, reflecting the May clouds, reminding you of the approaching rainy season. It feels like you are soaring among the clouds, and only the occasional small pebble or seashell, shining in the sunlight like the pieces of silver, reminds you that you are on the Earth. You don't need any drugs at that moment. It works better than LSD."

"Well, what is stopping you from walking in the sky here, Vasya? We'll pour more water on us and the floor will be wet. We'll walk and look at the clouds. The sky is, of course, behind bars, and there is no sea, but you can see the tops of some palm trees. Sometimes you can see flocks of green parrots flying overhead. It's no worse than a beach. Tell me, what's new in your cell?"

"Well... I had another dream about the cops, Vitya. When will this endless dream be over? Again I ran away all night."

"Well, I don't dream," Viktor says sadly, pouring the next ladle of water onto his head. "I close my eyes at night and the world switches off. I open them in the morning and it switches on again. No dreams. When my expert analysis comes in, I want to walk on a normal beach."

"Oh, I don't know, Vitya. Monsoon is coming, now I'm more worried about how not to rot in here."

"How can I manifest for the expert analysis to come by September? What do they write, Vasya, in your books about transurfing reality? What do I need to do to bring the analysis here quicker? I'm prepared to be here until fall; I will get pumped. My belly has gone now. I will learn English, and get out at the beginning of the season, born again – all the chicks will be mine. I have no desire to stay here in the season."

"The first thing to do, Vitya, is to believe and want it strongly enough. And now tell me, how is it that everyone is in here for drugs and you're in for dental anesthetic?"

"I got in the police's way. You know that they control all of the deliveries of drugs here. A gram of cocaine is sold for a hundred bucks, and I came up with my own powder. I bought amphetamine at the pharmacy, mixed it with ephedrine, and added some Novocain for taste. It didn't differ from cocaine. And the most important thing is that it costs five dollars per gram. The entire cocaine market almost collapsed. I sold it at half the price of the others. And, by the way, my powder is better than cocaine. You have to sniff cocaine every half an hour, and my powder works for four hours. So they decided to put me into prison, as the main enemy of the Goan economy. If they didn't add anything to the anesthetic, I should be released after the arrival of the export analysis."

"But, it's an outrage – going to jail for Novocain!"

"Here, Vasya, everyone who is connected to drugs serves time as a result of some sort of outrage. It is impossible to jail a smart drug-dealer honestly. Especially if he is a foreigner."

"So how did the police get onto you?"

"Well, I can only guess. Where did I sell my powder? In East End. Who runs East End? Tamir and his police cover. It was probably his team that grassed on me. When the police came to arrest me, I tried to play dumb, as if I didn't know anything, didn't understand English, and that I was a tourist. Pashish, their boss, dialed some number and gave me the phone. And there was a voice saying in Russian, 'Hey, you, that's enough playing dumb. You will serve some time and become a bit smarter.' So I'm serving my time and growing wise."

"It sounds like one and the same Russian sent us here, Vitya."

Chapter 14. Part Two. Outside.

Two weeks pass in a flash. I don't want to think about Russia at all. The parties, which are held almost every night, give me no choice regarding how to spend my evenings. Crowds of tourists prowl the streets of Anjuna, Chapora and Vagator, hoping to find the night's best party. It is hard not to join them. Quickly getting exhausted, I realize that I need to move somewhere further away from the center of the trance movement. So I move. I move to the northernmost point of Goa, to the place that various guides dub as 'the last refuge of hippies and freaks from all over the world.' I move to Arambol. Unlike Anjuna, in Arambol are people who have come here for a long time. Stretching their health over the whole season, they try to attend parties no more than once a week, only going to the coolest ones. By this time I have completely blended with this colorful and fun crowd, and don't differ from the other psychedelic tourists.

Replacing my shorts with an orange lungi[23], I spend my days hanging around in beach restaurants, meeting and talking to various interesting people. My shoulders are covered with a large bright yellow kerchief tied around my neck to protect from the sun. I don't need anything else in the way of clothes. The only thing I carry around with me is an orange bag containing a chillum, the keys to my bike, money, and an old broken camera, filled with a variety of drugs. In these restaurants, buying myself charas, MDMA and LSD without having to even go outside, I manage to sell half of what I acquire to newly arrived Russian tourists, fully recovering my money. I am sure that the key to successful sales is my appearance. Just like the freaks around me, I am covered with tattoos, several large pirate earrings hang in my ears, and I have dreadlocks. My dreadlocks are of course laughable, but I am proud of the three thin, matted braids that hang comically from my bald head.

Everyone I met refuses to believe that I have only been in India for a month. I am covered from head to toe with the attributes of a free life. Dozens of necklaces and charms made of the bones, fangs and claws of various exotic animals hang around my neck. I don't like the idea of returning home at all. I have finally found a place on Earth where I would like to live. The people who surround me are not like those I have been used to seeing since my childhood. They are real, genuine, and sincere. There are, of course, some complete idiots, but their number is as small as that of the normal people in Russia. There are a lot of things in Goa that attract interesting people from all over the world. Sea, sun, sex, fruit, music, drugs, freedom – all this is constantly available and you don't want to refuse it.

All of these things are self evident and complementary. But still, for me, the most important thing is the people. I really don't want to go back to an environment full of robot-like people! How can you voluntarily return from paradise – back to the sinful Earth? Compared to Goa, my homeland reminds me of hell. How have I lived for thirty years surrounded by my fellow citizens? Once again I will have to see their drunk, stupid faces around me. What can I talk about with these people? With

---

[23] Lungi - a traditional garment worn around the waist in India.

people who were brought up on the books of Darya Dontsova and Tatiana Ustinova[24]. I don't understand people who love Petrosyan's humor and live someone else's emotions, through endless TV series. My brain thinks feverishly without ceasing, looking for a way or a reason to stay in India. You need to think something up. Thousands of people manage to leave their business to come and stay here to live, in the land of promise. Or should I forget Goa and return to the hell that I've lived in all my life? But where can I take a pill to forget all the wonderful things that I have seen in only a month?

I am sitting in a small restaurant on the shore of the Arabian Sea, five meters away from me the gentle Indian waves slapping onto the rocks. The Sun is just beginning its short path from east to west. I am slowly eating a fruit salad, enjoying the beautiful view. A few meters away from me, on the beach, a solitary yogi with dreadlocks down to the ground, sitting in the lotus position, is meditating on the Sun, as it rises higher and higher. I wish I could meet and see off the Sun, eat fresh fruit, and communicate with great people my whole life, just like he does.

"Hi, Vasya. Have you been sitting here for a long time?" a tall guy asks me, interrupting the flow of my thoughts."

In front of me stands my Goan friend Arik, or as the natives call him, Ara. He has been living in Goa for four years already. Two meters tall, blonde hair, tanned, muscular body and smart, intelligent eyes – this is a brief description of this interesting person. And he managed to stay here, didn't he? Is it really possible to get into shape, eating only fruit and vegetables? Why do I have to miss my chance?

"What did you say, Arik?"

"I said, have you been sitting here for a long time, Vasya?"

"No, they've just brought the fruit, join me," I reply, not having fully returned to reality yet.

"I'm not alone. My buddy from Moscow has arrived. His name is Roma."

A standard Moscow tourist stands in front of me. A crew cut, shifty and uncertain glance, expensive western-style clothes, and a 'club tan' of a whitish-blue hue.

"My name is Vasiliy," I say, extending my hand to him.

"Have you been in Goa long?"

"A couple of weeks."

"Well, how do you like it?"

"I still don't quite understand what is what."

"I've been here for a little more than a couple of weeks, but some Israelis helped me to understand everything. I traveled with them for two weeks across India to Goa."

Roma, having examined me from head to toe, makes a surprised face.

"Actually, I thought you had been living here all your life, Vasya."

"You're kind of right, I've been sitting here thinking that I probably lived here my entire previous life. That's how comfortable I feel here! I have no desire at all to leave this place."

---

[24] Darya Dontsova and Tatiana Ustinova - modern Russian authors who are read by uneducated people, unwilling to think for themselves.

"So don't go," Arik interrupts us, pointing to the menu. "That's what I want: shrimps in sweet and sour sauce. I have been suffering the whole morning, wondering what to choose for breakfast. And when I saw your thoughtful face – I immediately realized that I needed shrimps in sweet and sour sauce."

"I envy you, Arik. You made a decision and left Russia."

"And what's stopping you from doing the same? Think something up. Use your head! Four years ago I also realized that I didn't want to live in Russia any longer."

"It's easy to say 'think something up.' I have a family, friends, and my favorite work in Russia."

"Why don't you bring it all over here, and live happily ever after? Vasya, let's go up to the hill tonight and trip. You will have a chance to think, and at the same time we will help Romka to move his assemblage point[25]: this poor fellow has been struggling for two weeks, not understanding what is going on," Arik says mysteriously, picking a strawberry out of my fruit salad.

---

[25] Assemblage point - a dynamic oscillating vortex of energy that exists within all of us. From the teachings of Carlos Castaneda.

Chapter 15. Part One. Inside.

I will see my Lena today. My heart is pounding, just like it did many years ago when I declared my love for her. Will she be able to understand me now? What an idiot I am. I'm terribly ashamed that I've ruined everything with my own two hands. Well, that's ok; I'll try to fix it. I have a head and hands; I will get out, start a new life. But where should I start? In Russia? No one is waiting for me there. What am I going to do? The era of legal money earning and self-employment has gone. I don't think that I'll be able to do some uninteresting job, working for someone else. Maybe I should conquer new lands? No money. A new life in Goa? Goa is dead. Nothing remains of the Goa that I found for myself five years ago. Maybe it is good that everything happened as it did.

Maybe fate is preparing a new surprise for me? Maybe it is making me ready for something new, something even more exciting. All of my old Goan friends have dispersed throughout the world. Some of them are in Latin America, others – in Thailand. Some are living in Bali, Vietnam, Cambodia, and others are hanging out in Nepal. Where are all the interesting people I met in this magical land? And where did all the magic that I found here go? Why am I surrounded by mugs again? Scum, grasses, drug dealers, loonies, alcoholics and drug addicts. What am I doing among them? My thoughts are interrupted by the sharp shout of the guard: "Vasiliy, come out, your relatives are here." I walk down the hall, as if on the first date in my life.

"How beautiful you are. I'm so sorry for everything that has happened."

"Don't worry, everything is going to be alright," Lena says in a quiet voice, hugging me tightly. "You've lost a lot of weight."

"You look great, too. I wish I could look at you forever. Just watch you and be silent. I want to tell you so much; but time is short, so there is nothing to say. We have only fifteen minutes a week for a date."

We sit opposite each other, and for some time we are silent. Our silent dialogue is interrupted by the voice of crazy Psyu, who for some reason waltzed in with my Lena. When she was silent, we didn't notice her, but Psyu speaks, taking away our attention and the precious moments to be together. As usual, she speaks loudly and very quickly.

First of all, her doped up brain gives a signal that she needs to say something, then her mouth utters sounds, and only after that, with a delay of a few seconds, Psyu realizes what she has said. It's impossible not to listen to her. During the few minutes of her verbal incontinence, she pours a bunch of unnecessary information into our ears.

"Next time come alone; I can't listen to her nonsense," I whisper in Lena's ear. "How is our daughter?"

"We are ok, it's just this damn crisis is screwing everything up. No one has any money, and everything is insanely expensive. The real estate market prices in Russia have fallen by half. It is just stagnating. It's absolutely unreal to sell our apartment now. But don't worry; your mom gave us a loan of six thousand dollars to get you out of here. But I don't know what I have to do."

"You don't need to do anything now, we just have to wait. Lena, can you imagine – these assholes planted twenty grams of MDMA on me. The drug was sent to Hyderabad for expert analysis. The judge will only start the case after the results of the analysis come back. And that's when we'll need the money."

"Where is the money that was in the safe? I left you five thousand dollars."

"All the money was taken by the police."

"Honey, why did you slit your wrists?" Lena asks softly, gently touching the scars on my wrist.

"An old prison trick. I heard that Russian criminals do it when the cops start doing something unlawful."

"Well, did it help, 'the old prison trick?'" Lena says smiling, gently stroking my hand.

"I don't know, but the chief of the drug police, Pashish, was a little scared, and out of the six thousand dollars that were in the safe, he left me one and a half thousand for a lawyer. He took the rest for himself and promised to help. However, I can only get that money after the case is closed, along with my passport and cellphone."

"Darling, what do you think, how long will you be in here?"

"Lena, I don't know. Everyone who has managed to get out of here was released not earlier than in a year and a half."

"Don't even think that you will stay in here for so long. I'll wait for you for six months at the most. And anyway, we'll get you out of here soon. Believe in it and visualize it. You know: if you think about something, then it comes true."

I can see my Lena's eyes fill with tears.

"Why did you get into this shit?" my beloved asks me with a trembling voice.

"I don't know. I guess I wanted to become a hero for you; to be the best."

Chapter 15. Part Two. Outside.

The Sun is slowly sinking into the blue ocean. It seems that the huge, yellow orange slows its progress as it touches the water. In this brief moment you can feel what time is. Flocks of parrots, seemingly scared of not seeing their Sun again, screech from the tops of the palm trees, the last to bid it farewell. Everything freezes, as if trying to delay the moment. But, despite the efforts of all living creatures, the huge star that gives us life quickly disappears below the horizon.

"Sunset is not over yet, the most beautiful sight will be soon," Arik says, picking up a drum.

Slowly, without hurrying, he begins to fill the space with pleasant sounds. We are sitting on top of a high hill, which offers an impressive view. It's the highest point in Arambol. Ahead are the vast expanses of the Arabian Sea. To the side, a string of Goan beaches stretches to the horizon like a giant golden road. From this point Arambol resembles living lava, consisting of hundreds of small houses, restaurants and rickety bamboo shacks. It looks like a load of multi-colored lava has flowed out of the green jungle and frozen, not reaching the water. I love this time. Fifteen minutes after sunset. The most beautiful time. The sky slowly becomes painted in pink. As if a mysterious lighting technician, hidden behind the scenes of the horizon, is slowly changing the color filters on his spotlights. It is as if all of the colors of the world come to life at this moment. Nestled in the hills, the pale green sunburnt jungle is painted a bright green color. The red, yellow and purple flowers in the bushes and trees that surround us glow brightly in the pink light. All of the colors are changing their hues, and, as if by the wave of a magic wand, they throw off the red Goan dust, becoming brightly saturated. The color of the sky gradually changes from pink to purple. Despite the fact that the Sun is no longer visible, there is still plenty of light. Roma, leaning his back against a large rock, is sitting in amazement with his eyes wide open.

"Fuck yeah!!! I've never seen such beauty," he says softly, closing his eyes momentarily in pleasure.

"This is only the beginning," Arik says, smiling enigmatically without ceasing to play the drum.

"Vasya, when will your drug start working?" Roma asks intently, looking like a child at an exotic flower he has plucked from a bush.

"Firstly, it is not a drug, but a psychedelic, or as it is called by the authorities a 'psychotropic drug.' And it's called 'lysergic acid diethylamide' or, for short – LSD 25."

"And what is the difference between a drug and a psychedelic?" Roma asks in surprise, not taking his eyes from the flower in his hand.

"You will get sick from drug abuse. From psychedelics: only psychological dependence and the expansion of consciousness."

"Well, when does your mind start expanding?"

"Didn't the sunset seem unusual to you? Or the flower in your hand, is it the same as always?"

"You're right, Vasya, there is something unusual about it. Each time I watch the sunset here: well, it's always as beautiful as usual. But, today is the first time I have seen such beauty... What else can I expect from the expansion of consciousness?" Roma asks, covered with a light sweat.

"Don't expect anything. Look around and listen; the LSD is working. Don't be afraid, and just let your perception restructure the way it wants. Look at the jungle swaying. As if it's not a jungle, but an extension of the sea on the shore. Look how the breeze creates waves in the treetops."

Watching Roma, I feel like the LSD has already been altering my perception for about fifteen minutes. My whole body feels the warm breath of the sea. The rich, bright colors of the altered outside world slowly began to merge into one indescribable flow with the music coming from Arik's drum. The music becomes tangible. Its vibration spills over me in rainbow fractals in all directions. The jungle is dancing with the sea, gradually losing its brightness with the onset of darkness. The sea begins to sparkle with billions of stars reflected on its surface.

"Look, the Moon is laughing at us today," Arik says, pointing at the sky.

"It's fantastic," Roma says softly, as if fearing that the new, previously invisible outside world will hear him and disappear in an instant. A crescent Moon hangs in the Indian sky. But it doesn't hang like an inhabitant of Russia can normally see it, i.e. vertically. It hangs horizontally, like the huge mouth of the Cheshire Cat, stretched into a smile across the sky. Two bright spots of light, Mercury and Venus, complete the picture, sitting in the sky exactly at the place where the Cheshire Cat's eyes would be.

"You see, nothing has changed in this world. The only thing that has changed is your perception," I tell Roma, leaning back on the green grass. "Have you ever thought about that?"

His face is shining. It is relaxed and satisfied. He is enjoying the surrounding reality.

"Say, Roma, what do you think, what is the meaning of your life? Have you thought about such things? Why do you live in this world?"

When Roma hears my question, something strange suddenly happens to his face. As if being afraid of being seen as he is now, he instantly changes his facial expression, putting on the mask of an average, slightly aggressive young man.

"Well, that... that... I... I love driving my convertible around the block... You drive, and all the chicks look at you," he blurts out abruptly, like a learned phrase.

"And this is the meaning of your life?" Arik says fearfully, having stopped playing music.

Roma's face instantly changes once again. Strange metamorphoses start happening on his face. It changes, as if trying to find a suitable mask, but nothing comes out. He clasps his head in his hands, closes his eyes and is silent. When he opens his eyes, we see a completely new person looking at us.

"I got it," he says in a whisper.

"I've been sleeping all my life. And today I woke up."

We never saw Roma in the guise of a dumb 'new Russian' again. That night the merry Moon took that stupid guy, leaving us a new man. A man with a truly expanded consciousness.

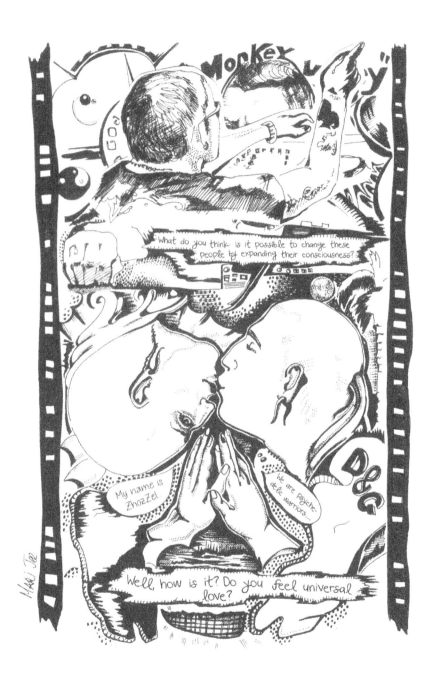

Chapter 16. Part One. Inside.

Viktor, cupping his hands, is standing quietly with his eyes closed, exposing his face to the still cool morning sun.

"Hey, bro," I shout to Viktor across the prison courtyard.

"Wait a minute, Vasya, I'm greeting the sun."

"You do that, and I'll say hello to the guys. David, what's new?"

"The same old shit, just another day," the old Iranian says, yawning and stretching in the sun.

"Right you are. The same old shit, but this day is going to be good, not as hot as yesterday. At night we'll sleep well. Hello, Adam, what's new with you?"

"Hi, Vasya. They'll take me to Delhi soon, and then – to Germany. It turns out that the German Interpol transferred a hundred thousand euros to the Indians for me. And there I will be sentenced to twenty years. The only good thing is that the conditions in European prisons are wonderful. TV, video game console, a refrigerator full of drinks, computer, and the Internet – what else does an officer in retirement need? The cells are equipped with all the amenities, in the bathrooms there are white tiles, the bed linen is clean. Bring it on! The rainy season is beginning here. It has been pouring for three days already. You could rot in here with such humidity. Nothing dries. The humidity is the same as in a Russian sauna."

"Yes," I agree, looking at the small pustules in the folds of my hands.

Your body is covered with moisture for twenty-four hours a day. All of your clothes stay wet and start to smell of mold.

"And here's our 'Al Qaeda,'" I point at a bald, long-bearded Muslim.

"Excuse me, Adam, I'll go and say hello to Ashpak. I haven't seen him for two days."

"Hi, Ashpak."

"Hi, my Russian brother."

"I haven't seen you here for a long time."

"I've been learning the Koran in Arabic, and doing gymnastics. I have no desire to walk in the rain. I lost four more pounds. A year ago my belly was like yours is now. And now look at it – you can see my abs."

"Well done, Ashpak, keep it up. Excuse me; I'll go and say hello to Count Dracula."

"Don't give up hope, Don Alexandro!" I greet the permanently-depressed Italian. "What's new?"

"Hi, Vasya, nothing new, everything is bad. No money, and progress is very slow."

"You just reek of bad energy, Milano. I'd rather go and talk to Viktor, before my mood is spoiled.

"So, have you finished greeting the sun, Vitya?"

"Yeah, now I can say hello to you. Hi, Vasya, what's new?"

"A rat came into our cell last night. It was huge, the size of a cat."

"It came to visit us too. It's not a rat – it's a Gus. That's what they call this creature here."

"I woke up last night because I felt something crawling on my feet. At first, still half asleep, I thought it was a snake. But after a closer look, I saw a really long tail and a nasty snout. I threw a bottle at it and woke up everybody in the cell. We chased it all over the cell, but couldn't catch it."

"It happens," Viktor agrees. "I once caught such a beast with a bucket. I kept it in the bucket for a bit and then let it go, I couldn't kill it..." without finishing what he is saying, Viktor abruptly dives to one side, lying flat on the ground.

I don't have time to understand what is going on. I stand with my mouth open, observing a strange scene. A dozen people, including Viktor, are crawling around on the floor, trying to snatch something from each other.

"Tobacco," Viktor rejoices, showing me a small plastic bag in which there is enough tobacco to fill a matchbox.

"It costs one rupee, and in prison it is more precious than gold. If you have tobacco, it means you have everything. This is the main currency here."

"But isn't it illegal here? Where did it fall from?"

"You see that fence, Vasya?" Viktor points to a wall covered with moss. "There is a road behind that wall. Those who are released throw us some tobacco over the wall sometimes."

"And the guards don't try to take it away?"

"Look at them, Vasya, what can they do?"

Under a rain canopy, four fat guards sit on plastic chairs. Despite the fact that each of them has a bamboo stick in his hand, it is unlikely they'd dare to take tobacco away from a prisoner, especially from Viktor or me.

"They barely move their asses. Why do they need another pain in the butt? Tobacco is useful here, even if you don't smoke."

"The next time I'll be more agile, and I'll snatch some, too. I would smoke it in the evening with great pleasure."

Chapter 16. Part Two. Outside.

"Will you smoke?" Roma asks me, holding out a neatly rolled joint. "Look what straight joints I have started making."

"Good for you, it's a pleasure to watch. It's not like stuffing a 'Belomor'[26]. You've reached the international level. It's only been a month since we met, and I already can't recognize you."

A completely new person sits in front of me, sipping fresh strawberry juice. Instead of a crew cut, a fashionable Goan mohawk is shaved onto his head. And in his ear there is a metal tunnel instead

---

[26]Belomor Kanal - traditional Russian cigarettes used for smoking marijuana.

of an earring. Nothing is left from the European clothes that he arrived in. Now it is difficult to determine where this young Aztec came from. His skin is tanned and his body has become lean.

"You've become a real Goan guy. Are you going to the party at 'Monkey Valley' tonight? Tamir is throwing a trance party."

"Well, if it's Tamir, then we'll probably have a good time. All the freaks go to his parties," Roma agrees, smoking his joint. "When he threw his first trance parties in Moscow, he was already considered the best DJ. No wonder that even then he was called the 'Rave Master'."

*

The 'Rave Master' is standing proudly behind the decks, holding the headphones with one hand, and choosing the disks for the next track with the other. He looks like a shamanic leader. His hands, covered with mysterious oriental tattoos, deftly play tracks, not giving the dancers a chance for a break. With a serious and wise look, he closely watches the dancing mass. A thousand different beautiful boys and girls dance captivated among the thickets of bamboo. Everyone is looking at him, transmitting their feelings into their dance moves. And he feels their vibrations. It is like he is hypnotizing all of them. Thousands of people move in the same shamanic rhythm.

"How will we expand our consciousness today?" Roma asks, screaming in my ear and dancing around.

"Let's start with 'Dymich,'[27] and after that we'll see. I'm saving the drops[28] for the morning."

Finding an empty seat next to a chai-mama, we sit on mats, sipping hot tea with spices, watching the people around us. MDMA crystals begin to dissolve slowly in our stomachs, covering our bodies with goose bumps of pleasure.

"Tell me, Roma, do you believe that it is possible that in our country too the majority of people will one day have kind, happy faces? Look at all these people who surround us now. They are not from another planet. And they can be happy."

"I don't know, Vasya, maybe one day, but not soon, I guess. The slave mentality has been engrained in our country for too long. Look over there, they are definitely Russians," Roma says, pointing at a strange couple dancing five meters away from us.

"That's for sure."

They stand out from all the other people dancing around in every respect. It seems like the man dressed in a tight white T-shirt with a 'D&G' logo has intentionally pulled his shorts of the same color up to his navel, in order to emphasize his big belly. His plump girlfriend, apparently believing that it's cool to be in matching T-shirts, shakes the logo of the well-known brand on her huge tits while dancing. Apart from them, there is no one wearing white here. The dancing people's clothes are of all different colors. Orange, yellow and black dominate, but no one else is wearing white. Their movements are also radically different from the movements of the people around them. It looks like they can only hear the top layer of the music, consisting of a single beat. The guy, marking time on

---

[27] Dymich - Russian slang for MDMA.

[28] Drops - liquid LSD-25.

the spot, looks like he is boxing an invisible enemy. His girlfriend, occasionally tugging at her vulgar short skirt, reminds me of a cheap whore. She dances clumsily, wiggling her big ass.

"What do you think, Roma, is it possible to change these people by expanding their consciousness?"

"And why should you expand their consciousness?"

"I don't know. I guess I want to make everyone happy. I feel sorry looking at them. Everyone around is smiling, and look at them: they can't even force a smile."

"You want proof of the theory of the psychedelic quantum leap," Roma says, smiling and putting his empty tea glass on the mat.

A few minutes later, we are sitting together with them near the chai-mama.

"My name is Zhyora, and this is my wife, Natasha. If you hadn't come up to us, we would never have guessed that you are Russians, too. You must have been living in Goa for a long time?" Zhyora asks, sipping from his bottle of beer.

"No, I also arrived recently; it's my second month here," I say, eyeing Natasha. The MDMA is already in full effect, smearing all the defects of her body in my mind's eye.

"We only came for two weeks. It's impossible to escape from Moscow for longer. In Moscow, I work for a construction company, and my Natasha is an accountant in a bank. And what do you do?"

"We are psychedelic warriors," Roma says, smiling. "The material world is currently not very interesting for us."

"We are actually in India for the first time. We still prefer Turkey. Usually, we go to Antalya with a big crowd, booze for two weeks, and return to work. We are tired of our colleagues; everywhere, no matter where we go, all of the conversations are about work. Any boozing eventually turns into a conference."

"So we decided to run away from everyone to India for two weeks," Natasha adds, once again adjusting her short skirt, baring a little triangle of her lacy underwear.

Under the influence of MDMA, Natasha no longer seems too plump. I struggle to drive the overwhelming lustful thoughts out of my head.

"And why didn't you change your clothes into normal ones?" I ask, hardly able to avert my eyes from her charms.

"What, don't you like our clothes? In Russia we always dress like this when we go clubbing."

"This is not Russia; look around – look how people are dressed. If you want to feel what Goa is, forget about Russia and its fashion. In those clothes they probably sell you everything three times more expensive. It's like you have a sign on your foreheads that says: 'We came here for two weeks. Our budget is five hundred dollars a day. Cheat us out of our money.' You are treated like walking wallets now, not as people."

"And where can we buy clothes like yours? You have cool boots."

"These are not boots, these are ninja shoes[29]," Roma boasts, wiggling the big toes of both feet.

_____

[29] Ninja shoes - Japanese knee-high boots made of cloth, with a flat rubber sole and a separate section for the

"I see that almost everyone here walks around in such shoes. I haven't see them in Russia."

"These are the best shoes for dancing in the open air," Roma says, stamping his foot on the dusty ground.

"Honey, please buy me a rum and Coke, and get something for the guys to drink. Boys, what would you like to drink?"

"We prefer tea," Roma says proudly, showing his glass.

"What, you don't you drink alcohol?" Natasha asks in surprise, again adjusting her constantly riding-up short skirt.

"Almost none."

"And how do you manage to be so cheerful? Is it the tea?"

"Tea, of course, also invigorates. However, today Roma and I ate a crystal of MDMA each. Do you want some?"

"What is MDMA?"

"MDMA is the main chemical element used to make ecstasy pills, it consists of crystals. Some Russian chemists, the Shulgins, invented it. Never heard of it?"

"No," Zhyora replies with surprise, carefully watching as I unfold a small plastic bag.

"Will we be tormented by a come down like drug addicts?" Natasha asks in a frightened voice, looking at her husband.

"Don't worry. Look at us; do we look like junkies? This is not a drug, it is a psychedelic."

"And what will we feel? We won't feel bad?"

"You'll feel love for everything around you, universal love."

"We like love," Natasha says, flirting and hugging her husband.

Tipping two doses of crystalline powder into a glass of tea, I give it to them.

"Well, what will be, will be. If we came to Goa, we must give it a try," Zhyora says, taking the first sip.

"I'll see you in an hour in the same place. Sorry, but I can't sit still any longer. I urgently need to dance," I say, putting on my big pink glasses. The MDMA burst of energy is so strong that I run up to the loud speakers. I want to let this energy out somehow, before I explode from happiness.

The incredibly beautiful music doesn't allow me to stand still. The people dancing around me draw the music with their bodies, moving unbelievably beautifully. Everybody has their own unique dance. It's not even a dance; it's a flight. It is simply impossible to stay in one place. Through dance I communicate with the others, moving around the floor to the beat of the music. The diameter of my dance movements stretches several meters now. Meeting the sparkling eyes of the dancing people, I understand that everyone here is saturated with love energy. I love this beautiful world, I love everyone. Tamir, behind the DJ booth, feels this energy and is revving up. Thousands of people feel unity with the whole Universe. Everything around is saturated with love. It seems like time has stopped, because it is irrelevant for love. Time only reminds me of itself through a dry throat and strong thirst. I should stop and get a drink. I see my new friends; they are also dancing, having merged

---

big toe.

into one long, passionate kiss. Their movements don't seem like the movements of two goblins anymore; their bodies feel the music deeply, and they move beautifully and harmoniously.

"Well, how is it? Do you feel universal love?" I say to them, drawing a big heart in the air.

"Yes," Zhyora and Natasha cry in unison, trying to shout above the speakers. "We got it. Thank you, Vasya, you're just a kind magician. It turns out it's possible to enjoy life without any reason. Life is beautiful and unique," Natasha shouts, twisting and dancing around Zhyora.

"I've finally managed to get rid of thoughts about my work," Zhyora adds, trying to show with his dance how he managed it. The eyes of both of them shine with overwhelming joy and happiness. I'm happy for them, because I managed to change their perception of this imperfect world. If I only I knew then what kind of a cruel joke fate had in store for them in the future. Their expanded consciousness would shrink unpredictably a few years down the line, changing their destinies.

"Listen, Vasya, sell us some of your powder," Zhyora says, hugging Natasha tightly around the waist.

"Actually, I'm not a drug dealer, but I have almost run out of money. If you give me two hundred dollars, I'll sell you my last two grams."

"Of course we will, no question. We came here to spend our money on our vacation. We'll be back in Russia soon, and we'll earn more. You live here; you need it more. Moreover, you do good work, helping people to wake up," Zhyora says, handing me two American bills.

"Look, Roma, how quickly people change."

"Yes, psychedelics work miracles on people. Still, Goa is an amazing place. For forty years people from all over the world have been coming here. And they still dream that someday the whole world will be ruled by love, not hatred."

"Look at that chick dancing to your right. I think she's from the same planet as you, and I think she wants to establish contact," Roma says, smiling and pointing out a girl dancing nearby.

Turning and focusing my sparkling eyes, I see an extraordinary creature: a beautiful young girl in a floor-length gypsy skirt, spinning to the rhythm of the trance music, with movements that remind me of a Mexican shaman. Big brown eyes, bushy eyebrows and, just like me, three dark dreadlocks on her clean-shaven head. Her perfectly slim body is moving so beautifully to the rhythm of the music that I can't take my eyes off her. She sees my fascinated gaze and blows me a kiss, inviting me to join her magical dance with a gesture. Once again time stops for me. Another DJ replaces Tamir and plays no less beautiful music. We keep on moving in circles across the dance floor, never taking our eyes off each other. The Full Moon is reflected in her large, bottomless brown eyes. I can't stop. I am very thirsty, but her gaze won't let me go, like a magnet.

"What's your name, wonderful creature?"

"Zhozel," she answers quietly, touching the lobe of my ear with her lips.

"And my name is Vasiliy," I say, breathing in the smell of her skin. The hair on my body begins to stand up due to this divine scent.

"Vashiliy?"

"Yes, Vashiliy, you can just call me Vasa. Where did you come from, beauty?"

"Uruguay."

"How did you get here? It's on the other end of the world?"

"And where are you from?" Zhozel asks, embracing my waist with both arms."

"Russia."

"Russia? Where is this country?" Zhozel asks in her broken English, pressing closer and closer to me.

"Well, how can I explain it to you, beautiful creature? Do you know such a country as Japan?"

"Yes," she nods, pressing her breasts against me.

"Do you know such country as Germany?"

"Yes."

"There is a large country between them, and that's where I live."

Suddenly the huge eyes of this beautiful bald girl fill with tears and she starts crying, throwing herself onto my neck.

"What? What's wrong?" I try to calm her down, not knowing what is going on.

"Why, why is the world so unfair? You see, all my life I've been waiting for you. Since my childhood, I have seen you in my dreams. Why were you born so far away from me?"

I try to reassure her, pressing her tightly to me. Like a little girl, she shudders and sobs in my arms.

"Let's go somewhere; I have a lot to tell you."

Forgetting about Roma and my new friends, I rush on my scooter towards the sea, cutting through the fog that has fallen on the road. The music doesn't stop, it sounds in my head, and it sounds from everywhere. Millions of cicadas sound to me like a trance rhythm. Even the motor of my scooter plays music; my head wiggles and the muscles of my arms and legs flex to the beat. Coming down to the sea, we drive along the water's edge, leaving a sparkling fountain of splashes. The Uruguayan beauty presses her warm body against my back, hugging my chest with her hands. The sea water, sparkling under the Full Moon, reflects the stars, which also dance to the music in my head.

"Let's stop here," my Uruguayan girlfriend tells me.

Stopping the scooter on the beach and without get off properly, we throw ourselves into each other's arms. Our lips merge in a long kiss.

"Will you stay with me?" Zhozel asks with hope, hugging me tightly. I can't lie to those eyes.

"Forgive me, but I love another woman. I have a family and a beautiful little daughter."

She cries in my arms again.

"I can't do this. My wife Lena is coming to Goa tomorrow."

Chapter 17. Part One. Inside.

"I need to go back to Russia," Lena says sadly, lowering her eyes. "Right now, I can't do anything to help you here, and there, in Russia, our daughter is alone, without us, staying with your mom. Everything will be fine. I called Tamir, and he promised to help when he gets back to Goa. Until that damn expert analysis comes, nothing can be done. Don't worry about us; we'll be fine. Think about yourself now. You need to take care of yourself, in order to survive. We'll be back in four months. I'll bring Vasilinka; she misses us, and I have to be there for her. I'll try to make some money somehow, and we will get you out of here."

I hug her for the last time, trying to remember her scent. She kisses me on the lips, and this moment that seems to last forever awakens in me something that I had tried to hide in the remotest corners of my memory. It's like an electric shock. The guards, who only see beautiful white women in the movies, stare lustfully at my Lena. For the last time, I cling to my beloved. The warden points at the clock; our date is over. My gaze follows her to the door. Before leaving, she blows me a kiss. Maybe it's better that she is leaving. My soul won't hurt from knowing that she is somewhere close by, while I sit in a cage, unable to touch her. The cell door closes from outside.

"How is your family?" Dominic asks me, turning down the volume of the screaming TV.

"They're okay," I say, opening the 'The Tibetan book of the Dead'. Buddhist literature always helps me to restore harmony with the surrounding world.

"Why are you so sad? Some problems with your family?"

"No, Dominic, everything is fine. It's just that the next visit will be in four months," I say, taking off the clean shirt that I normally only wear when I go to court. "But I'm not sad because of that. I'm sad because I don't know what to say to my daughter when I see her. How can I explain to her why I'm in prison? What should I tell her if she asks why her friends went to school, and she didn't? I don't even feel sad, I feel ashamed. Ashamed because I preferred my principles, my fucking psychedelic revolution, to simply being able to be with her. From her birth, she became my only motivation in life. After she was born, almost everything I did made sense. I knew that I was alive and that everything I did, I did it for her. Even taking drugs and exploring this uncharted path; I did it for her. Trying to go first and to protect her from future mistakes."

"But, if you think like that, then you have also been locked up for her. You made a mistake and are sitting here so that she will never repeat it."

I put on a prison T-shirt and slump down onto my place, staring at the high wall behind the barred window.

"I also sometimes feel sad about the fact that when my daughter grows up, the neighbors will point fingers at her and say, 'Her father is a robber; he robbed a gas station,' Dominic tells me, sighing. "But, we shouldn't think about that now; first of all we need to get out of here. Don't give up hope."

"Yes," I answer him, trying to calm my raging mind by imagining it as a calm ocean.

You can't be sad in prison, or you go mad. I need something to occupy my brain for the next four months. Of course, I will try to meditate as they describe in the Buddhist books, but I am not sure I'll be able to keep it up for long. What have I dreamt about for the last few years? Learning English, exercising, studying Eastern philosophy... that is what I'll do here. I have two two-liter plastic bottles. I can attach some handles to them out of rags and they will make pretty good dumbbells. The wall opposite my seat will make a great school board. Sharpening a pencil stub with my small piece of blade, I write on the wall in big letters, "I want improve my English." I am not going to waste my time; I don't have so much of it. Pushing aside my mat, I start doing push-ups, trying to recall the last time I did any. After recovering my breath for five minutes, I take a plastic water bottle, and start doing bicep curls. Well, I can do five push-ups and a hundred bicep curls with a two-liter bottle. Not a bad start.

Chapter 17. Part Two. Outside.

"How you have changed! You look great!" Both my wives say in unison.

"There were no tickets, so we bought two package tours for the two New Year weeks," Irina, my first wife, says.

"You look a bit tired. How are you doing, Ira?"

"After your move to India, I've had to deal with the business all alone. Nobody helps me now. I am tired... I'm tired of fucking Rashka[30]. We have to work more and more, but there is less and less income. The corporations have crushed small business entirely. Out of the ten stores that we once had, only one is left. Rent and taxes eat up almost all of the profits.

"Well, what about your personal life? Haven't you found a husband yet?"

"What personal life are you talking about? I don't have any time for relaxation. And anyway, I'm over forty now; who needs me at my age."

"Don't worry, we'll find you a husband. There are lots of interesting people here, in Goa. You are clever and beautiful; men are still going to be after you. Well, what's your first impression of India?" I ask, dragging a suitcase into the hotel corridor.

"Actually, it reminds me of a poor imitation of a decent resort," Irina says, pointing at a huge cockroach running along the wall.

"Although it's supposed to be a four-star hotel, in my opinion, it is difficult to give it even one star."

"Well, you should get used to it: this is India, everything here is fake. The Indians, due to their lack of a creative mindset, can only copy other people's ideas, and they copy them in their own way, as best they can. Thirty years ago, they were still climbing palm trees, and now they are building

---

[30] Rashka - a name given to Russia by Russians living in Goa.

hotels. Lena and I are going to head up north now, to Arambol. Give yourself time to acclimatize, get a good night's sleep, and then come and join us. You are going to like North Goa."

Lena and I race along on my scooter, away from the stupid hotels with their chlorinated swimming pools and air-conditioned rooms. We're going to the place where my modest bamboo bungalow stands on the edge of the ocean, where you can fall asleep to the sound of waves crashing against the shore just a few meters away from the window. We are going to a place where there are no drunken Russian mugs wandering around.

"It's so beautiful here," Lena screams in my ear, clinging tighter to my back. "I've never seen so many palm trees. And how fresh the air is here! Now I understand why you don't want to go back."

"Lena, you haven't seen the most important thing yet; this is just the beginning. The most important thing in Goa is the people. We'll be there soon and you'll see it with your own eyes. What's new in Rashka?" I scream, trying to shout above the headwind and engine noise.

"We need to do something about Hemp. Revenue is falling dramatically."

"What about the package I sent you from India. Is it selling badly?"

"Your package sold out long ago. Indian Hemp can help us out in the offseason, but the Indians don't make winter clothes out of hemp, and our winter is very cold. We need a serious supply of winter stuff. The suppliers haven't sent us the new collection yet. The rent swallows up all the profits. We urgently need to look for new suppliers or open our own production."

"Don't worry, I'll return to Russia in a month and think of something. I have a plan."

"I've really missed you. How do you live here? According to my calculations, you should have run out of money long ago. How do you earn a living?"

"Lena, I've realized that India is a wonderful country. You can easily live without money here. And any money that you really need, falls from the sky in the quantity you wish."

"What do you mean?"

"Well, for example: yesterday, when I ran out of money and had to pay the rent for the bungalow and scooter, I sold a couple of grams of MDMA – the money is enough for me to not only pay for housing and the bike, but it is also enough for a week of living without denying myself anything."

"Honey, isn't it dangerous to sell drugs?"

"I'm not going to sell drugs. I'll never touch any cocaine or heroin. And everyone sells psychedelics in Goa. Here, in impoverished India, the most serious problems with the police, for which the punishment can be up to ten years, can be resolved for as little as one thousand dollars. A crime for which you would be given five years in Russia, can be glossed over for a hundred bucks. India is a very corrupt country. The police recently raided a Russian drug-dealer, and he had a hundred grams of MDMA in a pile on the table. He gave the police one thousand dollars, did a line with them, and it was all worked out. In Russia, he would have been very lucky if the cops had demanded fifty thousand dollars. It's more likely that he would have been sentenced for at least ten years. If India's police start putting Europeans into prison, who is going to come here?

"And is it possible to earn a living legally here? After all, we have a young daughter. I want to be able to sleep peacefully at night. Vasilinka misses you too; she is with your mother now, and I told her that you would come home soon. When are you coming back to Russia?"

"Lena, I'm sure that I'll be back soon. But I'll only come back to resolve everything, and then I want to come back here. I don't know yet how I can legally earn a living here, but I've got some ideas. I've been searching for a place to open a restaurant, and I need at least a month to reach an agreement with the owner. We will have a restaurant on the beach."

The two weeks of the New Year holidays that year were the last in Goa's history when trance parties were held almost every day. Thousands of Russians, Israelis, British, and Japanese still prowled the streets of Goa in search of the night's best party. For two weeks, every night we moved from party to party, smoking hash and taking soft drugs, and during the daytime we lay on the beach, sipping fresh juice. Lena was happy, and so was I. We didn't want to leave at all. My first wife, Irina, was also fascinated by North Goa. Having escaped from the four-star hotel she had paid for in South Goa, she moved into a bungalow near us, without air conditioning, television, or maids; and she was blissfully happy. Thoughts about escaping Russia were also maturing in her mind, just like in mine. The thought that it wouldn't be bad to spend the rest of your life here in paradise, on the shore of the Arabian Sea.

For a whole month after the departure of my wives, I continued to live in Arambol. It was a turning point in my life. I woke up and went to bed with the thought of how to stay here forever. Over time, the parties ceased to be something exotic. I went to them like going to work. I liked making money, dancing and talking to interesting people. Moving all over North Goa, I met thousands of people. I was already known by all the Russians who lived permanently in the north, from Arambol to Anjuna. I sold my fellow countrymen LSD, mescaline, MDMA, ecstasy, charas. I didn't just sell psychedelics; I was a psychedelic preacher. When I arrived at a party, I chose my victims and worked on them the whole night. Sometimes they were loners, sometimes a whole crowd. I didn't care whether they bought something, because I earned at least a hundred dollars a day without putting much effort into it. I was interested in watching their transformation, the transformation of their perception of the world. I watched as within two weeks, notorious Russian gangsters turned into ordinary nice guys, and 'new Russian' businessmen who were previously unable to talk about anything but money, started discussing the meaning of life. On their departure home to Russia, many people thanked me for their awakening. They shook hands with me, promising to return. Everyone was transformed. Everyone became more human and more kind to some extent. Dozens, perhaps hundreds of such dedicated psychedelic preachers moved around Goa from one mama-chai to another, from one party to the next. Everywhere that at least one such preacher appeared, all conversations revolved around the psychedelic revolution, the expansion of consciousness, or the quantum leap in perception. Books by psychedelic professors and spiritual gurus propounding the expansion of consciousness through the use of natural or synthesized psychotropic drugs, were discussed everywhere. Hard drugs and alcohol were universally condemned.

People like me, psychedelic preachers, explained to people the difference between good and bad drugs, telling them the things that society tries to conceal, as society considers all drugs unequivocally bad. People who embraced the faith of the psychedelic religion, refused to return to their place in society. Having realized the futility of the endless pursuit of the Golden Calf or a happy future, people threw away their expensive clothes and cell phones, burned their passports and return tickets, preferring the simple life of a fishing village to the hectic life of a big city. If only we knew then whose toes we were stepping on. Society did not seem like a cruel monster capable of easily crushing anyone who tried to undermine its conservative principles. It seemed that it needed just a little longer, and our imperfect world would enter the final sprint in the race of evolution, where love and harmony would be the core values.

I returned to Russia in the middle of winter. Moscow met me with dirty snow and gloomy, worried faces. Having discarded all illusory problems, I shone, standing out like a sore thumb in a crowd of average Russians. Despite the cold weather, I wore a knitted Nepalese jacket that resembled a small rainbow from a distance, fluorescent orange pants, and I had a pink scarf around my neck. Over my shoulder hung a bag with a drum protruding out of it, and I had summer sandals on my feet. The smile didn't leave my face. Nobody could spoil my mood.

Dymkov, like all the other Russians I meet, greets me with a gloomy gray face.

"Tell me about your trip" he says without smiling, and pulls a pack of cigarettes and a little box of ganja out of his desk.

"I don't know what to tell you. I was on another planet."

"Did you fuck a lot of chicks?"

"You won't believe it, Dymkov; it was so good there that chicks didn't interest me at all. Well no, they interested me, of course; but only as interesting people, not as sex objects."

"You are getting old, buddy. When you and I used to visit prostitutes, they didn't interest you as people at all."

"No, Dymkov, it is you who is getting old. I learned to feel unconditional love. It's cooler than usual sex. What do you think of first after you sleep with a woman?"

"How to get rid of her, what else I can think about? You know, I have a family, kids."

"There you are. Well, I've learned to simply love everyone. For me, if I haven't slept with a girl she remains a mystery, the invisible Universe; and for you, everyone you have fucked is a thing of the past."

"It's obvious you took too many drugs in Goa. Let's have a smoke," Dymkov says, handing me a joint. "Chicks, drugs, Goa… I've got you. Let's talk business. Do you know what's going on with Hemp?

"Of course I know. But, I don't think there's any reason to panic. Don't worry, Dymkov; I have a plan. I know how to get us out of this crisis. We need to open our own production, and I'm ready to put together a business plan."

"And where are you going to get the money from, Vasya?" Dymkov asks me, suddenly serious, leaning back in the leather chair.

"What do you mean 'where from'? You said that Sam personally promised to support our project. Or is Legalize no longer of interest to him?"

"Legalize is Legalize, but in our corporation we have a rule: if someone takes money, they have to return it before asking for more."

"But it was clear from the very beginning that the project is new and risky, and that it would probably require additional investment. Besides, the main purpose of Hemp is not commercial, but political.

"Don't confuse politics with business."

"But it's not our business. I'm just a manager; you are a supervisor. Our business is to work. And theirs is to invest the dough."

"If we don't give back the money on time, the security service will come to your home and propose that you sell your apartment. And, if you object, they'll cut off your ear first, so that then you will run to sell your home yourself."

"No, Dymkov; we didn't agree on anything about my apartment. We need to get out of this crisis some other way. The business still works; it just needs upgrading. I am ready to sell my jeep and invest in Hemp.

"Well, that's more like it. Tell me, what's your plan?" Dymkov asks me, his face relaxing immediately, and passes me the joint.

"We have to go to Nepal. According to my information, they make a lot of fabric out of hemp there. We'll open our own production."

"Well then, you better get ready for a new expedition," Dymkov pats me on the shoulder approvingly. "Just stop smiling all the time, you're not in Goa now. Your cheerful smile ruins the working atmosphere."

After that, I managed to smile for another month. For a month, nothing could upset me. I continued preaching my psychedelic religion in Russia. I met with my friends and acquaintances. I called everyone to quit their businesses and move to Goa. Many people listened enviously to my adventures and dreamed that someday they too would abandon their stupid jobs, and go in search of the Promised Land. Some of them looked at me like I was crazy, as though I had taken too many drugs and gone completely mad. But after a while, I noticed that almost everyone was irritated by my happy face. Everyone raced around at high speed, pursuing a rich and happy future, pushing aside anyone who got in their way.

Happiness was somewhere just beyond the horizon. You only had to pull your socks up, and run for it. But no one managed to run with a smile. Happy, smiling people, like me, either relaxed you or irritated you. For exactly one month I managed to keep going on the energy I had accumulated in Goa. Then, unexpectedly, depression hit. The harsh Russian reality surrounded me like a heavy gray fog. It was as though my battery had suddenly died. There was absolutely nothing I wanted to do. I didn't want to go outside to see the faces of my disgruntled fellow citizens. I really missed fresh juice, fruit salads, freshly prepared seafood and the Sun, which for some reason didn't show up very often. Eating tasteless Russian food, I again gained the twenty pounds that I had lost in Goa.

I tried to give other people a smile, hoping to get at least a little bit of positive energy in return, but on meeting my gaze people either averted their frightened eyes, suspecting me of something bad, or responded to me with an evil grin. "Look, Petya, that dude is dressed like a rooster. He's probably a fag or a Hari Krishna," I often heard behind me. But then, finally, it was time to sell my car. I had money, so I began to prepare for a new expedition. It was an expedition from which I never returned, an expedition that radically changed my life.

Chapter 18. Part One. Inside.

"Today, another foreigner is checking into our 'five-star hotel'," Dominic tells me, tossing aside the newspaper. "Some Scottish guy was seized with three kilograms of charas."

"Nothing interesting. I'm neither hot nor cold about it. Today I broke a record: I can already do twenty push-ups. Now that's good news."

"Well done, Russian. You learn English all day long, do sports. How do you have so much vitality? I can either sleep all day or watch TV. I don't want to do anything."

"I can't understand how you Indians can sleep all day and all night. You slumber all of your life away. After all, if fate has thrown us into such a situation, we need to make the most out of it. Life is short. Every hour spent asleep is one less hour of your life. I've always wanted to have ripped biceps and to be fluent in English. And here I've got a great opportunity to realize my dreams. I can't fall asleep if I know that I haven't done anything useful during the day. A whole day of life is a priceless gift. I can't waste it; otherwise it seems to me that life is passing me by."

"I learned English at school, and I'm quite satisfied with my muscles," Dominic answers, examining his biceps.

"I learned English at school, university, courses – all to no avail. Without practice, I forget everything in two weeks. But here in prison, I have learned more words than during the rest of my life. Check what new words I know now," I point at the wall opposite me.

The wall within a radius of two meters from my 'bed' is covered with new English words.

"Improve, escape, effort, freedom, remain," Dominic reads aloud, smiling. "The entire prison lexicon. As for me, I have a slightly different approach to life. For me, sleep is also a continuation of life. And sometimes this life in sleep is much more interesting than reality. In a dream, I can enjoy all my feelings the same as in reality. And what feelings can I experience in prison? Mostly it is only suffering. Suffering because everything that gave me pleasure has been taken away. Even if I don't dream, I enjoy the fact that I can sleep now as much as I wish. What destiny has in store for me in the future, I don't know. Maybe all I'll dream about then will be to get a good night's sleep. Maybe I will lack the time to sleep, so its better that I sleep now, for the future. And I also love to fall asleep, having smoked charas. Have you ever smoked charas?"

"I don't even know what to answer. I can write a thesis about charas. Outside, a few years ago, I smoked a lot, ten grams per day. Last year, a couple of grams a day. And now, in prison, I haven't smoked anything at all for more than a month."

"Look what our David gave me," Dominic says, showing me a small black pea on his palm.

"What a surprise! Ah, David is a good doctor."

"Well, then, it's time to celebrate. I've done enough gymnastics for today. And as for my English classes; I'll take a break. We'll try to remind ourselves what it's like."

Breaking the little pea in half and lifted it to my nose, I slowly breathe in the magical scent. It is impossible to confuse it with anything else. Memories of the Himalayas, covered with endless fields of the miracle herb from which aromatic charas is made, instantly come to mind. Oh, why did this herb bring me here?

Having made a cone from a piece of notebook paper, on the model of the Russian 'goat leg'[31], I stuff it with a mixture of small pieces of charas and chewing tobacco, which is similar to shag in strength. The first pull burns my throat so badly I can hardly restrain myself from coughing.

"You have strong tobacco in India."

"Strong life, strong tobacco," Dominic answers.

The pleasant, familiar lightness strikes me first in the head, and then gradually spreads throughout my body. Leaning back against the cell wall, I become immersed in myself, watching how the reality surrounding me slowly begins to transform. The peeled walls become a nice yellow color. My brain, used to raging against the injustice of the world, slowly calms down.

"A small freedom," Dominic says sadly, also leaning back on the floor. "India's Independence Day is soon; maybe we'll be lucky and come under the amnesty. My lawyer prepared a statement for the judge. Maybe I'll be released on bail."

"It is unlikely. There is little chance," former policeman Chetsi interrupts our fantasies. "Those who are here for up to three years might get an amnesty, but we have no chance, we are serious criminals. We have a better chance of getting ten years than getting out of here."

"Police, stop whining. Don't listen to him, Vasya, everything will be fine."

"Don't give up hope!" our friendly killer Disay shouts to me from another corner of the cell.

Chapter 18. Part Two. Outside.

"Hello India, Hello Goa. I've missed you."

Once again, I'm running barefoot on endless Arambol beach. The blue sky is reflected on the sand, smooth and wet from the low tide. Once again, I'm running across the sky. My eyes are wet from happiness, and I can't understand whether I am crying or laughing. Happy like a child, I run trailing a large yellow scarf, which billows behind me like a flag in the currents of the warm Goan wind. I greet all the people passing me and they smile back at me with understanding. I'm back in paradise. Today, my friends from Rashka have arrived. The first of those who heard enough of my stories and, finally, decided to take a trip to India. I walk along the beach to the next village, to a cafe called Russian Sunset. I must help my country folks to see the Goa that I love.

"Hey, Valera, hello country folks!" I wave my scarf at a crowd of pale guys finishing up their duty-free alcohol in the shade of some low palm trees.

"Hey, homie," my tipsy fellow citizens extend their hands to me one by one.

"Welcome to the Promised Land. How was your trip?"

---

[31] Goat leg - in contrast to the classical joint, which is glued lengthwise, a Russian 'goat leg' joint looks like an elongated paper cone, into which tobacco is poured.

"We don't remember anything; we were boozing all the way. Now we'll have a hair of the dog and maybe then we'll remember something."

"Vasya, I don't understand: where are the elephants, where are the monkeys?" Valera asks, laughing and handing me a bottle of rum. "Will you drink with us?"

"No, thanks guys, but I don't want to drink in the heat, in the afternoon. However, smoking with you is a different story. I'll be happy to keep you company," pulling a tola[32] of charas out of my pocket, I give it to the guys.

"That's more like it. That's not a bad piece; that would go for around two hundred dollars at Russian rates."

"Yeah, and ten years in prison," one of the guys adds, laughing.

"Where will we go to smoke? Or can we do it right here?"

"Relax, guys, this is India; everyone smokes here. So smoke wherever you want. No one will say anything to you. And if the police bother you, give them ten dollars. This violation of the law doesn't cost more than that.

"To listen to you, this really is paradise. When will you show us Goa? Because in Russia, thanks to you, all everyone in the city talks about is India."

"You'd better change your clothes first, and get a bit of a tan. I am ashamed to appear with you like that in cool places."

"What's there to be ashamed of? We have normal, branded clothes. And we also have no problems with dough."

"Come on, don't be offended. You'll understand everything in a week's time. Now all you talk about is money, whores and business. And here, the values are a little different. To make interesting friends, you need to become interesting yourself first. You will soon understand everything. The closing party of the Baba Yaga Russian restaurant will take place in a week, so I'll be able to introduce you to the world then. For now: relax, sunbathe, there's no need to hurry."

"Listen, Vasya. We brought a 'micro oligarch' with us," Valera whispers in my ear, pointing at a guy with short hair standing nearby. "Show us the Goa you have been going on about the whole time, and we'll finance everything."

"Valera, why do you measure everything with money? The issue isn't about money, but your desire to see the best here. If you want to see, you'll see. And if you don't, I can't help you in any way. You'll only pay attention to shit."

"We will try to learn not to look at shit during the next week, but you should also not let us down, show us the party."

The week passed by quickly, like one long moment. Every day I bought samples of hemp products from Nepalese traders at the market, learned English, sunbathed, smoked, and enjoyed my life.

"We are going to Baba Yaga tonight, are you ready to see the real Goa?" I ask my Russian friends, who have managed to get suntans and undergo a transformation.

---

[32] Tola - an Indian unit of weight equal to 12 grams; among drug-dealers a tola is 10 grams.

"What, do you think it's time to introduce us to the world?" Valera says, laughing and showing off his tan. "We followed your advice and changed all our clothes. By the way, this is Oleg. He has been asking when we are going to see Goa the entire week. He's a micro oligarch. He is sponsoring all of today's goodies. He also likes smoking."

"Unless he is on a drinking binge," a man with a pleasant Russian face adds, extending his hand for me to shake.

"Well, if you're ready, let's get on our bikes and ride to Chapora."

Passing Mandrem, Ashvem, Morjim and Siolim, we drive on six motorcycles to the dusty and dirty, but fun and happy, town of Chapora.

"Here it is, the center of freaky Goa," getting off my bike, I tell the guys, who look around in surprise.

Hundreds of freaks and hippies from all over North Goa come to this small street every evening. There are no clubs, supermarkets, or beach, but for some reason they all gather right here. Both sides of the narrow street, which is covered with a layer of red dust, are lined with tatty little bars and restaurants. There is no luxury or glamour; it is not in demand here. Trance music sounds from almost every cafe. Charas is being crumbled at every table and chillums are cleaned continuously. Most of the regulars drink fruit juice, coffee or tea. Chillums pass from hand to hand and mantras praising Shiva are heard all around. A few of the best Russian representatives of Goan freak society stand near the entrance to Baba Yaga, dancing and talking.

"Are they really Russians?" Oleg points at them in surprise. "It's hard to believe. Where do they all hide in Russia?"

Unlike my friends, the guys standing near the entrance do not show any interest in the group of tourists that has appeared dressed in Goan outfits. Some of the freaks have long hair, some have dreadlocks. Some of them have fashionable Goan mohawk hairstyles. Their necks, wrists and ears are covered with the most incredible jewelry you can imagine.

"They don't live in Russia," I say, pushing through the crowd at the entrance. "Many of them migrated to Asia long ago, forgetting Russia like a bad dream."

"Well, I love Russia," Oleg says, sitting down at a table where the celebration of the closing of the season is in full swing. "I love winter, the Russian banya and Russian chicks."

We are sitting on the small flat roof of the first Russian restaurant in Goa.

"That's the owner over there, his name is Lyokha Zheltok," I point at a guy proudly sitting at the head of a large table.

"Look at that chick," Valera suddenly points at a Goan beauty who has appeared out of nowhere.

"Oh, that's Nadine. Do you want me to introduce you?" I suggest, smiling and waving to Nadine.

"Of course I do," Valera answers as if spellbound, not taking his eyes from her and downing his glass of rum. "Vasya, I think I've fallen in love. Maybe this is the last love of my life."

"Hi, Nadine!" I shout to her. "Come join us, I want you to meet my country folks. Let's drink to a successful end of the season!"

"To it not being the last one!" Lyokha Zheltok says loudly, wiping the remnants of cocaine powder from the tip of his nose.

***

"Where is Valera? I haven't seen him for a week. What have you done with our friend? Have you bewitched him?"

"I'm here!" I hear Valera's voice, as he sticks one arm out from a large pink hammock hanging on the porch outside the house.

"Valera, is that you? What happened to you? I don't recognize you. It's obvious that you fell into the hands of a Goan sorceress."

"We're on our honeymoon," Nadine says loudly, laughing and jumping into the hammock to join Valera.

"I'm happy for you. I have an interesting proposal."

"Don't tell me that you've brought more MDMA. We feel good now even without it," my friend says, disentangling himself from the beautiful girl's embrace.

Climbing out of the hammock, Valera smiles and extends his hand in greeting. At last, I can completely see the transformation that has occurred to my friend during the last week.

"You look like a Buddhist monk who took too much LSD," I say, looking at him from all sides.

Instead of his stupid hairstyle with a parting, Valera only has hair at the back, in the form of a small tuft, like Hare Krishna devotees have.

"You didn't want to put on a lungi for anything; where is your expensive Armani T-shirt now? I see you've already managed to get your T-shirt painted. I recognize the style of the artist, Vlad Lenka. Only his friends, real freaks, wear his trademark 'Los Uebanos'[33] T-shirts. People wait for weeks, or even months, for him to get inspiration so they can get a T-shirt covered with one of his paintings. I don't think this would have been possible without Nadine's magic. You're lucky, Valera. Wherever Nadine appears, the space around begins to change, like in a fairytale."

"Yes, that's me, a sorceress," Nadine laughs loudly, stretching her long, slender legs out of the hammock into the sky.

"Nadine, what do you think about going on a honeymoon to Nepal?" I say, looking at a beautiful composition of flowers floating in a large transparent bowl.

"I came here for adventure, so I'm ready to leave tomorrow," Valera answers, trying to free himself from Nadine's legs, with which she is trying to pull him back into the hammock.

"If Valera is going, then I'm in too!" the Goan sorceress laughs loudly again, pulling down the bright orange scarf wrapped around Valera's waist with her foot.

"We should hurry up, my visa expires in a couple of weeks."

"It's April, the end of the season; everyone's visa is expiring now. Almost everyone has already left. It's only us whose honeymoon is just beginning."

---

[33] Los Uebanos - a Goan slang term for junkies.

"And where is Oleg? I haven't seen him. Will he come with us?" I ask Valera, taking a large ripe mango from the table.

"No, Oleg won't come. He couldn't adapt here. On the fifth day, he couldn't stand it any longer, so he bought himself a ticket and flew back to his beloved Russia. He says Goa is not his place. He wants five-star hotels, whores and casinos. He is used to showing his status through money. Do you remember how he introduced himself to people at the Baba Yaga closing party? 'Hello, my name is Oleg, I have my own car showroom."

"Yes, unfortunately, there are people who are of no interest to others without money. Who cares here how much he earns? No one. So he felt that he wasn't interesting to anyone. It's Rashka where he is a king and a god. Everyone loves him and fawns over him. Russia is his place; the majority of the people there are like him."

The psychedelics that he took on the night of the Baba Yaga closing party scared Oleg. At that time, none of us had any idea that on his return to Russia he would decide to sell his car showroom and head off on a long trip to India. The psychedelic transformation caught up with him in Russia, forcing him to change his life.

111

Chapter 19. Part One. Inside.

"Welcome to our prison. My name is Vasiliy, I'm from Russia."

"James," the new lodger of our 'Holiday Inc.' hotel, as Viktor loves to call it, extends his hand to me. The short, round, hairy Scotsman looks terribly similar to the Russian Winnie the Pooh cartoon character. James tries to say something, but it is almost impossible to understand his Scottish accent. It seems like he is talking with his mouth full. Realizing that no one understands him, he smiles and goes off for a walk alone. Just like me, for the first week he walks around the outside of the prison yard at great speed, resembling a bear who has been caught in the wild and put into a zoo.

"Dobroe utro,[34]" Viktor yells across the prison.

"Dobautro," awakening prisoners answer him from different parts of the prison.

"Dobrautro," sleepy guards in turn repeat the to them funny-sounding Russian phrase .

"Hello, Doctor," I greet David, who is as usual stretching in the morning sun.

"Hello, Don Alexandro," I say, extending my hand to the smuggler from Sicily.

"Hi, Vashya," the Japanese 'Samurai' Yuki, who we nicknamed Suzuki, greets me.

These, and a few of my cellmates, are the only 'alive' people among the sixty inmates in our jail with whom I can somehow communicate.

"What's new, David?"

"I'm still alive," the old Iranian answers me, smiling and putting a pinch of chewing tobacco behind his lip. "I have already been here for a year and a half, so why am I so haunted by bad luck?"

"What's the matter, David? It's such a wonderful day, and you're in a bad mood."

"Vasya, you know that if the drug expert analysis doesn't come in a year, then the case is automatically closed?"

"Well, yes, that's not news," I agree, nodding my head.

"So, I paid a lot of money for this analysis not to come in time. I waited for a whole year and what did those jackals do? Two days before the end of the year period, the Goan police themselves went to the other end of India, Hyderabad, and collected my expert analysis. And the damn doctor that conducted the examination, besides taking my money, made a mistake in the analysis. He wrote that I had not five, but fifty kilograms of charas. That motherfucker put a comma in the wrong place. Now I will probably have to wait for another year. Why like this?"

"Because like that." I say, smiling and giving him a friendly pat on the shoulder. "Maybe you have such karma."

"David, and what did your expert analysis show?"

---

[34] Dobroe utro - 'Good morning' in Russian

"Who needs my cocaine? It's only eighty grams after all. It's not a commercial amount if it's less than a hundred grams. You can be released on bail with such an amount. The analysis showed a positive reaction. It was good cocaine, only the judge shows no interest in it. I can only be locked up for the charas."

"India is a strange country. You can be released on bail for two hundred and forty nine grams of heroin or ninety-nine grams of cocaine, and for ten grams of MDMA you can be imprisoned for twenty years."

After his traditional Sun Salutation[35], Viktor comes over and joins our discussion.

"Vasya, just think: two hundred and fifty grams of heroin or a hundred grams of cocaine can kill several people that are unnecessary for human society, clearing some space in overcrowded India. The population is almost a billion and a half anyway. Whereas ten grams of MDMA can make a few people happy, who could then give up their jobs, having finally understood that life is not for that. Who needs happy people in society? Society needs hardworking, frightened, dependent people who are ready to work for the rest of their lives for food and primitive pleasures. And what good is there in your psychedelics? When a 'social human' changes his consciousness, he starts to realize that making money is not the most important thing in life. That is why the laws are like that."

"Psychedelics promote personal growth, but prevent social growth," I agree, sighing. "But society also needs to evolve. Someday, we must develop into a fair, ideal society."

"Vasya, it's only you who thinks like that. Your idea is utopian; we will never achieve such a society. Remember the history of mankind. There have always been slaves and slave owners. Many centuries have passed, and has anything changed? Nothing has changed. Only the names of the regimes have changed. Socialism, capitalism, fascism, communism, democracy, liberalism – these are just names that conceal the essence of society. Any society, no matter how it's referred to, has always consisted of two classes. Slaves who need to give their lives for the benefit of the slave owners and slave owners who create laws and regulations so that the slaves work and don't flee. There used to be regular slavery, and now there is credit slavery. The names are different, but the essence is the same. They have just made the slaves' leashes a little longer, and have begun feeding them better. You want to make everyone happy, and that's why you're sitting here. You are a runaway slave, or rather all of us here are runaway slaves, who were caught and put into rehabilitation. So sit here and get rehabilitated, you fucking revolutionary," smiling, Viktor finishes his emotional monologue.

Chapter 19. Part Two. Outside.

We are crouching in the vestibule of an overcrowded Bombay-Gorakhpur train. I have only ever seen so many people in one train car in movies about the Nazis sending Jews to the concentration camps.

---

[35] Sun Salutations - Surya Namaskara, a common sequence of asanas, typically used as part of morning practice, although not only.

"What are we going to do?" Nadine asks us, putting on a discontented face. "It will take two days to reach the border and there are neither beds, nor seats. It's the end of the season, Monsoon is coming and everyone is running away from the rain. In India, ordinary people buy train tickets two months in advance."

"Well, Nadine, we only paid ten dollars for our three tickets," Valera says smiling, in an attempt to defuse the situation.

"So we have to crouch for two days; I need somewhere to lie down," Nadine huffs, intermittently tugging down her short skirt.

Besides us, a dozen people are sitting, standing or hanging from the bars in the vestibule of the train car. And, although the three of us are occupying a space where five Indians could sit, we are the only ones who look dissatisfied with our places. The rest of our fellow travellers stare with a melancholy gaze at the three strange white monkeys, speaking in an incomprehensible foreign language. More precisely, almost all of them are looking at Nadine. The bare shoulders and long, slim legs of the former fashion model draw the Indians' eyes like a magnet.

"Why are you dressed in a mini skirt? Haven't you seen how the local women dress?"

"They are going to devour me with their eyes. I can't stand it any longer." Our sorceress complains, snuggling closer to Valera. "Even in the sea, they bathe in clothes."

"Maybe they are seeing a white woman for the first time in their life," Valera says, trying to calm her down, and spreads a map of India on his lap.

I search for the nearest location where we can change transport.

"Ok, I think I've found the nearest town. Nasik, its population is one million people," I point a finger at a little dot on the map. "In a million-inhabitant city, there must be a more comfortable vehicle than the vestibule of a train car. We'll make a transfer and tomorrow we will be at the border."

Getting off at a reasonably large station two hours later, we begin to understand that the town of Nasik, tiny compared to the twenty-million-inhabitant city of Mumbai, has probably never seen white people before. Having visited the bus and train ticket offices, we realize that there are no tickets anywhere for the next two months. Stopping in the square in front of the station for five minutes to look at the map, we notice that a crowd has gathered around us.

"Valera, Nadine, take your attention away from the map for a moment, and look at what is going on around us." I feel like we are the main characters in some crazy movie. Noticing us, passing Indians stop and freeze, forgetting where they were going. It is like someone has pressed their 'pause' button. Some of them stand with open mouths, not believing the miracle that has appeared in their town.

"Are we really so interesting to them that they forget where they are going, and are ready to stand here and stare at us?"

"Don't flatter yourself, Vasya, they are staring at Nadine." Valera says, putting the map back into his bag. "It sort of feels like they thought that white people are only in the movies."

"Guys, they are not only staring at me. Have you seen yourselves in the mirror? In your bright skirts with weird hairstyles, you are like aliens to them."

Circling, the natives scrutinize us in silence, as if hypnotized. The shout of a policeman brandishing a short bamboo stick begins to disperse the crowd and shake them out of their stupor. After going around all of the taxi drivers in the station square, we understand that no one here speaks English.

"Valera, maybe you can do it. Go and talk to the drivers of motorcycles and rickshaws. Maybe you will manage to explain to them in simple terms that we have to get somewhere out of the city, preferably north," Nadine says, wrapping a scarf around her long legs.

"I'll give it a try; just make sure that our beauty doesn't get stolen," Valera says, smiling and heading towards the station square.

Left on our own together, Nadine and I sit on the steps, watching the passing locals. If it were not for the women's saris and dark skin, you could think that we were in Russia in the first half of the twentieth century.

"Well, here we are in the country of monkeys," Nadine says with a sigh, nodding her head towards the policeman standing not far from us and occasionally shaking the gawping passers-by out of their trance with a loud shout.

"Isn't our homeland a country of monkeys? Imagine some Indians dressed like we are, somewhere in Syzran or Kemerovo[36], on a square in front of a station. It is unlikely that they would meet even one English-speaking taxi driver. I think the situation would be the same. Here, at least the police protect us voluntarily. In Rashka, the poor Indians would be immediately cheated out of their money by train station crooks, cops and taxi drivers."

"I found one!" Valera screams joyfully from a distance, leading a short Indian. "He knows a few English words and I think he understands what we need. He has his own rickshaw and he promises to take us to some agency, where we can rent a car with a driver to reach the border.

"I know who have jeep," the driver mutters happily, piling our stuff into the old rickshaw.

Having driven for nearly an hour, we finally find ourselves in the only agency in the town, according to the driver, with a free car for hire.

"A hundred dollars," the owner of the office happily tells us with shining eyes, in anticipation of making a big profit. "We have a great jeep, one day and you will be at the border."

"You see, Nadine, there was no reason to be worried," Valera reassures her, moving our stuff towards the entrance.

After that, we only managed to leave Nasik two days later. For two days, we sat on chairs in the agency's small office, waiting for the driver to return from a wedding, and then – for him to bury his uncle, then – to repair some kind of a breakdown, then – something else. In the evening, we went back to the hotel to get some sleep and in the morning the same thing happened again. During our time in Nasik, we firmly grasped what the Indian 'fifteen minutes' means. India is a country without time, so there was no point getting indignant. In the end we were given a small Volkswagen Beetle, seemingly dating from the time of Indira Gandhi. We only reached the border three days later. It was good that we had charas with us: we smoked it everywhere and all the time. It was simply impossible

---

[36] Syzran or Kemerovo - small provincial towns in Russia.

to take in the reality around us in a sober state. The world that we saw from the window of our car was so unusual and strange that we could only begin to come to terms with it while stoned. Wherever we stopped, we became the center of attention for all the people within the zone of visibility. We were like aliens, whom everyone wanted to touch. They tried to speak to us in a strange language, to sell us something, and we just smiled in response. Of course, the charas helped with that. The border with Nepal opened up to us in all its Oriental beauty. It consisted of a standard small Indian street full of shit, garbage, and rats scurrying around.

The living stream of people was divided into two parts: a narrow current of individual tourists who stopped at the border guard post, which we joined; and a huge, colorful, streaming Indian-Nepalese mass of people that did not require documents to cross the border. The fact that we had crossed the border was clear from the dramatic reduction in the amount of garbage lying around. Having driven across the whole of the country, we realized that garbage is an integral part of India. In India, one can rarely find a habitable square meter of land on which there is no garbage or other results of human life. I have a feeling that Indians simply do not notice garbage. In contrast to normal Europeans, Indians don't hesitate to throw garbage on the floor. The Nepalese side of the border greeted us with a huge poster, on which two cupped palms and the inscription 'Namaste' were painted. As we understood later, in Nepal everything begins with 'Namaste.'

Wherever we went, any conversation began with palms pressed together at the chest, a welcoming smile and 'Namaste.' The fourteen hours of serpentine roads in an overcrowded old bus, together with chickens, goats and Nepalese people, was made bearable by the beautiful views of the Himalayas through the window. The highest peaks were somewhere far away. They appeared occasionally when we drove along large valleys, overlooking small green gorges. The base of the mountains could not be seen, but their tops, like magic white castles, hung above the clouds, causing us to experience child-like delight. The Nepalese with whom we had to share the bus's small seats were not impressed by the view out of the window, and, unlike the curious Indians, they hardly paid attention to us at all, preferring to nap for the entire journey. Exhausted and with swollen legs from sitting so long, we finally arrived in the capital of Nepal – Kathmandu.

"Well, we can finally devote ourselves to our honeymoon," settling down on the large hotel bed, Nadine forces a smile. "That's it. For the next few weeks: no travelling. I'm tired."

"I'll go and buy some charas somewhere, and you can search for your hemp as long as you wish," says Valera, lighting our last joint.

Having showered and dressed in a clean lungi, I go outside to see the capital of Nepal in the evening. Leaving our hotel and walking a few meters, I realize that I have finally made it to the right place. Practically across the street I see a sign saying Hemp above the entrance to a store. How long have I been looking for this hemp paradise!!! I need to make sure I don't spend all my money at once. I want to buy almost everything. No; no shopping today. Today I'll just familiarize myself with what's on offer. Thamel, the tourist district of Kathmandu, looks like a fairytale town full of kind little inhabitants.

It feels like two ancient civilizations – Indian and Chinese – mixed in this place, creating a wonderful symbiosis. Chinese pagoda architecture and bas-reliefs of Indian gods, Buddhist and Hindu temples standing next to each other, and the mongoloid facial features of half of the population. All this makes the city unique, unlike any other.

The intersecting streets surrounding our hotel contain thousands of shops, restaurants, travel and cargo agencies. After a few streets, I understand that Kathmandu can rightly be called the capital of hemp. In almost every shop you can buy something made of hemp. In Nepal, they make everything out of it: clothes, shoes, fabric, thread, souvenirs, jewelry and, of course, hashish and charas, which are unfortunately illegal now. During an hour's walk sightseeing, the street dealers approach me a dozen times, offering marijuana and poland[37]. I pass through the small streets, curiously examining a variety of unusual devices for smoking, eco-style accessories, and all sorts of other things somehow connected with hemp. I'm glad that I have finally found what I need.

But the most pleasant thing is that all it costs next to nothing. "Our Hemp won't die; Nepalese hemp is going to help," I think happily, heading towards our hotel. Back at the hotel, I am amazed to see a huge chunk of charas on the coffee table.

"Valera, have you gone nuts? Why did you buy half a kilo? We won't smoke that much..."

"Why won't we smoke it? We'll manage it easily. I actually only wanted to buy ten grams," Valera begins to make excuses. "But somehow I ended up buying this," he says with a smile, tossing the hefty chunk up and down in his hands. "I asked the price from a street vendor, and he muttered something in his own language, only one thing was obvious – he wants two hundred bucks. I figured that in Rashka ten grams cost a hundred bucks; it is clear that it's expensive for Nepal, but I wasn't going to haggle, I was tired after the journey. I gave him the money, and he took this brick from his pocket, gave it to me, and quickly disappeared."

"Good charas, by the way," Nadine chuckles cheerfully, kneading a big piece in her palms. "We'll sculpt figures out of it like out of clay."

Coming closer, I can see already completed sculptures of a smiling Cheshire Cat, a little girl, probably Alice, and a large mushroom with a fat caterpillar on the cap, which is also smiling. It's hard to believe it's all made out of charas.

"Join us, and try some Nepalese charas," Nadine says, smiling and breaking off a small piece from the cap of the sculpted mushroom. "The main thing is to determine which side to break it off of. If you take it from one side – you will grow big and get to heaven; and from the other – you will become small and sink right to the bottom."

---

[37] Poland - Nepali soft hashish.

Chapter 20. Part One. Inside.

A fortnight flies by like a day. Time seems to stop in jail. Every two weeks, the drug police come for me and take me to court. The court procedure usually takes less than two minutes. An elderly woman in a judicial robe worn over a sari looks up for a moment to ask only one question "Any complaints?" And you cannot complain, otherwise you can be transferred to a more restrictive jail. Today, I am taken to court in a small police jeep. Outside, it is pouring with rain. Indian cats scratch my soul with their sharp claws. My heart is pounding in the hope that this will be my last court appearance. Today the judge will decide whether to release me on bail or not. Again the same painfully familiar, shabby defendant's bench, and rusty fans overhead. Since I was first brought to the court, the yellow acacia outside has had time to blossom.

Today is my last chance to get out of here. Life goes on outside behind the barred window. People go about their business in a 2leisurely manner without considering the fact that they have freedom. They do not feel its value, they just have it. They can go wherever they want and do whatever they want. Somewhere outside, far away, are my girls. My daughter still doesn't know that I'm in here. How I would love to get out today, so that she never finds out that her father was in prison. The damp air smells of flowers and spices.

"Any complaints?" the judge asks without looking up at me.

"No, no complaints," I answer with bated breath.

"The application for bail is refused. The next trial is in two weeks."

Something cracks with a crunch in my heart. There is no more chance of getting out before the results of the expert analysis are received. For a whole month I had been hoping for a miracle, but it slipped away from me. No one has received the analysis earlier than in eight months.

The road to prison floats by, as if in a fog. I'm in the cell once again. There is absolutely nothing I want to do. Opening the English dictionary, I find a new word ideally suited to my state. "Frustration" – the derangement of plans and the destruction of hope.

Pramud yells from the next cell like a madman: "I'll get out and fuck her, I'll kill her, I want to fuck that nurse," the Indian, imprisoned for eleven grams of MDMA, shouts frantically.

He has already been waiting for his expert analysis for eight months. "He's probably gone completely nuts," I think, imagining myself in his shoes. I ought to pull myself together. I still need my judgment. Behind the jail walls, the Sun is setting. I have no desire to eat. My life force seems to have left me. By evening, I start to feel a light fever. Water drips from the tiled roof onto my bed in several places. From the window, gusts of cold wind envelop me. I gradually start to shake. I have no dry clothing at all. The whole cell smells of mold. I wrap myself in everything I have. My bones start to ache; it's almost impossible to lie still. I'm burning up. Please, anything but malaria. I can't be sick; I have a lot of unfinished business. Outside, my girls are waiting for me; they need me. I need to pull myself together and overcome this encroaching illness. Come on, protective neuropeptide system[38], turn on! Help me out; cure me, please! It is impossible to sleep. Time drags on and it seems that the night will never end. Morning finally comes. I have no strength to resist the illness and my body aches. I lie in a fetal position, wrapped in a wet blanket and various rags. All of my clothes are soaked through. At sunrise, I get a little better.

"Our Russian looks very bad," I hear Dominic's voice.

"He should be sent to the hospital," my neighbor Mudra hands me a cup of hot tea.

"Hey, guards, foreigner is dying," my cellmates bang on the bars. "This Russian looks very bad, take him to hospital or he dies here."

"Get dressed, you'll be taken to the hospital now," Disay tells me, giving me his dry shirt. "Grab your dictionary, you'll explain the doctor that you have a fever and the shakes."

I am accompanied by two security guards from the jail and put in an empty prison bus to travel to the Azilo state hospital.

"His body temperature is one hundred and four degrees, you will have to leave him here," a nurse explains to my guards.

I wonder how much is it in Celsius...

The Azilo hospital resembles a clinic for the homeless. Shabby, moldy walls, barred windows, old dilapidated equipment. A free hospital for the poorest Indians. In the hospital ward there are three old medical couches, partially covered with dried bloodstains. Someone screams in pain, someone else moans, in the hallway there is a huge queue. Almost all of the patients look like the inhabitants of Bombay slums. In frayed simple clothes, many of them have come for help barefoot. I am given a green hospital gown, smelling of bleach. Hundreds of disposable gloves, washed and yellowed from time, dry on a rope stretched across the corridor. I am led to a huge ward with fifty beds. People taking care of their sick relatives look curiously at the strange man who has appeared here for no discernable reason. Groans are heard from different beds. Someone screams as if in death throes. Next to almost every patient are relatives or friends. It smells of urine and medicine. On the neighboring bed, an old man lies connected to a drip. He looks like a prisoner from the Auschwitz concentration camp. He has almost no muscles and his skin clings to his thin bones. A woman lying on the floor under his bed, probably his daughter, is breastfeeding her child. Putting ancient, forged handcuffs with a chain on my feet, the guard fastens them to the headboard. An elderly nurse in a white paper cap with a red cross approaches the patients one by one, pompously carrying a tray with syringes. It's my turn to be pricked. Taking a syringe from the general pile, she quickly gives me an injection. I understand that everyone is injected with the same medication. I hope that they don't wash disposable syringes like they do with the gloves? After the injection, there is a pleasant drowsiness. I want to curl up, but my chained leg prevents me from doing so.

---

[38] Neuropeptides – biologically active compounds that are synthesized by nerve cells. They are involved in the regulation of the metabolism, affect the immune processes, and play an important role in the mechanisms of memory, learning, sleep, etc.

"Hey, guard, I want to relieve myself; take me to the toilet," I shout to the guards, who sit side by side on chairs.

A half-asleep guard lazily unfastens me and leads me across the room by the arm. Near the hole in the floor, is someone's unflushed shit and bloody bandages. Preparing to do my deed, I watch in disgust as a large worm wriggles towards my slipper. Horrified, I jump out of the toilet for fear that this parasite will have time to lay its eggs somewhere on my body.

"Don't worry; it's not a snake, just a worm," the guard reassures me, looking at the pink, hand-sized beast. Evening comes. Hospital attendants bring food. It's rice and pea sauce again. Just like in prison, everyone eats with their hands. After the scene I saw in the toilet, I don't want to eat at all. My two guards settle in to sleep on the floor, right under my bed. It is difficult to imagine a similar situation in the Russian reality. It is unlikely that Russian cops would agree to sleep under a bed – it is more likely that I would be put there. It's surreal. For the last half hour, two loud sets of snores have been coming from under my bed. The only distraction is to watch the rusty fan spinning above my head. The moans from different sides slightly subside. The idea that comes to me is terrifying. I want to get back home to my cell. Well, there you are. I unconsciously perceive the cell as my 'home'.

Chapter 20. Part Two. Outside.

Holding a rifle, the police officer looks at me with interest.

"Everyone except the foreigner, leave the bus!" he bellows at the frightened passengers. "And you, sir, can remain in your place, verification does not concern you," he says with a smile, hurrying the Nepalese with nudges in the side. Having spent almost all of my money in Kathmandu, I have decided to go to Nepal's second largest city, Pokhara. Nadine and Valera flatly refused to continue the journey, saying that they hadn't hade time to recover from the last trip across India yet.

While the police check the passengers' documents near the bus, I sit inside, examining its interior design. The Nepali bus is like a big, old toy. If the average Nepalese is nearly a quarter smaller than the average Russian, then their buses are correspondingly also a quarter smaller. Small windows, small doors, small seats. The interior space is carefully decorated with colorful wire, foil and rags. We stand at the latest checkpoint blocking our way. There is a revolution in Nepal. Driven into the woods, Maoist guerrilla groups sometimes make forays into small towns and villages, demanding tributes from civil servants. The passengers with the cheapest tickets climb down from the roof of the bus for inspection. In the luggage compartment, someone's goat bleats endlessly like a madman. In Nepal, tourists are treated in a special way: we are untouchable. We are the main source of their gross income, and it is understood on both sides of the Nepalese barricades.

My window overlooks a large valley, at the bottom of which there is a small, but fast river with rapids. Ganja, growing wild everywhere, pleases the eyes. All of the Himalayas are covered with wild-growing hemp. Near the checkpoint built of sandbags, right next to the road, I see a large bush, almost twice the height of a man. Whose idea was it to call this plant 'weed'? It's more like a small tree. The bottom and side buds have already been carefully cut by someone. The soldiers probably don't get bored here. You can come out from the bunker in the evening, cut some buds, smoke and contemplate the Himalayan peaks. What revolution? What guerrillas? Perhaps that is why their revolution has lasted for fifteen years. For decency's sake, they shoot at the sky once a month to demonstrate their guerrilla resistance and probably smoke again. Once hashish was the national product of Nepal. The best strains of charas were exported. The king controlled almost the entire production of hashish in the country. My neighbor in the bus, an elderly Nepalese man who spoke decent English, told me on the way that he remembered how a few years ago on Shivaratri[39], the King allocated a several kilograms of hashish to the babas, and everyone could smoke chillums for free near the entrance to every Shiva temple. According to legend, once upon a time, a sacred swan brought a cannabis leaf to the god Shiva, which he smoked and then understood everything. Since then, all believers in Shiva smoke in order to come closer to the divine.

Having loaded our chickens and goats back onto the bus, we drive away from the checkpoint. Smoking a joint rolled in my lap, I look out of the window, watching as our bus rides along the edge of a cliff, not reducing its speed on the turns. '1,200 Micrograms' plays in my headphones, a trance track called 'Hashish'. "On the seventh day, Shiva created hashish," the mysterious voice says and the magical mesmerizing music takes me away to my dreams and fantasies. Nepal is a fairytale country, a country of cannabis.

***

Pokhara meets me with flowering trees everywhere, a beautiful mountain lake and the snow-capped ridges of the Himalayan peaks. The white tops are so high in the sky that it seems like they are not mountains, but rather huge roads leading directly to heaven. To the place where the terrible god Shiva lives with his beloved Parvati. Mantras in praise of the gods over melodious music are heard from everywhere: from all the small shops and restaurants located along the lake. I love this country. I love Asia in general. I probably have more Asian than European blood in me. Although I have a Russian passport, am I really a Slav? Brown eyes, brown hair, Greek nose. During my youth, I had a terrible complex about my face. Although my parents are Russian, during my school years I was constantly teased with the offensive word 'churka'[40] and laughed at for my big nose. For some reason, everyone was interested in my nationality. This question was asked by friends, teachers, and neighbors. Almost all questionnaires included this stupid question. Girls preferred blue-eyed blonde guys and didn't pay any attention to me. Here in Asia, I finally feel at ease. I walk along the main street, enjoying the colors and sounds of Nepal, drawing up in my head the final touches to the plan not to return to my homeland. I don't want to go back to Russia.

"Hello, Lena, hello. How are you? Is everything okay? Have you received my Nepalese samples? What do you think of the specimens of hemp fabrics? Lena, listen to me carefully: I have a plan. I know how we can legally earn in Goa. We will open a restaurant in Goa and a Hemp store. Send the fabrics to the Saratov factory for them to sew a new collection of clothes. Find a replacement

---

[39] Shivaratri - the night of Shiva, a great Hindu festival.

[40] Churka - a Russian language, insulting nickname for people of Central Asia; in a broader sense – all non-Russian people, including the natives of the North Caucasus and Transcaucasia.

for yourself, a new manager for Hemp. Pack the summer collection that we didn't sell in the Hemp store and ship it to Goa. We'll sell it during the winter. And in three months, pack your bags, take Vasilinka, and come here. I'll meet you in Goa. Explain to Dymkov that we are not giving up on the business. Tell him that we will sell everything that is not sold in Russia during the season in Goa. Using that money, we will buy fabric in Nepal and send it to Saratov for production. Tell him that we will have our own production. Our Hemp won't be lost."

Chapter 21. Part One. Inside.

"How are you feeling?" a woman in an expensive sari wakes me up.

"Thank you, doctor. I no longer have a fever, and I want to go back to jail. I feel more comfortable there."

"You will get back to your cell only in the evening," one of my guards says. "The jail bus broke down," he adds.

"I don't want to stay here any longer. I'm ready to pay for a taxi, just to get out of here quickly."

In the cell, I have more chances of staying alive and healthy.

"If you're ready to pay thirty rupees for a rickshaw, then get dressed, we're going home," my guard proposes happily, as he also has no desire to hang around here until evening.

My appearance in the jail is accompanied by my friends' applause.

"How is your health?" everyone asks me, shaking my hand one by one.

"Well, I'll probably live."

"How did you like the Azilo hospital?" Viktor asks, dragging a bucket of water out into the exercise yard. "Welcome to the prison beach!" he yells across the jail, inviting everyone to pour cold water over themselves.

"You know, Vitya, our jail seems like paradise after that hospital. This morning, after the hospital, I even enjoyed watching an Indian TV show in my cell. It is much more interesting than watching a rusty fan spinning overhead. And what's new in the jail?"

"Pramud's AIDS test came back positive. And he has a wife and a little son. He says that he was probably infected in the hospital where he was treated for some illness. Look at him, he hasn't talked to anyone for two days, he just stares at one spot."

"Now I understand why he was yelling that he wanted to kill that nurse. I really thought he'd gone completely nuts."

"Hello, David, how are you?"

"Still alive," the toothless Iranian says with a smile and extends his strong hand to me.

"Tell me, David, what passport do you have? Iranian or Indian?"

"I am a citizen of India and I have an Indian passport," he says proudly, sitting down on the steps nearby. "All my relatives live in Iran. Forty years ago, when there was a military conflict with Iraq, I was sent to the frontline to die for my country; at that time, a lot of my friends were killed. Being young, I did not want to die at all. I took my weapon and ran away with some of my comrades. In Afghanistan, I sold my gun and came to India through Pakistan on foot. I started learning Hindi and English. At first I worked as a rickshaw driver and slept on the street. Then I married a Chinese student, she gave birth to my two children. Having saved a little money, I bought some land and built a restaurant. Now I have two restaurants in Hyderabad, my wife works in an expensive salon as a hairdresser. My children go to school."

"Then how did you end up in Goa, David? You could have lived happily with your family."

"Like anyone else who gets stuck here. Seven years ago, I came here on vacation for a couple of weeks and I liked it so much that I decided to stay. I began selling drugs. I thought I had found my paradise. Everything was fine until some Russian guy showed up. The police have would never have caught me if he hadn't given information to the cops."

"Who is this Russian?" I ask urgently, hardly believing in such a coincidence.

Rising from the steps, David takes a piece of paper folded four times out of his pocket and hands it to me. As I unfold it, my jaw drops in astonishment. A painfully familiar character looks at me from the printed black-and-white photo.

"Do you know him?" David asks in surprise, apparently feeling the same thing as I do.

"I'm here because of that bastard, too."

Chapter 21. Part Two. Outside.

If after the bustle of Rashka, calm Goa seems like a place of deep Shanti[41], then after Goa, Pokhara is like a magical place where there is no time. No one needs time. Pokhara is a city where no one is in a hurry. Why rush if you are in paradise? Fifteen years ago, Pokhara was a developed tourist destination, visited by thousands of tourists. Foreign and local investors put money into it and tourists also brought cash. Everyone was happy. But then, suddenly, the revolution came. Dissatisfied Maoists sponsored by the Chinese started to demand the king's abdication. The tourist flow plummeted, leaving hundreds of empty hotels, restaurants and bars. The main street that runs along the beautiful mountain lake is empty. Most of the tourists left, leaving Pokhara looking like an abandoned Swiss resort. Having visited the surrounding areas, I realize that this city is the best place to spend the five months of the rainy season. The rains here are not so frequent as in India, and the guerrillas only make themselves known by occasional forays into the administrative part of the city. But the most important thing is that housing, food and charas are two or even three times cheaper here than in Goa. Compared to Russia, these prices seem ridiculous. Now I understood that it is possible to not return to Russia at all. I had a plan and proceeded towards its realization.

I bought an old, non-operational laptop from a second-hand electrics store for fifty dollars, and remodeled it into a wonderful container for smuggling charas. I had very little money, but a great desire to stay in Asia. I was ready for anything. Having neatly packed a kilo of sweet, black Himalayan 'gold' into the empty laptop, I headed back to Goa. I had my remaining five hundred dollars in my pocket and a plan for a happy and carefree future in my head. I just had to quickly get together some initial capital. And initial capital, as I was taught in college, always had criminal beginnings. I crossed the border easily. No one searched my stuff. Not only had the customs officers

---

[41] Shanti - peace, tranquility. It's a very deep word. One may only understand it having visited India.

at the Nepal-India border never seen a laptop in their life, but they had never even seen a computer. And it really seemed like a white tourist was untouchable for them. This was an unwritten rule and I liked it.

Having crossing the border with a kilo of charas, for the first time in my life I really felt like someone. Back in Goa, I rented fifty square meters of beach for the whole season for five hundred bucks, and began to build a restaurant. Selling charas little by little, I used the money to buy bamboo, boards, plywood and tools. Hiring two assistants for the hard work, I toiled with them from dawn till dusk. Periodically rolling joints with my charas, I sawed, dug, and hammered nails. Working on the beach was fun and not really taxing. In a couple of weeks, the first restaurant in my life was finished – the first Russian restaurant on Arambol beach. Of course, it is difficult to call it a restaurant, as it was just a small construction with seven low tables, where one sat on soft mattresses that covered the entire surface of the wooden floor. It was more of a small chill-out zone serving food. But still, I proudly called it MY RESTAURANT. My restaurant resembled a large bird's nest made out of a long bamboo sticks attached to a palm tree at a height of three meters. Along with the piece of beach, I got a coconut palm tree growing in the middle and tilting towards the sea. Having dug in high bamboo poles around its perimeter, I covered them with a plywood platform that served as the floor of my place. The palm tree was left to grow in the middle, making a living roof with its huge leaves. So I got a two-story construction, where the ground floor was a shop and the first floor was a restaurant, which could be reached by climbing the almost vertical ladder from the back of the store. Everything was ready for the arrival of my girls. I hired a staff of five people to work in the restaurant and prepared a menu of Russian and Indian dishes. You could buy everything except alcohol. Alcohol was taboo; in my place, no one was allowed to drink any alcohol. You could smoke, take soft drugs, and eat hash cakes, but not drink.

Finally, the long-awaited day of my Lena's arrival comes. Clean-shaven with a nice-smelling aftershave, I stand at the airport an hour before her arrival with two garlands made of orange blossoms, traditionally worn by Indians around the neck on very festive occasions.

"Daddy, Daddy!" I hear the familiar voice of my little princess, who runs out of the crowd towards me with her arms spread wide.

"Hello, my beauty, I've missed you."

My four-year-old daughter promptly climbs onto my shoulders while I kiss my Lena.

"Dad, Dad, will you show me the monkeys?" Vasilinka shouts from above, pulling my ears.

"Of course I will, I have so much to show you."

Tearing myself away from a greedy kiss with Lena, I stand and look at my beauties.

"By the way, Vasya, I haven't come alone. This is Denis and Ilka. They are our first tourists."

Denis, a blond guy with a typical Russian face, extends his strong hand to greet me.

"I've heard about your adventures in India. And we decided to see everything with our own eyes. I'll be a tourist for about three months, and if everything is as wonderful as Lena told us, I am ready to work with you. To be honest, I don't want to spend winter in Russia, and I will do my best to stay here."

"And my name is Ilka, that's what everyone calls me," says a young girl of about twenty years with a naive, even somewhat childish face, giving me her plump hand.

"I also want to stay, but I don't know what I'll do. I've also heard a lot about Goa from Lena."

"We'll think of something. Get into the jeep. On the way, I'll give you the 'newly arrived tourist' lecture and then and we'll talk about business."

Having stacked the suitcases on the roof of the rented Indian jeep, we set off in the direction of North Goa.

"First of all, you need to change your European clothes. Secondly, you need a bit of a tan. More precisely, firstly you should get tanned and then buy clothes, otherwise with your skin color you will be sold clothes at three times the price. Locals treat a white, untanned person like a walking wallet. Ilka, what did you do in Russia?"

"I was a manager at Coca-Cola."

"And what happened, don't they pay enough? What drew you to Goa?" I ask with a smile, already guessing her response.

"They paid well. I even had a good company car. The only thing I did not have was a personal life with such a job. From morning till night I ran around doing business and in the evening I only had the energy to watch TV. And I'm young, I need to find a husband. And frankly, I'm disappointed in Russian men. In our country, there are more women than men, and all the men are spoiled. Russian men are not capable of elegantly courting a Russian woman, or they simply do not want to. Maybe here in Goa I'll meet a foreigner."

"Sure, you'll meet one. Goa is a magical place, where all wishes come true; the main thing is to have a clear idea of what you want. If you were a manager in Russia, maybe you could manage our branch of Hemp here? I've built a small store on the beach. The work is not difficult; you can swim and sunbathe, and at the same time sell things to tourists. And on Thursdays and Saturdays we'll need to organize a trip to the market. I rented two places there. It's not very hard work and in the meantime you will find a husband."

"By the way, Lena," I ask my beloved, "how's our Hemp in Russia? How did Dymkov react to my plan to open a branch in Goa?"

"To be honest, Dymkov was not very happy that I had found a new manager. In my opinion, he thinks that we want to slowly slip away from the project."

"He can think whatever he wants, we will continue our revolution and that's what matters. Everything will be ok. Now we'll sell all the remnants of the hemp summer collection that you brought here, we'll send him Indo-Nepalese hemp clothes, and he'll calm down. He'll even thank us for saving the Russian Hemp.

"Well, and you dear," I say to my wife, "what do you want to do here?"

"I don't know yet; I need to take care of our child. I am ready to do any work with a flexible schedule. I can deal with renting out our house. You wrote that you had rented a two-story house with eight rooms. We'll leave the second floor for ourselves, and I'll rent the first floor to tourists."

"And for you, Den, I have a separate proposal. I need help with drugs. But first, I need to take you to a party. If you like it, you'll earn well."

"I also want to work," my little daughter adds, hugging me tightly around the neck.

"Well, what will you do?" my Lena asks our little beauty with a smile.

"I'll walk, swim, play. You were young yourself once, you played and walked. It will be my job."

"Well, there's nothing you can say to that: the logic is solid," we agree, laughing.

Chapter 22. Part One. Inside.

"Hey, Ilka! I am so glad to see you here. Of all my friends, you're the first who dared to visit me. For some reason, all my friends fear jail like fire. Apparently, they think that if they smoke charas, they will be immediately locked up and put in here next to me."

"Hi, Vasya!" says a real Goan freak, kissing me on the cheek.

She has long, blond dreadlocks pulled back into a thick bun, a tattoo on her shoulder, and fashionable Goan trance clothes. The guards look curiously at this weird white girl who has dared to come to the jail.

"Oh, Vasya, how did you get in here? You didn't sell anything last year, you announced to everyone that you were now only doing legal business; and then you ended up in jail. What's going on?"

"I was set up. The police came to my home and brought 20 grams of MDMA. I got in their way. Or, perhaps, my karma caught up with me for some old debts, and I'm working it off now."

"And how long are you going to work it off?"

"I don't know, the prosecutor wants to give me from ten to twenty years. The lawyers assure me that six months after they receive the expert analysis confirming that I had the drugs, they will get me out. The problem is that no one has received the analysis earlier than in eight months."

"I see you're do not hanging your head while you are in here," Ilka says, smiling and touching my biceps. "You look great."

"I can't lose heart in here or I'll go crazy. You won't believe it, but I have no time for all my plans. All day long, I do gymnastics, learn English, play chess, read books. Now I embody everything I dreamed about. All dreams come true in India. I've lost twenty six pounds already."

"Do you have a gym in here?" Ilka asked with astonishment, making funny round eyes.

"I made a gym in the cell myself. I tied three two-liter plastic bottles together with rags. As a result, I have a good six kilogram dumbbell. Every day I lift six tons with each arm using the dumbbell, and I do a hundred and fifty push-ups – look at the biceps I have already," raising my sleeve, I show her my arm. "I've never had muscles like these in my life."

"Well done, you won't be lost. If you've managed to live in Asia for six years, then a year in prison will be nothing for you, everything will be fine."

"Thank you for your support, Ilka. I just want to get out of here as soon as possible. How long are you going to stay in Goa?"

"I don't know, maybe a month, and then I'll go north, to the Himalayas. A bridegroom from Israel is waiting for me there."

"Then your dreams are coming true. You've found a foreign husband in less than five years. By the way, Ilka, I saw you in an erotic and informative dream a week ago."

"Vasya, you're still your usual self, even in jail you think about sex. Tell me what happened in your dream," Ilka says, smiling.

"I dreamt of our first Arambol house. Do you remember in the first year we lived in a house with four rooms on our floor? Well, I dreamed that we were sleeping in the same room, but in different beds. And in the next room, my Lena was putting Vasilina to bed. You were already asleep, and I was tossing and turning, I couldn't fall asleep. Suddenly, you started to cry in your sleep. You cried like a child. You twisted your legs, but couldn't wake up. I called to you "Ilka, stop, you will wake up Vasilina!" Apparently you were having a nightmare, and couldn't wake up. I approached you, took your hand, and started stroking it to calm you down. Suddenly, you embraced me, put your arms around my neck and pulled me into your bed! I looked, and you were naked under the sheet. Before I could blink, you had already gripped me with your legs, and so deftly that I was immediately inside you. And as soon as I penetrated you, the door opened and my Lena came in. And at that very moment, you woke up and started pushing me away. You looked at me and said so seriously, 'What are you doing here, Vasya? Are you crazy, you took advantage of the fact that I was asleep?' And Lena was looking at me accusingly. I was trying to make excuses, saying that, well, I hadn't thought to do anything and that it was you who had seduced me in your sleep. And I was still inside of you. I understood that she won't believe that it all happened by chance. So I woke up with a sense of guilt and a wet spot on my shorts."

"Yeah, a very informative dream. You don't even need to visit Freud," Ilka says, laughing and giving me a friendly hug around my shoulders. "It is obvious, you haven't had sex for a long time."

"You have five minutes left," a guard interrupts our conversation, pointing at his watch.

"Listen, Ilka, I need your help. We've got an Iranian here, his name is David, and he can carry charas in his shorts into the jail. Once a week he goes to the hospital, and he is visited by his friends there. If you gave him some charas, we could smoke. Sometimes it gets so sad in here in the evening."

"I'll give it a try. Give me his phone number. And how do you manage to smoke in here?"

"Like anyone in prison: one keeps a look out while the other two smoke. I have also learned to chew tobacco in here. All Indians love it. I never thought that I would do it. You put tobacco on your palm, it is called pak-pak, rub chuna into it and put it behind your lip. It burns terribly, and then a large piece of skin on the inside of your mouth falls off."

"And what effect does it have? Is it so good that you are prepared to tolerate the burning sensation?"

"There is almost no effect. It's like your first cigarette; do you remember, a slight dizziness? Chewing has the same effect, it lasts for about fifteen minutes."

"But is it painful for your lip?"

"No, Ilka, it is not painful. The pain is here," I gesture with my fist towards my heart. "The main advantage of this tobacco is that the burning helps distract you from this great pain, at least for a while."

Chapter 22. Part Two. Outside.

"Vasya, it's New Year soon, can you braid me two dreadlocks?" Ilka asks me, laying a pink mixing bowl[42] and an elegant, recently purchased chillum on the table.

"What's with the sudden decision? Have you decided to become a freak? You sure you won't be sorry after? You have beautiful, blond hair and the dreadlocks will have to be cut out, because they can't be unraveled. In Rashka, you won't be able to get a decent job."

"You're like my father; it only remains for you to start lecturing me. I don't want to go back to Rashka, I like being here much more. What is waiting for me there? A boring job in an office and no personal life? Or an interesting job, for which you are paid a pittance. Or a Russian tyrant husband who is able to provide for me but with whom I have absolutely nothing to talk about. I'm young, beautiful and I want to live for myself. There will be a good party tonight, so I don't want to look like a tourist."

"Well then, sit down, young and beautiful, and I will braid your first dreadlocks, since you don't want to go back to society."

We're sitting in my restaurant, sipping juice and preparing our Ilka for a night out. The second floor offers a beautiful view of Arambol beach. The Sun is slowly approaching the horizon, reminding the night people that it's time to wake up. Hundreds of people, sensing the approach of the evening chill, are on their way to the beach to watch the massive burning ball cool down and sink into the sea. The heat of the day has subsided, and it is no longer necessary to seek shade. Someone is swinging poi[43], someone else is preparing a pole to perform a fire dance after sunset, by pouring kerosene on its ends. The bewitching sounds of drums are heard from all around. Trance music wafts from some restaurants. Some yogis meditate in lotus position. Practitioners of Chinese Tai Chi smoothly perform their movements near the water's edge.

Many people sit in small groups passing smoking chillums from hand to hand. Several Russians are comfortably sitting on mattresses in my restaurant, slowly sipping fresh juices. I wonder why this tradition of half-lying establishments with low tables didn't survive in Russia? It is more pleasant to spend time eating various tasty delights in a reclining position. Braiding Ilka's dreadlocks, I admire my daughter playing on the beach and building sand castles. Occasionally a warm, gentle wave reaches her sand castles and Vasilinka gets angry in an amusing manner, kicking the water with her little feet.

"I wish I'd had such a childhood and such a father," Ilka says, smiling and watching Vasilina. "Why wasn't I born in Goa?"

"If I could choose, I would also have chosen a childhood by the sea. I will try to do everything so that she grows up in Goa. I'll send her to a local kindergarten. Then to school. I want her to get used to freedom from childhood. Have you noticed what Goan children are like? Open, honest, easygoing. As a child, I was extremely shy when meeting strangers. In Russia, almost all

---

[42] Mixing bowl - a small plate for making smoking mixture.

[43] Poi - a type of juggling prop with balls on ropes that are held in the hands and swung in different directions.

parents are worried and nervous, and their children are the same. A child cannot be left unattended in a sandbox or he will be hit over the head with a shovel."

"Vasya, look, what's that?" Ilka says suddenly, pointing seriously at a noisy group of young Indian children. "What are they playing with?"

A few meters from my Hemp store, I see a small, grubby little girl of about five years old, who has tied a rope to the leg of a dead pig, and runs trailing it along the beach. Five other Indian beach children run after her, laughing merrily.

"Of course, it looks savage. But they have a different view of death."

"What do you expect, if Shiva, the god of destruction, is their main deity? A dead pig is just a toy for them."

"Hey, psychedelic bros," Denis says, smiling and coming into the restaurant.

"How's Goan life, Den?"

"Fine, as long as you don't think about the fact that the money is running out. When I think that I'll need to return to Rashka, I start to feel bad."

"But who is forcing you to go back? Look at all these happy people on the beach. Most of them made a choice to stay here. Are you any worse than them, or what? There's a party at Kerim Beach today; let's go, and I'll show you how you can earn money here."

Changing guard with the Sun, the Moon goes on patrol. The entire sky is densely studded with bright stars. Trance beats start to be heard from behind the rocks. There is something in the Indian tradition of gathering at Full Moon and dancing in praise of the gods. For some reason the best parties are at Full Moon. We are half-sitting, half-lying in my restaurant, waiting for some more Russian tourists staying in my house to turn up.

"Well, Ilka, your first dreadlocks are ready. What about a line of MDMA and let's head off?" I suggest, looking at the time on my phone.

Tipping a gram of Dimych onto a steel tray, I make eight equal lines with a plastic card. Having twisted a tube from a hundred-dollar bill, I sniff up two lines at once.

"Join me if you want," I pass the tray towards Den.

It seriously burns the inside of my nose, but I am willing to endure it, because this method of usage has its plusses. If MDMA is ingested, the effect is smooth, without any discomfort, but only after half an hour. If one sniffs it, after a few minutes a sharp explosion occurs in the head. It is this explosion that I want to feel now. Leaning back against the palm tree protruding from the middle of the restaurant, I start to feel how unwanted thoughts disappear instantly. The colors of the world, smearing slightly, become saturated with brightness, and everything is enveloped in the energy of love. Universal love for the world gently takes me away. The feeling of love and harmony is so overwhelming that I cannot even bring myself to piss in the sea. It is alive, with living creatures swimming in it. I cannot insult it with such behavior. I want to share this love with everyone. I want to save the world. After closing the restaurant, we head off into the dark in a joyful throng, along the beach towards the sound of magical music. Our hands are involuntarily dancing to the beat of the wafting sound. Hundreds of kilowatts of trance music boom from the rocks, forcing us to accelerate our pace. It is Full Moon, and the Moon, also dancing, lights our way. After a magical, hour-long walk, we find ourselves on a small, incredibly beautiful beach surrounded by high cliffs on all sides.

Fluorescent drapes, glowing in the dark, create the impression that we are on another planet. Oil lamps, used by the Hindu grandmothers for making tea, are lit everywhere. People sit and talk on mats in small groups around them. Taking one of these mats near the dance floor, we stop to rest for a while before breaking into the crowd of dancers. Around fifty beautiful people are tapping their feet to the rhythm coming from the massive speakers.

"Den, let's dance and meet some tourists."

There are only a few tourists, around twenty percent; the rest are all familiar faces. Tamir is working his magic at the decks.

"How does he manage to attract so many beautiful people?" Den asks me, taking off his shirt which is wet with sweat.

"Unlike other DJs, he personally hands out invitation flyers. He walks along the beach, at the night market, in places where freaks and other cool people hang out. He meets them and gives them his flyers. Look, Den, that group of tourists looks lost. Let's go and get to know them," I suggest, heading in their direction.

Three middle-aged men and two cute girls, drinking rum and Coke, sit on mats, looking bored.

"Do you mind if we sit with you?" I ask as we approach .

"Why not, there is no private property here. Sit down," says a guy in bright shorts, moving aside. "From your appearance, I understand that you are one of the locals. And its good to be friends with the locals. Let's get acquainted, my name is Alexander," the guy, who looks like he goes to the gym several times a week, says with a smile. "And please tell us 'newcomers' what is going on here. We have been to many discos around the world, but this is the first time we have seen such a well-dressed crowd. And the music is not like the House normally played in clubs. By the way, do you want some rum and Coke?" Alexander asks us, holding out a big bottle purchased in a duty free store.

"No, thank you, Alexander, we don't drink. We will order the best tea," Den says, pulling a chillum, safi and mixing bowl out of his bag.

"How do you do it? Even without alcohol, you are dancing while your are sitting here. We can't muster the courage to go out and dance without booze."

"For us, on the contrary, alcohol is a hindrance. It's not interesting to be on the low contours of perception."

"What do you mean?" leaning closer to us, a tough guy who introduced himself as Nikolay asks with interest "What are these contours and why is booze considered a low one?"

"If you want, I'll tell you."

"Well, go ahead, tell us, we have the whole night ahead, especially since we have another bottle," Alexander says, laughing.

"There was a professor at Harvard University named Timothy Leary. He devoted most of his life to the study of the impact of different psychotropic drugs that alter a person's perception of the world. He created a theory of an eight-contoured system. Well, according to this professor's theory, we can change our perception. For example, the first circuit of perception is the contour of insects. They want to get all the gain with none of the pain. It is a survival circuit. Heroin and cocaine addicts feel the same. In that state, they feel like they are the center of the Universe, nothing else is important to them. So in this state, their behavior is similar to that of an insect. They want to have fun and go unpunished. They are ready for anything just to get what they want."

"What is that pipe you've got there?" Nikolay interrupts me, curiously eyeing the chillum.

"Have you ever smoked charas?" I ask, wrapping the narrow end of the chillum with the piece of cloth prepared for the purpose.

"Well, actually we smoke hash and weed. But we have never tried to do it through a chillum. If you teach us, we will be happy to join you."

"Then watch carefully and repeat after us. Light it up, Den."

Puffing at the chillum, I enjoy the way Den loudly and melodically recites the mantra, "Bom Bolenath, Sabke Sath, Bom Shiva, Bom Shankar, Bom." Having inhaled strongly, I exhale the smoke for a moment with my eyes closed and, touching the chillum to my forehead, I pass it on to Den.

"One strong puff without touching the chillum with your lips and pass it to the person sitting on your right. Have you got it?" I explain, pointing at Den who is pulling as I speak.

While the chillum is passed from hand to hand, leaning back on the mat, I continue my story.

"The second circuit of perception is the animal contour. Alcohol helps us to get there. This circuit helps us to reproduce."

"That's right," our new friend Nikolay adds, pouring himself a glass of whiskey. "As soon as we get drunk we either want a woman or to get into a fight."

"That's right. We become like animals. In the wild, males mark their territory and fight, and the females raise their tails and walk in circles," I add, feeling another wave of universal love sweeping over my body. "Then there is the third circuit, the contour of domesticated primates."

"And who are these domesticated primates?" a girl sitting leaning on Nikolay asks curiously.

"That's us, 'domesticated primates' or 'Homo Sapiens.' In the evolutionary chain, we are between an ape and a conscious man. Psychotropic drugs, or psychedelics as they are called, suit us best. The marijuana group: hashish, charas, weed, and synthetic drugs: amphetamines, MDMA, LSD and their substitutes. Using them, we feel unity and harmony with the Universe. These drugs help us to understand who we are. As another psychedelic scientist and philosopher Robert Anton Wilson said, 'The problem of the transition from the third to the fourth circuit relates to the awareness of being a domesticated primate and the unwillingness to be one.'"

Exhaling the last puff, I feel the strong wave of a rush which causes my eyes to close and my body to tingle. Starting to clean the chillum, I pause my lecture for a moment to understand whether anyone is listening to me.

"And what should we do then?" Alexander breaks the silence, pouring more whiskey.

"Well, there are two paths," I continue. "Either you accept that you are a primate and live this primate life using alcohol as a catalyst. Or you make a quantum leap in perception. There was an American scientist – Terence McKenna. He devoted forty years of his life to the study of the evolutionary development of the human brain, and came to the conclusion that psychedelics influence a person as an accelerator of development. By studying the remains of prehistoric Neanderthals and Australopithecus, he concluded that the primate brain developed very slowly. However, during one short period of time of a few thousand years it tripled in size. And this period coincided with the end of one of the Ice Ages. During this period, the first humanlike primates ate a lot of plant food containing small doses of psychotropic substances. In this manner, over the past several millennia the brain was stimulated and developed, forming new areas responsible for speech and accumulation of knowledge."

"An interesting theory, but let's move on to practice. You have probably already done a quantum leap today," Alexander interrupts me, smiling. "Where can we try these accelerators?"

"They are not a problem to get it. What would you like to start with?"

"Well, if only we knew... I see you're professionals and I am ready to trust you. We haven't tried anything other than cocaine. But from your words – that's not quite what we need."

"Then I would advise your girls to try MDMA, and for you – a drop of LSD."

"What kind of drugs are these? We haven't heard of them."

"LSD was invented by Swiss scientist Dr. Albert Hoffman at the Sandoz pharmaceutical factory in 1943. He is 90 years old now; all his life he conducted experiments with LSD on himself and his relatives. And he is still alive and feels good, and is not going to die. MDMA was invented by Alexander Shulgin, a Russian American. You have probably heard of ecstasy, haven't you? MDMA is pure ecstasy without amphetamine additives."

"Well, come on then, give us some quantum accelerators. We want to dance like everyone else," says Nikolay, laughing and taking out some money.

"Den, smoke with the boys, while I go and fetch what they need. I'll be right back."

Moving 20 meters away from where we are sitting, I come across a dancing German named Nick. Nick is a true psychedelic warrior who, hiding from the German police, came to Goa 30 years ago and stayed here. With his huge earrings he looks like a shaman who has seen much in his lifetime.

"Hi, Nick. How are you finding today's party?"

"It's cool! So many beautiful people around. And the DJs today are the best. And how do you feel, my Russian psychedelic brother?"

"I'm fine. Nick, sell me a little acid and MDMA and I will feel even better."

"No problem, I always have a discount for regular customers," smiling, my German friend reaches into his pocket.

Having given him the money and smoked a chillum with him, I go back to our mat without stopping to dance.

"Here you are, these are your quantum accelerators," I hold out a small bag to my new comrades.

"What can we expect from this? We won't feel bad from a sharp acceleration?"

"It will be alright; the main thing is not to fear anything. If you have a clear mind, then everything will be beautiful and bright. And if you don't, you can experience a bad trip, but don't be scared as that is also useful. You only have yourselves to be afraid of; more precisely, your thoughts and intentions. If you have demons in your head, you will be haunted by devils everywhere; and if harmony and love prevail in you, you will see how beautiful the world around you is. Well, that's enough of the lectures, we'll come back and see you in an hour."

"Den, let's go and dance, a beautiful track is playing, I can't sit in one place any longer. Well, Den, did you get how easily you can earn a hundred bucks?"

"Yes, Vasya, now I also have a chance to stay here. It's good work to communicate with people and sell them psychedelics. And, as a matter of fact, it is not very risky if I only sell to Russians. There are no Russian cops here, so there is nothing to fear."

"For the next party I'll buy you different psychedelics. You can sell them and we split the profit. Deal?"

"Deal!" Denis says, shaking my hand and glowing with joy.

"Well, well, well! Roma, is it really you?"

Forgetting about Den, I rush to embrace my Goan friend whom I have not seen for almost a year.

"I heard that you were supposed to be coming, but I didn't know exactly when. Why didn't you call me, you son of a bitch. You look great! Did you come to Goa long ago?"

"No, I arrived yesterday afternoon, slept a little, and once again found myself in a fairytale. I've missed Goan parties. If only you knew how hard it was for me to be in Moscow without Goa. Vasya, I can't live there any longer. I quit my stupid office job, leased out my flat and came here as quickly as I could."

"I understand you very well, Roma. I had the same feeling when I was at home. But now, it's all over. I have realized my dream to stay here. I brought my family here, opened a restaurant. In the morning, we'll go there to drink juice. How glad I am to see you. So, it looks like we are going to light things up together again."

"By the way, about lighting things up," Roma says, as if remembering something, and takes a staff wrapped in a cover off of his back.

"Vasya, do you remember I was learning to swing a fire staff last year? I finally mastered it. Now I sometimes perform in Moscow nightclubs for money. In Moscow, a fire show is still something exotic. They pay pretty well. Sometimes it can be from three hundred to one thousand dollars per night. By the way, Vasya, do you know Hanuman?" Roma says, pointing at a guy dancing nearby. "He is from Nizhny Novgorod."

"Hanuman, this is Vasiliy."

A tall blond guy with a playboy appearance extends his hand to me.

"Hanuman, you have a nice outfit; minimalist style. Ninja shoes and orange shorts."

"I go everywhere like this. Here in Goa, I don't need other clothes."

Hanuman turns, and I see a big inscription 'Legalize' embroidered on his ass.

"Judging by the inscription, you must be one of us. Come on, I'll treat you to some MDMA."

"No, thank you, Vasya. I love cocaine. I don't like anything else."

"And I really thought that you were one of us, psychedelic people. I'm sorry, I can't treat you to coke, I don't sell it and I don't touch it myself."

"Well I, on the contrary, both sell it and touch it happily."

"Just don't argue about what is better and what is worse," Roma intervenes in time, unwilling to listen to our debate the whole evening. "Come on, I'd rather swing my staff for you."

Having pulled the staff out of its bag, Roma starts pouring the carefully wrapped ends with kerosene.

"Light it up!" he calls to Hanuman when ready for the fire dance.

The people dancing around us disperse, forming a living circle. Immediately catching the rhythm of the music, Romka starts turning the fire staff at a rapid speed, cutting the space around him, leaving a red and yellow pattern in the dark for a moment. I watch as Roma dances and swings his fire staff, and I can't believe that just a year ago he adhered to the notion that 'real' men don't dance.

"Dawn is coming soon, we should do some more. Let's go and snort a line of Dymich. I'll introduce you to our new friends," I tell Roma, who has stopped dancing.

"Roma, please meet Alexander. Today, he is trying LSD for the first time," I say, leading him to our place.

"We know each other," Roma says in surprise and extends his hand to greet Alexander. "In Moscow, everyone knows Alexander. He is the director of a large Russian television channel," Roma tries to tell me quietly.

But having heard us, Alexander adds with a smile, "In Moscow, I am a director, but here I am just like you – an ordinary man relaxing."

"By the way, thank you, Vasya. Today you gave us such an interesting lecture. And also thank you for the quantum leap."

"We have already been leaping for an hour without stopping," adds Nikolay, dancing next to us and laughing. "I think I realized a lot today."

"Roma, just imagine if Alexander, who manages a large media system and felt universal love today, and having become a little better, is then be able to pass on this love to the masses and change the world for the better. It depends on him what the whole country watches. And as he has changed today, then to some extent the changes will affect millions of people."

"People go mad, die, turning into

Cannon fodder, concentrates and oil,

Production waste, mausoleums and epaulettes

You see, the psychedelic army is expanding and growing..." Roma answers with a poem in a sing-song voice.

"Yes, Roma, the psychedelic revolution continues."

Chapter 23. Part One. Inside.

"Anybody medicine, anybody medicine?" I hear David's familiar low voice, coming down the hallway. David voluntarily occupies the position of doctor in the jail. Every morning and evening, he carries medicine, given to us for free by the Indian government, to the cells. When he reaches our cell, he puts the box of medicines on the floor, crouches, and carefully starts to rummage, watching the guards slumbering near the entrance out of the corner of his eye.

"Mr. Vasiliy, the doctor prescribed you some medicine," with a quick movement he inconspicuously throws a little paper bag through the bars."

"Thank you, David. I've been getting sick so often," I thank him with a smile.

"Disay, look what I've got," I shout joyfully, showing him two tolas of charas.

"What, is it a holiday today in our cell?" Dominic asks with a smile all over his face.

"Yes," I brag, showing off the two black balls. "There are only three of us who smoke in the cell: me, you, and Disay, so it should last us for a long time. We just need to think up a place to hide it. Sometimes the warden searches the cells for anything illegal, and if he finds this charas, they'll open a case, and then I'll definitely not be released sooner than in ten years."

Rummaging through my things, I find a bag of Indian toffees. Carefully removing the wrappers from four candies, I lay them aside and put the candies in my mouth. I mold four small bars from charas, wrap them in candy wrappers, and then show them to Dominic.

"Great idea, no one would think to unwrap all the candies."

Having warned the other inmates not to touch the candies, I put the jar with toffees in the most prominent place in the corner, where there is already a whole bunch of different packages and jars for public use.

"How will we smoke? The tobacco ran out," Disay asks me, rummaging in his pockets in a vain attempt to scrape together at least a pinch.

"Don't worry, we'll think something up. In Russia, in the height of Perestroika, all of the tobacco factories closed at the same time, and for a whole month people smoked anything that could be smoked. We, Russians, are accustomed to living in times of change, so we'll never be lost. As for me, at that time I tried to smoke black tea leaves. When you really want to smoke and there is nothing available, any smoke that can be inhaled will do. What do we have in stock? Peanuts, I think their husks will burn rather well."

Grinding a handful of dry husks in my palm, I make a mixture for smoking. One charas pea, a pinch of dry husks and I have a jail joint rolled from newspaper.

"That's fine, it can be smoked," breathing in the tasteless smoke, Dominic says and passes me the joint.

"It is very sunny today and our walk is in an hour. I haven't walked stoned for a long time, probably a couple of years," Disay adds, sighing.

"Hey, Chetsi, will you smoke with us?"

"No thanks, I don't smoke," the former policeman answers, keeping a look out near the door.

The lightness in my body again relaxes my muscles and thoughts. The wall slowly dissolves, and it seems that a pleasant sea breeze is blowing on my body. I'm free again, I'm lying on the hot sand and my little daughter is crawling on me, laughing loudly. My Lena and my friends are next to me. Life is beautiful and amazing.

Chapter 23. Part Two. Outside.

"Daddy, daddy, our parrots are gone!" my daughter tells me, weeping.

"What do you mean they are gone?" having looked from the balcony into a hollow in the palm tree to check for myself, I descend from the second floor of our house and yell our landlord's name across the courtyard.

"Francis! Come here, you son of a bitch. Did you take the parrots?" I ask the puny Indian, who abandons his pedigree bull and immediately comes running at my menacing yell.

"What parrots?" he asks, surprised, making his usual dumb facial expression.

"Do you see the palm tree growing near our house? At the beginning of the season, a big green parrot family settled in the hollow at the level of our window. They have been a part of our family the whole season: first they hatched, then fed their chicks, and now they are gone. There, you see, someone has smashed the hollow and stole the chicks. Look, the parents are flying around the palm trees, worried."

"I did not take them, for what I need them, I have bull. But today, I saw how neighborhood boys were fiddling with a ladder in the courtyard. If I find out that they did it, I will tear their ears out."

"Thank you, Francis," I thank the lean and wiry Indian of about forty years old in advance.

"Tourists come here, they need something exotic: where else can they have a shower and watch huge parrots eating guava from the window. In the evening, you can go out onto the balcony and see a family of eagle owls peeping from a hollow five meters away from you. In the morning, monkeys come here sometimes. It is like a zoo, you don't see this in Russia. You'd better try to get the parrots back; or we'll move to another house next season."

Francis is a classic specimen of an Arambol fisherman. It's highly doubtful that something could get stolen without his knowledge. I am sure he knows who took the chicks. He and his two brothers own three houses that form a typical Indian courtyard, full of pigs, chickens, dogs, cats, and a breeding bull, all of which they inherited from their father. Located on the edge of a palm grove bordering with the sea, the courtyard is densely overgrown with thorny bushes on all sides and so it is protected from intruders. So do not worry, my darling, we will find our parrots.

"Vasya, Vasya," Francis shouts, catching up with me on the stairs. "I cut down coconuts for you, they are at the entrance, 30 pieces. 300 rupees from you."

"What coconuts?"

"What-what, you asked me yourself."

"I asked you a month ago to cut down the coconuts above the footpath so that my family could safely get to the sea. After all, if a coconut falls on your head, it's certain death. Francis, look at the palm tree, the coconuts are still hanging as they did before."

"I cut down the palms on the other side, these have not ripened yet."

"And don't unripe coconuts fall on your head, or what?"

"They do, but very rarely. You can walk safely. I walk here every day and they have never fallen on me. Vasya, do not worry like that, you cannot run away from karma. So give me 300 rupees for coconuts."

"Okay, I will give you it in the evening if you return the parrots."

"Do not be sad, my girl, Francis promised to find our parrots. Will you come to the restaurant with me for breakfast?"

"Will you pull me through the waves on the way?"

"Of course I'll pull my little princess. Get your swimming board and come with me."

"Vasiliy, I made some fresh kvass[44], don't forget to deliver it to the restaurants after breakfast," my Lena shouts from the second floor. "While you have your breakfast, I'll finish making pastries. They have already called from the Tchaikovsky restaurant and ordered a hundred pieces. Oh yeah, Vasil, I almost forgot to tell you. We ran out of hashish for cakes. May I take some of yours?"

"Of course, dear," I shout back, lifting Vasilinka onto my shoulders. How I love my job! Have I really managed to do it? I don't need to get up early in the morning to clean snow from my car and warm it up after the night's frost. I don't have to meet with tax inspectors, I don't have to pay bribes to firefighters and the sanitary-epidemiological station, and I don't need to see the permanently disgruntled faces of my fellow citizens. I run along the edge of the sea, pulling a plastic swimming board by a rope, on which my daughter surfs, squealing with joy and leaving a cloud of splashes glittering in the sunlight behind her. How wonderful it is to have breakfast on the beach in your own restaurant! Depending on my mood, I pick one of the three breakfasts I invented.

Breakfast number one: potato pancakes with sour cream, tomato salad with garlic and cheese, pancakes with condensed milk, tea, and a glass of fresh pomegranate juice.

Breakfast number two: fried eggs, Greek salad, cottage cheese pancakes with chocolate cream, coffee with cream, and a glass of freshly squeezed orange juice.

Breakfast number three: oatmeal porridge with milk, cashew nuts and honey, sandwich with tender chicken, fruit salad of mango, papaya, watermelon, grapes and strawberries, and a glass of grape juice.

I usually start thinking about breakfast from when I wake up, carefully listening to my cravings. Which of the three should I choose today? It's a pity that I do not have three stomachs. Having had breakfast and collected the previous day's takings, we get back home close to midday. I load four seven-liter bottles of ice-cold kvass onto my scooter, put a box of hashish cakes into my backpack, kiss my Lena and set off to go do the rounds of the Russian establishments. In different

---

[44] Kvass - a traditional Slavic, sour low-alcohol beverage, which is prepared through the fermentation of malt and flour (wheat, barley) or dry rye bread.

parts of North Goa, fellow restaurateurs are always waiting for me. It's nice when your work is appreciated and loved. The owners and managers of different cafes and restaurants call me every day and order kvass, hashish cakes, and, at the same time, charas, MDMA and LSD for themselves for the night. Wherever I go, I am greeted with a smile, money and a rolled joint. By afternoon, I go home stoned, happy, and with pockets full of Indian money.

"Lena, life is good! I've brought a lot of money again. We need more cakes. Can you do another fifty by this evening?"

"What did your last slave die of?" my beloved answers, for some reason not sharing my joy, and pours herself a rum on the rocks in a square glass. "By the way, I want to talk to you."

"So, let's talk. What's happened?"

"Nothing's happened, I just want to ask you about your plans for the future. Tell me, dear, are you're going to sell kvass and cakes all your life like this?"

"Why not? I really like my job. Every day I earn a hundred dollars, it's good money."

"You think that a hundred dollars per day is good money?"

"Well, isn't it? We have everything. A driver takes Vasilinka to and from kindergarten. You and I have two of the coolest scooters, paid for in advance for the entire season. Leasing this house to tourists, we don't have to pay for accommodation. In our restaurant, we eat for free. Once a week, we go to a party where we can have as many drugs as we want. What are you complaining about?"

"Maybe you like selling kvass, but I'm tired of it. And what kind of job is that, 'kvass woman Lena.' I just started making money in Russia, and you brought me to this village, forced me to make kvass and accommodate tourists. I don't see any career opportunities in this work."

"Honey, what's wrong? You've probably had too much heat today. Firstly, no one is forcing you to work. Teach the Indians to brew kvass and make cakes, and just collect the money. And secondly, Lena, you must have forgotten that in order to live with the level of comfort that we have here, in Russia you need to earn not a hundred but a thousand a day. That means working hard from dawn till dusk. Look at the two-week tourists that come to us – they are exhausted and squeezed out like lemons, they can only dream of living like we do. They don't want to go back."

"Well, nevertheless, they leave and make careers. And no one really wants to come here to make kvass."

"Honey, what's wrong? We have a house full of tourists, things are going well, I would even say very well. Every day we eat fresh fruit and seafood. We have everything. Maybe you made a call to Russia again? What's happened, did your sister buy another mink coat?"

"How do you know about the coat?" Lena lifts her head in annoyance, turns away and pretends to be looking at something among the palms. "Here, you can't even find anything to spend money on. If you buy something fashionable, you look like a fool among these rednecks."

"Oh Lena, Lenochka, I see that I brought you here from Rashka too soon. You haven't got fed up with the city's shit yet. But I hope that in time, you will understand that we are living in paradise."

"Daddy, daddy, Francis returned the parrots! See, they are looking at us from the palm tree again," my little girl shouts happily, interrupting our discussion.

"Everything will be fine, my dear. Life in paradise continues."

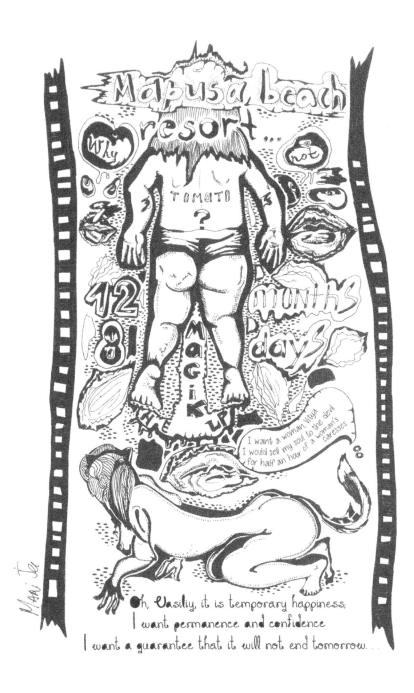

Chapter 24. Part One. Inside.

Putting aside the 'Tibetan Book of the Dead', I observe the behavior of a new tenant who has just arrived. Skinny, hollow cheeks, greasy dirty clothes, and obviously not being very picky when it comes to choosing a place, he positions himself near the toilet. Dominic's bowl is on a tank with water near the toilet and he pushes it away from the new tenant in disgust.

"Go and wash up, why are you sitting here? You can smell you down the hallway."

Frightened, the new tenant grabs a piece of soap that was given to him and, looking nervously at everyone, goes to the toilet.

"We better not contract tuberculosis or anything else from him," moving his mug closer to his corner, former policeman Chetsi says.

"Hey, Gandhi, you haven't got tuberculosis?"

"No, I'm healthy. I just have not eaten or washed for a long time," I hear the new tenant's voice from behind the door, speaking in fairly good English for an Indian.

"Dominic, do you know him?"

"Who doesn't know Gandhi? He must have been in all of India's jails. He spends all of his life in jails; he has neither relatives, nor a house. Now he'll get washed up, put on some weight, treat his sores – and in a half-year he will be released, as the rainy season ends. All his life, from May to November, he eats his full in jail."

"And what is he in here for?"

"As usual, petty theft. He stole a cell phone and got six months in jail."

Coming out of the toilet, Gandhi anxiously looks around, stares at me curiously and sits in his corner.

"Oh, you beast!" I hear Dominic yelling from the toilet.

Jumping out of the toilet with a broom in his hand, he thumps the new tenant on the head with the handle.

"I'm going to teach you how normal people live in the same cell!" Dominic shouts, striking the Indian's body and face. "You have only just come and you've already began to make a mess; weren't you taught to flush the toilet?!"

"I got it, don't punch me anymore, I won't do it again," huddling in the corner, the terrified Gandhi screams.

"Walking talk, talking walk, walking talk," a guard sings, mimicking a cell phone advertisement, and opens the door for us.

Finally, it's the time when I can speak Russian. Leaving Gandhi to wash the toilet, we slowly come out of the cell.

"Hey, Viktor!"

"Welcome to Mapusa Beach!" smiling, Viktor shouts back to me, as usual pulling a bucket of water out into the courtyard.

"Say, Vitya, I was embarrassed to ask before, why are your legs scarred?"

"That is a souvenir from the army. When I served in Afghanistan, I was blown up by a mine; instead of bones I have iron rods in my legs."

"If you survived Afghanistan, then you will also survive jail."

"Why would I need to survive here; it is like a health spa."

"Vitya, if it wasn't for your Russian face, you'd look like a veteran of the Vietnam War. Our Afghans don't have long hair, but you look like a character from a film about Vietnam veterans. The bandana on the forehead, the weathered and slightly wrinkled face, tanned skin. The last thing you need is an American flag in your hand, and a smile on your face. Then no one would guess that you're Russian. You also look like Homer Simpson in his youth. Have you watched the cartoon 'The Simpsons'?"

"No, I haven't watched TV for a long time. The last thing I watched was 'Only Old Men Go to Battle'[45]."

"Yes, you certainly are one of a kind. This is the first time I have met someone who hasn't heard of the Simpsons. One of the main characters, Homer, is shown in one of the episodes as a young man at Woodstock. Well, you would look just like him if you didn't shave."

Pouring a couple of buckets of water over his head, Viktor rolls up his shorts, turning them into a G-string, and lies down on a towel on the ground in the middle of the courtyard.

"Today, I am going to sunbathe. If you close your eyes and look at the Sun, you can vividly imagine yourself on the beach."

The Indians walking around leer at Vitya's bare ass and whisper among themselves.

"I think you are turning them on, Vitya. They've never seen a bare white ass before. And, in my opinion, they don't care what sex that white ass is."

"I don't care, I'm not in a Russian jail. No one will do anything to me here. And anyway, I am a crazy foreigner. If only they tried to do something to me..."

I squat nearby, in the shade of a wall covered with moss, and close my eyes.

"The buffet comes tomorrow, what have you ordered, Vitya?" I ask, imagining a bright juicy mango.

"This time, I wrote a huge list. My mother sent me some money, so I'll celebrate. Oranges, mangoes, bananas, apples, grapes, cookies, candies, nuts, jam, milk, soap and toothpaste," he lists, counting on his fingers, not opening his eyes. "We only live once. Soon I'll get my expert analysis – why should I economize?"

"What about vegetables?"

Viktor begins to laugh hysterically, grimacing and opening one eye.

"Vasya, I'll never understand the Indians. Can you believe it? You can order fruit, but not vegetables. Juice can be ordered; mineral water cannot. I have already written a statement to the

---

[45] 'Only Old Men Go to Battle' - an old Russian film.

prison warden and complained to the prison doctor that I need tomatoes, cucumbers and onions. Today, David and I are going to write a petition to the judge. Something like: 'I'm a foreigner and I do not have enough vitamins.' If the judge refuses to give us vegetables, I will declare a hunger strike. I will write a poster: 'Why not tomato?' and I will take it to court with me every time I go."

"Tell me, Vitya, what would you like to eat most of all right now?"

"I want raw oysters with lemon juice. I think about them more often than anything else; as for other things, I pretty much have it all."

"Well, I want a woman, Vitya. I would sell my soul to the devil for half an hour of a woman's caresses."

"No, Vasya, I would not give even a hundred rupees for a woman. I've had enough of women. All evil comes from them. Now, without them, I feel great. Nobody does your head in, no one bothers you; you can do whatever you want. If you think about it, we are sitting here because of them. I showed off in front of my girlfriend and ended up playing the drug dealer. I had everything: money, cars, drugs. All I wanted was to show my woman that I'm the coolest. And where did I end up? Here alone, and I don't know where she is or with whom. If I was offered a woman or an oyster, I would choose the latter."

"Looks like you have already got old," I laugh, wiping my face, which is sweating from the heat.

"Why am I 'old'? Everything is in working order. If the urge gets too strong, you can jerk off in the toilet at night. A sexual orgasm is a dubious pleasure; just a second and that's it. And then you stand there and think, 'Why am I doing this?' And an oyster – it is delicious, it gives pleasure for a long time."

"What are you chatting about, Russians?" David asks, coming up to us.

"We are chatting about the pleasures we have been deprived of – about women, about food. Viktor dreams of oysters. As for food, I miss pizza."

"I can get you pizza," the Iranian, sitting next to us, says with a straight face.

"Tell your wife to make a small pizza and bring it to me in the hospital. But the pizza shouldn't be larger than a pack of cigarettes, then I can easily carry it in my shorts into the jail," unable to keep up his serious tone, toothless David cracks up with laughter, "and as for women, everything is also very simple. You write a statement to the prison warden, that, well, you ask him to let you go home on Saturday and Sunday, and pledge to return by ten in the morning on Monday, and give your word of honor. You file a statement and wait."

"Get lost, David!" Viktor laughs, unrolling his shorts to cover his pink buttocks, which are slightly blushing from the sun.

"Vitya, and what would you want most of all from the real world now?"

"From the real world? Most of all, I want to get out, Vasya. Do you think that is a real desire or not?"

"To be honest, Vitya, in the near future it's impossible. Pramud has been waiting for his expert analysis for almost a year."

"I don't want to sit here for a year. But after serving a year, when I get out of here, I'll demand a million dollars compensation and file a lawsuit against the police. To serve a year for a pharmaceutical anesthetic, how is that even possible? I'm a foreigner, a disabled Afghan war veteran who came here on vacation as a tourist and lost everything. My business collapsed, my wife left me. My best years passed in jail, I want at least a million."

"Why are you fuming about it here in front of us; save it for the court. We know everything about you. Get out of here first and then you'll see what happens. You were actually put in here as an enemy of the state."

"Why, an enemy of the state?" Viktor asks in surprise, crawling closer to me into the shade.

"Well, let's think logically. The government makes laws: tell me what drugs can you legally have in large quantities to avoid punishment?"

"You can have up to twenty kilos of marijuana and get out on bail; but what has that got to do with it?"

"No, Vitya, I'm talking about synthetic, highly profitable drugs. You can have one hundred grams of cocaine in your pocket, and be released on bail in a couple of weeks. Why do you think that they have such laws here in India? After all, since the times of old man Freud, everyone has known that cocaine is a dangerous drug. However, it can be possessed in a large quantity here."

"Probably, to make it easier to sell."

"Right you are, Vitya. In this manner the state supports the sale of cocaine. They even organized a special service called the 'anti-drug police', that oversees this sphere. And what did you do? You almost brought down their whole cocaine market with your fake. The rumor about your magic powder quickly spread throughout Goa. I even heard tourists praising your powder: 'Everyone's cocaine gets you high for thirty minutes, and Vitya's keeps you up for four hours.' Who would lock you up for a legal pharmaceutical drug? Only those selling real coke whose way you got in. You even hit upon the idea of giving away business cards with the inscription 'Magic Help' to everyone at parties, where the old drug dealers sell their cocaine under police cover. You'll be lucky if the cops didn't plant real coke in your powder."

"But they wouldn't plant a hundred grams of coke, would they? That would cost ten thousand bucks."

"One hundred grams is very unlikely, but five grams they could. And then your case could be delayed for another year. So get out first, and then you can dream of becoming a millionaire."

"Well, can't I even dream?"

"It was you, Vitya, who told me – you have to dream about real things. And I'm just showing you a real possibility."

"Well I've had enough of it, this reality. Vasya, let's talk about something else. Everyday it is the same thing. All conversations are about possible realities, real and unreal desires. An ordinary man here in jail has only one desire – to get out quickly. Two years ago, there was a case where someone got his expert analysis in eight months. Someone got lucky. According to the law, if the export analysis doesn't come in twelve months and eight days, the inmate is released. So twelve months and eight days is our dream, we hope to get out in this time. And if the analysis comes back earlier, then it is our good luck. Whatever happens, you won't get out earlier than your own luck. You need to dream of getting out of here during this interval: from hope to luck."

Chapter 24. Part Two. Outside.

"Well, cyber gypsies, it's time to see the real India," I try to cheer up Lena and my friends, as we walk behind a huge cart stacked with luggage, on top of which my always cheery Vasilinka sits proudly.

Pausing for a moment to rest and wiping sweat from his face, the porter complains once again, asking us to give him an extra fifty rupees for the work. A passing elderly woman wrapped in a blue sari coos over Vasilinka and pinches her chubby cheek affectionately.

"Get your hands off her, you dirty cow," unable to stand it, my wife starts yelling in Russian.

Frightened by such aggression, the Indian woman quickly moves a few steps away and, judging by her look, is perplexed.

"Lena, what's the matter," Ilka tries to calm her, stroking her arm.

"I am fed up with these filthy Indians. Vasilinka will soon have sores on her cheek. All the way from Goa to Bombay, every woman passing by my daughter tries to touch her cheek."

"Well, what can you do, they have a tradition of showing their love in such a way. Your daughter is pretty and they like her."

"And don't they have a tradition of washing their hands!?" Lena shouts, no longer restraining her emotions.

"Why do you think they don't? Just like you, they wash their hands with soap and water," trying to calm my Lena, I put my arm around her waist.

"Don't try to pacify me; take your hands off me. It would be better if you bought us some plane tickets. I'll dig my nails into the face of the next person that touches my daughter. You say they wash their hands, then why is there dirt everywhere? If they were clean themselves, they would maintain cleanliness around them. I lived with these pigs for six months in Arambol. They shit where they eat. I'm tired of India."

"My dear, you were in Goa, and Goa is not India. The Goan Indians consider themselves more to be Portuguese. And they are all clean, compared to the rest of India. To consider Goans Indians is the same as to consider Tajiks Europeans."

"Well, thanks for reassuring me. What else should I expect from them? This is the last time I travel in India by train. Next time buy us plane tickets, or Vasilina and I will return to Russia."

"What's wrong with her?" Den, trailing behind, asks me in a whisper.

"Don't pay any attention, she will probably have her period soon, she is always furious a few days in advance."

"Oh, I get it now, my former wife was the same. Personally, I really like trains. Their restrooms are cleaner than in Russia. And the Indians aren't really such pigs. It's just that there is a half billion of them. So it seems that everything is dirty."

"Why are you telling me that, Den? You should tell it to my Lena."

"Oh, no, you're her husband and you must teach her; I don't want to become the enemy of your family."

"Lena, now we'll get on a train, and in two days we'll be in Nepal," I carry on with my efforts to appease my angry wife.

"When you called me to come and live in India, you didn't say that the rainy season here lasts for six months, and that we will need to move somewhere else for that time. You know, I'm tired from packing up all our things for monsoon. You were getting stoned with Den on the balcony, and I was packing everything into plastic bags, so that it doesn't rot before our return. Then I packed our luggage while you were sleeping after a party. I am tired. I hope that six months in Nepal will pass without me brewing kvass, Russian tourists and Hemp."

"Lena, look at everything from a positive perspective: the porters are carrying our things for us, and we have a personal chef, Krishna."

"Don't try to pacify me; this is my normal state. I'm just ready for anything," Lena says, finally forcing a smile and taking our daughter down from the suitcases.

Upon reaching the border, we face the first unforeseen problem: it is closed. There is another crisis in Nepal related to the revolution. Having unloaded all of our bags around the border guard booth, we stand watching as on the other side of the border several hundred Nepalese strikers with banners and red flags block the roads, demanding the abdication of the king.

"Well, don't be down. Come on, let's stay in a hotel. There is a good one a hundred meters away," I say, putting our things back onto the rickshaw again. "Don't worry, Lenok, in a few days the border will be opened. We just have to wait until the strike is over. I have MDMA and charas; let's throw a small party tonight and relax a bit."

The owner of the hotel, an elderly Sikh[46] with a black turban on his head, meets us at the entrance and immediately warns us that the strike might last for a week. Movement over land is completely blocked. But there is hope that if there are about fifteen people, a small plane will fly from the border to Pokhara.

Having checked into the half-empty, but comfortable small hotel, we stand on the balcony, sipping beer and watching the Nepalese strikers waving flags with strange symbols. There is an odd sign on the red banners: a sickle, hammer and scissors.

"Why didn't they depict a seven-pointed leaf on there as well?" Lena says hugging me, having finally relaxed after a line of MDMA. "I love you, Vasya, please don't take my moods seriously. Look how sweet our Vasilinka is sleeping. Maybe we should also get some rest?"

Two days later, the hotel owner wakes us up in the morning and gives us the good news.

"Get dressed quickly and come downstairs. In two hours there will be a plane; the next opportunity to fly away will be in two weeks. Everyone must give seventy dollars, and your chef – thirty-five. Sorry, but those are the rules; in Nepal foreigners pay twice the price for tickets." Having

---

[46] Sikh - an Indian nation of men who wear turbans, do not cut their hair or shave, and always carry curved daggers.

quickly packed our things and had breakfast, we jump into three rickshaws and attempt to cross the border inconspicuously.

"Vasiliy, I'm afraid of these idiots – I don't want us to get showered with stones."

"Why would they do that to us? They are protesting against the king."

"In Russia in 1917 they were also against the king, and you know how that ended."

"We need to drive for about forty minutes to reach a small airport. The airport is guarded by the military. Don't worry, we will be in safety soon."

An agitated crowd with banners and sticks appears in the main street in front of us. The enraged mob chants incessantly: "King, go out."

Our rickshaw driver quickly realizes what is happening and turns into a small alley. We ride in silence through deserted streets to bypass the crowd. I'm trying to defuse the situation with jokes, but Lena is not smiling, and presses little Vasilinka to herself.

"Well, here we are, safe," I say, watching the porters unload our stuff at the small airport.

We are flying with Yeti Airline.

"Do you remember the famous snowman living in the Himalayas? This airline was named in his honor. We will live in the country where the snowman lives."

Having passed the baggage inspection point, in horror I recall that I have fifty grams of MDMA and ten grams of charas in my luggage. But I am lucky and no one notices our contraband. Next time I should be more careful, otherwise I could end up in jail through my foolishness. I have never flown on such a funny plane before.

"Dad, dad, this plane is so small, like a toy."

"No, baby, it's a real airplane. The country is small and so is the plane."

"Look, Dad, that woman looks like an angel," Vasilina points at a stewardess dressed in a white sari.

"Why like an angel?"

"Because she is wearing white and she has a kind face."

After giving the passengers cotton balls to put in their ears, the angel-stewardess asks everyone to fasten their seat belts. The fifteen-minute trip would last fourteen hours by bus. We only need to fly over one big mountain. Taking off from the Earth, we fly over a large stunning gorge and it seems like we only just miss the tips of the treetops with our small wheels. Reaching its maximum height in order to fly over the ridge, the plane starts to descend. Ahead we can see Pokhara, conveniently located near a beautiful lake.

"Where are we? Where is your promised Nepali heaven?" dissatisfied once again, my wife grumbles, sitting next to me on a cart that is being pushed by a young Nepalese guy.

"Isn't this paradise? No big deal that there are no cars; you know that there is a revolution going on now and there is a strike across the whole country. And why don't you like the cart? We will be taken to our hotel for just one dollar. We would have to pay twenty for a taxi."

"So next time you go by cart, but Vasilina and I will go by taxi. See, people are laughing at us. Maybe we are the only ones crazy enough to come here at this time."

"No one is laughing at us, they are locals greeting us. They are very friendly here. Especially now that there are hundreds of empty hotels and restaurants. Now we are the only source of income for them. They will carry us in their arms. We will live in a palace. We'll stay in a hotel for a while, and then I'll find a palace for us. Would you like to live in a palace, my girl?"

"Of course I would, daddy."

"I promise you we'll have a palace."

"I hope that we will live without any fucking two-week tourists unable to wipe their own asses themselves without help, 'Lena, the hot water ran out; Lena, the electricity turned off; Lena, we have a spider in the toilet,'" mimicking the Moscow accent, my wife huffs, trying to force herself to smile at the people we pass by.

After staying for a few days in a hotel, getting a good night's sleep and eating decent food, we gradually start to get used to our new place of residence. The sea and palm trees begin to be replaced by the mountains and the lake. Instead of a scooter, I purchase three bicycles. A black one for me, a red one for Lena, and a small pink one for Vasilinka. Every morning, I get up and walk around the town, looking at dozens of homes in order to choose the best palace for us. After a few days, I finally find the house I had been dreaming of.

"Why did you rent such a large house?" Lena complains, annoyed that I made a decision without her. "Eight rooms, three floors, who will keep this palace in order? Me again? The Goan house was enough for me; I want to have a rest."

"Don't worry, Lena; why are you unhappy again? We'll hire a cleaning lady. You won't have to deal with this problem."

"I know your cleaners, they only see dirt if it is larger than a nut. Everything must be cleaned again after them. Who will do it? Me again? I need to take care of Vasilinka. And in any case, you promised that I could rest here."

"Take it easy; if I promised, I will do it. And I have already found a kindergarten for Vasilinka. Everything will be fine. I have always dreamed of living in a big house with a blooming garden, a large study, a dining room, and a huge roof where you can throw parties. Each room has its own toilet and shower, and decent, if old, furniture. And all this happiness for just one hundred and fifty dollars per month.

Climbing up onto the roof, Lena's mood improves, and she admires the view, fascinated. The Sun is setting behind a mountain, painting the sky and the lake surface in shades of pink. We sit on the tatty mattresses scattered across the roof.

"Here it is – happiness – and you let yourself get overwhelmed by mundane problems. Isn't the view from the roof more important than a cleaning lady?"

"Well, I agree, darling, I was a bit hasty – it's beautiful here."

"Have we found our happiness? We can spend our whole lives like this. How can you want to go back to Russia after this?"

"Oh, Vasiliy, it is temporary happiness; I want permanence and confidence."

"Lena, who in this world can give permanence and confidence?"

"Half a year on the beach under the palms and six months in the mountains is probably everyone's dream. I just want a guarantee that it will not end tomorrow. And now I don't feel this guarantee."

Having run around for a while, our child falls asleep right on the mattress on the roof. After darkness covers the Earth, thousands of fireflies light up everywhere, along with millions of stars. Isn't this paradise? I hug my beloved, who stares into the distance, already calm and relaxed. Nepalese music plays in the distance. A pleasant female voice sings about Parvati, the goddess of love and fertility.

155

Chapter 25. Part One. Inside.

"Dobroe utro!" Viktor shouts loudly in Russian across the jail. Stretching, he is the first to come out of the cells.

"Dobrautra, dobrautra," the guards and inmates make their daily attempt to pronounce what to them is a foreign tongue twister.

"What's new, Vitya? What news in your cell?"

"I came in my sleep last night."

"Well done, Vitya, you'll never be lost; I had diarrhea all night long."

"Well, Vasya, not bad news to start the day with; at least its something new," Viktor laughs, sitting down on the spit-covered steps.

"Hey, Russians, have you heard that yesterday a new Russian was put in the third cell?" a little Indian named Ishmael tells us.

"No, we haven't. That's great; new ears have arrived. We can talk about something new. You and I, Vitya, already have absolutely nothing to discuss."

"What do you mean; we haven't discussed who has what kind of shit yet," Viktor says, laughing and looking at the inmates coming out of the third cell.

Out of the cell comes one of God's creations, who I can immediately tell just by looking at him is going to be a disappointment. Squinting in the sunlight by the door stands a tall thin guy, who reminds me of a young Don Quixote who has just come out of the Auschwitz concentration camp. He has long, dirty hair and patched-up, tatty clothes.

"I think he has flipped out. It looks like we haven't gained a new companion," I try to explain to Viktor, but he doesn't listen to me and goes quickly to get acquainted with the new occupant of our obligatory health resort. Despite my concerns, I also decide to approach. Extending my hand to introduce myself, I immediately realize that my fears are confirmed. Instead of the usual handshake, Don Quixote touches my wrist with his wrist, which has a piece of ribbon wrapped around it.

"My name is Yelisei, and there is the power of Jesus in this ribbon, I always say hello like that. My visa expired, and I was arrested in Chapora. I would like to pick up my stuff, I really need it," Yelisei starts to talk quickly about himself without pausing.

"Stop, stop," Viktor interrupts him with a smile, "nobody is in a hurry here. And you have told us everything about yourself in one minute. If you are here, forget about your plans. Here, you will get washed up, put on some weight, and in a month you'll be released. Then you'll get your belongings."

"No, I urgently need to get them. My guitar is there, it will rot within a month; it is very important to me."

"Ok, I get it; having a new pair of ears around here turned out to be a disappointment. I'd rather go and talk to David," I say, heading to another corner of the jail.

"Do you Russians have an addition to your ranks?" David asks with a smile and holds out his palm with a pinch of chewing tobacco in it.

"Another nutcase who took too many drugs and flipped out."

"A lot of them have appeared here in Goa recently," David agrees, putting a portion of tobacco behind his lip.

"Look, Vasya, our Ashpak went to 'crack' the newbie. It's time for a show."

Surrounded by his boot-lickers, the bearded mobster whom all the Indian inmates fear approaches Yelisei.

"Well, tell us what are you here for?" he asks in pretty good English.

"Overstay, problems with my passport."

"I see. And we came to tell you about the rules in the jail. Do you know the jail rules?" Ashpak asks menacingly, enjoying the fact that he has found a potential victim.

"What rules? I speak English badly, I do not understand you," stammering, Yelisei starts making excuses.

"Our Ashpak is a classic jackal," I say to David, observing the newbie's behavior. "He has found a weak victim and is starting to press him. We should support our compatriot, even though he is crazy; I feel sorry for him."

"Ashpak, why are you talking to him? Look at him, he's crazy. This is not the passenger you need," Viktor cuts in.

Looking at us angrily, Ashpak goes about his business.

"Vasiliy, Viktor, you have a visit, your interpreter came," a guard shouts, coming to the door.

"Well, let's go and listen to what crazy Psyu has to say."

Putting on a T-shirt for decency, I go into the jail warden's room together with Viktor.

"Have you gone out of your mind, or what?" Psyu starts yelling immediately, without saying hello. "Have you decided to make a farce out of the court?"

"Psyu, calm down, haven't you had a sniff yet, or what? What court? What farce?" I interrupt her flow of verbal diarrhea.

"Yesterday, some of our embassy staff came and met with the Goan police chief, he told them how the day before this idiot gave a show at the court," says Psyu, pointing at Viktor.

"What did I do?" Viktor begins to indignantly make excuses, annoyed at being called an idiot. "Big deal, I wrote on my shirt, "I love drug police," I demanded tomatoes, that's why I wrote it to draw attention."

"And do you know that you may be accused of insulting and disrespecting the court?"

"And what do I have to do with all this?" I interrupt her, not understanding what is going on.

"Because for them, you two are like two Chinese people are for a Russian – the same person. And you have similar names and surnames: Vasiliy Karavaev and Viktor Koplenko. Do you want to be locked up for a decade? If the judge gets offended, he can easily give both of you ten years."

"But I didn't have drugs, I had Novocain in a jar."

"We'll know that when the expert analysis comes back. But he had MDMA," Psyu points at me.

"Calm down, Psyu, I'll talk to Viktor, he won't wear his T-shirt again."

"Who is the new nutcase that has been put in with you?" her mood changing quickly, Psyu changes the subject.

"His name is Yelisei, a crazy Christian preacher. It would have been better to put him in a psychiatric hospital and give him sedative pills for a couple of weeks. And they put him in here..." I try to tell her, but Psyu has lost the thought in her cocaine-scorched brain, and again changes the subject.

"Have you read in the newspapers about someone murdering women? A serial killer has appeared in Goa; he has killed sixteen girls. He robs and then kills them."

"Stop, stop," Viktor stops her, "we have had more than enough bad news; we are living among criminals. It would be better if you told us when we'll be released."

"You should be released soon. After two months, the chief of drug police will be changed. Pashish will head the criminal police now, and instead of him will be our man whom we have been 'feeding' for a long time. As soon as he comes, we will pull you out of here."

"Psyu, has anyone told you that you look like a Komsomol[47] party worker? So much fuss, and no results; mere promises of a happy future," Viktor says, laughing.

"Your time is over," a sleepy guard interrupts our conversation about nothing.

"That's all, I have to go. Have fun, guys. I'll come to see you again next week."

Psyu kisses us on the cheek and, with a wave of her hand, disappears out the door.

Chapter 25. Part Two. Outside.

"Five years ... You served five years for five ecstasy pills?"

"Yes," the skinny, blond guy named Gregory answers me with a smile, "five years and I was set free with acute tuberculosis. Now I am rehabilitating here, in the Himalayas. I spent five years as if in a dream. Only it seems to me that I was locked up not for ecstasy, but for five cans of stew."

"What do you mean?" I ask, driving away the flies that are trying to eat my scrambled eggs.

"Before I went to work on the TV show 'Up to Sixteen and Above', I worked part time as a night guard at a grocery warehouse. At that time, the Americans provided us with charitable aid in the form of stew. Of course, almost all of it was stolen and sold through commercial shops. They were stealing it by the truckload. I also stole a box of beef stew. I didn't eat it; I threw it on the balcony for a rainy day and forgot about it. And when I had already been sitting in jail for a while, my mother brought me a package. It was the stew that was lying on the balcony. Apparently, my karma caught up with me. Someone needed that stew back then. Punishment is imposed on us from heaven. I don't believe that I could be punished so severely for five pills. I was cured from tuberculosis only last year. I thought I wouldn't live to thirty-five."

---

[47] Komsomol - abbreviation for the Communist Youth movement of the Soviet Union.

"Grisha, was there really no way to get yourself out of jail? Your father is a famous TV sports analyst, known throughout the country. Your sister is known by the entire population for the film 'Red Riding Hood'. And you worked on a popular television show. How did it happen?"

"I just got into hot water. The authorities in our country decided to make an example of someone. Who needs to lock up major suppliers? They bring in money every month. So they made me the scapegoat. My arrest was broadcast on TV for a whole month."

We sit on the edge of Pokhara, in a small place with the amusing name, My Beautiful Restaurant. The few lunatics that have decided to spend the summer in dangerous revolutionary Nepal gather in this restaurant from morning till night. That summer was dangerous not because of the revolution that was taking place in Nepal; none of us even suspected the danger then. That summer was the last summer of a carefree existence for the various smugglers and drug-dealers who gathered in India and Nepal. That summer, the authorities of many countries drastically increased their efforts to combat drugs. None of us had any idea about it then. It seemed that we were just a few years away from the global legalization of soft drugs. The revolution didn't touch us at all. The only indicator of the revolution was that there were no lemons or cheese in the stores. Apparently, these were strategically important products. To the question, "Do you sell lemons?" sellers guiltily answered: "Sorry, sir, we have no lemons or cheese; there is a revolution in the country."

Having received from Lena the task of taking our child for a walk, I sit in the restaurant, stoned, and discuss Shulgin's new psychotropic drugs, while watching Vasilinka playing happily with some Nepalese children. Lyosha approaches the restaurant on his bicycle. Lyosha and his pregnant wife Larisa are staying at our house. They are our first Nepalese visitors.

"Hi, Lyosha," my little daughter, playing near the entrance, is the first to greet him. "I've go a pink bike..."

"Hi, Vasilinka, and I have a big black one with a luggage rack," Lyosha responds, smiling.

"What's new, how is your Larisa? Isn't she due yet? By the way, where is she?" Grisha asks, turning down the volume of the subwoofer, which is blaring trance music.

"It's still too early for her to give birth. In a few months we'll back in India and she'll give birth there. She is making vareniki[48] with Vasya's wife at home now."

Lyosha slowly detaches a large plastic bag from the luggage rack of his bicycle and sits down with us at the table under the open sky.

"Look, today I bought a kilogram of Nepalese hashish. I want to ship it to Rashka."

"Let's check it out first," Grisha says, smiling, and breaks off a matchbox-sized piece.

Old man Rico curiously rises from the neighboring table.

"Let me have a look, too," he says, holding out his bony hands.

'Psy Rico', a sixty-five year old Australian DJ, is a friend of another famous trance DJ, Goa Gil. Rico is a Goan freak of the first wave. Having tried LSD for the first time in 1968, he came to Goa and since then he has been traveling around Asia, preferring India, Nepal and Thailand. Once he grew marijuana in huge plantations in Australia and exported it to Europe, but now, being on a well-

---

[48] Vareniki - Russian ravioli.

deserved retirement, he prefers to play trance tracks and throw parties. Pulling from his pocket a small portable microscope, Rico puts a piece of hashish into it and starts examining it closely.

"Well, what do you say, Rico?" Lyosha is the first to break the silence.

"First-class stuff. It should cost about a thousand dollars per kilogram. It's not what they sell on the streets for three hundred dollars."

"I paid eight hundred dollars for a kilogram," Lyosha responds gladly, relieved that he didn't pay two and a half times the normal price in vain.

"Only it's not hashish or charas," Rico continues to explain without looking up, "it's poland, as they call it here. This method of preparation was brought here from Morocco by the first hippies. Prior to that it was collected by hand, like in the Indian Himalayas. This method is considered to be the purest. They take a large pot, pull silk over it, and beat flowers of hemp on it like on a drum. Cannabinol crystals go through the micropores of the silk, into the pot. Then they are collected, and they call it 'poland'. But that is how cheap, third-rate poland is made. You bought poland of the highest quality. You can see straight away that Europeans made it. Not through silk, but through perforated nylon."

"And how do you know it?" Lyosha asks, amazed.

"Ha! I have worked with ganga my whole life," Rico smiles slyly and hands us the microscope with a small piece of Lyosha's stuff.

"Look here, you see, there is nothing except the crystals, no garbage, it is clear that it was sifted through nylon. Its pores are half the size of those of silk."

"Let me see," burning with curiosity, I stretch out my hand. "That's beautiful! It looks as if diamonds were poured into the microscope. Indeed, only crystals, and the smell is really fantastic."

"You won't see this in Indian charas," Rico continues his lecture, enjoying his own knowledge. "Vasya, just imagine, the Indians work the hemp with their dirty hands for twelve hours, that's why you can find all sorts of different shit in Indian charas. Armpit hair, ass hair, trash, leftover food, and all of that abundantly drenched in Indian sweat," Rico laughs, placing the portable microscope back into his pocket. "That's why I love Nepal. Everything is cleaner here than in India, even the hash."

"It is a pity that not everyone understands that," Lyosha says, placing the kilogram chunk back into the bag. "Everyone is used to smoking charas advertised by the Jews; everyone wants cream from Manali. We're going to make charas out of this poland with my wife, we'll bring it to a marketable condition before shipping."

"How?" I ask curiously.

"It looks like halva now, but if you put it in the sunlight and keep it there for a couple of hours to heat it up and then compress it, it will turn from green and yellow to black, and it becomes soft, like plasticine. If it looks like that, then it will cost ten thousand bucks wholesale in Moscow, while you can sell it for as much as thirty at retail. We'll hide it somewhere and ship it next week via the post office."

"And how is it shipped to avoid any problems?" Ilka asks curiously, sitting next to us.

"We have already shipped it many times and so far everything has reached its destination successfully."

Having smoked Lyosha's first-rate poland, we are all silent for a while, lost in our dreams and fantasies.

"Does anyone speak Russian here?" standing at the entrance, a strange character with a Russian face wearing Nepalese clothes suddenly interrupts our silence.

"Yes, everyone speaks Russian here, except Rico," Lyosha answers, inviting our fellow citizen to join us with a gesture.

"Well, and I thought that there are only foreigners around here. I didn't expect to meet any Russians at this time. My name is Sasha."

"And what brought you here? Have you come to Nepal for long?" I ask, pulling out my chillum.

"I don't even know, I actually just escaped from jail," he says, sitting down sadly at our table.

"He's our passenger; it's clear at once," Lyosha says smiling and slaps him on the shoulder.

"I am from Goa, I escaped from Mapusa Jail."

"What did you do?" Ilka asks him in surprise, moving closer.

"It's long story, but to cut it short: I came to Goa on vacation for two weeks. Two weeks stretched into three months. I ran out of money; some Russian drug dealers proposed that I carry two kilograms of charas to Rashka, and promised to pay me well. So I agreed. I duct-taped the charas to my thighs, but I was too lazy to check it. The Indians had put iron screws in the package to add weight, so the metal detectors went off at the airport. They put me into prison in Mapusa. The prosecutor wanted to give me ten years. I served three months and decided to escape. I pretended to be sick in order to be taken to the hospital. And when I got out of the jail bus, I pushed the guard over and ran through a rice field. I ran into the jungle and hid in a thorn bush. I was sitting in the bushes for a whole day and night. I crossed the river and reached my friends' house. While I was staying with them, I received a credit card from Russia, I made a phony copy of someone's passport with my photograph, bought a train ticket with it and crossed the Nepalese border through the forest at night. That's how I ended up here."

"You are cool, Sasha," Lyosha interrupts him, admiring his heroic deeds. "And what are you going to do next?"

"I don't know yet. I have no passport. I am here illegally. Time will tell."

Chapter 26. Part One. Inside.

"Tobacco!" someone shouts, and I make a cat-like leap along with Viktor towards the center of the courtyard, tracking the course of the falling tobacco while it is still in the air.

A couple of dozen small bags are scattered on the ground. I manage to grab three. In confusion, hiding the tobacco in my shorts, I find someone's hand in my pocket trying to pull out a bag. Slapping the person's hand, I see an old Indian rogue jump back with an upset face. I even feel a little bit sorry for him. Being more agile, the youngsters manage to stock up the most on this strategic product. The old man is unlucky today; he is left without tobacco. Perhaps Suresh, who was released yesterday, kept his promise and threw us some tobacco over the wall from the outside.

"Let's go, Vasya, I'll introduce you to the new vacationer, he arrived yesterday," Viktor says joyfully, putting a few bags in his pocket.

"Yes, I read in the newspaper that a major exporter of drugs was caught. Three hundred grams of charas and two hundred and fifty grams of cocaine. Apparently, the drug lords grassed on a competitor to the Goan police again.

"Hello, my name is Vasiliy, I'm from Russia."

"And my name is Antonio, I'm from Greece," extending his hand to me, says a slightly stooped man with shifty, frightened eyes.

The Greek smuggler greatly resembles Mr. Bean from the English comedy.

"How were you caught, Antonio?" I ask, smiling, imagining that I am speaking to the English comedian.

"Someone informed the local police about me. I've been living here, in Goa, for twenty-six years. It's probably time for me to leave India. Once I found paradise here, I thought it would be enough for a lifetime, but nothing is left from the Goa I loved. All of the normal people moved away long ago. Some moved to Thailand, some to Bali, others live in Argentina. And here all you can find now are snitches and fools like me.

"First, get out of here, and then think about where and how to live," Viktor interrupts him rudely, mixing English words with Russian curses. "With what you have been put in here for, no one gets out sooner than in a year and a half. And a year and a half; that's if you're lucky. Ten years are more likely."

"No, I can't be in here for so long; my beloved girl is waiting for me outside. I love her very much; I'm willing to give everything to see her sooner."

"Now you have a great opportunity to check how much she loves you," Viktor says, soothing him and patting him on the shoulder.

"Has anyone tried to escape from here?" the Greek asks me hopefully.

"I had one friend. He ran away three years ago. He pretended to be sick and ran away from the hospital. He is still living in Nepal without a passport. But you won't manage to pull it off, Antonio. Any guard will catch you because of your belly. He'll catch you, and you will be given another six months for trying to escape. The judge will give you ten years, that's for sure. Start doing gymnastics. Personally, I run for forty-five minutes in my cell every day. I run and imagine the guards chasing me. At first, they managed to catch me every day, but now I manage to get away. I have already lost fifteen kilograms of weight. Antonio, you should accept the fact that for the next few years you won't get out of here. It's too early for you to think of an escape. First, you must try to get out of here legally. In a year, you'll obtain the result of the expert analysis of your drugs. Then the lawyer and the judge will start listening to the testimonies of the police witnesses. If you manage to prove that the witnesses are lying or do not remember you, then you won't need to escape. You'll be released after a while. And if the witnesses say, "Yes, this is Antonio, and we saw that he had drugs," then you will have a couple of months to prepare an escape. The witnesses are the crucial part in this thing. In the meantime, just relax and rest."

"I don't want to get ten years, Natasha is waiting for me," our Mr. Bean sighs sadly.

"Natasha, is she Russian or what?"

"No, thank God, she is not Russian. My first wife was Russian. I brought her charas to Moscow for four years. I know all your famous DJs. Everyone bought hash from me. Your Moscow is s a dangerous place. You can get banged up for five years for just a couple of grams of charas."

"I know all about it, Antonio. That's why I chose to live in Goa."

Chapter 26. Part Two. Outside.

"Why aren't you dancing, Den? Look at the beauty all around, jasmine blossoms, the starry sky, the Full Moon reflected in the lake like a mirror. The best trance DJs are playing now especially for us. And, most importantly, there are no tourists around, only friends. What else could you ask for? Maybe you want another line of MDMA?"

"No, thank you Vasya, I am already wasted. I can't differentiate between the fireflies and stars at the moment. Everything is floating and dancing in front of my eyes. I ran out of money and I don't know what to do. I don't want to return to Rashka, and I have no money for the tickets.

"Den, wake up, we are in Asia, and money appears when you really need it here. Don't be sad. If you really need money, I will help you to earn some. Do you remember Max, he came to visit us from Moscow; he bought half a kilo of charas from us?"

"Yes, I remember, if I remember correctly he put it in a jar with Indian honey and shipped it via the post office."

"Well, everything worked out. He earned five thousand dollars in one go then. I received a letter from him yesterday. He wants me to ship him two more kilograms. He will send me half of the money tomorrow. If you want, you can take over the business. We will split the profit in half. I prepare the package and you ship it. We'll earn five hundred dollars each. Good deal?"

"Yes, not bad work. You are helping me out again," smiling happily, Den pours himself a rum and cola. "This money will be enough to get me to Goa. And there I can earn easily."

"You see how everything happens in Asia. And you were worried. Let's go to the pool for a swim."

Having gulped down his rum, Den shouts, "I love you, Asia!" and jumps into the water with his clothes on, showering all the people dancing around it with a fountain of splashes. I wonder who came up with the idea of building a pool in the shape of Mickey Mouse's head, with an artificial waterfall, here on the shore of a lake in Nepal? I bet some American put his money into it and abandoned everything at the beginning of the revolution.

"Fox, how are you finding the party?" I shout to a smuggler from Ukraine who is swinging burning pois.

"Just great, all of the tourists in Pokhara are gathered here today. All fifteen people," he laughs loudly without stopping swinging the fire. "I love the Nepalese revolution; Vasya, look, there are only psychedelic drug-dealers and smugglers around us. It is unbelievable that it only costs twenty dollars per night to rent this place. Nowhere else there are there such places where you can throw a party for just twenty dollars."

"Fox, good job with coming up with the idea about fire. How many candles did you bring today?"

"There are one hundred and eight around the perimeter of the pool now. But I still have the same amount in my backpack. You know, Vasya, I love fire. Tonight is the most beautiful party that I have ever seen in Nepal."

"It seems you've jinxed it," Den says, coming out of the water and pointing at two approaching police officers.

"I haven't. Vasya, tell them where to get off, we are untouchable, we are tourists."

Scanning all of the people dancing around, the police come up to Andrey, who is puffing on a chillum.

"What is this?" one of them asks, pointing at the chillum.

"What is your business here? Get out of here. It is my religion, Bom Shiva, Bom Shankar, Bom," former lawyer Andrey says proudly, exhaling smoke directly into the face of the police officer.

"Ok, ok, don't worry, enjoy, relax," the policeman says and turns towards the exit.

"Oh, if only Russian cops were so obedient, I would probably not have given up my legal career."

"Look, Den, what beautiful girls we have," I point at Lena and Ilka dancing in swimsuits. Nothing beautifies girls like MDMA. Their eyes become shiny and slightly lustful. Their dance movements are liberated, and it seems that they are not dancing, but making love to an invisible partner. It is impossible to avert your eyes from our beauties."

"Vasya, isn't it dangerous to send a package from here?" Dan asks, taking off his wet clothes.

"Do you see Ilka dancing in the water? A month ago, she sent her grandma a pound of hashish to Rashka. Go and talk to her. By the way, can you see what a lustful look she has, according to my calculations she hasn't had a boyfriend the whole season," I wink, pushing Denis into the water.

"I love you," my Lena is yelling, trying to shout over the music from the speakers.

Passionately kissing me on the mouth, she grabs me by the arm and pulls me to the side of the cornfield bordering the pool.

"Honey, honey, I want you, take me right here, I'll go crazy if you don't take me right now."

Diving several meters into the cornfield, we rip each other's clothes off without stopping to kiss. MDMA enhances our senses, and we both moan loudly. Every time we touch, every time we kiss, we feel an orgasmic sensation, similar to an electric shock. It seems like the world has simply vanished. There is nothing but love; time has frozen, there are only the two of us in the Universe. We are completely naked like Adam and Eve, alone under the Full Moon; we taste the sweetness of the forbidden fruit. It's impossible to stop, our bodies move under the trance music, and it seems that the orgasm lasts forever.

"It can't be true, we must be in paradise," Lena whispers in my ear, holding me tightly with both arms.

"Let's go to the pool, they have probably lost us. Does everyone feel as good as we do now? Let's go for a swim in the pool."

Coming closer to the water, we see that no one is dancing; everyone has a frightened, serious face.

"Den, what's going on, what's the fuss?"

"Fox tried to set himself on fire."

"What?"

"It's true, go and talk to him yourself. You see, Ilka is wiping his face with vodka."

"Fox, what's wrong with you?" I ask, squatting nearby.

"I had a bad trip with this acid again; four drops is probably too much for me. I was swinging the burning poi, dancing, and bang – the whole world disappeared, there was only fire everywhere. And all of a sudden, the goddess Kali emerged out of the fire, came to me and said, "You should burn in the fire right now, to be born again purified." She told me that if I didn't set myself on fire, she would tell you to burn me. So I began setting myself on fire. I only came to my senses when the fire was taken away from me."

"It turned out that not everyone felt as good as we did," my frightened Lena whispers in my ear, "let's go and drink something, to take our minds off this horror."

"I haven't drunk for a long time, but I think now is the time."

"Dawn is approaching, it's time for booze," Alex Nicaragua shouts cheerfully, trying to defuse the situation, and continues to dance with a large bottle of rum in one hand and a bottle of Coke in the other."

"Nicaragua, fill the glasses. The Dymich is wearing off and we don't feel like ending the fun, and then there's Fox as well… tomorrow never come."

After drinking a bottle, we finally manage to forget about Fox.

"Tell me, Alex, why does everyone call you Nicaragua?" my Lena asks, inconspicuously putting her hand into my shorts under the table.

"Because ten years ago I tried to conquer Nicaragua. Have you heard of this country?"

"Well, how was it? Did you manage it?" I ask, trying not to give away what is happening under the table.

"I don't know whether I pulled it off or not. At that time, my father had a contract to head the development of some resources in Nicaragua. And he took me with him. Basically, they paid okay, but I quickly realized that we were doing bad things. At that time in Nicaragua there was a problem with drinking water. Different international funds allocated money for the development of water wells, so that the poor Nicaraguans wouldn't die of thirst. And local workers dug these wells, pretty much all by themselves, for two or three years. They paid something like a quarter of a million dollars from the funds for such a well. I visited various landfill sites and found an old Russian drilling machine. It was rusty without an engine or wheels. I bought it for a song, remodeled it, and began to drill. And I started to sell these wells for half the price. I immediately started making big money. As soon as I accumulated the first million dollars on my bank account, the Nicaraguan intelligence services came to my home and said that I had twelve hours to leave the country alive and healthy. And as for my bank account, they advised me to forget about it as quickly as possible. In Nicaragua, cocaine kings are in power, and I had no desire to argue with them. Since then, I've been known as Alex Nicaragua. And on arriving back in the motherland, I leased out my apartment and decided to go and live in Goa. I don't want to work any more. I'd rather dance till the end of my days."

"Hey, lovebirds, are you still fumbling with your hands under the table? Give me your glasses. I'll pour you some more rum," Alex abruptly interrupts his story, unwilling to think about the lost money.

The alcohol is rolling over my body with a pleasant warmth and mixing with the chemical vibrations of love. My perception of the world is floating; the alcohol helps my brain to forget all the unpleasant aspects of reality and immerses me in the illusion of a happiness where there is nothing except love. Somewhere very deep, my heart and mind are trying to tell me that something is wrong. That in addition to love, there is also reality, the harsh reality of the world. But the booze drowns the weak signals that try to break through the synthetic vibration of love.

Chapter 27. Part One. Inside.

"Vasya, have you heard that Yelisei declared his love today?"

"What love?"

"Love of God."

"Yes, the whole jail heard him yelling all evening."

"The warden came twice to try to calm him down. Yesterday, I gave him a little bit of charas and he flipped," Viktor says with a guilty smile.

"You shouldn't have done that. You can't give drugs to crazy people. He should be put in a psychiatric hospital, in a quiet place. He needs to be given tranquilizers in order for him to return to reality from his fantasies, and you arranged him a crisis in jail."

"Who said that he is mad? Are you a therapist?"

"Although I am not a therapist, a dozen of my friends lost their minds in Goa. I can see that he has the symptoms written all over his face. Five minutes of conversation were enough for me to understand that he has flipped out. He took too many drugs and now he doesn't understand anything. His logic is broken. I tried to talk to him. Such people lose their willpower, they can't stop, they devour all types of drugs, and then they can't understand where reality ends and fantasy begins."

"What do you mean: broken logic?" Viktor asks, stopping in the middle of the courtyard under the drizzling rain.

"Well. Take, for example, a cockroach. Tear off its leg and let it go. It will run away. From this example, it can be assumed that if a person loses his leg, then he or she will run on one leg. It's a classic example of broken logic."

"What's so illogical about that?" Viktor is surprised and tries to make a smart face. "In Afghanistan, I saw much more than that. If you want to live, then you'll run home even on one foot."

"I see, Vitya. When you stepped on that mine in Afghanistan, it looks like you didn't just injure your legs, but also your brain."

"Maybe," Viktor says, smiling, "but where is this line between madness and ordinary perception? Who sets it? Those who have weapons in their hands or those who are in power? So, to send me, a young guy, to die in a foreign country, isn't that crazy? Or to prohibit marijuana, which causes neither withdrawal symptoms nor aggression, and to advertise booze, which makes people go crazy from their hangover, on a nation-wide level, isn't that crazy?"

"Yes, I understand, Vitya, calm down, and I'm not angry with Yelisei, I just want to help him."

"Don't you think, Vasya, that you got into jail because you wanted to help everyone? Why do you try to impose your help, who asked you for it?" Viktor gets more agitated. "Have you decided to change the world for the better? Maybe you are playing Jesus?"

The Indians around us have hushed and watch curiously as two Russians argue over nothing.

169

"Yelisei gave me a very interesting book to read, about God, no nutcase would have understood it. After reading it, I realized last night why I got put into jail. I was supposed to meet Yelisei in order to read this book. My destiny led me to this book all my life. If anyone else had given me this book, I wouldn't have read it. But I saw how happy he was and decided to read it. It's called 'The Teachings of the Fire Spirit'. Now I realize that I have lived incorrectly my whole life. Now I know how to be happy. Do you want me to tell you?"

"No, Vitya, I do not. I think you are definitely out of your mind. Yelisei was taken to a psychiatric hospital, and you want to get in there, too."

"I don't deny that I'm crazy. And you're crazy. We all are crazy."

"That's it, you're pissing me off. Walk around on your own from now on. I can't listen to you anymore. I'd rather go and talk to normal people. I've had enough of you, when will they finally let an idiot like you out of here?"

Chapter 27. Part Two. Outside.

"Have you heard the news? Romashka[49] and Zont[50] were arrested at the post office yesterday," Lyosha tells us excitedly from the entrance.

"It can't be true!"

"Of course it can. Yesterday, after the party, they went to the post office to send a package. They didn't even change clothes. So they came to the main post office in trance outfits with stoned eyes. Just imagine the scene: two stoned freaks dancing without music, with a drum in one hand and a jar of 'Chavan Prashthi'[51] in the other. The main post office is always guarded by the police. So, the policeman looked at them, took a pre-prepared needle and, without thinking twice, stuck it into the jar and immediately pressed the alarm button."

"And what, they couldn't come to an agreement for money?"

"No, no agreement possible... They tried to escape and put up a fight. As a result, Zont's teeth were kicked out, and Romashka's arm was broken. Yesterday, they were broadcast on all of the Nepalese TV channels. It's such an unpleasant story. Especially considering the fact that I have a ticket to Rashka tomorrow. I'm carrying a pound of charas in my stomach. You don't think those guys will grass on us?" Vlad, whose nickname is 'Lenk', asks anxiously.

"What will they get?" I ask, thinking about the five kilograms of charas lying under my bed.

"If they go to jail together they could get four years each; if one of them takes the blame upon himself, he would be released in two years."

"They always give more for organized crime," Vlad says, putting aside a T-shirt on which he painted a huge smiling cat with five legs earlier this morning. "Let's stop talking about them. If they've been arrested, then so be it. There is no need to breed paranoia. Tomorrow, I have to go

---

[49] Romashka (Russian) - chamomile, here a nickname for one of the characters, Roman.

[50] Zont (Russian) - umbrella, here a nickname for one of the characters.

[51] Chavan Prashthi - a thick, honey-like Ayurvedic medicine.

through customs with a pound of charas and a smile on my face, so let's close the subject. Look at the funny cat I have drawn on my T-shirt. I have an entire collection of T-shirts called 'Five legged cats.' In Moscow, I'll sell T-shirts like this for two hundred bucks. I've got ten drawn already."

"And what about the 'Los Uebanos' series?" I ask, remembering the cool T-shirt he painted for Valera.

"Los Uebanos is last season's trend. For six months, I drew Los Uebanos T-shirts in Goa and sold the entire collection. I'll carry charas to Moscow, come back, and have enough money for another six months. In Nepal, I will draw five legged cats. And after the cats I have an idea: to paint Buddhist demons and hungry ghosts."

Vasilinka suddenly rushes joyfully into the room, and grabbing my and Vlad's hands, starts pulling us, trying to make us get up from the couch.

"Let's go to the balcony, the monkeys came back to harvest the corn again!"

"Come on, Vlad, it really is worth a look," I say, following my daughter.

We position ourselves in chairs on the huge balcony to watch the upcoming show of the struggle for the harvest. Ten meters from our house, a band of monkeys slowly comes down the side of the mountain in the direction of the cornfields. Having divided into two groups, the monkeys surround a small cornfield located on the hill. Seeing the approaching band, Nepalese peasants begin to shout loudly, waving their bamboo sticks. Apparently being accustomed to this turn of events, some of the monkeys try to distract the peasants by attracting their attention through screaming back at them.

"Look, the most interesting part is about to begin," I point at the second group of monkeys, which begins to slowly peel the ripe ears of corn.

Having noticed that the second group of monkeys is eating the harvest, the peasants abandon the left flank and run in a crowd from one end of the field to the other. The leader of the band gives a loud cry, and a dozen monkeys quickly climb to the top of the bamboo thicket, taking an ear of corn each.

"Why are the monkeys smarter than the peasants?" Vlad comments with a smile. "For hundreds of years the farmers have lived side by side with the monkeys, but they haven't learned how to protect their crops."

Vasilinka bursts out laughing loudly and claps her hands, cheering on the team of monkeys by shouting to them, "Come on. Come on, the people are getting closer!!" Having gnawed the juicy corn, the monkeys begin to throw the empty ears on the Nepalese peasants from above.

"Look how clever the monkeys are," my daughter points at the second group, which slowly begins to strip the ears on the left of the field.

The peasants abandon the right flank and run to the other end of the field in a noisy crowd. The left group of monkeys repeats exactly the same maneuver as the right group, and having comfortably positioned themselves in the tops of the trees, slowly eats the sweet corn. This is repeated a few times. Having eaten their full, the two groups slowly jump from tree to tree and head off into the jungle. The only thing the peasants can do is to count their losses, collecting the nibbled ears.

"Tonight's show is over. To be continued," Andrey says, laughing, and pulls a chillum out of his bag.

"What will we do today, get stoned or do nothing?" my Lena asks with a note of boredom.

"If you don't want to get high, you can clean the house," I'm starting to get annoyed be her constant discontentment.

"Don't quarrel again. Do you want me to show you the best ballet?" my little Vasilinka offers, trying to distract us from another brewing conflict.

"Of course we want to," smiling, we reply in unison.

"Then I'll change my clothes and give you a performance. Go down into the garden. And you, Daddy, turn on some slow music. Just not trance, please. I don't like trance."

"There it is: opposite thinking. The eternal problem of children and parents. I would like for her to grow up into a real psychedelic freak, and she loves ballet. There is one boy in her kindergarten, his father is a well-known Italian drug dealer, who can't stand the police and calls them all 'pigs'. So, once we were sitting in the Juice Center near the kindergarten, drinking juice, while our children ate fruit salads. And he asked his son, "Christian, tell me what do you want to become when you grow up?" "Daddy, when I grow up, I'll become a police officer, I will put criminals in jail, and everyone will be afraid of me." His father nearly choked on his juice."

"Vasya, and would you like your daughter to take drugs when she grows up?" pregnant Larissa asks me, stroking her big belly.

"That's a difficult question, Larissa. I have asked myself it many times. Of course, I don't want her to get hooked on drugs out of despair. But I want her to make a conscious choice herself. She's watching us now and making conclusions about what is good and what is bad. On the one hand, she sees our contented, stoned faces; on the other, she sees how we quarrel irritably in the morning until we have a smoke. It would be good if she simply didn't want them. But, if she consumed them occasionally and consciously, I wouldn't mind. Maybe I am living such a life so that she can see both sides of the coin. After all, drugs are not only 'bad'; they are, primarily, medicine. And, more often than not, medicine for the soul. I will try to raise her so that her soul isn't sick, and I hope that when she grows up she will prefer to take nothing at all. We are psychedelic warriors trying to change the world for the better, and she likes ballet. Maybe she will live in a different society. I hope that people will make a quantum leap in perception by that time. Maybe in the near future, people will move to the contours of higher perception, and then there will be no need for drugs at all. And if she wants to follow our path, I won't mind either. And I'll show her by my own example what kind of path it is and what the pitfalls are."

Downstairs, we sit in a semi-circle on the steps in the courtyard of our house. Between two large bushes with red flowers, my little princess starts dancing to slow music on an improvised stage, carefully imitating something she saw once on TV, 'The Dance of the Little Swans'. The doors of the iron gate to our yard open slowly, and I see five pairs of small black eyes curiously observing the unusual dance of the little white girl. Seeing them, Vasilinka pauses for a moment and invites them to come in with a gesture.

"Come in, sit down," my Lena says in a friendly manner, inviting the neighborhood children to enter.

Grubby and in tattered clothes, the children sit down next to us on the steps, mistrustfully. My daughter, trying her best with a serious face, attempts to repeat the dance of the dying swan. Becoming emboldened and realizing that nobody is going to hurt them here, the neighborhood kids quickly lose interest in the show.

"Give me money," holding out his hand, the eldest six-year old boy asks first.

Then all the children, having lost all interest in Vasilinka's show, start begging loudly for money, turning their backs on my daughter.

"Why have you come here? To see the ballet or to beg? Look, a little girl is trying her best for you," I point at my daughter.

"Money, Money," the little bastards scream excitedly, holding out their hands.

"OK, enough, if you do not want to watch, go away," I point at the gate severely.

Realizing that they won't get anything here, the children run away noisily, leaving the little dancer perplexed. A moment later, a hail of small stones falls on us from behind the fence.

"Why didn't they like my dance?" my little girl clings to me, crying.

"That's how this unjust world is. Not everyone can understand beauty," I try to calm her down.

Turning off the music, I hear that someone has pulled up to our gate by the sound of clattering gravel stones.

"What's wrong with you, you look like a ghost?" I say to Ilka, who is wheeling a bicycle into the yard.

"I just made a trip to call to Rashka, everything is very bad. The package with charas was arrested and my grandmother was taken to the police station for interrogation."

"Misfortune never comes alone. First our DJs, Romashka and Zont, now you. I am afraid that something bad will happen with our package." Lyosha adds, glancing at his pregnant wife.

"And I was going to go back to Rashka," Ilka says, rolling a joint with trembling hands. "What will I do now? I have run out of money."

"You can't go to Rashka for the next two or three years, and I am saying that as a lawyer," Andrey adds and hands her his lighter, "tell us in detail what happened with your grandmother."

"She received a notice from the post office that said, well, she can come to collect the package. She went to the post office, received everything with no problems, brought it home, and put it under the bed without opening it as I instructed her by phone. A week later, the cops came to her home with a search warrant. It turned out that they had sat in an ambush near the entrance for a week and waited for someone to come up and pick up the package. They searched everyone who went through the building entrance and looked suspicious. And, thank God, they didn't wait for me."

"Don't worry, Ilka. You didn't write your name when sending the package, did you?"

"No, it is not on there."

"Well, then, in a couple of years your case will be sent to the archive. They have no evidence that it was sent by you. So, in time, the case will be closed. What did your grandmother tell the cops?"

"She said that the package had been sent by her granddaughter's friend and that her granddaughter lives in India."

"Don't worry, Ilka, you'll get dreadlocks braided and become a freak in India. Now you have a good reason," Vlad says, laughing and trying to cheer her up.

"Well, what should I do, also become a freak without dough? After the arrest of the guys, I don't want to come close to the main post office with hash."

"Den, who is making you go to the post office? Get a bus ticket and go to India. There's no need to go to the post office. In Delhi Main Market there are hundreds of small firms engaged in shipping goods to Russia."

"We sent a package last year," Lyosha interrupts, "we put a kilogram of charas right on the bottom of the bag. The Indian who accepted the package found it and gave it back to us. He only scolded us with a finger and said that it was illegal. Take a bronze statue of Shiva, they are empty inside, stuff it with charas, sprinkle the top of it with pepper and other spices so the dogs don't smell it, and cover it all with epoxy resin. It is unlikely that someone will think to check whether there is something inside."

"Then I'll have to do it like that; I have no money at all. I'll pack my stuff tomorrow. And from Delhi I'll go to Bollywood[52]. Maybe I'll find a job there. They say they need Russians to do voiceovers for films."

---

[52] Bollywood - Indian Hollywood.

Chapter 28. Part One. Inside.

How can I go on living in Goa? Will I really have to leave? How can I live here knowing that he is somewhere nearby? What if I hire a hitman to kill him? Half of the jail would agree to do it for five hundred dollars. Anger and hatred overcome me, causing my body to shake. Grabbing a dumbbell, I pump it till exhaustion, ending up covered with sweat. It gives me some relief. Blisters appear on the calluses on my hands, but I feel no pain at all. Apparently, the adrenaline in my blood is off the scale. How did it happen that I was framed by my own people, by Russians? For the thousandth time I imagine my future release in my head. I walk through the Night Market or East End, around me are dozens of my friends and acquaintances, all shaking my hand to congratulate me and rejoicing at my freedom. And then I see him. How I wish that he had died or disappeared before my release, but he is alive and well, and his small, rodent eyes dart from side to side. He extends his hand to me, smiling, "Well, how was it in there? Have you wised up a bit?" he asks me with a smile. Once again, a flash of hatred and malice overcomes me, making my ears hum. I really want to shake his hand and say, "Thank you for this lesson. Thanks to you, I have become healthier, stronger, smarter. Finally, I've learned some English, read hundreds of books, got rid of unnecessary people and understood who was my friend and who wasn't. And most importantly, you helped me to get rid of the rose-colored glasses I was wearing when I arrived in Goa. The whole world is open in front of me again. I escaped from this trap and I can enjoy my life once more," but in my hands there is a heavy beer mug, and I slam it into his face with all of my hatred. His shattered front teeth and shards of the mug scatter in different directions. All that remains in my hand is a glass mug handle with razor-sharp edges. I hit him with it for the second time, right in the throat. The third is in the stomach. The fourth, fifth... Blood gushes from everywhere. There is so much blood that his face can hardly be seen. Returning from my crazed fantasy, I understand that I'm still in my jail cell. My teeth are clenched and my face is twisted with hatred.

"You should rest, hey, Russian!" Dominic pulls me out of my trance. "Do you want to be like Schwarzenegger? You've been lifting your dumbbell for so many months already, from morning till night."

"I was killing my grass again," I say, tossing the dumbbell made of plastic bottles onto the floor, "I can only manage to get rid of my aggression through exercising."

"If only you could see your face," Disay says, trying to lift the pound-weight plastic dumbbell.

"I know what kind of face I have. I see his face day and night. I dream of only one thing; his death. Because he's out there now, outside, enjoying his life. He snorts cocaine and believes that he is the king of life. And I am deprived of the most important thing: freedom. I can't be with my family. My daughter can't go to school here anymore; I can't live in peace knowing that he is somewhere nearby. He took my Goa away from me. If he had done it for the money that would be one thing… but he only did it to curry favor with the police. I wish I could forgive him, I dream about it. But, unfortunately, I still don't know how."

Chapter 28. Part Two. Outside.

Having taken my cell phone, money and MP3 player, and given me a badge with a number on it, the guard lets me into the jail. For the first time in my life, I am in a jail. Although I do not have anything illegal on me, I feel strange, unsettling emotions as if I were a criminal. I can't wait to leave this place. Passing a huge gilded statue of Buddha, I come to the meeting room.

"Hi, my psychedelic brother. How do you like the Nepalese jail?" I ask Romashka, reaching through the metal bars separating us to squeeze his hand.

"Nice to see you, Vasya. It's good you came to visit. It's not so bad here. At first I felt like an animal, but now I am used to it. The Nepalese are a non-aggressive people; it's manageable to be in jail with them. It's like some sort of cooperative called 'Jail' here. The state food is not that bad; rice, peas, vegetables. But it is also possible to cook yourself, and if you're too lazy, for ten rupees a guard will run to a nearby restaurant and buy everything you need. If you want to work, you can find a job. If you want to mess around, no one will say a word. Of course, they pay pennies, but it is enough for the Nepalese to buy goodies. The only problem is that this place is full of grasses. You can't openly smoke charas. Grisha from Pokhara brings me some weed from time to time, but I have to smoke it at night under the covers and exhale in a wet towel so that you can't smell it. And you, Vasya, what brings you to Kathmandu?"

"I'm here for a couple of days, the last time this season. I need to extend my visa and stock up on hemp. I want to buy hemp fabric and send it to Russia. You know, we have a store there."

"Yes, I remember your thing about the hemp revolution. How is Lena? How is Vasilinka?"

"We are all fine. We are going to Goa soon. Is there anything interesting here? How do you spend your leisure time?"

"In general, I'm ok. I read books, I've learned to swing poi, I do yoga, I lift a barbell every day. Look how cool I look now."

Rolling up his sleeve, Romashka shows me his muscular arm.

"Two years ago I was all broken. I couldn't squat or do push-ups. A year ago, I fell from the third floor. I was doing gymnastics on a hotel rooftop in Pokhara – I had been learning to walk on my hands for a year. And I became so good at it that I decided to try to walk on the parapet. I was fine once, twice. Then the third time my hand slipped. I fell headfirst from the third floor. My chin broke my ribcage, I damaged my spine, and my arms and my legs were broken. It was a miracle I survived. Well, now I feel better than before that fall. It is like I am in a health resort here."

"How long will you rest in this 'resort'?"

"I have a two-year holiday package. But that isn't much for two kilos. A week ago a Russian guy was released; he spent four years here for eleven kilograms of charas. He molded different figurines out of it, painted them and wanted to take them to Rashka. The Nepalese got him right on the border. It's a good job he hadn't reached Rashka, or he would have been given fifteen years. Under Nepalese law, they only give you four years if the amount of charas is between four kilograms and a ton."

"And what about your accomplice, Zont, has he been released?"

"I had to take everything on myself. They gave me less time to serve and he promised to help me with money. Although, of course, that son of a bitch fled immediately to Thailand. Well, God will judge him. You can't escape karma. What's new outside? How is the psychedelic gang doing?"

"As soon as you were arrested, everyone started having problems. Ilka's package was stopped in Rashka, so now she can't travel abroad. Lyosha and Larisa had a package detained in Belgium, and another one in Moscow. And I am wanted in Rashka."

"What for, Vasya?"

"I don't know exactly, I can only guess. I sent Den a couple of kilograms of charas to Rashka. A Moscow smuggler named Mohr ordered it. He had everything under control. At the post office his cops received the hash and retailers transported it across Moscow. He asked me to send a package to Moscow. After your arrest, no one here dared to go to the post office. So Dan had to go to Delhi and send it from there. And this summer, it looks like all of the post offices in Russia were equipped with X-ray machines. In short, his entire Moscow gang was arrested. And while he was on holiday in the Canary Islands with his parents, without thinking twice his accomplices grassed on him. He was caught right at the airport. Now he's under investigation. The cops are demanding two hundred thousand dollars to drop the case or they will lock him up for fifteen years."

"Well, what has that got to do with you, Vasya? You didn't break any Russian laws, did you?"

"I don't know what it has to do with me, maybe because he bought the hash from me. Maybe his accomplices grassed on me. I didn't send him the package, my name was not mentioned anywhere."

"How do you know you are wanted?"

"I have friends working in Sheremetyevo[53], they checked on the computer. They say that if I arrive in Russia, I will be arrested immediately at the airport. Moreover, for some reason I am wanted 'for fraud.'"

"So then you're a crook," Romashka says, laughing and pressing his forehead against the bars, "maybe some old debts?"

"I haven't ever been engaged in any fraud. In general, I always respected Russia's criminal code. I don't even know what to think."

"You can't go to Rashka in the near future; now you have a good reason."

"That's for sure. I'm just not sure whether to rejoice or not."

"Welcome to the prisoners of freedom club."

"Your time is up," a guard interrupts our conversation.

---

[53] Sheremetyevo International Airport, Moscow.

"Here you are, Romashka; fruit and a few books. Don't lose heart in here," I say, handing the package to the guards. "I'll probably see you next year. We are going to Goa soon."

My friend follows me to the corner with his silent gaze and smiles as we part.

I walk down the narrow bustling streets of Kathmandu, recalling Romashka dancing happily at the DJ console during our last party. How is it that people make such stupid mistakes that result in them going to jail? Why was he so relaxed that he started ignoring the basic rules of security? After all, it was possible to avoid it. Maybe it's because sometimes you get so fed up with everything in life that reality ceases to bring joy. Maybe Romashka wanted to get rid of this unsatisfying reality? As a result, he relaxed to the extent that he allowed himself to be sent on a vacation to jail. If reality satisfies you, then your brain does not allow such mistakes to occur. Perhaps people end up in jail when they subconsciously agree with it, realizing that reality is no better. Romashka may be a perfect example. In Russia he was a successful businessman in the oil business. But then something went wrong, his debts began to snowball, and he fled from his angry creditors to India. With no money at all, from scratch, he rose again, becoming a Goan drug-dealer. Stability and prosperity seemed to have returned, but fate still had a few surprises for him. First, his girlfriend left him and he couldn't come to his senses for a long time afterwards. Then some competitors grassed on him to the police. He got out of it for a thousand dollars and fled to Nepal, refusing to pay a monthly tribute to the cops and to grass on his friends. Then there was that stupid fall from the roof. He must have been tired of fate's surprises if he dared, without considering the consequences, to walk into a post office guarded by the police with two kilograms of charas, simply giving up on himself with the words, "Oh, whatever." I walk down the ancient Nepalese streets considering the vicissitudes of fate. The visit to the jail has shaken me, forcing me to immerse myself in my own problems. I ought to focus on legal business. I don't want to go to jail. Now I have to buy some hemp fabric and send it to Russia for our Hemp store. Although how can it be our Hemp, if I can't return home?

"Hello, John."

"Hi, Vasa. You're back in Nepal! I'm glad to see you. How's your Russian Hemp doing?"

"Quite well, how is your Nepalese?"

"Very well," says the ever-smiling American, owner of a large store of hemp products in the heart of Kathmandu.

"I'm here again, as I want to buy various fabrics from you, five hundred meters. Will you do it?"

"Of course I will, just let's go and have a smoke first, and then we'll talk about business. I'll do whatever you want, even send it to Russia for you," John says, laughing and rolling a huge joint made of the finest Himalayan marijuana mixed with the best Nepali charas.

"Tell me, John, have you always been involved in legal business? You have such a beautiful store. Did you manage to do everything legally?"

Leaning back on a sofa covered with hemp cloth, I puff on the large, neatly rolled joint.

"John, I've just visited my friend; he is in prison for two kilograms of charas. And my mind is now focusing on one thing: how not to end up in there too, as I sell a bit of charas in Goa."

"Oh, Vasa, Vasa," the American sits down next to me, slapping me on the shoulder. "Back in my time, I didn't just sell a bit of charas; I sold hundreds of kilograms of charas and ganja. I was just lucky enough that I met my future wife in India. Thanks to her, I was able to stop just in time. She gave me four children whom I love more than life itself. With the money from the sale of charas I bought a small factory for the production of nylon. If you buy high-quality poland or charas made out of it somewhere in Nepal, you should know that it was made with my nylon. Fabric and clothes made out of hemp – that's my hobby. In the place where I once bought hemp for export, I now buy its waste products: hemp stems and leaves. In the mountain villages, they make fabrics out of it almost by hand, and my wife develops designs and manages the clothing production. Thank God, I managed to earn enough money through charas; it will suffice for the rest of my life. I am not involved in hemp for the money; it's just not to get bored. And jail is par for the course if you're involved with drugs. You should always be prepared for that. If you don't want to go there, then drop it. Otherwise, before you even notice you'll find yourself there. Okay, let's not think about bad things. God saved me from jail and I hope He will also protect you. What do you want to buy this time?"

"I made clothes out of your fabric and everything has already sold out. So I'll buy the same thing as the previous time, as well as something new. I just need to make a call to Russia, and maybe I'll order something else."

"You can call from my phone, the Hemp company pays for all phone calls," John says, smiling and holding out his phone. "In the meantime, I'll bring some new samples."

"Hello, Dymkov, how are you?"

"I'm not bad. But as for you, Vasya, it could not be any worse."

"What's happened? Have they shut down our Hemp?"

"The shopping mall where our Hemp was located is closed for reconstruction; now there will be a grocery store in its place."

"But we invested fifty thousand dollars in the store! Where will we get another fifty thousand? And where are we going to open a new store?"

"Vasya, I don't know where you are going to get fifty thousand. You need to come back to Rashka urgently to sort out this problem."

"But didn't we find you a manager? A clever girl, she used to work for Benetton."

"Your manager is a total fool, you made this mess and it is you who must clean it up."

"Dymkov, maybe I would like to come back to Rashka now, but I can't, and I have no money. I've just ordered five hundred meters of fabric for you. And what about Sam, doesn't he support the Legalize project any longer?"

"Vasya, what the hell are you talking about, the Legalize project? Wake up! If you don't come back I will have to give the money back."

"Can't you do business without me?"

"Who is going to do it? Your stupid manager? I fired her. And you know what, I don't give a fuck about your Hemp. I have a nightclub, concerts, tours. Come back to Rashka and do your Hemp business, or sell your apartment, repay your debts and go to hell."

"What debts, Dymkov? It was you who was promised to be given this business; I was just a manager with a salary of eight hundred bucks. You know that I got involved in this project because of the legalization of marijuana. You told me yourself that the money is not important, the main thing is the political situation in the country."

"The political situation has changed. In case have you forgotten, Putin is in power now. Sam has already had half of his business taken away. Forget about the Legalize project; come back to Rashka and work your balls off just like the whole country does. I have nothing to add."

Chapter 29. Part One. Inside.

"Fucking cunt, if I sit here for another couple of months half a year will have passed. Can you imagine, Vasya? Six months of my life! The judge added another two months to my sentence today. When will that damn expert analysis come?"

"Are you sure that the expert analysis will show Novocain, not coke?" I try to wind up Viktor, who has just returned agitated from the court.

"Well, if the expert analysis shows cocaine, after serving my term I'll get out and shoot those assholes. They should be killed for this outrage."

"Hmmm, and isn't it a outrage to come onto their turf and start destroying their business, at the same time spoiling their reputation with your cheap imitation of cocaine?" I laugh, pacing around our walking area, "It would be better if you told me what's new in cell six."

"They are all in a coma. They gorge themselves on sleeping pills and sleep for days. And when they wake up, they begin raving. The Greek dreams of escaping all the time, although he wouldn't even be able to run fifty meters with his belly. The Italian is constantly whining that he is running out of money. The Scot is upset that he won't be able to support his football team, Celtic, during the European Cup. All Ashpak talks about is food. The Japanese guy says nothing. He just makes models of the prison furniture by gluing together empty matchboxes."

"Say, Vitya; what did you do after Afghanistan?"

"What did I do... What can young people do after a war in our country? I was a gangster. I was part of a racketeering gang that cheated businessmen out of their money."

"Don't you miss those days?"

"You know, Vasya, it was only fun at first. And when they began shooting our brothers, I went into business myself. My karma probably caught up with me in India; you can't escape from it. I don't believe that I'm here for pharmacy store Novocain. I feel it in my heart that it's for something else. There is some sin that I am apparently working off now."

"Did you kill someone, Vitya?"

"No, I didn't kill anyone, but five years ago I grassed on someone and he got a year in jail. In that sense, I feel my guilt. He owed me money. The amount was silly – just a thousand dollars – and I got him locked up for a year. It looks like I'll sit here for at least a year..."

"You're a strange man, Vitya. The fact that you extorted money from businessmen: isn't that a sin? Don't you feel guilty for that?"

"But they didn't give me their last money, and I provided a service, protecting them from other mobsters, risking my life."

"As for me, Vitya, I never wanted to be a gangster. Maybe I was raised differently. Tell me how does it feel to be a gangster? The sense of impunity must be intoxicating."

"Vasya, there was nothing good in that life, and I was intoxicated by vodka. I was boozing incessantly. I understood in my soul that something was wrong, but I couldn't do anything about it. And my heart ached from it constantly when I was sober. So I drowned the pain with drink, until I started smoking marijuana. When I started smoking I began to think, and realized in the end that I was wasting my life on unnecessary nonsense, on showing off. All my life I tried to impress people by being someone that I wasn't."

"You're not the only one, Vitya. I know many former criminals. All of them also boozed and caused havoc at first, but when they tried psychedelics they quit their criminal 'business', stopped drinking, and now they live a normal life, smoking quietly."

"That's right, but the state prohibits smoking marijuana, and advertises alcohol the whole time. Even here, in India, where hashish is considered to be part of a religious rite, the alcohol corporations lobbied for laws so that now it's not permitted to smoke charas anywhere. And a large bottle of rum costs only two dollars. You can be locked up for ten years for a kilogram of hashish. When I drank, I was like an animal. If I didn't have a hair of the dog the next morning, I felt so bad and so depressed that I thought I would die. And once you take a drop, your eyes fill with aggression and you're ready to grab someone by the throat over any little thing. Every day, like before an attack: a shot of booze and into battle. And when I went from being a gangster to a businessman, nothing changed. I drank in order to have enough anger to fight teeth and nail for every dollar. And so it went on, until one of my friends gave me LSD to try. I will never forget my first acid trip. I felt like I was reborn. The whole broken mosaic of my life came together in my head in a beautiful pattern. I quit the business, packed my things and went to Goa. It's good that I managed to buy a campsite on the shore of the Black Sea before Putin became president. More precisely, I bought a piece of land, for only six thousand dollars, and invested another fifty. I built huts with my own hands, and now it brings me in return fifteen thousand dollars per year. Why would I need more? I have friends in Moscow who still work their asses off. They buy one Mercedes after another, each of them has already built two villas, and it's still not enough for them. Their wives and mistresses each have several mink coats in their wardrobes, but they are still not happy. It became clear to me when I expanded my consciousness. You will never be happy in the endless race for money; there will never be enough. And life is short; it passes quickly. How many friends lie in the grave, having not caught up with the Golden Calf? But big money is not given easily, you must sink your teeth into it, protect it, showing the whole world your muscles, claws and teeth. It's just that in our heart we all are human beings, not animals. So we have to soak all of this world's unfairness in drink. When I realized all this, it was as though I was suddenly cut off from alcohol."

"Vitya, then why did you chase the Golden Calf again? Who forced you to sell fake cocaine?"

"Vasya, I don't even know how I got into this shit again. I guess I wanted to show off. Here in Goa, I had everything: a big house on the beach, a jeep, and enough dough. I wanted to become even cooler, so that my woman would love me more. So I decided to play drug dealer. I thought I would sell only to Russians. After all, here in Goa everyone has an expanded consciousness, we are all brothers. I couldn't even imagine that here, among our own people, there might be a grass."

Chapter 29. Part Two. Outside.

"Finally, we made it to the house. I'm so tired," flopping into a plastic chair, Lena puts her feet up on a suitcase. "Four days on the road, six stops, five months in Nepal – what kind of a gypsy life are we living? When will it end?"

"What's wrong with the gypsy life? Many people dream about traveling. And we have traveled across the whole of India and Nepal. Vasilina, tell me, do you like traveling?" I ask my daughter, who has already taken her Barbies out of her little pink suitcase.

"Of course, Daddy. When will our next new journey be?"

"You see: we like it," I say, rolling the last suitcase into the house.

"I don't mind traveling, but I need comfort, not trains and buses. Only airplanes and taxis. And in such a hot country as India, I need air-conditioned taxis."

"I'm surprised, Lena. Where did you get so much royal blood from? Your parents work as boilermakers in the Russian Far North. Five years ago, you not only didn't have a place to call your own, you had no money even to take care of your teeth. After Vasilinka's birth you worked for a year to repay your debts, and now you want airplanes and taxis."

"You know, my dear, that when I was fifteen I came alone from a damn provincial town to conquer the big city. All my life I dreamed of having my own house. And as soon as I got it, I am again forced to move from one rented lodging to another, and it's always either India or Nepal. That's not what I have been dreaming about all my life. And anyway, I miss Russia."

"Honey, you're just tired from the journey," I say, sitting down nearby on our little balcony. "Look around: there are palms, the Sun and the sea. See how happy Francis is because of our arrival. And what is there in Rashka now? Cold, mud, slush, plastic-tasting food. I promise you that when I have the money, we will travel by planes and cars. In a year or two, I will handle this situation with being wanted in Russia, and by then all the dust with Dymkov will probably have settled. Then we'll go to Rashka. So for now, enjoy India, especially since we've got no choice. A new season is ahead, we will meet new interesting people and have new adventures."

"Well, I am ready to suffer for a few years. Just tell me, when will we stop selling drugs? We carried two kilograms of hashish across the border, and I want to be able to sleep at night."

"Honey, I'll do my best for it to be the last time. We'll rent two houses this season. I'll expand our restaurant. Just be patient, soon we will do only legal business. And when we have the money, I will register a company here. Den will sell drugs this season. We'll send Vasilinka to school so that she knows Hindi, English and Russian from childhood. Ilka will help you with the housework, and in five years we'll sell our apartment in Russia and buy a house on the beach with the money. We'll live in it happily till we die. So take Vasilinka now and go for a swim in the sea. You will have planes and cars. We'll do it."

A few weeks later, having rested and swum enough, Lena stopped complaining about our gypsy life and I got down to my daily Goan duties.

After breakfast, I roll a morning joint and watch as the fishermen's dogs bark at a stray cow right in front of my restaurant, driving it into a huge puddle left when the tide went out.

"I'm coming to you for breakfast!" Hanuman shouts from a distance, throwing a stone at the dogs. "Hello, Vasya, I haven't seen you for a long time. Where did you spend the monsoon?"

"I'm glad to see you too, Hanuman. We went to Nepal, to Pokhara, for five months, and we have already been here for about a month. I finished building my restaurant yesterday and today you are my first customer. I see you are in your orange 'Legalize' shorts, as usual."

"These shorts are my style. When they wear out I buy another pair from the Nepalese. I love escaping from the police on my sports bike. The only thing the cops can see is my ass with the inscription 'Legalize'."

"Come into the restaurant, why are you standing near the entrance? I've just rolled a joint. How long have you been in Goa?"

"I have been here for about a month. I've wanted to visit you for a while, but I've had no time. Until all the drug dealers arrive, I am like hot cakes here. I'm making cocaine deliveries every day."

"I think it's a good sign that you're my first customer this season."

"Krishna!" I shout to one of my waiters, who is yawning at the morning sun, "Make breakfast number three for our customer, on the house."

"Hanuman, have you heard that they are going to throw a good party in Kerim today? Tamir himself is organizing it."

"I've heard. Everybody knows about it. He's the reason I won't go there."

"What wrong has Tamir done to you?"

"Nothing so far, only it seems to me that he grassed me to police."

"It can't be! I know Tamir pretty well. My Vasilinka goes to kindergarten with his daughter; I've talked to him many times. He can't grass or people will stop coming to his parties."

"Vasya, what does it have to do with your kids? You and your psychedelics bring in a maximum of a thousand bucks a month. Who would be interested in you? Whereas you can easily earn five thousand with coke; parties are becoming rare, so I have become a competitor for him."

"But Tamir doesn't sell; he is a DJ."

"He doesn't sell, but his pushers do all right. They sell and grass on competitors. You probably haven't heard that he pays the cops for protection every month. Yesterday, he came to me and said, 'Someone posted your picture on an Indian website, it says that now you are the main Russian drug dealer in Goa'. He also said that the police came to him and asked about me. They want me to come to them myself, and start paying them money. And if I don't come, they'll arrest me and throw me into jail. My whole life, I've never paid anyone for protection. I have always been my own protection. And if it was only about paying; I know these cops. They are eager to earn more stripes. They would force me to rat someone out; I have never been a rat, and I am not going to become one now. I need to get out of here, and the sooner the better. Especially since I know that there will be no parties in Goa any more. Perhaps they will allow two or three per season, but even those will be supervised by the police. And I decided to give up the coke long ago. Coke is like a swamp. You start with one line and it is impossible to stop. I'd rather go to Thailand; parties are thrown there four times a month and drug trafficking is punishable by the death penalty. So I won't be tempted to dabble in this dirty business. I would rather teach yoga there. Goa is dead and coke killed it. Be careful, Vasya, they aren't touching you now, but when all of the parties are shut down and competition between dealers is tough, you will be ratted out by your own people. Or you will be forced to rat on others."

"I think you're exaggerating, Hanuman. You probably have paranoia from the coke. If you don't want to go tonight, don't; but I'll be glad to go and have a dance."

The plateau on the top of the hill resembles a Martian landscape. The red volcanic surface extends almost to the horizon, in front stretches the endless sea, melting into the starry sky. It feels as if we are on another planet. A thousand elegant, colorful people dance to loud, beautiful trance music. It's good that I didn't listen to Hanuman this morning. I wouldn't have forgiven myself if I had missed tonight's party. Once upon a time in Goa parties were held on the beach. The local people and the freaks lived in harmony then, and no one got in anyone's way. The freaks bought seafood from the fishermen and fruit and vegetables from the peasants. Everyone was happy. Hippies and freaks sunbathed naked on deserted beaches, danced at the parties, smoked, and spent the money they earned by selling charas on the locals. Thriving quickly, the local population pulled down their primitive huts and built beautiful two- and three-story houses in their place. The strange, hairy white people were pleased to pay a lot of money to rent these houses, making it possible not to fish or grow rice. No one other than hippies wanted to visit wild and undeveloped Goa. All of progressive humanity preferred comfortable hotels and beaches with no cows or pigs on them. In Goan villages, there were neither cars, nor paved roads. There was nothing. The hippies helped the locals to open small restaurants, explaining why you need spoons and forks. They showed them how to cook European dishes and taught them minimum sanitary requirements. And the local people happily joined in dancing to the drums played by the white people at night. And just like thousands of years ago, the Indians danced happily in the Full Moon, thanking the Indian gods for the good harvest and the happy life that the foreigners brought them. And so it would have gone on if the Catholic Church hadn't come out against the satanic dancing. Since the time of the Portuguese, Catholic churches have been built throughout Goa. Even before the arrival of the first hippies, the locals started forgetting their Indian traditions and gods due to the influence of the Portuguese. Priests from Catholic churches preached the right way of life: a decent Indian had to work tirelessly all his life, producing more meat and fish, collecting more rice and bananas, building new homes, and acquiring all of the modern benefits of civilization. While all the time, of course, paying a tithe to the church in order to go to heaven after death. However, the philosophy of the hairy, happy visitors went against the philosophy of the Catholics. The younger generation of Indians preferred to be content with what nature and the white men gave them, and not to spend their spare time slaving away for a new refrigerator or an iron, which they didn't need in the first place, but enjoying life. Then Catholicism started a crusade against the evil influence of the happy, satisfied hippies. In the mid 90s, a political party supported by the Catholics came to power and the Minister of Tourism announced that Goa didn't need hippies and freaks any longer. "We need money for Goa, we need wealthy tourists who come for two weeks, not have-nots who cannot even buy a cup of tea," he declared on television and in the newspapers. From that time began a crackdown on parties. First, they banned them on the beach, claiming that the loud music disturbed the sleep of workers. Soon after, parties were also banned in the jungle and remote locations. From the beginning of the twenty-first century all parties are illegal in Goa. The organizers pay the police huge bribes, which can only be compensated through the sale of cocaine. And so coke started to be sold almost everywhere. Tonight's party is organized in the farthest northern point of Goa, away from beaches, populated areas and the sea. Despite the party taking place on a deserted stone plateau, nothing has prevented a thousand people who love freedom from coming from all over Goa in order to feel the vibration of love and harmony. This is the last place, the last bastion of freedom. There is nowhere else to run.

***

"Hello Tamir!"

"Hello, Vasiliy, have you been back in Goa long?"

"No, I arrived from Nepal just a month ago."

A genuine psychedelic shaman stands in front of me. More precisely: the leader of all of the Russian Goa trancers. Proudly strutting around the party, he greets every psychedelic warrior, every reputable freak. This is his fiefdom. A fashionable mohawk haircut, big earrings, 'X-Budu' written in large glowing letters on his back. In the past I couldn't have imagined that one day I would shake hands with the founder of the Russian trance movement. He has lived in Goa for eight years and there are rumors that he has been wanted in Russia the whole time, which makes him even more legendary.

"Well, Vasya, will you make your kvass this year? You make excellent kvass."

"Of course I will. I sold four tons last year."

"How's your daughter doing?"

"Well, we've started to prepare her for school, and now she will go to kindergarten together with your daughter. Tamir, look at the black gold I brought from Nepal," I say, pulling a piece of charas and a small magnifying glass with a built-in light from my pocket.

"Actually, I don't smoke Nepali charas. The Nepalese do not know how to make good charas. I prefer charas from Manali in India."

"Tamir, take a look through the magnifying glass; you won't find such a quality in India. Europeans made it in Nepal."

Contemptuously taking my charas, Tamir breaks the tola in half and starts examining it through the magnifying glass.

"Yes, you're right; it's the first time I have seen such pure charas. Apparently, the Europeans are working hard. Vasya, it has never occurred to me to examine charas through a magnifying glass," Tamir says, pulling a tola from his pocket. "Let's take a look at mine."

Examining his piece for a long time, he grins and puts it back in his pocket.

"No, it won't work to scrutinize charas through a magnifying glass, it is necessary to try it. Let's have a smoke. Although it is not as pure as yours, mine gets you stoned better than any Nepalese charas. But first, I will play, and then we will try it," he says, heading towards the DJ console.

I dance together with everyone else and my dance is like the final battle, into which I pour all of my love of freedom and hatred of the globalization that has come here. Around me are the same kind of soldiers, who believe in the victory of good and love over the evil of the modern world. Tamir stands before us. Watching him, I want to believe that we will win. We cannot lose our last fight. Because to lose is to surrender; to accept the rules of society, which sold itself to the corporations long ago. It seems as if we are dancing for the last time. I want to laugh and cry simultaneously. The joy of unity and a premonition of defeat. Several hours fly by in a flash. An Israeli DJ replaces Tamir at the decks. After a few minutes, a police car appears in the distance on the plateau. The music is turned off. With bamboo sticks in their hands, the police rush the dance floor, seize the sound equipment and generator, and arrest the DJ. "Perhaps they will accept a bribe? Perhaps the music will be turned on in the morning?" the same phrases are heard everywhere.

No one is leaving. The Indian grandmothers continue to make tea on their kerosene lamps. Sitting down on a mat, I order a sweet tea with milk and spices.

"Hi, Vasya," I hear a pleasant, familiar voice.

"Hi, Masha!"

Next to me on the mat sits a tall, slim Goan beauty with funny ponytails, like a squirrel. We don't know each another well. Our daughters go to the same kindergarten, so when we meet we usually talk about our children.

"How are you, Vasya? Where's your Lena?"

"Lena and Vasilina stayed at home. It gets cold at night now, and Vasilina needs be taken to kindergarten tomorrow."

"It's a sad party today. Vasya, for some reason it feels like it's the last one. By the way, this is my husband," Masha says, smiling and pointing at the guy sitting next to her.

Peering in the dim light, my jaw drops in surprise.

"And... Uh... You said that your husband is a musician, but I never would have imagined that he was one of the lead singers of Na-Na!"

"Alexey," the guy covered with stylish tattoos greets me and extends his hand.

Next to him, sit three other musicians from the super popular Russian pop group.

"I'm surprised to see you here, in the heart of the psychedelic movement."

"Aren't we people, or what? Do you think we relax to our music?" laughing, Alexey says, evidently imagining a party where he is dancing to his own music.

"Pop music is for making dough. It's too simple for a creative person to get pleasure from it."

"I thought that creative people only create because it brings them pleasure."

"Sometimes it's for pleasure, and sometimes you get pleasure because you are paid well."

"You're just some kind of cyberpunks! You sing stupid songs on stage, but in real life you enjoy trance music, and even come to Goa."

"Actually, there are only two of us in the band who understand trance music, the rest came with us for the trip. If you watch closely how we dance on stage, it becomes crystal clear who loves trance and who loves pop music. It is a pity that they are banning trance in Goa."

"Lyosha, it's a worldwide trend. House music is getting the green light everywhere, because no one needs freethinking, independent people. And the freaks that promote trance culture take psychedelics, expand their consciousness and therefore show a bad example. From the social perspective, there is only harm from them. The drugs they take are not the most commercial. You can't take a lot of MDMA and LSD, the brain won't take it and you'll go mad. Glamorous House music is another thing entirely. You need to snort coke and drink booze while listening to it. And coke only works for fifteen minutes, and then you want it again. And it is impossible to stop, so you need to drink in order to lessen the desire. Meanwhile, in order to buy cocaine and alcohol, you need to earn a lot of money. It is beneficial for society to support those drugs that encourage people to earn more and more. Therefore, trance is being banned everywhere. Psychedelics and trance make people freer and less socially adapted. Trance is not commercial music, and its cultural tail is not commercial at all."

"That's how dough triumphs over good," Lyosha says, laughing and hugging his wife. "In all ancient civilizations where natural psychedelics were used, it was always the prerogative of the elite. Shamans, chiefs and spiritual leaders had access to magical substances. In India, charas was previously only smoked by babas. In Mexico, the shamans ate mescaline cactuses. And in our pre-Christian Russia, the shamans of the north drank a brew made out of toadstools. Ordinary people can't be allowed to expand their consciousness. Who would work if they did?"

"Yes, Lyosha, and you can go crazy if you try to expand an unprepared mind."

"That's right," Lyosha agrees, looking at his watch, "it's getting very cold nearer to morning, we'll probably head home. Apparently, there will be no more music today."

Saying goodbye to the departing pop musicians, I move closer to the kerosene lamp to warm my hands. The day dawns. There are about a hundred of the most persistent freaks near the dance floor. Some are asleep, some smoke chillums, and some are simply unable to get up to go home. The first rays of the Sun break the horizon, giving the small, round clouds a pink color. It seems like there are thousands of pink balls in the sky. Have we really lost our last fight, is the party really over? An Israeli DJ with waist-length dreadlocks drives up to the dance floor on a motorcycle. Having detached a little generator from the bike, he quickly runs to the DJ console. It takes him several minutes to connect the wires, and the first rays of the Sun are met by a perfect trance track. As if by the wave of a magic wand, all of a sudden all of the remaining people at the party leap to their feet and begin to dance passionately. It feels as if it is the last dance in their lives. It seems like they are not dancing, but rather hovering above the ground. They jump high, trying to see the first sunrays over the hills on the horizon. I float above the ground too, and tears of joy stream down my cheeks. We have not lost our last battle. No one can take away our freedom.

Chapter 30. Part One. Inside.

"Hi, Masha. I didn't expect to see you here. I really thought that everyone had forgotten about me. I am very glad to see you."

The guards stare curiously at the tall beauty with squirrel-like pigtails.

"I'm glad to see you in good spirits, too. How did you manage to end up in here?"

"Masha, I have no idea. It's probably because I didn't believe that I could get locked up. I knew that the police were looking for me; I could have left everything behind and ran away, but for some reason I didn't. I didn't suspect that the cops wouldn't play by the rules. Right up until the end, I didn't believe that this could happen to me. While Tamir was in Rashka, one of his pushers set me up. Not even for the money, but just to curry favor with the cops."

"Yeah, I know everything. Lena told me. How are you doing in here?"

"To be hones, jail is good for me. I am reassessing my values in life, exercising, playing chess, and I'm thinking of writing a book. I've also gotten rid of unwanted people from my life. Here in jail, you quickly see who is your friend, who needs you, who wants you to get out as soon as possible. To some extent, I am even grateful to the guy who put me in here. How are you doing, outside? What's new?"

"I've recently returned from Bali, all the guys are there now. Do you remember Romashka who served a term in a Nepalese jail? He sends you his regards. He organizes all the trance parties there now."

"But Indonesia is a Muslim country, they have the death penalty for drug offenses, don't they?"

"You won't believe me, Vasya, but they sell legal stimulants in grocery stores. Just like ecstasy, but they are made of natural plant materials. Under their influence, you can dance all night long. Of course, marijuana is illegal, but the authorities turn a blind eye to smoking tourists. If you don't sell and don't smoke in public places, no one will touch you. And it's so beautiful there! Goa doesn't come close to it. I've been coming to Goa for ten years, and I can say that nothing has remained of the Goa it was before. I don't know why I came here again. Maybe because of my daughter, she loves going to school here, or maybe because of my friends. Many of my friends live here in Goa. But each year there are less and less of them. Many of them have gone to other countries. Recently, the police raided the Tereshkov place. They turned everything upside down and found nothing, but they talked about you. I don't know whether to tell you this or not..."

"Why not? You have already started, so go on."

"The police said that you will be released in a year and a half, not earlier."

"Oh, Masha, that's good news," I say, sighing, "because I could be given ten years. In Aguada[54], there are fifty people in for what I'm here for, and two of them are Europeans. And in a year and a half here, my spirit and my body will only become healthier. As my friend Viktor says, 'Me and Vasya don't get bored here. They fuck us and we grow stronger.'"

Chapter 30. Part Two. Outside.

"Hey Arik, you look like a ghost. What happened?"

"My Natasha died."

"What do you mean, died?"

"Just like that, the bitch just died. Yesterday in the hospital, without regaining consciousness, she croaked."

I look at my friend and can't believe my eyes. Having known Arik for three years, I have never seen him like this. An educated, intelligent man, this season he fell madly in love with a petite, weird girl. She was nothing out of the ordinary, with short hair, and almost half the height of the handsome, two-meter tall Arik. I had never seen him so happy before. It was as if he was flying on wings when he was around her, completely absorbed in this love. It seemed that he had been waiting for her his whole life and then he finally found her. And now, after such a tragedy, he stands in front of me and calls her a bitch. "Evidently, Arik has gone out of his mind," is the first thing I think on hearing his words.

"I opened my soul to her. I thought I had finally found my soul mate, and that bitch just croaked. She found a healthy, handsome guy like me, and croaked"

"Arik, what's up with your arms? Since you came into my restaurant, you haven't stopped scratching your arms and legs. You have already scratched them to sores. What's going on?"

"Vasya, because of this slut, I got neurodermatitis. I itch all day and night from nerves."

"Arik, I don't understand, you loved her so dearly, and now you say all these things. Have you lost your mind?"

"I haven't lost my mind, it was her who lost it. It turned out she was a fucking addict. She pretended to be normal. But she had problems with her head. That's why she died. She had AIDS, and came specifically to Goa to die. She knew that this season she would die, and didn't tell anyone."

"How can it be, AIDS?"

"So it is, she was a heroin addict. A year ago, her husband died of AIDS. And I believed her so much that I stopped using condoms. Then in the hospital I was told she had died of AIDS; I didn't believe it at first, I thought it was some sort of mistake."

"And what are you going to do now?"

"What can I do, Vasya? I've just had tests and I am waiting for the results. It's the third day that I haven't slept and I just keep itching. I hate that bitch. She laughed at me before she died, or

---

[54] Aguada - a village where a jail for dangerous criminals is located.

maybe she just didn't know what she was doing, but she looked normal. Three days ago, she suddenly fell into a coma, she lay there for three days, and then she died. Just like that."

"Don't lose hope, Arik, maybe everything will be ok. It happens, I've read about such cases."

"Vasya, what else do I have left to do? This is my only hope now. The doctors said that I need to undergo tests three times. Now, in three months time, and again in six months. So for half a year this nervous itching is guaranteed, but then we'll see. I'll go to the beach, meditate, do gymnastics. While I am practicing qigong I manage to forget myself. Although not for a long time, but I don't itch when I do it."

"I don't know what to say, Arik. I am stunned by this news. I will keep my fingers crossed for you."

Going down the stairs, Arik smiles at me, but judging by the incessantly moving muscles in his jaw, it's clear that it's hard for him to do so. "That man has a strange fate," I think to myself, watching him till he reaches his motorbike. Once, five years ago, he came to India as a convinced devotee of Krishna. And even earlier, long before India, while living in his native Chelyabinsk, he accidentally met those weird people who always seem to be happy. They were dressed in unusual clothes for Russians, more like Hindu outfits. Everything about them was unusual. The men shaved their heads, leaving a small braid on the nape, and drew a colored spot on the bridge of their noses. Many of them wore garlands of flowers around their necks. But most of all Arik was attracted by their unusual cheerfulness. They were always smiling and always seemed happy. That was what he needed most of all. Having been left at that time without his father and mother and with only one younger sister, he had quickly realized that the surrounding world was not as cozy and comfortable as it seemed in childhood. In this world, you have to fight to survive. Finally he met people who radiated cheerfulness and happiness. You don't need to fight for this happiness; you just have to believe these people. And he believed them. They proposed that he sell his apartment and go traveling with them to India, to seek a path of spiritual development. For three years he lived in ashrams, leading a monastic way of life. He practiced meditation every day, studied the scriptures and chanted mantras. But the happiness that radiated from his new friends started to seem ostentatious and simulated. Somewhere deep inside, he began to feel that there was something wrong, that withdrawal from society did not give him a state of inner peace. Gradually he became disappointed in this method of knowing oneself and the world. He left the Krishna Consciousness movement and settled in North Goa, in Arambol. After meeting European freaks, he started reading psychedelic literature, where our contemporaries proposed new, interesting, and at the same time rational ways of knowing oneself. For some time, he even became interested in psychedelic drugs, conducting experiments on himself in altered states. For a while, he regained peace of mind. But eventually he also became disillusioned with this method of self-development, preferring to change his mind through meditation, rather than using chemicals. We often argued, discussing books by Timothy Leary and Terence McKenna. He called them mad professors who overrated LSD, because they preached about the psychedelic revolution to the masses in an attempt to change the world for the better. I could not understand why Arik thought that the psychedelic path of self-development was only the destiny of the select few. In our debates, he tried to prove to me that in order to make a quantum leap in perception, it was necessary to have the required predisposition of the brain. Otherwise, unable to cope with the task, the brain may easily be damaged. He believed that at this stage in our evolutionary development, the majority of mankind was not ready for any leaps. I was an advocate of the ideas proposed by the psychedelic professors who believed that everyone could make a quantum leap in perception. I agreed with Timothy Leary, who claimed that if ten percent of progressive humankind would make their first quantum leap, setting an example for others, then all the rest of the population on the planet would wake up and start transforming, changing their attitude towards the world. In recent years, Arik did not go to parties at all, calling freaks 'jerks'. He preferred meditation, yoga, qigong and different martial arts. When he finally met his love in Goa, we, his friends, were immensely happy for him. It seemed that he had finally found the peace of mind that he had been seeking all this time. Today's news was a great shock to me. It was frightening to even imagine what kind of emotions were raging in his head after such a tragedy.

"Hey, Roma, I am so glad to see you! Have you come back to Goa? It is difficult to be without Goa for long, isn't it?"

"Yes, I have come for the whole season, returned to the Promised Land again," hugging me, says my friend whom I have not seen for six months.

"How is Moscow? By the white-blue color of your skin I can see that there is no sun at all at home."

"This time everything was much more interesting. I rented a piece of land on the Rublevskiy beach for the entire summer season, held trance parties, swung my fire pole, met lots of interesting people. This summer was very creative in Russia. In its death throes, glamorous Moscow gave birth to interesting creative projects the whole time. The Krishna Mira[55] club opened in Moscow, and all the glamorous Goans and their fans now hang out there. Many of them promised that we'll catch up here in the near future. Soon we will lure all the most interesting people to Goa and there will be only schmucks and cops left in Rashka."

"Good for you, Roma, only positive energy emanates from you, no matter what. Have you heard about Arik and his girlfriend?"

"Yes, such a terrible story. I have stopped talking to Arik for a while; he gives off only negative energy. I'll wait until he gains peace of mind again. His energy makes me want to hang myself. Vasya, I see that there are also interesting changes in your restaurant, I can't even recognize it. You bought expensive furniture and new mattresses."

"Yes, Roma, I had to stop selling hemp clothes. I have to adapt to the waves of globalization that are rolling even this far. I am putting the whole focus of my business on the restaurant now. There are lots of competitors, so I have to meet the demands of tourists. The whole idea of Russian Hemp collapsed without me in Rashka. I quarreled with my partner. As soon as I left Russia, I was immediately accused of stealing money and escaping to India. And now I have no desire to go back there to prove my innocence. And you have probably heard that I am wanted there now; I can't go to Russia."

---

[55] Krisha Mira ('Roof of Peace'/'Roof of the World') - a legendary Moscow club, run and frequented by a relatively progressive and bohemian section of Moscow society.

"I know about you and about Max, who got five years in jail in Moscow for a package from Nepal. I see you have started betraying your principles," Roma looks at me reproachfully, pointing at the menu lying near the table. "Have you started selling booze in your restaurant? You used to be a tough opponent of alcohol culture."

"Everything flows, everything changes," I repeat the Indian proverb with a sigh. "I had to buy a license for beer. But strong spirits are banned in my restaurant. Right now I believe that low-proof alcohol is not so bad. The owner of the land raised the rent and I need to earn money legally somehow. I can't sell drugs all my life. After all, my daughter is growing up, next year I'll have to pay for school."

"Yeah, well, don't make excuses," smiling again, Roman says and pats me on the shoulder, "everyone needs dough, and beer is not coke."

"By the way, have you seen the banner I hung in front of Hemp?" I point at a huge, man-sized photo of a hemp flower.

"Yes, I noticed that beauty a few meters away. Only in India you can advertise a restaurant with a hemp photo on the wall. Vasya, are you not afraid to attract the police through such advertising?" Roman says, smiling as he gets up from the table.

"I hung a 'No Drugs' sign for the police, and the most important thing is that it's true. No drugs in my restaurant, only psychedelics."

"By the way, my friends should be coming soon; they want to talk to you. And there they are, walking along the beach. I should wave to them so that they notice us. They have their own website dedicated to Goa, it's quite popular here, and they want to meet you."

"Vasya, this is Dima and Sveta. They want to put information about your place on their website. The fame of your kvass and wonderful hash cakes has spread all around Russian Goa. Now, Vasya, you will also be known on the Internet."

Smiling, a pretty, fair girl extends her hand to me, and then a tough-looking guy with small darting rat-like eyes holds out his hand.

197

Chapter 31. Part One. Inside.

"Open Mapusa Beach," I hear Viktor's familiar voice.

The doors of my cell open again. One hour walk again. And once again I have to walk in circles and talk about whatever, because we've already discussed everything many times. I know almost everything about his life and he knows everything about mine. Sometimes we argue ourselves hoarse about some nonsense like 'the duality of everything in this world' and part almost hating each other. But the next day we are again incredibly happy to meet for an hour to discuss the completely opposite opinion that was born during the night. We have only one hour to speak in our mother tongue, to exchange books or jail news. Today's top news is Yelisei's return from the psychiatric clinic.

"Vitya, have you heard the news? They say he escaped from the mental hospital and was caught again," I say, examining a huge dead rat killed by the guards during the night shift.

"Why guess? He is about to come out of his cell and we'll find out everything from him."

To the applause of the European inmates, Yelisei is the last to come out from cell number three, smiling and looking slightly overfed. He still has the same tattered old clothes on and the same long, unwashed greasy hair. The only thing that has changed is his hands: this time they are generously smeared with green disinfectant.

"Well, hello, tramp. Tell us, how did you find the Goan nuthouse?" Viktor asks first.

"Hello, boys."

Yelisei tries to rub wrists again instead of shaking hands.

"No, Yelisei. Apparently, you are not fully cured. Can't you give a human hand shake?"

"But I have Christ's power in the ribbon on my wrists, it is transferred to you, too."

"Never mind. Let's not argue about that. Tell us, what are these rumors about your escape?"

"I needed to get home. So I ran away from there. I said it here in the jail, that I had to pick up my stuff. But no one wanted to listen to me. While I was in the nuthouse, I demanded that they escort me home to pick up my things. I rent a room in Chapora and now it's rainy season, so if the things are not packed, everything will be lost. Moreover, I had my daughter there waiting for me in this stuff."

Accustomed to not being surprised by anything, Viktor and I silently exchange glances and continue listening to the flow of nonsense, amongst which sense may only be heard occasionally.

"The doctors didn't listen to me, they locked me up in a ward along with two local lunatics. One night, I broke off a piece of iron from the bed, used it to unscrew the four screws that fastened the bars on the window, and ran away. I had to wade through thorn bushes for a long time. They tore all my clothes and scratched my body. I came home, packed my things, put my daughter in my pocket, and made a joint. So I was sitting there drinking tea, when suddenly the police burst in and started shouting at me. They put me in the car and now I'm here again. Now I can sit here quietly for a long time, as my daughter is with me."

"And who is this daughter, for whom you were so eager to escape?" Viktor asks, his mouth open in amazement.

"Here she is," Yelisei takes a funny little doll from his pocket. "This is my daughter. Like all children, she was born as a result of a great love."

"Vasya, look what people do for love. And you and Antonio harp on about 'escape, escape.' If you want to escape, do it like this guy did. That's how people show their love, by risking their life. He may get an additional six months for the escape. You and Antonio love yourselves more. And if you love someone like that, no bars or walls will be an obstacle."

"Perhaps you're right, Viktor. Maybe I don't want to escape from here."

"Thank you, Yelisei. Thanks to you, today I realized the meaning of the phrase 'Fools are always lucky'," I say, holding out my wrist to him.

Chapter 31. Part Two. Outside.

"Hey, bro, tell me, who is Vasya here?" a tough-looking fellow with a shaven head asks me.

"I'm Vasya. What's the matter?"

"Well, finally, we've found you, we have to have a word with you. Where can we talk?"

"What's wrong with this place? Come up into the restaurant, sit down and we'll talk."

I interrupt my long observation of the capoeira dancers on the beach and prepare myself to once again communicate with 'messengers from the mainland'.

"I am not alone, I am with two chicks and my bro," the tough guy points at the two girls standing at the entrance in heeled sandals and a guy who looks like a typical train station conman.

"Why do you hesitate there at the entrance? Come in, make yourself at home, order juice while I talk to your friend."

"So, you are THE Vasya? We drove almost a hundred kilometers from South Goa to see you. We've heard a lot about you in Moscow. All the boys who come back from Goa talk about you."

"And what do the boys say?" I ask, smiling as I try to parody the style of 'gangster' communication.

"They say you have some kind of strong hash that you show under a microscope. And also, the boys told me that you make cakes with this hash. They say if you eat one such a cake it can get you so high that you don't need to smoke all day."

"Yes, your boys don't lie. I have excellent hash. The local boys call it 'from grandpa's cellar'. Fifty bucks for a tola."

"A tola - what's that? A local matchbox or what?" the second conman-looking guy says, looking through the menu.

"A tola is an India measure of weight equal to twelve grams, while the Goan tola is ten grams."

"We don't care, ten or twelve. We are satisfied with the price. Sell us a hundred grams to last us for two weeks, and about twenty cakes. How much do they cost?"

"One hundred," I answer with a smile, watching as their face-painted girlfriends in uncomfortably tight miniskirts sit on a mattress and look around slightly startled, covering their plump thighs with their expensive handbags.

"Isn't that expensive, one hundred bucks for a cake?" the conman asks, taking out a wad of money.

"One hundred rupees," I say, laughing, "they're three dollars a piece."

"Well... three bucks – that's damn cheap. Then we'll take fifty pieces; we have some more boys at our hotel. Today we'll feed everyone, let them enjoy it, as they can't afford such a thing in Rashka. And, most importantly, I almost forgot to ask. Do you have any Number One[56] by any chance? They told us in Moscow that you don't sell Number One, but we need it badly."

"That's right, I don't sell coke, but I have Dymich."

"What's Dymich'? We haven't tried it before."

"Dymich is MDMA, that's what we call it here. It is the basic element of ecstasy pills."

"No, we don't need pills, there are no parties here anywhere, where would dance on that? We want to snort some coke on the beach with vodka."

"Sorry, guys, then I can't help you, don't even ask. I don't go near coke, that is my basic principle."

"Listen, Vasya, what if we give you half of the money now, in the evening we try your hash, and if we like it, tomorrow we will bring the rest of the money and buy the same amount," the conman proposes, holding out the money.

"No, guys. I am not a bank and it's not my first day selling drugs. To give the goods and then wait for the money, that's not my style."

"Well, Vasya, don't be offended, he's kidding. Kolyan, give him all the money, don't you see he is one of us," says the tough guy, rising from the table. "Thank you, Vasya. We'll go because we've got a taxi waiting for us, and we have an hour's drive back."

Having packed everything for them in a package, I see how Arik, who has just come in with two guys, is watching us from the next table and smiling.

"Hi, Arik. How is it going? What's new?"

"So far, so good," the six-foot blonde says, smiling and fixing his long hair. "The first tests showed that I don't have AIDS, which is good news. But I need to give blood again after three months."

"You surprise me, Arik. Beautiful models must run after such a handsome guy like you, and you found a girlfriend half your height, a junkie, and with AIDS."

"Vasya, that's life. I must have such karma. I see that the boys are appearing in your place more and more frequently."

---

[56] Number One - a slang term for cocaine in Russia.

"Yes, Arik, normal people go to other countries, as there are no parties. Russian thugs have started coming here more often, and all they want is cocaine. But these are not the worst characters: the number of bard-nerds is constantly increasing. They need nothing but vodka. They get trashed and sing 'It's great that we are all together here today'."

"By the way, Vasya, these are some guys from my home, from Chelyabinsk. They are respected devotees of Shiva."

"Well, maybe not so respected, but we believe in Shiva," extending his hand to me, says a skinny, long-haired guy of about thirty-five to forty.

"My name is Zhenyok."

"Nice to meet you, Zhenya."

"And my name is Ivan," getting up, a bald guy with a simple Russian face extends his hand to me. "I'm still not sure what I believe in. In Chelyabinsk, all the guys believe in Shiva, while I am just observing for now."

"Nice to meet you, Vanya. Arkasha told me that you have a respected criminal kingpin who got all the lads hooked on Shaivism[57]," I say, sitting down at their table. "I also heard that all the lads in Chelyabinsk wear Shiva tridents on their gold chains instead of crosses, and they greet everyone by saying 'Hare, Hare, Mahadev'."

"Well, not everyone, of course, but most are like that," smiling, Zhenya points at the Rudraksha[58] hanging on his chest. "In Chelyabinsk we like smoking hash and sometimes we take psilocybin mushrooms. Vasya, do you have anything for sale?"

"Well, I would like some cocaine, I love coke," Vanya interrupts us, acting out the snorting of an invisible line of cocaine.

"I don't sell cocaine, Vanya. And I don't want to know anything about it, that is my basic principle."

"Why so?" Vanya asks in surprise, pulling a pack of Belomor Kanal from his pocket."

"Because it is a dangerous drug. Old man Freud wrote about it a hundred years ago. Besides, I'm not a drug dealer, and I don't want to spoil my karma with bad deeds."

"Well I, on the contrary, have always thought that cocaine is not a drug, and that there is no harm from it."

"I'm not going to argue with you. Your knowledge is based on personal experience, and I read a bunch of books before I first tried it. As for mushrooms, unfortunately, I don't have them. The yield is weak here in India and you need to collect them yourself. You never know what an Indian could put in the basket, he doesn't care. However, there is LSD, which is no worse and perhaps even better – it brings you brighter hallucinations. In terms of smoke, I've got two kinds of charas: Indian

---

[57] Shaivism - One of the four most widely followed sects of Hinduism, which reveres the God Shiva as the Supreme Being.

[58] Rudraksha - the seed of a sacred plant, from the Sanskrit 'Rudra' (Shiva) and 'aksha' ('teardrops') frequently used as prayer beads. Depending on the number of segments in the seed, they may cost from $0.1 to $10,000 apiece.

from Manali, it costs the same everywhere, a thousand rupees per tola; or two thousand for Nepali. Nepali charas is made by Europeans, you won't find anything purer than that."

"What? Do the Europeans collect it themselves?" Zhenya asks in surprise, pulling out a cigarette holder.

"No, of course not, the Nepalese collect the ganja, but the process of making charas is overseen by white people. Vanya, I would advise you to try Dymich instead of cocaine. It's more useful and more fun."

"What is it?" the bald Chelyabinsk guy asks in surprise.

"Vanya, have you ever tried ecstasy?"

"Of course I have, I love ecstasy. In Chelyabinsk if I can't get coke at a club, I buy four pills of ecstasy for the whole night."

"Well, Vanya, ecstasy is made of MDMA, but they also add amphetamine to make it cheaper, and then sell it. Whereas Dymich is pure crystals without impurities."

"Then we need a bottle59 of LSD, one hundred grams of charas and ten grams of Dymich – to try it."

"That's how we do things in Goa!" I say, laughing and reaching for the camera that I use to hide drugs in. "The thing is that I don't have that much on me now. Here you are, a little bit of everything, to sample. And write down my partner's number, his name is Dan. Call him and order as much as you need, he'll bring you everything. He will be in charge of the drugs now, as I've been too exposed."

"I'm a disco dancer, Jimmy, Jimmy, acha, acha..." the once popular in Russia Indian song starts playing on my phone.

"Here in India, everything is very often in sync," I say, pointing at the name on the display of my phone. "I just thought of Dan and here he is."

"Hello, Dan. What's up? I've just given your number to some guys from Chelyabinsk. Can you help them out?"

"Of course I can help. How much and what do they want?"

"They'll call you, they are Arik's friends."

"Vasya, have you heard that Seryoga was killed in a crash on his bike today?" I hear the agitation in Dan's voice over the phone.

"Which Seryoga?"

"The one who has lived on the first floor of your house for a month. Seryoga, his wife is Lena and their little son is Fedya."

"When has he managed to crash, if I saw him on the road an hour ago? He even nearly crashed into me, he was drunk as a skunk."

"Well, he didn't have time to drive far away."

Putting my phone away in my pocket, I sit for some time, staring at one spot and trying to remember Seryoga's face.

---

59 Bottle - one hundred drops of LSD, a hundred doses.

"What is it, Vasya?" Arik breaks the silence. "Has someone crashed on a bike again?"

"Yeah, a resident of my guest house has just died. I saw him alive an hour ago and now he's gone. Every year a lot of people crash and people still drive drunk."

Seryoga was a friend Andryukha Pineapple, the first tourist who stayed in my house during the first season. They were both heroin addicts, and for many years they had tried to get off this terrible addiction. Andryukha managed to do it first. When he visited a year ago, he easily switched to lighter drugs, started attending parties, and led a more or less healthy lifestyle. Having grown some dreadlocks, he successfully became part of the freak community and got the nickname 'Mr. Pineapple' for his love of bundling his dreadlocks on the very top of his head, making it look like a large pineapple. On Mr. Pineapple's advice, Seryoga also came to Goa with his wife Lena, both of them addicted to heroin. Having successfully gone through cold turkey they faced a new challenge – the emptiness, accompanied by the terrible boredom that formed in their heads. They usually filled this void with heroin, enjoying an illusory happiness. But they didn't want this drug any longer. And then they started to drink. They hit the bottle every day and heavily. An hour before Seryoga's death, I saw his eyes. Barely hanging onto his motorbike, he was driving in the middle of the road, his eyes as dull as those of a dead man. The reality of the world just did not exist for him. He was in his own illusory world. The surrounding real world simply didn't satisfy him.

***

I didn't go to Seryoga's cremation. I was not sorry for him, and I even felt some resentment or anger towards this person who was absolutely indifferent to the world around him. He didn't care that he could crash into someone, or kill himself. He didn't care about his wife Lena and his young son Fedya, who couldn't understand what happened to his dear daddy for a long time after the crash.

Chapter 32. Part One. Inside.

"Hello, daddy, is that you? Hi, I miss you. Why don't you come?"

"My dear daughter, if you only knew how glad I am to hear your voice! I really want to be with you, but I'm very busy. I have a lot of things to do and I cannot come now. Tell me what's new with you, and, actually, tell me anything."

"I learned to roller-blade. In Goa no one roller-blades, but here lots of people do it."

"Do you miss Goa?"

"Yes, I want to swim with you in the sea every day again. Mom says that soon we will go to Goa. And, daddy, I am taking classes in belly dancing, mom says I can shake my butt very well. I'll come and show you. And besides, mom recently told me a joke – oh, she is such a joker – that you are sitting in jail. I laughed and did not believe her. And I also learned the entire multiplication table. Remember when you drew the round things on the sand and we counted them? Now I know everything by heart. And what are you doing, daddy?"

"I am not wasting my time, either, darling. I exercise every day. I have become much stronger. I have lost my tummy, which you used to call the 'warm cushion'. I learn English every day. You helped me to translate from English the things I didn't understand, and now I understand everything and I can speak."

"You're cool, daddy. I am proud of you and miss you. Here, mom wants to talk to you, I'll give her the phone."

"Hi, sweetheart."

"Hi, dear."

"How are you?"

"We're fine, it's just that the money your mother gave us has come to an end. Everything is awfully expensive here, compared to India. But I'll come back to Goa and start selling kvass and cakes, and I'll be able to make some money. I wanted to tell Vasilinka that you're in jail, but she did not believe me. First she asked, "Has dad robbed someone?" And then she started laughing. "Dad could not rob anyone, mom, you are kidding." There is another fucking crisis in the country. No one has any money and I still can't rent our apartment to anyone. Once I do, we will buy tickets right away and fly to you in Goa. How are you? What's new?"

"Well, it seems there is nothing new. I finally cured the fungus on my back. I smeared my back with ointment for a whole month. Everyone who sits here for more than two months has a back covered in white spots. But in general, I have only become healthier. I miss you and often see you in my dreams. Well, my dear, we have to finish, the guards are showing me that our time has run out. Bye, I'll call you in a week. Take care of Vasilinka, I love you."

"Yeah, I've finished already, stop waving your hands," I scowl at the guard standing in the doorway.

Two guards escort me, leading me down the street in the direction of the jail. I have the right to make an international call once a week. Every Monday, as soon as I wake up in the morning, I write an application for an escort to accompany me to the international phone call office. In order to get an escort it is necessary to remind the warden about it every two hours, which makes him pretty angry. However, it is the only way to get what you want. If you don't keep reminding him, you can be left without a call. For the rest of the day after the phone call, I usually recollect the conversation and get upset about the fact that I forgot to ask or say something. I mustn't forget to get some sleeping pills from David. Otherwise, a sleepless night is guaranteed. Once a week, I walk down the street enjoying the fact that there are no bars over my head separating me from this beautiful world. Once a week, I can enjoy a variety of smells. It turns out that absolutely everything has its own smell. Before jail, I never paid attention to it, only differentiating good and bad smells. Actually, there are many shades of smell. Passing people and cars smell differently. Shops facing each other along the sidewalk also have different smells. But a particularly pleasant, fresh smell comes from the trees and flowers. Rain drizzles; the jail is up ahead around the corner. The guards yawn, paying no attention to me whatsoever and barely moving their feet, dragging themselves along next to me. Am I ready to push the guards away now and run headlong away from the jail, as Sasha and Yelisei did? Vividly imagining myself running down the street, I start to feel my knees shaking slightly. I guess I'm not as crazy as they are, or maybe I'm just a coward.

Chapter 32. Part Two. Outside.

"I urgently need to get out of Goa; Nick has been arrested."

"What Nick? Go where?" My Lena asks me fearfully.

"Nick, remember the German psychedelic veteran who always dances near the speakers at every party? He has a nice chillum in a snakeskin case."

"Yes, I remember that. I don't remember his face, but I recall a case with the head of a white snake. What has he done?"

"Well, he's done nothing; the police arrested him with three hundred ecstasy pills on him. He is sitting in jail now."

"And what has that got to do with you?"

"It has nothing to do with me; he's just my dealer. I've been buying everything from him recently. If the police press him now, he could tell them who bought from him. I'll go to Thailand for two or three weeks. Everything will settle down here, and if no one is looking for me, I'll be right back. In the meantime, I'll look for land, just in case Goa dies out in the coming years. Maybe we'll have to move to Thailand."

"You promised me that you would get out of the drug business…"

"Lenochka. First, I need to earn some start-up capital. I'd be happy to quit this business, but we need something to make a living with."

For some time we sit in our restaurant, silently watching as on the beach two black castrated bulls, tired of the hot sun, lazily butt one another, both of them unwilling to give way to the other. The heat slows down all living things. Dogs don't pay attention to cats, which, in turn, lazily watch big rats running right under their noses. Everything is trying to find some shade. Having clashed horns, the two bulls remain motionless for five minutes. Apparently forgetting the purpose of their confrontation, the right bull, sticking out his long rough tongue, starts slowly licking the face of his opponent, seemingly proposing that they part amicably.

"Hi, Vasiko, hello, Lenchik," appearing from nowhere, a young bald guy suddenly breaks the silence. "Can I get some soup?"

"Of course, Petya, come in, sit down beside us."

The tall, slim Ukrainian comes quickly into a restaurant and plops down on a mattress.

"Well, the drums clatter and the jerks gather," taking off his backpack, Petya says laughing. "I didn't come alone. I got myself a cat. Now I only move around Goa with it."

A little kitten, still shocked from a recent motorbike ride, stares at us from a completely transparent plastic backpack.

"Petya, you look like an alien from an orange planet."

For some time, we smile and admire Petya's orange outfit. A long orange scarf wrapped around his waist, hanging down to his ankles, a short orange jacket, ninja shoes with orange stripes in the shape of the 'Om' sign, orange glasses, and a fluorescent orange pendant around his neck.

"Vasiko, Lenchik, you cannot even imagine what a mess I've just got into. The police nearly arrested me just now. I will order a meal and tell you everything."

"Krishna, give me one cold soup with cream and pancakes with tea."

The kitten, finding its way out of the backpack, immediately starts playing with a piece of hash lying on the table, but having received a brisk flick of the finger from its owner, hides under the table.

"Now, listen. I decided to buy ten grams of coke; my friends should be coming soon. I asked around about who had the best cocaine. Well, of course, everyone said that Tamir has the best. I called him and he said that he is too busy at the moment to bother with it. But he gave me the phone number of some English guy called Murtinian. We agreed with this Murtinian guy by phone to meet at the gas station. I arrived and waited for him, and then he calls me and says that he can't come because his bike has broken down. And then he immediately calls back again and says he will come, but only for a little while, because he is in a hurry. He arrives a few minutes later and I try a snort. The coke is good, so I give him the money and he gets on his bike and leaves. As soon as I get on my bike, some suspicious Indian crosses my path and, getting off his bike, begins to wave some certificate. Realizing that he is a cop, I jump straight on my bike and rev the engine. And the bastard chases me. He keeps following me and won't leave me alone. I barely broke away from him. I thought I was going to crash on a turn. My hands are still shaking slightly. That is what can happen in Goa. Maybe I should go somewhere else for a while? What do you think, Vasiko?"

"You won't believe me, Petya, but I've just told my Lena that I want to go to Thailand for a while. Petya, why don't we go to 'Taika' together? We'll see Bangkok, visit the islands. And from there you'll phone your Goan friends. If no one is looking for you, you can return safely."

***

"What happened to you?" pulling the headphones out of my ears, I ask Petya, who is standing near the entrance to the airport.

"The day before yesterday, I drove a bit drunk and rolled my bike, as I careened off the road. But I got off well, only broke my arm. I thought I would have to cancel Thailand."

"Well, compared to Zhuzha and Seryoga Arambolskiy, of course, you got off lightly. The question is why were you drunk? You don't drink much. Didn't the guys give you an example by their deaths?"

"Yeah, Vasya, you're right. As you say: booze is evil. It's just that in the past we consumed drugs when went to parties, danced one night, or two, or three – it depended on how much you needed it – and then we went to bed. Now where can we go? Well, yesterday I snorted some coke with some pals. We were full of energy, but there was nowhere to put it. That's why we began to cover it with booze. And you know; in that state, no matter how much you drink, it seems like you are still sober. We got sloshed, set off to look for some fun, and I crashed. I'm lucky I wasn't killed. That's how people end up dying in crashes. I didn't know Seryoga Arambolskiy, but Zhuzha was my friend. There is a saying about men like Zhuzha, 'He was the life soul of the party.' Always happy and cheerful, he also didn't booze much before. And when the parties ended, out of boredom he made a moonshine distillery and began to make exotic hooch with banana, mango, papaya. So he died by degustation."

"I saw Zhuzha on the day of his death; he came to my Hemp with two girlfriends to eat Russian food. I couldn't even imagine that I was seeing him for the last time."

"This is a check-in announcement for the flight Goa – Mumbai," a female voice with a strong Indian accent sounds from the speakers.

"Well, Vasya, let's not talk about sad things, Thai adventures await us," Petya says joyfully, heading into the airport.

Mumbai, or Bombay as it was called before, left pleasant memories only because we got completely stoned on the way from the domestic to the international airport. In all other aspects it was an ordinary, dirty, crowded, large Indian city. But after a few hours, Bangkok met us with a pleasant female voice that meowed from the speakers that it was happy to see us on Thai land. The only trouble on this land was that according to their customs regulations, Russia and Ukraine were included in the list of sixteen countries for which one had to buy a special visa on entrance. After standing in line for four hours, we finally entered the land of former pirates and Siamese cats.

"Thailand is a country that has never been conquered," says Petya, coming out of the airport building.

And I felt it in the eyes of every Thai. Unlike other nations, Thai people are proud of their origins. They do not grovel and fawn in front of everyone they meet, like the Indians do. You get the feeling that Thais do not have an inferiority complex. India was conquered and fucked by everyone.

Moguls, Arabs, French, English... After India, where you get used to feeling special, in 'Taika' you quickly realize that you are a guest and that the Thais are the rightful owners of this country. We rush from the airport to the center of the capital in a comfortable, modern bus.

"Look, Vasiko, it's kind of the same Asia, but after flying only a couple of hours, we seem to be in the future. Multi-story roads, skyscrapers, modern cars, it is clean everywhere.

"That's for sure. And also, Petya, sniff the air – it smells of Thai spices and flowers. Almost like in India, but without the shit component."

"Khaosan Road," the bus driver announces, and when we go out onto the street we find ourselves in the former psychedelic center of Thailand.

I would describe this street where the majority of people travelling through Asia gather, as just like Moscow's Arbat[60] if it went through a psychedelic revolution and lost. Having walked a few meters, we immediately meet some Italian and Japanese freaks, friends from Goa. Once traveling on my bike across Russia, I drove from the Black Sea to Lake Baikal (7,000 km) and didn't meet any familiar faces. But here, in Asia, you can easily meet a freak friend, with whom you smoked together somewhere in Goa, Delhi or Rajasthan. Fifteen or twenty years ago you could buy any drug in any quantity on Khaosan Road, but now you can get ten years in a Thai prison for only a few grams of hash. It is surprising, but despite the fact that most of the people around are tipsy, no one emanates aggression or negative energy. The sounds of all kinds of music are heard from everywhere. Street vendors trade briskly, and a huge flow of tourists cheerfully moves from one establishment to another. In the street, you can buy everything a tourist or a novice freak may need. Every fifty meters, the street barbers offer to give us dreadlocks or weave our hair into colorful braids. I love Khaosan Road so much! At every small stall, they offer to make you a fake driver's license for any kind of vehicle, from any country, in just fifteen minutes and for only ten dollars. Dozens of tattoo salons invite you to get a tattoo or piercing. And, of course, the signs advertising the world famous Thai massage are everywhere.

"Maybe we'll go and get stoned first, and then we'll stare?" Petya asks, pulling out a piece of charas from under the plaster cast on his arm.

"Petya, are you crazy?! You brought hash into 'Taika'?"

"Not only hash, I also have a gram of Dymich and a gram of coke under the plaster," Petya says, smiling and holding in his palm the chunk that could get us twenty years in prison here.

"Jesus! You're crazy. Put it back now before the police see it."

"Come on, Vasya, why are you so nervous? We'll check into a hotel and get stoned. We are in Bangkok, dude!"

Having smoked and sniffed a line of MDMA, we go out for an evening walk along Khaosan Road. Thousands of lights in big and small lanterns refracting in a rainbow spectrum, mix with sounds and smells. I'm dressed in fluorescent pink trance clothes and Petya's are all orange; we probably look like two aliens who move by dancing and only stop to take a look at something bright and shiny.

---

[60] Arbat Street - a street in Moscow that is as famous as Broadway in New York.

"Well, Vasiko? Let's do a sex program? Check out all these girls walking around here," Petya points at two cute Thai girls in very short skirts.

"Oh, I don't know. Of course I want to, but I have never cheated on my Lena."

"Who is forcing you to cheat? You'll just use the mouth of a Thai girl once. Here in Southeast Asia, wives themselves bring geishas to their husbands, if for some reason they cannot satisfy their beloved. And you have a good reason. You're on a business trip, you're agitated; I don't think your Lenka would mind. Look how many beautiful women there are in the street tonight."

We sit on the curb, drinking delicious Thai beer and watch the tall, narrow-eyed beauties in short skirts. Seeing our hesitancy, a tall, slender Thai fairy of extraordinary beauty comes up to us and, in silence and with a smile, begins to walk around us.

"Look, Vasiko, she's very young, about eighteen. The nipples on her breasts are still pert. And what noble, refined features. Make up your mind Vasiko," Petya nudges me, not taking his eyes off her.

"Fifty dollars an hour, and I'm yours," the eastern princess says, smiling modestly and looking into our Dymich-stoned eyes.

"What the hell," I agree, taking the sorceress by the hand.

We follow the beautiful girl through some back streets to a brothel, located in a courtyard nearby. After paying the money in advance, I go upstairs with her first to the room, if you can call it that. It is slightly larger than the bed and behind its plywood walls the simulated groans of prostitutes may be heard.

"God, you have such a beautiful body. You should work as a fashion model," I say, watching as the beauty slowly undresses, exposing the small divine charms hidden under her clothes.

Standing only in silk panties, she gently puts a condom on my erect friend with her mouth, while giving me a gentle massage, touching my legs with her young breasts. After trailing her long, dark hair the length of my body, she suddenly devours me, and my skin feels her breath. Her perfect breasts fit snugly in the palms of my hands. I want the point of highest pleasure to never come. But I can't resist it and I feel that I am nearly cumming. Attempts to distract myself by looking at the ceiling do not help. I feel that the moment when all my nerves, having tensed, are about to give me divine pleasure, is very close. It's useless to resist. Slipping my hand under her lacy lingerie and hoping to touch her divine lotus, at the last moment I feel a wave of terror. In my hand, I feel a small dick.

"Let's get the hell out of here, Petya, this is not a chick, it's a transvestite," zipping up on the go, I shout to my friend who is waiting for his turn in a chair in the lobby.

"What do you mean a transvestite?"

"He has a dick in his underpants. And the tits are probably fake."

Bangkok is an amazing city, a city of contrasts. Coming out of an incredibly beautiful Buddhist temple complex, a few meters away you can watch a ping pong show, where ugly middle-aged women perform tricks with their overused genitals on a small stage.

"Petya, what are we doing here?" I say, watching as the Indian tourists in the front row, in the shadows, look longingly at the naked Thai woman shooting peas from a straw sticking out of her vagina.

"Vasiko, we are doing the Thai cultural program. To be in Bangkok and not see a ping pong show is like going to Moscow and not seeing the Mausoleum."

"Why couldn't they hire beautiful young girls for the stage?"

"Vasiko, is there a young girl lying in the Mausoleum or what? Nonetheless, all the foreigners go there to look at the old, dead man. If you don't like overused chicks, watch the Indian tourists at the front – it's also a show."

"That's the only place I've been looking for quite a while."

"Vasiko, look, she has stuck a cigarette in there. And she can even drag on it," Petya says, poking me in the side, his draw dropping in amazement.

When the naked woman lying on the stage with a cigarette in her vagina notices that the nearest table is out of beer, she pulls out the cigarette, which is covered in mucus, and puts it out in the ashtray standing on the table, while illuminating the faces of the elderly German tourists with a flashlight. A few minutes later, the bartender brings more beer for the confused krauts, and having turned off the flashlight above their table, gives a sign to the naked woman on the stage to go on with the show.

It is difficult for a European mind to understand the contrasts of Bangkok. Thai law stipulates the death penalty[61] in the form of an injection of cobra venom in the neck for the sale of even a small amount of drugs. At the same time, a concentrated stimulant that works like an amphetamine is advertised and sold everywhere. This concentrated drink is banned for sale everywhere except Thailand. Since ancient times, the country's population has traditionally consumed a variety of herbal stimulants in order to work tirelessly. Thais are one of the most hardworking people in Asia. And after visiting lazy India, it catches the eye. Through traveling and reading books, I have realized that each country has its own drug. Russia is firmly alcoholic. Since the time of Peter the Great, our rulers have got the people hooked on booze at the state level, turning them into drunken scum, ready to work all day in order to get drunk in the evening and forget themselves. India smokes hash and charas, because they, like the Kagor wine of the Russian Orthodox religion, are practically a part of God. And that's why the whole nation doesn't hurry. Muslim countries such as Afghanistan, Pakistan, Iran, and Syria, consume opium on a massive scale. This drug is also a part of their religious practice, and therefore the people of these countries do not want to do anything, constantly being in a state of divine Barakah[62]. American Indians traditionally consumed psilocybin mushrooms and mescaline cactuses. They quickly evolved spiritually, but they were easily conquered and destroyed by the Spanish, because of

---

[61] In a few years the death penalty will be replaced with imprisonment for a hundred years. An amnesty is given once every three years on the King's birthday, reducing the term to 25 years.

[62] Barakah or Baraka (from Arabic: بَرَكَة) in Islam is the beneficent force from God that flows through the physical and spiritual spheres as prosperity, protection, and happiness. Baraka is the continuity of spiritual presence and revelation that begins with God and flows through that and those closest to God.

the lack of craftiness that is so critical for survival. The barbarians of North European countries drank a decoction of toadstools and, going berserk, rushed fearlessly at their enemies and so conquered new territories. For many centuries, residents of Latin America have warmed their blood with coca leaves, making them more fit for work and aggressive. Knowing the flipside of any drug, you can attempt to explain the abnormal behavior or tendencies of any nation. The use of psychotropic stimulants always leads to an increase in libido, or, in simple terms, under the effect of a stimulant you always want to fuck. The effect of stimulants on the development of the Thai nation is evident immediately. Perhaps that is why Thailand is called the country of sex tourism. Prostitution, homosexuality, transvestites, pedophilia, any sexual perversion – everything is legal, semi-legal, or can be obtained by paying a small amount of money. When we buy tickets to Koh Phangan island, we get acquainted with the owner of the tourist agency, an elderly Jew who left the USSR thirty years ago and spoke Russian tolerably.

"Why would you want to go to Koh Phangan? The trance parties are controlled by the drug police there, and there have been no illegal parties for about ten years. I know where you can find pedophile villages in Thailand. I can sell you a ticket to one of these villages at a cheap rate. There you can rent a girl or boy for a couple of weeks for a few pennies. I do not advise you to take one over eight years; usually by the age of ten they already have the whole complex of sexually transmitted diseases. Poor peasants from the neighboring villages give their children to brothels themselves, because they are unable to feed them. By buying such a child, you give him a chance not to die of hunger. At the age of twelve, they are kicked out of the brothels into the streets like expired goods. And only a few of them survive to adulthood. Unfortunately, this is the harsh reality of Southeast Asia."

"No, thank you," we say in unison. "We have our own children, and we do not feel like having such an experience at all."

Having traveled by train across Thailand and crossed over to Koh Phangan island, we are finally in the land of former pirates.

"Well, here we are, at the famous Full Moon Party," Petya tries to shout over the music, and pulls the gram of Dymich from under his plaster cast.

"But I think we're the only freaks here. Petya, look at the way everyone is staring at our ninja shoes. It seems like everything is trance here: the music, the design, the only thing that is a bit strange is the people."

"Yes, the majority of the people here are sex tourists, they don't care what music they dance to."

Having poured the gram of Dymich into a bottle of water, I gulp down half of it at once.

"Vasiko, I see you are going for it?" Petya says, taking a few sips.

"I want to feel the energy of this island today, I want to do it properly. I have fifteen minutes to examine this reality," I say, flopping onto the soft grass.

"They decorate the parties very well. Just like in Goa, at Hill Top, the palm trees are colored with fluorescent paint, the only thing that is different is that the local artists also worked on the boulders sticking out of the ground. Everything is expertly done. Fluorescent fractal figures braided from yellow and green threads, high-quality batiks with psychedelic paintings. However, what are these rosy-cheeked figures with plastic buckets in their hands doing here? Why are they constantly drinking out of them?"

"Vasya, they are the usual two-week European tourists. You must have got out of the habit of seeing normal tourists in North Goa. They drink alcoholic cocktails: vodka, rum, whiskey, cola, sprite and ice. There is one liter in a bucket. It costs as much as an ecstasy pill."

"And how much does ecstasy cost here?"

"As much as it does elsewhere, pills go for the same price everywhere: from Moscow to Europe. Maybe a quarter less, but no more."

"And do all these people prefer a liter of booze to an ecstasy pill?"

"Vasya, wake up, we are in the twenty-first century, the time of the psychedelic revolution was in the past century. Society prefers alcohol to all drugs."

"Petya, I must be going crazy. I can't get my head around society's choice. It seems to me that the whole world has gone mad. What can all these people think about when they hear trance music? They don't care what kind of music they move to on the dance floor. To be honest, the MDMA is starting to bring me up. Let's go to dance," I call Petya, who is sprawled on the grass, "Come on, let's show them some real Goan freaks."

"No, Vasya, somehow I still feel too uncomfortable to dance among these perverted mugs, I would rather lie here a bit longer."

"Well, I'm off, I desperately want to get on the dance floor."

Before even reaching my destination, I abruptly start to feel the world around me begin to transform, adjusting my perception to only positivity and vibrations of love. The drunken mugs don't stand out any more. My perception refuses to see them. I see the world only from its best, most beautiful side. I am wearing pink trance pants and a yellow fluorescent cape like a psychedelic Batman would have, which follows me as I move quickly among the dancers. It seems like I am soaring above the dance floor, watching the movements of my body. It is as if my body is trying to draw a huge hieroglyph across the radius of the dance floor, and to decorate it with the colorful traces that my glow-in-the-dark clothes leave in the air. This giant hieroglyph is visible only to me. I repeat this hieroglyph over and over again, making magic passes with my hands in an attempt to understand the meaning of this sign. The music is so beautiful that it seems that if it were to stop right now, I would probably die. It's impossible to stop. Pausing for a moment to sip some water, I discover that I am immediately surrounded by several transvestites, who insistently try to grab my dick or pinch my ass. Each of them, competing with one another, offers me to go private with him in the nearby bushes. For the first time in my life, I'm in a position where the majority around me has a different sexual orientation. Having grown up in working-class neighborhoods and raised on concepts like 'real men aren't fags', for the first time I don't know how to react to this invasion of my personal space. But the solution is found fast. Why should I need aggression, if there is dance? Dance is like a dynamic meditation, in which all of the factors that annoy me break down into molecules. Only the most beautiful things are left, flowing around me at high speed. All of the negative dissolves into a white light. The feeling is that I'm in a racing train and someone colored everything behind the window with fluorescent paint. The world seems both very bright and vague at the same time. At some point, I realize that I don't exist any longer in the usual sense, in the way I am used to perceiving myself. The self to which I am accustomed does not exist; there is the realization that I am a part of this beautiful world. I am a particle of the Earth, and not even just of the Earth, but of the entire Universe, and not just a particle – I am the Universe. And there are actually no parts at all; there is only the Universe – harmonious, living, pulsating. From the awareness of the integrity of myself and of the Universe, I begin to experience an immensely powerful orgasm. Not the simple kind of physiological orgasm that a person experiences during the peak of sexual pleasure, but an orgasm a thousand time stronger, that has nothing to do with sex. Shivers run continuously throughout my body, and it goes on and on. Convulsions of huge pleasure roll over me to the beat of trance music. It's not me who is controlling my body now; the Universe is dancing through me.

"Vasya!" Petya yells in my ear, trying to get through to me, "maybe it's time for you to rest a little? From the side, it seems that you've been having a continuous orgasm for about thirty minutes. Let's go and lie on the grass, or you'll pass out. You've taken almost a gram of MDMA tonight. This dose could easily knock out an unprepared, normal person. It's dawn already and you have been dancing non-stop all night."

His words of reason gradually bring me back to my senses.

"Petya, you right are, my body needs to rest."

We stretch out on the trampled green grass, eating two ripe, juicy mangos. My hands continue to move to the beat of the music. Sometimes I catch myself thinking that I even drink and swallow to the tune of the music. The orgasmic waves continue to run throughout my body periodically. As it begins to get light, I notice that the crowd surrounding me has completely changed. Drunk from the night before, the sex tourists lie asleep in the arms of transvestites and prostitutes, and out of nowhere on the dance floor there have appeared beautiful people dressed in elegant trance clothes. With sunrise comes the heat. The smiling DJ, who appears to be in a daze from happiness, turns up the volume and gives sign to a Thai standing near a tap that supplies water to lawn sprayers, which are mounted on braces between the tops of palm trees over the heads of the dancers. The pumping crowd merges into a single happy cry, expressing the joy of the Victory of light over darkness.

"Hello, lads, what brings you here?" I hear a familiar Russian voice.

Near to where we lay, dancing and smiling joyfully, are Vlad Lenk, Fox, Alina, Zont, and our Nepalese-Australian psychedelic old man, DJ Psy Rico.

"Fancy meeting you here, that's unexpected!" Petya exclaims, rising from the earth and wiping the mango juice off his hands onto the grass.

"Time really flies; the last time I saw you was in Nepal six months ago. You are the only living people for us now. Petya and I had started to think that we were the only freaks here. Since evening, it seemed that only perverts gather here."

"Vasya, the freaks only come to the parties in the morning. In the evening it's simply unbearable to have to look at all the drunken perverts," says Vlad, sitting down nearby.

"I've already got that. When will you come to us in Goa? Vlad, you haven't been to India for a couple of years. Don't you miss it?"

"To hell with Goa and Rashka. I have found my Paradise – it is Koh Phangan. I am satisfied with everything here."

"And I bought a load of different electronics on credit in Rashka for a total of twenty thousand bucks. I sold them quickly and came here," Fox's always-cheerful girlfriend, Alina, interrupts us with a smile. "Now I have a good reason to stay here forever."

"Alina, what do you think about India?"

"There are only drug addicts, alcoholics and grasses in India. I don't want to go there anymore. Alex Zheltok barely managed to escape, and he was the first Russian restaurateur, a well-known character in Goa. Someone just grassed on him. It's good that his people warned him. A warrant for his arrest had already been issued, but he managed to get out of India almost at the last minute. And Hanuman? He was wanted by the Goan cops when he came here. Our own people, Russians, grass to the police."

"Alina, I think you are slightly exaggerating. I live there and everything seems calm. Of course, there are less normal people, but Goa is still alive. You say that Russian informants work for the police. Do you know even one by name?"

"Vasya, you are so naive, when you go back to Goa, rack your brains and think a bit. Whom haven't the police touched for many years? Why are other people banned from throwing parties? Who holds the best parties? It's likely that he is that one. However, you can't touch such people, because all of the dirty work is done by their pushers. And they always come out as clean as a whistle."

"Those are the laws of this business," Zont adds with a smile, pulling a rolled joint from his pocket. "And here, there are no grasses for now. Here the passengers are more serious too, because your life is at stake. They'll shoot a grass without blinking."

"Vlad, what do you think about Rashka? Has it been a long time since you were in the motherland?"

"Vasya, they are grassing on each another in Rashka too. For that reason I stopped taking charas there; now I bring it here."

"You're a desperate man; you could get the top punishment, an injection of cobra venom in the neck."

"Vasya, don't you worry, I have a profitable connection with God, he protects me," Lenk says, smiling and pointing at the sky.

"And how is Hanuman doing here? I saw him at the beginning of the season, he left Goa with paranoia."

"We see him from time to time. He gave up cocaine, exercises, teaches yoga to tourists, reads a lot of Buddhist literature; he doesn't go to parties anymore. But as for us, you can regularly see us in the morning, either here or in some other cool places. You came to the right party. Vasya, let's go, I'll show you some really serious guys. Suckers don't come here in the morning, only serious characters come out at this time. Do you see that group of guys with dreadlocks dancing on the right over there? They are Dominican boys, very serious passengers. They control the supply of cocaine. I advise you to stay away from them. They do not sniff coke themselves, but they'll kill any competitor, even though they look like ordinary freaks. And there, can you see the guy in the pink robe, rubbing up against a young boy? Although he is a fag, he controls the red light district in Amsterdam, with all the prostitutes and drug dealers. He doesn't even touch drugs himself, but he does serious deals. A dozen 'camels' work for him. He has had some more plastic surgery, and now he is resting on the island. Although he looks as if he is forty years old, in fact he's about seventy. Look how he is hitting on that guy."

Pausing, I watch as a stout man in a pink hat and a long, knee-length pale pink robe is trying to pull a skinny young man. The young man pretends not to notice that the strange man dancing next him is hitting on him. The guy pretends to scrutinize the DJ and lazily swings one hip.

The old pervert stands back to back with the young man, as if looking at something in the opposite direction, and begins to swing one thigh, occasionally slightly touching his buttocks to the young guy's. After a few minutes of such foreplay, he takes the young man by the hand, and they are dancing in sync, still looking in opposite directions.

"That young fag didn't play hard to get for long," Lenk laughs and leads me across the dance floor.

"And do you see those serious Thais over there, not smiling or dancing? They are the local boys. They sell ecstasy, Dymich and ganja here."

"Well, and we are the Russian mafia," adds Zont, smiling as he walks next to me, "we sell Nepali charas and LSD. Everybody knows each other here, and there are no grasses. No one pokes their nose into anyone else's business. Vasya, do you know why? Here, in the country of former pirates, no one will joke around. They'll bump you off without hesitation, and then throw your body into the sea. Because everyone knows: the price at stake is their lives."

For a while we dance in silence, looking at the different characters gathered in the morning at this place. Zont is at the DJ console, playing his favorite morning trance music.

"How is Romashka doing in Nepal? Have you heard anything, Vasya?" Fox asks me, stomping his foot to the trance beat.

"I guess he is still in jail, he was given two years."

"What about you, Fox? Have you asked Zont whether he is helping Romashka? When I last talked to Romashka, he was angry at Zont. You know that Romashka took the blame upon himself; while Zont, as soon as he got out, immediately ran to Thailand, even though he had promised to help."

"What do you mean 'help'?" Lenk cuts into our conversation. "It seems to me that Zont has flipped. Firstly, after jail he stole Romashka's girlfriend. Vasya, I will show you her later. She is a former Israeli sniper; she was shot in the leg during the war. She leads a wonderful life on her state pension here. Well, she is now pregnant with Zont's child. And Zont takes between three to five drops of LSD per day; I've been afraid of him recently. Sometimes he talks nonsense, confusing reality with his hallucinations. He proposes either cheating the Dominicans out of money or shafting the Thai carriers out of ecstasy, and sometimes he starts yammering something about God. He has definitely gone out of his mind, it will come to no good."

"That's not surprising considering how much acid he takes," I say, scrutinizing Zont's insane face at the DJ console.

"Vasya, do you remember Andrey Red, the former lawyer? He hung out with us in Nepal? He flipped because of acid too. First, he accused us of being fags, then he had an obsessive-paranoid idea that everyone wanted to fuck him, so he began to run away from everyone. In the end he fled to Sri Lanka. Now he is on the booze. Vasya, I think that our Kazan friend Andryukha just saw too many fags while tripping, there are loads of them here, and after that his feminine side twitched."

"What do you mean?" I ask Lenk, watching as the fag in the pink robe touches the young guy's ass.

"Well. We all have the Yin and Yang, feminine and masculine. There is no person who is a hundred percent man or woman. Men can be gentle and affectionate, and women can be brave, like the Amazonians. Depending on the amount of masculinity or femininity, we feel a belonging to homo- or hetero-sexuality. Andryukha's balance twitched. Rather than accepting himself as he is, he was frightened and invented an unseen enemy in the form of a global homosexual conspiracy. Recently, I've been reading the work of a German nineteenth century philosopher, Otto Weininger. His book is called 'Sex and Character'. He convincingly explains the reasons for all sexual deviations, describing the basic problems of gender relations. The only pity is that this guy, who wrote such a work, hung himself at the age of twenty-one after refusing to accept the imperfection of sexual relations."

"Vlad, I'll definitely borrow this book from you to read. In Goa, we have a character with similar symptoms too, Vanya Chelyabinskiy. After gorging himself on acid, Dymich and coke, he started accusing us of some sort of conspiracy. It seems he grew up as a regular tough guy, but he came up to me once at a party and asked, 'Vasya, I don't why, but each time I look in Freak Stephen's eyes, I get so sexually aroused. Maybe he wants to fuck me?'"

"Vasya, we had the same shit here with Andryukha. These guys don't know where to draw the line with drugs; their minds explode. Only a few become normal again."

Chapter 33. Part One. Inside.

Slouching on the stairs, I watch as the Japanese guy and the Nepalese guy walk along hand in hand, like husband and wife.

"Vitya, I still find the concepts here in Asia rather strange. In our Russian jails, everything is much tougher. Nobody cares about your sexual orientation here, and in fact, no one makes any conclusions if two men walk around holding hands."

"Vasya, why aren't you running circles around the yard? Have you calmed down a bit?" says Viktor, smiling and pointing at the Scott.

"I eased off a bit," I say, laughing as I watch our Scott, James, walk past at high speed.

"Not too long ago you were walking around angrily in in circles too."

"The weather is good today, I don't feel like walking in circles. I'll sunbathe a bit."

We lie on the steps in front of Viktor's cell and idly observe what is going on around. After a long stay in the small cell, any new actions draw your attention like a magnet.

"Vitya, they resemble monkeys so much," I point at a group of young robbers who are focused on picking lice out of each other's heads. "I have watched monkeys do that in nature many times. I really don't want to catch lice while I'm in here."

"Vasya, don't be afraid and everything will be fine. And if you think about it, you can be sure that you'll catch them."

"Viktor, you've started thinking like an Indian," I say angrily, looking at the white marks left by fungus on my shoulders. "I've been trying to get rid of this fungus for two months. I contracted it from these monkeys, but I didn't think about it at all."

"Vasya, have I told you that I have half Indian blood?"

"No, you haven't. How can that be? Do you have Indian relatives?"

"No, it's not about relatives. It's just that a year ago I was seriously hooked on drugs here. Back then I used everything: coke, acid and Dymich. I completely stopped paying attention to my health, I didn't take care of my body. I ate bad stuff and my intestine ruptured, resulting in septicemia of the blood. I barely survived. They put me in hospital for surgery here in Goa, and I received a blood transfusion. Some Indian donated blood. Since then I've had Indian blood. Vasya, I really began to look at many things differently after the transfusion. Maybe because I was almost at the death's door, or maybe I got some information along with the blood."

"Vitya, I've noticed that. I will only walk in slippers on the spit-covered floor and I watch where I step, but you happily walk barefoot on spit and snot and don't even think about it. And your philosophy is like that of the Indians, 'There is no yesterday and no tomorrow, the only existing time is today'. Vitya, you probably know that in the Hindu language there are no words for 'yesterday' and 'tomorrow'. There is only the word 'today'."

"Of course I know. Not only do I know it, but I can also feel it," Viktor laughs, tearing a wing from a fly he has just caught.

"Look, Borish has also come to warm himself in the sun," I point at the Turkish artist, who looks like John Lennon. "Hi, Borish!"

"Dobra vodka!" the ever cheerful young Turk responds, greeting us.

"We haven't seen you in a long time."

"I have recently begun to sleep in the daytime and draw at night. I have depression. I've been sitting here for a whole month and there are no changes or news about my case."

"Oh, Borish, stop it with your 'depression'. No one has ever been in jail for more than a month for a visa overstay of six months."

"I'm still afraid. Felix got three years for this."

"Do not compare yourself to Felix. Firstly, Felix is African. About a hundred of them live here without visas, and secondly, his visa expired three years ago, and he also has one escape from the police. And you should be released today or tomorrow. You'll pay a fine of three hundred dollars and get out. Yelisei had a six month overdue visa too, and in addition an escape from the psychiatric hospital, but he paid a fine and was set free."

"Yelisei is crazy, it's easier for the judge to get rid of such people, as there will be less problems. But I am normal, or so it seems to me," Borish laughs, making a face like an idiot. "I don't like the fact that my lawyer didn't appear in the court twice."

"Borish, where did you find this lawyer?" Viktor asks in surprise, crushing the sentenced, wingless fly on the floor with his finger.

"Ashpak, your jail mobster, gave me his number. He said that he is the best lawyer in Goa. I paid him my last thousand dollars. He hasn't appeared in the court for a month. So I'm nervous because I have no more money."

Chapter 33. Part Two. Outside.

"Hi, Mulik. Finally, at least one of my old friends came to Goa. How long has it been since we last saw each other?" I say, hugging my friend.

"Hello, Vasya, I am glad to see you, too. We haven't seen each another since you left Rashka. You look good. By the way, this is Lucy, my girlfriend. We came here together."

"Nice to meet you," I extend my hand to a tall blonde with big blue eyes and a long dark-blond braid.

My friend, a scrawny man almost a head shorter than her, looks like her little brother. I've known Valera, nicknamed 'Mulik', for ten years now. Long ago when I had my tattoo saloon, he worked for me, piercing people's ears, nostrils, navels and other unusual places for money. Mulik, just like me, happily consumed soft drugs at that time and visited all the parties and open airs together with our crowd. At that time, we especially liked psychedelic fishing. Having bought a gram of amphetamine and a pack of weed in the evening, we used to get in my boat and sail along the creeks all night. We would find some extraordinarily beautiful island or bay and listen to intellectual music, talk about religion, philosophy and world order. Mulik, just like me, was fond of psychedelic literature and spent his free time reading books by Wilson and McKenna. We discussed books, sniffing a line of amphetamine from time to time, all night long. And in the morning at early dawn, stoned and high, we caught big pikes and perches, getting terrific fun from all of this. Having heard my stories about the Promised Land on my return from India, Valera, like most of my friends, had a great desire to go to Goa. But unlike all the others, he did everything he could to get here.

"Well, tell me, Mulik, how did it happen that you had to flee from Russia with a someone else's passport?"

"Vasya, I still can't fully believe it, everything was like in some dream. Since you had gone to India for good, I started dabbling in drugs. Nothing serious: ecstasy, amphetamine, weed. I helped my party-going friends get everything they needed. I was mixed up with it for two years without any hassle. And then, somehow my sales turnover increased to ten thousand bucks a month without me noticing. My customer network grew so rapidly that I began to deliver drugs from morning till evening. I was living the good life. I thought that I would earn a little bit more and then go to Goa to retire. I just needed to earn one hundred thousand bucks, buy some real estate, rent it out, and live here happily on the money. But one day the cops came to my house and showed me a video, or rather three different recordings made with a hidden camera, where you could see me selling ecstasy. They took my goods in the sum of ten thousand bucks and said, 'And now, brother, you will work for us. Now you have to pay us every month and grass on your friends one by one. Otherwise, we'll lock you up for ten years.' And they showed me a list of names and surnames of all of our psychedelic bros who hung out in the clubs. The cops took my passport and gave me a week to bring them ten thousand bucks for the first time. It was then that I decided to flee the country. I have a bro in Russia who looks like me. I pierced his ears, gave him centimeter wide tunnels, trimmed his beard – in a word, I made him look like me, and then photographed him. With this photo, he went to the visa and registration office and got an international passport. And then I crossed three borders with his passport: first I lived in Ukraine for a while, hoping that the cops would forget about me. But a month later I found out that the police had started looking for me and submitted my name to the all-Russia wanted list. Then me and Lyuska decided to get a ferry from Ukraine to Turkey, and they nearly caught us at the border. The border guard kept going on about the shape of my skull, saying that it was different in reality and in the picture, but Lucia saved the day. She made up a story about an operation on my skull, which I allegedly had following a car accident. As there was a long queue at the harbor, the guard gave up on us and let us cross the border. So we found ourselves in Istanbul. There we ran out of money while we were waiting a week for Indian visas. I had to sell my laptop and camera. And as for the Turkish and Indian border guards, we are like the Chinese to them – we all look the same. So we crossed the border quickly without any questions. No one examined the photos in the passports. Vasya, we have already been waiting for you for about a week in Goa, your Lenka said that you went to Thailand. What is it like there?"

"Well, Mulik, it's good, but it's too early for us to go there. Although everything is pretty cheap, you spend twice as much money. There is a wide range of pleasures you can spend money on. It is in India that you don't have anywhere to spend your cash, but in Thailand there are so many temptations that it is impossible to resist. But, most importantly, the people there are not like here. Here you feel at home, and there you feel like a guest. To earn money there through drugs you need huge balls, because you risk your life, and our bollocks have not grown that big yet. Look, there is a gypsy on the beach trying to sell something to a fat white tourist. You see, he's scared and doesn't know how to get rid of her, and he is ready to buy anything for her to just to get her to go away. In Thailand all of the tourists are like that, there are very few freaks."

"Vasya, we realized that Goa is the place for us in just a week. We will live here now. By the way, Vasya, do you have any work? We borrowed some money from your Lena, we need money desperately."

"Don't worry, Mulik, we'll find you a job. You can be the manager of my restaurant if you want. It's not big money, but I am ready to give you half of the profit, if you do the job instead of me. The main income here is the same as everywhere else – from drugs. You can earn five hundred dollars legally, and if you go to the parties, then you can earn about a thousand bucks."

"I wouldn't like to sell drugs again, but I have no choice. When is the next party?"

***

Arriving at Paradiso on eight scooters, we park, and I once again explain to the newly arrived tourists how to get into the club without paying money.

"Your clothes and hairstyles are freaky, so you do not have to pay anything," I say to my friends, who stand in a semicircle. "This is our culture, trance music is our life, people like us brought trance to this land. Fuck these damn Indians, we are not paying them anything. If we – the freaks – don't come here, then who will go to their club? Fishermen and peasants? They can make money on the two-week tourists," I indignantly tell Mulik, forgetting that almost all of my tenants, who are only staying for two weeks, are with me. "I'll go in first, then you make serious faces and walk in."

After going into the club first and not paying a penny, I watch as Mulik and the other newly arrived tourists hesitantly mumble something to the guards. A minute later, the whole crowd turns towards the cash desk to pay for tickets. Despite their trance clothes and trendy Goan haircuts, they fail to trick the skilled security guards, who can tell the difference between tourists and the freaks who live here just by looking at them.

"Well, what went wrong? Couldn't you tell the guards convincingly that you live here and that the party is your home? That's all, my tourists; I leave you here. Enjoy, dance, and if you run out of drugs, find me or Dan on the dance floor."

"We told the guards everything, but probably not as confidently as you did," Mulik's girlfriend says guiltily.

"Don't worry, you'll pay a few times, and then you will learn how to get in for free. I will go and say hello to the Chelyabinsk lads. They are no longer two-week tourists; at least I can talk with them about something."

"Well, then I'll go and show Mulik the club," says Dan, heading to the chill-out, where the chai-mamas sit.

"Hey dudes, you are partying hard today," I say to the three guys stripped to the waist.

"Yes, today's party is cool. Today our homeboy Shelsik is playing, do you know him?" continuing to dance, Zhenyok shouts in my ear, trying to be heard over the music from the speakers.

"Of course I know him, he's from Tamir's crowd. Shelsik is a very good DJ."

"Vanya, how are you?" I say to a bald guy, dancing with fucked-up eyes.

"Vasya, I'm fine. And as for your conspiracy with Kirill Morozov... I understood about it long ago. But you won't manage it," Vanya tells me, leering, evidently thinking that I understand what he means.

"Ok, I got it, Vanya. No more questions for you."

"Zhenya, is he still going out of his mind?"

"Yes," says Zhenyok, smiling and turning his back towards Vasya. "Although it isn't funny at all, but we can't do anything about it. Vanya is suffering from paranoia from the drugs. He accuses everyone of being involved in a conspiracy. We've already told him to take a break for at least a week, but he doesn't listen to us. He takes something every day. By the way, Vasya, this is my friend. His name is Sergey, he is a Chelyabinsk Shivite too."

"Nice to meet you," says a guy with a simple Russian face, extending his hand to me. "I want to thank you very much."

"For what?"

"We stocked up on your drugs from Dan yesterday; I have never seen such quality. It seems that all the drugs we get in Chelyabinsk are already diluted."

"Sergey, thank you for your kind words; I consume the same drugs, so I buy the best. And dilution of drugs is not my thing. Let's go and have a chillum," I suggest, turning towards the chill out.

"No, we can't do that now, we have already taken half of a gram of MDMA; it's already impossible to stop. By the way, what a fantastic track is playing now. We'll come and find you later when it eases off."

"By the way, Vasya, who is that dancing near the speakers?" Zhenyok asks me, pointing at a white-haired old man jumping about like a youngster.

"Oh, that's Oleg from Odessa, he has already been jumping about here for eight years."

"Vasya, we have been watching that gray-haired old man dancing for a while, and he is always near the speakers. He is also constantly spinning iron balls in his hands. Do you know what they are?"

"That's how he meditates; you see, he is in a trance. Zhenya, why are you asking about him?"

"Oh, it's just I saw how the police dragged him out of the club at the last party by the hair. We thought they would send him down, but here he is jumping about again. No party happens without him."

"Okay, party on, guys, I'll go and take something too. See you later."

Approaching our mat, I see Dan is making lines of MDMA on a plate with his driver's license.

"Does anyone want some?" he asks, addressing all those sitting around.

"Oh, what is it?" asks Olya, a cute girl of about thirty who has recently started living in our house. "I have only tried cocaine and ecstasy."

"Well, if you have tried them, then you sure can have it. This is the purest ecstasy in your life."

Having snorted a line, I immediately take a smoking chillum from the hands of Lyokha Sponsor.

"Khatam, Lyokha, You need to clean it." I say, pulling a safi and stick out of my bag.

"Vasya, I'm about to explode. Clean the chillum for me; Tamir is at the decks now. In the meantime, I'll go for a dance. Just don't leave it unattended; it's my favorite chillum," Lyokha yells as he runs off.

Putting the chillum in the middle of the mat, I start to wrap a safi around the carved stick made of mahogany.

"Vasya, why are they staring at us? Are they cops?" Mulik says, pointing at two suspicious Indians in black trousers and lacquered leather shoes.

Coming closer to us, one of them bends down and picks up Lyokha's chillum.

"Who is the owner of this chillum?"

Realizing that they are police, no one dares to take responsibility for the contents of our table.

"What's the problem?"

Getting up, I try to snatch Lyokha's chillum from the hands of the Indian cop. Out of the corner of my eye, I see that Dan manages to brush away the few remaining lines from the plate with his hand.

"Come with us, we need to talk to you, we are the police."

As we leave the club, the policeman immediately starts searching my pockets. As long as they don't open my old Kodak camera, packed with enough drugs to get me ten years in jail.

"What is this?" the cop shows me the tola of charas that he has found in my pocket and which I hid there as a distraction for just such cases.

"This is illegal in Goa, we have to arrest you."

Having found the camera in my bag, he shakes it near his ear, not daring to open it.

"Sir, you must come with us to the police station."

"Maybe you'll take money?"

"No, sir, we have to arrest you," the second cop tells me with a serious face, grabbing me firmly by the elbow.

I start to put on a show, the final of which is already clear. I have to bluff that I don't have much money, and agree to go to the police station. They won't take me there, anyway. Fifteen minutes of negotiations on the way to the police station and I manage to buy my freedom for fifteen thousand rupees.

"There, take it, there is only thirteen here," I stretch out a bunch of crumpled bills, knowing that I only have seven.

The policeman, returning me the chillum, puts the money in his pocket quickly without counting it and, having hastily shaken my hand, walks away.

"Well, thank God; we were already thinking of going to the police station to rescue you."

"Thank you for covering for me," Dan tells me, getting out another gram of MDMA. "If I was taken instead of you, I would not have got away with it; you can find pretty much everything in my bag."

"Dan, how many times have I told you to buy an Indian camera for five dollars and stash everything in it. The days when you can store everything in your pocket are over. And you, Mulik, buy one too, it is for your own safety."

"Hey Vasya, what's the fuss? I saw how you were taken away by those two. Were they police?"

"Hi Ibrahim, everything is ok," I extend my hand to a scrawny freak with bulging eyes and long black hair pulled back to his crown.

As always, a bunch of beautiful young girls is hanging around Ibrahim, waiting for him to start smoking freebase[63] or unpack one more gram of cocaine. Ibrahim does not sell drugs in Goa. He is an ideological preacher of cocaine here. Having read somewhere that the Mayans predicted that the end of the world would take place in 2012, Ibra began preparing for it. He stopped leading a normal, social life, and began looking for a way to spend the remaining time before the end of the world rationally. Having tried all kinds of drugs, he realized that cocaine is all he needed. After talking to Ibra for fifteen minutes, no one could doubt that he sincerely believed in the end of the world as predicted by the wise Mayans.

"Vasya, did you give the cops a lot of money?"

"Just a little, Ibra. About two hundred bucks in total."

"What did they find?"

"One tola of charas. I always have one in my pocket as a distraction for them, so that they don't search deeper. It's relatively cheap to buy yourself off for a tola, whereas in my camera I have two hundred drops of LSD, ten grams of Dymich and thirty grams of hash. If I was taken to the police station, they could open the camera there."

"Well, I wouldn't have given more than twenty dollars for one tola," Ibra says, boasting and stroking the thigh of a young sorceress sitting next to him.

"That will do, Ibra, don't rub salt into the wound, I would like to forget about it as quickly as possible, as I could have gone to jail, but you keep reminding me about it."

"Do you want to some freebase? It's on me."

"Oh, Ibra, Ibrahim, I have asked you a thousand times not to offer me or my friends your devilish drug. I have not met anyone who, having tried it, would refuse to try it for a second time. But I have seen dozens of people like you, who smoke it every half an hour, day and night. And when they don't have freebase, they experience bouts of paranoia and manic depression. You not only want to die by 2012, but you are also dragging young people along with you."

---

[63] Freebase - 'crack', crystalline cocaine.

"You're right, Vasya," Mulik chips in, trying to calm me down. "While you were dealing with the cops, I tried freebase for the first time. The feelings are very nice, but they last only ten minutes and then you want more."

"It's not just 'nice', but devilishly pleasant," Ibra adds, smiling. "One drag and straight to hell. It's the best feeling in the world. As if you become the center of the Universe and everything is spinning around you and only for you. Vasya, what is preventing you from getting the thrill of crack every half an hour? Sell divine coke and you will always have the thrill. There is no future. Tomorrow never come. In 2012, the Sun, having increased in size one million times, will explode and swallow the planet. Enjoy the present day. Shelsik is coming over. He will support me, he knows more about the Apocalypse."

Ceasing to preach, Ibra points to a guy with a severe, rarely smiling face who is walking in our direction.

"He is going to ask me about Number One again."

"Hello, psychedelic bros, do you have any Number One?" not even having said hello properly, Shelsik immediately asks Ibrahim.

"I've run out of coke," Ibra begins making excuses with a serious, unhappy face.

"And I never had it. You know, Shelsik, I don't touch it because I don't like it. I can get you first class Nepalese charas; you have never tried anything like it," I say, holding out a soft tola, flattened into a pancake.

"No, Vasya, I have my own basic principles, I don't smoke Nepali charas. The Nepalese don't know how to make it. I only smoke charas from Manali. By the way, how do you find the new music? Or were you zoned here and didn't hear anything?"

"No, of course not. The music today is very cool, you and Tamir are the best DJs and your music is the best," Ibra's girlfriends begin making compliments.

"Thank you girls. Come next week, I'll be playing again. Well, now I'll go and snort some Number One somewhere. Keep on partying."

"I'm going to go for a little walk, too," Ibra says, standing up. Three cute girls in short skirts quickly leap from their places to follow him.

"Vasya, Vasya, I feel so good right now, like never before," running up to me, Olya suddenly grabs my arm. Her eyes look like those of a naughty slut during orgasm. "Vasya, I felt so good until a guy bought me a bottle of beer. I think he slipped something into it. I am so scared, stay with me, don't leave me alone."

"And why do think that he slipped you something? Did you see it with your own eyes?"

"No, I didn't, it's just he looked into my eyes in such a way that it made me scared. I don't know what to expect. I read in the books that it happens, people get spiked with different substances. What will happen to me now?"

"Olya, nothing is going to happen to you. In the most extreme case you could get fucked in the bushes somewhere at your own request."

"Well, I'm not afraid of that."

"Well, if you are not afraid, then go and dance before that guy who treated you to a beer finds someone else."

"Thank you, Vasya, you've calmed me down, now I feel better than ever!" kissing me on the cheek, Olya runs away, waving her hands.

"In my opinion, just like Vanya, she has had enough drugs. Do not sell her anymore, Dan."

After the night's adventures I don't want to take anything else now.

"Does anyone want some rum?" I say, pushing aside a glass of unfinished tea.

We are the last guests in the club and sit lounging on big leather sofas near the bar. The has already risen, forcing us to move into the shade. All of our group, being drunk and stoned, is still having fun, half-sitting, half-lying, not wanting the party to stop. The music was switched off long ago, but the bartender is still happy to serve us drinks. Chillums are puffed non-stop. Sprawling on a sofa, I hug Lena with one arm and Ilka with the other. Here it is, the Indian nirvana, a celebration of life that never ends. And even if death comes soon, it is not the end, because we are young, drunk and happy. 'Tomorrow never come,' repeats in my mind like a flash of enlightenment. And all this is covered with waves of MDMA, causing pleasant goose bumps throughout my body.

"Who is that pointing at us from the second floor?" Ilka asks laughing, drunk and merry and trying to focus her vision. Shelsik is standing on the club's roof terrace explaining something to an Indian, gesticulating and occasionally pointing at our group.

"Don't worry, Ilka, he is one of us; that's DJ Shelsik. And as for the Indian in the lacquered shoes; I've seen him somewhere before," I explain in a drunk, slurred manner.

"Let's go to our balcony and throw an afterparty," someone with no place in the shade on the couch proposes.

"We'll smoke now and then go," smiling, Dan lights another chillum.

It becomes very hot.

Chapter 34. Part One. Inside.

"My girls will be coming soon. Time flies... almost half a year has passed already. Vitya, they say that the season has started outside – the first party took place at Hill Top."

"Vasya, what sort of parties are they?" Viktor asks angrily, ceasing to swing his hand-made jail pois. "From six to ten in the evening; they're for kids."

"Vitya, this is our reality today. You only start dancing and it's time to go home. Parties at Hill Top used to be held for two or three days in a row. And what kind of party can it be, where ninety percent of the crowd consists of Indian tourists who don't care what music they jump about to. You can't dance with them normally. They stand in front of you and scrutinize you, pointing their fingers."

"Well, fuck those parties, I am fed up with them. When I get out, I'll think about whether to go to them or not. There is no freak community any more."

"Vitya, tell me what would you like the most? What would you do if you were released now?"

"I would buy oysters and eat them raw."

"Well, Vitya, I wish I had your desires."

"Vasya, I would also swim in the sea. And visit my mother, but not for long, just for a couple of weeks. She is old, she doesn't know I am in jail; she thinks I'm in the Himalayas learning English."

"Well, I don't want any food. I'm used to the food they serve here. And if there is nothing else, then you can even get pleasure from rice and peas. Especially when you are very hungry."

"I agree, Vasya. But I still really want oysters."

"I'm starting to feel hungry, Vitya. Let's stop talking about food. Tell me this: aren't you afraid of loneliness?"

"Vasya, I used to be afraid of it, but now I am not. All my life I was afraid of being alone and did everything I could to end up alone. Of course, I didn't do it on purpose, that's just the way it turned out. All my life I had a pain somewhere here," poking his chest, for a while Viktor looks like a hero volunteering to go off to war at the front. "And now when I am left alone, nothing hurts. All my life I wanted to get rid of this pain, and I could only manage it when I was as drunk. And here in jail, I've realized that all my life I didn't have love, but rather a sense of ownership. Our stupid sense of ownership and self-importance are to blame for everything. We want to own everything. For the last ten years I had a girlfriend. I thought I loved her, and I was sure that the feelings were mutual. But as soon as the police arrested me, my beloved took my hidden stash of three thousands bucks and fled to Thailand, leaving me here alone. At first I was very sad that everyone had abandoned me. I sat here for three months until you got locked up. Not one bitch visited me. And then I felt an extraordinary lightness. Lightness from the fact that I didn't need to take care of anyone. And no one has to take care of me. Nobody will take care of me better than I can. And I realized one more thing in here: no one forbids me from loving everyone that I love without possessing them. And now I love my girlfriend from a distance without owning her. So what do we have? I earned the three thousand that she stole in order to spend it on her; it's just that I wanted to spend the money the way I considered correct. I thought that I earned the money so that she would love me more. But love cannot be enhanced by money. You can only get someone to love you by loving them unconditionally; there is no other way. When you don't try to possess a person, but just love them, then that person loves you simply for that. Vasya, all my life I was scared of losing what I possessed. And now I do not want to possess anyone; I want to live for myself. All my life I lived for someone else, and now I just want to love and don't want to demand anything in return. And, first and foremost, I want to love myself. Because if I don't love myself who will want to love me?"

"That's all true," I agree, having waited until Viktor has finished his emotional speech. "But apart from unconditional love there is also conditional love. Every woman needs to be courted and be wooed. Every woman wants to be possessed."

"Yeah, and she wants to be the only one that is possessed," Viktor adds, mysteriously raising his index finger into the sky. "And that, Vasya, is not love, that is where this stupid sense of ownership is born. After all, we are all alone by our nature. We came into this world owning nothing and we'll leave it the same way. So in this world it's better to love without possessing or demanding anything. After all, once we possess someone or something, over time this love fades away. After that, our hearts start to hurt, sending us signals that we are do something wrong. I only ceased feeling this pain here in jail, when I had absolutely nothing else to possess. Vasya, the first few months I sat here and was very angry with my girlfriend; the anger almost ate me away from within. It was only when I was able to let go of the grip of ownership, that I started to enjoy my love for her. And now when I think of her, I love her, not hate her. Maybe she is somewhere with someone else now. But when you love, you are ready to give everything, just for the object of your adoration to be happy. That's why, Vasya, I am not afraid of loneliness. We are all alone on this planet, and I've understood that it is much more pleasant to love than to be loved."

"It may sound funny, Vitya, but here in jail I have also started feeling relief in my heart. When I was outside, I suffered from insomnia, I drank too much, it seemed that everything around me was wrong. Neither the nor the sea, nor the people close to me − nothing pleased me, and I wanted to be alone more and more. I realized that I was doing something wrong. I was living not quite right. I dreamt of learning English well, I wanted to get muscles, to get rid of my belly. I dreamt of writing a book about my psychedelic revolution. But I never managed to do the things I wanted. I always had time for some nonsense, and I constantly put aside my dreams for later. Although I lived near the sea, I only swam in it once recently. I was so fed up with all kinds of pleasure that nothing made me happy. And for the last couple of years my Lena wanted to return to Russia. And I held her here. I wanted everything my way. I wanted to be a hero, to be loved by everyone even more. And to be loved, you must give people the things they want. But, Vitya, I gave what I wanted to give just like you did. I wanted my daughter to study at a school that I couldn't go to, and now she likes the Russian one more. I wanted us to live where I wanted; I wanted everything to be my own way. After all, I am God, I know better. My heart told me that everything wasn't supposed be like that, but I didn't listen, I drowned it in drink before I ended up here. You won't believe me, but sometimes I imagined myself in jail."

"Vasya, I did too."

"And here we are, Vitya. Here in Asia they are right: thoughts and desires are material. They just don't materialize immediately and not exactly in the way you want. Here in Asia, one needs to know exactly what to desire and picture it vividly. And as for us, Vitya, we didn't know what else to wish for. Nothing pleased us, so we ended up here. Vitya, doesn't it seem to you that when everything is going well and your soul is at peace, it becomes boring to live? There is no heaven without hell, after all. Do you remember, a month ago I gave you a book by Milan Kundera? I miss the unbearable heaviness of being. And when I feel unbearable lightness, I just want to hang myself. It's not the way out — loneliness and unconditional love. I want contrasting feelings. How can you love without knowing what hatred is like? I want the whole spectrum of feelings, not only those that you are allowed to have now. I knew one lonely person who loved everyone unconditionally and he seemed to be happy. You used to see him at all the parties. They called him Oleg from Odessa. He lived here before you came to Goa. He was an old man of about seventy, with long white hair and a gray chest-length beard, and he always danced with iron balls in his hands. He loved everyone. In monsoon, he hanged himself in Arambol and left a suicide note. He wrote that everything in this life had become clear to him and he was bored. He wrote that he went to another dimension."

Chapter 34. Part Two. Outside.

"What if we go to Nepal together?"

"No, dear. You went to Thailand, and I want to go to Russia."

"It's always the same, Lena," I comment, spreading avocado and black caviar onto a piece of bread. "We just manage to earn a bit of money and you start wasting it straight away. You know, five thousand bucks here in Goa is like fifty in Russia. You can live here on this money for a season, denying yourself nothing. If you and Vasilinka fly to Russia and back, this sum of money will be enough for two months at most, even if you save on everything."

"You won't talk me out of it, honey. I've missed Russia."

"Lena, dear, I worry that you'll like it, and you'll want to stay there," I playfully try to influence her decision in any way I can.

"Oh, please don't be so dramatic. I'm not just going for a vacation, I'll try to lease out our apartment and find out about you being on the wanted list. Don't worry; I'll be back in two or three months. I'm tired of Goa. I'm tired of tourists who can't do anything by themselves, like dim-witted children. I'm tired of you dealing drugs. All of that makes me restless. I'm tired of your friends, who are not showing themselves in the best light here. Valera Mulik and his girlfriend lived here with us, ate with us, went to parties with us. But when it came to work, I had to do it all on my own."

"Lena, I agree. Mulik did a weird thing. He found out where I buy drugs, found out my client base and left, having borrowed money. The truth is, I think he didn't stay to work with us for a different reason. It is unlikely he will become a competitor. After the incident with the Russian cops he is constantly paranoid. He has no wish at all to fall into the hands of the police. I understand him. Yet the story with the death of Sergey Chelyabinskiy affected him. He doesn't want to sell drugs anymore. And I understand that."

"Tell me honestly, Vasiliy. Was it you who sold MDMA and LSD to Sergey before he died?"

"Thank God, no. Lena, I thought many times about whether his death was my fault. The last time I saw him, Sergey himself offered to sell me a hundred grams of MDMA. He met some Israeli drug dealers and even helped me to get MDMA. We bought fifty grams each. I didn't sell mine in a week, but he and his friends snorted all fifty grams. It's not surprising, his reason failed him after such an amount. And when he ran out, he stripped naked, got on his bike, drove to the bridge in Panjim and jumped into the water. They fished that asshole out, and he leaped back in again in headfirst, shouting 'I am Shiva'. He was only found three days later."

"Maybe, you will stay?" without hope I ask Lena, who is packing her bag. "We would fly to Nepal. No trains or buses. I promise. We'd have a ball with five thousand bucks."

"I know, Vasiliy, but I've had enough. In the evenings we would get stoned and watch the monkeys stealing corn. Or we would fuck in a cornfield, high on MDMA. You would once again rent a Nepali palace teeming with rats and I would have to keep house."

"We had a housemaid, Lena," I make an attempt at indignation.

"Screw Nepalese and Indian housemaids! No matter how much you pay them, you still have to redo everything after them. They are wild, like monkeys, they are more trouble than they are worth."

"Dear, what do you have against sex in a cornfield? I thought it wasn't bad."

"It's romantic to fuck in a cornfield once, just like on the beach. I don't want to fuck in a cornfield or on the beach anymore. I don't want to fuck for the next three months. I want to miss you. I'm tired of you and your psychedelic revolution. That's all. If you don't want to spoil the farewell party before we leave, don't keep on at me. I've made my decision. Vasilina and I are going to Russia."

***

"Hello, Olya, long time no see," surprised, I address our former tenant who disappeared a couple of months ago. "We thought you had left already, or had overdosed and flipped out. We wanted to throw your stuff away. And in any case, you look a bit weird, Olya."

"What's so weird, Vasya?"

"Do you think that men's trousers and a vest five sizes too big for you is okay? And where are your shoes?"

"I like walking without shoes. Why are you nit-picking? We are in India."

"I'm not nit-picking, Olya. I just get the feeling that you are flying at the moment."[64]

---

[64] ...you are flying at the moment. - the original Russian version features an untranslatable play on words: "to

"Vasya, and aren't you flying too?"

"No, Olya, I am sane. My family is flying to Russia now. I saw them off yesterday. They are probably about to land in Moscow now."

"It's good, Vasya, that you didn't throw my stuff away. I came to take it to the post office to send to Moscow. By the way, you haven't put any drugs in my stuff? I will check everything."

"Are you nuts, Olya? Why would we put something in your stuff? We wanted to throw it away. So take your belongings and go to the post office," I say irritably, placing the large bag at her feet. "I can call a cab for you to leave faster. See you next season. I hope your mind comes back to you in Russia. I'm going for a walk along the beach, I love walking along the shore alone in April."

"Francis!" I shout to the owner of the house, who is washing his bull, tied to a palm tree. "Help my tenant, call a cab to Mapusa. She wants to go to the post office," going down the stairs quickly, I run away from crazy Olya.

I really like walking along the beach in April, especially in the early morning. But even now, when the is getting warmer, as I approach the sea I again experience an excitement similar to that which I felt here the first time. The endless beaches seem to hypnotize you with their beauty. All the way to the horizon there are no annoying tourists. Only the fishermen, returning from fishing in their old wooden boats, slightly disturb the harmony of wild nature. But somehow they also fit harmoniously into this beautiful landscape that has not changed for hundreds of years. The music of the crashing waves is occasionally interrupted by dogs barking and the abrupt cries of the fishermen's wives, who noisily share their husbands' catch. The fishermen silently untangle their nets, throwing small mackerel or Goan flounder, pomfret, into baskets. What happens here, in Goa, with people's minds? Why do so many people go crazy here? I wonder after my recent meeting with Olya. Where is the line between madness and sanity? Why do people go over the edge? Or maybe I'm crazy too but I just don't realize it yet?

"Hi, Vasya!" The loud shout of a fisherman interrupts my thoughts. "Fresh fish, new fish, come here, check it out! Do you want to get it roasted in our restaurant?" my friend, Ganesh, says to me, showing me an extraordinarily beautiful fish.

Pulling it out of the basket, he demonstrates a fish shaped like a perch, but larger, two palms in length, with a coloring unusual for the area. It is bright lemon yellow with blue stripes, and looks like the cartoon fish Nemo. I wonder how it got here? I have only seen such fish on TV programs about coral reefs.

"Only one hundred rupees," the joyful Indian fisherman offers me, pointing at his restaurant.

"I wonder: what is your fish called?" I ask, looking at the Goan goldfish with fascination. Stumped for a couple of seconds, Ganesh looks at the fish with a silly expression, not knowing what to say. But the desire to get a hundred rupees saves him.

"Color fish. Yes, its name color fish!"

---

be in flight" can mean to be going mad in Russian slang, but also has the usual aviation-related meaning. Vasya uses the first meaning in relation to Olya and the second when referring to his family travelling by plane to Russia.

"OK, Ganesh, you've persuaded me. Just tell me, have you ever caught such a fish before? Maybe it is not edible?"

"No," he shakes his head, making an innocent face. "But my father told me he caught such a fish once, he said it was very tasty," the fisherman begins to look for excuses, fearing that I will be afraid to try the new fish.

"Okay, you win," I say, sitting down at a plastic table in the empty shack under a coconut tree. Why not have a second breakfast? All the more so, because I don't want to go back and talk to crazy Olya. It's unlikely that she has left yet. Why do people no longer feel the line, after which there is no way back? I continue thinking about Olya, waiting for the unusual roasted fish. Drugs surely have a reverse side. The comedowns give us a sign that we need to stop. The body tells the brain that it's over: it's time to rest. After all, we live in the information age. You can surf the Net to find out everything about the drug you take. You can also find out in advance how much of a substance you can take without harm. Of course, I'm no saint; I can take ten doses in one day, and I enjoy taking more the next morning. But you have to be able to stop. Or, as a last resort, there is alcohol: you can get drunk and fall asleep. I have been practicing this lately. However, to be on drugs more than you sleep is real madness. If you like to have a blast, then you need to be able to rest as well. Those who didn't live to the end of the season, or cuckoos like Olya or Vanya: how long can they go on blasting non-stop? They haven't sobered up for several months. The poor brain of such a tripster simply overheats and crashes, like a computer. I don't understand them. I can't look at any drugs after a day of psychedelic experimentation.

"Your fish," says the fisherman's wife, smiling and putting the tray in front of me.

"I hope it is not a puffer fish…" I think, smiling, and take the first bite.

*

"Vasa, Vasa!" Francis cries to me, having seen me from a distance. "What happened here! What happened here!" unable to find words, the owner of our house waves his hands.

"What is it, Francis? But speak slowly, I don't understand your ten-word English."

"I called a car, as you asked, for your friend. I called my brother. He has a beautiful car, red car. He took her to the post office, she sent a package, and they returned. My brother says 'Give five hundred rupees,' you know, Vasa, it's not expensive, it's friends price, and she gave him a shirt button, and said that this button is worth more. She said she give no money. She went up to your balcony, stripped naked, and started to laugh, tearing a blanket to pieces. My neighbors, my children see all that. Decent Catholics live here, and here is such shame. Then she put on your ninja shoes, wrapped herself in the blanket and ran towards the sea. I think she's crazy. Don't take her here again."

"Don't worry, Francis, I got your point. Go and wash your bull, someone is calling me on the phone," I say, taking the phone out.

"Hello Pasha, I'm glad to hear from you," I greet the consul of the Russian Embassy in Bombay. I met Pavel in my restaurant at the beginning of this season.

A nice guy dressed according to the latest trends, I would never have believed that he works at the embassy if he hadn't given me his card. Pavel is a real FSB[65] officer. He doesn't take drugs or smoke, but he isn't averse to drinking. Basically, he looked like an ordinary guy. He has helped my friends in difficult situations several times, and so he knew my phone number.

"Hello, where are you now, Pasha? Are you in Bombay, or have you come to Goa for a weekend again?"

"Vasya, I have no time to come to Goa now. You know, my work is to send crazy and dead fellow villagers back to the motherland. This season has been hotter for me than ever before. Four corpses in the past two months. Addicts going crazy almost every day, one after another. I sent one Russian to the motherland just last week. He took too many drugs and happily burned his passport. His parents came to take him away, and he dug his heels in. He said 'I will not go; I want to stay and live in Goa'. We had to add sedatives to his cola. At last, we managed to send him off. Vasya, I am calling you on business. Today I spoke with a Dutch businessman who runs a large advertising agency in Moscow. He has been living in Russia for ten years already. He says he lost his Russian girlfriend in Goa. He spoke to her on the phone, and he realized that she had gone crazy. She also said that she didn't want to go back. She started to go to parties and went off her rocker. Have you heard of her? Her name is Olya."

"Tell me straight, Pavel, are you watching me with a satellite telescope? She fled in my ninja shoes in an unknown direction half an hour ago."

"No, Vasya, you are not of the required caliber to follow you via satellite," Pasha laughs into the phone. "If you find her, call me at the embassy, I'll give you the phone number of the Dutchman, he is ready to pay dearly for someone to send her home."

"Okay, Pasha, I'll try to find her, and I'll figure out how much it will cost to transfer her to Bombay and send her to Russia. I still need to talk to her first, maybe she won't listen to me."

Switching off the phone, I stand in silence for a while, figuring out courses of action. I ought to call Igor Tereshkov, he is the only Russian left in Anjuna. He might have heard about Olya.

***

"Hello, Igor! Have you seen a crazy Russian girl in Anjuna? Her name is Olya."

"Hi, Vasya. Yes, I did a few days ago, I barely managed to kick her out. She has seriously flipped out. I lent her a thousand rupees; when you find her, tell her to give it to you. Someone saw her in Morjim with an Englishman. They say she is living in some yellow house by the sea, near the Glavfish restaurant."

"Thank you, Igor, for the information. I'll do my best to find her."

Getting on my scooter, within fifteen minutes I reach the neighboring village and start asking the fishermen about a yellow house by the sea.

"Hello!" I address an Englishman sitting on the yellow balcony with a joint in his hand. "I'm looking for a very strange Russian girl, her name is Olya. Do you know her?"

---

[65] FSB (Federal Security Service of the Russian Federation) - the principal security agency of the Russian Federation.

"Yes, I know her. She lived here for a week. She stole a gold chain and my trousers. She left her dirty rags and fled. She's crazy; she needs to see a doctor. She is said to be in Arambol with some Russians. When you find her, tell her to give my chain back."

"Thank you, I'll tell her," I respond, getting back on my scooter.

The central beach of Arambol, down to which the only main road leads, is a gloomy place at the end of the season. The rare bamboo restaurants that are still working sit bored among the empty gaps left by those that have already been dismantled, until recently their noisy neighbors. If you look at it from the sea, Arambol beach currently looks like the mouth of the crazy old freak lady who begged me to give her some money when I got off my scooter. She wore dirty, torn clothes, and had tousled hair and an absolutely crazy stare. She smiled at me, baring her toothless mouth, in which the rare yellow teeth were surrounded by rotten black cavities. In one of the remaining seaside restaurants, old and faded to yellow in the during the season, I see a crowd of Russians noisily drinking warm vodka, apparently brought from the motherland.

"Hi guys! I'm looking for a Russian chick. She's off her trolley a bit; she has flipped out. Her name is Olya."

"Is she a girl wearing men's pants? I know that bitch. If I catch her, I'll kick her ass," says the drunkest man in the crowd, waving his hands. "I'm the keyboardist of Splean[66], she took my expensive camera, gave it to someone, and ran away. If I see her, I'll kill her; all the pictures from my two-week vacation are on there."

"Calm down, Splean keyboardist," I clap the drunken guy on the back. "She needs to see a doctor, she's cuckoo. You probably didn't think about that when you fucked her. And now you think about your camera. Forget it. You should have thought of it earlier."

"I saw her today at the small beach," says his friend lounging on a chair, barely moving his tongue. "If you find the camera, tell me, I'll make it worth your while."

"Okay, but I saw her in the morning; she had no camera," I say, heading towards the small beach.

Having walked for just five minutes, I see Olya, who is pensively tearing off white flowers from the bushes along the path.

"Hi, beauty. Have you had enough of running? Maybe it is time to go back home to Russia, isn't it?" I try to speak in a caring tone, afraid she will escape again.

"If you say so," Olya says, smiling childishly, and takes me by the hand like a little girl.

"Do you have your passport, Olechka?" I ask with hope, dreaming of easy money. But not having heard the answer, I am already thinking of the pain in the ass that I will have to deal with.

"No, I haven't. I threw it out. My visa had expired, anyway."

"That's great, Olechka. We'll have to get a new one. It will take at least a week. We will need to go to the police station and the embassy. Come on, we'll buy you some clothes first. It doesn't suit such a beautiful girl to walk down the streets like that," I try to speak as playfully as possible. "And then we'll call your fiancé, he promised to send us money to bring you back to him."

---

[66] Splean - a popular Russian rock band.

"You have been living in my flat for three days already, Olya, and I still don't understand whether you are playing the fool or not. Tell me, Olya, how did it happen that you, a clever girl, a psychology graduate, has gone crazy? You must be smarter than me."

"I don't understand myself, Vasya. I'm normal. And everyone says that I'm crazy."

"How can I consider you to be normal, if I have to hide the knives and scissors from you? How many times have you promised me not to touch your hair? But, as soon as I turn my back, you try to cut it off with anything at hand."

"Vasya, what's wrong with wanting to cut off all my hair?"

"I don't mind, Olya. Cut your hair however you like when you get home. And anyway, what the heck are you doing? You cut off a tuft while I was talking on the phone and began to set it alight in my cup of tea."

"And where am I supposed to do it?" Olya asks, making a surprised face, as if everybody burned their hair in cups of tea.

"Olya! What do you mean 'where?' Why are you doing it, if I asked you not to in my house? And tell me: why did you take the camera of the honorable Splean keyboardist, and where did you lose it?"

"I took it to take photos. What's wrong with that? It's just that an Indian man came up to me on the beach and said that he was ill with some contagious, fatal disease. I gave him the camera and the gold chain."

"But, Olechka, think about this – is it okay or not to give someone else's things to the first person you meet?"

"What is wrong with it, Vasya? That ill man is in more need of money than I am, or that musician."

"Olya, don't you think that the Indian man lied to you?"

"I don't care, my boyfriend is a Dutchman; he is a millionaire. He's in love with me and will send planes and helicopters to rescue me, so I'll be alright. Think whatever you want about me. Anyway, he bought you too."

"Does he know that you lived here with other men? Or do you have an open relationship?"

"I don't care, Vasya, I don't love him. I love nobody. I can only let someone love me. In fact, I don't want to go back, at all."

"I've got your point, calm down," I agree, regretting that I raised the subject. "After today's visit to the police station, I finally realized that you don't care. If I had not bribed the police chief, we would have never obtained a reference to get you a new passport. They could even have fined us for your insulting behavior. Why did you pull your T-shirt over your head in the chief's office?"

"Was he staring at my tits?"

"Did you decide to show them to him?"

"No, I decided to hide my face, so I pulled my T-shirt over it."

"And why did you flatly refuse to wear a second shoe? Why did you go to the police, wearing just one shoe?"

"Vasya, haven't you read the fairy tale about Cinderella? Can't I be Cinderella in Goa?

"That's it, Olya, you are starting to drive me crazy too. And stop walking about in my shirt with no panties on the balcony. The downstairs neighbors are decent Catholics; they are already shocked by your behavior. I have someone on the phone, I'm going to talk. But beware: I am keeping my eye on you. Don't you dare pull any stunts."

"Hello, Pavel!"

"Hello, Vasiliy, how is our cuckoo?"

"She's not causing too much trouble; I just hope I don't go bonkers from her. On one hand she appears to be normal, but on the other she seems to have lost her mind somewhere at a party. I've gathered all the references about the loss of her passport and will fly to you in Bombay tomorrow. I phoned her sponsor, and agreed to restore her docs and transfer her by plane to Moscow for a thousand bucks. He has already transferred the money to me."

"Did the private detective from Bombay meet with you, Vasya?"

"Yes, he dropped by. He asked about Olya. But I don't understand, why were we both hired? I said to her sponsor-fiancé that I would find her and transfer her. Why was the Indian hired?"

"Vasya, you will never understand what millionaires want. He just has tons of money, so he plays it safe. He must love this fool a lot."

"Pasha, you should have seen the performance she pulled in front of the Indian detective. I just asked her if she wanted the Indian to escort her to the plane. The whole village heard her mad shriek. She tore off her clothes and ran naked along the roof. I followed her and thought I would fall to my death. And the Indian, seeing this show, grabbed his shoes and ran away. I have not seen him since."

"Well, Vasya, hold on! I understand you. I work with mad people, too. I hope you will have no more performances like that. See you tomorrow at the embassy, bye!"

***

"Olya, we are about to land now, please, promise to listen to me. And let's agree that you won't play hide-and-seek in the toilet again."

"I did not hide. I just wanted to wait for the plane in the toilet, as no one was staring at me in there."

"Yeah, but we nearly missed the plane. It was a good thing I found an English-speaking woman and sent her into the toilet for you. We have to stay in Bombay for just a couple of days and then you'll go home to your mom, or to your boyfriend, as you wish."

***

"Olya, please stop, we'll be run over by a car!" I shout on the run, trying to keep up.

We are running along the central separating strip of a bustling Bombay highway. The oncoming cars are honking their horns and flashing their lights. Olya is running effortlessly ahead, smiling. With a red face and carrying bags full of female junk, I follow her. Sharply crossing the street and almost being hit by a car, she speeds up, outrunning me by a hundred meters, and runs up to the Taj Mahal five star hotel. Out of breath, I run into the elegant foyer and see her booking an expensive room, lounging in a chair, as if nothing happened.

"Please, stop. This girl is crazy," I try to explain in my broken English.

"Vasya, I won't go anywhere from here. Call my fiancé; let him send more money. I'll only stay overnight here."

"Hello, John? It's Vasya. We are currently in the Taj Mahal. The cheapest room here costs three hundred and fifty dollars a night. Olya says that she is not going anywhere. Are you ready to send more money?"

"Okay," I hear the short answer on the phone.

"Olya, you have a good friend. But, if I were him, I would have got rid of you a long time ago. You haven't gone bonkers. You are just a moody, naughty girl who doesn't know how to keep herself amused. I got you pegged."

"Vasya, think what you want but I always do everything the way I want. And now I don't want to go up in the elevator with these Indians."

Having waited until the huge luxurious elevator arrives, Olya is the first to run in and blocks the passage for a group of Indian men in expensive suits standing near the elevator. She starts to shout, "I will not go up with these monkeys. Get out of here! I am a white woman."

Ready to sink into the earth, I resort to hand gestures to explain to the Indian men near the elevator that I have nothing to do with her, that she is crazy. Hiding my face in shame, I enter the elevator sideways.

"I'm fed up with you, Olya. I'm going to lie on the floor. And you can enjoy the gorgeous bed. Just know that I am not going to sleep. If my eyes are closed it just means that I am having a rest. Don't you attempt to pull any stunts. I'll have an eye on you all night long."

"Good morning," I slowly wake Olya, who is sleeping like a baby. "Come on, beauty, let's make the final leap. Now we're going to the police, get a stamp, then consul Pasha will give us a duplicate passport, and that's it. Tomorrow you'll see your mother."

"You know what, Vasya. Call the embassy, let them to come here, and let the police come here too. Tell everyone that I went to the gym," Olya says quite seriously, slowly putting a white robe ostentatiously onto her naked body.

"What should I do with you, Olechka? You don't want to obey your boyfriend. Maybe you'll listen to your mother? Shall we call her?"

Dialing the Moscow number, I turn to the window in order not to see how Olya is sitting in a chair, legs wide apart, exposing her charms with no shame. Outside the window, near the pool below, a few Indian men are peacefully sunbathing in loungers. I wonder why they do that? Any European would envy their natural tan. Most ordinary Indian people, on the contrary, hide from the and buy various creams that allegedly whiten the skin, hoping that the color will get closer to that of a white man. These are forward-thinking, rather odd Indians.

"Olya, come here, I've got your mother on the phone," I say, turning to the empty room.

The door to the hallway is wide open, a white terry robe lies on the floor.

"Tatiana Petrovna, I'll call you back later. Your daughter has just run out of the room, completely naked."

As if I didn't have enough on my plate! Shit, a naked cuckoo has run away from me in a five star hotel. What am I being punished for?

Having walked around all sixteen floors without finding her, I go to the reception to surrender. I somehow manage to explain my problem. I ask the administration for help. Having listened to me carefully and showing no emotion, the manager calls the security service to help me. I have to explain it all over again, primarily using hand gestures:

"I am her escort and she is mentally ill. I'm not crazy, and I'm not her friend. I was paid money to put her on a plane. She ran off naked in your hotel. Here she is," I show them a small photo of Olya. "Help me to find her."

Walking again around all sixteen floors with the security guards, we still do not find her. The doormen standing near the entrance say that no naked girls ran out of the hotel. Having spoken to the internal video surveillance service by radio, the security guards report that there is a video from a camera in a corridor, where she is seen running into the open room opposite, which the maid accidentally forgot to close.

"Madame, open the room immediately!" a female guard shouts at the door, dressed all in black.

Opening the door with a spare key, the entire crowd burst into the room. I am the first to see Olya sitting naked in the bathroom, shaving her pubic hair. Not daunted at all, Olya takes a sip of whiskey from the bottle standing next to her, as if her personal security guards were standing in front of her.

"You have to leave our hotel immediately. You cause too much trouble."

"But we need to stay overnight somewhere, we are willing to pay and I promise this will not happen again," I try to explain to the unsmiling security chief.

"No, that's your problem. There are no rooms for you in our hotel."

We pack our stuff quickly, and have to leave the elegant five star accommodation. Having spent all day in different offices, in the evening we finally collect all the references allowing Olya to leave the country.

"Olya, I get the impression that you have been messing with me all day on purpose," I address my ward, who has put her long legs on me. Look, the cab driver is not watching the road, he is just staring in the mirror at your thighs. In the morning, you ran naked around the hotel, then you again hid in the toilet in the immigration office, then you played hide-and-seek in a corridor of the embassy, and now you are driving this Muslim cab driver crazy. We are going to a cheap hotel, we will not be allowed into an expensive one. We will sit there for a day until you leave. You will not run away from me again. I am coming into every toilet with you."

***

I've been prowling round the back streets of Bombay for several hours, trying to find Olya, who ran away from me again.

"Hi, Zhenyok!" I shout in surprise to a Goan friend, a DJ, walking down the same street. "I am glad to see you! What has brought you to Bombay?"

"I was staring in the movies, Vasya. I made some money, and now am going back to Goa tomorrow. Why are you so agitated, Vasya? What has happened?"

"Zhenyok, help me out, I am in such a mess. I am making money here in Bombay too, but I have my own movie. I was paid money to put one cuckoo on the plane; she's another Goan flip-out. Everything would be okay, except she is a bad case. She has caused trouble all the way. Today we were kicked out of a five star hotel. I went with her to the police, got all the stamps for her departure, bought her a ticket to Moscow, even agreed for a flight attendant to escort her to the plane. We arrived in Colaba check into a hotel, and while I paid the taxi driver, she once again ran away from me. I have already informed the embassy and the police, and took a photo of her to the hotel that we were thrown out of. Night is falling. There are slums all around here. It will be very bad if she is not found. She will be made into mincemeat, as she is a pretty blonde, and a lustful whore on top of that. She has no money, no documents, nothing with her. Let's go, maybe we'll meet her somewhere. I have tramped around several blocks for the last three hours."

"Well, if she is a pretty, lustful blonde, we could search for her," Zhenya agrees, smiling.

"Zhenyok, she's crazy. You can't fuck crazy girls, and don't smile like that – she needs help."

I hear the Indian ringtone of one of my phones in my pocket.

"Hello... Thank you, we'll be there in five minutes. Zhenyok, they called from the Taj Mahal, and urgently asked to take her out of there. They say that she is in the restaurant lying on a couch and does not want to leave."

Reaching the hotel in five minutes, I again stand in front of my cuckoo. A security guard nearby tells me that she starts shouting loudly if anyone tries to touch her. A bill for one and a half thousand rupees lies on the table next to a half-eaten piece of cake and a bottle of wine.

"Whom should I pay the bill to?" I ask, getting the money out.

"Do not pay anything. Just take her away quickly and never come back. An international conference starts here in fifteen minutes, we don't want any police, just leave now."

"Olechka, let's go, darling," I'm trying to establish contact, speaking as gently as I can.

"I'm not going anywhere from here," she says quite aggressively. "I'm going to stay in this hotel as long as I want."

"Zhenyok, could you try?" I whisper in the ear of my friend, who stands stunned next to me.

"I've had no experience of meeting whacks before. I can try."

"Hey girl, may I get to know you?" Zhenyok joins the crazy show. "Why are you so sad? May I sit next to you?"

Ten minutes later, hand in hand, they walk through the lobby like a normal couple. They are talking and smiling.

"Zhenyok, nicely done! How did you manage to do that?"

"Even mad women like affection. You've scared the poor girl."

"Listen, Zhenya, if you are so good at it, perhaps you could accompany her. I'll give you five hundred bucks. Put her on the plane tomorrow evening. I have all the documents ready and the tickets are bought. Just stay with her until the flight. I can't, she is driving me crazy. I would fly to Goa at five in the morning. I'm allergic to her already. I need urgent rehabilitation in Goa."

"Vasya, let's do as follows. I'll stay with her until four in the morning. If contact is established, I am in. But if she starts to play up, I'm sorry, babysit her on your own. Now go to bed, Vasya. I'll call you in the morning."

The ringing phone saves me from two male nurses chasing me with a straitjacket in my dream. In the darkness of the room, I can see Zhenya's number flashing on my cell phone. Has she run away again?

"Hello Vasya, come down here, I'm waiting in the street. Contact is established."

As if nothing had happened, Olya stands near the entrance, making eyes at me and smiling.

"Thank you, Zhenyok. Am I really going to fly home to Goa? It's four o'clock in the morning, my plane leaves in an hour. Where have you been all night?"

"We walked around the hotel. She is a good conversation partner. Her mind wanders occasionally, but that will pass in Russia."

"Here is the package with her documents, Zhenyok," I say, squatting near the entrance of the small hotel. "Sit down near and listen carefully. This is a reference from the Arambol police that she lost her passport. This one is a reference from the Pernem police that they have no claims against her. This is a reference issued by the Panjim police that they do not mind her leaving. This reference is from the Bombay police that the fine for her expired visa has been paid. This is a reference issued by the embassy confirming her identity. This is the plane ticket. I'll give you some pocket money and five hundred bucks for the work."

Looking around and making sure that we are alone on the deserted street, I pull out a wad of cash.

"At the airport, find a flight attendant from the Russian airline, and give her Olya and the documents. Have you got it?"

Having counted the money, I give him a wad, but instead of answering, I see how his expression changes, trying to tell me something. At the same moment, someone from behind snatches all the money from my hands and starts to run away quickly. "Is it Olya again?" is the first thing that comes to my mind. But the receding silhouette does not look female.

"Stop, stop!" Zhenyok shouts, trying to seize the robber, who appeared out of nowhere. For a split second my brain considers whether to run or not. On the one hand, it is night, Bombay slums, it's risky, and it's not so much money, just a thousand dollars. But, on the other hand, I spent a whole week with crazy Olya. I need rehabilitation. I need my money back.

"Stop, you bitch!!!" I shout, kicking off my sandals as I run.

Speeding up and reaching the corner, I see the son of a bitch trying to jump into a car with an open door, which is already starting to drive off. For a moment imagining I am a bear, I do two huge jumps with a wild roar and land on the frightened robber. Remembering Filipino soldiers, I make the mad shout of an alpha male and, grabbing my enemy's neck, I start to strangle him, demanding my money.

"Money! Fucking monkey, give me my money!" I shout like crazy in the silence of the deserted street. Having heard my cries, slum dwellers start to come out from garbage cans and cardboard boxes, like in a horror movie. Struggling to breathe, the Indian robber casts my money aside. Also just like in a movie, a gust of wind from nowhere spins my valuable paper, for which I decided to risk my life, in a small tornado. Several pairs of eyes immediately begin to sparkle at an easy target in the empty Bombay street. Looking each of them in the eye for a moment, I snarl with such a mad cry that they realize I am ready for anything, and none of them dares to come closer. Giving a kick in the stomach to the failed robber lying in the street, I collect all the money and quickly run to his accomplice sitting in the car. Still in a frenzy, I bellow so loudly in his face that he gets five hundred rupees out of his own pocket in fear and hands them over to me.

After settling accounts with Zhenyok and calling a cab, fifteen minutes later I go to the airport with the sole desire of getting to Goa as soon as possible. I ought to call Olya's mother and say that the mission is accomplished.

"Hello, Tatiana Petrovna? Hi, meet your daughter tomorrow. I did my job. My friend will put her on the plane today."

"Vasya, how can I ever thank you?" I hear the elderly woman crying into the phone. "God bless you."

"Don't thank me. Her friend paid me enough."

"Then I will light a candle for you in the church tomorrow."

"Everything will be fine with your daughter. The most important thing is to not let her take any drugs, they are no good for her."

Chapter 35. Part One. Inside.

"Hello, my children," a young priest addresses us, coming out into the courtyard.

Behind him several limping nuns appear. An old cross-eyed Indian woman of about seventy years, wearing glasses with very thick lenses and dressed in a Catholic robe, smiles broadly, greeting all the prisoners walking around. The second, younger sister of about sixty, with no defects on her face but lame in one leg that is shorter than the other, appears last, carrying a bag with gifts. This absurd picture reminds me of some crazy comic. The first sister's huge lenses magnify her eyes so much that she looks like a giant chameleon, with huge peepers looking in different directions.

"Today is apparently Monday, if the circus has come here," says Antonio, sitting alongside me on the steps.

"What's new, Mr. Bean?" I address our Greek.

"Why do you call me Mr. Bean? I really hate it. Please do not call me that anymore."

"I won't, you just look an awful lot like the main character of the British TV series. Why are you so sad, Antonio? Does this nickname piss you off so much?"

"Oh, if only... I've been scammed again," says the Greek, sighing and making a Mr. Bean face. "Vasya, I have to kiss my freedom goodbye for the coming year, at least."

"Who has scammed you? What happened?" I ask with sympathy, ready to hear another sentimental story about how the world is unfair towards Mr. Bean.

"Mafia, Goan state mafia. The judge, the lawyer, the chief of the drug police, Pashish, and the prosecutor. They studied together here, in Goa. They grew up together and now they work together. Pashish captures you, the lawyer takes your money, the judge and the prosecutor get bonuses, and everyone is happy. First, Pashish takes all the drugs and money. The bulk goes into the pocket of the drug police chief. He shares it with the son of the interior minister, who covers for him. The police chief takes the drugs to the most famous drug dealers, the grasses, who then sell them. Pashish sends the minimum amount of the remaining drugs for analysis to Hyderabad, in order to get another star on his epaulettes for doing a good job. Then we pay the lawyer five thousand bucks. Some of it certainly goes to the judge, some of it to the prosecutor. If the money is not paid, you get ten years for sure. There was an Israeli named Daniel. He thought he was clever and hired a lawyer from Bombay. The lawyer muttered something in the prosecutor's ear, the prosecutor explained everything to the judge and, eventually, the Israeli was sentenced to ten years in prison for two kilos of charas, while his cellmates, Nepalese men, were released despite having twenty kilos. If you want to get out of here, Vasya, you should make everyone happy. The government should be happy with your sentence of from a year to three years. The witnesses should be happy with the five hundred dollars they earned. The police should be happy with the money they received from the drug dealers. The prosecutor, lawyer and judge should be happy with their good salary. And you should be the happiest person, because you are not hurled into prison for ten years. Vasya, do you realize that this is kidnapping at the state level?"

"Antonio, I've heard the story you've just told me a dozen times from each drug dealer. Tell me, who conned you out of your money? How did that happen if you're sitting in jail?"

"The cops conned me out of it, Vasya. Those bastards know I have money. They offered me to perform the expert analysis of my cocaine much faster than in a year, for six thousand bucks. They promised that they would check the purity of my nose powder at the same time. I know that my coke is sixty percent diluted with paracetamol. In such an analysis, my two hundred and fifty grams would turn out to be a hundred. And a hundred grams would allow me to be released on bail. I handed over the money to the police through my friends, and yesterday, when I was taken to the court, I was talking with my investigator. Do you know what he told me? 'Forgive us, Greek brother, but we won't succeed in releasing you sooner than in one year. We have already spent your money. We also love cocaine, and it is expensive now.' They tried to reassure me by promising that I will be set free in a year and a half or two. But I need to get out as soon as I can. My love, Natasha, is waiting for me."

"We've seen your Natasha, she's an attractive girl. The guards always stare at her when she comes to visit you," Viktor shamelessly buts into our conversation. "On the other hand, Antonio, you'll test her love. If she waits for you, you will appreciate her more, and if she fails to wait, she is not worth a dime."

"That's enough, Viktor. I can't listen to your philosophy any more. I get enough of you in the cell. I'd rather go talk to the priest."

"You don't like Catholics," says Viktor to the departing Greek, laughing.

"It is better to talk to them than listen to you."

"Why does he react to you like that?" I ask, moving a step downwards, in order to sit in the sunlight.

"Vasya, he is angry with me, because I call him Mr. Bean when we are in the cell and I constantly wind him up. Has he already told you how he was conned?"

"Yes, he has."

"But in fact it is not the first time he has been conned. The cops feel that he still has a stash of cash. Nobody wanted to appeal to the Court of Cassation for two hundred bucks. But he agreed, despite the fact that the lawyer warned that there is one chance in a hundred. Our Greek is really strange. Vasya, can you imagine that he faces ten years in prison, and yet he worries all night that his car stereo may be stolen in Greece. He left his car in front of his house in Greece a week before he was arrested."

"It will pass with time, Vitya. In the beginning, I also worried about how I would live in Goa with that bitch who set me up. I sweated all night long, thinking about how I am going to make money. I was endlessly thinking about how my girls are living there without me. And now only one thought remains – I wish not to get ten years. Ten years is almost the end of life. All other problems are simply ridiculous compared to that."

"That's right," Viktor agrees with a sigh. "I am afraid of ten years, too. What if the police added cocaine to my Novocain?"

"So you are still going on about the same old thing, Viktor," I begin to get agitated. "To give you ten years, the cops should add at least one hundred grams, and that would cost ten thousand dollars. Why would they want to do that? They may add five grams at the most. If the analysis concludes a positive reaction to cocaine, write a statement requesting that it be checked it for purity. After serving twelve more months, you'll get the second analysis and will get out of here. I hope I will be outside by that time. Don't worry, Vitya, I'll bring you deliveries from the outside."

"Vasya, why should I serve two years for a jar of Novocain?" Viktor starts getting angry with me, as if I put him in prison.

"Vitya, you would have been given five years for the pharmaceutical amphetamine you're selling if you had been in Russia. And here, the police didn't even attach the few grams of amphetamine that they found to the case. So pray that they don't add anything to your 'coke'. Nobody is going to give you ten years. Do you see the smallest man in the group of blacks sitting there?" I point at the corner where our seven black friends usually hang out. "He was detained with eight hundred and fifty grams of cocaine. Nobody but him knows how many he actually had. In this case, it would cost them nothing to add a hundred grams to yours. However, you are not worth so much money. Nobody needs that."

"That's it. I'd rather go talk to the Catholic priest, Vasya. I'm tired of listening to your nonsense. They are going to hold competitions. I'd rather watch them, as I won't be able to sleep at night again after talking to you."

"Okay, don't get mad, don't give up hope," I shout to Viktor, who goes to the other side of the prison.

Borish, who is walking nearby, sits down next to me in Viktor's place.

"What's new, Borish?" I ask the young artist. "Why are you sad, my Turkish friend?"

"Why would I be happy, Vasya? My girl lives in Turkey, and I've been stuck here for two months already. I was planning to get married, but the lawyer that Ashpak recommended doesn't really make any effort to get me out of here."

"Don't worry, Borish, you will be released any day now, and you'll go to your beautiful Bulgarian girl. I have something to ask you, Borish. My girls will come to Goa soon and my daughter will celebrate her birthday. She will turn eight. Would you be able to draw her portrait, if I give you a little photo?"

"Of course I can, Vasya. I'm an artist."

"Okay, thank you, so I'll at least be able to give her some gift. I have a lump of hashish to pay you as an advance."

"Thank you, my Russian friend. Here, in prison, this lump is worth more than gold. I'll exchange half of it for tobacco and coffee, and I'll smoke the other half tonight. Vasya, is there anything new in your cell?"

"Our cell was searched today. They were looking for a mobile phone again. I almost got into a fight with the guards. They wanted to take away my self-made dumbbell. I have a good dumbbell, made of two six-liter bottles. The prison warden burst into our cell today with the guards, the entire cell and all of our stuff was searched. It was good that I had hidden my hashish in candy papers and they didn't unwrap them. The warden saw my dumbbell and ordered the guards to take it away. And you know, Borish, at the moment my dumbbell for me is like my wife. I can't fall asleep if I don't lift twelve tons a day. It is the only important thing I have now. I grabbed it with both hands and shouted like crazy: 'I won't give it! I will bite or cripple anyone who tries to take it away!' I was alone against five guards with sticks. I was standing in a corner, with my arms around the dumbbell, my knees were shaking, and I was baring my teeth at them. I was lucky that my inmates stood up for me. They said 'do not touch this Russian, he does exercises with this dumbbell, and does not bother anyone. He may go mad without this dumbbell from having nothing to do, God forbid." In short, the warden took pity on me and did not take away my last joy. It's good that the new prison warden is a nice old man, but you didn't see the previous one. He was transferred to the jail in Vasco. He was like an energetic vampire. If he doesn't do something nasty, the day has passed in vain for him. I remember Lena brought me a rubber mat so that I wouldn't have to sleep on the concrete floor. Well, that bastard only gave it to me two months later, after I had been hospitalized with fever. He would have definitely taken my dumbbell away. And yet, today we have a piece of good news, even two. Viktor gained us the right to buy vegetables, through the judge. He wrote different petitions for six months, went on a week-long hunger strike, and complained to the doctors and the judge. All of the judicial structures heard his phrase 'Why not tomato?'. Tomatoes, cucumbers and onions will be delivered to us on Monday. And another piece of good news is that I managed to get us mayonnaise delivered on the sly. It was a different problem with the mayonnaise. The guards who take the orders have never tried it and never seen it. I somehow managed to explain what it is to them. I fought for mayonnaise for two months, and I won. So we have a good day next Monday. We'll finally eat a salad. At least some vitamins. I can't look at rice and peas any more. Borish, look at the circus the priests have put on, you can only see such things in India!"

Stopping speaking, we watch in amazement how, having divided the murderers, robbers and rapists in two groups, the priest organizes a children's competition in the middle of the walking area. On the count of 'one, two, three', one Indian criminal from each team runs from his side, trying to be the first to grab an old slipper, lying in the middle. The winner gets a plastic cross on a string.

"The Pope has stretched his tentacles even here. In my opinion, it is unfair to give people religion, denying them the right to choose," the Muslim Borish says to me, sighing.

Chapter 35. Part Two. Outside.

"Arik, it's getting hot in Goa again, monsoon is about to begin."

"Yeah, Vasya, it's time to move to Nepal. It's nice there now, not so hot. I've missed the Himalayas."

"I'm so fed up with Indians, Arik. They are so full of themselves and haughty at the end of the season. Theirs is a slave mentality, for sure. In September, when they are cash-strapped at the end of the rainy season, they are ready to kiss your ass for ten rupees. Yet in April-May, they are as proud as baboons. They act so full of themselves.

"Well, what did you expect, Vasya? The Portuguese used them as slaves for so many years. They have an inferiority complex."

"That's right, Arik. Take Francis, the owner of our house, for example. He brought us two plates of rice with chicken on his daughter's birthday. I said to him: 'Sit down with us at the table,' and he refuses. He and his wife sat on the floor and watched, from the bottom upwards, how we ate. But Francis is not poor. He owns two two-story houses, a motorboat, five motorbikes, a breeding bull, his own rice field. Do you know, Arik, how they live in the rainy season? The four of them sleep on the floor in a small room. And do you know why? They don't want the other rooms to wear out. Although judging by local standards they are well-off peasants, they live like slaves used to live a hundred years ago. Francis came to me at the beginning of the season. He is an adult man, but he stood and cried like a child, 'Vasya, lend me one thousand dollars, I need to bribe the police, my second house was built illegally, they could demolish it. I will pay back in two weeks.' I chased after him for the whole season, asking for my money back. I only managed to write off the debt by agreeing with him that it would be payment for the house rent for the next season. However, he still raised the rental charges by one third, the bloodsucker."

"Yes, Vasya, you can tolerate the Nepalese and Indians for six months only, and then it becomes unbearable. I've missed the Nepalese, too, Vasya. Their thick layer of smartassedness hides a humane attitude underneath. Meanwhile, the layer of Indian smartassedness covers their slave mentality, and then a humane attitude lies beneath that."

"It's good that we are going to Nepal without my wife this time. My girls are already in Russia. They are probably eating sausages and meat dumplings by now. You know, Lena really did my head in when we went to Nepal by train last year. She wasn't happy with anything, she frowned the whole time. Why is she so haughty? It would be a different matter if she was from a wealthy, cultured family, I would understand her resentment, but she has neither education, nor money. However, she is arrogant like an aristocrat. She is not satisfied with trains. What kind of people travel by train? The have-nots just like us. So the Indians treat us as equals, what else can you expect? But my Lena pictures herself as a white princess. She imagines that somebody is looking at her funny, or thinking wrongly about her. It will be easier without her. Some people lack pride, and some have too much of it. Why is the world so unfair?"

"So, are we going to Nepal without women this time, Vasya?"

"No, Arik, Dan is coming with his woman. He found a woman with a child. Her husband is serving time in an Indian prison for a kilo of hash. She is a former Krishna devotee, like you. So, we'll be going with them. I just wonder, what on Earth is Dan thinking about? He is penniless, but hooked himself a chick with a kid. I can feel that I'll have to provide credit to his family. He came to me yesterday and complained that he was short of money. He danced the entire season at parties instead of earning money. He says to me: 'What should I do, Vasya? I only have the money to get to Nepal.' Arik, I wanted to travel to Nepal by plane. But, apparently it's not on the cards. I had to buy a hundred grams of MDMA from crazy Psyu with my last money. I'm going to throw parties in Nepal and Dan can sell; you have to help your friends. We'll last till the next season somehow. I myself have money for only a month. If the money runs out, I'll exchange MDMA for food," I say, laughing and pulling my travel bag out.

***

"The same people in the same place," Arik says, laughing and taking his backpack off at the entrance to My Beautiful Restaurant.

"What's up, Grishanya! Another Nepalese summer in Pokhara?"

"Hi, Lenk! Half a year has flown by. Six months ago, we were leaving and you were sitting here. We have come back, and you are sitting at the same tables. Did you come back from Thailand recently, Lenk?"

"I returned a couple of weeks ago. The rains started in Thai, so we moved to Nepal."

"Vasya, have you heard about Zont?" Lenk asks, suddenly stopping smiling and exchanging glances with Grisha.

"No, I haven't. I haven't heard anything about you since I went to India. What happened?"

"He covered himself with gasoline in Thailand, and set himself on fire."

"What?!" jaws dropping in astonishment, Arik and I exclaim almost simultaneously.

"He either flipped out and committed suicide in a state of delirium, or someone helped him. His charred body was found right in the middle of the street. He took a few drops of LSD every day during his last days. His head wasn't working right. Reality and illusion became all mixed up."

"Well, are you all right, Grisha? How was your season in Nepal? You didn't go nuts from loneliness?" I ask the visibly thinner, hairy brother of Little Red Riding Hood[67].

"Same old, same old, Vasya. I spent the entire winter in Pokhara, I did nothing for six months, and didn't leave Nepal. I took tuberculosis tests. The doctors say I am completely rehabilitated. I want to fly to Russia, but I don't know how."

"Have you stayed here without a visa for six months already, Grishanya?"

"Yeah. On top of that, Vasya, my passport has expired," laughing nervously, Grisha responds, adjusting his glasses like the rabbit from the Winnie the Pooh cartoon.

"Grishanya, isn't it dangerous to live in Nepal without a visa?"

"I visited Romashka in prison, Vasya. Five people there are serving two-year sentences for expired visas. However, I have already done time. I have nothing to fear. It's no big deal to eat at the government's expense for a few years."

"How's Romashka doing in jail? We'd better visit him."

"He's okay. He's gets treated for scabies or lice from time to time, just ordinary prison stuff. He always has charas. He is doing time like a king, getting high every day. And where is your family, Vasya? Have you come without your girls?"

"Lenka and Vasilinka flew to Russia for a couple of months. Dan has arrived with his wife and child instead."

"When did he settle down to married life? He was a bachelor last season."

---

[67] Little Red Riding Hood - a famous and very popular Soviet movie. Grisha's sister, Yana Poplavskaya, played the lead role.

"He'll come here a bit later, Grisha. He settling his family in and then I'm sure he'll come. You can ask him yourself how he ended up with a wife and a five-year old child."

"Look at this character coming down the street! He must be a Chechen," Lenk says, sitting back in an armchair, having felt the approach of something new and interesting. "Maybe at least something will cheer me up today, as nobody, except for us, has come in here the whole day."

Vlad Lenk, a big guy with oriental facial features and a small beard, now resembles a genie that it is unlikely that anything in this world could cheer up.

"I feel new blood and new ears," rubbing his hands and grinning, says our genie, getting prepared for a conversation with the Chechen.

Trusting Vlad's authoritative statement, we also make ourselves comfortable, waiting for something that could somehow add variety to the everyday life of Pokhara. Coming closer to the tables in the open air, the new character with the face of an ordinary Caucasian stops in front of the entrance and examines us for some time, as if deciding whether to come in or not. Dressed in a sleeveless sports shirt, shorts and sneakers, resembling a newly-arrived tourist, he is first to start talking.

"Hi there, lads! I see you live here," hunched over in the manner of a Russian criminal, the Chechen, who has somehow appeared in Nepal out of nowhere, says to us. "Have you seen any darkeys here lately?"

"And who do they call darkeys here, in Nepal, I wonder? This is something new," fighting down a smile, Vlad Lenk asks seriously, like a teacher.

"Well, sort of like me, Chechens."

"So, are you a Chechen?" making a surprised face, Grisha joins in the game.

"Well, I am not a Chechen exactly, I am half Ingushetian."

"I've been living here for two years, I've seen people of different nations, but this is the first time I have seen a Chechen. So this is what you Chechens look like. My name is Grisha. I'm almost Nepali, although I'm from Moscow. Nepal is not a place where Chechens go for vacations. What is your name, my Chechen brother? Sorry, there are no Nazis here, I cannot call you a darkey."

"My name is Marat."

"How old are you, Marat?"

"I'm twenty five. My father sent me here to get away from mafia showdowns. He is a big cheese in the Chechen government; he distributes land plots. And now the situation in my homeland is not calm. Enemies from another Chechen clan want to kill him. He and one Arab built a big hotel in the United Arab Emirates, and the Arab conned him out of his money. I got my education in the Emirates, lived there for ten years, and visited that Arab many times. He seemed like a normal Arab, and then turned into a vulture. He sold the hotel behind my father's back, and decided to hide. So my father's people had to abduct the Arab's brother and transfer him to Chechnya. They sent me here to hide and to undergo treatment at the same time."

"What's the matter with you? Do you have tuberculosis, too? Grisha interrupts, showing interest.

"No, I don't have tuberculosis. I have one little sin; I like heroin very much. I've loved it for many years."

"You don't have AIDS?" Grisha asks him again, for some reason taking an interest in his health.

"No, I don't have AIDS. Should I?"

"No, you shouldn't. It's just that a Russian chemist lives here, in Pokhara. He is also the son of a famous person, the head of the Moscow institute of chemistry. His dad sent him away here, to Nepal, because he really loves smack. The son is a burnt-out junkie, and an AIDS sufferer on top of that. Thanks to his good education, he can cook any drug in the kitchen. I think you'll get acquainted with him, maybe you'll even be friends."

"Guys, could you help me find a gun? I have no problems with cash, I'll pay as much as necessary."

"No, brother, although there's a revolution in Nepal, we will not look for a gun for you," Vlad answers on behalf of all of us, pulling a piece of hashish out of a beautifully carved box. "Peace and love. That's our philosophy. Sit down with us, Marat. Have you ever smoked a chillum?"

"I like hash, but I've never tried a chillum. I'll smoke it with pleasure, if you teach me."

"Then, watch us and repeat. There are two main rules when smoking a chillum: don't touch the chillum with your lips and don't talk while it is in your hands. Marat, here is a piece of hashish, crumble it up while I dry a cigarette."

"Lenk, listen, where is our psychedelic old man Rico? I haven't seen him for ages," I say to Vlad, remembering my hashish teacher.

"Vasya, don't ask me anything else. I don't know anything about him and I don't want to," Lenk starts complaining, while drying a cigarette with a lighter.

"How is that, Lenk? You've been the best friends for many years, haven't you?"

"He stole a girl from me, Vasya. I was having a beautiful love story with a young lady" shyly lowering his eyes, Lenk says, while mixing tobacco with hashish. "I lived with her for six months on Kho Phangan, I fell head over heels in love with her. I thought I'd finally found a normal girlfriend. My love ended when we had a quarrel once after we had got high, I don't even remember what it was about. I think it was because a transvestite gave me a blowjob at a party. And she went to Rico for the night to spite me. She came back in the morning and said she had fucked him in revenge. Couldn't he have resisted, the old bastard? A pussy turned out to be more important to him than his friend. I don't want to know him anymore. If he shows up here, I'll move to another restaurant, I don't want to see him."

"Yeah, Vlad, it has been an eventful year. Maybe it's because it's a leap year? My whole life passes from one leap year to the next. I have experienced a crisis every leap year, all my life. In the following year a new idea is born, then comes its blossoming and implementation. Then it slowly fades away in the third year, and the fourth brings a crisis again. I hope I can survive this leap year."

"Yeah, and I wish to know the things it's preparing for us in the future," adds Arik with a sigh.

"Om Mani Padme Hum," Lenk breaks the silence, loudly pronouncing the mantra of compassion.

Everybody stays silent for some time, lost in their own problems and memories.

"Well, thank you, my Chechen brother, you have cheered me up," Vlad says to Marat, standing up. "I will remember about darkeys and guns in Nepal for the whole day. I'll go and pack charas, I need money for the leap year."

Chapter 36. Part One. Inside.

"Hi, David. How are you?"

"No mom, no dad, no whiskey, no soda, just vodka and Red Bull," laughing, the toothless Iranian answers, narrowing his eyes due to the bright sunlight.

"David, Russia is neighbor to a country called Azerbaijan. Your accent and appearance reminds me of an Azerbaijani."

"I understand the Azerbaijani language, it is almost like Iranian. I know a total of about twelve languages. I am an international drug dealer."

"Tell me then, international David, you know everybody. Do you remember German Nick, the old Goan drug dealer?"

"I remember him very well. He served twenty months here. I had just been locked up and he was about to be released. We were together for a month here. Vasya, why do you ask about him?"

"David, I know him very well, too. He was my first drug dealer. I used to buy all my drugs from him. That's why I ask. What quantity of drugs did he have when he was arrested?"

"Three hundred grams of charas and three hundred ecstasy tablets. He was charged under the same article as you, 21C, from ten to twenty years. He had the same lawyer as you and I have. Don't worry, Vasya, the lawyers will get you out of prison. You'll serve twenty months at the most."

"Vasiliy, visit!" a guard shouts.

As if having received an electric shock, I jump up from my place, forgetting what I was talking about. The wait is finally over. I run to the entrance joyfully like a child, to see my loved ones.

"How I am glad to see you! Vasilinka you are so big. You've become a head taller. Let me kiss you all."

Here is the only thing I've been dreaming about for six months. Why is the world structured so that we do not appreciate the things we have, and we only regret losing them when they are gone? How did it happen that I put at risk the opportunity to be close to my loved ones in the name of my illusory ideals and basic principles? We silently look at each other for a while. Little Vasilinka's palm tightly squeezes my hand. I don't even want to talk about anything; I just want to watch. My mother is first to break the silence.

"We told Vasilinka that you were a hero when you saw a girl being beaten up by hooligans and defended her. You had to beat the hooligans badly, they went to the hospital and you were put in prison. But the police will soon work the matter out and let you go."

"So it was, mom," I say, lowering my eyes for a moment.

"Oh, daddy, daddy. How could you?"

"Forgive me, daughter, I will soon get out of here and we'll have a ball together."

"I forgive you," sighs my little princess, hugging me around the neck.

"Tell me, daughter, do you like going to a Russian school?"

"I really like it. I understand everybody, and I have a lot of friends."

"There's probably no chance to make a freak out of you," I say, smiling, and kiss her on the cheek.

"No, dad, I won't wear dreadlocks like freaks do. I like Barbie. And I like to listen to different music. We were at Tamir's. His daughter Surika will go to school this year. And I'll study at home with mom."

"Yes, we were at Tamir's," Lena interrupts us, gently touching my cheek. "For some reason he is not doing anything to get you out of here."

"That's it, Lena, that's what I was afraid of. He was my last hope. When the drug police chief Pashish came to arrest me, the first thing he said was that only Tamir could help me. He gave me a phone with Tamir's number and said to call him. But Tamir was in Ukraine then. He said that Tamir was the best Russian DJ, and his good friend for many years. He said he knew Tamir's daughter Surika, and knew that she and our Vasilinka went to the same school.

So I waited for six months, thinking I could get out of here with Tamir's help. Six months passed, the police asked the court to extend my term. If someone had spoken to Pashish, I could have been released on bail. So Tamir was my only hope, and now I have nothing to hope for."

"So, how long will you stay in here, son?" my mother asks anxiously, stroking me on the head with a warm hand.

"If none of Pashish's friends will speak for me and things shape up in my favor, I will serve a year or a year and a half. If the lawyer makes a mistake, I will serve from ten to twenty years. Crazy Psyu succeeded in getting her Murtinian released for thirty thousand bucks. He didn't spend a month in prison. Surely it should be possible to get me released for five thousand? I have already done six months. The case was so simple with Murtinian. The policemen just forgot to come to take him to court on the fourteenth day when his term was to be extended. According to the law, if your term is not extended, you can be released on bail on the fifteenth day. Many ways to get out of here could be found, if there was someone to intercede for me."

"Vasiliy, in addition to Tamir not wanting to speak for you, he also started to stand up for the bad guy who brought you here," Lena says, looking sideways at our daughter and winking at me. "Don't forget, Vasya, the bad guy works for Tamir. He has no reason to save you."

"There is still a small chance to try to free me through Vova. When I was transferred to the court, I asked the policemen how I could get out. They told me, 'let the one who came to visit you in Panjim prison at night come to talk with Pashish. The car had a prominent number plate, 001.' And that car belongs to the son of someone from the authorities, the son of one of the ministers of Goa, one of Vova's friends. If Vova refuses to help me, he is a bastard. After all, when I was arrested, I could have paid the police off with Vova's money, but he convinced me not to give them the money, saying that the police did not have a warrant for my arrest. He promised that if I were put into prison for a day, his friend would quickly pull me out. The police brought me Vova's MDMA. Shouldn't he at least have some sort of conscience? After all, I am doing time in here instead of him."

"Darling, I'll try to speak to him, but Vova is unlikely to do something for you. He has been scared since you went to prison. He doesn't respond to phone calls. If he wanted to help you, he would have done it long ago. He is afraid you will grass on him. Maybe he hasn't got any money either at the moment, just like us. Just one thousand is left from the six thousand dollars your mother gave us. And we need something to live on here. Be patient a little longer. The season is starting, I'll start making kvass and selling hash cakes. I'll earn some money and try to get you out of here."

"But still try to find Vova. As a last resort, I have many friends, relatives, my ex-wife. They will help, if I ask. I'll be able to borrow the money; just get me out of here before I go bonkers. Prison is a serious test for the mind."

"Hold on, Vasiliy, we will do our best to get you out. By the way, I have good news for you. We will visit you twice a week. I had to pay the lawyer five thousand rupees, but I think it's worth it."

"What a penny pincher that lawyer is! He has already received fifty thousand from us and did nothing, yet he still takes money for getting a permit for additional visits. Well, to hell with the money, I will earn more. How are you going to make it without me? You yourself need money to live on. And here I am, a burden on you."

"Don't worry about us, dear. I leased our apartment in Russia, so five hundred dollars are dripping in every month. Focus on your health and taking care of yourself."

"Your time is up," the warden interrupts us, pointing at the wall clock.

Giving Vasilinka a good-bye hug, I enjoy every second, trying to remember these moments. I imagined how I would hug her so many times over the past six months. I lived without my daughter for six months. She is the only thing of real value they have managed to take away from me. Everything else can be earned or bought. But depriving me of the opportunity to watch my little princess growing up is a very severe punishment. Can't they see somewhere in the heavens that I have already paid off my karma? How long will I be punished? Is it possible that everything I have done in my life, thinking I was doing good things, turned out to be the ravings of a crazy idiot? Did I really sin so much to deserve ending up in here?

"I'll see you in two days, daddy," says Vasilinka, hugging me with her little palms.

Lena kisses me so passionately I want to push her off. For so long I have tried to forget those lips and to get rid of the memories that frequently cause me to suffer sleepless nights. How can I explain to her that the pain of having everything taken away from me is so strong that I'll have to lift my prison dumbbell until I get blisters? Only the physical pain will help me forget those lips for a while. When I'm outside, I will always kiss her as passionately as she is kissing me now.

"Lena, the guards are staring at us, you're in India," I say, stepping back and breaking apart our little freedom.

"Everything will be fine, son, I believe in you," my mother whispers in my ear, hugging me tightly.

Chapter 36. Part Two. Outside.

"Go on in," I open the door for my beauties. "This is your house now."

"Wow, it's so beautiful!" yells my Vasilinka and makes a running jump onto the sofa in the main room.

"How do you like your Nepalese apartment? I walked around the whole of Pokhara for an entire month. Everybody offers huge houses with shabby furniture and rats running around. No one has small, high-quality housing. This apartment is the best in Pokhara. If you don't pay attention to the Nepali toilet bowl, on which you have to squat, you could think we are in Switzerland.

"Thank you, dear. You've done great this time. A huge main room, bedroom, dining room, kitchen, TV. It's everything I need," hugging me around the neck, my beloved kisses me sweetly on the lips, which have been thirsty for tenderness for three months.

"I also want to kiss daddy!" my daughter shouts, climbing me like a tree. "My first tooth fell out in Russia. It didn't hurt," she shows me a funny gap in the row of small teeth.

"Lena, you have noticed the kitchen, the TV, but you didn't pay attention to the most important thing. There are large windows all along the perimeter of the apartment. We have a three-hundred-and-sixty-degree view from anywhere in it. You can look at the top of the Himalayas, or at the lake, it's up to you. Let's go to the balcony, I'll show you the most beautiful part."

"It would be better if you told me what the story was with crazy Olya. I understood from your letter that you fucked her."

"Lenochka, you are the same as always. Did I write to you that I had something with her? The fact that I slept with her on the same balcony does not mean anything. She just couldn't sleep alone in a dark room.

"And was her running naked on the roof also a coincidence?" my wife asks, with her hands on her hips and a stern face.

"Lena, come on. I earned a thousand bucks on her; I did not sleep with her. Let's go and have a look at our balcony. Vasilinka can ride a bicycle there. It's the same size as the main room."

"Daddy, I've never seen so many colors," my baby shouts, running out first onto the balcony covered with constantly flowering Nepalese bindweed.

"Yes, it's impressive. When we got to the house, I noticed that the entire third floor was covered in purple and scarlet colors, like a greenhouse. But I thought that the owners of the house lived there."

"Just like in India, the owners here divided the first floor into six smaller rooms and they occupy one of them. They made a two-room condominium of the same size for foreigners."

"So, you say you did not sleep with crazy Olya. Well, I had a wonderful time. I went to open airs in Moscow and Samara. I was also surrounded by a bunch of crazy guys. One guy told me a joke. I was laughing so hard I almost fell out of bed," my honey starts teasing me.

"Well, you seem to have put on weight," I respond. "You must have eaten sausages with meat dumplings every day."

"I put on a little, just five kilograms. But I promise I will ride a bike here, and lose the weight in a month. Will we have a housemaid here?"

"There was one, but she ran away yesterday. I tried to teach her how to wash the windows; I wanted everything to be beautiful for your arrival. I bought washing fluid, clean cloths and newspapers. Here they wipe the window with a dirty rag and think it is clean if you can see through it. I showed her how to wash them, and she said to me: 'I could wash the windows of ten houses in this time. If you need such cleanliness, wash it yourself,' she turned and walked away. I was washing all fifteen windows all day yesterday. But look what a nice view there is through them."

"It's good that you washed the windows, you're my smart cookie. However, I like the large refrigerator most of all. We can stock up at the market once and not worry for a whole week."

"The large fridge is definitely down to me. When I first came here, there was none. I went to the owners of the house and said: 'Do you want to get all the money for five months at once? Buy a fridge.' The old Nepali was pleased to see such money. 'Yes, I do,' he says. 'I'll buy you any refrigerator.' 'Just buy me a good, big one; it will remain yours anyway.' The next day he brought me a fridge, smaller than a stool, the cheapest one. Even a bottle of beer didn't fit into the freezer. I had to go to the store and pay extra to exchange it for a bigger one."

"I love you, darling. This time you did everything for us. I don't want to live here in a huge house; this apartment is the best I have seen in Nepal."

"And the location is convenient. Five minutes from the kindergarten, five minutes from the lake. Five minutes on foot to get to everything you need."

"Vasiliy, you talk as if we were in paradise. It's a pity that there is nowhere to go in this paradise. When I think that I'll have to spend three months here, depression sets in immediately. We are going to do each other's heads in; there is absolutely nothing to do here. There are so many interesting things in Russia, and what is there here?"

"Can't we just enjoy paradise, and just live?"

"Vasya, when I was fifteen I moved from the fucking town of Labytnangi to the big city, having dreamt of living in a metropolis. I lived in a hostel, in rented apartments. I sunk my teeth into life in order to achieve my dream. As soon as I started to succeed, as soon as we purchased our own house, you took me to the ass end of the world, where the only entertainment is looking at a mountain lake, or going to a party by a cornfield."

"Calm down, darling, there are no parties here now. Globalization has reached this place too. Parties are banned now. Two Russians are currently serving time in jail. The drug police came to their hotel. Two kilograms of charas were found in a German's room. The German escaped through the window and all his accomplices were put in prison. They tried to throw parties here. Now trance parties are illegal in Pokhara."

"You see, Vasiliy, there aren't even any parties here. I feel like the wife of a Decembrist[68]. Everything is beautiful, of course. I appreciate that you found a good nest before we arrived. But we'll

---

[68] Decembrists - members of the Russian nobility opposition movement and various secret societies of the second half of the 1810s - the first half of 1820s, who organized an anti-government uprising. They were exiled

start to have fights again. Twenty-four hours together, without rest. You will do my head in with your lectures on spiritual development and quantum leaps in perception. And there is nowhere to run away from you. Meanwhile, my friends in Russia each have two mink coats already, drive jeeps not bikes, go to fitness clubs and large supermarkets, where you can buy anything, not only what's available."

"Lenochka, tell me, what do you need a mink coat for? It's warm here all year round, flowers bloom all year round, and you have a bicycle instead of an exercise bike. If you don't want to ride your bicycle, a cab costs ten cents here. Although you are right that there is nowhere to go. I met you at the airport in a large jeep. I remember your love for jeeps; I rented it especially for you, my love. And the products in Russian supermarket are all half-plastic, the fruit and vegetables don't taste right, they are genetically modified. Do you remember Igor Gandhi? He was once the largest supplier of soybeans for almost all of the meat processing plants in Moscow. He doesn't eat anything produced at those plants, as he saw with his own eyes how it's made. All of the sausages are eighty percent produced from genetically modified soya. Have you ever seen pink meat after cooking? It should be grey and tough, like that of a wild animal. But it is full of chemicals that should be stored in jars with the inscription 'Attention - Poison'. And it's not just the case with meat, my dear. The entire Russian food industry substitutes natural ingredients with chemicals. Whereas here you can still eat natural food, grown without fertilizers. Even the sausages that the natives make here are much safer than any Russian ones, because they don't know about chemical additives. Nepal has everything for enjoying life. You won't find anywhere else such a peaceful place with a budget of one hundred dollars per person, per month. Rich people come from big cities to Nepal, because they know how to appreciate the state of relaxation where you don't need to hurry anywhere. Other people can only dream about admiring the Himalayas for months. And if you can't even find peace in your head here, you won't find it anywhere. You won't find it in the city, or on a desert island. You are always dissatisfied with something. Apparently, it is an integral feature of all women. You're always lacking something."

"It is you, my dear, that can bliss out anywhere, because you've already had your full of everything. But for me Pokhara is like a prison. Like staying three months in a Nepali jail."

"Lena, jail is in our mind. If you get rid of it, then you won't care where you are. You'll get a buzz from everything. You should be able to enjoy everything you have at this moment of your life. Even in prison or a scrapyard you can be even happier than in Hollywood. Look at the people here. They are happy, everyone smiles. And you want supermarkets."

"Mom, dad, why have you started fighting again? We've just arrived, and you are already rowing."

"No, daughter, we are not rowing. Your mother and I are just discussing where it's better to live, in Russia or in Nepal."

"Daddy, you'd better go and smoke a chillum on the balcony, you will be kinder. Mom will unpack our things, and I'll make toy cakes for you."

---

for life to do hard labor in Siberia and their wives willingly went along with them. In the city of Tobolsk there is a monument to the wives of the Decembrists.

"Don't be mad at me, darling," embracing me gently again, Lena whispers in my ear. "I'm just tired after the overnight flight, I need to rest for a couple of weeks, to acclimatize, and I'll calm down. Everything will be fine. I'm going to sort out our things, and you listen to what is happening in Russia. Don't be offended, my dear; you've placed everything very well, but I will rearrange it all in my own way."

"Okay, my dear, but don't you be offended if I have to ask you when I need to find something in the apartment."

"Just memorize where I put things."

"Well, it's difficult for me, darling, to memorize where everything is, if it's not me who put it there. And in general, it seems illogical to me the way you place things," I say, feeling that I am starting to get agitated. "I would never have the idea of putting a glass jar with detergent on a narrow windowsill. It could fall off and break. It is not logical! It would be more logical to put it on the floor."

"And I think, my dear, that it is not logical to knock it off. You would have to be an elephant to knock into it."

Staying silent for a while, I watch with disappointment as my two days of work arranging things logically goes to waste.

"Well, okay, rearrange everything how you want. Tell me, what else is new in Russia, except for your girlfriends' mink coats?"

"I received a summons in your name from the police. Your father went to sound out the situation and found out that your accountant, Vlad Sernov, who worked for you for the past five years, had stolen your money. To be more precise, he stole the state's money that you gave him to pay taxes. It turned out that he cut that money in half. He paid one half, and shared the second half with the tax inspector, his buddy. Your accountant is a former tax inspector. They stole your taxes for many years and made fake invoices on a computer for you. An audit caught them after we had gone to India. However, they shifted the blame onto you without hesitation, and the tax police opened a fraud case against you. You owe the Russian state half a million. In addition, penalties are accrued on a daily basis. Our apartment was seized; we can't sell it now. The bailiffs are threatening to put it up for sale. If you arrive in Russia and show your passport to the border guards, they will press a special button and the cops will come for you with handcuffs. They will hold you until they resolve everything. How long it will take is up to the court to decide."

"That's an interesting piece of news. I don't know whether to laugh or cry. I thought Vlad was my friend and I didn't take receipts from him when I gave money for taxes. One pleasant fact is that I haven't been charged with a drug case. I don't know how many smugglers bought charas from me for export. I thought that it might be to do with Max or Ilka. We'll settle this problem. Tamir couldn't return to Russia for eight years, but we'll sort this out in a couple of years. We'll earn more money and pay off all our debts. We just need to buckle down a bit, but it's not a problem. I'm full of energy and I think that we will earn even more money next year. Sasha Venus did an excellent advert for me with his book Goa Syndrome, as I am portrayed as a positive character throughout the book. It tells of our restaurant, the psychedelic revolution, and our kvass. Andrey Loshak showed my interview nationwide on the NTV[69] program 'Reporter is My Profession'. Reporters from CentrNauchFilm[70] also came here to film a documentary. Three Russian TV channels did different programs about our restaurant, and five magazines published articles. We are now the face of Russian downshifting. It will attract even more tourists. And if we earn enough money, we'll repay all our debts and will be able to put an end to selling drugs."

"It would be good if we could," Lena sighs, placing an incredible number of makeup jars on the table. "Sasha's book Goa Syndrome is spoken of well in Russia. There are a lot of different reviews in magazines and on the Internet. He managed to describe our first season very well."

"Yeah, Lena, everything began so nicely. Who could have imagined that it was the last season for all the freaks and hippies? Now there are only nutcases, drunkards, drug addicts and losers left in Goa. But, nevertheless, many people have read Goa Syndrome and will come to see the Promised Land next season. After all, everybody thinks and believes that the Goan paradise is still alive. Everything is going be all right, darling. Let the freaks and their trance go to hell, we'll make money from the tourists and swim in the sea."

"Vasiliy, I hope everything will be as you say, as we don't have another way out. Tell me, honey, what's new in Nepal, since last year?" Lena asks me, carefully moving the pile of my things from the right shelf to the left shelf of the wardrobe. "You can skip the part about the neighbors' calving cows and pigs. It is unlikely that anything has changed during a year in Pokhara."

"We have the following news here. A new character appeared, his name is Marat. He jacked up for two months so intensively that he began to look like a skeleton. He is totally spaced out. He rented a motorbike, got high, and forgot it somewhere. The Nepalese men forced him to buy a new one. He tried to protest, but they beat the hell out of him. He bought them a new motorbike, and two months later he remembered where he had left the old one. If he asks you to lend him any money, don't. He'll blow it on drugs and won't pay you back. He owes the whole of Pokhara. Another new Russian loon came here, his name is Akam. He sold his shared apartment in Moscow and wants to set up a business renting out canoes and inflatable boats when he gets to Goa. You will recognize him at once; he looks like Shurik from "Kidnapping, Caucasian Style[71]". I even feel a little sorry for him. I'm afraid he will be scammed out of his money before he reaches Goa. Like any good nutcase, he thinks there are only good people around. In general, everything is just the same. All of the drug dealers that lived here last season have converged on Pokhara. They are having a rest here and doing their business."

***

"Good morning, darling," I wake my sleeping Lena with gentle kisses.

"Mommy, wake up," Vasilinka, who woke up first, kisses her on the other cheek. "Daddy will walk me to kindergarten today, will you come with us?"

---

[69] NTV - Russian television channel.

[70] CentrNauchFilm - a Russian non-fiction film studio.

[71] Shurik from Kidnapping, Caucasian Style - the lead male character in a 1967 Soviet comedy film dealing with a humorous plot revolving around bride kidnapping, an old tradition that used to exist in certain regions of the Northern Caucasus.

"How can you wake up so early?" Lena stretches without opening her eyes. "I have a headache after yesterday's rum and coke. Heat up the porridge for Vasilinka; it's in the fridge. I am awake already."

"Well I feel great, my love. Darling, you've been living here for a week and you still can't get used to waking up with the Sun. Maybe we should stop drinking in the evenings?"

"Listen, don't start spoiling my mood with your moral preaching first thing in the morning. Take Vasilinka to kindergarten, go and see Lenk and do your tai chi workout with him, have breakfast at the restaurant, have a smoke, and then come back. Just don't do my head in. I'm going to sleep some more. Vasilinka's stuff is on the table."

I walk along the small, deserted street, holding my daughter's hand. It's not hot yet; the Sun hasn't had time to dry the dew on the green leaves. The air still smells of the night's freshness and blooming jasmine. The Creator painted this land in a bright palette. Almost all of the bushes, grass and trees are covered with flowers. The riot of colors gives you the idea that this must be what paradise looks like. My little princess, picking the most beautiful flowers as we walk along the road, holds a bunch with unusual colors.

"How do you like your new kindergarten, daughter?"

"I like it, Daddy. There are even two non-Nepalese children, like me. They are half Nepalese, to be precise. Katrine has a German dad and Nepalese mother. And another boy has a Japanese mother and Nepalese father. They are fluent in English, and I love playing with them."

"Vasilinka, look how beautiful everything around is!"

There are no cars, so the green around us is not covered with dust like in large cities, where there are almost as many vehicles as people. All of this green mass blooms all year round, painting the world with all colors imaginable. Passing by a tree covered with white bell-shaped flowers the size of a bottle, we stop to admire them.

"Daddy, look at these big bell-flowers! I have never seen any like them! Look, there is another tree, all covered with small bright purple flowers."

"Look, daughter, how green the rice is growing in the field. And can you see the women in crimson saris working there? Tell me, isn't it incredibly beautiful?"

"Yes, Daddy, Nepal is like a fairytale. Everything is bright and colorful. When mother and I arrived in Russia, everything was like in a black and white movie. And people there don't say hello on the streets and don't smile at each other."

After walking a few meters, we stop again and observe three huge snails, about the size of my fist, creeping slowly along the asphalt road.

"The biggest one must be the daddy-snail, the smaller one is the mummy, and the last one is me, their daughter," my little beauty says, laughing loudly.

"Well, here we are. Look, all your friends have already arrived while we were looking at the snails. Listen to the teacher, and I'll go do tai chi with Lenk. I'll come for you in the afternoon."

Walking along the deserted road to Lenk's place, I meet a few locals whom I see for the first time. Despite the fact that I might never meet them again, each presses his hands together at his chest, smiles and greets me, saying the Nepalese word 'Namaste'. Coming into the courtyard where Lenk lives, I see him sitting in the summerhouse, holding a joint in one hand and a brush in the other, painting on a T-shirt stretched over a pillow.

"Namaste, Lenk," I greet him in Nepalese, pressing my hands together at my chest. "I've come to do tai chi with you. Are you ready to take me as a student today?"

"Namaste, Namaste, we'll finish smoking this joint and then go up to the roof. There, in the shadows of the trees, it won't be hot for another hour. Vasya, do you know what the Nepalese word 'Namaste' means?"

"It must be a greeting."

"Vasya, 'Namaste' means 'I see God in your eyes,' or 'the divine within me bows to the divine in you.' Aren't the Nepalese people forward-minded in this regard?"

"Sounds nice. I'd never thought about it."

"You know, Vasyan, inspiration has come to me. I've been drawing for two hours. I have been working on one T-shirt for a whole month. I'll sell it for five hundred bucks, not less. Look at these Buddhist demons," Lenk shows me a white shirt, almost completely covered with a beautiful, delicate pattern, through which the faces of Eastern deities can be seen. "I woke up at the crack of dawn today with a terrible desire to paint. I neither washed, nor had breakfast. I took a brush and have been painting the entire morning."

"Yeah, your shirts are outstanding. Each is like a unique picture. There are more layers of paint than background. And all of the decorations are so fascinating that they look like patterns up close, and resemble dragons or demons from a distance."

"Vasyan, sometimes I manage to sell shirts like this for five hundred bucks, and sometimes I give one in payment for my debts. I am always in debt, like any normal artist. I actually prefer to give them as gifts to people who understand and appreciate the work of an artist. Any jackass can buy Armani or Brioni without hesitation, as thousands of the same jackasses wear the same clothes. The clothes that I paint are unique, guaranteed. People who appreciate my gifts also provide me with some free services, or give me something. I like giving more than selling."

We finish smoking the joint in the overgrown summerhouse and go upstairs to the roof of the second floor, and watch from above as a hardworking Nepalese man mows the neat lawn around his house.

"Vasya, I love Nepalese people for that. An Indian man would prefer to sleep and throw garbage in front of the entrance. And these people are like ants, they do everything beautifully."

On the roof, we stand in a place where the high bamboo thickets cast dense shadows.

"Vasyan, now I'll teach you to stand like a tree. Repeat after me. Feet shoulder width apart, knees slightly bent, arms in front, fingers at eye level and stand like this, contemplating the space between your palms. Stand like this for as long as you can and try to think about nothing. I stand like this for thirty minutes in the morning and evening. Advanced Taoist monks stand like this for two hours a day.

Having stood for five minutes, I realize that this exercise is perfect for me. This gymnastics and meditation is just right for lazy people like me. Having stood for a few more minutes, I begin to feel that I've broken into a sweat and that my knees are shaking. It takes all of my effort to keep my arms, which feel like they have been filled with lead, parallel to the ground.

"That's it, Lenk. I can't do this anymore. It feels like I have been doing gymnastics for half an hour."

"Well, then, wait for me, I'll finish in half an hour," says Vlad, still staring at one point, and smiling only with the corners of his lips.

Having sat down on the mattress lying next to me, I suddenly feel a strong wave of bliss and euphoria sweep through my body. Leaning back against the concrete parapet, I observe how harmonious Vlad looks. Covered with oriental tattoos, he looks like a futuristic twenty-first century Buddha against the background of green bamboo and Himalayan peaks.

"Vlad, I get the impression that you are sitting on an invisible Zen horse. How you look has just blown my mind, so that I think I have understood why you get a buzz out of doing these exercises every day. Not only do you keep your muscles in tone, but you also relax you brain as well. For ten minutes, Vlad, I also managed to switch off my brain, which is normally like a broken record, ping-ponging some endless nonsense around my head. For a whole ten minutes, I could feel the frailty of the whole world. I felt like a small part of the Universe that is taking a bit of care of itself, keeping this body in tone. Creating this tone in my muscles, I felt how my restless mind calmed down, immersing me in a state of bliss. Just like you are now, I was standing and smiling at the world."

"Vasyan, if only you knew how long ago the Taoists got the point. They have even cooler gymnastics. It's called Baguazhang. The exercises were invented by shamans; we still have a long way to go. When I succeed in keeping the upper Tan Tien for two hours in tree pose, I'll go to China to look for a Baguazhang teacher. Drugs are not the only thing to get a buzz out of in this world. There are many more interesting things in Asia. However, why be a hypocrite: I am guilty of loving drugs, but I try hard not to abuse them," Lenk says, beaming, without moving a muscle. "Well, Vasyan, that's enough gymnastics for today, let's go to a restaurant and have some breakfast. I'm in a creative mood. I want scrambled eggs for breakfast, fried with fresh white cheese on a bun, pancakes with honey, a cup of coffee with milk and a glass of mint tea. I weighed one hundred and sixty kilograms five years ago, and now I weigh only a hundred. Surely I can treat myself if I have good inspiration in the morning. Vasya, if you want you can come every day and we'll do exercises together. I wake up at seven o'clock in the morning here."

"Where shall we go for breakfast, Lenk? My Beautiful Restaurant or Be Happy'?"

"Let's go to Be Happy today, Vasya. Let's put on the Ritz. Breakfast is half a dollar more expensive there, but it's more delicious by a whole ten dollars. And there are no Russian junkies there, only decent people. I have had a creative mood since morning; I will deny myself nothing. Vasya, if earlier the cream of the psychedelic underground hung out in My Beautiful Restaurant, now there are only drug addicts, AIDS sufferers and nutcases. I can't understand how it happened."

On the way to the restaurant, dozens of pullers-in try to invite us into empty establishments. Having entered the Be Happy restaurant, where my family was pretty much the only customers during the previous revolutionary season, I see the joyful owner busily serving several occupied tables. Here my Lena taught the chef to make mashed potatoes instead of disgusting potato paste. The restaurant started to serve potato flapjacks, beetroot soup and other Russian dishes. The walls are decorated with photos of enlightened old men smoking chillums in different poses, as well as my daughter's drawings depicting the owners of the restaurant. The drawings of the Nepalese grandfather and his two daughters, son and mother are childishly absurd and funny, but it's touching that the owners still keep them hanging on the walls of their restaurant six months later. These people spend most of their life in the restaurant. Having seen us from a distance, the older daughter of the householder beams and quickly spreads a new tablecloth over our favorite table.

"Vasya, would you like me to show you how to distinguish between a genuine psychedelic warrior and a fortnight passenger?" Vlad asks me, sipping mint tea. "Look, two teas have just been brought to that table. The man who is taking his time and slowly stirring the sugar in his glass, admiring the Himalayan peaks appearing from behind the clouds, is French. He is a seasoned smuggler. He brings a kilogram of cocaine in his stomach from Colombia to Paris at a time. He closes a couple of deals a year, and then meditates here in this relaxed way. The man sitting next to him is Akam. Look how quickly he stirs his tea. He seems to be short of time. Tea is splashing into the saucer from his cup. However, in reality he has nowhere to rush. Akam is a really weird guy. He sold his room in Moscow for thirty-six thousand bucks and is walking around telling everybody about it. The poor bastard is at a loss to know what to spend the money on. His mental development is like that of Pinocchio, although he plays the flute well."

A cow passing by the restaurant, as if interested in our conversation, pauses to eye me, Akam and the French smuggler in turn.

"Some crooks will definitely con Akam out of his money, one hundred percent. I even feel sorry for him, but bollocks to that. Here is Arik," Lenk says, dramatically switching to another topic, pointing to a tall man with a cheerful sun umbrella walking along the road.

"Arik is also our passenger. Look, he is walking and enjoying every moment," I say to Lenk, sipping tea.

"Hi, there, Ara! Why are you shining today?" I say, handing my leftover toast to the cow, which has come close.

"Hi Vasya, Hi Lenk. I took the final test yesterday. I don't have AIDS! That fool died six months ago. She failed to take me with her. To mark the occasion, I suggest smoking a chillum and ordering a fruit salad with ice cream," Arik says happily, flopping into a plastic chair.

"What will we smoke on such an occasion? Pokhara is the only place left on the planet where you can do that in a restaurant on the main street," Lenk says, smiling and slapping his palm on the snout of the cow, which is trying to draw near to our table for a second serving.

"You won't catch me fucking without a condom again! I believe nobody now! Cheers to rubbers!" Arik says, raising a glass of tea. "By the way, Vasya, I have something to ask you. I recently received a letter from some Goans in Moscow; they say that there is currently no LSD there. The entire capital is covered in cocaine, but there is no acid anywhere. I know you have a couple of bottles left. They have already transferred the money to my card. Would you like to earn some dough? You'll only need to send them a package. Buy some nonsense for five hundred rupees for show, pour the acid in a bottle of eardrops, and send it. It's not necessary to write your surname in the sender info for a small package. So you risk nothing. If the deal is successful, you can sort me out later."

"Arik, you see how everything happens in time here in Asia! As soon as I am short of money, the heavens send me more. Bom Shiva!" I shout, praising the gods, exhaling a great puff of sweet, fragrant smoke. "A thousand bucks is just what I need right now, I lent my last six hundred to Dan."

**

"Hey, Dan. A week has passed; you must have come to repay your debt. Man, you don't look yourself. What's wrong? A delay with the money? Don't worry, Arik helped me earn a grand, so I can wait for another month."

"No, Vasya, I came for another reason. I have decided to get out of the business. Here are your two kilograms of charas back," says Dan, lowering his eyes and putting the package on the table. "I don't want to carry it across the border."

"Dan, it's up to you, of course, but I bought you charas with my last money. You will have to provide for your family in India. What are you going to do for a living?"

"Five hundred bucks is too little for such a risk."

"Dan, but I have no more money. The more charas you bring to India, the more you will earn. We already agreed, didn't we?"

"I changed my mind," Dan says, still looking at the floor. He hands me a small package. "Here's your MDMA. Ninety grams. My girlfriend and I took ten grams. I don't want to sell drugs anymore. I have drug dealer paranoia already, I see police everywhere. I'm leaving for Bombay tomorrow."

"And what about the six hundred bucks you borrowed from me for a week, Dan?"

"You can consider that you paid me six hundred bucks for bringing your MDMA across the border to Nepal."

"Dan, but I did everything for you. I had money for living and I have a business in Goa. I invested my last money in drugs for you. You understand, Dan, that you are ripping me off now? I thought you were my friend. I put my head on the block for you when you scattered MDMA on a tray in front of the police at that party. If it hadn't been for me, you would be sitting in a Goan jail now."

"Do this business by yourself. I don't give a shit about your friendship."

"Well, then, goodbye forever, Dan. I don't want to even know you. I will take everything across the border without your help. And you are acting like an asshole and a coward. I have nothing more to say to you."

"Think whatever you want. Bye Vasya, bye Lena," Dan says without looking up, leaving the room.

"So, Vasiliy? My trip to Goa by plane has gone down the drain. Again those fucking trains and buses. With a bag of drugs, on top of that," Lena says indignantly, angrily closing the door behind Dan. "We need to return to Goa soon, and once again we have no money."

"I'm such an idiot! Dan asked me to lend him three hundred dollars, and I gave him the last six hundred."

Chapter 37. Part One. Inside.

"Why have you been so preoccupied lately, Vasya?" Viktor asks me, peeling a green orange.

"In a week it will be six months since I've been in prison, Vitya. The prosecutor will soon extend my term for another two months. I'm trying to think of a way to influence him to avoid this extension."

"There you go again, Vasya, dreaming about the impossible. Forget that nonsense. Everybody would love to influence the prosecutor, but there is no chance. It would be better if you ate a slice of orange and dreamt that they will bring ripe oranges next time."

"Vitya, how can it be impossible if someone has already managed to get out of here for money?"

"The last time was three years ago. Then parties were still being held all over the place. The police didn't have the instruction to imprison foreigners and you could bribe yourself free for a thousand dollars on the spot. It was later that the minister of internal affairs stated through the media that there were no more drugs in Goa."

"Yeah, and do you know why he did that?" I say, wincing at the sour orange. "He must have done it so that his son and that drug dealer Apollo could freely sell drugs in Goa. All of the last parties took place under the protection of the minister's son. Vitya, you must have seen him many times. Only a few people know who his dad is."

"Why did they close all the parties down then?" Viktor asks, rubbing his legs with the orange peel.

"Other forces closed them down, Vitya. Those who wanted to take the minister's place. Look at the words that start newspaper articles about the drug dealers: 'The Interior Minister said that there were no more drugs in Goa. However, yesterday the drug police arrested a major Nigerian drug dealer with two grams of cocaine.' All of the newspaper articles about the arrests of drug dealers contradict the words of the minister about the absence of the drug business in Goa. All of the major drug dealers continue working under the cover of this minister's son, without any fear. They jail idiots like us. 'The police arrested two major drug dealers, named Winnie the Pooh and Mr. Bean," smiling, Viktor points at Greek Antonio and Scotsman James walking around the yard.

"The newspapers have had some interesting articles recently. Someone began digging around about the most influential drug dealers. According to the journalists, only three of them remain in Goa: Tamir, Apollo and Idu. I wonder how this story will end?"

"It will end with nothing, Vasya. They'll pay off the reporters and that's it, no more articles. All of the old drug dealers say that they make monthly payments to the chief of the drug police and sell the minister's son's drugs. Who will dare to touch them? A snake can't bite its own tail."

"A snake can bite its own tail. Well, bollocks to this politics! Vitya, what do you think – is it possible to fool the local cops? When I did my time in Panjim prison, Pashish proposed that I grass on a drug dealer and promised to assist in my release. What do you think, if I offer to grass on someone, will I be released on bail, or not?"

"It's not good to grass, Vasya. Grasses are like homos; if you agree once it means forever."

"I'm not going to grass on anyone, I want to fool the police. If I am released, I will run away immediately to Nepal. I'll make myself a new passport; I have people in Russia who can do this cheaply. Some other friends will get me a visa at the Indian Embassy, and others will arrange the entry and exit stamps. It will be no problem to leave the country. All I need is to be released."

"Vasya, who is going to believe a smartass like you? You already considered the cops to be fools once, and now you're sitting here. First you would have to grass on someone and then they would think about whether to free you or not. They could also add another charge to your case just to mock you."

"Vitya, but the police offered both of us freedom for thirty thousand bucks."

"Who knows; maybe they were just trying to cheat us out of our money."

"Yeah right; Murtinian was released, and we are still sitting here. Vitya, what if I use something larger as bait? For example, if I say that there is an MDMA lab in Goa. That they have MDMA worth one million dollars."

"But who is going to believe a smartass like you? Here, in prison, every other person tells such stories. Everyone wants to get out."

"Well, everything depends on me, Vitya. If I lie convincingly, they will believe me. Once I am released, in two days I'll cross the border to Nepal and show India my bare ass like Rico once did. To hell with India and all its police and their pet drug dealers. There are so many beautiful countries to live in. I'll go to Vietnam or Cambodia, open a restaurant on the beach, and make a fresh start."

"Get out of here first, dreamer. No one will believe your stories about a lab and a million bucks. If that were true, you would have been bought out of here for thirty thousand a long time ago. But you are a pauper, just like me, the same as all the others sitting around us. The last hope – codename 'Tamir' – has evaporated, and now you are filling your head with nonsense. Your brain will explode with all this raving. I understand that your girls came to see you and now you can't get your mind off this nonsense about how to get out of here quickly."

"Vasiliy, visit," a guard shouts, opening the door for me.

"There you are. Go, Vasya, and speak with your loved ones. Maybe you'll feel better for a while."

"Hi, girls! You've got suntans so quickly. I really don't want to talk about business; I would prefer just to look at you," I say, kissing everybody in turn. "You are so beautiful. We have only fifteen minutes. Lena, you have the most important information, so you speak first. What did Vova say about my case?"

"Your Vova is an asshole. He doesn't want to give us any money for a lawyer. Even though when you got locked up, he promised to hand over five thousand bucks. He is afraid to go to speak to the police with the minister's son. Or maybe he just doesn't want to."

"What a bitch! Well, what am I supposed to do then? I'll take care of my health and learn English for the next year and a half. There are no other options. Then we'll consider the topic closed. Tell me, how are things going for you here?"

"Mom and Vasilinka are having a wonderful time. But I want to go to Russia," says Lena sadly, lowering her eyes. "Nothing makes me happy, Vasiliy. I don't want to do anything here. I don't want to make cakes or kvass. I don't want to do anything. God damn this India. All my illusions about Goa have finally disappeared. I hate India now," my Lena says, almost crying. "We'll probably stay here for a couple of months and then leave. At least I will be able to something in Russia, whereas here I don't feel like doing anything. Whom should I try to do something for here in Goa? For the mugs that surround us now? There are only assholes left here. Your brother is coming to Goa soon. He'll stay here with your mom for several months after my departure. And I think Vasilinka should go to school. The annual fee for the local school was raised from two to five thousand dollars. We do not have much money. More precisely, we have no money at all."

"Lena, sell my laptop, the air conditioner, washing machine, sell everything you can, and go back to Russia. I understand you. Someday I will get out of here and come to you. The main thing is wait for me. Maybe it will be for the best if you leave, as my heart breaks when I look at you. It will be easier to survive in here without you."

Chapter 37. Part Two. Outside.

"Hi, Vasya; hello, Lenk. Are you getting stoned again after a workout?" Arik greets us, having just come into the restaurant.

"Why not get stoned in the morning, if there is nothing to do? Ara, why are you so serious first thing in the morning?"

"I have a problem because of you, Vasya. Your package arrived in Moscow yesterday; there was no LSD. There was all the crap you bought to add weight, but no bottle. They have already asked for their money back. So we got ripped off. Sorry for bad news in the morning."

"Arik, and what do I have to do with that?" I push away my uneaten pancakes, feeling that my appetite has instantly evaporated. "I took the acid to the post office and sent it. Why should I be responsible for it not getting to Moscow? Maybe they are tricking you, Arik?"

"No, they aren't tricking me. They are my friends; I have known them for a long time."

"Maybe the cops took it?"

"If the Moscow police had found it, they would have been arrested immediately. Vasya, did you compile a list of the contents when you sent the package?"

"No, I didn't. You don't need a list or a passport when sending small packages."

"Maybe the local police are onto you?" Lenk asks, pulling my pancakes towards him. "Vasya, you have to go to the post office and find out what happened, or return the money," Arik says seriously, eyeing someone far off behind me.

"It's kind of scary to go to the post office with such a matter after Romashka, but don't worry, I'll figure it out. It's not likely that the Nepalese police have ever seen LSD. Look, Arik, it looks like your Chelyabinsk buddy is coming down the street," I point to the approaching bald guy.

"All that was missing was seeing him, Vasya. It's definitely him. And I was thinking: 'why does that bald head look so familiar'? I think it's already too late to hide, he has spotted us."

"Hello, boys. Did you think you could hide from me in Nepal?" the guy asks us with a serious face and crazy eyes.

"How did you find us, Vanya?"

"One guy, Marat, told me where you could be found. He borrowed five hundred rupees from me. He is about to come here now, too."

"Oh, shit!" Lenk clutches his head, chewing the last pancake. "Breakfast is ruined; we need to move somewhere before Marat comes."

"How is life in Chelyabinsk?" carefully hiding my nervousness, I ask the strongly built bald guy with bulging eyes.

"I'm fine. I only wish I could have a Coca-Cola chair on top of the mountain and a juicer on the beach, so that the women would put out more often. I'm quite reflective, because my kundalini has twisted in the wrong direction. However, I understood everything about your conspiracy. You wanted to drive me out of Goa, but I have found you, even in Nepal."

"That's it, Vanya, stop, I can't listen to this. You know that you need a psychiatrist."

"I was at the doctor's in Chelyabinsk. He prescribed me some pills. But they don't help, because it's all about my kundalini."

"It's not about your kundalini, Vanya. You should stop taking drugs. You'd better stop smoking, too."

"On the contrary, I came to Nepal to smoke charas, Vasya. It helps me to twist my kundalini energy back."

"Hey, adzur[72] give us the bill, we're leaving," Lenk says to the owner of the restaurant, hurridly wiping his lips with a napkin.

"Where are you going, guys? I wanted to talk to you. Marat promised he'd come now."

"No, I'm sorry, Vanya, I need to go to the post office to sort something out."

"And I feel I need to do gymnastics urgently," Lenk says, getting up from the table.

"Well, maybe you will talk to me, Arik? Should I sit and talk to myself here, or what?"

"I don't feel good, Vanya, I'd better go and get some sleep. Bye, guys, talk to you later. See you tonight."

Coming out of the restaurant, I see Vanya mumbling something to himself with a serious, lonely face.

***

---

[72] adzur - a Nepalese junk word to replace any word. Indian people sometimes jokingly refer to Nepalese people as 'adzurs'.

"Thank God you're back from that post office," Lena says with a sigh, opening the door for me. "When will you give up the drug business? Max is in jail, Nick is in jail, Romashka is in jail. Do you understand that you went to the post office to ask about drugs that you sent to Russia? Do you realize you could have ended up getting arrested like Romashka?"

"Well, not exactly. Don't worry, dear. Everything went well. The Nepalese would have never thought that there were two hundred doses of LSD in a sealed bottle of eardrops. It was even fun. I went into the post office and asked, 'Where are my eardrops I sent in the package?' And they said, 'We beg your pardon, a new rule came into force a month ago. Now you cannot send medicines without a prescription. Your drops are in Kathmandu, at head office.' The post office personnel apologized to me very politely and said that my bottle would be delivered by the first plane to Pokhara. So I'll get my drops tomorrow."

"What if they found out there were two hundred doses of LSD there? What if you are arrested tomorrow?"

"Lena, we are in Nepal. They don't know about any drugs except charas."

***

"You were deceived here, too. You said we would have a compartment on the train," my Lena says, almost crying, seating Vasilinka on her knees. "I'm so tired, when will it be over? First we spent fourteen hours in that fucking bus; I thought it would fall apart on the road. When it rained, water poured down on me from holes in the roof. Then there were the Maoist guerillas. When they attacked our bus driver and began to beat him up, I thought we were going to be taken hostage. Then in bloody Gorakhpur Vasilinka cried all night from earache, I thought I would go crazy. After all, there are only self-taught vets and no hospitals within a radius of several hundred kilometers. And now it turns out we were sold normal seats instead of the promised compartment."

"Well, at least the car has air conditioning," I try to calm down my wife, who is ready to explode with resentment and indignation. "The travel agent in Nepal swore that those tickets were for a compartment. It's not my fault, Lena."

"Vasiliy, we are carrying two kilograms of hashish, one thousand doses of MDMA and five hundred drops of LSD. Do you realize what a mess you have got us into? And last night in Pokhara you hung around the house tripping on acid, instead of helping me to pack our things."

"Lena, you know I didn't get high deliberately. When I received my LSD 'eardrops' at the post office, I decided to immediately pour them into another container. I spilled half the bottle on my hand. It was concentrated acid and instantly absorbed through the pores in my skin. It was a good thing I had the sense to wipe the acid off my hand with a handkerchief, otherwise I would still be tripping now. Grisha in Pokhara put my acid-soaked handkerchief in some water and takes a sip every day. I think I was extremely lucky. One Israeli told me that he spilled a hundred drops on his hand and was tripping for three days."

"Vasiliy, it seems to me that lately the word 'lucky' and you have been in different parts of the world."

"I'm sorry, honey, I really want to save you from all these unexpected troubles. It just happens like that, by accident. By the way, look: I believe we aren't the only Russians on this train. I bet those white people loading their belongings are also Russians."

"Hello, fellow countrymen," I address the couple, who pass by with big suitcases.

"Are you Russians, too?" a guy with a round, simple-minded face asks in astonishment. "Are you going to Bombay, too? That's good, it will be fun to go together."

Having happily taken the free seats in front of us, they are first to introduce themselves.

"I am Vitalik. This is my wife, Lena, and this is our son, Kirill."

Being thirsty for communication with a Russian their own age, our children immediately start playing some kind of a game, screaming and jumping from one shelf to another.

"We have been living in Goa for three years," says Vitalik, putting his arm around his wife's shoulders. "Together with an Indian guy we run a restaurant in the south, in Palolem."

"We have a restaurant, too. In the very north of Goa. It is called Hemp. Have you heard about it?"

"Are you the Vasya described in the book Goa Syndrome?" Vitalik asks in surprise, laying food on the table.

"That's me. More specifically, that was me three years ago. A lot has changed since then, and Goa is not the same as it was. I'm all white and fluffy in the book, but now, in real life, I can't go back to Russia because I'm wanted by the police."

"Not for fraud, by any chance?" Vitalik asks with a smile, pulling out a large pack of Nepalese potato chips.

"How do you know about the charge? It wasn't mentioned in the book as far as I remember."

"I don't know, I just presumed. I have been wanted on this charge in Russia for several years, too. I worked as a real estate agent in a large Moscow-based company, even though I'm from Belarus. Several years ago, my passport expired and I had to return to Belarus. I asked my boss to give me leave to go home for a couple of weeks, but he flatly refused to let me go. He said I was the backbone of the whole department. He advised me to get a new passport made quickly through his friends for three thousand dollars. I agreed. And at that time, the Chechens carried out a terrorist attack. Do you remember the Nord-West musical? The terrorists seized the theater, something did not work out, and a lot of people were killed. Well, the terrorists had the same fake passports as I had. At that time, I had to fly to Sochi and was arrested at the airport. I gave the cops three thousand bucks to let me go; I didn't want to be hurled into prison. I returned to the office, picked up thirty thousand bucks and quickly left for India. The truth is I spent them on cocaine in a year, but now I am a restaurateur. My passport expired two years ago," Vitalik says, laughing. "My wife and Kirill crossed the border legally, and I walked along a forest path."

"You are the man, Vitalik! My passport will also expire soon. I have no idea what to do. It looks like I'll have to make my way through the forest next time, too. However, I have an idea to fake a permission from Sai Baba so I can live semi-legally in India for a year. And then I'll have to break through to Nepal."

"Vasya, I've been crossing the border to Nepal without a passport for two years already. You saw the mess there is at the border. Vasya, it seems to me that we have met here for a reason. Such coincidences only happen in India. Two dudes of the same age return from Nepal in one wagon, their wives have the same names, their children are of the same age, and they are both wanted for the same charge. They both moved over here from Russia at the same time. You run a restaurant in the north of Goa, and I run one in the south. Maybe you also love to play chess?"

"Vitalik, you won't believe me, but I just wanted to suggest that we play chess! I love the game."

"Vasya, I have some ideas about opening a large restaurant. Come visit us, in Palolem, you'll like our place."

"I'll come for sure, Vitalik. I have been thinking lately of exploring new lands. I have stayed in Arambol for too long. Look, our children are already playing together. Set them up."

Chapter 38. Part One. Inside.

"Checkmate, set them up again," Viktor laughs, wiping raindrops off the cardboard on which a chessboard is painted. "I've listened to your story, Vasya, and I want to ask you. Just don't get offended. Are you an idiot or a fool, Vasya? To escape from the police with their money, and then to go back home a week later just because you had your first crop of shrooms."

"I don't know, Vitya. I have asked myself this question many times over the last six months. I must have been an idiot, indeed. I didn't return home just because of the shrooms. I wasn't sure that I had the police on my tail. I thought that the local bandits were trying to rip me off. Just in case, I changed my motorbike, bought new clothes, and even shaved off my beard and mustache. Although, to be honest, the main motive for my return home was the psilocybin mushrooms and hydroponics. I worked day and night for three months, experimenting with different methods of cultivation. It's not so easy to achieve a crop under Indian conditions, especially on an industrial scale. And when the first mushroom grew after many failed experiments, I could not give up my work. You know, Vitya, growing shrooms is not like making fake cocaine from dental anesthetic. Mushrooms are like children, they require attention and care."

"Vasya, do you realize that you were lucky that the police came on that day, rather than a couple of weeks later?"

"Yeah, there would have been thousands of shrooms in a couple of weeks."

"Then the police would have had no reason to plant MDMA on you."

"You're right, but they don't have an article for shrooms, nobody has been put in prison for them."

"But you can easily be locked up for psilocybin, which the shrooms contain. You can get ten years in prison for fifty grams of synthetic psilocybin. Do you realize that a thousand doses of magic mushrooms on a daily basis would seriously undermine the LSD market in Goa? Someone supplies wholesale quantities of LSD here. If you'd had at least a couple hundred of those mushrooms, they would have been sent to Hyderabad for analysis and you would have been charged with cultivation and production of drugs on an industrial scale. And that's from ten to twenty years in prison."

"I am looking at ten to twenty years anyway, Vitya. My friends, who are experienced shroom pickers, Andrey and Natasha, told me that you can't sell magic mushrooms. You may give them as a gift or share them, but you must never sell them. The shrooms could take offence. These guys have been growing shrooms at home for ten years already. They told me that mushrooms are a mysterious form of life: neither plant, nor animal. The Mayans worshiped these mushrooms, considering them to be the flesh of God. I've also read on different Internet resources that you can't sell mushrooms."

"Vasya, then why did you decide to arrange a whole plantation at your place?"

"Well, first of all, ten thousand bucks every month is not bad money. And, secondly, by growing so many mushrooms you could force LSD out of the drug market in Goa. How many people have gone crazy from LSD in recent years? The Russian Embassy itself sends around a dozen loonies back to the homeland every year. Whereas, I've never heard that someone went crazy from shrooms. After all, mushrooms are a natural product. They are legally sold in smart shops in many European countries. Maybe the LSD they have been making recently isn't as pure? I don't know. Maybe the substitutes are of poor quality, but every year I want to take LSD less and less. My shrooms were pedigree: Cambodian cubensis. The police did not even indicate the quantity in the report. They just wrote: 'Article 20A, cultivation of marijuana and psychotropic mushrooms.' In fact, Viktor, I would have had a couple of kilograms of hydroponics every two months."

"Vasya, that would have been another ten grand every month. What would you have spent so much money on?"

"I would have spent it on the revolution," I laugh, imagining myself as a psychedelic Lenin.

"Vasya, when will you stop playing at revolutions? You already have a gray beard."

"Probably never, Vitya. Throughout the ages there have been people who are dissatisfied with all of the shit that surrounds us. I belong to that category of person."

"Vasya, the final destination for all dissatisfied revolutionaries is the same: either the cross, or imprisonment."

"There is no other way, Vitya. We either agree with the shit around us, or oppose it. You have been agreeing with it your entire life, and you had no peace in your heart as a result. You hit the bottle and took dope because you didn't have any other choice. I have hated seeing the shortcomings of the world since my childhood, Vitya; I didn't learn to ignore them. Therefore, my life path is to oppose these shortcomings. Anyone who can't bear to agree with all the shit of this world makes his own revolution. I wish that cocaine, which blacks bring to Goa in their assholes, would disappear from the market. I wish that real freaks would come back to Goa. I wish I could return to the paradise I found here a few years ago. It would be good if people ate natural mushrooms, not LSD of unknown origin, and if they smoked high-quality weed, not charas mixed with dung."

"So, Vasya, your revolution is aimed at switching people from poor-quality drugs to high-quality ones?"

"No, it doesn't, Vitya. Drugs are a protective response to the injustice of society. Society wants everybody to be slaves of consumption, whereas the right drugs cure this infection. Corrupt governments say they are trying to protect the public from drugs, but they are actually doing everything possible to switch people onto other, more harmful, destructive drugs. How many years has there been a war in Afghanistan? Who needs this place in the middle of nowhere with nothing but opium poppies? Afghanistan is the world's main heroin supplier. Nobody fights against heroin; everybody tries to gain control over its production. Alcohol and tobacco companies advertise their drugs on the state level. Nobody cares about the people; there is nothing but lies and hypocrisy all around. How can we oppose these transnational drug dealers, if they have power, weapons, money and the law, which they create to protect their interests? How can the common man oppose them, if everyday an avalanche of false information from the media falls on him? The average person is no longer able to think for himself. 'Big Brother' thinks and makes decisions instead of him, preventing all freethinking. And only the right drugs and appropriate consumption can help you expand your consciousness and drop out of the game imposed by society. There is much injustice in modern society and that is what I refer to as 'shit'. I don't urge that we fight against it to the bitter end; that would be utopia. I believe that we need to oppose it, so that society can change, evolve, and not stand still."

"There has always been the shit you are talking about, Vasya."

"Yeah, there has always been a lot of shit. However, our attitudes to it are different. You don't care. You know how to live with it, but I can't."

"Vasya, do you realize that you rub people's noses in their shit with your revolution as if they were mangy cats?"

"But it's a great opportunity to clean up their shit and get better, Vitya."

"Did they ask you to rub their noses in it? You should be the first to completely get rid of it and then you can teach people, you fucking Trotsky. You should say straight that you wanted to make money, but you fuck with my brain, talking about revolution. I am square with you: I have earned money all my life and have never cared what is on other people's minds. I never thought that someone could have revolution or opposition in his head."

"Vitya, you measure everything in dough. Of course I need money; everybody needs money. I'm not saying that I'm a saint. But a man as an individual should oppose the system. After all, any social system pursues one goal: to crush our individuality and make slaves out of us, so that we work our whole lives like robots, without thinking about why we are living."

"But, Vasya, the system will also always oppose the revolutionaries like you. How many people have died or gone mad because of your 'right drugs' in recent years? Don't you feel responsible for that? Don't you feel it was your fault, directly or indirectly?"

"I don't know, Vitya. I still haven't understood whether it was or wasn't my fault. The people who had problems as a result of psychedelics show the other side of the coin by their example. Psychedelic drugs are, first and foremost, medicines. How can I be guilty if people take these medicines and go over the top? The psychedelic revolution is like a mirror, in which society sees its flaws and then changes. If there is no opposition, there will be no development of society. Society needs people like us. By opposing the shit, we prompt society to cleanse itself. Vitya, have you heard about the Aum Shinrikyo sect? Do you remember they released gas in the Tokyo subway a few years ago?"

"Yes, there was something like that. Are they also psychedelic revolutionaries?"

"Time was when I didn't understand why they had done that. No one knew why a blind, crazy sectarian organized an attack that killed many innocent people. But I understood everything after reading 'Underground' by Haruki Murakami. Thousands, millions of people around the world live like robots, trading their life for worthless, but supposedly valuable paper. They often produce unnecessary things, and convince each other of their necessity. The meaning of their life boils down to work for the sake of work. 'I woke up as usual at 06:45, I left my house at 07:30, I walked into the first door of the penultimate subway car at 07:45, as usual for the last fifteen years. I felt that I was starting to die of poisonous gas at 08:15, but I didn't go home or to the hospital, I crawled to my office, to the factory, to my work, to ask my boss for leave to go,' is how all of the victims in this book described that terrible day. They died in their hundreds like poisoned cockroaches. Some became disabled, but they still walked or crawled to their job because they were used to doing it their whole life. So the insane, blind old head of the Aum Shinrikyo sect is no worse than Che Guevara or any other prophet who didn't spare his own life trying to save people from self-destruction. Unfortunately, he only found one way to shake up people's minds. By poisoning people in the Tokyo subway, he showed them who they were. Society has turned people into a mindless mass with only one goal: to live in the name of society."

"Vasya, that's why society has locked you up in here. And when you get well, you will be released. One more thing, Vasya: throughout history people like you have caused problems for others. For example, one man lives and doesn't bother anyone, everything is good in his life. And then a revolutionary smartass appears and starts telling him how to live his life. Have you ever seen how soldiers proudly march on parade? It looks nicely because they like doing it. And you laugh at them; you call these people robots and feel sorry for them. And they don't need your pity. They are satisfied with their lives, so they succeed in everything, and you don't."

"I stopped trying to teach people long ago. I'm finished with preaching about psychedelics, and I'm in prison in any case. Those who march nicely don't come here in pursuit of the meaning of life, and their souls don't hurt when they bomb and shoot civilians for oil or other monetary interests of the state. But those whose hearts hurt from the injustice of contemporary life, they find me and ask me to sell them medicine for sick souls. After all, psychedelics were first invented as a medicine and used to be sold in pharmacies. But instead of giving people information about the dangers of abuse, society began to prohibit not only the substances, but information about them as well. Thank God, they haven't started controlling the Internet yet. However, many resources are not available in China, and in Russia, too. Vitya, do you know how I bought the book 'Storming Heaven: LSD and the American Dream' in Russia a few years ago?"

"No, I don't. Are there problems with buying books now?" Viktor asks in surprise, looking at me as if I were crazy.

"Don't you know that many books are banned now? 'Medical Marijuana', 'Club Culture', 'Storming Heaven' and many others are banned, due to allegations of drug propaganda. The fact that people pass on their knowledge about drugs is considered to be propaganda. People tried their best, accumulated information, performed experiments on their brain and body, and then those people wrote books to pass on their knowledge to others. Meanwhile, society simply prohibits heretical literature, like in the times of the Inquisition. They could print on the cover: 'This book contains information on drug propaganda. It is prohibited for children under thirty-one.' But no; heresy must be banned, people must have no alternative. I went to a bookstore in Russia and said that I wanted to buy the book 'Storming Heaven: LSD and the American Dream.' The shop assistant tells me, 'We can't sell this book; we can be fined for such literature.' I was just about to leave, but the shop assistant caught me at the entrance and said, 'However, you can leave an application for this book, and if we find it, we will call.' I wrote down my phone number and went out, ready to head home, when the shop assistant caught me up again on the street, looked around, and said, 'Come with me, I have what you need.' He took me into a back room, opened a door to another room, and I saw all these prohibited books lying there on the table. 'Choose,' he says. 'Just don't tell any strangers you bought them here'."

"Yeah, Vasya, you bought the book like a communist worker bought the *Iskra* newspaper[73] in 1917. I had no idea everything was so sad with censorship in our country."

"Vitya, do you think that the state cares about people, that it is worried about them going crazy and jumping off bridges, when it bans books about drugs? The state is afraid that its citizens won't go to fight for oil money anymore. Society is afraid that people won't want to work hard at chemical factories, getting milk to compensate the harm to their health. Society is afraid that citizens will become disillusioned about its major religion called 'The Golden Calf'."

"Well, who would work then?" Viktor asks, standing up from the steps.

"Those who want to work, will work, Vitya. You can't take away a field from a peasant for anything, and the workers in our country slogged away at plants and coalmines for almost nothing during Perestroika. If a person needs to work to survive, he will want to work. But when society reminds you on a daily basis through the media that you are a loser if you don't have the latest model of TV, refrigerator, or cell phone, it's deception. And society is afraid that its citizens will become smarter and will not want to service its palaces and luxury Mercedes."

"Vasya, you really are a crazy fanatic. They were right to lock you up in here."

"Maybe they were right, time will tell," I agree, sighing. "However, you still don't know everything about me, Vitya. The time will come and I will tell you why the police threw me in here. But now it is too early for you to know more."

Chapter 38. Part Two. Outside.

"Hi there, Zhyora, I haven't seen you for ages," I extend my hand to a tall, strong guy, lying on the floor near a low tea table.

"Hello, Vasya. I haven't been in Goa for three years; time flies."

"Where's your wife?" I ask my old friend, looking around the bar.

"Natasha and I broke up a year ago. I have come alone for the whole season this time, or perhaps for my whole life. Vasya, do you remember the party where we first met three years ago? My whole life changed after that party. Then I understood everything. I understood that I was living the wrong way. I realized that I was surrounded by the wrong people and that I was not doing what I wanted to do. And now I have finally got rid of the anchors that have always held me. I quit my boring job at a construction company. I got rid of my wife, who loved my money instead of me. Now I'm really free."

"You look good, Zhyora, much better than you did three years ago."

---

[73] Iskra ('Spark') - a political newspaper for Russian socialist emigrants, established as an official organ of the Russian Social Democratic Labor Party. Initially it was managed by Vladimir Lenin.

"Vasya, I have lost thirty kilograms since then."

"Yeah, Zhyora, then you looked like a hog, and now you're a real psychedelic warrior. Just there is nowhere to fight now. All of the parties have been closed down. The cool people went to other countries.

"What is this then? What's wrong with this party?" Zhyora asks me in surprise, pointing to the space around us in the bar.

"This is Psy Bar, it's not a party."

"But, Vasya, it's the only place where you can listen to trance and dance all night in Goa."

"Yeah, you can; quietly though," I agree, lying down on a mattress. "The Estonian guys are clever cookies, they opened the nicest trance bar in Goa. You can either dance or lie around, as you wish. Most people lie around."

We recline on mattresses on the floor in a small room. The walls are covered with large cloths, painted in fluorescent colors. Outer space landscapes glow beautifully in the dark.

"Vasya, I've worked out that Psy Bar is now the best place to trip in Goa. I've already taken a drop of LSD," Zhyora says with a mysterious smile, reclining and shaking his arms and legs in time with music.

"It doesn't seem like you're tripping, Zhyora."

"I have been taking these drops every day here, for a month. A drop of LSD for me is like a bottle of beer now."

"Be careful, Zhyora. So many people have already gone crazy from acid. Don't consume it every day. Last season, the owner of this bar, Ilya, took too much acid and started attacking people. He was lying in a nuthouse here, and then he was finally sent home."

"Don't worry about me, Vasya, I won't go nuts, I have a strong mind. How about you? Have you been in Goa for long? When was the last time you went to Russia?"

"That's a difficult and strange question. Two weeks may be a long time for some people. I have been living here for three years, but it seems like a week. I haven't been home since I opened my restaurant here."

"Is there nothing drawing your back to the homeland, Vasya?"

"This is my homeland now. My daughter goes to first grade at school here. And I can't go to Russia; I'm on the wanted list there."

"Are you wanted for drugs?" Zhyora asks, professionally rolling a nice smooth joint.

"I hope not."

"What do you mean?"

"What I said. Although I didn't violate Russian laws, a few drug dealers connected to me were locked up in prison there. And, at the same time, the tax police opened a case for tax evasion against me. However, I was put on the wanted list for fraud. Now my brother in Russia is trying to deal with the case. He went to the police with my passport and said that he was me; it's good that we look similar. He was not arrested immediately. He gave a written undertaking not to leave, so he – or more precisely, I – can't leave Russia. According to my documents, I'm under house arrest in Russia now. And my passport here expires in three months. If my brother Lyokha goes to court instead of me and manages to close the case before the passport expires, then a new one can be issued and sent here. Then I'll be free again, but I can't currently travel out of India."

"Well, maybe it's for the best, Vasya. You have a reasonable excuse to live in India, many only dream of that."

"Hi, Mishanya," I extend my hand to the bartender approaching us. "Misha, this is my friend Zhyora. He and I had a ball at a party three years ago."

"We have already met, Vasya. He buys acid and charas from me every day here."

"By the way, Zhyora, look at Mishanya. He is the only character out of all my friends who managed to get back in the swing after a strong acid flip-out. Last season, he and Ilya sold LSD almost by the glass and hit it themselves pretty heavily. Ilya is still being treated by psychiatrists in Estonia, but Mishanya recovered on his own. Bravo."

"It's true. We had the gloves off last season," Mishanya laughs, tucking his long, wavy hair behind his ears. "The only thing is, I lost my passport while I was flipped-out, Vasya. My brain is back in place, and I don't know what to do. My visa expired a year ago."

"You'll think of something. Don't worry," patting him on the back, Zhyora tries to cheer him up, for some reason putting a handful of shells in his glass of cola. "How are things in your Hemp, Vasya?"

"Everything is okay, Zhyora, all clear. Do you remember Dan, my partner? He conned me out of money in Nepal, I don't even want to know him any more. But I've found a perfect new partner this season. His name is Sanya. I'm so glad that I met him. Although he is a young guy, he is very responsible. Now I am working at normal pace at last. I work one week, and have a rest the next. We halve the profits. Now I can happily hang out here, in Psy Bar, all night long. I don't need to go to work tomorrow."

"Vasya, you talk as if you worked at a factory."

"You won't believe me but the work was like a holiday for me only during the first year after opening the restaurant. When I began to sell spirits in the second season, the holiday turned into work. Work still remains work, whether it is at a factory conveyor belt, or in a restaurant on the beach. It may be difficult to believe, but I'm fed up with sitting on the shore all day long. I hardly ever swim in the sea. And, sometimes, in the working week, I go home for half an hour, in order to be alone at least for a while. It's not the people I wish to see that come to my restaurant. Earlier, I was embarrassed to take money from clients, because the people were interesting. Everyone was like a new Universe. We could talk for hours on any topic. And now, I have nothing to talk about with the new tourists. They come in, sit down, and drink beer from morning till night. Or they play with words. I say to them, 'Let's go to a party at East End. Let's show them that we are still alive, that we won't trade in our freedom for anything.' And they answer, 'No, you go alone, it's more fun to play with words. Guess what word starts in 'a' and ends in 's'?'[74] Then they start squealing with delight. If you heard, Zhyora, what they talk about. I just don't understand them. They are just the same as our politicians. They

---

[74] No, you go... what word starts in 'a' and ends in 's'? ('ass') - The Russian original contains and untranslatable play on words, the phrase hinted at in the word game is the equivalent of telling someone 'to fuck off'.

seem to be talking about something, but they aren't actually talking about anything. With them it's the opposite: I want to con them out of their money for their arrogant stupidity. I'm so bored I started playing chess. I sit and play chess with tourists all day long. I called all the best people to come to Goa, but instead, just dorks and dickwads came. I can't understand why it happened like that. Zhyora, you have no idea what sort of morons come here. One of them has got into the habit of coming into my restaurant. I don't know how to get rid of him. An AIDS sufferer, alcoholic and drug addict. He's like a normal person when he is sober, but as soon as he gets a little drunk, he runs to a pharmacy to buy amphetamines. He gets off his face and starts bugging people. If you throw him out of the restaurant, he catches people near the entrance and tries to do their heads in with his raving. Mishanya did pretty much the same last year. Tell me now, Mishanya, why did you break a street musician's flute over his head last year?"

"Oh, I don't know, Vasya, everything was in a fog. I remember a man walking down the road playing a flute. And the music wasn't trance-like at all. I had just taken a couple of drops and his music didn't fit into my trip. So I smashed his flute over his head. I feel embarrassed about it, Vasya. I haven't taken acid since. That was the last straw. I behaved like a lout the whole season. Some Indian guys wanted to stab me. It's lucky they missed. When they stitched up my arm in the hospital, I nearly beat the doctor up."

"I've had an eyeful of people like you, Mishanya, and I don't consume LSD any more, either. And I only take any other chemical drug once a month at most."

"Well, guys, I haven't reached that understanding yet," says Zhyora, pulling five hundred rupees out of his pocket. "Do you have any acid for sale?"

"Out of stock. New acid will be tomorrow," Mishanya throws up his hands with a serious face, as he watches Zhyora whispering something into his glass.

"I have. I can sell some to you," I say, producing a black LSD trip.

Chapter 39. Part One. Inside.

"Dobroe utro, Mapusa!" stretching himself in the sunlight, Viktor loudly shouts 'good morning' in a drawling manner in Russian.

"Dobrautro!" the inmates and guards shout in broken Russian in response from different sides of the prison.

"Is it you again?" Viktor laughs, extending his hand to me.

"Yeah, it's me again," I smile at him, happy to have someone to talk to.

"Well, my prison friend, let's go and fuck each other's brains."

"Count me in. But let's agree on one thing: we orgasm at the same time. If I don't cum in your brain, I won't sleep all night."

"That's settled," I say to Viktor, shaking his hand. "Where shall we go today, from Arambol to Ashvem, or from Ashvem to Arambol?"

"Let's go to Morjim today, Vasya. The puddle near the sewer will be our sea, your cell will be Arambol, and my cell will be Morjim. By the way, you may congratulate me, Vasya. Today marks eight months in prison. Fucking Nirma washing powder[75]. The entire prison laughs when they see a washing powder commercial on TV. Nobody has ever served eight months for common washing powder."

"It's still not the end, Vitya. Only the Creator knows how long you will stay here. Vitya, you'll go down in the history of Goa as the man who served a year for washing powder."

"Even the police call my 'cocaine' washing powder. Sometimes it seems to me that I've already gone mad, Vasya."

"I feel the same sometimes, Vitya. Look at those two idiots going around in a circle. I think they don't even realize they are in jail. We'll also walk like that in time, I guess."

For a moment, we stop and look at two mentally ill Indian men walking around the same way we do, but lovingly holding each other's hands, as if they were husband and wife.

"Why were they put in here and not in a loony bin? How could the judge not see they are mentally ill?"

"Do we differ from them, Vasya? Is the only difference that we don't hold each other's hand? We are loonies just like them. We wanted to teach people something, but lost our brains somewhere at a party long ago. Sane people are not locked up."

"Vitya, do you know how that ever-smiling creature got in here?"

---

[75] Fucking Nirma washing powder - when Viktor was being arrested, the police put the dental anesthetic found at his place in a Nirma washing powder package.

"No, I don't. He must have stolen an ice cream or some chocolate. What else could he do with such a face, Vasya?"

"Vitya, he took a stone and began battering the wall of a Christian church. He broke something in the church, and was put in prison. Many people lose their minds on religious grounds. Do you know what Desai said to me yesterday? He's been here for three years. He says that a Russian sat in my cell before me. His name was Zhyora. I couldn't fall asleep last night after his story, I was thinking about karma."

"What does that have to do with karma, Vasya?" Viktor asks in surprise, overtaking the two idiots going round in a circle in front of us.

"I knew that Zhyora. He flipped out a few years ago. He was a sound guy, but overdosed on LSD and went bonkers. He climbed the Arambol hill and broke the Christian cross, which the Catholics installed some time ago."

"I remember him, Vasya. The Indians crippled him well."

"'Crippled' is not the word for it, Vitya. He was nearly stoned to death. He was in hospital first for three months, and then served a few months here in prison."

"And what does that have to do with karma, Vasya?" Viktor asks, not even noticing that he has stepped on a piece of cat's shit with his bare foot.

"I sold him LSD on the night he went bonkers. He wanted to pay me the next day, but he obviously didn't. I learned from the newspapers about what had happened to him that night. Many of the newspapers had hysterical headlines: 'Crazy Russian breaks the cross in Arambol, abusing the Catholic Church.' But, Zhyora appeared pretty sane that night. He driveled a bit, but he was on an acid trip after all."

"So what? Do you worry about it, Vasya? If you hadn't sold him acid, somebody else would have sold it to him."

"You are right, but the thing is that it was me who offered him to try psychedelics for the first time, five years ago. He expanded his consciousness according to the standard scenario. He quit his job first, then broke up with his wife, and then came to live in Goa. I had no idea that his consciousness would let him down so badly. Or, maybe I'm crazy, too, and I just can't understand it?"

"Of course you are! If you could hear yourself talk, you would have understood that a long time ago. At least I ended up here for money, Vasya, whereas you are just a crazy psychedelic revolutionary who wanted everybody else to go crazy, too."

"Perhaps, you're right," I sigh, remembering Zohar's face. "I spoke with Desai about Zhyora. He said that he was a total madman who was muttering about some energies all the time. 'I,' he said. 'ask that crazy Zhyora, why you break the cross? Whom did it bother?' And Zhyora says, 'I wanted to help the people. Good energies are coming from the sea, but they can't enter Arambol because the cross does not let them. So I had to break the cross to let the good energies come into Goa.'"

"Viktor, to be honest, I would also have loved to break down that cross, because it spoils the whole view. Zhyora wasn't scared; he broke it. After all, everyone has his own faith in God in his soul. How many Indians, Muslims, Jews and other people believing in their own religions look at that hill and see the cross on it. And the cross is a symbol of someone else's faith, not theirs. That's how interfaith conflicts arise. Faith should stay in the soul, not in symbols. It's a good job that Jesus was crucified on the cross, and not impaled. What a terrible symbol that would have been! Can you imagine, Vitya, a statue of Jesus impaled on Arambol hill? Even though I was baptized, for me the symbol of a cross with a crucified man always reminds me of martyrdom. Why should such a terrible sign be displayed? In our Orthodox religion, crosses are placed on churches and at cemeteries. But Catholics put them everywhere; concrete crosses all over the place without any reason. It's a pity that it all ended so sadly with Zhyora; he was still out of it even six months later. Pasha, the consul from the Russian Embassy, told me about him. Sasha Shanti bought him out of prison and sent him to Bombay, and he began to raise hell at the embassy. He said, 'I don't want to go back to Russia, I am a former paratrooper. And paratroopers don't give up so easily.' He was taken from the embassy to a nuthouse in Bombay. I don't know how it all ended. He could still be sitting in the nuthouse. That's the story. Someone breaks crosses, and someone tries to put them up. There is a character in Goa, his name is Mr. Ptichkin. He's an Orthodox believer, an intelligent guy over fifty from the first generation of Soviet black marketeers. He decided to promote the Orthodox religion in Goa. He ordered a heroic wooden Orthodox cross from a carpenter. He humped the cross onto his back, like Jesus, and pulled it up the hill. He dragged that cross for half a day. Then he spent another half a day installing it. Then, when he was finished, the police came, broke his cross, and hurled him into prison for a week. They said it was illegal to put a cross on Indian land without special permission. Criminal proceedings were even initiated against him. Fortunately, he got off with a fine. Strange coincidences occur here, in India. German Nick was the first to do time in my cell; I used to buy LSD wholesale from him. Then Zhyora, who went off his rocker from acid, was sitting in this cell. And now I am sitting here, the one who sold him the acid. Maybe it's my karma. Maybe this is the very thing that I am in here for. But God is my witness; everything that I did was done with good intentions. I wished no evil. I wanted to help people."

"Vasya, I hope that it will mitigate your punishment up there," Viktor says, pointing to the sky.

Chapter 39. Part Two. Outside.

"When will the film adaptation of your book be released, Sasha?"

"I don't know anything, Vasya. Don't ask me about the movie. Ask Buslov any questions about the movie," laughs the always-cheerful Sasha Shanti. "Vasya, I came to you to eat Russian okroshka[76], and you attack me with questions that I don't know how to answer."

"Krishna!" I shout to my waiter, who is chasing a soccer ball on the sand in front of the restaurant. "One okroshka!"

"Sit down and talk to me, Sanya. You'll get your okroshka; I brought fresh kvass today. What's new in your life? How is your book selling? You must be pestered with questions about the movie."

---

[76] okroshka - Russian cold soup made from kvass, cucumber, radish, dill, egg, and meat.

"Vasya, the book is selling very well, but I really don't know anything about the movie. The director Buslov bought the rights to my book."

"Well it's clear, Sanya, that the information about a movie being shot based on your book was put out to boost sales. It's no joke to sell a hundred thousand copies. And the majority who read the book will come here to check out whether it's true that Goa is the fantastic country you describe. Do you remember, Sanya, three years ago we were sitting here and figuring out how to sell something to the two-week tourists here?"

"Yeah, I remember that, Vasya. You came up with the story that The Beatles once visited the old banyan tree. I was working as a guide in a travel agency. The poor tourists suffered from not knowing what to spend their money on. Things have changed so quickly over the years."

"You, Sanya, wore a mottled lungi[77] then, just like I did, not fashionable Goan clothes. My idea worked. Three years later, new guides lead their victims, fair-skinned, sunburnt tourists, to the old banyan tree to show them the place where the legendary Beatles allegedly sat and smoked a chillum. And they sincerely believe it. And after the program on NTV was released, the whole of Russia knows about Arambol and The Beatles. And not only Russia: NTV is broadcast to the whole world via satellite. When I was in Nepal, I switched the TV on and just stood dumbfounded. The 'My Profession is Reporter' episode about downshifters[78] was on. Can you imagine, I turned on the TV and saw myself giving an interview here, in Hemp, talking about what a paradise it is in Goa. That's how easily legends are born. The reporter, Andrey Loshak, made a good advertisement for Goa with his program. Now Beatles fans travel to Goa. However, if I could use a time machine and go back, I would advertise Goa in a different way. If I find a new promised land now, I won't tell anyone about it."

"I don't regret writing my book, Vasya. Even though people blame me for the Russians spoiling Goa, due to the fact that all the dregs of society allegedly started coming here after the book was released. Goa is large; there will be enough space for everyone. If it more dregs appear in one place, it means they have gone from somewhere else. If I hadn't written the book, someone else would have written it. But, Vasya, you remember how everything was different here before."

"Yes, Sanya, of course I remember and I understand you perfectly. You wrote the book because you couldn't not write it. You're in love with Goa, just like I am. I also wanted to tell the entire world that there is a place where good people live well. I gave interviews to various newspapers and magazines, hoping that the best people would respond to my call. Of course, there are less interesting people here now, but Goa is still the best place on Earth that I know."

"Your okroshka with sour cream. Chego izvolite barin?[79]" Krishna says, smiling and mangling the Russian language, offering a tray of food to Sanya.

---

[77] lungi - a traditional garment worn around the waist in India.

[78] Downshifter - a person living a simpler life to escape from the rat race of obsessive materialism, focusing their life goals on personal fulfillment and relationship building, instead of the all-consuming pursuit of economic success.

[79] Chego izvolite barin? (Russian) – 'What else can I offer you, your mightiness?'

"It was a cool idea to teach him Russian, Vasya."

"I told him to call my friends 'Your mightiness', Sanya."

"Vasya, judging by Krishna's happy face, your restaurant business is doing well, isn't it?"

"I don't know what to say, Sanya. I sit here all day long, watching the tourists and thinking only one thing: when will my working week be over? I'm tired of selling drugs. I still haven't succeeded in making my living legally. My restaurant brings me one thousand bucks a month at most and I give my partner half. Five hundred bucks a month was enough to live a normal life three years ago, now it is not enough. Everything gets more expensive every year. Selling drugs gives me another grand a month. However, my drug dealer paranoia is growing as a result of this business. Therefore, the money doesn't make me happy. The police can come and check on me at any moment."

"What partner are you talking about, Vasya? I thought you opened the restaurant alone, didn't you?"

"I took on a partner this year. He once tried to open a restaurant in Mandrem, but something went wrong. Here, look, he brought some fresh ideas," I show Sasha the green linen cloths stretched above his head.

"Hemp is much better decorated this year," Sasha says, pulling closer the bowl of okroshka brought by Krishna.

"Although he is young, he is a savvy guy, one of the new generation of freaks. Look, there he is playing with his year-old son on the beach," I say, pointing to a thin, pimpled guy. "He is very young, twenty-one years old. His name is Sasha, too."

For a while we silently observe as the guy with blond, rare dreadlocks builds fairytale castles out of sand, while his naked chubby kid persistently tries to break his father's creations.

"Do you remember, Sanya, how we used to meet and tell each other about the wonders of India that we witnessed almost every day? We talked a lot about the moments of synchronization that occur so often here in Goa."

"I haven't noticed such things lately, Vasya. Goa is changing and we are changing, too."

"Miracles haven't happened to me for a long time either, Sanya. The last time a moment of synchronization occurred was a few months ago, in Nepal. Do you remember, Sanya, I told you about the falling leaf in Pushkar? There was total silence in the street while a palm leaf was falling. As soon as the leaf touched the ground, a bell tolled somewhere at the very same moment. And everything burst into sound again."

"Of course I remember that, Vasya. I changed the story a little and described it in my book."

"Well, Sanya, a similar story happened to me for the second time in Nepal. Lena and I were walking in Kathmandu. There is one place there; it's called 'Seven Corners'. The street breaks seven times like a ladder. Sanya, imagine a small, crowded street in a big Asian city. Street vendors trade briskly, everyone is trying to attract customers in his own way. I hear the 'Om Mane Padme Hum' mantra coming from a music shop. Builders are repairing a small building, banging their hammers on stone. Someone is sweeping, someone else is talking on the phone. We're going along this street in a bicycle rickshaw, there is a noisy cacophony around, and only the Buddhist mantra with a charming female voice pleases me. That mantra brought back three-year old memories of Pushkar. I recalled the falling leaf then and thought: could I have imagined it in Pushkar? Maybe I was just too stoned. And as soon as I questioned my memories, I suddenly felt absolute silence around. We had just passed one of the corners of the street. Sanya, it's hard to imagine. The street is crowded with people, everyone is doing something but they are not emitting any sounds. The music stopped, the builders stopped making a noise, the storekeepers went quiet. I could only hear the creaking pedals of our rickshaw and no other sound. Those few seconds of silence seemed like an eternity to me. Looking around at the people, I realized that no one noticed or paid attention to the silence. And then I met the eye of an old beggar sitting on the sidewalk next to a tray decorated with flowers. He held an iron Shiva trident in one hand, and a little bell in the other. And when his gaze met mine, I realized that he could also hear the silence. Smiling at me, he hit the bell with his trident, saying 'Om Shankar', and the street was again filled with sound. I had the feeling that nobody had noticed that silence except for me, my Lena, and the old man with an enlightened face. There were a few seconds of inexplicable silence that occurred just at the moment when I recalled the leaf in Pushkar. I haven't experienced any miracles since then, Sanya. We used to tell each other such stories about the things we had witnessed at least once a week."

"Yeah, Vasya, something is changing; either in us, or in India. Somehow paradise and the miracles that take place in it are becoming commonplace, and we simply don't notice them. Vasya, I have been thinking recently of opening a restaurant in Ashvem. The material world draws you in tightly, leaving no place for miracles."

"Sanya, I want to sell my Hemp. I want to open a large restaurant in the south of Goa, in Palolem. I want to start earning money legally. A buddy from Palolem has invited me to start up a new business with him."

"But there are no freaks there, Vasya. How are you going to live there? There are only two-week tourists, whom you hate."

"Sanya, I'm not ashamed to take money from tourists. It's a pleasure for me to con those mugs out of their money. I want to live here, in the north of Goa, and earn money in the south. Look at the people on the beach, here in the north. I don't want to take money from them. I want to chat with them, make friends, love them. Although there are less and less each year, such people still prevail. And on Palolem beach you only get mugs like directors of meat processing plants and car-care centers, with their wives and fat offspring. They come here to booze; you can't talk to them about anything. However, they have so much money that they throw it left and right. So I'm thinking of selling my restaurant and opening a new one for the tourists. I will work on a rotational basis. I'll work one week in the south and then I'll come up north to have a rest for a week. Do you want to buy my restaurant, Sanya? I'll sell it for five thousand dollars."

"No, Vasya, I want to build my own, on the beach. I want to work as a DJ there. I have picked a place in Ashvem. I'm thinking of opening it next season."

"I think a show is about to start. Look, Sanya, a representative of the new Goan generation is coming."

"Hi, Vasya. I need LSD. Will you sell me a drop?" a skinny guy with absolutely mad eyes says to me as he approaches.

"Listen to me, dickwad. I've told you in Russian many times, I won't sell anything to you anymore," I say, getting up from the table and preparing for the worst.

"You're an asshole, Vasya. I want to be friends with you and you don't understand. I came into this world to save you."

"Save yourself first, you moron. Get out of my restaurant," I start shouting loudly.

"I won't go anywhere until you sell me some acid."

"And I'm going to give you a bamboo massage," I say, pulling out a bamboo pole prepared for such an occasion from behind the counter.

Having stepped a few meters back, the off-his-face degenerate stops in front of a table at which a young pregnant woman is sitting. Snatching a glass of juice from her hands, he throws it at us. The glass breaks with a crash against the wall behind us.

"Why are you staring at me, you big-bellied beast?" the whacko starts yelling at the innocent woman.

"All right, my patience has run out. I'm asking you for the last time: Get out of my restaurant!" I yell at him, swinging the stick above my head.

"Vasya, I want you to hit me," the madman begins to laugh hysterically, approaching me.

I give him a hefty smack around the face with the stick.

"Hit me again!" Laughs the crazy dork with wild eyes.

"Here you go!" I inflict a series of blows to his head and body.

Apparently finally feeling the pain, the nutcase runs towards the sea.

"That's it. Did you see, Sanya, what it means to have a restaurant in North Goa? I don't want to do any business here. Why should I put up with these dorks for ten cents? And I don't want to sell drugs. Our revolution has been lost, Sanya. I don't want to confront such idiots. I don't want to change people's minds anymore, let them be born idiots, live like idiots and die idiots."

"Calm down, Vasya. Sit down, drink something. Why did you fly off the handle? So he's an idiot, what's the big deal? They are everywhere here. Do you think there are less of them in Palolem?"

"There are idiots everywhere, Sanya. The idiots there are almost the same as those here, only in Palolem they are of the alcohol format. They get loaded and behave the same way. The only difference is that they have money there. I will wash off all the shit they pour on me in their drunken delirium with their bucks later. And what can you get from this cuckoo? He came in, spoiled the mood, flung mud and fled. He's not just an idiot; he's also got AIDS. Do you think he cares about condoms when he's fucking freak girls here? People like him should be isolated from society. I don't know how to communicate with them. Although; I've also forgotten how to speak to drunk people, too. Now I am trying to familiarize myself again with these circuits of perception. Last year, the mayor of some provincial town, Saratov or Syzran, visited Palolem. He got drunk on vodka and started messing around with the waiters. First he hits them in the face, and then stuffs a hundred bucks in their pocket, laughing just like that madman."

"Yeah, Vasya, I understand you. But don't worry so much, that's the way of the world. Assholes are sure to turn up in any nice place."

293

Chapter 40. Part One. Inside.

"Look, everything is changing so rapidly around," I point at the facade of a building made of concrete and tinted glass.

We drive in a small police jeep from the court to the prison, looking out of the window at the changes to the surrounding world that have taken place in the last two weeks.

"European-style renovation," Viktor answers smiling, chewing a salted cucumber. "The ethnic charm is disappearing, Vasya. Don't the Indian people realize that the soul of the building is lost? They can build such beautiful buildings in the Hindu and the old Portuguese style."

"You'd better eat some meat, Vitya, otherwise I'm going to finish it all while you're gazing at the buildings."

"I haven't eaten such a delicacy for a long time," says Viktor, putting a piece of boiled beef tongue and a salted cucumber in his mouth at the same time. The Indian police officer sitting next to us screws up his face, watching how we eat the tongue of his deity[80].

"Do you want to try?" Viktor says with a smile, offering the cop a piece of boiled beef tongue.

"No, no," the middle-aged Indian with a star on his shoulder straps says with his face screwed up in disgust, moving even further away from us.

"Well, as you wish. All the more for us," I say, enjoying the forgotten taste.

For the first time in the past six months, we are not eating rice with peas and stewed radish, but real, tasty, homemade food. I must ask Lena to cook shrimps for the next court hearing.

"It's so delicious, I'm about to explode," Viktor says with his mouth full, spitting crumbs. "Shall we have a drink, Vasya?"

"Open the package, there are two bottles of coke in there somewhere. Lena poured one of them half-full with rum. Take a gulp, but don't breathe on the guards as they'll smell the booze on your breath and won't allow Lena to give me a package for the next court hearing."

Quickly opening the warm bottle of coke, Viktor sprays all four policemen with the sweet fizzy liquid.

"It's not that one, Vasya, there's no rum in here."

"I'll open it myself, or we'll be left without a drink, otherwise," I say, taking the bottle from Viktor.

---

[80] Deity - a cow is a sacred animal in India.

I slowly open the bottle and take the first sip. The strong alcoholic drink rolls throughout my body with a warm wave.

"Open the jar of caviar," I say to Viktor, eating a cucumber pickled by my Lena. "Viktor, it's fantastic!"

We are driving in a jeep with policemen from the court to the jail, getting sloshed on rum and eating caviar, spooning it out of the open can with our fingers.

"Look what Lena gave me with the care package," I show Viktor a small handkerchief.

"What is it?"

"It's a gram of MDMA."

"What do you mean, Vasya?"

"I had ten grams of MDMA in my house. I knew the police would come for me, so I poured everything into a small bottle of vodka. It would never have occurred to the cops to try an open bottle from the fridge. Yesterday, Lena soaked this handkerchief in some of the vodka and then dried it out."

"So what, Vasya? Are we going to eat this handkerchief?"

"Why do we need to eat it? Use your brain, Vitya. When we get to the prison I'll put the handkerchief into a jar with water, we let it soak for a few hours, and then we drink the water."

"Not a bad plan, Vasya. But what are we going do in the cell when we are high? Run round? We have no music and no chicks, just bare walls."

"You'll close your eyes, Vitya, and you'll have chicks and music, while the bars and walls will disappear."

"I guess you're right. What do we have to lose? Nothing, except prison. We must try. There aren't so many amusements in prison to pass up on some drugs. Let's be happy for a while."

"Did you ever see a TV program about downshifters, Vitya?"

"You know, Vasya, that I don't watch TV and I don't read newspapers."

"I don't have a TV either, Vitya. However, I watched a quite good program on a satellite channel in Nepal. All of the interviewees were either former or current drug dealers. About ten of them gave interviews and all of them said on camera that Goa is paradise on Earth. Boris said he taught yoga, while everyone knows him as the main seller of psilocybin mushrooms in Goa. Tamir said he was the chief consultant on any issue. However, drug police chief Pashish told me that Tamir is the only real Russian mobster in Goa. Lyosha and Larisa, who opened a kindergarten in Morjim, once sent kilograms of charas from Nepal to Russia. Lyosha was once a well-known drug dealer in Moscow, with the nickname 'Frenzied'. He is also a psychedelic warrior like me. He also believed in a quantum leap in perception. He went to Russia for a month, consumed a drop of LSD and went crazy. He stayed in a nuthouse for a long time. He didn't come back to Goa. His Larisa ran the kindergarten alone for a while and raised their small son, Fedka. When she returned to Russia, she was arrested too, and got five years of probation. When I was interviewed, I said that I sold kvass to make my living. And now I am serving time in jail because of that 'kvass.' Vitya, how did it happen that I used to get a thrill out of life in Goa, and then: bang! I'm dead sick of everything. Suddenly I became bored with life. And that boredom relaxed me so much that I made the critical mistakes that led me here."

"Here we are! Get out, final stop – prison," shouts the driver of the jeep, winking at me in the rearview mirror.

"Finish eating your food, and get out. You can't bring anything into the prison. You have three minutes to finish eating," a policeman says to us strictly, darting a contemptuous glance at our boiled tongue sandwiches.

Chapter 40. Part Two. Outside.

"Look who decided to show up! Finally, at last someone who is truly alive, not like these goblins," I point at three tourists drowsy from beer and the hot weather, who have fallen asleep on mattresses right next to the table. "Hello guys!" I happily shake hands with my old Goan friends. "I'm glad to see you! It's rare to meet real people in Goa. You've made me happy by showing up."

"Hello, Vasya!" my friends hug me in turn: Petya Kievskiy and Vasko, a skinny Moscow Rastafarian with long, almost waist-long dreadlocks.

"Petya, you are dressed completely in orange, as always."

"Yeah, Vasya, you know orange is my color," smiling broadly, the tall, bald Ukrainian guy answers me.

"Petya, where is your kitten, the one you carried everywhere with you in a transparent backpack last year?"

"He has grown up, the beast. He no longer wishes to sit in a backpack. He now lives with some Indians. I've adopted a dog. Look," Petya points at a small ginger mongrel chafing on his calves with its tail between its legs. "It's coming down at the moment. We gave it LSD yesterday and it was chasing dog demons in the yard. It also has an expanded consciousness now. Vasiko, do you have anything tasty in your restaurant?"

"You know, Petya, I am not Indian; I don't serve shit with spices."

"Then mashed potatoes with a cutlet for me, two cutlets for my dog, a glass of pomegranate juice and cottage cheese pancakes with sour cream."

"And I'll have a vegan okroshka and potato flapjacks," adds my namesake, known as Vasko.

Pressing a button nailed to the trunk of the palm tree growing in the middle of the restaurant, I hear a loud ring in the kitchen.

"What's this innovation?" Petya asks me in surprise, calming down his dog, which was frightened by the loud noise.

"I did this for the comfort of my clients, Petya. Now you don't have to shout to call a waiter, you just go up to the palm tree. I nailed a doorbell button on the tree for that purpose."

"Vasya, and you complain that you have lost interest in your work? You spend time here like a king. You've made a podium this year and surrounded yourself with mattresses. You sit the whole day watching the sea, playing chess, drinking fresh juices, and eating the most delicious food. I'm sure you pig out on crabs and oysters every day. What have you got to frown about, Vasya?"

Having come running at the sound of the bell, my Nepali waiter Krishna hurriedly writes my friend's orders down in a notebook.

"Would you like something to eat, sir?" Krishna asks me helpfully, adjusting his apron.

"I have no appetite this morning, bring me a glass of cold kvass," I say, turning to my friends again. "Krishna, don't forget to put a couple of mint leaves in my glass. Petya, this year I made a podium instead of the second floor in my restaurant because the Goan government banned two-story restaurants on the beach. As the son of an engineer, I'm capable of building a solid construction. In the first season, I was the first in Arambol to construct a two-story building out of bamboo. The Indians saw the crowd of people rushing to my place, and built second floors out of thin plywood everywhere. Their constructions were so fragile it became dangerous on both the first and the second floors. So the authorities banned everybody from building second floors. As for oysters, crabs and natural juices, I've eaten a bellyful of them for three years. Now I prefer Russian traditional cuisine."

"I know you have a chillum. Let's smoke while we're waiting for the order?" Petya says to Vasko, taking out a piece of charas.

"Yeah, guys, I have a chillum. But I won't smoke it with you," Vasko says with a serious face, tying his dreadlocks in a large bundle.

"Why not?" we ask almost at the same time, surprised by our friend's strange behavior.

"Because you eat meat. I only smoke chillums with vegetarians. It's a vegetarian chillum."

"But we don't touch the chillum with our lips when smoking," I say surprised, hearing that there is such a thing as a 'vegetarian chillum' for the first time.

"I'll roll a joint for you, we can smoke that together. Guys, I'm sorry, but I believe that those who eat meat defile my chillum."

"Well, roll a joint at least," I say, sighing and twisting a finger by my temple behind our Rastafarian friend's back.

"I think everybody is slowly going bananas," Petya adds, smiling and watching how our vegan is prepared to engage in a debate over the horrors of eating meat with a completely straight face.

"Vasko, you are a fascist vegan. All meat-eaters have become your enemies. I've seen a lot of vegans in my life, and I myself didn't eat meat for six years. Judging by my experience, someone who really doesn't want to eat meat, does not react to someone enjoying meat in front of him. And those vegetarians who dream about pork knuckle at night, are usually indignant towards meat-eaters, and come up with different stories, such as a vegetarian chillum. In fact, Vasko, you want meat, it seduces you, and you resist this temptation in your own way."

"Okay, forget about meat, Vasya. I've brought bad news," Vasko says, rolling a joint.

"What happened? Vegetarians are outlawed now?"

"Get lost, Vasya. A Russian girl was arrested this week at Goa airport. She put three hundred grams of charas in her bra, got high on something, and walked smiling through border control. She was detained there."

"That's not news, Vasko. I know this girl. She bought a bottle of LSD and that charas from me. When I sold it to her, I even warned her, saying, 'Don't even think of taking it to Russia.' 'Don't worry,' she said, 'It will all be used in Goa.' And she flew to Russia the next day. Some people – they put ten years of their life on the line for three hundred grams of hash."

"Well, Vasya, she bought that stuff from you, but told the police she bought it from a Russian called Vasa with dreadlocks on his head. Tamir told me that. The police asked him whether he knew either 'Vaska' or 'Vasa' with dreadlocks. And there are just two 'Vasas' with dreadlocks – you and me."

"I'm bald. I only have three dreads on the back of my head."

"That's what I'm saying Vasya, you and I need to lay low for a while."

"Well, I, on the contrary, have come with good news for you, Vasya. And I believe my news is just on time," Petya interrupts us, giving a cutlet to his dog under the table. "I want to travel a bit. Let's go to the Andaman Islands for a couple of weeks? I understand you need to hide for a while. The last time we had a ball in Thailand, and now I suggest having a rest on the Andamans. You can wait till your drug dealer stuff simmers down. Vasko, will you come with us?"

"No, I'll lay low here, in Goa. I have nothing to be afraid of. I didn't sell anything to that chick."

***

"The buses are finally over," says Petya, leaning back in the comfortable chair of the airplane flying from Chennai to Port Blair.

"Twenty-four hours by bus. Petya, I will never travel in a sleeper bus with an Indian next to me again."

"Why, didn't you like the Indian, Vasya?" Asks Petya's girlfriend Marina, laughing.

"I didn't want to tell you what had happened to me at night while you were asleep. Well, okay, I'll tell you."

"That's an intriguing start," says Marina smiling, pulling the Air India magazine out of the backrest.

"I was asleep at night on the bus, and I dreamt that a beautiful girl on the beach at night was undressing me, unbuttoning my pants, putting her cool girl's hand inside and beginning to caress me. She goes down on her knees and opens her mouth... And something wakes me up at that moment. Half awake, I open my eyes and see that a hand from a nearby chair has crawled into my pants under the blanket and is stroking my dick. At first, as much as I regret it, I thought it was you, Marina, but then I recalled you were sleeping on the other side. I flinched, and the Indian immediately removed his hand back under his blanket. I rubbed my eyes and looked, but the Indian seemed to be sleeping. I thought that maybe it was just a hallucination or a dream. But in the morning, when the Indian got off at his stop, that bastard came to my window and blew me a kiss."

"Why did you frighten him away?" Marina says, laughing cheerfully. "You could have closed your eyes and returned to your beauty on the beach."

"Marina, I would like to see what you would do if some Indian man put his hand up your skirt at night."

"It depends on the kind of an Indian man and how nicely he did it," Marinka continues laughing, thumbing through the glossy magazine.

"My goodness! Vasya, look!" interrupting us, Petya shows us the Indian Airlines magazine.

"I don't understand..." Marinka says slowly, opening her mouth in surprise.

On a big, half-page picture, I see myself, Petya, and my Lena dressed in elegant orange clothing, standing at the Flea Market.

"When did a photographer catch you?"

"Judging by the length of the three dreads on the back of my head, this is our first year in Goa," I say, looking at the photo.

"And look, boys, the article says, 'Earlier on, people went to Goa to pray in temples, and now it's full of parties, freaks, drugs, and prostitutes.' Apparently you, dressed in orange clothes, happy and smiling, are the embodiment of evil, preventing people from visiting churches," Marina says, smiling.

"I think it's a good sign for our little trip to see our faces in the magazine of the airline we are flying on," I add, biting off a piece of hash cake, caringly prepared by my Lena.

***

As the darkness begins to fade, the yellow substance resembling flour to the touch starts to become saturated with white and turns into the most beautiful sand I've ever seen. The incredible fairytale animals that crawled out onto the beach at night turn back into huge, beautiful seashells and large pieces of coral. The huge dragons and dinosaurs turn into giant trees with the approach of the Sun. Torn out of the ground with their huge roots during the last tsunami, they lie on the beach, polished white by the wind and sand. Two elephants majestically pass by the enormous roots, while a fire burns down. Enjoying this beauty, we swing in hammocks strung between palm trees. The DJ has already put on smooth chillout music, and we see how the people who have been dancing all night on the beach slowly begin to disperse. The elephants slowly waltz away to go about their business somewhere. We feel like we are in paradise.

"I haven't been to such a beautiful party for a long time," Marina says, watching fascinated as an elephant scratches its hip against the huge roots of a tree lying on the shore. "It's good that you are only permitted to stay on the islands for one month."

"Why do you say that? I'm just thinking about how to move here," Petya asks in surprise, having stopped the hammock swinging with his leg.

"Petya, if it was permitted to live here longer, all of the Goan freaks would move here. Compared to Goa, it's paradise. And if the freaks came here, the crazy tourists would follow them. Parties would be banned, and the elephants would not be able to walk along the beach because of all the sunloungers."

"Marinochka, it's an untouched paradise compared to Goa, that's for sure. While I was swimming in the sea, I saw a giant turtle floating in the water for the first time in my life. It hovered slowly, like a mysterious alien, looking straight into my eyes."

"Yeah, Vasya, the local underwater world resembles the Red Sea, but untouched by tourists," says Petya, lighting up a joint.

"Boys, when I dive into the water, it seems like I am in a huge, well-maintained aquarium. In Goa, the water is cloudy with cellophane bags floating in it. That's why I like the fact you can only stay a month here."

"Well, tripsters, are we going to spend tonight on another beach?" Petya asks us, examining the beach we spent the night on.

"Of course, I want to see as many beaches as possible in two weeks," Marinka says cheerfully, jumping out of her hammock.

We have been moving along the beaches of Havelock Island for three days already, without renting a room. It's far nicer to spend the night on the beach in a hammock, strung between palm trees, than in a stuffy bungalow.

"Well, the LSD drops have come in handy today. I really thought we'd have to take them back," says Petya, drawing an 'Om' with a stick in the sand.

"Petya, I never thought we'd end up going to a trance party on the Andaman Islands. I brought them along, just in case."

"It's so beautiful, even if there had been no drugs we would not have missed them."

"Vasiko, we must be the wrong sort of drug addicts. All normal dopers increase their doses and how frequently they partake. And we do it the other way round. Bro, do you remember how we used to take everything and anything three years ago?"

"We must have eaten our fill, Petya. When I came here from Russia, I really wanted to try as many psychedelics as possible. They are expensive in Russia, and you can't relax the way you can here. There are cops everywhere in Russia and they are ready to send you to prison for just one joint. My daily dose of smoking charas has reduced three-fold during my three years in India. I consume MDMA once or twice a month, and take LSD every six months. It's difficult to say no to a good trip in Russia, because you never know when you'll get the next one. And here, when you have a stock of drugs to last you for the next few years, you don't want to take them too often. We must have made our quantum leaps; psychedelics can't offer us anything new. It's a pity that not all our friends reached this understanding safe and sound."

"Maybe we haven't reached it either?" Marinka says, laughing loudly again. "Look around, boys, we are in paradise. Maybe we died and everything around us is heaven, or the last dream of our minds."

Chapter 41. Part One. Inside.

"Vasiliy, Budram, Vassu, Paju, Chetsi: you have five minutes to pack your stuff."

Holding a list, a guard recites our names through the bars.

"Transfer to another prison, pack your things quickly and don't ask any questions."

Having just smoked a big chunk of hash, I stand and look at the guard, smiling stupidly. What kind of transfer? I should be released soon; it must be some kind of mistake.

"Dominic, is it a joke?"

"No, Vasya, it's not a joke. You're being transferred to a larger prison. It's called Vasco."

"And what about Viktor, James, Antonio, David, Alexandro? Am I the only foreigner who is moving?"

"How should we know, Vasya?" former policeman Chetsi answers, collecting his things quickly.

"I won't go anywhere alone. I go where the foreigners go."

"That's right, Vasya. You can fight for your rights, unlike us. They wouldn't dare beat you," Dominic says to me, trying to give me moral support. "You are a foreigner, so demand the embassy and your lawyer."

The warden starts to swear in the corridor, pushing the prisoners who are ready for transfer towards the exit. Twenty people will go to Vasco today. The sluggish attempts of some prisoners to resist are suppressed with stick strikes and the jailer's loud cries. Prisoners I know that pass by the door tell me that Viktor's cell, along with all the foreigners, is refusing to move. Several passing Indians, having heard that, also try to go back along the corridor to their cells.

"Hey, mera dosts[81], pass this note to Viktor," I shout to them, poking a piece of paper with a short letter through the bars, saying 'Hold on until the guards use force, I'm with you, Vasiliy.'"

The additional police squad that has arrived for the purpose leads Chetsi and Paju out to the prison bus.

"I refuse to go," I say to the warden, sitting on my belongings. "If my friends go, I'll go, too."

After a few minutes of waiting near the bars, I see the police squad coming back down the corridor, followed by my European friends walking in a row.

"That's it. All resistance has been crushed. It looks like I must say goodbye to you, too," I say, shaking hands with my cellmates who will stay in Mapusa prison.

I am the last one to leave the jail. Unlike the others, I not only carry stuff in my hands, but also on my shoulders. A bundle of two pillowcases filled with my books hang around my neck. Viktor helps me drag another bag with prison junk.

---

[81] Mera dosts (Hindi) - my friends.

"You're like a bourgeois with all your sacks. Look, the Indians have one or two small packages. Whereas you are covered in bags and are dragging your dumbbell, as well. Couldn't you have at least poured the water out? It would have become twelve kilograms lighter."

"I didn't think of that in the hurry. I had just smoked some charas in my cell, Vitya, and then the transfer was announced," I say, opening the bottles tied to one another. Having poured the water out, I am the last one to get onto the bus, accompanied by my friends' applause. If not for the uniformed guards, you could have thought that a group of cheerful friends had gathered to go on a picnic. The bus sets off, and the hubbub of twenty drug dealers and thirty guards lulls. Many of them look out of the window, saying goodbye to the place where they spent more than a year of their lives. I've lived here for six months. So long, Mapusa Lock-up Jail. The prisoners observe the scenery outside, keeping silent all the way. After only an hour's drive, we pull up to a gloomy building with huge black gates.

"This facility is more serious than Mapusa," an Italian says grimly to an Iranian. "Those who've been sentenced for up to three years, or whose trial is lasting a long time, do time here. Furthermore, the former warden of Mapusa is now the warden here."

"Did you hear, Vitya, what the Italian said?"

"What?" Viktor asks, coming back to reality and staring at the black iron gates through the window.

"Do you remember there was another warden in Mapusa three months ago? He didn't allow you to order tomatoes, and didn't give me my rubber mat."

"I remember that vampire. Is he waiting for us here now?"

"Yeah, Vitya, you've guessed it. Welcome to the kingdom of Dracula," I say, entering the new prison. "There is one positive thing: I hope we'll be put in the same cell," I add as I unload my packages with prison stuff.

Spotting a large, life-size mirror in the hallway, many of the prisoners gather around it immediately, looking at their reflection in turn. I haven't seen my reflection for nine months. "I think I look great," Viktor says happily, grimacing in front of the mirror.

Our group, consisting only of foreigners, is the first to go upstairs to the second floor. A large covered walking area is surrounded with five cells with barred doors. A long time ago, I watched many different movies where the protagonist goes to prison. Imagining myself in his place, my heartbeat always quickened and I experienced a slight fear. Having found myself in a real prison, I understood that everything is much easier than in the movies. I was worried that I would show my fear somehow, but now I don't have any at all. Indifference is the only thing I feel. A vast indifference towards everything, as I've been already deprived of everything really important to me. I don't have anything other than a few packages of things smelling of prison and mold. Dozens of curious eyes look at us through the barred windows from different directions. Opening the iron door, the guards let us into a cell four times larger than we had in Mapusa.

"Welcome to our prison," someone's voice is heard from the corner of the cell. My name is Andy. I'm the cell boss," a tall, thin Hindu says, offering his hand to greet me.

Having shaken hands, we put down our bags of stuff in the middle of the cell and sit in a semicircle, looking at the space around. The same yellow, shabby, fungus infected walls. There are six small, barred windows above head level.

"Vitya, if you stand on tiptoe, you can see the sky and some industrial buildings. It's a beautiful view here, compared to Mapusa. We should settle in, Vitya. How many of us are in this cell?"

"Twenty," Viktor says, thrusting his bag of junk into the gap between two board beds.

"Vitya, if only you knew how much I've missed a bed," I say, spreading my rubber mat on the floor.

"Vasya, I love sleeping on the floor at home," Viktor says, throwing someone's greasy pillow straight onto the concrete.

Noticing a nail stuck into the wall just above my head, I happily realize that I will now have my own furniture. I won't have any more problems with storing my stuff. I tie a rope made out of a rag onto the nail, and attach three old toothbrushes to it. Using the brushes as hooks, I hang the bags with my belongings on them. That's it, I've settled in. One more thing to do is to put my pile of books in the corner. The door is opened as loudly as it was in the previous two prisons, making many of the prisoners flinch. The cell boss, Andy, quickly turns the TV volume down, and all of the cell's tenants stop what they are doing and squat in rows in the middle of the cell.

"You sit down, too," he says to us. "They'll count us."

Our old friend, the former warden of Mapusa jail, appears at the door surrounded by six guards. We see the same nasty face and one more new star shining on his shoulder straps. The warden starts to count us without a word in absolute silence, pointing his finger at each of us.

"Dobroe utro![82]" Viktor breaks the silence loudly and clearly, speaking in Russian.

"Dobrautra![83]" the warden answers in his high, homosexual voice, with the only Russian phrase he knows.

"We should write a petition to be transferred back to Mapusa," James whispers to David. "It will take three hours to go to court and back every time. We need to get back to the old prison."

"I like this place more, I'm not going anywhere," Viktor expresses his opinion; as always, the opposite of that being voiced.

Chapter 41. Part Two. Outside.

"Well, is everybody ready?"

"Yes!" two groups of children of about Vasilinka's age answer in unison.

"Stand in line, eight kids in each group. On my whistle, the first two climb into a sack and jump all the way to that chair, where Ilka, oh sorry, Olechka, is waving to you. The team that is first to jump to the finish will receive a big bag of prizes.

---

[82] Dobroe utro! (Russian) - Good morning!

[83] Dobrautra! (broken Russian) - Good morning!

Lyosha, a former Moscow drug dealer also known as Frenzied, is coping perfectly with the role of children's party host. Having given up his criminal business a couple of years ago, Lyosha and his wife, Larisa, opened a small Russian kindergarten in Goa. Larisa bore him a son, Fedka. Lyosha quickly and easily got into the role of 'mustached nanny', being happy to teach and play with the children. It was much nicer to work with children than to sell drugs. Today, Lyosha is on form with the children, working off the money he owes me after the last drug deal we made a year ago.

Having smoked a chillum with me before the competitions, he is in good spirits, talking and playing with the children as if he were the same age as them. The kids love it. They are playing and fooling around with him, and squealing happily. All of Vasilinka's Goan friends have come to her birthday party.

"Did you ever dream of having such a birthday party when you were a child, Lena?" I hug my beloved wife.

Together with the other parents, we watch our children having fun on the beach.

"I don't remember any of my birthdays as a child. Our family didn't throw big parties on birthdays. I remember how mom and dad took us to the sea. I remember how my dad dragged ten suitcases, my sister, my little brother and me. I never even dreamed of having a birthday like this."

Having fenced off a piece of beach in front of my restaurant with colored flags and ribbons, Lyosha holds different competitions, entertaining the happy children who are dressed in a variety of colors. The children of Goan freaks are the most beautiful and the most cheerful kids I've ever seen.

"Vasilinka is a princess today," my Lena says proudly, holding my hand.

My daughter has been brought up from a young age surrounded by freaks who are always cheerful and happy, and it is easy for her to connect with any adult or child, just like it is for all of her Goan friends. At her age, I behaved completely differently with people. It was very difficult for me to get to know someone and until I went to school I preferred to go for walks with my mother. Being used to addressing adults with the words 'missis' or 'mister' since childhood, I felt uncomfortable when addressing elders by their names when I became an adult myself. Such concepts do not exist for my daughter. Despite her age, she is free to address everyone by name, considering all of them her friends. I did not want her to have the same social complexes as I had, and maybe that's why I wished most of all that my little princess would grow up and get her education in Goa. All of her school friends and even her class teacher, an elderly Englishwoman resembling Mary Poppins in retirement, have come to her birthday party.

"Daddy, daddy, two Indians are asking for you over there!" Vasilinka says, pointing to the beach, having run up to me.

"Judging by the patent-leather shoes and black trousers, the cops have arrived," I whisper to Lena.

"Daughter, I'll go and speak to these men, they must have come to congratulate you. Go and play with your friends over there," I say to my daughter, heading towards the two creeps waiting for me.

"Do you have permission to throw this party?" a chimpanzee-faced officer asks me.

"Which party? It's six o'clock in the evening, are you mad? Children's music is playing quietly. Can't you see that it's a children's birthday party? Balloons and colorful hats – does a trance party look like that? There is their class teacher. The parents aren't dancing. Everything is decent. It will be over in a couple of hours and everyone will go home."

"And why is part of the beach fenced off with colored flags?"

"They are holding children's competitions," I say, beginning to run out of patience. "Who is this fence bothering?"

"Stop the party right now, or we'll call in a police squad. An illegal party is a serious offence. Remove the fence from the beach immediately; it's state property," a small policeman standing next to chimpanzee man begins to huff, puffing up like a baboon.

"Go to hell, call whoever you want, I won't stop anything. Do you see the guy with the Rottweiler over there? He is Tamir Akhmedov. His daughter has also come to the children's party. If you try to disturb the celebration, we'll let the dog loose on you."

"We'll call the police chief now, and we'll see what you will do when the police squad comes here," the police chimpanzee says, starting to dial a number on his cell phone.

"Go ahead, make a call, and don't forget to tell him that Tamir Akhmedov and his daughter are here, and wait for the squad to arrive. If you don't know who he is, ask your boss," I say, going back to my restaurant.

Having talked about something for a few minutes, the Indians walk away silently.

"Well, Tamir, let's smoke a chillum while our children are playing?"

"Why not, Vaso? I've already prepared the chillum," he says, pointing at a beautiful Italian chillum lying on a table. "I haven't been to Arambol for a long time, Vasya," the most famous Russian trance DJ says to me, pulling a piece of charas and a beautiful mixing bowl out of his pocket. "I stopped visiting this place when they started banning parties. We threw the last trance party here, in Arambol, five years ago. I haven't been here since then."

"Well, you're back at a party in Arambol, although it's children's party. Freak tourists used to live in our house, Tamir. We often went to your parties. And now, almost all of our ten rooms are occupied by domesticated half-freaks with families. All of them have kids and rarely go to parties. In front of us now we see the children of psychedelic love."

After smoking and cleaning his chillum, Tamir approaches the children.

"So, kids, listen to me. I'll show you a fun contest," he shouts loudly with a Jewish accent, immediately attracting the attention of all of the children. "The winner will get a prize from me."

"What a great guy Tamir is," Masha, the former wife of a singer in a Russian pop group, says to me. "He's a professional entertainer. He hosts the best events for both adults and children. Do you remember, Vasya, how he held a birthday party for his daughter at the Lotus Inn, by the swimming pool? There were lots of children there and he showed them tricks. All of the children squealed with delight. He loves children, and they also respect and obey him."

"Masha, I remember that children's party most due to the fact that Tamir came up to me and said, 'Vaso, let's go into the bushes and smoke a chillum. My mother has come from Russia and I don't want her to know I smoke charas.' It was very touching and quite funny. A forty-something-year-old DJ, the leader of all of the Russian trancers and a real psychedelic shaman, taking care of his elderly mother so movingly. He didn't want her to worry about him."

"Antoshka, Antoshka, let's go and dig potatoes..." a children's song from one of the cartoons from my childhood is heard from the speakers. It's funny to see how a group of adults, dressed in the most unimaginable Goan clothes, dances to this music, watching their children playing. Some smoke chillums, some sip mulled wine. Almost all of the children resemble their parents in hairstyle or clothes. The Greek DJ Theo has given his son a Goan mohawk, which turns into a plait on the back of his head, just like he has. Masha has dressed her Alyonka in a bright crimson color, the same color as her own dress. Vasilinka has fifty thin braids interweaved with colorful ribbons, the same as my Lena.

"Sanya, where did you get the same freak vest for your son from? He's just one year old!"

"I bought it at the Night Market. I bought the same one for both of us. Isn't it cool, Vasya?"

"Yeah, it looks nice. By the way, I want to talk to you. What are we going to do about the restaurant, Sanya?"

"What do you mean?" my partner asks me in surprise.

"Do you remember, Sanya, I told you that I wanted to sell my restaurant three months ago? Well, a tourist has offered me five thousand dollars for it. But I'm ready to sell it to you first, Sanya, as my partner. I will sell it for the amount I invested in it."

"That's pretty expensive, Vasya. You aren't selling the land. You are selling furniture and refrigerators. They've become pretty worn out in three years."

"Sanya, I've managed to create a well promoted brand in three years. Worn out though they are, the restaurant equipment will serve for another few years. Google 'Hemp, Goa', and you'll see how many links, photos, and information there is about my restaurant. Someone has even posted a picture of my establishment on Google Maps. It's a well-promoted place; there are always people in there. You'll get your money back in just one season. Is that really expensive?"

"Vasya, I don't believe that someone will give you five thousand bucks for it. In my opinion, your tourists are running their mouths off. I'm ready to work with you again next season."

"No, Sanya, I'll open another restaurant next season. Well, I warned you, don't be offended that I haven't sold it to you."

"I have another problem now, Vasya. I'm going to Nepal next week. Will you work instead of me?"

"Of course I'll work instead of you, Sanya, no problem. Just come back before we close, as it will be difficult for me to dismantle the restaurant on my own. Besides, you need to take your fridge and furniture before the rainy season starts, as the restaurant will have a new owner next season. And give me a thousand bucks before you leave. I need to pay salary to the cooks and waiters."

"I have no spare cash now, Vasya. You know, my wife and I bought a land plot in Goa, we're going to build a house. I'll give it to you when I get back. Deal?

"Okay, Sanya, no problem. Have a safe trip to Nepal, see you in a month."

Chapter 42. Part One. Inside.

"Viktor, look what I brought from Mapusa," I show him six yellow rubber balls, each the size of an apple. "My Lena brought me them half a year ago. I wanted to learn how to juggle. But the warden didn't allow me to play with them in the cell for some reason and took them away for safekeeping. And now the same warden lets me bring them into the cell."

"He probably wants us to get used to them, and then he'll take your balls away in order to get double satisfaction. Vasya, stop digging around in your things, let's go into the corridor and play tennis with these balls. There are high ceilings, it should make a good tennis court," Viktor suggests, trying to adapt his thick notebook for studying English in order to use it as a tennis racket. "It will be awkward to play with a notebook; wait, I'll make a racket from a book."

Having grabbed the first available book, Viktor runs out into the large exercise hall, which is the size of a badminton court. While I reflect on the fact that the Dalai Lama and Buddhists all over the world would not be against someone playing tennis with a book with his picture on the cover as a racket, Viktor is already pounding the ball with all his might, rejoicing loudly like a child. The sound of a shattered lamp and Viktor's cheerful scream of "Goooooaaal!" are heard from the hall a few seconds later. Having stepped out into the corridor, I play with him for five minutes. Unable to bear it, Viktor runs away to the cell to bring a second ball.

"Vasya, here you are, take a ball. Sorry, but you don't play tennis right. I'd rather play squash against the wall."

"Look who's talking, Vitya! Have you seen yourself in the mirror? You remind me of a giraffe on a tennis court." I rage at his unjust accusation against me.

"And you run around like a little elephant, Vasya. I don't like waiting for you to come back to the starting point with the ball."

"Well, okay, Vitya. That part of the wall is yours, and this is mine. We'd better play against the wall; it doesn't care how we hit and run. In my opinion, it's more fun in this prison than in Mapusa jail," I say to Viktor, loudly returning the ball towards the wall with the book with the Dalai Lama's portrait. "We've got our own personal tennis court and a walking area without bars overhead in this prison. If James and David are allowed to move back to Mapusa, I won't go with them, Vitya. I like this place more. Staying in Mapusa is like sitting in a cage. James and David need to go to the court regularly, their cases are already under consideration, but my case won't be opened sooner than in six months. I'll stay here. Anyway, they won't be transferred back for a couple of months at the earliest, so I should try to learn some English from James while he's my neighbor. Just think, Viktor, if someone asks me, 'Who was your English teacher?' I'll answer: 'My teacher was a real Scotsman.

Although nobody could understand him due to his accent and the fact that half of his tongue was missing."

"That's a cool description for an English teacher," Viktor says, laughing, without ceasing to beat the ball against the wall.

"Vitya, do you know how he lost half of his tongue?"

"He said something about a fight and that someone bit it off, Vasya. But, you know, it's impossible to completely understand his Scottish. It's a strange story, though. How is it possible to bite someone's tongue off during a fight? Was he kissing someone, or what?"

"I don't know, Vitya, we should ask him for more details."

"Why do you want to know, Vasya? Do you want to find out his sexual orientation? Ignorance is bliss. Look, 'sexy' has come," stopping playing, Viktor points with his racket made out of the *Tibetan Book of the Dead* at a guard with an obvious homosexual orientation who has just appeared in the corridor. Passing by three young Indians prisoners, the guard doesn't miss the opportunity to feel up their asses.

"Vasya, I think he likes you," Viktor says, smiling and watching how the guard, having moistened his lips in a vulgar manner, heads toward me, swinging his hips like a woman.

"Just what we needed."

I begin to hit the ball with the book twice as hard, demonstrating my aggressive attitude. Having waited until I miss the ball, the guard immediately appears in front of me. Making eyes at me and coming quite close, he tries to grab my dick. Having successfully dodged aside, I knee him in the balls; not hard, but with relish.

"Well, fag, have you understood that you can get a knee in the balls from me?" I say in Russian with an aggressive tone. "I am not an Indian or a fag, so don't touch me."

Having realized he shouldn't hit on me, 'sexy' quickly transfers his attention to an Indian standing near the window.

"Are they all nancy boys in here?" I say to Viktor, who is laughing merrily.

"The voice of the jail warden is like a girl's, and it seems to me that his deputy also has abnormal sexual inclinations. He touched my ass in his office yesterday. I also had to show him my teeth"

"Vitya, have you heard the voice of the guard who was on duty last night?"

"It's awful, Vasya! When he speaks, you could think that a ten-year-old girl was talking. God forbid being born with a voice like that. How did they manage to get a job in prison?"

"I had a dream about that last night, Vitya," I address Viktor, who has again started playing tennis against the wall.

"One hundred points!" Viktor shouts loudly, looking through a small toilet window. "Wait, Vasya, don't tell me about your sexual phobias, I'll get the ball out of the toilet."

Viktor comes out after a few seconds holding the ball, from which a thread of some sort of mucus hangs, with two fingers.

"It's jail, man," Viktor says, holding the ball under the stream of water in the sink with disgust.

"So, Vasya, what dream did you have? Let's go to the cell and you can tell me. I'm sweating like a pig from playing for half an hour. The court is closed for today. Come on, let's have a smoke while everybody is out walking."

Pulling the plastic jar with candies out of my bag, I pour all the sweets on the floor.

"It was a good idea to disguise the hash as toffee, you'd never find which one is the prize," Viktor says smiling, taking off his vest soaked in sweat.

Having crumbed some charas into a bong made out of a plastic bottle and foil, we take several big puffs.

"Well, tell me about your dream," Viktor says, stretching out flat on the cool concrete floor.

"I had a strange dream. I didn't want to tell you about it, but after that incident with the 'sexy' guard I will. I dreamt last night that I went into the guards' room and I saw them, dressed in German Gestapo uniforms, fucking James brutally, while he said to me, crying, 'Vasya, I was forced to. I didn't want to. I resisted as best I could.' And I said to him, "I need to escape from prison before someone fucks me too.' And then we ran through some slums all night, fleeing from the fascist guards who were chasing us.

"Well, Vasya, I think you've started developing homophobia," Viktor says, smiling and rolling across the floor towards a spot under the fan.

With a nasty clang of the iron latch, the door to our cell is opened noisily. Our inmates have returned from their walk, covered with red dust and wet with sweat. Some have prints from a soccer ball on their shirts. They first go to their plastic water bottles, eagerly swallowing the cooling liquid, not paying attention to the odd sediment floating in it. James looks the most cheerful.

"Hey, 'Celtic'[84]", how many goals have you scored today?" Viktor asks the fan of the Scottish football team.

"I scored three today," huffing and puffing, James answers as he sits down onto the floor, looking like a big, tired Winnie the Pooh.

Rolling onto his back, big, fluffy Winnie flops near smiling Viktor, enjoying the pleasant coolness coming from the concrete floor.

"Guys, I don't think I have played football for twenty years," says our plump Scotsman, dripping with sweat. "I've lost fifteen kilograms in six months. I didn't think I'd ever play football again in my life. I've got a lame leg. I was in an accident, drunk as a skunk, a year ago here in Goa. I broke my leg and went deaf in one ear."

"So, you're deaf on top of everything else, James!" Viktor says, laughing loudly, looking at our puzzled English teacher. "Well, Vasya, we have a great teacher. A deaf, lame Scottish smuggler with half a tongue."

"Tell us, James, how did you manage to lose half your tongue in a fight?" I ask him, unable to hold back a smile. "Were you kissing or what?"

"Yeah," James says, embarrassed. "Something like that."

---

[84] Celtic - a Scottish football club.

"I don't believe it!" Viktor smiles, lifting his head from the floor, having apparently recalled the 'sexy' guard.

"I haven't told anyone this story, but I'll tell it to you Russians. Me and my ex-wife, the mother of my son, used to have a lot of fun together when we were young. One time, we snorted a load of coke and hit the bottle. And then we had a huge row over something. I leaned in to kiss her, and she grabbed my tongue between her teeth, and almost pulled it out by the root. The funniest thing occurred the next day, when my mom and my brother came to visit me in the hospital. My mother said to me, 'Show me your tongue, son,' and I pulled half of my tongue out of a jar and held it out to her. She broke into tears, and my brother killed himself laughing. I always keep it a secret and don't tell anyone that my wife did it. You are the first ones I have told. I hope you and my ex-wife won't talk about it."

"What have you read in the newspaper, Alexandro?" I address our Sicilian Italian, who is lying on the floor.

"A new model of motorbike has been released. Look what a nice bike!" he points his finger at a bad quality black-and-white photo in an Indian newspaper.

We stare at the new motorbike in silence for a while, remembering our biker youth. An old Indian doing time for rape who pretends to be mad, breaks our silence.

"And what about Volkswagen?" the rapist nicknamed Churchill, who resembles something between a monkey and a caveman, asks us out of the blue.

"How does Volkswagen come into the picture, Churchill?" Alexandro asks in surprise. "We are discussing a motorbike, there is no Volkswagen here."

"I just wanted to keep the conversation going. Volkswagen is a good German car, and Indian cars are bad."

"Why do you think that, Churchill?" I ask with a smile, watching the daily crazy comedy.

"It's because Australian bananas are good, big," the old ape-man points to the length of his forearm, up to the elbow, "and Indian bananas are small, the size of a finger. However, India is now a good friend of Russia, and isn't friends with Australia. In Australia, the local residents beat Indian taxi drivers. Meanwhile, India has bought weapons, planes, rockets, and machine guns from the Russians."

"That's it, Churchill, stop doing our heads in! Turn off your broadcaster or change the channel to another topic," Viktor yells at him, being the first to get fed up of his nonsense.

"Do you have a cookie?" Churchill asks, quickly switching to another topic, making a plaintive face. "Let me wash your clothes? And I could do a foot massage for you, if you give me some jam."

Having crouched swiftly on all fours, Churchill starts massaging James's feet attentively, occasionally looking into his eyes.

"No, Churchill, get off, I don't need your massage. Wash my T-shirt and shorts though," the Scotchman says, throwing his dirty, sweaty T-shirt at him.

"And wash my sheet and blanket," I add, having remembered that they haven't been washed for three months already.

"Here is the advance, Churchill," Viktor says, giving the old rapist a candy.

Watching us through the bars, the guard nicknamed 'sexy' stops pawing the young Indian boy standing next to him, and thrusts out his hand to Viktor.

"Take some candy too, fag," Viktor says, holding his hand with a toffee out to the guard. Having grabbed Vitka's elbow through the bars, 'sexy' instantly kisses his hand.

"How is this even possible, Vasya? A prison guard is ready to kiss my hand for a candy."

"It is India, man," the Italian says with a smile, shrugging his shoulders.

Chapter 42. Part Two. Outside.

"I'm fucking tired of this shit. I've finally finished dismantling the restaurant," I say, pouring cola into a glass of rum. "Today we can say that another season in Goa has finished. Four years in Goa have passed like one day."

"Honey, I fully support you in your new project," Lena says, gently massaging my head. "At last you sold that fucking Hemp, but the most pleasant thing for me is that we are moving away from fucking Arambol. All of the normal people moved to live in Siolim long ago. Honey, I really like our new house! Even though it's a long way from the sea, there will be no pigs running around and no disgusting fishermen. It takes just fifteen minutes by car from our house in Siolim to get to all the places that we need to go. Fifteen minutes to Arambol beach and fifteen minutes to Mapusa market. We'll only need to wake Vasilinka up half an hour before school. And the people living in Siolim are all decent. As we are renting a floor in the house of the panchayat's[85] engineer, the whole place is equipped with modern furniture, has marble floors and an elegant kitchen. I'll love you even more, if you buy me a washing machine," Lena says laughing, sitting a couple of steps above me on the stairs leading from the balcony to the roof.

Lena blows me a sexy kiss, slightly parting her legs, and quickly covers her white panties with her short skirt.

"You have deliberately not had sex with me for a whole month to force me to buy you a washing machine, Lena," I say, slightly offended, but unable to resist the sexual magnetism of my beloved.

"I haven't had sex with you because you have been in a terrible mood for the last three months. And your jokes have been stupid recently. I understand that you have had showdowns with whackos, you closed the restaurant, and your partner Sanya hasn't come back yet, the snake. You had to dismantle your restaurant alone. I understand, dear, that you are nervous because of all these problems. But why do you bring these problems home? Vasilinka and I haven't done anything wrong. And I told you about a washing machine long ago. If you want me to be less tired and more affectionate with you, then buy an automatic washing machine. I took Vasilinka to Ilka's for the night on purpose today, as I've missed you. Pour me some more rum and cola," Lena says, playfully parting and closing her legs under her pink skirt.

---

[85] Panchayat - village council in Hindi.

"Stop teasing me, Lenochka! I'm leaving for vipassana the day after tomorrow, so it would be a good idea for us to make love tonight. I won't see you for ten days."

"I promise you, honey, we'll have fun, if you don't get boring and spoil my mood again today."

"Lenochka, do you see how beautiful the Full Moon looks against the background of the palm trees?" I say, sitting down on the step next to my wife. "The view is just like a postcard."

"Oh, Vasya, I can't imagine you doing vipassana. After all, you'll have to sit in the lotus position ten hours a day for ten days. And the most unbearable thing, in my opinion, is that you're banned from speaking for ten days."

"You know, Lena, I wouldn't have imagined myself keeping silent for ten days, either. But I am so tired of everything lately that I believe that being silent for ten days will be good for me. Nothing gives me joy me recently. I would like to experience some new sensations. Maybe the people around me are different, or I have changed, but some kind of boredom is eating at me. I started to down rum with you every night because of these blues, although I didn't drink at all before."

"Come on, stop going on about alcohol. Don't drink, if you don't want to. Just don't spoil my erotic mood," Lena says in a huff, adjusting her skirt. "It would be better if you smoked a chillum instead of giving me a lecture on female alcoholism," Lena says, frowning and pouring rum into her glass. "Go, Vasil, do vipassana, meditate. Maybe it will ease your mood a bit. However, I think it's nonsense to sit and meditate for ten days. It would be better if you thought about your new restaurant in Palolem for ten days. I want you to succeed in this business so much! I don't want to make anymore kvass or cakes."

"Lena, an Indian woman from Arambol prepares kvass for you. You only need to drive around the Russian restaurants once a week, and collect the earnings. Ten different Russian places buy our kvass. You're my kvass queen. You should be proud that your kvass was shown throughout the whole of Russia on TV. Five different magazines wrote about our Goan kvass. Even Sanya mentioned your kvass several times in his book 'Goan Syndrome'. Nadine makes cottage cheese and is proud of being 'Holy Dairy Mother Double Queen'."

"Well, my dear, I don't want to be the kvass queen, and your Nadine is not an example for me. If you call me that one more time, you won't have sex with me at all," my Lena says aggrievedly, turning her back to me. "I'd rather be the wife of a top restaurateur instead," my beauty winks at me playfully again.

"I'll do my best for you to become the wife of a successful restaurateur. I expect to earn thirty thousand dollars a season. Lenochka, just imagine: four hundred Russian tourists a day stay in the five star hotel in front of our new restaurant. And there is not a single decent place nearby. They will leave all their money at my place! I sold my Arambol restaurant for five thousand. Vitalik will add five thousand bucks, and we will build a palace out of bamboo for ten grand. Nobody will have a restaurant like it. One thousand meters of land are not the same as fifty square meters of Arambol beach. Vitalik and I met for a reason on the train. Heaven gave us a chance to start a new life. I'll make money honestly, without any drugs."

"Are you sure, Vasil, that your new partner won't let you down, like Dan and then Sasha did?"

"Lenochka, Dan conned me because of drugs, and I believe that Sasha will turn up. Maybe he has a valid excuse for getting lost and not coming back for two months. I don't think he will quit Goa because of the thousand dollars he owes me, having left his used furniture and old refrigerator. And even if he disappears, his equipment will come in handy in the new restaurant."

"Just be careful with Vitalik, Vasil. He's a former estate agent and he conned his company out of thirty thousand bucks."

"In my opinion, you are exaggerating your fears, Lena. He has nowhere to go from Goa, he doesn't have a passport. I doubt he'll want to con me."

"Why doesn't he pay back the hundred bucks he borrowed six months ago?"

"Lena, calm down, he'll cover the money he owes when we build the restaurant. Don't worry, he has money. Look how they live. They have a big jeep and a classy house with air conditioning. Crooks don't show off like that."

"Everything will work out, dear, I believe in you."

Lena kisses me gently on the cheek, putting both arms around my neck.

"Honey, I'll work in the restaurant in the south of Goa for a week, and come here to you to relax in the north for the next week. All problems related to work will be left in the south, and here I'll be a good husband and a model father. I believe that this schedule will be the most suitable for us. After all, Lenochka, we argue about some nonsense every day. Just think about it, we're living in paradise, but there is a feeling that paradise without hell slowly becomes hell. So we invent different problems to resolve and then get a buzz out of arguing."

"Oh right, my love, so we quarrel about some nonsense do we? Is it really that difficult for you to clean the crumbs off the table after you have had a meal? Or do you leave them on purpose every time, to spite me?"

"Lena, please, don't start preaching, or I'll leave for Palolem right now. You moan every day. I always clean up after myself, but you're always nit-pick and find what I don't see. You're the only person that sees microbes of dirt."

"Vasil, there you have a classic example. And we have the same story every day. We'll only benefit from being apart for a week. And if I miss you too much, dear, I'll jump in the car and get to you in two hours. The main thing is, don't take a mistress, because I'll come and tear all her hair out."

"Calm down, dear, I'm going to work there, not to have a rest. Lena, it's an interesting thing how the attitude towards time changes here in Goa. To spend a couple of hours in a traffic jam in Moscow seems like no big deal, but two hours seems to be a huge distance here, where it takes fifteen minutes to get anywhere you need. Listen, sweetheart, let's go for it tonight to mark my leaving for vipassana and unpack a gram of MDMA?"

"I don't need to take Vasilinka to school tomorrow, I don't need to make kvass. Why not? We haven't taken anything for more than two months. Let's arrange a party tonight. Vasil, shall we invite some friends to have someone to talk to?"

"Let's invite Andrey and Oksana. I haven't seen them for ages. They're good company."

"Hello, Andrey, are you busy now? Lena and I have decided to have some fun on the occasion of my leaving for vipassana. Come with your wife to our place. Just bring a couple of bottles of Coca-Cola and a couple of bottles of rum. Meanwhile we'll unpack a gram of MDMA. We're waiting for you, see you soon."

***

"So you decided to do vipassana?" the short, muscular guy with huge tunnels in his ears asks, going upstairs to the balcony.

"Yeah, Andryukha, I am ready for vipassana. Hello, Oksana," I kiss his pretty wife, who has appeared after him, on the cheek. "We've decided to throw a house party on the occasion of my departure. I have to speak my full before ten days of silence. Come into the house, there are lines of Dymich for you on the glass table. Lena and I have already snorted ours."

"We guessed that from your sparkling eyes," Oksana says, laughing and putting bottles of rum and cola on the table.

"This Dymich kicks in so quickly, I can already see the stars in the sky dancing to the music," Lena says to me, leaning on a mattress lying on the balcony. "Vasil, tell me, why can we only forget our petty grievances, which stop us from simply loving each other, when we are high on Dymich? How do people who don't take anything manage to live without arguing?"

"Lenochka, I am now experiencing the same feelings I had when I fell in love with you. It's a pity that domestic problems get in the way of these feelings. Do you remember how we met in the Rock Bar?"

"Of course I remember, honey. I didn't think then that I would marry you."

"Whereas, as soon as I saw you, I immediately realized I had fallen head over heels in love with you."

"The love stories have begun, huh?" Andrey says smiling, sitting next to his Oksana.

"We always only talk about love when doing Dymich," Lena says flirtingly, her eyes half-closed in pleasure.

"Vasya, I am starting to feel the music deeply," Andrey says, leaning back in the armchair. "You have good trance, Vasya. The only thing is that the Dymich is really stinging my nose so far. But I'll catch up with you soon and will enjoy, too."

"I like to talk about love when I'm coming up, too," Andrey's young, beautiful wife says.

"When I'm on Dymich, I think about unconditional love," I say with half-closed eyes, eagerly staring at my wife's beautiful legs. "All topics and thoughts boil down to this, when I'm high on MDMA."

"What do you mean by unconditional love, Vasya?" Andrey asks with closed eyes, resting his head on his Oksana's lap.

"As far as I know, Andryukha, there are three kinds of love: erotic, friendly and universal. Well, universal love is the ultimate expression of love, when you love someone without a sense of ownership, for no reason, when you enjoy love without asking for anything in return. After all, it is possible to just love, without any conditions."

"Yeah, too bad you only enjoy this kind of love in the early days of being together or under the influence of MDMA," Oksana joins our dialogue, caressing her husband's hair.

"When on Dymich, Vasya and I love fucking in different, unusual places," Lena says, flirting, stroking her nails gently on my leg. "We've done it in a thousand different places: on the roof, on the beach, in the hallway, in a cornfield. Do you remember Nepal, sweetheart?"

"Of course I remember, honey."

"You had multicolored ribbons interweaved in your dreadlocks, Vasil, and you resembled an alien in my trip. During sex, it seemed to me that I was being fucked by an alien from another planet."

I passionately kiss my Lena on her hot, moist lips, watching out of the corner of my eye how Andrey kisses his Oksana, with his eyes on my Lena.

"I want you badly now," my Lena whispers in my ear. "Maybe we'll go to the bedroom for half an hour?"

"Do you want to get new sensations, my love?" I say in a whisper, kissing my beloved's neck. "Let's make love in front of Andrey and Oksana."

"That's a terribly exciting suggestion," Lena whispers, watching our friends kissing. "But no complaints later. You won't reproach me later and say that I came up with the idea?"

"Darling, I promise it's going to be a kick! I feel like I'm going to explode with excitement, the main thing is that our friends don't object."

"Hey, sweet couple, stop for a second, we want to offer you a surprise," I say to Andrey and Oksana, who are kissing to the music. "Do you want to watch how we make love?"

"Wow, that's quite an offer!" Oksana says with surprise, smiling and adjusting her skirt, revealing part of her underwear.

"I do. That tops everything I've seen," Andrey says, preempting Oksana's response and opening his mouth in surprise.

"We haven't done it before, either," Lena says, pushing me towards a mattress lying on the floor in the hall. Slowly undressing and covering each other with kisses, we move in time with the music like two snakes, intertwining in amazing poses. Every kiss, every touch, echoes with a burst of orgasmic pleasure in the brain. The adrenaline rushing through our blood due to the realization that we are doing something forbidden multiplies the satisfaction a thousand times.

"Look," my beauty whispers in my ear, "Andrey and Oksana are making love, too."

Struggling to focus my vision, which is blurred from Dymich, I see Andrey making love to his Oksana beautifully and tenderly on the balcony.

"They're so beautiful!" Lena says to me, passionately looking at the naked couple, harmoniously moving on the floor.

"Let's invite them to our mattress?" I suggest to Lena, who tenderly presses herself against me.

"Won't you regret it later?" my beloved asks me, staring into my eyes.

"You're so beautiful to me, I love you very much! I love you with universal love. And if you get satisfaction, I'll get ten times as much from this, no matter what you do."

"Andrey, Oksana!" I shout to my friends. "Why are you lying on the floor, come to our mattress!"

Intertwining in various poses, we sometimes touch each other, moaning with pleasure. It's already impossible to determine whose moans are heard. The candles burning in the dark help hide the embarrassment that arises occasionally. Waves of pleasure, enhanced by Dymich, roll through our bodies, making us bend brokenly and emit sounds of pleasure. The space around us doesn't exist; it has dissolved in our bliss. I have the feeling that we are protagonists in an erotic fairytale.

"I'll go and snort one more line of Dymich," I say, having come to my senses a bit, leaving my beautiful woman lying next to the two intertwined, naked bodies.

"I hope you don't mind, Vasya?' Andrey asks me, putting his hand on my Lena's thigh. Having met my beloved's gaze for a second, I smile amicably and nod.

"I'll take a line, too," Oksana says, leaving her husband next to my beauty. Having quickly snorted a line of crumbed crystals each, we plop down onto the couch, absolutely naked, watching our soul mates merging into one.

"Look, they do that so nicely," Oksana whispers, pressing her naked body to me. Another wave of pleasure fills me, running with shivers from my heels up to my nape, making my hair move.

"I've never experienced such feelings. I feel as if I were making love to her, and at the same time watching from the sidelines."

"Yeah, it's a great feeling, Vasya," Oksana says, having looked up from our loved ones for a moment, stroking my chest with her nails.

"When you truly love someone, nothing can keep you from enjoying this love. Look, my Lena is so beautiful. The fact that she's with your Andrey now doesn't diminish my love for her one bit. It's amazing, but I'm not jealous. I feel only love. If my Lena feels good now, I'm even happier."

"I am experiencing the same feelings, Vasya. I'm also pleased to watch your Lena making love to my Andrey. Shall we join them?"

"Let's go," I say, taking Oksana's hand. "I guess we've all gone mad. However, I really like what we're doing. It must be the highest manifestation of love. We'll probably never forget this night. Tomorrow never come."

***

"Shall we take one more line?" I offer Lena, closing the door behind Andrey and Oksana.

"Just the last one for today," Lena says, standing naked with her hair loose in the morning sunlight.

"Well, did you like this night?" I say, smiling and pouring some crystals onto the glass table.

"Darling, although I feel a bit embarrassed, while I am still high I like everything. But when I start to come down, I feel I shouldn't have agreed to this experiment today. I feel somehow uncomfortable. Now it's like I'm in a different reality."

"Honey, I adore you, I love you, and I'll never reproach you or condemn your behavior today. On the contrary, I'll always thank you for your understanding. Its rare that a wife makes the gift you've made me today."

"Sweetheart, just promise me that when we come down and are sober, you'll never discuss this topic, otherwise I'll be terribly angry and have complexes."

"This Dymich really stings the nose," I say, making a cocktail of black rum and kvass.

"Honey, I'm leaving tomorrow and we will both have time to think about what we've done tonight. I don't want you to feel remorse. Remember, I'll never condemn you for this night. Let's go to bed and enjoy the last wave of love for today. I love you, honey."

"I really love you, too."

Chapter 43. Part One. Inside.

"... Lena, try to borrow money against our apartment, I'll get out of prison, we'll sell it, pay off our debts and start all over again. I love you, sweetheart, and give you the right to make your own decisions and assume responsibility for them," I finish reading aloud the letter that I have prepared to hand over to Lena during her last visit before she leaves for Russia.

"Churchill!" Mario shouts to the old rapist, pointing at the window separating us from the hall, where the guard is dozing in a chair.

'All clear,' Churchill answers with a gesture, keeping his eyes on the guard.

It only takes a second for Mario to jump on the shoulders of Suresh, forming a human pyramid, and quickly hide the cell phone behind a lamp bolted to the wall near the ceiling.

"I understand, Vasya, that you've just had a spat with your Lena on the phone, so your letter is written in an offended mood, but it's not right," Viktor says, drawing the Sun on his bedspread with a pen.

"How is it 'not right?" I ask irritably, ready to fiercely defend my point of view.

"Vasya, as I've understood from your letter, you don't want Lena to sell your apartment in Russia without you. Am I right?"

"Yes, I'm against it," I say, becoming even more irritated by the fact that Viktor is trying to evaluate my personal affairs. "My mother gave her six thousand dollars to get me out of jail, and she simply wasted the money for seven months, didn't earn a penny, and now doesn't want to do anything. I face ten years in prison, and she has just told me on the phone that she won't borrow any money from anybody for me. I'll manage to get money without her help. I still have a lot of friends. The problem with our apartment is that I am its formal owner, and Lena has asked for a power of attorney in order to sell it. I don't mind. I'm ready to sell our three-room apartment to pay for a lawyer, and then buy a one-room apartment and register it in Vasilinka's name. I'm simply afraid to trust my Lena with financial affairs, because my wife will again squander all the money, and I'll get ten years in prison. She can't just have money, she always spends it on some unnecessary stuff."

"Vasya, I believed my whole life that I thought about love, but in reality I cared about money. You have to let your wife go, all of your problems are caused by a sense of ownership. You aren't worrying about her now. You are worrying about how she will manage the money without you knowing."

"Vitya, I have no sense of ownership, just common sense," I say, seething with anger at the lack of understanding.

"Vasya, I look at you as my mirror image," Viktor says, laughing like an idiot, trying to parody me. "Our lives are pretty much the same. We were tourist traders in Turkey at same time, we've both had two wives, and we're almost identical psychedelic revolutionaries. I sold speed[86] to squeeze cocaine out of the market, while you sold MDMA. And our way of life led both of us to prison," Viktor begins to laugh hysterically now. "I used to love, adding the word 'if', the same as you do. But you need to love without this prefix. You blame your Lena for selling all your laptops, refrigerators, air conditioners, and not wanting to do anything here in Goa. Did she want to live the life you gave her? It's you who like delivering kvass and selling drugs. Maybe she's not that kind of person, and you can never change someone to fit you. She's not your property, even if you have a stamp in your passport."

"Viktor, but we've always had a democratic relationship. We even had group sex once."

"It doesn't matter what kind of sex you had, that's your business. You just have a huge sense of ownership. Vasya, don't you realize that it's not love if you don't give her what she wants. Your own conscience will torture you. With my second wife we also had a democratic relationship. I allowed her to go fuck a black guy sometimes, and she didn't mind me bringing girls home. After I was locked up in here, she visited me for a month, and then took the last three thousand dollars and moved to Thailand, leaving me here alone, without any money. I was also angry for the first four months, but then I realized that I had earned that money for her, but only wanted to spend it as I saw fit. And she spent that money how she wanted. So it turns out that I was angry for nothing all those four months. I could have been happy the whole time. Whereas, I had a headache instead. Everything is due to that damned sense of ownership. You, Vasya, should give your Lena the full right to be in charge of her life and your property. Then you'll do your time much more peacefully, and nobody will bother her. She's the mother of your daughter; let her be responsible for her life. You worry that she won't be able to earn money without you, because, as far as I've understood from your words, she does everything wrong. And have you given her a chance to do something on her own, without your guidance?"

"To be honest with you, Vitya, I've always thought in advance that she will fail, no matter what she starts to do."

"Who could do something good, if they are constantly supervised and criticized? And as far as I already know you, Vasya, you seem to think that everything that is not done by you, is done wrong. I am exactly the same."

"Yeah, you're right, Vitya. It's almost impossible for somebody to implement my ideas well. I'd better write a new letter to my Lena. I'm going apologize for being in prison and not giving her the things she wanted. I'll let her do what she wants to. Especially as I can't do anything to influence it now anyway."

"Write it later, let's go and have a smoke. Look, our friends have already gathered," Viktor says, pointing at the bong that David has prepared.

---

[86] Speed – amphetamines

Crawling after Viktor onto James' nearby bunk, I see how some of the inmates who don't have access to our cell's exclusive smoking club watch us with envy.

"What was that?" I exhale the strange, plastic-tasting smoke.

"Welcome to the world of freebase," Viktor says, smiling devilishly and taking the bong from me. "I deliberately didn't tell you, Vasya, that it was crack, so that you could feel what it was on your own, without anyone's influence."

"I've refused to take this serious drug for a long time, Vitya. But, apparently, today it's time to try it. What should I expect from it?" I ask Viktor, being slightly nervous and leaning back comfortably on the floor.

"Nothing. It resembles nothing. What do you feel right now?"

"I smoked hash with you before that, so I feel good anyway. I don't feel any change."

Viktor, getting ready to enjoy the onset of the crack, also leans back comfortably on the floor, using a plastic bottle for a pillow.

"After all, what incredible surrealism surrounds us! Vasya, just look where we are," Viktor gestures to the space around us with his hand. "We are at the very bottom, in prison. And we are smoking the most expensive drug."

"And I'm looking at Sunny and thinking: he is a Sikh, and if he ever found his girlfriend with a lover, he would kill both on the spot. He is unlikely to ever understand our talks about unconditional love and democratic sexual relations. You'd never be able to convince him that a sense of ownership and love are incompatible. In my opinion, Vitya, we are two loonies, from whom society has isolated itself."

"Vasya, we aren't loonies, we are the chosen ones. Do you remember how mad Yelisei visited us in the Mapusa for a month? He gave me an interesting book to read. It said that if you have realized what divine love is, it means that you are one of the chosen. Let them say I'm crazy, but I won't be the same as the majority of people, who prefer a sense of ownership to love.

"Vitya, you really are either enlightened, or a crazy cuckoo. Although they are probably the same thing, as there is no line dividing enlightenment and madness."

"They may think I'm crazy," Viktor says with his eyes closed, "but at least I've understood how to live in this world. You should radiate love and listen carefully to what your heart says. When we listen to it, we do the right things. And when we do everything right, our heart doesn't hurt, and our conscience doesn't torment us. And if nothing gnaws at you from within, you can really enjoy this life. And then you don't need to take something in order to run away from a reality that doesn't please you. And you don't need to drown the signals from your anxious heart with anything. Come on, let's take another puff," Viktor suggests, again starting to creep closer to David. "You feel so good on this drug, but only for ten minutes," Viktor says, exhaling the strange smelling smoke in my face and closing his eyes in pleasure.

"I don't feel anything, Vitya," I say, trying to detect any changes in my mind. "I must have been so stoned on hash that I can't feel the crack."

"Vasya, if you expect something out of the ordinary all the time, you won't feel anything at all. Let's chat about something abstract. Tell me, Vasya, why did you get a tattoo in Sanskrit on your arm?"

"I've already told you, Vitya, that these are the Buddha's words, 'Anicca vata sankhara.' It means that no sankhara lasts forever. Sankhara is kind of a scratch on our mind, which remains from our strong desire to either have or not have something. It's like the inscription on King Solomon's ring. When unresolvable problems appeared in his life, he turned the ring and read the inscription aloud to himself, 'This too shall pass.' My tattoo is a kind of eternal beacon that always reminds me that everything in this world is an illusion. I got it when I came back from vipassana. Then, for the first time I felt so good that I didn't want to change my consciousness with anything. Vitya, can you imagine – ten days of silence seemed to have cleansed me. For the first time in the last fifteen years of my life, I didn't take anything, didn't smoke, ate healthily, and spoke to nobody for ten days."

"And how much did that pleasure cost you, Vasya?"

"It cost me nothing, Vitya. There are vipassana centers in all countries, and it's free everywhere. This organization has been working on donations for two and a half thousand years. If you like it, you can donate as much as you wish. For the first time in my life, Vitya, I felt that I had had a rest from myself. It's such a thrill when you don't screw anybody's brains and nobody screws yours, as if you were in paradise! There is a beautiful garden, full of flowers, extraordinarily beautiful buildings like in a Buddhist monastery, with gilded pagodas, a great vegetarian buffet, and a private room with a shower and toilet for every meditator."

"And all of that is free of charge?" Viktor asks in surprise, watching as the inmates around David take turns to smoke crack.

"Yeah, believe it or not, Vitya. The thing is that it gives you such a kick for ten days, that you want to give them all your money so that they can continue doing such a good deed, helping people to understand the reasons for the distress of their soul and to get rid of it."

"Well, did your vipassana help you, Vasya?"

"You know, Vitya, I went home to Goa as if I had wings. I thought that I should convince Lena to do the same meditation, but, unfortunately, there was the opposite effect. Before I left for vipassana, Lena and I experimented with group sex, and I went to meditate the next day. Meanwhile, Lena was tortured by remorse for ten days. She was on my back for two weeks after my return from vipassana. We quarreled every day. She was about to go to Russia then. I tried to explain to her about unconditional love, but she didn't want to understand me. I didn't drink or smoke for two weeks and we couldn't reach an understanding. One day, I broke down and got plastered. I scoffed some meat and got high on charas. That's when the harmony finally came back to our family. We stopped quarrelling and had sex again. I realized then that couples need to have an equal level of spiritual development. I had flown away from reality to higher contours of perception, and Lena grounded me. From then on I went along with my sweetheart to explore the lower contours of perception. Lena and I had wonderful time there. I thought that having explored the lower contours, we would go further along the path of spiritual development together. However, these lower contours have brought me to the very bottom. Only the Azillo prison hospital, followed by the cemetery, are lower."

"Vasya, without experiencing the bottom, you can't come to know heaven," Viktor says, offering me the bong with the next portion of freebase.

Exhaling the cocaine smoke, I finally feel a wave of sensations, Along with a feeling of numbness in my gums, my brain suddenly experiences a crystal-like clarity of perception and a powerful adrenaline rush. I suddenly feel like superman.

"I think I've understood why people like cocaine. After taking a puff, I felt like the center of the Universe. This feeling is like the highest level of pleasantness. That's the only way I can describe this state."

"It is this state that aware people are willing to give everything for. Why do you think I asked about your tattoo, Vasya?" Viktor says, handing me an album with pictures by our artist Borish. "I want to make a full back tattoo. You're right, Vasya, a tattoo is like a beacon that you send into the world in search of like-minded people. I want a tattoo of my god. I want to get the Sun completely covering my back. Borish has already drawn a picture for me. There are several different suns in the album; I just need to choose one. We are going to be released at the same time, in March. I want to open a tattoo salon for him. He is a professional tattoo artist, you know. I'm going to buy all the equipment in Thailand, rent a house for him, and let him work. He's a born artist."

"Oh, Borish, Borish, poor wretch. Ashpak really set him up with that lawyer. I've never heard before of someone being sentenced to seven months in jail for a six-month expired visa. Even Yelisei was released after just a month despite his escape from the nuthouse. They say that Ashpak is going to be transferred here, to Vasco jail. He has let down a lot of people during his three years in prison, not just Borish. They say he threw sulfuric acid in somebody's face here in prison, and all of the skin peeled off. Ashpak is the only thing people talk about in every cell, from morning till night."

"To hell with Ashpak. Don't we have anything better to discuss while we are coming up? Tell me instead who did your Buddhist tattoo in Goa. Was it Max and Akula from Tattoolab?"

"No, it wasn't. I only dreamt about being tattooed by them. Unfortunately, it was done by the wife of my former friend. I had an old friend, Andryukha, who I knew for fifteen years. We started studying psychedelics together. We traveled on motorbikes all over Russia. I can't even remember how many women we fucked. It was him I called when my wife and I decided to try group sex. I wouldn't trust anybody else with my beloved. At that time he had bought a tattoo machine for his wife, Oksanka. He invited me many times that season, 'Come any time, we'll do you a tattoo free of charge, my Oksana will practice on you.' Many tattooists offered me a free tattoo that season. What could be a better advertisement for a beginner tattooist than the tattooed restaurateur of a famous Goan restaurant? When I came back from vipassana I had one thought: how to make sure I remembered this knowledge for the rest of my life. Then I recalled their offer and went to them immediately. His Oksana tattooed me all night long, although an experienced tattooist would have done it in a couple of hours. And she did it so-so – not very well. I was most afraid of getting some Sanskrit like the writing in Russian on Chinese goods. I really went into one about calligraphy. I searched for a good Sanskrit font on the computer for a week. As always, everything turned out as I had feared. My tattoo reads 'Anicca vala sankhara', although it should be 'Anicca vata sankhara.' It's nonsense, of course, because nobody understands ancient Sanskrit these days, but I was still a bit upset. And then, Andryukha called me the next day and said, 'Give me a hundred bucks for the job.' I had a row with him, but gave him the money. We haven't talked to each other since then. However, that wasn't the reason for losing my friend. He must have been jealous of his Oksana's attention towards me. So that's my tattoo, vipassana and group sex experience, Vitya," I say, settling down to sleep on my bunk. "I think I've understood the problem with freebase, Vitya, and why it's almost impossible to refuse it, if there is any left. Ten minutes of ultimate satisfaction are followed by a hard, fast return to reality."

"That's right, Vasya, I have been lying here thinking about only one thing for half an hour: whether we'll smoke any more," Viktor says, asking David in gestures.

"Vitya, I've been thinking about that, too. But I'd better sleep now."

"Running for nothing," I say in my broken English to my Russian friend, putting on my eye mask with the 'Aeroflot'[87] inscription. "Good night, my friend Viktor, see you tomorrow."

Chapter 43. Part Two. Outside.

"So, Vasya, we've been left alone?" Vitalik says, inhaling a thick cloud of charas smoke. "The monkeys came to the balcony again last night. Look, they've left a load of shit, the bastards. Shall we play chess, Vasya?"

"Yeah, with pleasure," I say, kicking the monkey poop from Vitalik's balcony. "We'll have to spend a couple of months together on this balcony. It's stuffy in the room, Palolem is empty and we have no other place to go."

"But we have hash, rum and chess. We'll be alright!" Vitalik says, handing me a bong and striking a match. "It's amazing how similar our lives are. Our wives have the same name, they flew to Russia on the same day without agreeing on it in advance, and they will both come back to Goa in exactly two months."

"Vitalik, and we both have expired passports," I say, recalling a freak who served three months in an Indian jail for an expired passport. "We'll have to hide out in the rainy season. We shouldn't be seen by the police. We need to build the restaurant, not do time in jail."

"I don't think it's risky to go out to buy food once a week," Vitalik says, setting up the chessboard. "The season will come and there will be a lot of foreigners again. We'll be safer then, as now we are the only two white men in the whole district. The cops could check our passports. I love the monsoon. I love getting stoned and watching the rain all day long. Vasya, I just wanted to ask you to lend me some money. Will you give me five hundred bucks? I owe you five hundred already and if you lend me another five hundred, I'll invest a grand in the restaurant construction on you behalf. My wife left me no money at all."

"I have exactly five thousand bucks for construction of the restaurant and a grand to live on, Vitalik. Of course, I'll lend it to you, but how will you pay for your accommodation for all these months? Your apartment alone costs five hundred dollars."

---

[87] Aeroflot - one of the largest airlines of the Russian Federation.

"Don't worry about me, Vasya, I'm a professional estate agent. I owe the owners of my apartment rent for six months, but that's is my problem."

"Well, Vitalik, if you've managed to scam an Indian by not paying him rent for six months, you must be a born realtor. The Indians usually charge for six months in advance."

"I'm not only a realtor, Vasya; I am a professional scammer," Vitalik says, cutting a piece of ripe mango with a knife. "I also owe about five thousand dollars for the motorbike and jeep. We'll open the restaurant and I'll repay my debts. Scamming Indians out of money gives me pleasure."

"Do you have the money for construction of our restaurant?" I ask seriously, starting to doubt Vitalik's decency.

"I don't have money for the restaurant either. But don't worry about me, Vasya, I'll find the money in time. I don't have my own money. However, my wife's father has about forty thousand bucks. He is an FSB colonel in St. Petersburg."

"And what about your restaurant in Palolem, Vitalik? You said you invested ten grand in it." I ask, moving a pawn on the chessboard.

"That was also my wife's money, not mine, Vasya. We invested the money, trusting in Indian fairytales, but our restaurant didn't bring any profit this year. I now hope that the Indian, my ex-partner, will return me a thousand bucks in a couple of months. I sold him my share; let him work for food, I need income. However, he has been doing my head in for three months already. He can't manage to scrape together the money. He says he has no money at the moment. But don't worry, Vasya. We'll find the money in time. My wife is pregnant. She'll give birth here in October. I think her father will definitely send some dough on the occasion of his grandson's birth," Vitalik laughs, opening a bottle of rum. "Don't worry about me, Vasya. Tell me instead about the problems you have had recently in the north. Your Lena said you had a fight with your ex-partner?"

"Yeah, she's right. Just imagine, Vitalik, my partner got lost somewhere at the end of the season. He legged it, owing me a grand. The other day, the bastard appeared and said, 'Give me back my fridge, and a couple of tables and chairs.' And I responded, 'What about the money, Sanya? You owe me a thousand dollars.' Do you know what he says to me? 'Sorry, Vasya, but we've bought some land. We're going to build a house, so there will be no money in the near future. And in any case, Vasya, I know you have problems with your passport. 'If,' he says, 'you don't give me my fridge back, I'll call the police. If you don't want to be locked up, forgive me the debt and give the refrigerator back.' Our family was just preparing to have a dinner. My nerves snapped there, I grabbed a microphone stand that we were using instead of furniture in the hallway, and smacked him with it. I nearly threw him off the balcony in a fit of anger."

"So? Did he notify the police about you?" Vitalik asks me, putting me in check.

"I was one jump ahead of him."

"How? Did you go to the police to file a complaint about him with your expired passport?" Vitalik says, removing my rook.

"More or less. Thank God, my friends helped me. I have a buddy in Siolim, his name is Vova. He has an Indian friend, a former coke dealer. Or maybe he still deals, who knows. He works in the Goan government now; his dad is a minister. So, he has high-level connections in the police, he can solve any problem. At the request of Vova, he and a policeman visited my partner and explained to him that it was wrong to do what he had done. You can't come to a person's house and blackmail them. They got him to sign an acknowledgement that he wouldn't ever approach my house. And I paid them three hundred dollars for the service. That's it, Vitalik. Partners have already conned me out of money twice here in Goa. I hope nothing like that is going to happen with you?"

"Checkmate again, Vasya," Vitalik laughs, sweeping the pieces into a pile. "Don't worry, that won't happen with me. I'm not going to let you down. Everything will be fine. Shall we play another game, Vasya?"

"No, Vitalik, I'd better go and do my tai chi practice and meditate. It's unreal to win against you, anyway. Let's take another puff before I do gymnastics."

329

Chapter 44. Part One. Inside.

"Fuck, man, my brain is gone," Viktor suddenly shouts loudly in his broken English, getting up from the floor after staring silently at one point on the ceiling for thirty minutes. "New Year is coming, the whole world is busy preparing for the holiday, and my only entertainment is to watch a lizard catching flies on the ceiling. When will it end? Judging by the fact that Prasad, Vasu and Chetsi got the analysis of their drugs only after twelve months, I'm going to celebrate this New Year's Eve here. It looks like I have no chance of getting the analysis before February 16. February 16 will mark a year since I was arrested."

"Vitya, you seem to have lost your spirit. You've been lying around and doing nothing for a whole week already," I exhale heavily, lowering my dumbbell after pumping my bicep. It would be better if you lifted dumbbells for a while, maybe it would get rid of your blues."

"I don't feel like doing anything, Vasya."

"Are you so worried about New Year, Vitya? You shouldn't be. We'll celebrate New Year's Eve right here, no big deal! Look what a crowd has gathered, the cream of society!" I smile, starting to lift my hand-made dumbbell again.

"Chetsi and Vasu from Colva are lucky that they will celebrate New Year at home. Theirs is a strange story. They brought a kilogram of heroin from Kashmir, were jailed, and waited for the expert analysis for a year. However, the analysis showed that it was mint powder, not heroin."

"There are rumors that the army did everything they could to get them off," I say, grunting and dropping the six bottles of water tied together onto the floor. "Vasu is a soldier and Chetsi is a policeman, you know. I don't believe they were sold mint powder instead of heroin. Vasu served in Kashmir, and transported pounds of heroin from there, and Chetsi sold it to local drug dealers through the cops. The new people are power hungry and evidently want to take control of this market. But whoever who runs the military's drug supplies, magically turned heroin into mint powder."

"What does it matter, if they are outside, while you and I are sitting in here?" Viktor says sadly, lying down on the floor again.

"Don't hold it against me, Vitya, but I'm glad I won't celebrate New Year alone in here."

"I'm not holding it against you, Vasya. I'm even flattered that someone is glad I'll just be with him this New Year's Eve. Usually, everyone needs something from me, but you, Vasya, are just pleased that I'll be near."

"Vitya, frankly speaking, I can't imagine how I'm going to manage to stay here alone, without you. Who will I talk to? Who will I tell about my dreams?"

"The same way I lived in a cell alone with twenty Indians, not knowing the language, for the first three months until you were arrested, Vasya. You'll get used to it. Man is like a beast, that gets used to anything."

"Look, Viktor," Churchill says, appearing suddenly and holding out a newspaper. "Ashpak is mentioned in latest newspaper."

"Fuck off, Churchill!" Viktor starts yelling, throwing an empty plastic bottle at him. "How many times have I told you, you old monkey, that I'm not interested in the news from the newspaper? Don't show me any newspapers anymore, they never cover any good news."

"Give it to me," I say, taking the *Goan News* from the old rapist. "The famous gangster Ashpak, after a week stay in Vasco prison, was delivered to the Bambolim hospital in a serious condition, with stab injuries following a fight he provoked in the prison."

"Ashpak is not long for this world," I say, returning the newspaper to Churchill. "Someone attempted to kill him twice during his week's stay in our prison. Furthermore, there are rumors in the prison that the top inmates got an order from the police to kill him. They say that whoever kills Ashpak will be released on bail the next day. He crossed a lot of people here, in Goa. He borrowed pots of money from the local have-nots, by intimidating them. They took revenge against him yesterday. Can you imagine, Vitya, how zoned out you have to be to organize an attempt on your witness's life from prison. His gang of cronies butchered the witness in broad daylight, when he went to give evidence against Ashpak."

"Well, Vasya, he got payback yesterday," Viktor says, pulling out his notebook for English classes from under his pillow. "As soon as Ashpak was transferred to the jail, our electrician, who is doing time for murder, tried to smash his head in with a hammer. Ashpak's head was stitched up, a week hadn't passed, and the young guy who pours the tea stabbed Ashpak three times with a huge kitchen knife. He is hard to kill, but you can't escape from karma, it always catches up with you."

"The same thing will happen to him in all of Goa's prisons," I say, laying my English notebooks on the bound-together bottles of my dumbbell, like on a desk. "Maybe I should also study some English with you, Vitya. My hands are covered in blisters from the dumbbell. Gymnastics is over; it's time to study English. Have you taken my pen, Vitya?" I say, eyeing what Viktor is writing with.

"Vasya, you do everything according to your schedule. Gymnastics, English, chess. Here is your pen, Vasya. I've changed my mind; I won't study. I'm no longer in the mood. I can only do something when I'm in the mood; I can't do anything well if I don't feel like it. I look at you, Vasya, and I can't understand how can you do everything according to a schedule? I'd rather lie around and wait till I want to do something."

"For me Vitya, it's the only way to avoid going mad. And I don't understand how you can lie around like that and do nothing for a week. I would have gone mad already."

With a clank of the lock the cell doors fly open, and eight guards, led by the warden, quickly enter.

"Looks like there is going to be a shakedown. They'll search for mobile phones again," I say, covering my desk made of dumbbells with a towel.

Asking no questions, the guards promptly begin to shake out old plastic bags and newspaper clippings onto the cell floor. A large pile starts to form in the center of the cell.

"Whose are these things?" The warden starts yelling wildly, holding a cell phone that has been found.

"That is my stuff, but it's not my phone," a young man named Shugar tries to clear himself.

Swinging his whole arm, the chief guard gives him several loud, powerful slaps, making the boy slide down the wall.

"And what is this? Whose is it?" the warden points at my bottles tied together with a rag handle.

"It's mine," I say with my fists clenched, ready to strike back immediately if anyone tries to touch me.

"It's not allowed," the warden says in his disgusting high voice with a nasty smirk.

"Sir, I use it as a table to study English, please let me keep it."

"Take away!" he roars, indicating my dumbbell to the guards.

Having pushed me back, the guards take away my only pleasure, my dumbbell, which has helped me to avoid madness for the last seven months. Leaving the whole cell turned upside down, the guards, happy with their trophies, go to check the next cell.

"My hard physical training must be over. Shall I start writing a book? What do you think, Vitya?"

"Try to, I started to write in Mapusa, too, but gave it up."

Sitting on the pile of my things, I take down the photo of my daughter that I have stuck to the wall next to my place.

"Thank you, Viktor."

"What for, Vasya?"

"For talking sense into me here in prison. Earlier, it hurt to look at the photos of my girls. Now my heart is high, since I have really understood what love without possession and a sense of ownership means. Here I'm looking at my little princess and I know that she loves me and is waiting for me somewhere far away. Just as I am waiting for her. And if I hadn't listened to you when I wrote my last letter to Lena, I would have experienced remorse and resentment instead of love now. Now I look at my baby and feel only a pleasant melancholy. But I can't escape from this melancholy. This is my reality. I can't influence it now. I know for sure that someday I'll get out of here and see my girls again. I'll always feel this melancholy whenever I am apart from them... Oh... We have one month left before New Year."

Chapter 44. Part Two. Outside.

"We have one month left before New Year, and you still haven't opened. Normal restaurateurs have been working since October," my Lena says, braiding Vasilinka's hair.

"Lena, I don't know what to do, I am badly lacking another three thousand dollars. I can't open the restaurant without them."

"Vasil, I've already borrowed seven thousand dollars for you. We have nobody else to borrow from. How did you and Vitalik estimate the budget of your restaurant, so that it turned out to be twenty thousand instead of ten? We still need to pay a thousand for school, and we're short of money."

"This is India, Lena. It's impossible to estimate everything here. On the plus side, nobody has such a beautiful restaurant. We just need to open it. The money will appear immediately."

"Dad, what will be the name of our restaurant?" Vasilinka asks, twisting round on a small chair.

"USSR, daughter."

"Dad, what is USSR?"

"That is how Russia was called some time ago."

"Daddy, I already want to see your new restaurant so much. When will we go to Palolem? And I also want to see Vitalik and Lena's little baby."

"Stay still!" Lena bawls at Vasilinka. "First we need to braid your hair, and everything else will be later. Tell me, Vasil, why don't Vitalik and his wife borrow any money? Why is virtually the whole restaurant built on our money? You are going to halve your profit, aren't you?"

"Lena, you know that their second child has just been born. They spent a load of money on the birth, and his former restaurant partner conned him out of money. They owe six months' rent for their apartment. They say they have no more money. Everyone is experiencing hard times at the moment. Another crisis has hit Russia. I'm terribly stressed. Debts are piling up and there is no sign of income yet. One thing calms me down. If I succeed, I won't need to sell illegal substances," I say, looking sideways at curious Vasilinka. "According to my calculations, I can earn sixty thousand dollars per season. Four hundred fat Russian vacationers will live in the five-star Intercontinental hotel in front of our restaurant, every day. They pay five thousand bucks for a two-week holiday and bring the same amount with them to spend here. They'll have no other place, except for ours, to spend their money in. They won't be able to eat the disgusting, highly spiced food prepared by fishermen. And we'll offer oysters, crabs, okroshka, shchi[88], Russian salad... We'll offer everything a typical Russian needs."

"Honey, try calling Valera."

"You're right. Bring me my phone, daughter. Valera has a lot of rich friends; maybe one of them will lend me money. And bring me your school notebooks as well; I want to look at your marks. If Valera doesn't give me the money, I'll go bankrupt. I don't know what to do then."

"Hi, Valera, how are you?"

"I'm fine, Vasya, I'm fine as always. We're sitting on the roof of our house, smoking a chillum. Life is beautiful."

"Valera, I know you have no money, but I desperately need three thousand bucks, maybe you can advise me where I can find them? I remember that your rich friends from Samara, who organized a sapphire mine in Sri Lanka, came to visit you. Have they already left for Sri Lanka or not yet?"

"They left a week ago, Vasya. Do you lack money for opening your restaurant again, Vasya? When will you finally open it?"

---

[88] Shchi - Russian cabbage soup

"Valera, everything is almost ready, only the finishing touches are left. The chefs have already started preparing food for us. We only have to get a license and buy spirits."

"Vasya, aren't you afraid that people won't come to you?"

"Why won't they come if they have no other place to go to?"

"Don't you watch the news? Bombay is on fire, some flights have been canceled."

"Valera, what do you mean 'Bombay is on fire?'"

"Exactly what I said. Al-Qaeda is carrying out terrorist acts again. Everything is serious this time. The railway station is ablaze, the famous Leopold restaurant has been blown up, and the five-star Taj Mahal hotel is also on fire. Over a hundred people have already been killed and terrorists with guns run the streets. It is broadcasted on all the global news channels, Vasya. And you don't know anything, as you're busy with your restaurant."

"I don't even know what to say, Valera. It's a whole thousand kilometers to Bombay."

"It's a whole thousand kilometers for you, but it's only a thousand kilometers for the tourists who come here."

"Crazy Olya and I once stayed in the Taj Mahal, Valera. And the Leopold restaurant is the only place in Bombay where you could have a decent meal. Is the Indian shanti really over?"

"It never actually existed here, Vasya. You don't read the newspapers and don't watch the news. The terrorists are blowing something up in every state, every day. You probably don't know that there was a blast here in Goa, in Margao."

"No, Valera, I didn't hear anything about Goa, I should begin reading the newspapers. This is the second time that terrorist attacks have been carried out in a place we have visited. I remember, Valera, that day when you came out of a shop near the Hare Rama hotel on the Main Bazar in Delhi, and it exploded five minutes later. A lot of people were killed then. If you had stayed there five minutes more, I wouldn't be talking to you now. To be honest, I wished that somebody would commit a terrorist attack. Three years ago, that could have saved Goa from rising prices and the flow of non-trance tourists. But now that I myself need these wrong tourists, someone in heaven decided to scare them away from me."

"Vasya, our thoughts are material, and time is thick, like a mango smoothie. We must be very careful before we wish something, especially in places of power, like Goa," Valera says, laughing into the phone. "I can't help you with money, Vasya, but I will give you advice. Call Punin, who lives in Morjim."

"Is he the guy who was once the producer of Metal Corrosion[89]?"

"Yes, Vasya, that's him. He's not likely to just give you money, but he might buy a stake in the business. Sell him one third. You'll solve all of your financial problems in one sweep. But be careful: he is as cunning as a fox, and he is hooked on methamphetamine as well. You should talk with him in the evening, but not too late. By nighttime he can't understand anything. And he is always mad like a dog in the morning."

"Thank you for the advice, Valera. I'll think about it, Bom Bolenath."

---

[89] Metal Corrosion - a popular heavy metal rock group in Russia.

"Bom Bolenath," Valera answers in the Goan style and switches off his phone.

"Daddy, what has happened? Why have you become so serious? Is something wrong with your restaurant?"

"Everything is okay, my princess."

"Well, if everything is okay, daddy, then look at the essay I wrote for my English class," Vasilinka says, giving me her notebook.

Reading her essay, I begin to smile and even laugh at the end, having forgotten about my problems for a while.

"Daddy, why are you laughing? What's so funny in my essay?" my little girl says aggrievedly, puffing out her cheeks and putting her hands on her hips.

"Everything is fine, just the topic of your essay is very interesting, 'My favorite restaurant.' Lena, I don't remember us having such topics in the second grade in the USSR. I was 16 years old when I went to a restaurant for the first time; the Soviet Union had already collapsed. What kind of topics will you have in the eighth grade? 'My Flight to the Moon'?"

"She has such topics, Vasil, because she goes to a decent European school, not to a plain Indian one," Lena says, getting down to braiding Vasilinka's hair again.

"I think this topic was given because the children of restaurateurs, DJs and drug dealers go to the school. Lena, have you seen what a funny mistake Vasilinka made?" I say, pointing at the copybook, wiping away my tears from laughter. "My favorite restaurant is the Ivon's Nepalese restaurant. My favorite dish there is pig with garlic sauce."

"What's so funny, dad?" my baby starts puffing her cheeks even larger, taking offence.

"Nothing, Vasilinka. You'll understand when you grow up. 'Pig' means a live pig in English, while 'pork' is the meat we eat."

336

Chapter 45. Part One. Inside.

"You're such a pig, Viktor! Why didn't you hang your jar of honey on the window at night? Do you see how many ants there are? There is an ant path across the whole cell to your place."

"Vasya, they like honey, too," Viktor answers, smiling and stretching himself out on the floor.

"Your ants are really pissing me off. Vitya, you don't live alone here. One day you leave your jam open, another day you don't put away your candies. I don't like ants running over me."

"If you don't like it, then you tidy up yourself," Viktor says, turning over on his side, covering his head with a sheet again.

"Why am I punished like this? There is only one other Russian in the whole prison, but he is a pig and an idiot. I've realized why the heavens sent you to me, Vitya. You are my mirror. I behaved just the same way with my Lena. I never understood why she was so indignant when I forgot to tidy away crumbs from the table or wash my dishes. I always had the same philosophy as you. I always thought that the cleanliness around me maintained itself. And now I understand why Lena sometimes wants to kill me."

"Okay, stop bitching, Vasya. Tell me instead what we're going to do today. Shall we get high in the morning, or go and play tennis," Viktor asks me, popping his pleased, smiling face from under the blanket.

"Let's get high, Vitya. It's Sunday after all."

"Let's go and smoke in the toilet, Vasya. We only have a little hash, and these have-nots also want to smoke," Viktor points at the young robbers, rapists and murderers lying on the floor.

"What will they say to us, if we get high without them? I don't care what they want. They never give us anything. They're just hang around, begging for something every day."

"Vasya, I think that if we smoke in front of them, we have to break them off a bit.

"Vitya, don't you think that you show them your weakness, by revealing your kindness? They believe that if you are good, it means you are afraid of something."

"How can you think instead of them, Vasya? How do you know what they think?"

"Vitya, it's just that my life experience tells me that you shouldn't do good to people who don't understand what good is. Every time I've done good deeds for such people, it ends up with them ripping me off. If you want I can tell you how I was scammed in relation to the restaurant in Palolem. I was very kind then. I tried to radiate 'peace and love' energy to the outside world."

"I'll listen to you carefully, Vasya. Let's go to smoke in the toilet, I can't smoke when someone is staring at me."

"No, Vitya, I won't go to smoke in the toilet, you might drop the hash in the toilet bowl again."

Having pulled the bong out of the garbage bag and put a few crumbs of hashish on the foil attached to the plastic bottle, I hand it to Viktor.

"Relax, Vitya. Smoke."

Several pairs of eyes eagerly watch how I light the hand-made bong for Viktor. Having taken three good puffs, we lean back on our rubber mats on the floor.

"The same hands, the same legs. Vitya, is it really me lying around on the floor in jail? The day before yesterday I smoked hashish that had fallen into the toilet bowl, yesterday I ate an unwashed pineapple together with the skin, that had been cut up on the floor. Some imperceptible changes are occurring in my consciousness. New Year will soon come. This time, Vitya, exactly one year ago, the events that led me to jail began to develop rapidly. Vitya, I think the time has come to tell you the whole truth about how I got here."

"That's an intriguing start. Will I hear something new from you today? Do tell, Vasya."

"I built the restaurant in Palolem a year ago. I thought I would finally give up the drug business. I started to set up a legitimate firm and found a partner, a clever guy. However, this clever guy started to rob me before the restaurant had opened. I began to check the receipts for expenses and discovered that he had stolen three thousand dollars from me, without even starting to work. Moreover, he not only robbed me, but his wife as well. I don't know what he spent that money on. Maybe he spent it in cocaine or on repaying old debts. It turned out that he owed everybody. According to my calculations he had about twenty thousand dollars of debts, maybe more. Meanwhile, we lacked ten thousand dollars to open the restaurant. And then I came up with a plan. I convinced Vitalik that we should sell a third of our business to a wealthy Russian named Punin. Punin didn't come alone; he brought Dima Lucky with him. That very Dima, whom I owe my stay in here to. They agreed to invest money in our restaurant, and offered me ten thousand dollars for one third of the business. And it so happened that I caught my partner Vitalik in the next theft at that time. We had a big row with him. My partner, without pausing to think, went to Punin that evening. They snorted cocaine all night long and, in the end, decided to oust me from the business. Vitalik came back the next morning and said that he had sold my stake to Punin. Meanwhile, the terrorist attacks hit Bombay, and tourists were afraid to come to Goa. So, only twenty five-star Russian holidaymakers arrived instead of the expected four hundred. In addition, the global crisis started and everybody abruptly became short of money. I wasn't too angry that my stake was sold under those circumstances. Of course, I lost about three thousand bucks, but it was nothing compared to the sums everyone lost back then. The entire world economy seemed to be about to fall apart. Large corporations, banks, and small businesses went bankrupt. I experienced very strange feelings when I took my money from Punin. I understood that they had scammed me, but I was very grateful that he had saved me from a terrible pain in the ass. I had no desire to work with a partner who stole from me again. Punin and Dima Lucky opened the restaurant together with Vitalik from Palolem. They worked for a month and got nothing but losses instead of super profits. They wanted Vitalik to return the money for their share, but he had nothing but debts. Not wanting to invest more money in an unprofitable business, Punin and Dima left Vitalik to deal with the restaurant and went back to North Goa, to Morjim. That's when Dima nursed his first grievance against me. Every time he met me somewhere, he accused me of conning him out of money by selling him the unprofitable restaurant."

"How does kindness to the people around you relate to your story with the restaurant?" Viktor asks me, spreading mango jam on a cookie.

"Vitalik wouldn't have stolen my money, if I hadn't been too kind to him. I saw what sort of a man he was, and he himself confessed that deceiving people brought him joy. I should have been strict with him. I should have kept an eye on him the whole time; whereas I, like an idiot, began to trust him with everything, believing that good is answered with good. So he took advantage of my kindness, the same as my previous two partners. I stepped on the same rake three times here in Goa. I don't believe in being kind to people anymore, it's a fairytale. Of course, you can show your kindness and love to people who know how to appreciate it, but there are not so many people like that, unfortunately. Most people who can't appreciate kindness perceive it as weakness and try to use it, whenever possible. Kindness provokes people into committing crime. The majority thinks that if you are kind, it means you are weak and it's easier to take away something from a weak person. That's why I suggest smoking here, not hiding somewhere. We can treat the guys to a crumb in the evening, but we can smoke without them in the afternoon. We paid our own money for this hash. It would be better to treat James or David to a smoke when they come back from the court. I like those people, while these primates and have-nots annoy me," I point at the robbers sitting in the corner, delousing each other.

"Dima Lucky wanted to scam me out of my money then. He thought he would muscle in on my profitable business on the cheap, but it turned out that he conned himself out of money, by forcing me to sell my restaurant to him."

"Khana agya, khana agya![90]" our cellmates begin to shout in unison, having seen a guard coming to our door.

"Let's get some food, Vasya. You can finish your story later; the door is about to open. I'm so hungry, as if I had been working all day long."

"Well, another half a day has passed," I say, hunting out my iron plate among the twenty others lying on the floor under the TV set.

The guard watches lazily as the first, hungriest prisoners start to appear from different cells, carrying their plates and mugs.

"Viktor, do you want me to show you a serial killer?" I ask, going down the stairs leading to the kitchen.

"I beg you, Vasya, please don't do that. Why do I need to know that? It's much easier for me to speak to people when I have no idea what they did."

"As you wish, Vitya, but he is one of the five Indians who distribute the food. He has a mustache, but I won't show him to you," I say, smiling and watching Viktor grow angry. "Just imagine, Vitya. He killed eighteen girls just to steal their jewelry."

---

[90] Khana agya, Khana agya! (Hindi) - Food is coming, food is coming!

"Why do you say this to me before a meal, Vasya? There is no past and no future here in prison. There is only here and now," Viktor says, giving the serial killer his mug to get some pea soup. "Thank you," Viktor says to the carelessly smiling maniac, moving further along the line, unaware that a monster hides behind this ordinary, human smile.

"Viktor, would you believe me if I told you that my friends and I organized an MDMA production laboratory?"

"I won't be surprised by anything after hearing that you had managed to grow psilocybin mushrooms in Goa. How much MDMA did you make, Vasya?"

"We only had the chance to make the first half kilo before I was arrested. But we had the chemicals for ten kilos," I say, putting my plate on the floor next to my deckchair.

"Ten kilos!?" Viktor shouts loudly in Russian, clutching his head. "That's a million bucks! Vasya, why did you tell me that? I've only just decided to never deal drugs again. And what is the production cost of one kilo?"

"Nothing. You'd better eat, your rice is going to get cold," I say, smiling and watching Viktor imagining a million bucks with his mouth agape. "The entire laboratory with the consumables cost six thousand dollars. Vitya, I decided to tell you about it all for a reason. I called my Lena yesterday, and she said that those friends have contacted her through the Internet. They didn't surface for half a year, and now they say they want to sell MDMA in Goa. They should have produced five kilos in half a year."

"It's an interesting offer, Vasya. But how are you going to sell it? You're sitting in jail."

"They suggest burying a pilot batch in a certain place, and then sending a photo of this place by e-mail to the person who agrees to sell it."

"So they are even ready to accept payment after it is sold?!" Viktor clutches his head again. "Vasya you are a tempter, you're pushing me back into the drug business again. Who would be able to sell such a large quantity of drugs in Goa, Vasya? Nobody, except Tamir."

"Yeah, but I don't want to talk to him, Vitya. Dima, who put me behind bars, worked for him."

"Vasya, try calling crazy Psyu then. She knows everybody. She hangs out with Tamir, and her husband is the oldest cocaine dealer in Goa. They all threw a party in East End together. She might be able to give you some advice. And why don't your friends help you with money, Vasya? Why don't they try to get you out of here?"

"I don't know, Vitya, I'm very angry at them. They promised to pay my lawyer fees, but they don't even send me money for food. They must be afraid that I'll grass on them. They might not have any money, either. The most important thing is that they managed to find an unlimited supply of safrole oil in India. It costs only fifty bucks per liter, whereas four hundred grams of MDMA can be produced out of one liter."

"Vasya, do you realize what a mess you have got into? How can you say that it was me who undermined the Goan cocaine market with my fake coke? The police have completely ousted MDMA from the market; they've jailed all the suppliers. It immediately became a third more expensive than cocaine. I used to sell MDMA for six thousand rupees whereas coke cost four thousand, before I ended up here. All the tourists began to only buy cocaine."

"MDMA disappeared throughout Goa after you were locked up. Can you imagine that? Nobody had it; it couldn't be found anywhere. I was the only person who had it, and I sold it for two thousand, not six."

"Vasya, do you realize that you crossed the government? The cops decided to sell their cocaine, and you come along with your ten kilos of MDMA. You could easily be killed for a million. Vasya, you were lucky that the cops only planted twenty grams on you, they could have just killed you."

"Why do you worry about me so much? You could have been shot dead for your fake cocaine as well. Anyway, you'd better eat your rice, it's already cold," I say, dipping a flatbread in the spicy pea soup.

Chapter 45. Part Two. Outside.

"Your visa expires in a week. Take Vasilinka and fly to Thailand immediately. I've arranged that you'll be given a new five-year Indian visa there."

"What about you, Vasil?"

"Don't worry about me, my brother Lyokha will send me a new passport next week."

"Will he really succeed?" Lena says, taking a break from putting Vasilinka's textbooks in her schoolbag and hugging me joyfully.

"He has almost succeeded. My brother went to the court twice instead of me. Neither the judge, nor the cops realized it wasn't me. It's good that we look alike. He just called me and said that I was sentenced to pay a fine to the tax service. My mom helped me again and paid the fine. Now they only need to get a passport and send it to me. I'm no longer wanted in Russia. My brother filed the documents for a passport on my behalf. If everything works out, I'll try to leave India across the Nepalese border."

"How will you cross the border, if your passport and visa expired six months ago?"

"I have an idea, Lenochka. I want to make a fake permission in Photoshop as if I had spent all this time at the ashram of Sai Baba. I'll try to break through with these documents. I think I'll manage it. My ex-wife Irina will meet you in Thailand and help you receive your visa. Irina says it's possible to make a five-year Indian visa for Krishna devotees now. Irina will give you special Krishna devotee clothes. You'll wear them when you go to the embassy. I'll arrive in Thailand ten days later. Now I will take Vasilinka to school and buy tickets to Thailand on my way back, so you can pack your things."

"Daddy, are we going to school by motorbike? Hooray!" My daughter screams happily, clapping her hands. "I want to sit on the back like an adult. Only children sit in front," my baby says haughtily, making what she considers an adult expression.

***

"Hi, Svetka, I'm so glad to see you!"

"Vasya, is it really you? What brings you to Nepal? I haven't seen you for ages. Well, welcome to my restaurant!" says the Russian beauty, who for some unknown reason decided to live in Nepal, opening the door with one hand and adjusting her blond hair with the other.

"I've heard a lot about your restaurant, Sveta. I've seen lots of links about it on the Internet, 'The first Russian restaurant in Kathmandu.' You have a beautiful place," I say, looking around the hall, bathed in the bright morning light.

"I painted all the walls with fluorescent paint myself. The restaurant is empty in the morning, all of the customers gather in the evening. Sit down at any table, I'm going treat you to solyanka[91]"

Having disappeared behind the kitchen door, she leaves me alone in the large hall with huge, ceiling-height windows. Through the windows I can see a noisy Nepalese street, which is slowly waking up after the cold night. I hear Svetka explaining to her Nepalese chef what to do, speaking a mix of English, Nepalese and Russian swear words.

"You'll have to wait a bit, Vasya. The chef had added his spices to the solyanka again. I made him prepare a new batch."

"I'm not in a hurry. Don't worry. Moreover, as a restaurateur, I understand you perfectly. It's easier to teach a monkey to cook European food than to teach an Indian or Nepalese. I trained my chef for three years. And the bastard still can't resist sometimes, and adds his spices, thinking it will be more delicious his way. How do you cope with running it alone, Svetik?"

"I hang on by the skin of my teeth. The most difficult thing is to fight against Nepalese stupidity. Sometimes I want to kill them. One day they start to prepare a fruit salad with a knife, without having washed it after chopping onion. Another day they try to cook old ingredients. But the most striking thing for me is that they really don't understand why I yell at them. 'What's the big deal if strawberries smell of garlic? At least they don't smell of shit.'"

"I understand you very well, as a restaurateur understands another restaurateur."

"By the way, tell me, Vasya, what was the story with your restaurant in Palolem? You wrote to me that my ex-husband had conned you out of your money."

"I don't know who was conned in the end, Sveta. Dima Lucky bought out my stake in the business, without my agreement, and then lost the restaurant. My ex-partner in the Palolem restaurant really turned out to be a professional scammer. First, he robbed me, and then he scammed Dima and Punin out of their money. I have finished my restaurant business in Goa. I'm fed up with being a restaurateur. Now I want to sell visas. It's complicated for Russians to get an Indian visa now, and I have connections in Thailand. I can sell a package of documents for a five-year visa for fifteen hundred dollars. I already have a queue of people wanting to get visas in Goa. Many of them have already paid the money in advance. Even Tamir asked me to get a visa for him. I'm going to eat in your restaurant now, and then I will go and buy tickets to Thailand. My two wives are waiting for me there now."

"What do you mean 'two'?" Sveta says, pushing a nice steaming bowl of hot solyanka, which has been just brought by a waiter, nearer to me.

---

[91] solyanka - a traditional Russian soup.

"My first, ex-wife, Irina, and my current wife, Lena, are now waiting for me to break through the border."

"And how do you manage to get along with two wives? Don't they quarrel with each other?"

"My first wife is like my sister now, we have a great relationship. After we divorced, we had a joint business for a long time. We shared a boat, car, and shops. I don't like conflict; we remained friends after we broke up. Even after my Lena had given birth to Vasilinka, we often spent time together."

"But don't they quarrel with each other, Vasya?"

"No, Svetik, they don't have any outright quarrels, but they're constantly squabbling behind my back, voicing all their issues to me. Lena calls her an old hag, and Irina, gritting her teeth, tolerates her foolishness, trying not to react. But when we are all together, everything is fine, and I'm happy with that. Irina, being tired of business in Russia, came to India a few years ago in pursuit of happiness. After a two-year search for Indian shanti, she made friends with some Krishna devotees, and now she lives in Thailand. She has already helped get a five-year Indian visa for my Lena."

"I thought my Dima and I would remain friends after the divorce, I even left him my motorbike in Goa. However, he has been a swine to me recently for some reason. I wrote him a letter, asking him to help me. He could have at least come here for a month, to lend me moral support while I was opening the restaurant, but he replied, 'Start fucking the Nepalese; let them help you.' I did no harm to him in any way. His brain has completely melted from cocaine. I'm happy I left India. I've been living without cocaine for a year already. I prefer it. How is Tamir doing in Goa? Is he still working with the cops?"

"I believe he is, judging by the fact that nobody bothers him. He and Dima are now kings of the cocaine market. Tamir throws parties in clubs and Dima Lucky sells coke. Everyone involved in the sale of MDMA has been locked up. It's not on sale anywhere now. But nobody bothers those who sell cocaine for the cops."

"Be careful with them, Vasya. There is no concept of 'us' and 'them' in the cocaine world. It's a dirty business. When you are coked up, you are the center of the Universe and all other people are a waste of space for you. When I last spoke to Tamir in Goa, he sent Dima Lucky and the police to Palolem. Dima had to shop some Iranian competitor. The police promised them complete immunity afterwards. There isn't as much cocaine in Nepal, so life is calmer here. But how did you cross the Indian border, Vasya? You wrote that your passport and visa had expired. Did you make your way through the forest?"

"No, Svetik, I couldn't go through the forest. I wouldn't have been allowed to travel to Thailand without an entry visa to Nepal. I made a fake permission on the computer, allowing me to stay in India for six months. Then, taking my new, clean passport and this permission, I went to cross the border at six o'clock in the morning. I deliberately went there when it was still dark, so that the border guards couldn't have a proper look at the seal, made with a color printer. I gave the documents to the border guards, and although they could feel that I was nervous, they couldn't find fault with anything. They said, 'Give a hundred bucks, you have no registration.' I gave them a hundred and ran immediately to the Nepali side, before they looked at my papers under a lamp."

"You got off lightly, Vasya. If you had been caught, you could have been sentenced to five years in prison."

"The gods must have saved me. I was on the wanted list in Russia for three years, I lived without a visa in India for a year, and now I've become legal at last. Now I'll get a five-year visa and won't have any problems for a five whole years."

"You are lucky, Vasya, whereas I feel absolutely exhausted. It's hard to run a restaurant alone. Stay with me. You're an experienced restaurateur; we'll halve the profit. What do you need Goa for? All the decent people have already left, anyway."

"Thank you for the offer, Svetik, but I've had enough of the restaurant business. Moreover, my experience has shown me that business partnerships only lead to no good. You need to be friends with good people; money spoils all relationships. I'd rather sell visas in Goa. No restaurant will bring me as much money. Your solyanka is so delicious, Svetik, I would stay here longer, but I have to go and buy tickets. Thailand and a new life are waiting for me tomorrow!"

***

Hello, Khaosan Road! Good evening, Bangkok! Thailand, I love you so much!

Finally, I am a fully legitimate citizen of the world. I have a passport and a five-year Indian visa. But the most important thing is that I can now move wherever I want. I've earned five thousand dollars in a week by just receiving orders for Indian visas via the Internet. I'll live in India in November, December and January. Of course, I'm tired of India, but it's much better than Russia. I've had enough of the restaurant business. I'll make money in India and spend it in Thailand.

"Life is getting better," I embrace my Lena, eagerly kissing her on the lips.

"Daddy, I really like Thailand, too," Vasilinka shouts loudly, climbing up me, trying to reach my neck. "You look great in your new hat. Can I wear it for a bit?"

We are taking a leisurely evening stroll along Khaosan Road, doing window-shopping and buying different kinds of multi-colored shiny stuff. My baby is sitting on my shoulders, proudly holding my red German hat onto her head. Around my neck I have a Tibetan mala with a skull made of yak bone, decorated with six large sapphires.

"Daddy, you look like a real pirate, I love you very much," my little princess says, kissing me on the top of my head.

"Honey, you look nice in those zebra glasses. You look like a drug dealer on vacation or a pimp at work in them."

"Thank you for the compliment, darling, but I hope we will finally manage to give up the drug business this time. However, I think I'll keep the drug dealer image. I've always liked looking bright and unusual. Nobody else has glasses like these. Our parents wore such glasses when they were young."

"Lena, look! Is that crazy Psyu coming towards us?"

"Yeah, it's her. I think it's already too late to hide. She has spotted us."

"Hello, Karavaevs! Where is your other wife, Vasya? How was your rest on Ko Phangan? When are you leaving for Goa? Murtinian and I decided to buy visas from you," Psyu jabbers several questions quickly, in one breath.

"Wait, Psyu, I can't respond to several questions at once as quickly as you. Let's go to a nearby restaurant and talk."

"Three beers, one milkshake and ten different kebabs," I order from a young Thai waitress in a very short skirt, barely covering her charms.

"Honey, the food is so delicious here! And their beer doesn't resemble that Indian Kingfisher piss," my Lena says, taking a small chicken heart from a kebab with her teeth.

"And I like the local girls. Most local women in India are ugly for some reason. The pretty girls are probably hiding somewhere. If there had been such waitresses in Goa, I wouldn't have become a drug dealer, we would have had a queue for our restaurant."

"Where have you lost your senior wife? I need her," Psyu asks, licking beer foam from her lips.

"Irina stayed on the islands. If you want to talk about five-year visas, talk to me."

"You've monopolized the market quickly. Murtinian and I want to get such visas. What should we do, Vasya, to become the proud owners of a five-year visa?"

"Everything is very simple. Just give me fifteen hundred dollars and your passport details. I send them to Irina via e-mail and she prepares a package of documents, making you a student of Ayurvedic yoga classes at the Indian Krishna Institute. You'll have to dress neatly and go to the embassy, and we'll give you special beads. With these beads you'll be classified as an elite Krishna devotee, of the highest rank. And then you and Irina will go to the embassy, to an appointment with the Indian consul. There your documents will be signed, and you will become the happy owner of a five-year X visa a week later."

"And what does X mean?" Psyu asks, pouring some of the delicious Thai beer out of my glass into her own.

"Psyu, it means that you become a resident of India under this visa, and you can renew it in five years. Having received it, you almost become a citizen of India."

"When can I give you the money, Vasya? I want to become a resident so badly."

"The sooner, the better. I have a waiting list of a month. But since you're already in Thailand, we'll make you a visa through the buddy system, without waiting."

"Let's have another round of beer to a successful deal. I'm happy I met you here. I'll bring you three thousand dollars today. Make visas for me and my Murtinian. By the way, how was your rest on Ko Phangan?" Psyu says, clinking her glass of beer against mine.

"I really liked it!" my daughter interrupts me, licking off the mustache left after her strawberry milkshake.

"What did you like the most, little beauty?"

"I liked the supermarket, you can buy so many interesting things there, unlike in Goa. I also liked the beaches, everything is very beautiful, and there are pools where you can swim for free everywhere. My daddy said we will sometimes live in Thailand now."

"Yeah, Thailand is not an Indian trash hole!" my Lena says, hugging me and Vasilinka playfully. "Now we have Thailand for resting and India for working."

"The criminal case against my Murtinian was closed in Goa a few weeks ago. He couldn't go back home to his beloved Britain for three years. It cost us thirty grand to get him out of prison, after he was arrested. They found a kilo of cocaine and one hundred grams of MDMA at our place. It's all over now. If we are issued five-year visas, it will be possible to think about Murtinian's retirement. He is already sixty-three years old. Drug dealers rarely live to such an age."

"And how old are you, Psyu?" Lena and I ask at the same time, amazed by the age of her husband.

"Why do you ask a not very young girl such a vulgar question? I'm twenty-eight," Psyu answers, flirting and adjusting her highlighted hair. "We're going to be married. We'll register our marriage and hold a wedding in Goa. We need to hurry up while he is still alive, otherwise he won't have anybody to leave his legacy to. Why are we only talking about me and Murtinian? Tell what you did on Ko Phangan. Did you go to any parties? Who did you see? Did you try yaba[92]?"

"You're chattering so quickly, Psyu! How does your Murtinian understand you? I've never met any other person in my life, Psyu, who could talk as fast as you. You remind me of Woody Woodpecker. But I think you're even more hardcore. We didn't go to any parties, Psyu, we were tired of everything. We had a family vacation. No drugs, no dancing. Just zoos, shopping, and strolls along the beach. We had a wonderful time. From the old guard I only met Vlad Lenk. He gave me three grams of hash the very first day, free of charge, for old times' sake. Hashish is five times more expensive here than in Goa."

"I should hope that he didn't take money for such crap! He swallows a kilo at a time, when he brings it here."

"How do you know that about him, Psyu?"

"I know everything about everybody. I graduated from the FSB school for a good reason," Psyu laughs, waving to a waitress.

"Lenk is a desperate man. He plays roulette with death every time he flies to Thailand. They make no bones about it here. A couple of weeks of investigation are followed by an injection of cobra venom in the neck. Although, actually, they used to have the death penalty here. The laws have been changed recently. Now the judge sentences you to a hundred years in prison and reduces the penalty by twenty five years once every three years, on the king's birthday."

"How is Lenk doing now?"

"He's fine, he lives with a Russian girl and her small son. He doesn't go to parties anymore, he says he is disillusioned with freak culture. He is getting more and more interested in tai chi and yoga. He doesn't take any drugs."

"By the way, Psyu, what do you know about MDMA? Why has it disappeared? You can't get it anywhere. Only cocaine is sold in Goa."

"It's because the police got instructions from above, so they jailed all the Dymich suppliers. Vasya, what do you need it for? It's more profitable to sell coke. Do you know how much cocaine its fans snort per night?"

---

[92] yaba - a Thai stimulant

"I know, Psyu. That's why I don't sell it. It is a serious drug. I don't want to be responsible for the crippled fates of the people who take it."

"Do you think your favorite MDMA is not a serious drug? Do you know how many people have gone bonkers because of it?"

"MDMA is not a drug, it's a psychotropic agent."

"Vasya, just don't start talking to me about the psychedelic revolution. I heard enough about it in Goa five years ago. Your time has passed, Vasya. Now it's the time of cocaine. But a little MDMA is still left for dinosaurs like you. Murtinian said that half a kilo would soon come to Goa. However, the price of MDMA is now a third higher than cocaine. Demand creates supply and supply is controlled by the cops. That is the law of the drug market. When you get back to Goa, Vasya, call me, and I'll help you to get MDMA."

"No, thank you, Psyu. I hope to get out of the drug business completely if I succeed in selling visas."

"Dream on. It's not so easy to give up the drug business."

"I'll try and I'll succeed. Anything is possible if you want it enough."

"To legal business," Lena says, raising a glass of beer.

"To good business," Psyu says, clinking glasses.

"To good luck," I say, hugging my girls.

Chapter 46. Part One. Inside.

"Well, have you talked on the phone? What did Psyu tell you?"

"She said that we caused a lot of trouble for her."

"What do you mean? How can we cause trouble for her from prison?" Viktor asks in surprise, trying to catch an ant running into his groin.

"Vitya, if only you had heard how she yelled at me. She says that the police began to come to their home after I offered her MDMA by phone. Psyu says her Murtinian gave the cops fifty thousand rupees. Psyu also said that she doesn't want to deal with us. I called my Lena, she says that it looks like Psyu has gone completely nuts from the coke. Maybe Psyu now thinks that any problems happen because of us. Someone met Murtinian in Chapora and he said that it was a normal police raid on old drug dealers. They found a tola of hashish and fined him a hundred bucks. But Psyu evidently thought I wanted to shop her."

"Forget about it, Vasya, she was off her nut long ago."

"Easy for you to say, Vitya. Your sentence is one year at most. The analysis of your Novocain will arrive and you'll be released. Meanwhile, I don't know how much time I'll stay here. I need money to get out of here and I don't have it yet. And I have no way of earning it. Psyu won't come anywhere near me now. When I called her the first time, she was very interested in the Dymich and promised to find me a buyer. She started to ask me about cocaine, whether I knew where to get it. She talked to me very calmly on the phone. And today she started yelling at me all of a sudden."

"Vasya, it was probably Murtinian who turned her around. He must have told her not to get involved in the drug business. So she got paranoid. Who needs to eavesdrop on your phone conversations?" Viktor says, arranging the chess pieces on the board made of matchboxes.

"Anyway, it serves me right. The heavens sent me to prison so I could think hard about drugs, and I tried to sell them from prison again. That's it. I've had enough of the drug business. I don't want to step on the same rake a second time. Alexandro, leave me two puffs, I'm all worked up."

"That would be a good nickname for you: 'twopuffs'," the Italian says, handing me a rollup made of notebook paper stuffed with chewing tobacco.

"Strong life, strong tobacco," I say, screwing up my face from the coarse smoke and returning the prison cigarette. "This tobacco tastes awful, it's worse than shag."

"Smoke more, why do you take only two puffs?"

"I'm not a junkie like you, Alexandro, two puffs are enough for me. If I take three, I'll soon smoke like you, from dawn to dusk. Two puffs give me a kick like hash. I use the placebo effect. I imagine this is charas and get off from memory."

"Well, Vasya, do you feel better? What else did crazy Psyu tell you?" Viktor says, moving his bishop made of a piece of soap along the board.

"Another thing she said, Viktor, is that I am a fool."

"Yeah, I know that from how you play chess."

"Psyu says that if my MDMA comes onto the Goan market, she will personally make every effort to get me locked me up for ten years."

"Did you tell her about the laboratory, Vasya?"

"No, I didn't, Vitya. Thank God, I'm not that stupid."

"You're still pretty stupid; check!" Viktor says, happily removing my knight from the board.

"Psyu also said that I was locked up in jail as a competitor. I'm a fool. I still hadn't got it after being here for six months. Back in Thailand she mentioned half a kilo of MDMA. Murtinian must have explained to her that their product must be sold first. So she went crazy."

"You'd better forget about your MDMA, Vasya. You could be killed, or jailed in Aguada for ten years."

"The chain of events is finally taking shape in my head. My cellmate Dominic told me that when he worked for Apollo they bought cocaine from Murtinian. And they saw Tamir there several times. Do you see what that means, Vitya? Psyu, who was the first to come to the prison, allegedly to help us, is the wife of the main drug dealer in Goa. The people whose sellers locked us up as their competitors, bought cocaine wholesale from him. In my opinion, Psyu was deliberately sent to us to find out whether we were going to shop anyone."

"Yeah, it's a strange coincidence. You've turned out to be a fool again, Vasya: checkmate. You have no chance of beating me. Set them up again."

"Vasiliy!" Churchill yells as he comes running, holding out his hand with a newspaper. "A Russian girl was raped again in Goa."

"Fucking Churchill, you've brought your crime news again! There is no escaping you," Viktor says, pulling his English notebook out. "I'd rather learn English, Vasya. And you teach Churchill a lesson in political awareness."

"Churchill, give me your newspaper, I'd rather know the bad news than see the world through rose-colored glasses. Those glasses brought me here to jail. 'A nine-year-old Russian girl was raped in Arambol.' That's the third rape in the past three months, Vitya. All of the victims are Russian girls. What a bastard he must be to rape a child! Here you have the other face of Goa. They recently climbed down from the palm trees," I say with utter hatred, staring at the old rapist.

"Vasya, why do you tell me all this? I'm a human being, too. Why are you grinning, you old monkey?" Viktor barks at Churchill, crouched next to us. "What's funny about raping a child, huh? Anyway, why did you rape a mentally retarded woman?"

Churchill mutters something in return, smiling stupidly, obviously not feeling any guilt.

"Vitya, just look at this monkey. His ears are as hairy as my mustache."

"I've already asked you, Vasya, not to read me the bad news. For me it's easier to speak with these monkeys if I don't know what they did. Why do I need to know, for example, that the bald man sitting in the corner is an AIDS sufferer, who raped and infected a five-year-old boy? And that jerk who I played at tennis yesterday, raped his four-year-old daughter. The cross-eyed asshole, sitting opposite, fucked a sixty-year-old, legless woman. Churchill raped a mentally retarded woman. I know everything about them, Vasya, but I try not to think about it. It could turn out tomorrow that I will have to spend ten years with them. Get out of here with your newspaper, Churchill."

"Okay, Vitya, don't get so steamed-up! I'll read you the good news. 'The wall cracked in one of the cells in Aguada prison. Thirty drug dealers, sentenced to long terms, will be temporarily transferred to Vasco prison."

"Well, that's not news, the whole prison has been talking about it for a week already. New ears will come soon and at least we'll have someone to talk to. The drug dealers are the only smart people among all these stupid thieves, rapists, and murderers."

"We are more likely to be new ears for the Aguada prisoners. They are sitting there for ten years and they have something to tell us."

"Are we having a shakedown again?" Viktor says, pointing at the warden who has appeared at the door, surrounded by five guards.

Taking out a list of prisoners, the jailer announces loudly: "You will be moved to different cells tomorrow. David, Andy, Mario, James go to cell number ten. Vasiliy and Viktor go to cell number six. All the rest go to cell number twelve, first floor."

Chapter 46. Part Two. Outside.

"It's a pity that they don't play trance music at the Night Market anymore. The freaks used to dance near every bar before, music could be heard everywhere."

"Whom should they play it for? Just look around, there are only Indians. Maybe for them?" Igor Tereshkov points at a couple of plump Russian tourists, who must have arrived a few days ago, judging by their tan.

"I don't understand, Vasya, do they really think they look cool? Why does he need to pull his Adidas shorts up to his navel? And does his chick really think that her tight, short skirt makes her fat cellulite thighs more appealing? Such people are everywhere now. I don't understand, Vasya, whether the world has gone mad, or I'm wrong in the head."

"Igor, it also seems to me that the world has gone mad. When I first came to the Night Market, I looked like most normal people did. There were far less stupidly dressed tourists than freaks back then. Even those who came here to have a rest for two weeks, knew they were in the center of the trance movement, they knew where they were, and why. Meanwhile, these people who are walking around here now are more likely to listen to songs like Vladimirskiy Central[93] and have never heard of trance. The Night Market was the last outpost of free people. After the parties were banned, you could meet and hang out with the like-minded people who came here from all over Goa once a

---

[93] Vladimirskiy Central - a popular Russian criminal chanson song.

week. Where are those colorful, cheerful people now? Look, we are the only people that look like freaks."

"Don't I look like a freak?" Sheribon says with a drunk smile, standing next to us

"Sorry, Sheribon, I forgot about you. You definitely don't look like a tourist," I say, putting my empty glass on the table, cluttered with beer bottles.

"Sheribon, you'd better go and buy us some more beer," Igor says, giving him a five hundred rupee note.

"Vasya, do you want a line of coke while that windbag goes for the beers?"

"No, Igor, you know I don't snort coke."

"Well, I'm going to have a line, Vasya," Igor says, opening a metal box with a mirror inside.

Not paying attention to the dozens of people standing around, Igor pours a little mound of white powder onto the mirror. Having elegantly made a couple of lines with his credit card, he snorts them both at once through a tube made out of a rolled-up a one-thousand rupee note."

"You must save a lot of money on clothes, Igor. Your body is almost completely covered in tattoos. You're always half-naked whenever I meet you. But, thanks to the tattoos, it seems like you're dressed."

"That's why I love Goa, Vasya," Igor says, rubbing the leftover white powder onto his gums. "In Russia, I would have been arrested for such a look long ago. When I go back to Russia, I take out my earrings and try to wear a shirt with long sleeves. And what about you, Vasya? Aren't you afraid of selling drugs looking like that? You look like a drug dealer. Decent people don't dress like that."

"Igor, I have allowed myself to look like this since I gave up selling drugs. Now I sell visas."

"Well, well, let's see how long you will manage without the drug business. Your new business will last three months, and it will be shut down. Do you think there are fools sitting in the Indian Embassy? I've found out through my own channels that the visas that are currently being issued in Thailand are being given out by the old ambassador. He retires in three months. He has nothing to lose, so he is reaping his reward. And when the new ambassador comes, he will turn the tap off. However, I'm very grateful to you for the visa, Vasya. I didn't even dream that I could get a five-year visa. You started this up at just the right time. My one-year visa has just expired. You've rescued me for the second time already."

"Vasya, is it already the second time that you have done a visa for Tereshkov?" Sheribon interrupts us again, coming up with bottles of beer. "All of the Russians at the market are speaking about you, Vasya. Everybody wants to get such a visa, but no one has the money. Vasya, make me such a visa on credit, I promise I'll pay you back in a year."

"No, Sheribon, I don't work on credit, especially with your sort. As for Tereshkov, I helped him to make a passport a year ago. Someone stole his passport back then. Pavel, my friend the consul, worked at the Russian Embassy at that time. Of course, the embassy told Igor to get a new passport in Russia. I called Pasha in Bombay and asked for help. I said that Igor had trouble with bandits in Russia and he couldn't go there now. So they made him a new passport in just three months. And he didn't need to go back to Russia. Oh, Anton has come to the Night Market!" I point Igor towards the approaching 35-year-old guy, dressed like a tourist who has spent a month in Goa.

"Hi, Antokha! How's life? What's new? You don't seem to be too cheerful today."

"Life is wonderful, Vasya, but something is wrong with my business."

"What's happened?" The ever-curious Sheribon interrupts everyone.

"Hi, Sheribon, nothing serious has happened. I bought six motorbikes to rent out at the beginning of the season, and I was such a fool that I trusted the Arambol Indians."

"You must have registered everything in their name, am I right?" Igor says, laughing and looking condescendingly at Anton.

"Let me guess, Antokha. The Indians say they don't know you and don't want to know anything."

"Yes, you're right, Vasya. When we bought bikes with my money, they promised to halve the profits, and now they don't want to know. They promised to beat me up if I approach them again."

"Take it easy, Anton. It's an everyday occurrence here. Come to my house tomorrow. I have some Indian friends who settle various issues for dough. We'll think of something."

"Okay, I'll come to you tomorrow. I'd better go, Vasya, and get a beer as well, see you later."

"Who is he? His face reminds me of a Russian cop," Igor asks me, watching the unfortunate businessman leave.

"He is a cop. You have a professional eye, Igor. However, he is a former cop. I met him at the embassy in Thailand. He used to help people get out of prison for money in Russia. He had good connections with the police. He didn't share some money with someone, and his cop cronies shopped him in the end. He is on the all-Russia wanted list now, facing ten years in prison. He can't go back to Russia. He's not having much luck recently. In Thailand, the street vendors managed to con him out of eight hundred bucks."

"How did he manage to let that happen, Vasya? He must be a real sucker."

"Igor, do you remember the fake driver's licenses they make for ten bucks on the Khaosan Road in Bangkok?"

"Of course I remember. I myself bought two licenses there."

"So, Antokha asked them, 'My dear crooks, can you make me a fake passport?' 'Of course we can,' the kind Thai swindlers said. 'Give us,' they said, 'three thousand bucks.' He left them eight hundred bucks as an advance payment and two standard passport photos. They promised to make him a New Zealand passport. Nobody ever saw them again."

"That's a funny story," Sheribon says, pulling his chillum out of his pocket. "Look, guys, there's a dude over there that looks like a crazy Russian Benny Hill. Where do such characters come to Goa from?"

"Sheribon, that's Akam. Hey!" I shout to the Russian spitting image of Benny Hill, wandering through the crowd with a vacant stare. "What brings you here? You wanted to arrange a kayak rental business in the south of Goa, didn't you? Or have you changed your mind?"

"Hi, Vasya. I failed. Nobody needs those fucking kayaks in Goa. And anyway, I've come here to say goodbye to everybody, I leave this place forever tomorrow."

"What happened, Akam? When I saw you in Nepal last time, you were much more enthusiastic. After you sold your Moscow apartment, you've got the money to live the high life here in Goa for the rest of your days. Why do you need those kayaks? Live and enjoy life."

"I was scammed out of my money. I have nothing now. I worked for two months to buy a ticket to Moscow."

"How were you scammed? Were you robbed or what?"

"No, Vasya, I was a fool. I trusted a scammer. He told me stories about us opening a company to sell apartments here. And I believed him. I myself gave him thirty-five thousand euros. He was supposed to buy the first real estate. He took my money and disappeared with it. And I have no relatives, no friends, no one in Russia. Now I have nowhere to live, either. So I think I'll go to a shelter for the homeless when I get back home. I'll look for a job. I'll try to start a new life in my fifties. Goodbye, guys, I doubt whether we'll see each other again."

Watching Akam go, we stand in silence for a while, assessing the mess our friend has got into.

"Such stories happen. He has lived to his fifties, but he has no brains. Shall we smoke?"

"These aren't the times to smoke chillums in public places, Sheribon. It would be better if you rolled a joint. The police have been patrolling this area recently, you know."

"I don't give a shit about the police, I'm in Goa," Sheribon, emboldened by alcohol, says loudly and gives me the prepared chillum. "Bom Bolenath!"

"Hell yeah, you're right. We're in Goa, light it up!"

"Bom Shankar," Igor says, lighting the chillum.

Chapter 47. Part One. Inside.

"Just look at their faces, Vasya. They are all in a state of nirvana. No one is nervous; no one is in a hurry. We've got a good New Year present. Thirty drug dealers from Aguada are now living in our former cell. It feels like the heavens have sent them to us on purpose, as an example."

"I become horror-stricken when I imagine myself in their shoes," I say to Viktor, standing in line for my portion of food.

"Today we'll be given a piece of chicken on the occasion of the New Year. Jingle bells, jingle bells, jingle all the way!" Viktor sings, beating time with his empty mug on his palm. "It'd be better if you didn't think about Aguada, Vasya. Why do you pull this reality towards you? Think less and you'll sleep better."

"No more need to pull it towards us, Vitya. Aguada has come itself," I point at the Indians in prison white shirts and blue shorts, standing in the queue ahead of us. "Just look, they all have clever, intelligent faces, unlike our cellmates. Compared to our prisoners, the Aguada inmates look like they have been preserved. They move around the prison like ghosts. They have to wear the same clothes for ten years. They have to look at the same faces of their cellmates for ten years. Vitya, I'm already tired of you after eight months. And they tolerate each other for ten years. Oh Lord, I've understood everything; I won't sell drugs. I've understood your sign. I don't want to spend ten years in prison," I say, holding out my plate for some rice from an Indian in dirty clothes, sweaty from the heat. Having scratched his balls and then placing some rice in a measuring cup with the same hand, he drops my portion onto the plate and offers it to me with a smile.

"Vasya, now everything depends on how sincerely you have recognized your sins. Have you understood that revolutions, including the psychedelic variety, do nothing good to people?"

"Viktor, as God is my witness, everything I've done in my life, I've done only with good intentions. I've never intentionally wished anybody harm."

"Right, and ten kilos of MDMA are equal to a hundred thousand doses. You wanted to feed the whole of Goa with your ten kilos. Do you realize you were stopped just in time? How many people could have gone crazy or jumped off a bridge like Sergey did?"

"Vitya, but how much good could have appeared in people."

"Well, now all your sins and good deeds are being weighed up in heaven," Viktor says, giving his mug for spicy soup to the psycho who killed eighteen girls.

As we walk in silence to the cell with our meal, we examine the Aguada inmates walking ahead of us. No despair, no hopelessness. They have accepted their punishment and now live outside of time. Putting my plate with food on the floor, I take half an onion that I tucked away in the morning, out of my box.

"Vitya, look what I have."

"We have a perfect New Year lunch, Vasya," Viktor says, sitting cross-legged on the concrete floor next to me. "Vasya, save your onion for dinner, we'll add some variety to our New Year's rice in the evening."

"Vitya, the priests will come today in the afternoon, they'll throw a New Year party. Have you seen how Borish painted the hall on the first floor?"

"Yeah, Borish is awesome, he made little figures for the Nativity scene, and wrapped a dry tree with cotton wool. It looks like a real New Year tree. It will be the first time I celebrate the New Year in such a way," Viktor says, cutting the onion in two halves with a rusty iron lid. "Will we be given some extra food, I wonder? We donated a thousand rupees for some reason. David promised he would cook mashed potatoes with chicken in the kitchen for us."

"Yeah, Vitya, I would really love to eat something without Indian spices."

"Oh, I don't know, Vasya. The guards don't allow strangers to come into the kitchen after the attempt on Ashpak," Viktor says, gnawing a chicken bone in coconut gravy with relish.

"Vitya, wash my plate today, and ask for anything you want in return. I feel slightly drowsy after the chicken," I say, stretching and sinking into a pleasant slumber.

Having closed my eyes, I feel how the ants, taking advantage of my weakness, cease bypassing my place and now meanly run over me while going about their business, tickling my arm and neck unpleasantly. I could relax if I were sure they are large ants. But sometimes squads of their smaller relatives with painful bites run along their paths. Running over my body, those bastards don't miss an opportunity to nip me, leaving itchy bumps on my skin.

"Large ants, please chase away the little ones from me, I promise I won't kill your sort for that, and you will be allowed to run over me in peace. And in the evening, if no one bites me, I promise to put a candy that I've been hiding from you in a plastic jar, on the windowsill for you."

"What will you give us if we bring you MDMA?" a senior ant asks me, having stopped near my ear. "We know where there's a lot of MDMA. If I order my ants, everyone can take a small crystal on their way back. If you open the jam jar which you tied up in two bags, for the night, we'll bring you a gram of MDMA in the morning."

"It's a good offer, but what am I going to do with it here? My Lena once delivered me Dymich, my cellmates and I spaced out for several hours, and then the tough depression came. I don't even know whether I want MDMA."

"We can bring charas to you, but we'll have to crumble it into small pieces in order to push it through the holes in the wall. It's a lot of work. You can order us a jar of honey in exchange for the charas."

"Look, ant, can I think it over for a couple of weeks? Vitka and I have smoked charas every day for a month; I have ceased to feel it. I should take a break from smoking. I think about Aguada all the time when I'm stoned. I really don't want to get ten years. I need some kind of drug to forget all my problems and to not have depression as a side effect from it. I need a kind of drug that makes me want to live life to the full, but doesn't cause addiction. The best option will be a powder to make me fall sleep and to wake up just before I'm released."

"We have such a drug, Vasya. Here is a crystal, eat it and you'll fall asleep. We'll wake you up just before your release. You owe us a packet of cookies, Vasya."

"Thank you, ant. I'll give you all my cookies. Just tell me, why does this crystal taste like onion?"

"It's because it is made of onion extract, infected with ergot. You're going to fall asleep now, and we'll wake you up when the time of your release comes."

"I think it is starting to work, I'm falling asleep. Bye ants, see you before my release."

"Wake up, Vasya," Viktor shakes me, holding half an onion near my nose, let's go to the first floor, the priests are going to hold a New Year concert there, and I couldn't wake you up, you bastard."

"I had such a good sleep after lunch," I answer him, stretching on the floor. "Vitya, I dreamed that the ants started to carry drugs to me in jail."

"It's still early for you to think about drugs. Put on a clean T-shirt, and let's go down. Our cellmates have been preparing sketches for a whole month. Come on, let's watch."

"Vitya, do you think a T-shirt with the face of Dr. Gonzo from Fear and Loathing in Las Vegas will be okay?" I ask, putting on a T-shirt with several cuts on the back.

"Vasya, don't you have a shirt without holes on the back? There will be priests, after all."

"Why don't you like my shirt? They are artistic cuts and it's not as hot in it as a result."

"Put on what you want. But look, the other inmates are all dressed in the white shirts that they wear to court," Viktor says, waving his hand at me. "Catch me up, I'm going down."

"Hi, Borish! Happy New Year!"

"Good vodka, Happy New Year," the Turk, the very spit of John Lennon with a beard, shakes hands with us.

"It's an unforgettable New Year; it's so surreal," Borish says, pointing at the space around. "One hundred and fifty prisoners sit on their haunches and watch two killers acting out a scene on the topic of 'New Year and crime.' You get the impression that none of these people could have committed any crimes. Look how pleased the young Indian over there is. Do you see the hole painted on his shirt and a monster looking out of it? It's a good T-shirt; it fits his character perfectly. He and his partner broke into a private house, killed a security guard, then raped and killed the mistress and her two small children. And now look, he is so happy that he is clapping his hands."

Three murderers, a rapist and two drug dealers, with serious faces, begin to sing a New Year song in chorus on the stage.

"Have you watched 'The Snowball Tree'[94], Vasya?"

"Yeah, Vitya, I also just remembered the Evening Bell[95]," I say, watching the criminals singing.

---

[94] The Snowball Tree (Russian: Kalina Krasnaya) – a famous Russian movie, starting with a scene of criminals singing onstage.

"Look, the priests have started to hand out the presents, the concert is over, apparently," Viktor says, holding out his hand to take a present as the pastor approaches us.

"A bar of soap is a well-timed New Year's present, Vitya, taking into account that I dropped mine in the toilet bowl yesterday."

"There is toothpaste as well; I've just run out of it," Borish says, happily waving the plastic bag with a Christmas tree on it.

"Those who have received your gifts, go back to your cells!" A guard shouts, pushing the joyful criminals towards the exit.

"Do you have anything to smoke, guys?" the Turk asks hopefully, accompanying us up the stairs.

"No, Borish, you won't believe it, but we have neither hash, nor a single pinch of tobacco. Vitya and I have one nitrowhite pill for the two of us, which we are going to snort instead of champagne before going to bed."

"Well, okay, happy New Year to you, I'll have to smoke peanut shells," our Turkish friend waves his hand to us through the bars, saying goodbye.

"Apparently, we'll have no chicken with mashed potatoes today. They fooled us with that donation."

"Vasya, stop moaning. It's New Year's Eve. Be happy for the warden, he's probably eating our chicken at home and remembering us with a kind word."

"Yeah, I know his kind word. 'Wow, I've conned those Russians pretty well, may they eat their thin broth, and I'll have a good rest on their money.'"

"Look, Vitya, Russia is on the TV news," I say, powdering the sleeping pill with an iron mug. "Someone made a wall-length piece of graffiti in Moscow."

'Awaken your spirit' the Russian letters on the side of some building shine on our prison TV screen.

"Well, Vasya, we've seen our homeland, we may consider that we've celebrated the coming New Year."

"Now we'll have the performance 'Put your spirit to sleep,'" I say, making two lines of powdered sleeping pill on an iron plate.

Having snorted my line, I lie and watch a young robber, who accidentally shot off his partner's finger during a robbery, preparing tea over a candle in the toilet.

"We'll have tea now and nighty-night!" Viktor says, pulling out a packet of cookies.

"A sleeping pill starts working quickly through the nose. We'll fall asleep in half an hour," I say, leaning back on my rubber mat. "I wish you a happy New Year, Viktor."

"I wish you a happy New Year, too, Vasya."

---

[95] The Evening Bell (Russian: Vecherniy Zvon) – a popular Russian song.

Chapter 47. Part Two. Outside.

Having put a syringe with liquid mycelium into the jar with grain, I hear the unpleasant sound of the doorbell. Oh hell, it's such a bad time, I will have to re-disinfect everything again. Having taken the gauze mask and rubber gloves off, I unwillingly go to open the door.

"Vova, is that you?"

"Yeah, who else could it be? Open the door! Vasya, you look like a mad professor in that surgical suit. What a smell there is in here, we'll get caught because of you," Vova says, screwing up his face and hitching up his trousers, although they are already pulled up to his navel.

"What's up, Vova?"

"Vasya, I think that the first batch of MDMA will be ready in a couple of weeks."

"I just don't get it, Vova. You've been telling me the same thing for three months already. One day your distillation device crashed, another day the nitroethane ran out. How much money have you already invested in the laboratory?"

"Five thousand bucks have already been spent. But we still lack one thousand."

"Vova, don't ask me to lend you anymore. You already owe me two thousand. I myself have already invested a grand in mushrooms and hydroponics. I need to have some money to live on until the season starts."

"You must have money, Vasya; you're selling visas after all. You said that Tamir had paid you an advance for four visas."

"Yeah, he gave me five hundred bucks, but five-year visas are no longer being issued in Thailand. I think my visa business is over. It couldn't last for long. I have already sold fifteen visas.

"Okay, then think about who we can sell two hundred grams of MDMA to? We'll buy chemicals with that money. It should be enough for ten kilograms of MDMA. By the way, what have you managed to grow? Show me," Vova says, heading towards the room for psilocybin mushrooms.

"Stop!" I shout, grabbing him by the arm. "First go and wash your hands with soap. Vova, the grains are finally covered with mycelium, and you could bring an infection. I can do without that. I've got everything sterile in there, like in an operating room."

"What about Dima Lucky, Vasya? Did you do a visa for him?" Vova asks, lathering his hands with liquid antibacterial soap.

"He is such a jerk, Vova! The entire Russian Goa is already laughing at his unsuccessful trips to Thailand. Just imagine, that moron bought tickets to Bangkok, and forgot to get a Thai visa in his passport."

"But Thailand doesn't require visas anymore, does it?"

"It doesn't require visas from normal countries, but Dima Lucky is a citizen of Belarus. So, that moron flew to Thailand, and the border guards obviously sent him back. Then he tried to bribe a Thai official. The story ended up with him being arrested, put on a cargo plane, and sent back to India."

"What a smell you have in here, Vasya. Did you spill some bleach or what?" Vova says, coming into the poorly lit sterile room. "All three floors in the block smell of your bleach, Vasya."

"Vova, I chlorinated every square centimeter of the room from floor to ceiling. What else should it smell of in here? Nothing will grow without chlorination. Listen, Vova, I chlorinated the grains for a whole day last time, and I got a mold from the agrius family instead of mycelium. I was interested what kind of mold it was, and why it grew instead of mycelium. I surfed the Internet and saw that I had got a very strange mold. I began to learn more about it in order to find out how to deal with it, and read that this mold has a close relative called nigera. It is the same color, but a different shape. This nigera grows in countries with a hot climate, and it is considered to be the worst poison in the world. In 1961, a hundred thousand Turks died from it in a week. It was highlighted on the Internet that if you find such a mold, you must inform the authorities and write a will immediately, as you will die in a week from liver failure."

"Vasya, have you decided to poison the whole of Goa?"

"Don't worry Vova, my mold is only a relative of that nigera. I myself was so scared at first, I vomited in the toilet. A week has passed and I'm still alive. Vova, do you remember the story about the archaeologists who opened the tomb in the Pyramid of Cheops? All of the people who entered it first, died a week later under mysterious circumstances. Well, nigera caused that. Do you want me to tell you about the experiments that were carried out with that mold in space?"

"No, Vasya, tell me next time. I want to discuss one more issue with you. You'd better move from here. We'll get busted because of your bleach. The chemicals in our laboratory don't have such a strong smell as your mushrooms."

"Vova, I have been thinking about doing that. My girls will soon go to Russia for the summer. I'll move all my mushrooms and hydroponics to my house."

"What about your hydroponics? When will the Goans finally get to try decent marijuana?"

"Let's go to the other room."

"Should I wash my hands again?"

"No, Vova, hydroponics is an easier case. The equipment is more complex, of course, but you don't need such sterility as with mushrooms."

"Yeah, it has a futuristic look, it's much prettier than the room with mushroom jars," Vova says, squinting from the glare of the powerful lamps. "Why do you need these corrugated silver pipes, like in a spaceship?"

"It's an extraction fan. Nice, huh? And in the plastic trays is a solution of fertilizer. Air is fed from a compressor to saturate the water with oxygen. The marijuana grows in expanded clay pots over the trays. Holes are drilled in the pots, so the roots hang down into the solution. There are 250-watt lamps above the plants. Ganja grows poorly at temperatures above thirty-five degrees. So I had to stretch an extraction fan from each reflector lamp to the window. In addition, the whole system is on a timer. It's switched on and off when required. And if the electricity is cut for some reason, then everything keeps working automatically, on battery power."

"Yeah, the hydroponics system looks more serious than the mushrooms."

"Vova, that's not actually true, I've been working with the mushrooms for two months already. I have to work every day with a gauze mask on my face and sterile gloves. If one hostile bacterium gets into the grain, two days of work goes to waste. Meanwhile, there are three hundred thousand different bacteria around us. They're just waiting for conditions to breed. I had begun to lose hope, but just recently my grains in sterile jars have finally been covered with fungus. I only need to learn how to sterilize the straw now. If the straw and grain are mixed successfully, the first mushrooms will appear in two or three weeks. I'll have pedigree Cubensis mushrooms. Nobody will buy LSD after them."

"Vasya, just don't start going on about your psychedelic revolution."

"I'm not talking about revolution right now. I will be able to harvest thousands of them every day. And I'm going to sell each mushroom for five dollars. One such mushroom gives you a kick like one drop of LSD. Cubensis mushrooms are not like wild magic mushrooms, which you have to eat a hundred of."

"Not bad profit, Vasya. It would be good to prepare mushrooms, MDMA, and hydroponics during the monsoon. And having got prepared for the season, we'll shut down the business till next year. We could earn a lot of money. We won't be able to sell that much here, in Goa, Vasya. We'll have to organize deliveries through the ministerial line to Bombay. Twenty million people, can you imagine how much money that is? It's not Goa. I spoke with the minister's son, he promised to help us with contacts and a police cover. Do you know what connections he has in the government?"

"Vova, I don't know about the government, but he really helped me solve a problem with my partner, who blackmailed me when I didn't have a passport. The policemen stood to attention in front of him, as if he was their chief."

"If we perform deals through him, we'll have a safe cover."

"Let's go to the kitchen, Vova, I have some beer in the fridge. I'll continue to tell you the story about Dima Lucky."

"Vasya, what are these flasks and syringes lying next to the beer in your fridge?"

"Don't worry, Vova, liquid mycelium is stored like that. It's my mushroom gene bank. Millions of mushrooms could be grown of it. Here, have a beer," I say to Vova, removing foil from one of the flasks. "Look, it's so beautiful."

"Vasya, you have strange taste. It looks like snot, floating in water."

"Vova, you don't have a clue about biological beauty. When you have made several months of unsuccessful attempts to grow such 'snot', and then you finally succeed, this beauty is like a child to you. It's simply a miracle, when you manage to grow liquid mycelium from mushroom spores. All my flasks are sterilized in the pressure cooker. I rub the gloves with spirit every minute. The room is sterilized with a special antibacterial lamp, in addition to chlorine. I carry out all operations above a hot oven. It's not an easy task to grow psilocybin mushrooms on an industrial scale in the local climate."

"Stop telling me about your mycelium, I'll lose my appetite for the beer. Tell me what happened next with Dima Lucky."

"Oh, yeah. Upon arrival from Thailand, Dima flew to Belarus, finally got a Thai visa, and called my Irina in Thailand. She said to him, "Buy a one-way ticket. Thailand is celebrating New Year now, and no one knows exactly when the Indian Embassy will open after the holidays. But Dima Lucky thought with his stupid head and bought a round-trip ticket with a fixed date. He must have decided to save money. Well, it happened that he didn't have time to get a visa because of the holidays. He arrives in Goa tomorrow. He called me from Thailand and threatened me with trouble. He says it's my fault he was left without a visa."

"Are you going to return that fool the money for the visa?"

"Bollocks to him! I'll give him his fifteen hundred bucks back. The problem is that he wants me to pay him the money for the air tickets. He says it's my fault he flew to Thailand for nothing, twice."

"I'm afraid he might get you in trouble, Vasya. This is the second time you are dealing with him, and again you end up with problems. You agreed to make a visa for that jerk, as if you hadn't enough of an example with the restaurant in Palolem. Be careful with him."

Chapter 48. Part One. Inside.

Having run out onto the stage, an Indian ballerina with a fold of fat on her stomach takes a step and hides her face theatrically behind her hands at the appearance of the 'black swan'.

"Look, Vitya, it's the 'Swan Lake' ballet by Tchaikovsky on TV."

Not reacting to my words and keeping his eyes fixed on his notebook, Viktor continues copying the English dictionary into it.

"Vitya, don't you want to watch 'Swan Lake' performed by Indians?"

"No, I don't. I want to complete my dictionary before I'm released. Soon I will have been here a year and the expert analysis still hasn't come. I don't believe that the police added cocaine to my powder, so I will get out soon. I need to finish the dictionary."

"Vitya, are you going to copy all twenty-five thousand words into your notebook?"

"No, I don't need about fifty per cent of the words in the dictionary. For example, why do I need to know such a word as *ipecacuanha*, 'vomit root'? Half of the dictionary is full of such unnecessary words. I only copy those I may need later. When I get out of here, I don't think I'll study English. I'll have no time for it there; I'll be busy with life."

"Vitya, is it really not interesting to you to watch plump ballet dancers in saris pretending to be swans to the music of Tchaikovsky, barefoot, without ballet shoes?"

"Vasya, it doesn't interest me at all"

"Well, at least have a look at the faces of our cellmates. It's a show in itself to watch those savages staring at the TV set."

"Vasya, I'll repeat once again that I'm not interested. I'm not going to do anything except study English now," Viktor says, not wanting to even look out of the corner of his eye at the space around him. "I will have been here for one year on February 16, and it's unclear to me why I am still in prison."

"Relax, Vitya, you'll be released soon, whereas my prospects are much more uncertain. If I'm lucky, I'll be released in a year, and if not, I'll be hanging around in Aguada prison for ten years. Shall we have a smoke, Vitya? I'm already shaking from the energy you are giving off. You're straining at the leash to get out, and I'll have to stay here alone. Let's have a smoke, Vitya. If you calm down then I'll be able to calm down, too. David gave me a lump of hash today. It's small, but it will be enough for the two of us."

"Okay, Vasya, I'll leave my English for a while. Crumble it and I'll prepare the bong."

"Look at the surrealism surrounding us," I say, exhaling a cloud of sweet smoke. "Just look at those failed robbers, watching 'Swan Lake' with their mouths open in astonishment."

"Yeah, we have the theater of the absurd around us, that's for sure," Viktor says, smiling and exhaling his portion of smoke. "They remind me of clowns with serious faces. Look at Powan, the skinny, tall guy, wearing thick-lensed glasses. That's Mukhan standing next to him. He is four feet nine inches tall and has hairy ears. And then we have their third mate, that one with a moronic expression who is picking his nose now, nicknamed Meradost. They are like the Russian comedy trio, the Coward, the Fool and the Pro. I can't imagine these eighteen-year-old boys doing an armed raid on a jeweler. The funniest thing is how they failed. The tall one accidentally shot Meradost's finger off."

Having heard the familiar name, Meradost, a young Indian moron sitting a few feet away from the TV screen, smiles happily at us, waving the hand with the mutilated finger.

"I think they've got tired of watching the ballet, now they'll switch channel."

A few minutes later we watch, smiling, as the skinny four-eyed guy with a serious face pokes a stick into a hole in the TV, trying to reach the channel changing mechanism, the button for which has long since been lost.

"I think its time for Shaktimaan."

"Shaktimaan! Shaktimaan!" joyful cheers are heard from different cells.

Rejoicing at the prospect of watching the next episode of the show, a wild mixture of the 'Teletubbies' and 'Superman', criminals, murderers and rapists of all ages stop what they are doing and draw nearer to the TV, like small children.

"Vitya, what do you think: how big are their brains?"

"Slightly bigger than a walnut, I suppose," Viktor says, pulling out Shakespeare's 'Othello' in English from a pile of books. "Six months ago, I wouldn't have believed that I could read this book. I didn't speak English a year ago. I'll call my mother in Russia next week to boast about reading Shakespeare in English. May she be happy for me in her old age."

"Vitya, as far as I remember, you haven't told your mom anything about prison. She thinks you are chilling in the Himalayas. Your mother is an educated woman. She'll understand what's going on immediately. She'll say, 'Son, I've known you for fifty years. You had bad marks in English at school. You would only start reading Shakespeare in English if you were in jail.'"

"You're right, Vasya. Although she is old, she's a clever woman. I won't tell my mom about Shakespeare for now."

"Look, Vitya, Churchill is examining the photos of dug up corpses again. Do you want to have a look?" I ask, smiling, knowing Viktor's answer in advance.

"Reading Shakespeare will be a more interesting occupation for me," Viktor says, looking up a new, unfamiliar word in the dictionary.

"Well I saw them yesterday, Vitya. It's a real horror. The police officers took those photos at the scene. The headless body of a naked woman and two children's corpses with their stomachs ripped open. That man over there, wearing a shirt with a monster on it, raped a woman before killing her," I point at the guy, who is laughing happily at the stupid jokes in the TV program. "The photos make Churchill's mouth water, I think. Just look at him, he gets a kick out of looking at a naked, dismembered body."

"Vasya, why are you telling me all this again? Perhaps you also get a kick out of it?"

"Vitya, I'm writing a book, and I want to describe all this. I'd like to share my life experience so that other people don't repeat my mistakes. I want to do at least some good in my life. Vitya, I thought you enjoyed listening to the next chapter of my adventures that I write during the day."

"Yes, I look forward to the continuation of your show every evening. But, please, read me the chapter about dismemberment when we are outside. How can I talk to these monsters after your stories? We are all equal here, in prison. I have to share food with them and smoke one cigarette between us. Churchill washes my clothes and that young murderer is the same age as my son. I'm a living person. I cannot hate them, even though I want to very much. They are facing life sentences anyway, and your stories only promote hatred and despair."

Chapter 48. Part Two. Outside.

"I haven't swam in the sea for six months. The tourists who have broken away from cold Russia to come here probably wouldn't understand me. Today it's the first time in six months that I feel a burning desire to swim in the sea. Today I feel as if I have come to Goa for the first time. I want to run along the deserted beach, to laugh and cry with joy. I want to collect beautiful seashells and build sandcastles, wallowing in the warm shallow water. Romka, do you want a line of MDMA?"

"Right now? In the middle of the day?"

"What's stopping you? The season is over, the tourists have left your Sunset. I've already snorted a couple of lines this morning."

"I can see that: running along the beach, collecting seashells. You're obviously high," Romka says, mocking me playfully, standing on the veranda of the Russian Sunset campsite. "Vasya, where did you get MDMA from? Did you make it yourself or what? Nobody has had it for several months already."

"No, I didn't make it myself, but I gave the idea to my chemist friends. This morning they brought me the first trial batch of the purest MDMA. The cocaine period is over in Goa. Soon MDMA will again become cheaper than coke. Dymich in unlimited quantities will be everywhere now."

"Well, then I'll turn on some music, we'll make a presentation," Romka says happily, placing his acoustic system on the porch of the house, which stands on the seashore. "By the way, Vasya, do you know that today is the Day of the White Crystal Wind, according to the Mayan calendar?"

"That's a good sign, I think," I say, turning the trance track 'Ecstasy' up louder. "We've been living in Goa for five years already. Time flies. Roma, do you remember when you first tried LSD on Arambol hill?" I ask, scraping the powdered pink crystals into lines with a credit card on the glass table.

"Of course, I do, Vasya. You and Arik arranged an unforgettable psychedelic trip for me. My whole life changed after that night. My beloved, the enchantress Camilla, appeared in my life. Now I do interesting creative work that brings me great pleasure. I live in a beautiful house by the ocean. I am surrounded by interesting people and I don't want to go back to my old life, where I drifted through a dreary day-to-day existence."

"Romka, your Sunset turned out to be an excellent project!" I say, feeling another wave of pleasure starting to roll from the bottom of my stomach to the top of my head, making me shudder. "This house has had four owners over the years I've been living in Goa. So many people have expanded their consciousness here. So many parties have been thrown here on the beach. Your Russian Sunset is a cult place. The first Russian owners, Vlad and Mariika, began to promote this place five years ago. Bamboo bungalows once stood in front of the house, the bar was open around the clock, and you could listen to music all day and all night. Famous people came to stay with them: the owners of corporations, TV channels, Muz TV[96] celebrities. The following season, Sasha and Natasha tried to add some aestheticism to this place in their own way, banning tourists from snorting cocaine. Then, Valentin and Ksusha ran the place for two seasons. Then the new generation of cocaine youth began to come, snorting lines of coke off their laptops. This season, you and Camilla put your creativity into the place. Now it's forbidden to eat meat here, and all your visitors are fascinated with the Mayan calendar. It was a good idea to demolish all the bungalows. Now you have a gorgeous view of the sea from the veranda."

"Vasya, I wish we could make the music louder and dance non-stop for a couple of hours. I'm really starting to come up," Roma says, dancing on the sand and taking out a mixing ball and a lump of hash.

"The times have changed, Roma. You can't play music up loud, even in the daytime. The police will come and arrest you, and then open a criminal case for noise pollution. By the way, how did the story with Greedy's arrest end? And why was he arrested? What did he have to do with anything?"

"I still don't understand it, Vasya. Camilla and I decided to organize a creative festival at the end of the season. Just to gather all the Goan fire artists, jugglers, dancers and drummers, and make a kind of convention, with no drugs and no alcohol. We managed to bring together around a hundred creative people of different kinds. The police went in circles around our house for two days. They couldn't find fault with anything. The only commerce was that we sold vegetarian salads; that's it. Well, they arrested our DJ, who was playing relaxing music softly in the daytime, on the third day. And Greedy was arrested because he was the only person from our crowd who had a business visa. He was accused of 'illegal organization of a party'. Greedy spent two days in jail; we only just managed to get him out on bail. Now he's not allowed to travel abroad, he's under investigation. The Police said, 'This will be a lesson for you, Russians, so that you don't arrange anything on our land without the knowledge of the authorities'. Why am I telling this to you? Look, there's Greedy himself with two beauties. Ask him yourself, and I'll go up to the second floor to my sweet Camilla, she's about to wake up. Vasya, I feel such a surge of love and tenderness from the MDMA, I just can't sit here while my love is waking up without me. I should be the first one to wish her a good morning. I'll be back in half an hour!" Romka shouts to me on the run, smiling, his face beaming with synthetic pleasure.

---

[96] Muz TV - a Russian music TV channel.

"What's up, Greedy! What beautiful girlfriends you have! Hi, girls!"

"Hi, Vasya! Why are you so happy first thing in the morning?"

"Today is the Day of the White Crystal Wind according to the Mayan calendar. MDMA has again appeared in Goa."

"Well, what can I say to that, Vasya? Pour us some too, then. I am sure my enchantresses won't be against it," Greedy says, hugging his cute girlfriends.

"Of course we won't. If today is the Day of the White Crystal Wind, we must celebrate it in the right way," the red-haired enchantress says, laughing happily, taking a tube rolled from a banknote off the table. "By the way, there will be a party at East End tonight. Will you come with us, Vasya?"

"I have no choice, babydoll. Of course I'll go with you. Will you snort the MDMA or shall I mix it with some water?"

"No, Vasya, I don't like snorting, my nose itches then, I'd rather drink it," the tall blonde with a bunch of long, thin braids says, dancing around a palm tree. "Make a line for Angela, she has a trained nose. Russian Sunset is such a wonderful place, you always meet everybody here. We met Greedy here yesterday. He has a strange nickname. I would call him Generous."

"He is only generous to gorgeous girls," I say, laughing and crumbling the large crystals on the table.

"I woke up today with a hangover and thought 'where can I get something for the evening?' I started to wake Valera up, and he said to me, 'Why are you fussing, Snezhana? Everything appears of its own accord in Goa. Let's go to Sunset, we'll think of something. We are bound to meet someone there.' We come here, and here you are Vasya, like a kind magician, pouring out your magic crystals. Do you have good MDMA?"

"Girls, you won't believe it, but this is the first time in the five years that I'm involved in selling drugs in Goa that I can safely say it couldn't be any purer. I give you a one hundred percent guarantee."

"That sounds convincing when you say it," Greedy says, watching Angela screwing up her nose after snorting a line. "Vasya, let me try a line too, if we are celebrating the Day of the White Crystal Wind."

"How did your story with the police end, Valera?" I ask, staring through my rose-colored glasses at Angela's young, firm ass."

"Wow, your powder packs quite a pinch," Greedy says, grimacing and rubbing the tip of his nose with his hand. "It hasn't ended, Vasya, I'm still under investigation and the case is open. The thing is that Roma didn't pay any money to the cops before holding the event."

"Well, what's that got to do with you, Greedy?"

"Romka leased the house in my name. I was the only person here who had a business visa. So, I am accused of being the main organizer. My lawyer says that in two years I will be sentenced to pay a two hundred bucks fine."

"But you held a non-commercial event," I say, rolling a joint and struggling to focus my vision.

"Vasya, who cares whether it was commercial or not? The cops want to get money from everything. However, on the other hand, the Indian state provides me with a free visa for the duration of the trial. Such cases can last for two or three years here. They can't lock me up. In the meantime, I'm pleased to go to court once a month to get a free visa. So I am happy, even. Whatever God does is for the best. Oh, Vasya, I feel high already. I've just now noticed how beautiful my girlfriends are. Look at the blonde one, she's dancing so charmingly under that palm tree," Greedy says, leaning against the house and pointing at Snezhana, several feet away. "She must be coming up now, too."

"We got so plastered yesterday, Vasya, I don't even remember whether I had something with her or not. But I won't miss my chance today. Did I see Romka fleeing to the second floor when we arrived? Did you give a line as well, Vasya?"

"Of course, I did," I say, smiling and passing the crooked joint that I have finally finished rolling to Valera. "Romka is proving to his Camilla that he loves her more than anyone else, and then he'll come down."

"Hurrah to the Day of the White Crystal Wind! Let's swim in the sea!" Snezhana shouts, unbuttoning her colorful bra on the go.

"I love swimming in the sea with naked gorgeous women, especially when I am coming up," I shout to Greedy, running towards the deserted beach.

"Pull yourself together, Vasya. You have a wife and child," Valera laughs after me, settling down comfortably in a hammock stretched between two trees.

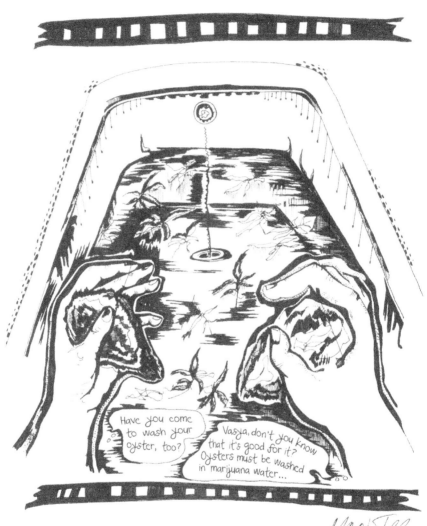

371

Chapter 49. Part One. Inside.

"Next stop Lenin Avenue," a pleasant female voice says. The tram slowly picks up speed, tapping out the rhythm of the city's trance with its wheels.

"Dad, we have to get off at the next stop," my little daughter pulls on my hand. Dirty snow banks, hunched under their own weight, line the road. It smells of spring and exhaust fumes. The people crowding near the exit remind me of zombies from a horror movie. Their faces do not express any emotions. Putting a mask of indifference on their faces, they are wrapped up in their own concerns. It is unusual to see my fellow citizens around me instead of Indians. Even their dull faces do not overshadow the joy of holding my little princess by the hand. The tram's doors open unusually loudly, making me wince. I've heard a similar sound of doors opening somewhere.

No! No! Anything but that!

"Counting," I hear the guard's disgusting voice while still half asleep.

I wake up here again. My cellmates, already dressed, sit crouched in rows in the center of the cell. Only Viktor and I remain on our bunks, wrapped up in our blankets like mummies. A new guard, waving, tries to make us get out from under our blankets and sit in the center of the cell.

"Fuck off, monkey, I'm a foreigner. Dare touch me and I'll give you a hard time," I say angrily to him in Russian.

Having asked his partner something in their language, he listens to what the other says for a while, which includes the word "foreigner" repeated several times. Sitting on the floor, I close my eyes again, trying to remember my dream.

"Dobroe utro!" still half asleep, I hear Viktor shouting to the whole cell.

"Dobrautra!" the guards repeat, like parrots.

This means it's six o'clock in the morning now. You can lie on the floor and to try to catch the end of your dream. If you're lucky, you can sleep soundly for a couple of hours. I want to fly away from this reality so much. Covering my head with the blanket, I intensely try to recall the end of my interrupted dream. I'm back in cold Russia, the smells of the last days of winter emerge from my memory. The brooks are about to start flowing and the first green leaves will soon begin to break out of the swollen buds on the trees.

"Daddy, shall I show you what I drew at drawing class today?" Vasilinka asks, taking a plastic bag with copybooks from my hands.

Pulling a package out of the bag, she unwraps it slowly, rustling noisily.

"Churchill! You motherfucker, stop rustling your bag! I fuck your ass, let me sleep," I hear Viktor's irritated shout next to my ear.

Silence settles over the cell for some time. I'd really like to go back to my dream. I beg my mind to take me back to my daughter. She's about to appear next to me, stretching out her little hand to me, but I hear a painfully familiar mumbling somewhere far off. That bloody pedophile has started reading his damned Bible out loud again. I wonder, what is he asking God for every morning? Does he ask not to be given a life sentence? Or does he ask for a miracle to happen, and for everyone forget that he raped a five-year-old boy and infected him with HIV? If it was someone else who was muttering his prayers now I would be able to return to my dream, where I could be with my child.

'You can tell a man by his friends,' a wise phrase uttered by someone, pops into my mind. This cell is full of scum. Murderers, robbers, rapists, maniacs. Who am I, then? Can I really be the same crazy primate as they are? Oh great Morpheus, take me in your arms, give me at least an hour to stay in the world of dreams and illusions. Along with thoughts about Vasilinka, the image of a monster sitting in the next cell who raped his four-year-old daughter comes to mind. Apparently, I won't see Vasilinka again today. There's silence for a while. I hear sparrows chirping outside the window, enjoying the new day. There are green trees and shrubs everywhere. A white bath, filled with clear water, stands on a lawn lit by the bright Sun. I am holding a small bundle in my hands, it must be my child. Folding back the edge of the bundle, I see a giant oyster in my hands. Suddenly, Tamir appears near the bath. He is also holding a similar package. Coming closer, I see that the bath is half filled with marijuana and is overflowing with water. Beautiful hemp buds lie on the bottom beneath the clear water.

"Have you come to wash your oyster, too?" the famous trance DJ asks me.

"Won't that harm the oyster?" I ask, watching Tamir putting his bundle into the water.

"Vasya, don't you know that it's good for it? Oysters must be washed in marijuana water. Come closer and try bathing your oyster."

"Your breakfast, sir," I hear Viktor's voice, pulling me out of my dream. "Vasya, I guess your wives didn't bring you breakfast in your bed as often as I do."

"Thank you, Vitya, you're my best wife," I say, smiling, and get out from under the blanket. "Who will bring me tea in bed once you're released?"

"Just let it be over!" Viktor says, picking the soft part out of his little bun. "We ate all the cookies yesterday, what will we have for breakfast?"

"Vitya, I have one onion left from dinner. We can make one sandwich with onion, and another with just salt."

"Well, that's not a bad to start to the day."

It will be sunny today, as the shadow of the barred window is clearly visible on the opposite wall.

"Vitya, what will we do after breakfast? Will we play tennis or learn English? Or will we go for a walk with the others?"

"It would be nice to sunbathe, Vasya. I've become as white as a vampire without sunlight. I believe we haven't gone for a walk for a couple of months already. We could take our rubber mats and sunbathe. Let's have breakfast first, and then we'll see. Vasya, you're planning things that may not happen again. We could not be released for a walk today, or I could fall on the slippery floor in the bathroom, hit the back of my head, and you'd have no one to go for a walk with. It's not a bad idea to go for a walk in the fresh air for an hour. But I badly want to be free after a walk, so perhaps it's better not to go for one. Vasya, maybe we should have a smoke this morning?"

"That's a good proposal, Vitya. But I've decided to learn English. Let's read and write a bit, and then smoke."

Having taken a sip of hot tea with milk, I open the fresh morning paper brought by Churchill.

"Look what the newspaper says," I address Viktor, who is dipping his roll in his tea.

"Just don't read me anything about murders," Viktor says, putting the last piece of bread sprinkled with salt into his mouth

"Can I read to you about a murder of fruit?"

"What fruit?" Viktor asks irritably, fearing that I'll give him negative information again.

"Mangoes, bananas, apples. The newspaper says that twenty tons of carbide ripened mangoes have been seized and destroyed in Goa in the last week. It turns out that the Goan 'farmer-monkeys' came up with the idea of collecting unripe fruit so that it will keep longer. A few days before sale, they dip the fruit in a carbide solution and it ripens instantly."

"Carbide is very harmful to health, isn't it?"

"That's the story the newspaper is covering, Vitya. A special separate police unit is engaged in seizing poisoned fruit. The journalists report that almost all fruit wholesalers use this horrible method. Two farmers have already been jailed for a couple of weeks, and criminal proceedings have been initiated."

"Vasya, I thought I ate natural fruit in Goa."

"I realized long ago, Vitya, that India is not the cheapest, as I thought before, but actually the most expensive country. Everything that is done properly costs more here than anywhere else in the world, because there are few clever people here and most of the population are monkeys. Goods that seem to be cheap are actually made ass-backwards. The newspaper also says that India has bought a large batch of cereal, vegetable and fruit seeds."

"What does that have to do with you, Vasya? Have you decided to become a farmer?"

"Vitya, only the state can sell seeds in India, that's the problem. The Indians bought genetically modified seeds from the Americans. The newspaper says that almost all vegetables, fruit, and cereals in India will be genetically modified within five years. All advanced countries are fighting against this, while India does the opposite. Genetically modified products are cheaper than natural ones in all countries. Governments compel manufacturers of such products to inform the consumers about it, but India is proud of it."

"Why do you care?"

"When I came to India, Vitya, I thought I had found a place on the Earth where I could eat natural products for the rest of my life, and it turned out that I was deceived. I am thinking about my future more and more. I don't want to live in India. What can I do here? I was locked up for the drug business and I don't want to do legal business with these crooks. All the stories about foreigners who have tried to do business here always end sadly. Once a business becomes profitable here, the kind Indians come along with sticks and ask you to leave their land. The Indians have never invented anything new. How much energy was invested in them by the English, the French, the Portuguese? How did that turn out? Everything belongs to these monkeys now. How many people have been scammed out of their money in Goa? At first, they allowed foreigners to buy property in Goa, and now the newspaper says that a new decree has entered into force. Visas for foreigners will only be issued for two months. The natives will again seize on the cheap the beautiful houses built with love by white people. I don't believe the Indians any more. My friends, who are smarter, went to other countries long ago. I'm not happy with the prospect that fruit and vegetables will have a plastic taste here soon, just like in Russia."

"What are you thinking about, Vasya? You are facing ten years in prison, and again you are worrying about the future of the world. Get out of here first. While you are here, you should have only one motto, 'Here and Now.' Live, enjoying every moment. You have neither a future nor a past now."

"If we are speaking about 'here and now', Vitya, we should think about how not to catch head lice from our cellmates. Look, the two rapists over there are combing each other out. They resemble monkeys so much."

"Have you looked at yourself in the mirror, Vasya? You are the same sort of monkey, just a white one. You've only just recovered from scabies."

"That's right, Vitya. I'm a white monkey, as people do not sit in cages. By the way, Vitya, do you know that my neighbor to the right, that seventeen-year-old four-eyed guy looking like a mug, an A student, has also begun writing a book? He told me yesterday very seriously that he had had seventeen girls before he was jailed. When I was his age, Vitya, I had also had seventeen girls, maybe even more. My mother had the *Otto* fashion magazine with photos of girls in their underwear. I dated them all in the bathroom every day. I doubt he could see a woman's tits, let alone other things. Look at the tattoo he drew with a pen, he was copying mine for half an hour yesterday."

"He's the same age as my son, Vasya," Viktor says, sweeping the place where we had breakfast. "But mine is playing football in his leisure time, and this one is coloring in children's books with crayons. The place is clean. Well, Vasya, let's go to school?" Viktor announces loudly, laying our exercise books and dictionaries on the floor.

"Vitya, how can you learn English using your method? I just don't understand. You copy out about one hundred words from the dictionary into your notebook every day, but memorize only five percent of them. You're writing new words every day. Don't you think you waste ninety percent of your time?"

"Well, I don't understand you, Vasya. You copy out twenty words a hundred times. I can't imagine how you can do the same job a hundred times. It's terribly boring. That's probably the reason why you succeeded in cultivating mushrooms. If I'm not interested in something, I quit it immediately. I've listened to you, Vasya. That is real madness how many times you sterilized your flasks, cans, grain, and straw, again and again. How long did you say you did it for? Did you do the same thing for three months until you cultivated your mushrooms?"

"Yeah, Vitya. I patiently did almost the same thing for three months until my first mushroom grew. I was arrested on the day it sprouted."

Chapter 49. Part Two. Outside.

"When will your mushrooms finally sprout?" Vova asks, throwing the latest bag of pinkish crystals onto the table. We have already made almost half a kilo. We could cook a kilo of this stuff every month.

"Vova, I think our first harvest will be ready in a week. I've found a way to cultivate mushrooms on an industrial scale, while surfing the web. One botanist posted a dissertation on mushrooms and hydrogen peroxide. I've been experimenting for a whole week, Vova, and I think I've succeeded in peroxidizing the rice straw. I've finally managed to infect the straw with millet covered in mycelium. I am waiting for the first mushrooms to appear any day now."

"How are the sales of MDMA, Vasya?"

"Vova, I've sold twenty grams to my friends. But who will buy half a kilo now? I can't even imagine. The season ended a month ago."

"Vasya, we need to come up with some idea. We need money urgently. Now we have the opportunity to buy all of the necessary chemicals, while they are on sale. The backstreet safrole oil factory was shut down in Vietnam. A courier delivering nitroethane was arrested in Bombay. That moron dropped a bag with a glass bottle at the station. Thank God, he thought to tell the police that he needed nitroethane in order to make firecrackers. All of the chemicals used in synthesizing MDMA are also used in the production of high explosives. Throughout the world, these chemicals are under strict state control. Meanwhile, in India, some people manage to steal the necessary reagents from chemical plants. Therefore, we urgently need to buy as much as possible. We may not have such an opportunity later. We can produce ten kilograms in a year. Do you realize how much money we could earn, Vasya?"

"Yeah, Vova, I understand. Sometimes I get scared thinking about the kind of game we've started to play. Do you realize, Vova, that the state is lobbying for the sale of cocaine and heroin through corrupt politicians? According to their law, cocaine and heroin are the safest drugs. You can safely keep two hundred and fifty grams of cocaine and one hundred grams of heroin at home and you won't be jailed for it. But MDMA could be the main problem for the sale of hard drugs. If there is no MDMA on sale, then people will start to buy cocaine. Heroin is for local have-nots, while cocaine is more for wealthy tourists. You need ten times as much cocaine for a night, as its effect lasts for only fifteen or twenty minutes. The effect of MDMA lasts for four hours. At the beginning of the season, the police arrived from Bombay and detained the main MDMA supplier, the Israeli Ida. He was released a month later, but MDMA immediately disappeared from Goa after that. And its price skyrocketed. Where have you seen that cocaine costs a hundred bucks and MDMA costs a hundred and fifty bucks per gram? And they don't bother the old cocaine dealers, who continue safely selling their coke."

"Vasya, stop going on about your psychedelic bullshit. I don't care how people earn dough. If I could make coke, I would make it instead. You know I don't take anything at all, and I don't like drugs. It would be better if you thought about who could buy our Dymich. We have prepared two hundred grams. If we can get in touch with Tamir, we can sell a lot with his help."

"Vova, can't your minister's son find us clients?"

"I asked him about that, but he is staying silent. It's not his level to sell two hundred grams. He will be interested when we prepare ten kilos. Tamir is the caliber we need. The only thing is that it's dangerous to work with him. His police cover from the parties is in opposition to our minister's son."

"We won't get in touch with Tamir in the near future, he is in Ukraine at the moment. I'll try to talk to him when he comes back at the start of the season. He's unlikely to do something bad to me. Our daughters are friends and are in the same class at school."

"Vasya, put your thinking cap on. Where can we get money? Otherwise, we can't do anything till the start of the season. Do you have any friends still living in Goa who could buy two hundred grams?"

"Vova, what do you think about Dima Lucky? He works for Tamir. Shall we offer it to him?"

"Vasya, he tried to scam you out of your USSR restaurant!"

"He tried, but an attempt doesn't count. He forced me to sell him an unprofitable restaurant. It's still not really clear who was scammed. I am personally grateful to him for it. I don't think he'd dare to turn me over to the cops without Tamir's knowledge."

"But he could try to con you out of money."

"Well, Vova, I'm not such a mug to get conned during a deal. Everything should turn out fine if he pays in advance. I have a meeting with him today. He's coming here soon to get his money back. He wasn't issued a five-year visa in Thailand in the end. He came back with a three-month visa. I took fifteen hundred dollars for a visa from him a month ago. I've promised to return the money. I'll try to offer him MDMA instead of money. He might agree."

***

"You've come at last!" I hold out my hand to Dima, who is climbing down from his yellow sports bike.

The strongly built man squeezes my hand, apparently wishing to show his strength.

"You're a swindler, Vasya. Have you brought me my money?"

"I've brought you your money, but why am I a swindler?"

"I believe, Vasya, that I flew to Thailand twice because of you. And I ended up without a visa."

"Dima, how should I know that Belarusians can't visas on the Thai border? You're Belarusian; you should have found everything out in Belarus in advance. I sell five-year visas to India and my clients get them in Thailand. Everything else, Dima, doesn't bother me. Here's your fifteen hundred dollars back. If you hadn't bought a ticket from Thailand to India, as you were told not to, and had instead stayed in Bangkok for a week, you would have a five-year visa now. By the way, I can give you MDMA instead of money, if you're interested."

"I don't need your MDMA, Vasya, give me the cash."

"As you wish, but I have MDMA for sixty dollars per gram," I say, giving him fifteen green notes.

"Where did you get MDMA, Vasya? It can't be found anywhere," Dima asks, looking at me from under his eyebrows, starting to show an obvious interest.

"Dima, I helped some chemists to get hold of some safrole oil to make MDMA from. They've sent me the first batch from Ukraine," I lie on the go. "MDMA goes like hot cakes for one hundred and fifty dollars per gram. If you want, I can give you a gram to try. I still have a hundred grams."

"I'll ask around," Dima says gruffly. "But, Vasya, I still consider that you owe me money for my pointless flight to Thailand. We'll talk about that later. I have no time right now. Give me your tester."

"By the way, I'd almost forgotten, Dima. I've prepared a consolation present for you. I saw one girl had this thing, and I immediately realized that I had to beg her to give it to me for you. You suffered in Thailand because of your country."

"What do you have in your bag, Vasya? Show it to me," Dima asks curiously, getting ready to mount his bike.

"It's a Belarusian flag. Standard size. You can't buy it anywhere here," I say, smiling and giving him the package.

"Are you mocking me, Vasya?" Dima says irritably, taking the bag with the Belarusian flag and the MDMA tester.

"No, Dima, I'm not mocking you. I'm sorry that things happened the way they did. You are the only one out of fifteen people who did not get a visa in Thailand through me. Maybe you can compensate your losses through selling MDMA," I say, barely holding back my smile.

"I'll call you today," Dima says without a smile, climbing on his motorbike.

379

Chapter 50. Part One. Inside.

"Give me a cigarette, my friend, but there's only silence in response, my friend did not return from the court yesterday[97]," Viktor sings, smiling and packing his things. "It's hard to believe, Vasya, that today marks exactly one year of my imprisonment for a jar of Novocain. Can it be true that I will really be released today?"

"You should be released. Today is the last day, and there has never been a case when the expert analysis didn't come within a year. The result of the analysis must come today. It's unlikely that someone added cocaine to your powder, Vitya. So, pack your things. You'll come here after the hearing to collect them, and will already be lying on the beach by evening."

"Vasya, I think that I will have to take a nitrowhite sleeping pill before the court hearing, so that my heart doesn't burst from happiness when the judge says that I am free. I may run up and kiss her in the heat of madness. I could be arrested for insulting the judge."

"I don't want to take sleeping pills with you, Vitya, but I'll have a smoke in honor of your release with pleasure. Only God knows when we'll next smoke together. Here is the last piece of hashish, you crumble it and I'll peal this orange. I also have some strawberries, Vitya. My mother delivered me some food yesterday."

"Yeah, thank your mom for the fruit," Viktor says, assembling our smoking device from a plastic bottle, foil and a pen.

"Vitya, nobody in the world loves us as much as our moms do. My wife, while she was still in Goa, came every other time at the end, and constantly moaned that it was difficult for her to drive to see me once a week. She didn't want to go around the restaurants to collect the revenue from sales of kvass. She didn't even have to prepare the kvas, which was made by a specially trained Indian woman. When she left for Russia, she said she would only wait for me for six months. I'm happy that my mom and brother arrived in Goa. My mom travels to see me for three hours by bus with a backpack full of fruit, and she is always happy to see me."

"And where are your thousands of friends, whom you talked to me about constantly, Vasya?" Viktor says, handing me the bong.

"I don't know what to answer you, Vitya. Everyone has their own troubles and problems, they've all got lost somewhere."

"I know what the problem is, Vasya. Drug dealers do not have friends. You are surrounded by cronies, beggars, clients, buyers, and whores. All sorts of people, but not friends. It's because you sell them oblivion. No matter what drugs it may be, good or bad, psychedelics or opiates, all these

---

[97] Give me a cigarette, my friend, but there's only silence in response, my friend did not return from the court yesterday - paraphrased lyrics of a famous Russian song, with the word 'court' replacing 'battle'.

drugs disconnect them from reality for a while. And then, when their effect ceases, we live with the memories of them. And it doesn't matter how often you use them, every half an hour or once a month. Everyone who buys drugs wants to lose connection with the reality they are not happy with for a while. People waste their lives making money, and then give that money to a drug dealer to get a few hours of illusion. Drug dealers take part of their lives. Who will like them for that? Everyone just fakes love and friendship in order to get a cheap illusion. People only like drug dealers till they are under the influence of drugs. You are lonely, Vasya, just like I am. It's our reality. Where are they, the friends who are willing to blow up the wall, or to arrange an escape, to get you out of here? Vasya, you have your mother and daughter; they really love you. They do not need anything from you. Whereas everyone else has some selfish purpose."

"I've just come up with an idea, Vitya," I say, exhaling a big puff. "There is some truth in your words, I just don't want to believe that I am a drug dealer. I've never considered myself to be a drug dealer, although that may be my illusion. I want to ask my brother, while he is still here, to put up announcements in the Russian restaurants in North Goa. My photo with the heading 'HELP!' and the wording below: 'Friends, I need your help.' I'll write that I was arrested in a trumped-up case and that I'll have to sit here for ten years if I don't find the money for a lawyer. I'll say that I feel bad and lonely here, without money and support. So, I'll see, Vitya, whether I have friends or not. I won't have another such chance to check my friends. My illusion about the members of the united Russian psychedelic colony coming running to help their fellow countryman at the first call is falling apart. Vitya, my open letter will confirm or deny your statement that I am a drug dealer."

"If I were you, Vasya, I wouldn't do that. It sounds like begging. Wouldn't you feel awkward to beg for money from people?"

"Well, first of all, it's not awkward, because I've really run out of money. I can't even buy cookies, let alone hash. And I'm not even talking about the lawyer. Where can I get ten thousand dollars to pay for his services? I just don't know. I hope that my Lena will sell our apartment by that time. Secondly, I am writing a book, Vitya, and I would like to understand and describe everything that is happening to me. My book is my confession. Maybe, the heavens have sent me here, to prison, in order to understand myself. Look, Vitya, what a beautiful orange I have," I say, holding the pealed fruit on my palm, lit by a bright ray of sunlight falling through the small window. "I think it's a good sign. You'll be released, Vitya, the orange is proof."

"You're stoned again, Vasya," Viktor laughs, breaking off half of the orange. "An orange is always a good sign, especially in prison. An orange is a symbol of freedom."

"Look, there's an article about drug dealers again," the old Indian rapist with hairy ears hands me a newspaper.

"Vitya, look, there were arrests at the Curley's trance bar. The owner of Sonic Cafe was detained," I say, reading the Goan crime news. "The article also says that only Ida, Apollo and Tamir remain at large."

"Well, Vasya, now they have the official status of drug dealers," Viktor laughs, tying his pants with a rope made out of a towel. "The opposition party must be digging around about them, because the interior minister himself provides cover for the Goan drug dealers. Nobody dares bother them."

"Vitya, how many kilos have you lost in a year?" I ask, watching Viktor fixing his loose pants.

"I've lost fifteen kilos, and I am very happy. I hope I'll buy some new pants tomorrow."

"Viktor!" The loud voice of a guard is heard echoing in the empty hallway. "Bus to Mapusa court."

"I'm coming in five minutes, I'm almost ready. Well, it's time to go now," Viktor says, putting a headband made from an old T-shirt on his forehead.

"Vitya, you look like a veteran of the Vietnam War. Long, gray hair, held up by a rubber band around your forehead, two-months of stubble, and a shirt with psychedelic mushrooms embroidered on the chest."

"Vasya, I was arrested in these very clothes last year, after the Arambol freak carnival, when I returned home while tripping on acid. Just imagine, Vasya, if I am released today, the cops will give me my cell phone back, and there is half a trip of LSD under the battery from last year's carnival. Today, the carnival will be held again in Arambol. Just imagine, I can take the half trip that I didn't have time to take at the last carnival, close my eyes and find myself tripping again at the same carnival, only a year later. I'll have a sort of year-long trip."

"Not a bad trip, Vitya. When you're outside, have fun at the carnival for me. I don't think I will take food at lunch for you today. Good luck to you, Vitya. Look, our cellmates are ready to say goodbye to you. I'll wait for you to come after lunch for fifteen minutes to take your stuff. I'll say goodbye then. I'll gather your things in a bag, and write the phone numbers of friends and my mother on the cover of your dictionary. Good luck!"

Chapter 50. Part Two. Outside.

"Are you ready, Vova?"

"I'm always ready."

"Then everything is going according to plan."

"Vasya, I'll stand at the appointed place in thirty minutes. Boyana will meet you. You'll take the money from Dima and give it to her. Then you'll get on your bike and drive along the path to my car, take the bag with MDMA from me and give it to Dima. Just watch carefully what is happening around you. It takes three minutes on foot to get there from the place where you'll wait for Dima Lucky."

"I'll get to you by bike. I promised Dima I'll be back within two minutes. He'll come with an Englishman. The Englishman will give me five thousand bucks and Dima will stay with him as a guarantee that I won't run off with the money. I'll give Dima two hundred bucks for that later. If everything turns out well, the Englishman will be ready to buy another hundred grams. See you soon, Vova. I'm going to get ready, I've just woken up. I was sterilizing straw all night long again. The first mushrooms will sprout in a week."

"So long, good luck. I'll be waiting for you at the appointed place," Vova ends the conversation.

***

It would be good to have a smoke before leaving. However, it's a serious deal, I shouldn't get stoned now. I'll relax after I close the deal. It's the first major deal. A thousand bucks is not a big sum to earn for such a risk, but, on the other hand, I haven't invested my own money. On the plus side, we'll soon have ten kilograms of MDMA. Then I'll hit the jackpot. What should I wear, smart or casual clothes? I'd better be fancy dressed. Today, it's necessary to look like a real drug dealer. You can expect anything from Dima. Let him think that I'm not afraid of anything. Red zebra print hat, horn-rimmed glasses, bright Caribbean shirt, and Ali Baba trousers. Well, I'm ready. It will be good to get there a little early, to check that everything is okay. What have I forgotten? Oh, I haven't looked at my pets today. How are my mushrooms doing? I'll just have a look at them and leave then. God, what a pleasant mushroom smell! I would like to admire you all day long. My first mushroom should appear in a week. I'll say goodbye to you for a while. I'll sell the MDMA quickly, and come back to you. I need to infect some straw for you today.

Having reached the appointed place, I see the Englishman waiting for me.

"Hi, John, and where's Dima Lucky?"

"I don't know, he promised to come," the elderly, lean Englishman says, smoking a cigarette nervously. "Vasya, have you brought the goods?"

"Hold on, John, you will get the goods. I just have to call Dima. His phone is turned off for some reason. How will we close the deal without him?"

"John, have you brought the money?"

"Yes, I have, look," the Englishman shows me a wad of money, pulling it out of his pocket with trembling fingers. "But I won't give you money in advance without Dima." Dima hasn't come to the deal, the son of a bitch. He is sure to ask for a cut later. The girl is about to come and I am supposed to give the money to her. What should I do? The deal could be scuttled because of one idiot. Well, John, we'll do without Dima. Here is Boyana. "Have you brought the MDMA?" I ask Vova's friend, watching how an Indian standing not far away is staring at her.

"No, I haven't. Vasya, what did you and Vova agree on? I have to take money from you, and you have to take MDMA from Vova's car now," Vova's Buryat friend says petulantly in Russian.

"What should I do, Boyana? Dima Lucky hasn't come, and this one," I point at the Englishman, who is standing nearby and not understanding anything, "doesn't want to give the money in advance. I can understand him though. He's afraid for his bucks. Well, okay, no guts no glory," I wave my hand. "Everything seems to be calm around, there's nothing suspicious. Boyana, go back to Vova's car. I'll drive to him, take the MDMA, give it to the Englishman and take the money. John, stay here, I'll bring you the goods now," I say, mounting my red scooter.

I chose a good place for the deal. A car cannot not pass here, and the junction consists of three paths. If something happens, no one will catch me, or find me in these reeds. But there should be no 'ifs'. Everything will go smoothly.

***

"Vova, give me Dymich," I say, not getting off my scooter and holding out my hand to the open car window. "Dima Lucky hasn't come, the Englishman is afraid to give the money in advance. But everything seems to be quiet; there are no strange dudes around. He showed me the money. I'll give him the goods and bring you the money in a couple of minutes."

"Here you go," Vova hands me a package with pinkish crystals. "Just no delays, Vasya, come back soon. I'll get nervous otherwise."

"Everything will be okay, Vova. I'll come back in two minutes."

***

"John, I've brought the goods, I just don't like that dude over there," I nod towards an Indian wearing sunglasses, sitting on a bike five meters away from us. "Come on, let's drive away a bit."

Having driven off about fifty meters, I stop and look in the mirror of my bike. The Englishman is slowly walking towards me, holding the bag with money with both hands. A strange car with blacked-out windows stands at the crossroads. Maybe I should drive another ten meters away.

"John, why are you standing there? Get on your bike and drive up here," I wave to him. Why are you so slow, Englishman? Drive fast, give me the money, and then take your time. I don't like that Indian staring at me from the other side of the road. It seems like he's going to leave, he is getting on his bike. I must have paranoia. It's not cool when I imagine that every Indian is a policeman. I have paranoia for sure. Yeah, he is leaving. But why is he staring at me like that? All Indians are curious like monkeys, so he stares. I'm dressed too bright for him, that's why he is watching me. John has finally reached me on foot.

"Put your money here," I shout nervously at him, pointing to the open side pocket of my pants.

I should start the bike, take the money, and get out of here. Vova must be rattled already.

"From hand to hand," the Englishman says, trembling, holding out the money hesitantly.

"Here is your Dymich, give me your bucks," I say, abruptly snatching his bag with the money.

Giving the bike full throttle and accelerating sharply, I drive out from the tiny street onto the bustling intersection. Fuck me, is this a frame-up?! The Indian who was staring at me, having driven off some distance, turns around and tries to ram me head on. Is he a cop? I should get out of here. Happen what may, even if they shoot at me. Looking in the rear-view mirror, I see the car with blacked-out windows driving up to the Englishman. Another Indian in sunglasses on a scooter is trying to reach the intersection, but a car that won't let him past forces him to slow down.

"Will you dare do the same, cowardly monkey!" I scream at the cop driving towards me.

I must somehow outwit him, otherwise he'll drive into me head-on. He is a cop for sure. He waves some document at me.

"Okay, I give up, I'm stopping," I shout to him, switching on the left-turn signal.

Seeing that I am going to stop at the edge of the road, the policeman brakes. Noticing a space that has formed between the traffic and the policeman, I accelerate sharply and drive into this gap. "Thank God I have a high-speed scooter," the first thought comes to mind, when I start to speed up and get away from the place where I was almost caught. "I'm doing a bunk, gods save me just once!"

I repeat the words of the famous Russian song without pause, like a prayer. I see in the rear-view mirror that the Indian who was trying to ram me is turning around, and is apparently going to chase me. What should I do? I can't go to Vova now as the lab is at his place. Should I throw the bag with money away? The cops may be waiting for me at the next intersection. No, I won't throw away the dough. I must come up with some idea. I notice that my hands and knees are shaking from fear. "Don't panic," I urge myself, biting my lower lip. I should zoom through the next intersection in high gear, and then, a hundred meters further on the left, there is a path that nobody knows. I'll lose my pursuers there. "I'm doing a bunk, gods save me just once! " I shout loudly, shooting through the busy unregulated crossroad in front of the Siolim church at maximum speed. I should drive into the jungle and bury the money. If they catch me with no money, nobody will be able to prove anything. Leaving the bike near the path leading up the hill, I run up, scratching my skin on the prickly bushes that treacherously try to detain me, catching me with their thorns. "I have to pull myself together, the main thing is not to forget this big tree," I think, burying the money in its roots.

"Hello, Vova, we have a problem, I was almost arrested. Come to the short cut leading to Saligao, right now. You'll see my bike by the side of the road, give me a honk, I'll come out of the jungle. Don't ask me any questions, it's not paranoia. I'm waiting for you."

Not wanting to talk for long on the phone, I interrupt his flood of questions, which are irrelevant now.

I have no time to put the phone back in my pocket and I hear it ringing again. "There you are, motherfucker," I look at the number shown on the display: Dima Lucky.

"Hello, Vasya, I'm sorry, I was five minutes late. Some Indians are hassling our Englishman here, they are demanding money from him. Where are you now?"

"Dima, what are you asking me about? I've just got away from the police, who your Englishman brought. And I'm wondering why you yourself did not come to the deal."

"I was delayed, Vasya, my bike broke down. It's good you got away, Vasya. But don't worry; they are not cops, just local bandits. They wanted to grab the MDMA from you. I've just spoken with them. They took the Dymich from the Englishman. Let John get himself out of it; it serves him right. It's his loss; he brought the tail with him. Where are you now, Vasya? I want to come to you."

"What does it matter where I am, Dima? I need to get out of here for a while. I don't believe you, Dima."

"Vasya, I had nothing to do with it. I am also thinking of getting away to northern India, to the Himalayas. I don't like this situation, Vasya. I am asking you where you are because you owe me two hundred bucks, for bringing you a client. We did the deal; you earned your money. When will you give me my dough?"

"Not now, Dima. See you in the Himalayas. Don't call me on this number any more," I say, switching my phone off.

"Catch me if you can".

MARITEE

Chapter 51. Part One. Inside.

"It's five p.m.," the toothless Iranian David says, looking at the photo of Dima Lucky once again. "Vasya, I have a big favor to ask you, when you are outside, don't touch Dima. Leave him to me; it will give me great pleasure to settle accounts with him. He's fond of cocaine, before he dies I want to rub his face in it. Let him die of it. For three years, I have been rotting behind bars because of him. I also know the Englishman, who came to you along with him. That Englishman loves heroin as well, he also brought the police to me, and was sniffing around for ages in order to grass me up. But I've known about him for a long time, he shopped a lot of people to the police. A friend of mine is doing ten years in Aguada jail thanks to that English bitch. I will settle the score with this Englishman for my friend. I could not live calmly, knowing that those two bitches are hanging about in Goa. Who will respect me if they remain unpunished? I am a professional drug dealer. I love my job. Viktor will be released from prison today, he must be receiving his passport and phone at the police station. Soon he will come here to take his stuff."

"David, I have already guessed about Viktor. You are the tenth person who has come to me and said sympathetically that Viktor is likely to be released. As if I couldn't live without him. I have already taken Vitya's pillow. I gave his mat to my neighbor."

Suddenly, the majority of my cellmates who were dozing on the floor, jump up on hearing Viktor's loud shout, in order to be the first to hear the good news.

"Good afternoon!" Viktor shouts loudly in Russian before entering the corridor.

"Well, here he is. He came to take his stuff," I say to David, ready to hug Viktor for the last time. "Well, Viktor, is it freedom?"

"Fuck freedom," my hairy, bearded Russian friend says with an idiotic laugh through the bars.

"What happened?" several cellmates ask in different languages at the same time.

"I'll tell you what happened. The result of my expert analysis has not come yet. They gave me eight more days; they don't want to release me as not guilty. In eight days, I should be released on bail as a suspect. I'll have to pay two thousand bucks to the state as a deposit, so that I don't run away from India. All previous prisoners who were waiting for the results of the expert analysis, got their reports in one year. But I haven't got it for some reason."

Having opened a door to the cell to let Viktor in, the guard slams the iron bars shut again.

"Welcome home, we've missed you," David holds his hand out to Viktor.

"I didn't take dinner for you, Vitya. Or rather took your portion of fish and already ate it."

"I don't care about dinner. I'm full. I ate with the police officers at the restaurant on the way back from the court. It is only possible in India to pay the guards a hundred rupees and to go with them to a restaurant in front of the prison."

"Vitya, we have to take your mat back from our neighbor."

"I see that you have already helped yourself to my stuff," Viktor says, laughing and kicking my former torn pillow.

"Vitya, I can give you a cup of tea, it's cold but sweet, and there are also two kinds of cookies. You can crunch on one of them with the tea. You can dip the other in the tea and eat it wet. I have nothing else to alleviate your grief."

"I could do with a cup of tea, but I can't understand one thing – why I'm still here. The cops say they have a legitimate eight days to file the charge sheet. But it seems to me that they intentionally lost my expert analysis, because those bitches know that there was no cocaine. That's why they lost my papers. The Italian said that his friend has lived in Goa for four years. He is restricted from travelling abroad. He was released on bail, and his expert analysis has still not come yet. For four years he has been attending the court twice a month, and nothing happens."

"Well, Vitya, you wanted to live in India, that's your free visa for the whole period from the state."

"It's good," Viktor says, giggling foolishly. "But I want to see my mom and dad, they are old already."

"After your release in eight days, you will go to an Internet café and talk to your parents via web camera."

"Vasya, I have never used the Internet. I don't even have an email address. My dad surfs the Internet all day long. You won't believe it, but I have no idea how to use it."

"Wow. This is the first time I have seen a man who has never used the Internet."

"That's the way I am, Vasya, I'm unique. Looks like I will need to master the Internet outside," Viktor says, wrapping his pillow in the old T-shirt that he has just taken off. "Well, there's nothing for it; let's get stoned!"

"Well, why not?" I agree without hesitation, reaching for Vitya's glasses case, where our daily dose of charas is kept.

"By the way, Vasya, I learned some news from the police, another Russian guy will join us soon. Do you remember Kostik, the owner of Sky Bar?"

"Of course, I do. Was he arrested for selling cocaine?"

"I wish he was! He killed a taxi driver and is serving time in Panjim prison now. He got into a fight with a taxi driver, who died later that night of a brain hemorrhage."

Chapter 51. Part Two. Outside.

"Finally, you have come."

"What happened? Tell us, Vasya."

"Somebody just almost scammed me out of the money," I say to Vova, looking around. "I guess it was the police, but I ran away. I took the money, handed over the goods, and managed to escape from under the noses of six police officers, who were stunned by such impudence. Four of them were in a car and two rode scooters."

"And I thought that you wanted to scam me out of the money. You said you would be back in two minutes and disappeared. Did you get the money?"

"Yes, I covered it with earth under that tree. Dima Lucky just called me and said that it was not the police. He said that gangsters wanted to screw me. Vova, what will we do?"

"First of all, dig the money up, and then you have to hide for a couple of weeks. It means that Dima shopped you. But to whom? If it was gangsters then we can settle it. If it was the police – you need to leave the country. If it was the police, the first thing they would do is visit the owner of your scooter. It's good that the owners don't know you. Vasya, I will go to them today and give them your scooter back. The owners are my good friends; they will tell me if the police visit them. I'd risk my life on their honesty."

"And I, in turn, will send someone home after a few days to gather information. If nobody is looking for me, it will be possible to go back home in a week. Vova, here are your two hundred grand and fifty for me," I say, brushing the red Goan earth off my hands. "If the owners of my house say that the police are looking for me, then my mushrooms are lost. My first mushroom sprouted today. "

"Vasya, are you crazy? Your life is at stake, and you are thinking about mushrooms. Vasya, you urgently need to change your image. Shave off your moustache and beard, get some other glasses, buy new clothes, and throw your red hat away now. I will take the money to the bank. You get on your bike and go along this road to Parra. Do you know where DJ Yura lives?

"Of course I know, Vova, but he has overstayed for a year. He is unlikely to allow me to stay at his place. He doesn't even turn the light on in the evening, he is so afraid of the police."

"Vasya, why didn't he buy a visa? He doesn't look poor. "

"Vova, his passport expired, and the Russian Federal Drug Control Service caught him, he barely had time to escape to India. He has been wanted in Russia for three years. And he has been living here with an expired visa for a year. He's got paranoia, he sees the police everywhere."

"Will he let you stay in his house for a few hours, Vasya?"

"I think he will."

"Ok, then go! Shave your beard, take some clothes, and I'll be there in an hour. We will go and buy you some new clothes. Vasya, you will have to live the life of an ordinary tourist for a while. And on your way to him, think about a place where you can hide for a couple of weeks. See you in an hour at Yura's place. Don't worry, everything will be fine. It's good that you ran away from the cops. You are a brave guy. And the sticker on your bike is cool," Vova says, pointing at the 'Catch me if you can!' sticker on my scooter. "Just think of faces of the cops when they saw this sign disappearing with their money. Don't call Dima Lucky anymore. I give you a 100% guarantee that it was his tip-off. He got even with you for the Belarusian flag."

Chapter 52. Part One. Inside.

"Electricity finish, fucking Pakistan took our electricity," a voice in the darkness says.

Various strange sounds are heard from different cells. Someone has started to meow, someone barks like a dog, and someone else mimics a baby's cry.

"Vasya, what surrealism surrounds us," I hear Viktor's voice in the darkness.

"It's not surrealism, Vitya, it's a sort of madhouse. And it's murderers, rapists and robbers that are meowing and barking. I feel like I am in a zoo, not in prison. If only you knew, Vitya, how much I've missed the darkness. I've been sleeping with a light switched on for nine months. It's a kick to just be in total darkness for a while."

"Just imagine, Vasya, we're now in complete darkness in a locked cell with ten killers and two homosexual rapists. Is this really happening to us? It's not a dream?"

"It's strange, Vitya, but I don't feel any fear. I can't believe that the people who are sitting around us now could cause us any harm. They are more like children who are being punished for misbehaving. It's hard to believe that they did such terrible things. Russian criminals look different. They look like beasts, whereas these ones just look like monkeys. They were naughty, did something wrong, and now they sit here. They scratch their heads and ask God every day why he let them commit their crimes."

"I agree, Vasya, most of them got here because of their natural stupidity."

"It's a pity, Vitya, that you haven't seen the serial killer from the first floor. He really has the eyes of a beast."

"Why is it a pity? On the contrary, I am glad that I haven't seen him. Tomorrow I'll be released and I'll never have the opportunity to see those eyes, and I'm extremely happy about it," Viktor says, rustling a plastic bag in the darkness in search of matches.

"In theory, Vitya, you have to be released tomorrow. A year has passed, the judge gave them eight days to draw up your charge sheet. By law, you have to be released tomorrow. A week has passed quickly, like a couple of days."

The electricity switches on abruptly and the TV comes on loudly, causing everyone to jump and screw up their eyes. The entire jail joyfully welcomes the electricity with applause and monkey cries. We are also pleased that the electricity has come on, because electricity means, above all, that the fans spin continuously on the ceiling. During the fifteen minutes of total darkness without the fans my shirt has become covered in sweat as if I was in a sauna.

"It's so hot without the fans, Vitya. God forbid that they break, we could get heat stroke."

"It's India, Vasya, anything can happen here. We must be ready for anything. I'll go to the toilet and pour water over myself, I am as wet as a frog," Viktor says, hanging a towel around his neck. "And also, Vasya, we have run out of matches. How will we smoke?"

"We could ask our cellmates."

"There's no point asking them. You know that these have-nots can't even buy matches, let alone tobacco."

"Vitya, go and pour water over yourself, we'll think of something regarding fire," I say, wiping my body with a damp towel. "Churchill, you said you had some kind of fish oil? Pour me a bit in a medicine bottle cap," I say to the old rapist with hairy ears.

"I've got the oil. But it was used in the kitchen for frying fish. If you want to put it on your hair, you'll smell like fish."

"Indians put oil on their hair. I need it for something else. I want to make an oil candle. I'll stick a wick made from a piece of cloth in the medicine bottle cap, pour oil into the cap, and set it alight. And Vitya and I will be able to light our bong from it."

"Vasya, will you give me a cookie if I pour you some fish oil?"

"Of course I will, Churchill, but only when the buffet comes in a week. I'll buy cookies and give them to you. Now I have nothing."

"Well, Kulibin[98], have you made fire?" Viktor says to me, coming out of the toilet with a piece of soap attached to a string.

"Vitya, why have you tied a string to the soap?"

"It's always falling into the toilet hole, and it is convenient to pull it out with the string."

"Vitya, I've prepared an oil candle. Now I am trying to get fire from the mosquito coil. We need to blow up a piece of coal. I'll put a sheet of oiled paper on it. We'll have fire soon," I whisper, gently blowing on the tiny red spot of light.

The small black dots that appear on the sheet of oiled paper are gradually framed by a red pattern with a scorched hole in the middle.

"Well, I lit my candle. Now it's necessary to protect it from the fans," I say, covering the little flame with one hand, and feeling with the other to find a spot in the corner without air movement.

"It's a sizzler today," Viktor says, taking out the piece of hash hidden in the glasses case.

"Heat doesn't break your bones. It's far better to clean your karma from sins in an Indian jail, than to clean your tarpaulin boots from clay in a Russian jail. Vitya, do you remember I told you about my buddy, who escaped from the Russian cops through Turkey to India?"

"Vasya, are you talking about Valera Mulik?"

"Yes, I am, Vitya. He flew to India using his friend's passport. I called my Lena in Russia today and she told me that he was eventually arrested there. The trial lasted for only two weeks and he was sentenced to five years in prison. Imagine, Vitya, he lived on the run for three years, and then decided to return to Russia for some reason. He lived in great comfort here, and then something pulled him back to the homeland."

---

[98] Kulibin - a Russian mechanic and inventor.

"Is he a complete fool, Vasya? To go back while on the wanted list. He even didn't have his passport."

"Vitya, he quietly flew from India using his friend's passport again. He successfully passed the border control at the Moscow airport and got caught for a trifle. He bought a train ticket using his old passport. And now there is a unified computer database everywhere. He was arrested somewhere near Saratov, while he was sleeping peacefully in his compartment."

"Yeah, Vasya, many Russian Goans are doing time in our prisons now. They get used to freedom and relax. You won't be put behind bars for a kilogram of hashish here, while in Russia you could be sentenced to five years for a small lump."

"Do you remember Telescope, Vasya?"

"Of course I remember him. I sold him two hundred grams of charas for export to Russia five years ago. He stuffed the hash up his ass and passed two border controls with flying colors. He was arrested with hash in St. Petersburg a while ago. One of his friends paid him back a debt in charas. He put three hundred grams in his pocket and went on the Metro. He was arrested during a random search at a passport check[99]. He won't be coming back here in the near future."

"I heard that story from someone. I feel sorry for Telescope, he was a nice guy. It is one thing that we were earning money, but he didn't deal, he simply loved smoking himself."

"How can I take a puff from your candle, Vasya? The flame is small. If you tilt the bong the hash falls out. And if you tilt the candle, fish oil drips onto the hash."

"You need four hands to smoke like this. I'll hold the candle and direct the tip of the bong. You hold the other end and smoke through the tube. Just be careful not to put the flame out, otherwise we'll have to waste a lot of time to getting a new one. By the way, have you heard, Vitya, that Idu and Apollo have been arrested recently? Everyone thought that they were untouchable. But they have found themselves in jail, too. Their police cover didn't help them."

"The whole prison is gossiping about it," Viktor frowns, exhaling a stream of bitter smoke into my face. "Chewing tobacco is just disgusting. It's a hundred times worse than our wild tobacco."

"I don't have anything else, Vitya. This tobacco matches our life. Come on, you hold our construction and I'll smoke."

A guard who has approached the bars, smiles while watching me smoke the bong.

"Churchill, take a pack of soap out of my bag and exchange it for tobacco with the guard, I'm busy right now. You see, he is waiting for me near the bars."

The old rapist happily jumps up from his seat to fulfill the assignment, knowing he will get a packet of cookies for his work."

"Vitya, do you remember Sergey from Chelyabinsk, who jumped from the bridge?"

"Are you talking about Sergey, who bought MDMA from you before his death?"

---

[99] Passport check - the police check the passports of passengers at random every day in the Metro (subway) in Russia.

"Yeah, but he bought his last fifty grams from Idu. It looks like Idu will also have to work off his karma in prison. There must be a serious re-division of the drug market taking place. He paid the police chief, Pashish. Who could have thought that the Israeli drug mafia would be arrested?"

"Well, who is next?" Viktor asks, leaning back on his bunk.

"Tamir is the only officially recognized drug dealer from those listed in the paper who is still at large. If he is not a fool, he is unlikely to return to Goa. They say that the new police team that has replaced the old one is not corrupt yet. Moreover, there are two squads of anti-drug police now, both spying on each other. Pashish can't provide any cover for Tamir now. Pashish has been suspended from the position of drug police chief. He was given another position in another town. When the cops took me to the court, one pair of guards said that Tamir is a good friend, while the other asked me to give him information on Tamir, saying he is a big fish and they will catch him sooner or later. Just imagine, Vitya, if you're released tomorrow and there are no drug dealers around. What will you do?"

"Vasya, don't tempt me. I won't sell drugs anymore. I'm fed up with drug dealing. I just wish to be released tomorrow."

"Don't worry, Vitya, it's your last night in jail. By law, you should definitely be released tomorrow."

Chapter 52. Part Two. Outside.

"I've been stuck in here for four days already. I have something to ask you, Greedy. The mushrooms in my house are about to sprout. We must save my mushrooms."

"Vasya, you've convinced me once and for all that you are completely mad. I will be arrested if I go to your house. The police must be patrolling near your house day and night. You ran away with their money. Vasya, do you think the cops will simply forgive you for taking five grand from them?"

"Greedy, it was not an organized operation. They just wanted to con me out of money. No one has come to the owner of my scooter. If it was a real police case, the cops would first approach the owner of my bike to find me. Nobody is patrolling near my house. I sent someone there to check the situation out, everything is all right. Marinka, a friend of my wife, went to my place with her son yesterday. I told her to tell the owners of my house that I have gone for a rest in Palolem and asked her to feed the fish in my aquarium. You know, I've got piranhas in the aquarium in my house. Well, Marina said everything was quiet yesterday. Nobody was waiting in ambush near my house. The owners said that nobody has been asking where I am."

"Do you have any drugs at your place?"

"I had a bottle of acid and a few grams of Dymich, but Marinka took everything away. Now I have just a couple of marijuana plants and psilocybin mushrooms at home. But it's not a criminal offense according to local legislation. My mushrooms could die. They are covered over. I am afraid they may suffocate. I am very worried about them. The covering should be carefully cut off with scissors, but the scissors and hands should be sterilized with spirit first. I have a large bottle of spirit on my table. Be a good soul: go to my house this evening. Besides, we'll be able to check again whether someone is spying on my house. If anything happens, you can say you've come to feed the fish."

"What about your marijuana, Vasya? Should I water it?"

"No, you shouldn't, Greedy. Don't worry about the weed, it can grow without me for another month. Everything is on timers. The compressors switches on when necessary, and the light is turned off at the right time."

"Okay, Vasya. I'll go this evening and save your mushrooms."

"Greedy, feed my piranhas at the same time. I have some meat in the refrigerator. Those poor things must be starving by now."

"Don't worry, Vasya, everything will be okay. What does Dima Lucky say about this whole story with the cops?"

"Dima says he is innocent. He blames it all on the Englishman, but I don't believe him. When I talked with him the last time, I told him I was leaving Goa. I haven't spoken to him since. I believe it was his honeytrap. My plantation should be transferred to another location as soon as possible. I have already agreed with someone from Arambol. If everything goes well, I'll move the mushrooms and weed to his place next week and go to the Himalayas for a couple of months to wait until everything settles here."

"Are you going to move everything to Anton's place?"

"How did you guess, Greedy?"

"He is the only Russian who stays here in the rainy season, as he's not allowed to leave. Aren't you afraid, Vasya, to trust a Russian cop to look after your marijuana and mushrooms?"

"He's not a cop now. He was once, but now he's on the run. If he returns to Russia, he could be sentenced to ten years in prison. Cops and criminals are all equal here, in Goa. We all are human beings, we all like drugs."

Chapter 53. Part One. Inside.

I really don't want to open my eyes. I have been lucky to have nice dreams all week long. Every night I meet with my family and friends. I go to great trance parties. I snort MDMA, drink beer, and eat fried meat. I really don't want to see that idiot, Viktor, right now and hear his terrible English accent.

"Vasiliy, your breakfast. Would you be so kind to give me ketchup please," I hear the voice of Viktor, who, racking his memory, makes huge pauses between words and doesn't trouble himself about pronouncing them correctly."

"Vasiliy you want breakfast?" he continues to speak in broken English

"That's it, I'm waking up, Vitya," I say, pulling my sleeping mask off my face. "Why on Earth is it you again? When will my daughter wake me up again? When will you be released, Vitya?"

"I don't know," Viktor says, smiling a silly smile, giving me a cup of tea.

"Who does know, Vitya? You don't know anything, that's why you're still here. You are unsure about everything. When you are asked any question, you always answer, 'I don't know,' or 'Maybe yes, maybe no.'"

"What are you so geared-up about, Vasya, first thing in the morning? Didn't you dream about MDMA last night? And anyway, Vasya, let's speak English as we agreed yesterday."

"Vitya, it's because of you that I have started to say sometimes 'What can to do' instead of 'what can I do.' The entire prison corrects your wrong phrases, and you just laugh like a fool. Go to hell with your English, Vitya. Learn it first, and then speak it. Instead of conversational English, you have begun to learn aristocratic Oxford phrases, pronouncing them with a country bumpkin accent. The Greek, the Italian, and the Iranian have already told you that the Shakespearean phrases you're memorizing are only used by the Queen of England. You should learn simple phrases first."

"What if I go to England from India, Vasya? What if I have to talk in polite company in England?" Viktor says, spreading ketchup on a roll.

"Oh right. And what are you going to talk about? Are you going to tell them that Russian criminal chanson should be mixed with trance? Are you going to advise them that the high from ephedrine is softer than the high from amphetamine? Someone could only talk to you about nothing. You don't read books or newspapers, you don't watch movies, and you can't distinguish between good and bad music. You should stay in Chapora, near the juice center, and chat with the other dorks like you under the banyan tree. They know nothing, and don't see their future, either. The only thing is that you won't be able to talk with them for long, Vitya, as they'll tell you to get lost pretty quickly."

"Why would they tell me to get lost? Because I know rare English words and freaks from Chapora don't?

"Words aren't the point, Viktor. Your stupid manner of communication is the point. You always have the opposite opinion during a conversation. You don't care what you talk about, you just want to wind up the person you are speaking to with your conflicting opinion, and then laugh at him. No one wants to talk to you. You laugh like an idiot and don't even notice when you offend people. You've already driven me crazy with your conflicting opinions. I wake up every morning with the thought that I'll have to look at your stupid grin and listen to your nonsense all day."

"Have you looked in a mirror, Vasya?" Viktor says angrily, pouring instant oatmeal and cocoa powder into his warm tea.

"Yeah, Viktor, thank you for the mirror. Thanks to you, I've realized that you're like my clone, just ten years later. I met my clone in prison, and he turned out to be an asshole. I refuse to notice in myself everything that irritates me about you, Vitya. That's why I thank you for being such an asshole. I can only acknowledge all my flaws after seeing them in such an exaggerated form as you are demonstrating. I can change for the better thanks to you. You are bad example for me. By constantly making errors, you save me from them. You refuse to see your future and that's where all your uncertainty comes from. When you radiate the energy of uncertainty to the outside world, you get the same thing back. I cannot see my future, either. I have accumulated too many problems in my life. And I will have to solve them after my release. Like you, I don't know what I would like to see in my future. However, thanks to you, I'm starting to realize that seeing my own future is my main goal now. I have to carry out this difficult work every day. It's the only way I can materialize my desires. If I am sure about what I want to have in my life, I'll definitely achieve it. When I'm taken to court twice a month, I look out of the window at the living world and realize how many difficulties I will have to overcome upon my release. I have no money and no job, just huge debts. As of now, I can't see my future in Russia, or in India. But I will work on myself. I don't want to live in uncertainty, like you do. In Russia, I will have to prove to Dymkov that I don't owe him anything, whereas he claims I owe him thirty-five thousand dollars in relation to Hemp. Another thing is that I have to borrow at least ten thousand dollars somewhere in order to get out of here. In addition, I'll have to provide for my family somehow. So when the guards bring me back to jail from the court, I feel more comfortable here. Here, I feel as if I am protected from all my problems. I am fed and guarded. I have free medical care. I do what I love doing. I learn English, play chess and tennis, write my book. I sometimes catch myself thinking that I don't want to go back and face the challenges awaiting me outside. But that is wrong. Despite all my problems, I want to get out of here, and I know for sure that I will succeed. You can't give up and admit defeat by life's difficulties. Having realized this, I have started to imagine my future in a positive way. I will deal with all my problems. I just wish to get out of here as soon as possible. Sometimes it's difficult to see our future, but that's the only way I can influence it, I don't have any other way. Three killers have been released recently. Each of them, in spite of everything, believed every day that he would get out of here. Mario was under investigation for three years and was released, despite the fact he killed his girlfriend. Sunny and Baloo also got out even though they killed two people. They never said, 'I don't know', or 'Maybe yes, maybe no'. They clearly saw their future in freedom and were eager to get out of here. They never radiated the energy of uncertainty, unlike you, Vitya. It seems that you don't want to get out. I get the feeling that you have given up. You're like a fatalist. You have lost heart and are now waiting until everything is over. But your life is at stake. You understand that you were treated harshly. You should have got out of here two months ago. You've been hanging around here for fourteen months. I will have been here for a year in two weeks, and you still can't manage to get free, saying, 'I don't know' and 'maybe.' I've said goodbye to you ten times already."

"I can't help it if the circumstances around me are like this," Viktor says, not taking his attention away from eating swollen cereal flakes from his cup of tea. "Everybody else gets it right, Vasya, and I get it ass-backwards. A year has passed but the expert analysis has not come. So, I must be released on bail. If the analysis comes and shows a positive drug reaction, the judge starts a trial. But my analysis hasn't come, and I wasn't released on bail."

"Vitya, it happens like that because you don't want to see your future. If you had got on the ball in advance and had paid your lawyer, then everything could have happened differently. But you held off as long as you could and this is the result. Everyone who wanted to get out of here has got out already, and you're still in jail. You do everything in your life differently to other people. Moreover, you do so not based on logic, but because of your opposite opinion. Everybody writes an application for a phone call in the established form, 'Dear warden, could you let me make a phone call...' And you just scribble four words on a piece of paper, 'for me need phone.' Everybody gets permission, whereas you are allowed to call last in line, a week later. Everybody tries to get information from their lawyer as early as possible in order to consider their next move, but you wait for a week until you're allowed to make a call. When they go to court, everyone dresses neatly and has a shave; whereas you, like a hippie, put party clothes on and go to the court unshaven. Do you understand that you are treated like a rich fool here? You never remember the date of your next court hearing. You don't even ask the lawyer why you are still here. You were too lazy to write a letter to get permission to go to the bank and withdraw money from the ATM in order to give it to your lawyer for two weeks. I get the feeling you don't want freedom. Your idea of freedom has been narrowed down to a single desire, the desire to eat an oyster."

"Eating oysters is not my only desire, Vasya. I also want to swim in the sea and go to visit my mother in Russia for a week."

"Is that all? All your desires? Maybe you should have more of them? Then you'd get out of here quicker."

"What should I do? What will change, Vasya, if I start dressing like everyone else, start shaving and calling my lawyer the whole time? Is it my fault that at first the judge's husband was ill and she took sick leave to care for him? Then he died, and the judge did not work for two weeks. Then it was the damned Indian New Year and the court again didn't work for two weeks. Then the judge refused to release me, arguing that the police allegedly had a preliminary analysis that the showed I had cocaine, although nobody saw this piece of paper. The next two weeks I was waiting to be transferred to the Court of Appeals, and now the verdict has been put off three times for two weeks each time."

"Yesterday was the deadline, Vitya. Do you remember what your lawyer said? On April 12, he will send an assistant to the prison with good news for you if you are released on bail. If nobody comes, you have been rejected. Today is April 12 and nobody has come with good news. According to the law, it means you'll be sitting here, Vitya, until your analysis comes."

"But it will come one day, Vasya."

"Viktor, you tried to fuck the system, and now it's fucking you in response to you selling fake cocaine. An Italian lives here in Chapora. He has already been waiting for his analysis for four years. In my opinion, they just lost it. The Goan police won't allow your analysis to come with a negative cocaine reaction now. They'll take great pains, but won't allow another scandal to occur. The drug police chief, Pashish himself, along with six officers, has been sitting in jail for a month. They all face ten years in prison. Their application for release on bail has already been rejected. Did you read yesterday's newspaper? Oh yeah, you don't read newspapers. Well, twenty-eight kilos of hashish have disappeared from the seized drugs warehouse. Do you know what the drug police chief, Pashish, said when he was arrested? He said that white termite ants ate the hashish. That's what it says in the newspaper. First, Chetsi and Vasu's expert analysis somehow showed that they had paracetamol instead of a kilogram of heroin. Later, Ram-Ram got his analysis, which showed mint powder instead of a kilogram of heroin. All of the newspapers covered that. Can you imagine what will happen if your analysis also shows you had anesthetic powder instead of cocaine? Another few police officers will follow Pashish to prison. Their lives are at stake. They all have good connections. It's a piece of cake for them to lose your analysis. Meanwhile, no one will cancel a ruling of the Court of Appeal in the next five years."

"What about the Supreme Court? I will lodge an appeal with the Supreme Court."

"Viktor, you are in a country with a population of over a billion people, while there is only one Supreme Court for the whole of India. The Bombay Court of Cassation has three hundred thousand pending applications. The Delhi Supreme Court must have at least a million. Here in Goa, which is not as densely populated, you waited for the Cassation Court's ruling for almost a month. You'd wait in the queue for the verdict of the Supreme Court for five years."

"What can I do? Should I put my head in a noose, Vasya, or what?"

"Nothing can be done now, Vitya. It's too late already. Now you can only hope for a miracle. But they also occur frequently in India. It could happen any day, you just have to wait for it. I have to follow the same path, but I don't want to repeat your mistakes. They say the arrested drug police chief will soon be transferred to our prison. He's been sitting in Panjim jail for a month already."

"Can you imagine, Vasya, if he is put in our cell?"

"It could easily happen. We're in India. Can you imagine how happy I would be to see the menace of all the drug dealers, the drug police chief Pashish himself, sleeping next to me on the floor and eating the same soup as I do. I would like to ask him what he sent for analysis, MDMA or some other powder. Vitya, I hope he did not send the drugs. Just think about it. He took my money, sold my hundred grams of MDMA through Apollo, and put me behind bars. For the hydroponics growing in my house, I am only subject to a ten thousand rupee fine. What's the point of sending twenty grams of MDMA for analysis, if nobody had it at the time? It was worth two thousand dollars. I believe, Vitya, that he sold my MDMA and swapped it with some other powder, the same as he did with Vasu and Chetsi. I don't think he held onto one hundred grams for two weeks, waiting for me to come back home. I ran off with their money. Their operation was not planned, it was illegal. They had to get their money back. They must have sold all my Dymich and swapped it for some other powder. They made about ten thousand dollars in total on me. If they wanted to jail me, why did they send away my boxes with hydroponics? They could have just sent my package with Dymich. But no, six police officers carried my boxes with marijuana saplings and jars with mushroom spawns. They sent half a jeep full of my boxes for analysis, knowing that everything would result in a fine of only ten thousand rupees. My charge sheet doesn't even specify the amount of mushrooms and marijuana. It just says 'minimum.' If my weed were dried out, I would have had only ten grams. Any amount up to one kilogram is considered to be the minimum.

"When I was arrested, Vasya, the police found three hundred grams of charas and didn't even attach them to the case. When they rubbed my Novocain on their gums, they were very happy when they felt them going numb. They really thought they had found a jar of cocaine. They sent it for analysis, and just kept the charas for themselves."

"It's because they wanted to screw you over, Vitya. They didn't fuck Chetsi, Vasu or Ram-Ram, they just took their heroin worth twenty thousand dollars and the same amount of money. And you, Vitya, had Novocain and didn't pay them any money at all, and secretly undermined the coke market, as well. You crossed them, so they decided to send you to jail. They won't manage to keep you here for long, but the trial could last for three years. It will be a lesson for you to be smarter. But I am in the opposite situation. I believe, Vitya, that the cops took my Dymich and money for themselves, and sent a small amount of weed and mushrooms for analysis in order to punish me."

"I wish it were so, Vasya. I really want you to have a negative analysis. However, nobody except for Pashish knows what was sent there, and he is in jail now."

"Who could have thought, Vitya, that the most famous, untouchable drug dealers, Idu, Apollo and their entire police cover, would end up sitting in jail? Apollo is a piece of work, a real drug dealer. He managed to record his conversation with Pashish on video, when the police brought him confiscated drugs for sale. However, Apollo must have not thought that his ex-girlfriend would post the video on YouTube. All the local newspapers have been covering the story every day for two months already."

"Let's play chess, Vasya, to hell with these politicians."

"Let's play. Just tell me, Vitya, what will you do if the chief of the drug police is put in our cell? It was him who locked us up."

"If Pashish is sentenced to ten or twenty years, it will be like a life sentence for him. Vasya, do you remember the faces of those thirty drug dealers, sentenced to ten years, who were transferred from Aguada to our jail for a month? They won't let him live a single day. They will tear him to pieces. Of course, I will be pleased to see Pashish sitting on the floor and chewing the same thin broth as I do," Viktor says, setting up the chess, "but I don't intend to kill him. His karma has already punished him well. I don't care whether he's sitting in jail or not. You've been harping on about the future all morning, Vasya, but I don't want to think about the future. I'm already tired of thinking about it. I have no future now; time has stopped. I used to wait for a certain date, wishing that time would pass. I used to think that I would be released when it came. But now I am not waiting for any date. I could be released on any day in the next five years. I just need to sit quietly till the damned analysis comes, and its not clear when that will be."

"Moreover, Vitya, there are forces that don't want your analysis to come as their life is at stake."

"Well, what do you suggest I should do, Vasya? Should I hang myself like Andy did? Or should I poison myself with sleeping pills, like the Englishman who was serving time for murder?"

"First of all, Vitya, you shouldn't give up. You must fight for your freedom and be sure of victory. Andy hung himself because he had been jailed for life. The Englishman was a hired killer; he spent half of his life in prison. He was sentenced to twenty years when he was fifty, so it was the same as life imprisonment for him. Neither of them could see their future, so they gave up. But we, Vitya, must fight. I will have been in prison for a year in a month's time. If my analysis doesn't come, I suggest we go on hunger strike. Your application for release on bail was rejected because the police allegedly had a preliminary analysis. I want to talk to my investigator to make sure he doesn't invent any preliminary analysis for me. I'll offer him money and he might agree. I have to use any opportunity. I won't give up and just wait like you. And if I am released on bail, then you should also be released. The newspapers also reported that Pashish was asked during his interrogation how it happened that the kilo of heroin taken from Chetsi and Vasu turned out to be mint powder. Pashish replied that at that time the police lacked portable laboratory reagents, so the kilo of heroin was sent to Hyderabad without the conclusion of a preliminary analysis. Vitya, if I am released before you, I'll definitely ask the judge how it happened that Vasu, Chetsi, you, and I were arrested at the same time, but they didn't have a preliminary analysis and we somehow did. I'll raise such hell when I get free, they will regret it. If necessary, I will pay someone to get your analysis from Hyderabad. I'll approach the embassy; they have to help. It's an outrage and against the law that you are being held captive here. After all, the consuls from our embassy ordered two big articles in the Indian newspapers, '*Two Russians imprisoned illegally for a year*', and '*Police chief arrested for trumped-up criminal cases and drug racketeering. Two Russians illegally arrested on false charges.*' I hope that the judge reads the newspapers. We should kick up a fuss if my application for bail is also rejected. At the same time, we'll need to file a complaint with the Court of Cassation. It will be good if we have already been on hunger strike for several weeks by that time. We could be released then."

"You know, Vasya, I don't want to go on hunger strike. I love eating. A hunger strike won't have any effect anyway. We'd die of hunger before the men at the top decide to release us."

"I don't understand you, Vitya. Is it the spirit of contradiction speaking in you now, or don't you give a damn about your life?"

"Vasya, you're mistaken if you think I don't give a damn about my life. I just don't believe in hunger strikes; it wouldn't have any effect."

"As you wish, Vitya, but I'll struggle for my freedom till my last breathe, I'll clutch at straws. I'll use all methods, both real and unreal. I refuse to say, 'I don't believe'. I BELIEVE. I believe in getting out of here as soon as I can, any way possible."

"It's good that you believe, Vasya. You go ahead and live with your faith in tomorrow, and I'll live for today. It's too early for you to get out of here, Vasya; you still haven't learned to play chess yet. When you can beat me every time at chess, I'll sign your release form. As for now, set the pieces up again; checkmate. Live for another month before you go on hunger strike, Kasparov[100]."

Chapter 53. Part Two. Outside.

How beautiful life is! A sunbeam bursting through the gap between the two thick curtains and moving along with the rising Sun, has managed to reach my face. It's time to get up. Everything is so fine in my life. I don't want to get stoned in the morning at all, as it's impossible to have a better mood. Grabbing the remote control, I turn on a Shpongle track. I love waking up to trance music. You can lie around with your eyes closed for another fifteen minutes. Your brain still remembers your dreams and the beautiful music decorates them, overlapping them with its patterns, adding a joyful, positive tone. If you know how to wake up to music, you can spend the rest of the day in a good mood. It's so nice to enjoy the coolness of the morning in your room, knowing that it's stifling, scorching weather outside. I should be grateful to my mushrooms and marijuana, as I recently bought an air conditioner especially for them. Opening my eyes, I see two narrow beams of light cutting the room's twilight in half. The beam coming from the window merges with the bright strip of light coming from my hydroponics room. If these two beams have joined, it's time to get up. What should I do? Should I look at my mushrooms or marijuana first? How have they spent the night without me? Or should I have a look at the chamber with grain first? Mycelium should have covered all the grain during the night. But I should probably feed the piranhas. After all, they are the most living of my pets. Or should I get stoned first thing in the morning after all? I feel as if I am brimming over with happiness today. No, I decided to only get stoned after sunset. There are too many pleasant things that I should do today responsibly. The straw has been sterilizing all night long in hydrogen peroxide, and the fresh grain was prepared and disinfected in the evening. I have to inoculate a new batch of jars with grain, which is a responsible task. In short, I have a lot to do; it will be enough to keep me busy till evening. What should I do first though? It's so nice to do your favorite work. Throwing off the blanket, I get up and make my choice. The first thing I want to do is look at my mushrooms. Wrapping a white towel around my waist and putting on a surgical gown, I anxiously open the plastic box with mycelium. Yes!!! Yes!!! Yes!!! I've done it!!! At the bottom of the box here are ten rollers, resembling Ostankino sausages[101] but made of grain and straw. Thanks to the mushroom mycelium, the mixture of grain and straw is snow-white. The largest sausage is covered with small dark balls; primordia, future mushroom caps. But the most beautiful thing is a mushroom that has sprouted from a little mycelium living in one of Vasilinka's teacups. Having spread his cap proudly, he towers alone over the whole mycelium. Here it is, my first-born! I never thought that I could be so proud of a mushroom. The feelings are similar to those experienced when your child is born. Three months of experiments later, and I finally see the real fruits of my work. Antokha should come from Arambol today and take the mycelium to his place. I should prepare the hydroponics equipment for him and the

---

[100] Kasparov - Russian (formerly Soviet) chess Grandmaster, former World Chess Champion.

[101] Ostankino sausages - a type of sausage in Russia.

first batch of rooted clones of pedigree Dutch marijuana. I wonder how it's doing, my favorite? I haven't seen it all night. Opening the door to the secret room, I finally disperse the gloom in the bedroom. Three bright 250-Watt lamps hang on chains from the ceiling. They could illuminate the whole house, but are only used for two White Widow moms, two months old, and their twenty clones. You are so beautiful! I'll give you to Anton today. He has already bought an air conditioner for you, too. He promised to take care of you and love you the same way I do. You and the mushrooms will live in Arambol; I'll only keep the moms. The mother plants will give new clones each month, so I'll visit you often, bringing your young clone brothers and new mycelium. I've dreamt of having such a grow-room for a long time. I must look very funny. A crazy professor talking to his plants, which are connected to wires, hoses, ridged pipes, thermometers, humidity sensors and timers. A 150-liter tray bubbles with chemicals around the clock, feeding the dangling roots with an oxygenated solution. Well, what do we have in the grain chamber? Wow!!! The grain in all ten jars has been completely covered with mycelium, white as snow. The thermal heater shows twenty-nine degrees Celsius. The air conditioner sensor displays exactly the same number. Nature is amazing. If you decrease the temperature by only three degrees, the mycelium starts to sprout mushroom phalluses, ready to open in order to release their spores. But it's too early for you to appear. First you need to be mixed with straw so that we have many phalluses, and the phalluses are big. One good phallus can cost five dollars, while a medium-sized mushroom can be sold for two or three dollars. And how many changes you'll have to make to human minds! Thanks to you, humanity may soon reach the barrier of the quantum leap in perception. And I will finally have money, making it by doing work that I love. I'll deal with you after breakfast. I should give breakfast to my piranhas, first. There was a frozen chicken leg somewhere in the fridge. As I open the door leading from the bedroom into the living room, I am hit by a wall of hot, dense air. The difference in temperature is about fifteen degrees. Feeling that hot air is flowing into the room, the air conditioner's sensors make the magic device switch on and carefully protect my pets from the destructive heat with its cold air. If it's so hot in the room, what temperature is it outside? I don't want to go outside at all. What am I going to eat for breakfast? Opening the refrigerator door, white, icy vapor hits me in the face. The oysters I bought yesterday evening that are now lying on the top shelf will be perfect for me and my piranhas. The tightly closed shells tell me that the oysters are still alive. "Good morning, my liquid mycelium!" I address the bottles standing on the shelf for eggs. Ten bottles sealed in foil, awaiting their time. Each of them contains a small jellyfish, that looks a lot like snot, a few droplets of which can give birth to a new mushroom body. I've been sterilizing the boiled millet all night long for you, I'll deal with you in the evening; this is the most important work. I need to protect you from the three hundred thousand enemy bacteria that float in the air and will try to kill you. It's not easy to protect you. Different molds and parasites grew instead of you a lot of times, but now I have a sterilizing lamp. I shouldn't forget to cover the aquarium with a thick blanket, as this lamp may not only kill bacteria, but the piranhas as well. If you stare at this lamp for ten seconds, you are guaranteed a burnt face and cornea. Still, no enemy bacteria will survive! Yeah, I should throw a piece of peeled oyster to my piranhas. Here they are, my lovelies, they have come to meet me, nuzzling their terrible jaws against the glass aquarium. An Indian tune coming from my cell phone interrupts my internal dialogue.

"Hello, Vova, it's a great morning today, isn't it?"

"Are you got stoned already this morning?" I hear Vova's familiar, husky voice.

"Why do you say that? Not at all. I only get stoned after sunset now. I've got too much responsible work."

"What's new, Vasya?"

"Vova, the first mushrooms have sprouted!"

"Well, I heard this news from you yesterday."

"No, Vova. It was the first, test mushroom, which sprouted yesterday. Today they've started to appear on an industrial scale. We'll collect the first harvest tomorrow or the day after."

"That's good news. What about the police?"

"Vova, I've been living here for a week already. No one has come. The police did come to visit my neighbor a couple of weeks ago. On the day I ran away from them, they visited Alik. They checked his passport and left. It seems like it really wasn't a police operation. They just wanted to con me out of my money. They picked on the wrong guy, Vova," I say, watching two hand-sized fish tearing an oyster to pieces with their sharp teeth as it falls to the bottom of the aquarium.

"That's good, Vasya. Has Dima Lucky appeared or called you?"

"He has appeared, the bastard. He reached out to me through social networks yesterday. He says he's innocent and blames the Englishman for everything. He asked me to sell him a hundred grams of Dymich."

"What did you answer, Vasya?"

"I wrote that he is an asshole. I wrote he should have had my back at the meeting, rather than be late due to some alleged mysterious circumstances. I wrote to him that I will only work with him on a pre-payment basis now. Cash in advance, Dymich in a week. I told him a story that the MDMA is now being sent from Ukraine and it is not available here."

"You said the right thing, Vasya, but I don't think we should have anything to do with him anymore."

"I think the same thing, Vova. Especially as he's unlikely to give us the money in advance. Well, what about the laboratory?"

"Everything is fine, we've been working all night. I promise we'll have a few kilograms of MDMA at the end of the season."

"Come to my place this evening to have a look at my mushrooms, Vova. I also want to talk to you about one project. I've found information about Finnish mini breweries on the Internet. If we invest twenty grand, we could become the beer kings of Goa. Normal beer isn't on sale here, in Goa. You can only buy bottled urine. Vova, I've sold four tons of kvass this season[102]. Do you imagine how much good unfiltered beer could we sell here? It costs almost nothing to produce, and it's relatively simple to make. Ten years ago I used to brew such beer all year round at my home."

---

[102] Kvass this season - kvass is a drink made from bread that is similar to beer and resembles beer even more if left to ferment too long.

"Okay, Vasya, tell me everything when I come in the evening. It would be better if you smoked in the morning, you're overflowing with enthusiasm."

"You're right, Vova, I am full of enthusiasm. But I'm not going to smoke now. I don't want to turn into a vegetable. When everything is turning out well, it's so nice to work and live. Okay, Vova, see you tonight, someone is knocking at my door," I say, putting a live oyster into my mouth. "It must be Antokha. He is coming to take the seedlings away; I'm transferring all of my agriculture to his place today."

"Is that you, Antokha?" I shout through the door, turning the lock.

"It's the police, Pashish. Open the door, we need to talk to you."

407

Chapter 54. Part One. Inside.

"Hey, Russians! Why are you talking through the bars?" Italian Alexandro addresses us, holding an iron cup.

"Hi there, Milano, this is my new friend. His name is Sasha, just like yours."

Putting his mug of tea on the floor, Milano squats down next to me.

"Have you read the newspaper? An Englishman was found dead. He overdosed on heroin. His name was John. Could it be your grass, Vasya?"

"It could be him. David has been at large for over a month already, he promised he'd immediately get even with all the grasses. I wouldn't be surprised if they find a Russian who died of a cocaine overdose. A black guy was found dead on the street after Antonio was released. The jail rumors say he was the informant who got the Greek locked up."

"What will you do with your Russian grass, when you get out of here, Vasya?"

"I don't intend to do anything, Milano. If I meet him, I will thank him. I've learned English and improved my health thanks to him. I've realized who loves me and who doesn't. I've got rid of an unnecessary ballast of questionable friends. The most important thing is that I've seen the other, real Goa. Now I no longer have the rose-colored spectacles that I wore for the last six years. For the first six months I thought about how to get even with Dima, but what would it give me? I believe that you can't escape from karma. I'll even warn him and tell him that David really wants to get even with him. David is an intense, Iranian, criminal dude. He won't be able to sleep if he doesn't get revenge. I believe that all of the participants in my case got their just deserts. The policemen who arrested me have been in jail for two months already, the Englishman is snorting heroin in the afterlife now, and Dima Lucky is now in complete uncertainty. I don't think he sleeps soundly at night. And anyway, I don't have any desire to take revenge on anyone. I want to live peacefully and sleep well outside."

"I'm not going to take revenge on anyone, either, Vasya. I want to try to go back and live in Italy. However, I can't even imagine my life there. I've been living in India for twenty-five years. What about your new friend, Vasya? Has he been in Goa long?" the Italian says, pouring half of his tea into my cup, pointing at Sasha, who is sitting behind the bars.

"Milano, you won't believe me, but he arrived in Goa just a couple of months ago for the first time. He also had his own sort of psychedelic revolution in Russia. He has been making methamphetamine in Sverdlovsk for the last five years. He came to purchase chemicals and was arrested for an expired visa. He told me his plan for the psychedelic revolution yesterday. He's a real anarchist. He can also make explosives from nitrate and sugar. He says it would cost almost nothing to blow up the central police office building. He just needs sugar, nitrate, and red phosphorus for the detonator. All of these chemicals are used by terrorists throughout the world. All these ingredients can be easily bought in stores here, in India, the same as in Russia. Sasha says that after several major government buildings are blown up, the government would be as meek as a lamb, trance parties would be allowed again, and normal life would return to Goa. Sasha says that all previous generations of psychedelic soldiers were stoned freaks and feeble hippies, showing no resistance to society. He says that all the local psychedelic gurus are just cowardly runaway slaves, while more serious people should oppose society, otherwise we will all be made slaves again. So, my new jail friend is a real psycho, as you can see."

"You, Russians, are all psychos in your own way. Although, there are anarchists in all countries. The authorities in Ibiza once tried to shut down the parties, but the major drug dealers financed a new anarchist terrorist organization. After several bombings had been carried out in Spain, the authorities softened the sentences of arrested drug dealers. The parties were allowed again in Ibiza, and now it is a flourishing resort, which gathers young people from all over the world, who come to dance and do drugs on vacation there. This is how terrorists and anarchists appear. A man comes to have a rest here and is locked up for a year. It's quite natural for him to desire revenge. Your friend may have the future of Goa in his hands, Vasya, and you were worried you would have no friends after Viktor was released."

"It is what it is. They have already released all the foreigners, even those who were arrested after me. You are going to be released today. However, Sasha has been convicted, and I have not. We can only communicate a few minutes a day and only through the bars. All convicts live on the first floor, and those under investigation live on the second. We can only speak for a while when we go downstairs to get meals."

"Sanya, why are you keeping silent? Say something to the Italian. He's one of us, a Sicilian smuggler. His name is Alexandro, your namesake."

"Hi, namesake," Sasha says, grinning from ear to ear, holding out his strong hand through the bars.

"Doesn't your friend speak any English, Vasya?" the Italian asks me, smiling at Sasha in response.

"He knows English pretty much the same as Viktor knew it sixteen months ago. Absolute zero."

"What is your Italian speaking about? Translate, please, Vasya, till I can speak English a bit better."

"The Italian is asking the same thing. Sanya, you resemble Viktor very much. He was my neighbor before you came. He was released on bail a month ago. He was locked up for dental anesthetic for fifteen months. When he came to jail, he didn't speak English at all, just like you, but he was able to read Shakespeare in English by the time of his release."

"Vasya, why is the Italian so gloomy? Why was he locked up in here?"

"Alexandro, my friend asks when you'll be released?" I say smiling, tapping our Sicilian on the shoulder.

"Vasya, I just can't believe it. Is it really my last day today? I've served twenty months already. The judge gives me all the documents today, and I get out of here. The police could not prove my guilt, but invented a new rule. If they lack evidence, the suspect is given a small sentence, a year, so that he can't ask for compensation from the state. And since I have been under investigation for almost two years, they release me tomorrow. They gave me a little punishment to please everybody. The state is happy about being seen to punish me, the cops are happy because they've taken away my drugs and money, the lawyers are also very happy because they got five thousand bucks. And I am the happiest of all as I haven't been sentenced to ten years."

"Alexandro, my new Russian friend asks why you are so gloomy, and not happy about your release."

"I am happy, I just took too many sleeping pills this morning. I've been reduced to a nervous wreck. I've been taking ten pills a day lately. I hope I will get rid of this stupid habit outside."

"Yeah, Milano, you should give that up. You've been looking like a living ghost lately. You're pale and unshaven, and you move slowly around the prison with your eyes always half-closed."

"Vasya, do you think it's a joke to be locked up in Indian prison for ten years? I've got up and gone to bed with this thought for almost two years. It's like a death penalty for me, since I'm fifty-two years old. If I was sentenced to ten years, I would hang myself the very next day, like Andy did."

"Well I love life, Milano, and I feel very happy lately. I know what my sentence will be. I'll be here for another year at the most and that's it. I don't allow myself to think about ten years. I have food, which I've got used to, I get stoned on charas in the evenings. I have my own servant, Mustafa, who washes my clothes and brings me tea in bed in the morning. I read books, learn English, play chess and tennis. The most important thing is that I don't have to think about how to make a living."

"Vasya, you're crazy. You're just the same as your former friend, Viktor. How can you say that you are happy? You are in prison, and you face from ten to twenty years. You can say that you have accepted this reality and agreed with it, but you can't be happy! Viktor kept saying that he was happy. Now it's you. You have viral schizophrenia. I am sure that this Russian will insist that he is also happy in six months. He was sentenced to a year in prison for an expired visa, but he sits there smiling, without a clue what I am saying to him now. The blacks are sentenced to three months in prison for a six-month overstay, while he was sentenced to a year for a month overstay. Only a complete idiot can stand up during a trial at the Indian court and shout in Russian: 'Long live the Indian court, the most humane court in the world!'[103] He was given a year just because of his contempt of court. Viktor also asked the judge to issue a permit for tomatoes, wearing a handmade T-shirt saying 'I love drug police'. As a result, he served fifteen months for dental anesthetic."

---

[103] 'Long live the Indian court, the most humane court in the world!' - the catch phrase from a popular Russian movie where the main character says this during the court hearing.

"What is this Italian going crazy about? Is he saying something bad about me? Translate what he saying about me, Vasya."

"Everything is okay, Sanya. He has prolonged, lifelong depression. He's on sleeping pills now, and he jabbed a vein for five tears when he was outside. To be more precise, he's been on something all his life. He is happy to take, inject, or snort anything he's offered."

"He doesn't look like a junkie. I'd say he's in his forties, Vasya. He's muscular and flat-bellied."

"What good do his muscles do him, Sanya? He is in his fifties, but he still hasn't learnt how to be happy. He doesn't believe that I'm happy right now."

"I still can't understand how you can be happy. I sat in Mapusa jail for a month before I was sentenced and I realized then that I was in the shit. There can be no happiness in prison."

"I have no alternative, Sanya. You can be happy and enjoy every day, or be miserable like this Italian. There is no third option in prison, or outside either. I'm not going to moan around the clock like this Italian. I've thought about ten years in prison many times already, Sanya. It's not the end of everything. I'm not going to put my head in the noose. If you don't learn how to be happy in prison, you have been doing time in vain."

"Well, Vasya, I'm happy I wasn't sentenced to three years like Idu was. He only had one day of overstay."

"Don't compare yourself to Idu. He and Apollo got seven police officers locked up. The drug police chief himself is serving a sentence in Panjim prison. The Indian special services managed to do that. Idu is basically the main Goan drug dealer. It's difficult to lock him up for drugs; he could get the minister put in jail then as well. The minister, or rather his son, who controls the drug market, is a member of the ruling Congress party now. Sonia Gandhi, Rahul Gandhi, and Priyanka Gandhi rule the country now. The police can't put a blot on their names. That's why Idu was jailed for his visa. But he will soon get free anyway. I've been living with him in one cell for a week already. He'll serve a year and then be released by the Court of Cassation."

"Are you talking about me in your language, Russians?" the Italian, sitting on his haunches nearby, interrupts our conversation.

"No, Milano, we are talking about happiness. Sanya says he's happy in his own way, too. Do you see how he is smiling?"

"You're definitely all madmen, you Russians. How can you be happy in prison? Everything started to fall apart when you started coming to Goa in the mid-nineties. I've lived here for twenty-five years. Everything was so wonderful before the Russians came. I thought I had found my own paradise. The whole paradise was destroyed as soon as the Russians came. They offered three hundred bucks, where the Europeans gave a hundred. It's because you got money for free during the times of change, after the Soviet Union collapsed. You don't know the value of money. Like barbarians, you burst onto the scene here and acted like you owned the place. You can't string two words together in English, but you have the ambitions of Julius Caesar. If something goes wrong, you immediately start to fight for your rights using your fists. Three months ago, a Russian named Kostya ended up in a bad way. He killed a local taxi driver for no reason. Now, all Indian visas are only issued for a month. It's because of you, Russians."

"Hey, Mussolini[104], so you're a Nazi or something? Why are you having a go at the Russians? First, Kostya killed the taxi driver by accident. You know yourself how aggressive they are sometimes. He fell from Kostya's punch and hit his head on a stone. He died a day later, after all. That could happen to anybody. Second, what has it got to do with us, your prison friends?"

"It's got nothing to do with you. I'm not a Nazi. Just nobody likes Russians in Goa now. Wherever the Russians appear they put an end to everything. You are like savages, who have run away from the forest. You fill all the space around you immediately, ignoring the fact that someone else was here before you. You and Viktor take food without waiting in line, despite the fact that everyone else stands in line and waits.

"Milano, it looks like you've completely lost your mind. It's good that you are being released today. Viktor hasn't been here for a month already, but you still remember how we reserved a place in line for each other. Tell me, if there was another Italian here, would you stand separately in the line for food? Whoever comes to get food first, reserves a place for the other one."

"Italians would never do that. I am me; a friend is a friend. You have to think about those around you. We are all sitting in one prison and we all want to eat. Well, Vasya, don't be offended, I will go to pack my belongings. I am gloomy because I'm getting outside today and only I have money to live for a week. I have no mom, no dad, no work, nothing. I'm afraid to be involved in the drug business now. The time of the free drug business is over. Now it's too criminal. My new life begins tomorrow, Vasya. I'm afraid of new adventures."

"I'm not offended Milano, I don't like Russians, either. I agree with you that Russians have killed Goa. But I'm a different Russian; I don't want you to include me along with all Russians. I am me. And give up your fears about your new life. You will go outside and everything will be okay, fate will give you a few more pleasant surprises. Think positive and stop taking those sleeping pills. Before you leave, come to my cell to say goodbye. I will miss you."

"Why has the Italian gone away? Was he offended?"

"No, Sanya, he wasn't offended. He has gone to pack his things, he's being released today. He doesn't like Russians in general, and I agree with him."

"Why doesn't he like Russians? Has he been holding a grudge against us since World War II, or what?" Sanya asks, smiling and passing me a cookie through the bars.

"What is there to like us for? We are wild like Arabs. If it wasn't for oil, we would still be eating cabbage soup with a straw shoe. We came into money only recently and don't know its value. Russians squander money everywhere, undermining the interests of others. We're used to living in total chaos. For a hundred years this chaos has reigned, ever since the royal family was shot dead. We are all brought up in the spirit of chauvinism. Although Russia fights against Nazism and chauvinism, it is drummed into our heads that Russians are the best, while the rest of the world are second-class assholes. Take, for example, the mail.ru website, one of Russia's most popular e-mail providers. It's

---

[104] Mussolini - Italian politician, journalist, and leader of the National Fascist Party, the founder of fascism.

definitely controlled by the state. Either the state or the FSB have a stake in all the large media companies. Well, the latest news is posted daily on this website. When you're outside, read the comments below some of the news. It's like Nazis wrote those comments. Of course, every website should have moderators to identify offenders and remove them. But the titles of these comments are not deleted, they sound like calls for action. Every day you will see such calls to beat Jews and expel Tajiks from the country. And that's the state-controlled media. If you look at the way the news is presented, you will notice that nationalism is covertly promoted everywhere. A whole generation of Russians is growing up, thinking that they are somehow superior to other nations. And these Russians do not hesitate to treat other nations as second-class people. The English language is taught in schools in most countries from the very first grades. For them, if a person does not know English it means that he doesn't have a basic primary education. Foreigners can't understand that our borders were closed for seventy years. We didn't learn foreign languages because we had no chance to use them in the future. For them, we are wild, uneducated, rich barbarians, demanding that everybody be afraid of us, respect us, and speak Russian. I hope, Sanya, that the recent economic crises will teach our citizens to appreciate the money they earn. The Italian is right; we've spoiled everything in Goa. We are too lazy to learn fifty English words and to find a good apartment in Goa. It's easier to go to the Indian owner of the house where an Italian lives and offer three times higher rent, outbidding him. That happened with Milano's house, so he's not been very fond of Russians since then. He's a cool dude, in fact, he came to Goa from Amsterdam by bus for the first time twenty-five years ago. The bus was called the Happy Bus and traveled to India every three months. It took a month to reach India through Greece, Afghanistan, Pakistan and Iran. The bus was stuffed to the gills with synthetic drugs and drove to Goa with thirty happy hippies on board. The Italian has seen things in the last twenty-five years that you'll never see. His generation of freaks helped wild Goa to make the quantum leap in perception. He remembers the time when today's millionaires, the owners of hotels and restaurants, were climbing palm trees and collecting coconuts with bare asses. There was no normal transport, no paved roads. Not everywhere had electricity. Just a half an hour drive into the neighboring state you can see how Goa looked fifty years ago. In the mid-nineties, the Israelis came here en masse, but they knew how to count their money, they quickly began to hassle the Indians, forcing them to provide more benefits for their money. But Indians are lazy because of their hot climate. They quickly got irritated by the never-satisfied Israelis, who constantly demanded more and more comfort. All the money invested by the Israelis was expropriated by Goan residents through both legal and illegal means, including through limiting their stay in India with a three-month visa. And then the Russians came and the prices doubled within three years. At first the Indians liked the Russians for their generosity, and then they started to drive the Russians, just like the Israelis, out of their spheres of influence. The Russians tried to stand up for their rights here, so the Indians began to dislike us, too. Goans only like those who don't demand rights to anything on their land. And they are right in their own way; it's their land."

"Why do they make me clean the cell, Vasya? I am a foreigner. They don't force me, of course, but they say I'll have to sweep the floor in the cell next week. That's not in accordance with the thief's code of conduct, is it? Or am I wrong? Tell me."

"Sanya, if you don't want to clean the cell, you should find someone to clean, sweep, bring you tea, do everything for you."

"Vasya, do I really have to bully someone? Won't they beat me? There are twenty men in the cell and I'm alone."

"If you have no money at all, then you'll have to bully. But if you can buy a pack of biscuits worth five rupees for the guys to have tea every day, they will find you a beggar to serve you till the end of your sentence."

"I have no problems with that, Vasya, I have money. But I don't know how to put it on my account. I have a passive income of fifteen hundred bucks per month. I've had a great time in India, huh? I went abroad for the first time in my life, enjoyed two months of holiday, and was sentenced to a year in prison!"

"You, Sanya, are just as unique as Viktor. He had to serve fifteen month for a jar of pharmaceutical anesthetic, and you were sentenced to a year in prison for a one-month overstay."

"Was Viktor declared not guilty? Although I don't know him, I've realized he was famous here. All the guards are constantly saying 'good morning' in Russian to me, some even call me 'Viktor'."

"Sanya, it's because you do look a bit like him, although we all look the same to the Indians, just like the Chinese do to us. Two prisons have learnt Viktor's greeting 'dobroe utro'. The whole prison woke up every morning to his loud cry. He even signed his statements 'Viktor, dobroe utro'. He fell foul of the drug police mafia, while trying to sell fake cocaine. He mixed pharmaceutical amphetamine with anesthetic. He nearly brought down the whole cocaine market with his cheap price. He waited for the results of the expert analysis for fourteen months, although he should have been released in a year according to the law. Then the findings came, stating that no drugs had been found, but the chemical formula of this anesthetic is the mirror image of that of cocaine, even the name of the formula is 'stereo isotropic of cocaine.' Upon receipt of the analysis, the judge took a month to decide what he should do with Vitya. This substance is not on the list of banned drugs, but the name itself sounds very suspicious. So, the charge was changed from 'selling cocaine' to 'producing cocaine.' The prosecutor alleged that this stereo isotropic, which is sold for twenty bucks per kilo at any pharmacy, is part of cocaine. His lawyer only just succeeded in getting him out on bail for five thousand bucks. The police, meanwhile, sent his powder to Delhi. There, having performed a repeat analysis of the 'stereo isotropic of cocaine', whose only effect is numbing the gums, they decided to include it in the list of banned substances. Two weeks ago, the newspaper had a long article saying that a strange Russian drug dealer who was released on bail is continuing to sell a lethal new drug called 'stereo isotropic of cocaine', which has resulted in several deaths already. The police asked the prosecutor to issue a warrant for Viktor's arrest again. Then the police came to his house and asked him for a thousand dollars to avoid being arrested. They told him that if traces of pharmaceutical anesthetic were found in the body of anyone who died of an overdose, he would be sentenced to twenty years in prison. Of course, Viktor gave them the money and disappeared the next day. Nobody has seen him since, he hasn't called anybody since then. His girlfriend says that it's like the Earth swallowed him up. He didn't come to the court hearing twice, and the judge issued a warrant for his arrest. His passport was kept by the police and he hadn't ordered a new one. He could have been killed by the police or drug dealers, or maybe he is hiding somewhere. Now that he's on the all-India wanted list, even if he is sent a new passport, he still won't be able to leave the country legally. If he is caught, he'll face from ten to twenty years. If he crosses the border with Nepal illegally, he won't be able to leave Nepal legally, either. He'll be locked up in a Nepalese jail for that, and then he may be extradited to an Indian jail for ten years. His story is not over yet. He's a fool, he should have ordered a new Russian passport immediately, and then fled with it before he was put on the wanted list, but now it's too late."

"Why did he start sell his powder again, Vasya? Is he really an idiot?"

"Sanya, he didn't sell anything. The police just decided to punish him. The whole story with the 'stereo isotropic of cocaine' was completely made up by the cops. Viktor refused to accept the rules of this state's game, so he was screwed. You are here too, not because you had a one-month overstay, but because you mocked the judge."

"What's wrong with my phrase, 'Long live the Indian court, the most humane court in the world!'"

"It may sound funny to you, Sanya, but it seemed offensive to the judge. Now you'll sit here and think for a year, so that you are afraid and respect them next time. If you pray to your gods, your sentence may be reduced by a few months by the Court of Cassation."

"Well, Vasya, I've found myself in a fairyland. I read that here in India there are miracles everywhere and complete legalize, but now I see that there is just chaos and lawlessness. I need to find a good lawyer, but I don't know how. I've been asking to make a call to Russia for the three weeks already. But something always happens. One day the paper finishes. Another day the phone is broken. On yet another day there is no electricity or the warden is ill. Every day they tell me, 'Tomorrow, tomorrow, tomorrow...' I'm going to crazy soon from this 'tomorrow.'"

"Hang in there, Sanya. It really is an amazing country, where the language has no such words as 'yesterday' or 'tomorrow.' There is only 'now.' It seems that the Indians only vaguely understand the meaning of these words. They have their own perception of time, which Europeans can't understand. It's difficult to get used to, but you need to accept it as soon as possible, or you'll go mad within a year. If you really need something urgently, Sanya, then you have to go on hunger strike. They respond quickly then. You'll get everything you need on the fifth day. My lawyer told me some time ago to prepare five thousand dollars for me to be released on bail. First, I waited for a month for the judge to give me a permit to go to the bank with two guards. Then, for another month, the warden told me I would go to the bank tomorrow. I got tired of listening to his 'tomorrows' and went on hunger strike. I made a sign saying, 'No ATM - stop eat.' I sat in the middle of the cell and held this sign in my hands while we were counted. Three days later, I went to the bank. However, it turned out at the bank that only a thousand dollars can be withdrawn from a card per day. I kept going to the bank for over a month till I got the whole amount. I called my lawyer and said that the money was ready. The lawyer came a week later and the warden told him, 'There is no cash.' It turned out that it is prohibited to keep such a large sum of money in the prison, so the warden gave it back to the bank.

And for a month my lawyer hasn't been able to get my money from the warden. India is a wonderful country, a country without time."

"Vasya, there was a black man in my cell. His name was Obi. He went completely nuts within six months. At first I couldn't understand why he had imagined that all the cellmates were following him and talking about him. When he had been sentenced to seven years and moved to Aguada, the cellmates told me that his name, Abi, means 'now' in Hindi. The word 'now' is one of the most frequently used words among the Indians, and Abi, just like me, couldn't understand a word in English or Hindi. He was paranoid. Everybody was saying his name all day long. He started to suspect everyone of plotting against him.

"Sanya, he went nuts a long time ago. If he had been normal, he wouldn't have raped an Australian chick. So now he has seven years to restore his mental health in Aguada, if he doesn't kick the bucket sooner. Lots of people break down in Aguada and take their own lives. I'll never forget Andy's eyes when he said goodbye to me. He was sentenced to life imprisonment for murdering an elderly Englishwoman. He told me in broken Russian that he would see me soon, and hung himself in the closet the next night. After all, Sanya, just like Russia, you can't understand India with your mind. It's a country where the state prison service gives you special free coconut oil for your hair every week. Maybe you've noticed that absolutely all Indians put special oil on their hair at least once a day. However, it's prohibited to buy mineral water. No matter how many times I have requested it, I have always been denied. I just can't grasp with my mind how my lawyer can simultaneously be the lawyer of the arrested drug police chief, who detained me fifteen months ago. We are transferred together to a court hearing sometimes. Just imagine how absurd it is: first, the lawyer tells the judge that I am a law-abiding tourist, who was jailed because of a dishonest police chief who sold drugs and planted them on me in order to blackmail me. Now this corrupt policeman is under investigation in Panjim prison and cannot testify against me. But fifteen minutes later, the same lawyer, defending the former drug police chief, tells the judge that his client is a man of crystal-like honesty, who was the victim of a plot by evil drug dealers. And the fact that there is a video capturing how the police chief sells drugs to the drug dealer Apollo, is a ridiculous coincidence. The video is just fun and is not considered to be a crime. The fact that twenty kilograms of drugs disappeared from the police warehouse is not his fault either. They have a letter from zoologists saying that white termite ants love eating drugs more than anything else. According to the documents, all of the seized drugs that disappeared from the warehouse were eaten by ants. Do you realize what kind of absurdity happens in the court, Sanya? It's not even a madhouse, it's Holy India. As of now, all the drug dealers arrested by Pashish have been released. Some were released on bail, like Viktor. Some were acquitted, like Iranian David, who was detained with five kilograms of hashish. A total of twenty people have been released. Even a black guy with a kilogram of cocaine, the last person arrested by Pashish, was released after serving only six months. I am the last one, Sanya."

"What about you, Vasya? Why have you been sitting here for fifteen months already?"

"I have to blame my psilocybin mushrooms. There are three drugs in my case. MDMA, marijuana and psilocybin mushrooms. The analysis of the MDMA has come, the result was positive. The examination of the marijuana was also positive. However, the examination of mushrooms, or rather one mushroom, hasn't come yet. It will most likely never come. I cultivated these mushrooms at home, Sanya. The first and only mushroom sprouted, and I was arrested. Just imagine: the police sent the package with my mushroom by train to the other end of India, to Hyderabad. The package was in the Indian heat for at least two weeks. The mushroom had enough time to go bad, dry out and turn into ashes twice. The experts in the laboratory must have just thrown away the rotten stinking mycelium as a misunderstanding. But the judge cannot open the case without this analysis. To be more precise, he couldn't. My lawyer argued with the prosecutor at the last court hearing. It seems like the prosecutor doesn't really know the law. He had been refusing to exclude my mushrooms from the case for two months, saying that I can be jailed for ten years for one such mushroom. However, at the last court hearing, the judge got tired of listening to his ravings. She got up and brought him a book of the law, stipulating that the maximum penalty for psychotropic mushrooms is a two hundred dollar fine. In short, the mushrooms were somehow removed from my case. On Monday, the judge finally opens my case."

"What are you facing for the grass and MDMA, Vasya?"

"People are rarely jailed for marijuana here, Sanya. You can get ten years if you have more than twenty kilograms. If you have less than one kilogram, you have to pay a two hundred dollar fine. As for the MDMA, I face from ten to twenty years. But I'm sure I'll be released soon. Have you heard the story about how the drug dealers Idu and Apollo got seven police officers locked up?"

"Everyone in the prison has heard that story, Vasya. Everyone can hardly wait until those policemen are transferred to our prison."

"They won't be transferred here, Sanya. They may be released on bail tomorrow along with Apollo, due to insufficient evidence. They can't be jailed. If the cops are jailed, they will drag the minister to prison as well. The whole system would have to be jailed then. And if the minister has been paying even more senior officials, the whole government would need to be jailed. It's called corruption. All of the people who were arrested by police chief Pashish over the past three years have been already released under various pretexts. I am the last one who is still in prison. But I won't stay here long. My lawyer said that on Monday the judge will finally open my case. The doctor who carried out the analysis of my MDMA in Hyderabad will come here in three weeks. Since there was no analysis of the purity, the lawyer will ask the doctor how he can be sure that I had twenty grams. Maybe I had just one gram of MDMA and nineteen grams of mint powder. And since the analysis has already been carried out and the MDMA destroyed, no one can determine the exact quantity now. So, I will be released on bail in a month."

"Vasya, what are you going to do next?"

"I don't know, Sanya. I have two options: either to escape from India through Nepal, saying goodbye to this fairyland forever, or continue with the case for two more years until I am declared not guilty."

"Vasya, India really is a fairyland, nothing is the way it's supposed to be. If you were in Russia, you would have been quickly sentenced to ten years, within two weeks, and would have been sent to chop wood somewhere in Siberia long ago. Here you can be involved in a case for three years, trying to prove that the police are idiots. By the way, Vasya, do you know that the ex-tourism minister is sharing a cell with me? My cellmates call him Mickey Mouse."

"How could I not know this, Sanya, if all the newspapers have been covering it for the last two months? They report that the former minister, Mickey Pachuta, also used to be involved in the drug business, all of the drug dealers know him. A few years ago he went into politics, laundered all his black money and become a very important person. He was locked up for murder. The rumor goes that he killed his mistress. She got pregnant and he poisoned her with rat poison. He's the second minister to be arrested. Another one is sitting in the neighboring prison for the rape of a Russian girl. He's been there for six months already. He faces ten years in prison. They say he will be transferred here soon. If yet another minister is locked up in relation to Apollo and Idu's case, there will be three ministers in prison. All miracles are possible here, in India."

"My minister cellmate is not very talkative, Vasya. I asked him in Russian yesterday why we are sitting in the same cell if he was the tourism minister and I was a tourist. Maybe it's a sign? He didn't answer me, just muttered something and turned away. Many things are not clear for me here, Vasya. Today I saw my cellmates shaking the TV set. It had a bad picture, so four of them turned it upside down and began to shake it. I can't even imagine why they did that."

"You can't understand India with your mind, Sanya. But when you live here longer, many things become clear. For example, your cellmates shook the TV set because a lizard might have climbed inside it. Lizards like to settle in TV sets. We had the same thing recently. Your logic and all your life experience are no use here. You shouldn't try to understand India with your mind. Many things blow your mind here, but they exist all the same. I really want to have the possibility to come to this country. I don't want to run, burning bridges behind me, like Viktor did. I want to close my court case; it's a completely trumped-up charge. But I've missed my girls so much. I am worried that I'll give up and go to Russia. But let's wait and see. I paid five grand to my lawyer in order to be released on bail. I will still have to pay almost the same amount to close my case. I have no more money, no job, and no desire to sell drugs again. I don't even have the money to flee to Russia. Sanya, I will have to start living a new life when I'm outside, my future is completely unclear."

"Why don't your friends help you? Can't they collect money to get you out of here?"

"I have no real friends, Sanya, because I'm a drug dealer. The whole time I thought I was a psychedelic preacher, but it turns out that I'm a drug dealer. Nobody likes drug dealers. I tried to organize a campaign to raise money to pay for my lawyer. My brother put up posters with my photo and a call for help all over Goa. Not a single bitch responded. I thought I had thousands of friends ready to come running to rescue me. Only my mother made the effort to find the money to get me out. I must be the one to clear up my own mess. I lost my revolution. I have to start to live from scratch now. Now, every day I wait for the warden to come and say, 'Vasiliy, go out.' Then a new story will start, and Buddha alone knows what it will be like.

Chapter 54. Part Two. Outside.

"Open the door, we're from the police, we need to check your passport."

"One second, I'll just get dressed. Wait a minute."

Okay, just don't panic, maybe they really do want to check my passport and that's all. I should turn off the lights in the hydroponics room and hide the small lump of hashish.

"I'm coming," I say, trying to make my voice sound as calm as possible, and opening the door.

As if not noticing me, two Indians in civilian clothes enter the house, smiling, looking around the room curiously. Having shown me his police ID card, Pashish haughtily plops down on the couch, putting his feet on the coffee table.

"Gotcha! Did you think we wouldn't find you if you shave and change your clothes? You're a very smart guy, but we're not idiots. Bring our money here."

"What money? What are you talking about? You must have got me mixed up with someone else?"

"Okay, stop clowning around! Show your passport to my officer. Maybe you have a problem with your visa?"

"I have no problems with my visa, I'll show it to you. I have a five-year X visa. I have registration. What do you want from me?" I say angrily, opening the iron safe in the wardrobe.

Seeing the open door of the safe, the second police officer jumps up immediately and thrusts out his hand, trying to grab a wad of money lying inside.

"Hey, hey, slow down! It's my money!" I yell at him, closing the door abruptly. Having almost got his hand caught in the safe door, the young policeman runs back to his chief, lounging on my couch.

"Chief, he's got a bundle of money in there. What shall we do?"

"Well, Vasiliy, stop fooling around. Call your accomplices, let them come, we'll have a talk. Otherwise, we'll arrest you right now."

"I don't understand what you're talking about. I'll call my lawyer."

"Call whoever you want, you have five minutes."

Trying my best to keep calm, I dial Vova's number, hiding with the key to the safe in a glass with Vasilinka's pencils with my other hand.

"Hello, Vova. We have big problems. Two policemen are sitting in my room right now. They are demanding money and that my partner come. What should I do?"

"The main thing is to stay calm, Vasya, don't panic. We'll think of something. Win some time, I'll try to contact the minister's son. Ask the cops to show you the warrant for the search and your arrest. If they don't have any papers, it means they are just trying to cheat you. Call me again in two minutes."

"Okay, Vova, I'll try."

Putting my phone on the table, I stare at the police chief for a while, trying to figure out what he's up to do.

"Well, Russian, have you called your accomplice? Now give me your cellphone."

Chapter 55. Part One. Inside.

"You need a cell phone? I'll give you a cell phone, bitch. Have you decided to make tension for me? I'll make you so much tension that you'll regret it."

Pulling a cell phone out of his underwear, Idu hits it against the iron bars dramatically. Several split pieces pierce his palm, making a bloody pulp.

"Idu, you've violated the law. A cellphone in prison is a gross violation. I have to open a file on you," the warden shouts in his nasty voice, in front of the astonished guards who stand silently.

"You're not a prison warden, you're a taxi driver. Until recently you worked as a taxi driver at the market. What sort of problem can you make for me? I'm in prison already. I was sentenced to three years for a visa that had expired by one day. You want me to be an obedient, good boy after that? I'll bring you a broken phone every day, so that every day the newspapers will report that Idu has a cellphone in prison. I will do that until you are fired from here. Eight mobile phones and three articles in the newspaper were enough to get me transferred from Aguada to this prison. I'm a big drug dealer, in case you didn't understand. I have a lot of money, so much that you can't even imagine. In spite of all your threats, I will always have a cellphone, charas, cigarettes and everything I want in my cell. I've been living in Goa for twelve years already and I know your whole corrupt system. I've been paying all of you, from ordinary policemen to a government minister, for twelve years. Everybody: Bollywood stars, politicians, civil servants and businessmen, have been buying cocaine from me for twelve years. I've got dirt on everyone. You, Indians, are all corrupt."

"I'm not corrupt, and I don't need anything from you, Idu," the warden says, lifting his chin arrogantly.

"What did you say? You are not corrupt? Do you think you have earned those three stars on your shoulder straps honestly? You are a former taxi driver, and your wife, who works in the administration, helped you to get the post of the warden because her father is a judge. You have to serve at least twelve years to get each of your stars, while you're just thirty-five years old. I am a professional drug dealer. I served in the Israeli army for three years, I saw death many times. What can you or your guards do to me? I'm ready for anything. When I was in Aguada, I fought with the warden, I fought with the guards, I fought twelve prisoners at the same time. For a long time I have been afraid of nothing."

Throwing the smashed phone at the feet of the guards, Idu splashes almost everyone with drops of blood from his injured hand.

"Calm down, Idu. We're not going to do a complete check today. After Hitler escaped, we have to check all the cells," the senior guard is first to break the silence, trying not to show his fear.

"I spit on your checks. You can come every day, I don't care. It's Jewish New Year today. Jews all over the world give apples covered in honey and different sweets to their neighbors and friends. I just asked you to buy some sweets using my money and give them to the prisoners. You've spoiled my holiday. You allowed the Muslims to give sweets to everybody on Ramadan. The Shivites hand round sweets in all the cells on all Hindu holidays. But you haven't allowed me to make my fellow cellmates happy on the Jewish holiday, which happens only once a year. You were the first to make tension for me, so remember: I'll make it for to you from now on."

"Idu, but we let you bring apples and honey to the prison," the warden starts to speak again, as if apologizing, fastidiously wiping a speck of Jewish blood from his trousers with a piece of newspaper.

"I gave those apples to the convicts from the first floor, and you, boss, know that perfectly well. I asked you to buy more sweets using my money so there would be enough for everyone, and you forbade it. You forbade it without good reason, just to make trouble for me. So, remember this day, you're going to have troubles from now on."

"Idu, it's just a misunderstanding. I didn't understand you; that's all. You can threaten me and do what you want; I'm not afraid. It's my job to be the warden. You're not the first and not the last."

The warden turns around and leaves our cell, accompanied by eight guards. Having slammed the barred iron door shut, the last guard shrugs his shoulders, as if apologizing for the inconvenience. Left alone in our small cell, the three of us assess the damage in silence. Three overturned sleeping mats, the bedclothes turned inside out, shards of the broken phone, and everything splashed with small drops of blood.

"Should I bandage your hand?" Nepalese Bim is first to break the silence, holding out a small white towel to the Israeli.

"It's okay, Bim, the injury is only slight. However, waving my hand around dripping with blood was spectacular. They won't bother us in our cell now. Well, what are you staring at, you Nepalese chump? Make our beds quickly and clean the cell. You'll wash Vasiliy's bedclothes tomorrow; I spattered them with blood, too. And now the Russian and I are going to smoke a bong."

Pulling the prepared bong and a coconut mixing bowl with crumbed charas from behind the TV, Idu hunkers down next to me.

"Well, Vasya, how did you like my speech today? They've decided to make tension for me. I've had to take down more serious guys than that in my life. I grew up in the most crime-ridden neighborhood in Israel. When I was six, I found a hand grenade while playing in the yard. When I was twelve, I found a buried gun, while I was burying stolen candies in a neighbor's yard. I started to sell drugs on the street when I was fourteen. I served one year in an Israeli prison. My elder brother served twenty-four years. My father was from a family of Moroccan drug dealers. I know how to cut people like our warden down to size."

"You didn't go too far with your threats against the warden?" I ask, taking the bong. "After all, the warden himself has a lot of problems now. After Hitler escaped, our prison is checked constantly."

"What is that to us, Vasya? We are serving our term, bothering nobody and not attempting to escape. Vasya, when I was locked up in Aguada for three years, I realized that if the government has decided to fuck me, I won't miss any opportunity to fuck the government. In Aguada, they also tried to make tension for me, but I drove the warden crazy. He found a cellphone, charas, and cigarettes in my cell every day and seized everything. However, the next morning I had everything again. I bribed the entire prison staff, except for the warden. After the newspaper published the latest article saying that Idu uses a telephone and the Internet, and smokes drugs in prison, the warden got rid of me by having me transferred here. If he hadn't done that, I swear he would have been fired. Now the warden of this prison knows he shouldn't get funny with me, no matter what. He decided to check my cell! Let him grow some balls like I have first, or at least some like the escaped Hitler had. That Hitler is a piece of work, of course. He dug a tunnel with an iron spoon for a whole year. His cellmates knew nothing about it. Every night he removed a tile in the toilet and slowly picked at the stone wall. He spent twenty-three years in prison. He escaped three times; that was his fourth escape. When he escaped for the first time, the first thing he did was to kill a witness, and he received another life sentence. He has nothing to lose. If he is caught I'm sure he will start to dig a new tunnel the next day. I respect such people. He's a real criminal, the same as I am."

Throwing the bloodstained towel at the Nepalese guy, Idu roars at him, as if he were his slave.

"Oh, you stupid Nepalese chump, why are you smearing blood all over the floor? Wipe it with a cloth. Are you afraid of blood or what? Do the Nepalese have a different color blood? The Nepalese probably have yellow blood," Idu says, laughing loudly, watching Bim fastidiously wiping red drops from the floor. "Why are you staring at me, Bim? If it wasn't for me, the warden would have hit you with a stick on the back in honor of Hitler's escape. Who pays you money, who buys food for you, who gives you charas in the evening?"

"Idu, why are you swearing at me? You're a big drug dealer. You've bribed the entire Goan government. And I'm a little drug dealer, I have just thirty-five kilograms of charas in my case. My balls are not as big as yours, I'm not as brave as you, but my blood is not yellow."

"Okay, Bim, don't be offended. I'm kidding, you're a good servant. I just got all steamed up after the row with the warden. You know me, I'll have a smoke and calm down."

Having remade my bed, I lie and watch Bim preparing dinner, cutting tomatoes and onions with a sharpened spoon for a salad. I hear the unpleasant meowing of the ever-hungry prison cat coming from the corridor, waiting for its portion of fish near our door. Someone starts calling Idu from a neighboring cell, repeating his name continuously, like that cat: Idu, Idu, Idu...

"Hey, Idu, give us a piece of hashish, we have tension," I hear the lamenting voice of Suresh.

"That's it, stop!" Idu roars loudly so the whole prison can hear him, making the cat and Suresh shut up. "I'm fed up with you. Don't I have tension, huh? Am I a shop or supermarket for you? Everybody needs something from Idu. Why did nobody bring me a bucket of hot water this morning? Nobody will ask for anything from me today. Has everyone understood?" Idu shouts at the silence again. "If someone asks for something today, he can forget my name forever. Making tension is Indian style. Vasya, in my twelve years of living here, I've realized that everyone makes tension here.

Look at that shabby cat, it's exactly like any Indian on the street. It appears not to bother you, but by begging for food constantly it creates a small amount of stress that evolves into large tension sooner or later. Dogs on the streets, beggars, wandering cows, monkeys – everyone in this country is trying to make tension to get what they want. They lack the brains to get what they want in a rational way. They don't have enough brains or big enough balls to get what they want, that's why they create tension all the time. This is the way India has been mooching at the expense of other countries for more than a thousand years. Mahatma Gandhi, without using weapons, drove the English, who tried to impose their own order here for several hundred years, out of India using this method. Indians make tension professionally, causing a white man to slowly go mad. But I've got their number, Vasya. We must be the first to begin making tension, and do it all the time and everywhere. You can protect yourself from their tension if you create minor problems and stress for the people around you, both with and without reason. I've got enough charas hidden in the cell for a month, even if the three of us were to smoke it every half an hour. I also have another two cellphones hidden. And today's incident with the Israeli New Year is just my excuse to start making tension for the guards. Today I showed them that I'm crazy. I'm absolutely sure that nobody will bother us with a check in our cell again."

"Idu, aren't you afraid that the warden will complain to the judge?" I ask, peeling a large yellow orange.

"Vasya, what can they do to me? I'm already in prison. The government failed to catch me selling drugs, and locked me up for three years for a one-day overstay. By order of top policemen from Delhi, an officer whom I had bribed every month wrote a whole list of drugs in my charge sheet, which were allegedly found in my car. He arrested me, apologizing and promising that I would get out in a year. The police authorities from the capital instructed him to jail me, threatening that otherwise he would be jailed. I gave him a year to overturn my case. If I don't get out in a year, I swear on my mother's life that I'll order a hit on this officer and the two witnesses, from prison. If they lied to me and I get ten years, I'll drag half the Goan government with me to prison. Thank God, I have enough dirt on them. My whole house is crammed with hidden cameras and microphones. If you only knew, Vasya, who came to my house. But I can't tell you about that. I can only say one thing. The whole state system in India is corrupt from top to bottom, and many people like cocaine. So I want to sit here the same way as I lived outside, with no one bothering me or making tension for me. As long as I'm here, I will make tension for the system."

"Idu, you remind me of Che Guevara. He also opposed the system and fought for freedom. He was offered the post of minister, but he chose to go against the system and died in the forests of Bolivia."

"Vasya, I am a modern Che Guevara. Since my early childhood, I have understood how the system tries to make slaves of us, and I have opposed it since then. Let the system think that it has punished me. I have permission to visit a private doctor seventeen days per month. Every other day I go by my chic car to visit the private doctor, accompanied by three guards. I give thirty bucks to guards and I can do whatever I want to. I make love to my girlfriend in the doctor's office two or three times a week. I don't eat prison food. My sister sends me parcels with good kosher food from Israel every week. Let the system think that I am deprived of everything, like other prisoners. But I actually now feel safer than when I was at large. I am guarded, fed and served. Meanwhile, I continue fucking the system, organizing deals over the phone. While I am here, in prison, I promise to fill Goa with drugs. If you have bought MDMA, ecstasy, LSD or cocaine in Goa during the last ten years, you should know that ninety-five percent of it was my drugs. All of the MDMA and LSD that you bought for sale came from my wholesalers. I've sold thousands and thousands of different drugs in Goa. Everything in Goa is built on drug money. Hotels, roads, bridges, electricity... There was nothing here before. So now the system thinks that it has punished me by locking me up? I will get out of here after serving a year at most, and then I will litigate to the bitter end, demanding compensation for each day I spent in prison. When I was arrested by the Bombay police, my charge sheet said I had fifty grams of cocaine and one hundred grams of ecstasy. After I had spent only two months in a Bombay prison, these drugs became mint powder and pills for diarrhea. Yes, I spent forty thousand dollars, but I did my time like a king. The biggest Bombay mafia, led by Chet Rahul and Mickey Rajan, supported me. Imagine, Vasya, a large room in which two hundred people live. At night, when everyone went to sleep, only two narrow passages remain on the floor. Well, I had a triple-sized spot that was sectioned off and five people serving me there. Someone washed my clothes, someone made tea, and someone fought for me. I had my own small gang, and I had everything I wanted. Now, in our prison, I also already have people loyal to me in each cell. I will have the strongest gang here in a few months."

"Idu, why do you say a few months? You are already considered to be the most respected passenger in the whole prison. I've been sitting in different cells together with a bunch of Indian beggars for sixteen months. Only you have helped me to move into this little VIP cell. It's far more comfortable if there are just three of us. Thanks to you, I now sleep not until six, but until ten o'clock in the morning. Thanks to you, I always have charas, tobacco and fruit. And anyway, Idu, you're like my wife, you make the Indians wash my clothes and bed linen twice a week. There were periods here in prison, when I did not wash my things for two or three months. You have no desire to do anything, when you are told you will get out of here in a week. You just want to throw away all your prison stuff and get out of here wearing only shorts and with the release certificate in your pocket. Thanks to you, I have become a normal, white man again. Soon I will be released on bail, and I will leave like a normal person, not a savage, after all these months of being here."

"Vasya, when will you finally get out of here? You've been waiting for your release every day for a month already. You should have understood long ago that you could await your release for ten years here. You need to learn how to live day by day in this reality. But you, Vasya, have been sitting here in your dirty, smelly clothes for almost seventeen months, expecting to get out tomorrow."

"Idu, I still can't get used to the Indian prison wisdom 'Tomorrow never come'. Every time my lawyer says that I will be released tomorrow or the day after. First, I waited for the analysis of the MDMA for a year. Then I waited for four months for the doctor who performed the analysis to come. The doctor told the judge that there was a positive reaction to MDMA, but he couldn't name the exact amount of the drug as he hadn't performed an analysis of the purity. I would have been already released if it hadn't been for the Ganesh festival, which lasted for twenty days. Now I'm waiting for my lawyer to get another six thousand dollars from my mom. After Viktor escaped from India, my lawyer demands full payment in advance. Viktor called my wife from Moscow. He said that he had escaped across the border with Nepal. Then he went to the Russian embassy and said that he had lost his passport. After serving three weeks in a Nepalese prison, Viktor got a certificate from the embassy and flew to Moscow. So now I have to pay the full amount to my lawyer because of him. I just need to be given a letter of guarantee from a local resident, and I will be released. My Indian friend Ganesh promised that he would prepare all the documents soon. However, his wife gave birth recently, so my release next week may be put off again. When I was locked up, the lawyer said that I would get out of here for four thousand dollars. I have already paid eight grand, and I'm still here."

"Don't worry, Vasya, you're not alone. Everyone who wants get out of here pays the same amount. James and Antonio paid the same."

"Movies, movies, movies are going to start," Nepalese Bim starts shouting happily, settling comfortably on his bunk near our feet.

"I wonder what Bollywood fake they will show us today, Vasya? In the six months I have been here I've seen Indian fakes of almost all Hollywood movies on TV, from the Indian The Matrix to Fight Club. Judging by the beginning of the film, we'll be shown the fake of Tarantino's Four Rooms today."

"Bim, have you ever heard of Quentin Tarantino?" I ask the Nepalese, fascinated to watch the moment when the protagonist bets his finger that his lighter will light on the first attempt.

"What is twenty Tarantino?" the little Nepalese asks in surprise, not getting distracted from watching the TV for a single moment.

"Vasya, who are you asking about Tarantino?" Idu says, smiling, and begins to crumble another batch of charas. "I bet my finger that no Indian in this prison has ever heard of Quentin Tarantino and will probably never hear of him. Why do they need Hollywood here, if Bollywood makes fakes of any movies every day? They don't understand and they are not interested in movies without Indian dances and tear-jerking love stories... What are you going to do outside, Vasya?"

"I don't know, Idu. I've thought about it so much, getting ready for being released, that I'm tired of these thoughts. If I were outside now, I don't know what I would live on as I have no money. It looks like I will have to again deliver 'medicines' to mentally ill people, at least in the beginning."

"Vasya, I hope you will start to work now without any bullshit, with no psychedelic revolution. Cocaine will help you to remedy your financial situation very quickly. Pop down to Colombia, buy a kilo for a thousand dollars, pack it nicely, bring it here and sell it for a hundred thousand very quickly. Now you know all the holes in Indian legislation. You can safely carry one hundred grams of cocaine, knowing you'll get out on bail. Now you know that if you have ten thousand dollars, you're safe from ten years in prison. You'll spend twenty months here at the most, and then get out. There are no normal drug dealers outside now. Tamir, if he is not a fool, is unlikely to come here again. If Dima Lucky comes to Goa again, I will help you to make such troubles for him that he has not even dreamt of. Vasya, I have contacts that nobody else has. If you work for me outside and listen to what I tell you, you'll quickly earn your million dollars. Vasya, have you ever stabbed someone?"

"No, I haven't, Idu. I've never needed to, thank God."

"It's a shame you don't have this experience, Vasya. You'll have to go through this practice. When you are released, you will have to cut Dima Lucky's face. If you don't do it, you aren't a drug dealer, and nobody will be afraid of you and nobody will respect you. If you meet a man with a scar on his face in Israel, you know he is a former police informant. The drug business is no picnic. You should be feared, not loved. Of course, you can sell one or two grams and live like a cowardly rabbit, fearing that someone will shop you. But, in my opinion, Vasya, fate has brought us together for a reason. Stop playing with toys, kidding around is over. It's time to become a grown man."

"Idu, you're right that the time of playing children's games is over. But I don't want to make a million on drugs. Iranian David was with me in the same cell and was always asking how to earn a million quickly. He sat here under investigation for five kilograms of charas for three years. He was acquitted, released, and caught again with two kilograms of hashish three months later. He will soon be transferred to our prison. This time he didn't even have time even to earn the money for a lawyer, so he is likely to go to Aguada for ten years."

"That's what I'm talking about, Vasya. You shouldn't sell two kilograms; you should sell tens and hundreds of kilograms. One deal should bring enough money to bribe the police and pay for the services of a lawyer. Vasya, if you are released on bail next week, you will be able to go to Russia in five years at the earliest. The cases of those who are released on bail move very slowly in the court. So, when you get outside, get ready to cling to life with tooth and nail, as I have done since my childhood. Otherwise, run away from India forever, like Apollo and Viktor did. And if you run away, you'll live in your Russia till the end of your life, fearing that Interpol will find you and send you to an Indian jail for ten years. Apollo is already wanted by Interpol. In a couple of years, Viktor is also likely to be sentenced to ten years in absentia and put on the international wanted list. If you don't want to be on the run for your whole life, listen to my advice, Vasya. Learn to fight for your truth, whatever it may be. You always have to fight to the death. You are thirty-seven years old and you are still playing at revolution. Now your revolution will entail staying alive when you are outside and not being locked up again. Or you can give up the drug business and continue writing your book, maybe someone will buy it. And while you are here in prison, Vasya, enjoy your last days of peace. Here, have a bong, you revolutionary, Bom Bolenath!"

Chapter 55. Part Two. Outside.

"What's all this crap on your table?" the policeman says, screwing up his face, pointing at the oyster I opened few minutes ago, ready to die in my stomach. "Do you Russians eat them raw, like the French?"

"Do you want to try?"

"God forbid! We fry them before eating them in Goa. Let me see your cellphone. Who is Vova?" Pashish asks, looking at the display of my phone, stubbing his cigarette out on the glass table.

"He's my interpreter, I'm not good at English. He'll call my lawyer, and we'll try to settle this misunderstanding. In the meantime, please show me your documents, and the permission to enter my house and ask your questions that I don't understand."

"It looks like you don't understand who I am ,Vasiliy. I am Pashish, here's my identification. I don't need any other documents," the police chief says, smiling, pulling a cell phone out of his pocket. "Here, Vasiliy, look, it's Tamir's phone number . He's my good, old friend, I know everything about you. I know that your daughter's name is Vasilinka and that she is in the same class as Tamir's daughter. I know that you've been selling cakes with hash and some sort of your traditional Russian drink, kvas or kvus, in Arambol for a long time. You shouldn't have started to play with the big boys. If you refuse to cooperate, I will fuck your life. If you don't understand the whole seriousness of your situation, call Tamir. You may call from my phone."

"I can't call Tamir because he is in Ukraine now. He's my friend, I think he'll help us to sort out this misunderstanding when he is back in a couple of months."

"I can't wait that long. Tamir is the only Russian who pays me. If you're so stubborn and unwilling to cooperate, then get dressed, take a toothbrush and a towel, and we'll go to prison."

"What do you mean, prison? Are you crazy or something? Show me the warrant for my arrest and the search."

Standing up from the sofa silently, Pashish approaches the table.

"I believe you take us for fools, Vasiliy. Do you think that I didn't see how you put the key to the safe in the glass with pencils? Basically, we don't need anything else from you. Rahul, call the squad, we're arresting him," Pashish says, smiling and putting the key to my safe in his pocket.

"I'm not going to go anywhere, show me the warrant for my arrest," I say, sitting on the floor and getting ready to resist the two policemen.

"Vasiliy, I'll show all the papers at the police station, now stop jerking around. I'm not going to lay a finger on you. The six police officers who are coming up the stairs now will deal with you. That's it, Vasya; the games are over. You face from ten to twenty years in prison."

Epilogue.

At nine o'clock in the evening on October 21, I finally heard the phrase I had dreamt about for a year and a half:

"Vasiliy, pack your things and come out, you are released on bail," the guard said, opening the door for me.

I said goodbye to my former enemy and partner in the Hemp restaurant, whom I had forgiven and even made friends with to a certain extent, while walking during my last week in prison. It was symbolic that he was sentenced to three months for... a visa! Just a few years previously he demanded money and threatened to shop me to the police, who could have locked me up for an expired visa. Thanks to prison I was able to forgive him. He was put behind the bars a few days before my release. Saying goodbye to my cellmates, I mentally asked the gods to forgive these people who had committed such terrible things and had to share this time and space with me. A human being is a weak creature, able and inclined to make mistakes. Not everyone can proudly call themselves a Human Being. All of us, each and every one of us, has his or her place in the endless chain of evolution. Sometimes we think we deserve more and then our cunning mind can justify all of our actions, protecting our ego. We frequently break the law or commit a crime, thinking we are doing a good deed. Saying goodbye to my cellmates, I realized that most of them, just like me, are caught in the trap of their egos, constantly justifying themselves and their actions. Most of them, just like me, consider their stay in prison to be a big misunderstanding: how did it happen that God allowed me to end up in prison?

When I got outside, I realized that I had the opportunity to start life from scratch. I had no money, no job, no home, and no family. I had to start all over again. Already after a few days, I knew that I didn't want to be involved in the drug business anymore. My accomplices in relation to the MDMA laboratory disappeared without a trace, although they left me a lot nonetheless: the chance to live a normal, legal, law-abiding life. Having made my choice to no longer be involved with drugs, I began to notice how the space around me started to transform. On the first night I met a character mentioned in this book, Lyokha Sponsor, who donated me some money.

The next day I met a friend who is also a character from this book, Roma, who gave me the key to the apartment where I lived during my first month outside, while I came to my senses. My friends who had distanced themselves from me in recent years, again began to become close. I was very happy when another character from my book, Andrey, having read a few chapters posted on Facebook, sent me financial support, insisting that I not deal in drugs anymore. I want to say many thanks to Eduard and Mikhail, tourists who came to visit me and gave me money for the publication of the book. My friend Andrey and his wife Natasha also supported me financially and emotionally, helping to edit the book. It was nice to know that I have friends and I am not a drug dealer, scorned and hated by everyone.

When I went to my first trance party after a break of one and a half years at the Hill Top club, I was severely disappointed to see what the trance movement in Goa had become. Drunken, junky freaks stuck in Goa danced dismally on the spot, surrounded by Indian youngsters off their heads on cocaine and alcohol. I saw how the new generations of Russian tourists, who had come to Goa for the first time, were enjoying what was happening. This mess seemed like a celebration of life to them. But the last straw that finally deprived me of hope was a scene I witnessed in Chapora, the former center of the freak movement. We were drinking rum near a small, old cafe, where all the battle-seasoned freaks usually hung out. A car with blacked-out windows drove up to the entrance. A well-known trance track could be heard coming from the car. Lowering the window, the driver shouted something to the old, heavyweight freaks standing near the entrance. The way they reacted made me think that he was probably their old friend. Greeting the driver in turn, they started talking to him like good friends who have not seen just for a couple of hours.

Approaching the car, I looked into the window out of interest. It was a police officer, the one who drove me from the prison to the court twice a month for a year. Waving at me amicably, he congratulated me on my release and advised me to take it easy and enjoy life. This blatant integration of a government representative into freak culture boggled my mind.

I found out from the newspapers that two months after I had been released on bail, drug dealer Apollo fled through Nepal to Latin America, where he was soon arrested by Interpol. My cellmate, Italian Alexandro, to begin with spent his time doing heroin. He was as thin as death the last time I saw him near the Juice Center in Chapora. But a few years later I found him on Facebook and he looked pretty good in his photos. Our cellmate, Japanese Yuki, was arrested for drug smuggling in Indonesia and is likely to be sentenced to death. The new police chief, who jailed his predecessor Pashish for his ties with drug dealer Apollo, was also arrested for ties with drug dealer Idu. Greek Antonio, after he had been released on bail, quietly died of a heart attack in his sleep three years later, the criminal proceedings against him not having been closed. A few months later, my friend Alex Nicaragua, who had introduced me to India and was the first of my friends to visit Goa, died of a methamphetamine overdose. When he was being cremated in the open air, I watched his remains burning down and smoked a chillum in his honor, thinking that it was probably the end of another period in my life, the period of experiments involving the chemical expansion of consciousness.

A couple of months after my release, the freedom that I suddenly found myself in totally blew my mind. I was bursting with happiness in the evening, and struck by infinite melancholy in the morning. My family no longer wanted to come back to India, and I could not leave the country. 'Who am I? What's my purpose in life?' Every morning as soon as I woke up, these questions were first to come to mind, disturbing me and not letting me enjoy my freedom or my life. In order not to go mad, I tried to do whatever I could. I earned my first honest hundred dollars two weeks after my release, selling a bag of oysters, the same thing that Vitya and I had dreamt about so much in prison, to some tourists. I arranged oyster parties, tried doing barbecues, helped tourists extend their visas, gave lessons in Thai massage, tried writing articles, worked as a tour guide, and even starred in an Indian movie.

But none of that gave me peace or helped me to find harmony with myself. Yoga turned out to be the real salvation for me. It not only helped me to become calm, but also freed me from my growing depression. I am very grateful to my yoga teachers Olga, Tatiana, and Mikhei, for the free lessons they gave me. My second wife Lena didn't want to come back to India and I had to divorce her. In March 2013, I got married for the third time. For all of the six years that I've been restricted from travelling abroad, I've made my living by selling my books. I continue writing, as I'm quite good at it, judging by the reviews of my readers. I have already published four books and now I am working on the fifth. Slowly but surely, I have moved from the guna of darkness and passion to the guna of goodness[105]. I hope that this guna will protect me during my trial, which will last for about seven years. The lawyers reassure me, promising to win the case, as the charge was completely fabricated by corrupt former police officers. But the closer my sentencing approaches, the more unpleasant I find it to recall my article. From ten to twenty years is almost a death sentence. Now I am a law-abiding citizen, and I hope with my whole heart that I will never have to go to prison and write the continuation of this book there.

---

[105] guna of goodness - a guna is a concept from Samkhya philosophy, which means 'virtue, merit, excellence', or 'quality, peculiarity, attribute, property' depending on the context.

Arambol, Goa, India, November 13, 2015

If you liked my book and you are ready to read the continuation of this story, I'm happy to announce that my next book will be released soon. It was written during the monsoon and is titled *'LSD-52. The Oyster Has Opened'*. Yes, 52, not 25, because 25 was in the book you're holding in your hands. It is set in Goa in 2052. There you will meet the same characters, in both the present and the future, after they have undergone a transformation of consciousness through time and new chemicals. A group of psychedelic chemists and researchers who continue work on a new psychotropic substance that was not finished due to Albert Hofmann's death, come across an intermediate formula that radically changes a person's perception of the world. All of the people on our planet fall under the influence of this new psychedelic – the harmony serum. A perfect harmonious society arises. People discover new areas of their brains and new opportunities. Society and the individual make a quantum leap in perception. However, the non-conformism hidden in the DNA of certain characters you met in this book prevents them from finding peace, even in heaven on Earth...

In my book, 'Goa. Confession of the Psychedelic Oyster', I examine the problem of the transition from the third to the fourth circuit of perception, described by R.A. Wilson as 'the awareness of being a domesticated primate and the non-willingness to be one'. In my next book, I try to look at the problems that may arise during the transition from the sixth to the seventh circuit, when a person faces the choice between merging his/her 'I' with the divine and being alienated from God. Having made a huge evolutionary journey, a person can say that he or she becomes a god. What choice will mankind make in the future? Will we go back to where we came from, or become new gods? Will it be a disembodied conscious form of existence in the DNA core, or the infinite bliss of the realization of being a particle of the divine? Will it be the ability to create new worlds, filling them with particles of ourselves, or the endless chain of rebirth?

Made in the USA
Monee, IL
02 October 2022

15035542R00243